I0641315

FAME AND FORTUNE TELLERS

A young man's meteoritic rise to stardom

A novel by Todd Netland

Copyright 2014 by Todd Netland; All rights reserved, re-edited 2015, 2017.

Fame and Fortune Tellers
A novel by Todd Netland

Printed in the United States of America

ISBN-13: 978-0692316771
  10: 0692316779 (Todd Netland; Rainbow Rose)

The author guarentees all contents are original and do not infringe on the legal rights of any person or work. No part of this book may be reproduced in any form without the permission of the author.

Unless otherwise indicated, all Scripture quotations are from the Holy Bible, *King James Version 1611*.

What people are saying about *Fame and Fortune Tellers:*

"Todd Netland is a student of the Bible. He has great knowledge and understanding. He has a fantastic revelation of the end-times. I, Pastor Willy Vega, really enjoy his book and recommend it to those that are students of the Word and have the revelation about the end-times."
--Pastor Willy Vega; Recovery Pastor at Free Will Baptist Church in Concord, California; founder of "Get Real Ministries."

"It's a fabulous book!!!"
--Michele L. Knowles

"This is an amazing book. Please buy a copy....it's good."
--Catrina Calloway

ACKNOWLEDGMENTS

I would like to express my thanks to my mom, Jane Netland, who gave me some very valuable constructive criticism on this novel. Thank you, Mom, for doing such a wonderful job in raising me, as you had a tough job dealing with my autism as a kid, a teenager, and even as a grown man. Thanks goes also to my dad, Edwin T. Netland who was a wonderful dad, who is now having a ball up in heaven, playing golf and worshipping Jesus. Thanks also to you, Christine Soto for your suggestions and encouragement on this manuscript, and for being such a wonderful Christian and prayer warrior! Also, thank you so much, Michele Knowles for your wonderful encouragement and input on this book. Also, thank you, Paula Paul John for your valuable suggestions on editing this book. And last but not least, thanks goes to my beloved wife, Wendy Flagg-Netland for putting in your two cents of advice on this novel!

TABLE OF CONTENTS

1. The Encounter 11
2. The Gig 21
3. The Revolutionists 35
4. More Open Doors 47
5. Onward and Upward 69
6. Spiritual Vitamins 79
7. The Worms in the Big Apple 101
8. Excursion into the Spirit World 119
9. The Mysterious Mansion 137
10. Trouble for Eric Burns 147
11. The Easter Sermon 157
12. The Fight at Mills College 167
13. The Evil Agenda 176
14. The Summer of '74 186
15. The Last Chance 217
16. The Prayer Vigil 253
17. Behind the Curtain 287
18. Into the Pit 306
19. The Valley of Time Travel 311
20. The Circle of Celestial Celebrants 341
21. Epilogue 375

DEDICATION

I dedicate this book to Jon and Mimi Stemkoski who are such great leaders of the group, *Celebrant Singers.* I can truly say that the time I spent as a keyboardist with the *Celebrant Singers* during the 1990s and early this century were truly the happiest years of my life except for the year-and-a-half I've been married to Wendy. The musical arrangements of that group are truly magnificent—and it has really been neat to see all the people who have come to Christ through this ministry!

PREFACE

In 1976, I accepted Jesus into my life as Lord and Savior. In the spring of 1977, I started writing this book that you are now reading. I wrote about one hundred hand-printed pages—and then, just like many tyro golfers who are poor putters, I didn't follow through. I put my novel on the shelf, and over the decades, hardly gave it a thought. My mind was fixated on my career as a Christian musician trying to "take this world for Christ."

In 2006, I became part of an intercessory prayer group that met at our church from 6:00 to 7:00 every weekday morning. Chris Soto was the leader of that group. One morning toward the end of 2009, one of the ladies in the prayer group told me about a dream that she had had the previous night concerning me.

She asked, "Did you write anything between the years 1974 and 1979?"

"No," I promptly answered. (This novel was not even on my mind.)

Well, I went home to my little apartment, and a little later, it dawned on me, "Wait a minute! I *did* write something during that period of the 1970s when I was a freshman at Cal State Hayward."

Then and there, I decided to "dig the old wells again," and started to revamp my manuscript, keeping the things that I felt were good and junking the things that were not so good. Over the next several months, I typed a rough manuscript of the book you are now reading. Over the years, I have edited and re-edited this manuscript to attempt to bring it to the highest standard of excellence as I possibly could. My prayer is that this novel may lead many people to Christ, edify and uplift many Christians, and bring them into a more intimate walk with Jesus and with the Holy Spirit. Also, my hope is that you will experience many hours of just plain good old entertainment as you peruse this book.

Todd Netland

FAMOUS LAST WORDS

"Let's roll!" *–Todd Beamer.*

"I hope I haven't bored you." *--Elvis Presley's parting words at his last press conference.*

"I'm shot!" *–John Lennon.*

"Tis well!" *–George Washington.*

"This is the last of earth. I am content." *–John Quincy Adams.*

"Be of good comfort, Master Ridley, and play the man. We shall this day light such a candle by God's grace in England, as (I trust) shall never be put out." *–Hugh Latimer.*

"Jesus, give me Your love. I love You, Jesus. I love You." *–Mother Teresa.*

1.

THE ENCOUNTER

September 30, 1973 was a pleasant day for the two couples on Highway 50 who were driving home from Lake Tahoe after a fun-filled weekend at Harvey's Resort Hotel. The sunlight glistened against cars, trucks, and motorcycles on the beautiful highway running through the heart of the Sierra Nevada Mountain Range in the eastern part of California, while the drone of motors resounded across the mountainous expanse. Signs showing the distance to Sacramento and San Francisco were interspersed on various sections of the busy road. The canopy of cloudless, cobalt blue sky blended in with the countryside, which was covered with gorgeous green coniferous trees and red rock formations. This scene painted an enchanting, dazzling, and panoramic picture of magnificence.

The more things change, thought Randy Miller to himself, *the more they stay the same.*

Randy, his wife Lila, and a couple who were their best friends, had just celebrated Randy's thirtieth birthday with a weekend of golfing, gambling, and partying. Randy was a fairly swarthy man with dark brown hair and brown puppy-like eyes. He was five feet, nine inches tall and fairly thin. His attractive wife was thirty-two years old and five feet, six inches tall with dirty blonde hair and sparkling blue eyes. Mike and Donna Applebaum were cuddled up together in the back seat of Randy's 1972 blue-and-brown station wagon. Mike was thirty-two years old with jet-black hair and a goatee beard. He had brown deep-set eyes. His wife, Donna, had flowing brown hair and beautiful green eyes. Mike was five feet, eleven inches tall, and Donna was a petite five foot, three.

Randy mused over his gambling escapade at Harvey's Resort with a sardonic smile of resignation. He had put a quarter into a slot machine and won a very small fortune of fifty dollars. Over the next hour, he had lost all of it to the money-guzzling slot machine after putting quarter after quarter into the hungry coin eater. He wound up with a loss of one dollar and twenty-five cents. *How right Lila was,* thought Randy to himself when she had advised, "Quit while you're ahead." It seemed like this same scenario happened to him every time he went to a casino in Nevada.

11

Randy was a moderately accomplished musician. He could play the piano fairly well, sight-read music, and improvise, but by no means was he a virtuoso. He had started playing the piano at age nine. He had an adequate tenor voice that was never either sharp or flat—he had perfect pitch—but it was not polished like Bing Crosby's voice was. He had taken up the guitar at age eleven and had become pretty good at that. He also had composed some music, both classical and pop. He was the choir director at Campolindo High School in Rheem Valley, California.

First period started out with Men's Chorus at 8:00 A. M. This was followed by A Cappella Choir at 10:00, Girls' Chorus at 11:00, Madrigal Singers at 1:00 P. M., and Girls' Choir at 2:00. It seemed like every year, he had rowdy men who would goof off half of the time, tease and torment the substitute choral teachers, and shape up just in time for an important concert. Randy smiled wryly as he thought of the day last spring when he had had a commitment that had kept him away from his classes. The men had been especially rambunctious that day. One music folder was ripped up, the window to the piano practice room was broken, and to top it off, Ray Palmer had pulled a very obscene prank that had totally offended and embarrassed the female substitute teacher. The next day, Randy had come very close to having him suspended, which would have led to his expulsion from Campolindo High School. As it happened, he finally escaped the penalty of expulsion by the skin of his teeth.

The girl choir members were easier to handle. The A Cappella Choir and Madrigal Singers were even easier to handle, except it seemed like there was always a shortage of tenors, and the sopranos had a tendency to send the whole group flat.

Randy played the piano on weekends at Shakey's Pizza Parlor in Lafayette. This brought in a little extra money via tips and free pizza. He was holding his own financially, yet he never seemed to be able to get ahead. Every time he got a raise, inflation would wipe out his real monetary gains. He had just enough money to feed, clothe, and house his family in a middle-class neighborhood in Orinda, California and have the luxury of a vacation trip once or twice a year. *Yes,* thought Randy, *things haven't changed in ten years.* In about thirty-five years from now, he would be able to retire.

"Hey Mike," said Randy. "Wouldn't it be great if we could make more money than what we do right now, say a million bucks?"

"I don't know, Randy. It isn't very easy to become rich today. Gas shortages, beef shortages, skyrocketing prices this summer. I think things are going to get worse before they get better. My big brother, Sid, has enough trouble trying to put his son through college with the high prices of education these days."

"Well, still, Mike," continued Randy. "It would be a nice thing if I could have a whole bunch of money so that I could buy a great big mansion with a swimming pool with a diving board and a ten-foot-high slide. I would have a

Steinway grand piano in my living room. That old upright piano I have now hasn't been tuned in eight years."

"Are you kidding?" giggled Lila. "The way you gamble, you'll never get ahead! You can't stay away from those slot machines long enough to chug down a can of beer."

"You know, that reminds me," said Donna. "I was looking at my horoscope this morning. The word for my sign, Pisces, warned me against risky bets and investments. I suppose," she laughed, "if I had put my quarters into one of those slot machines today, we woulda' had to sell Randy's car and hitchhike all the way back to Contra Costa County!"

"My reading for today was more optimistic," said Lila. "The word for Aquarius says, 'Days of sunshine and happiness are right around the corner.'"

"Oh come on you guys!" bantered Randy. "You know all that astrology stuff is a bunch of hooey! Horoscopes are just a passing fad that will die out in a few years just like that charlatan, John Brinkley, did early in this century with his quack electrical 'cure' to restore virility using radium-laced water."

"I remember that, Randy," said Mike. "He didn't cure anybody. Instead, he did a whole lot of harm."

"You know, Randy," said Donna. "There just might be something to this astrology stuff. Remember: the moon has quite an effect on our moods as well as on the ocean tides. It could very well be that the stars have the same effect on us. Everything in our universe is interwoven together."

"I still say it's all a bunch of gobblygook."

"You're just skeptical because you're a Libra!" teased Lila. "Libras are naturally skeptical and tend to be worrywarts!"

"Say, what's Randy's horoscope for today?" queried Donna.

"Let me see," responded Mike. "I have the newspaper right here. Uh-um. Let's see. Oh, here we go. The reading for Libra says, 'An opportunity for popularity and financial increase is knocking at your door. Be on the lookout for new and unexpected encounters with people you have never met before. They will be the gateway to great riches.'"

"Ah, fiddlesticks!" exclaimed Randy. "You know all that phony baloney is just a gimmick to make money off of suckers like us. Besides, people have always had an interest in knowing the future."

"Well, love, it might be true," said Lila. "Look what the sign said about you today. Isn't that what you want, to get ahead?"

"Yes, honey, but you don't make it to the top through astrology or fortune telling. You make it to the top through a lot of hard work, a lot of talent, and a little bit of luck. However, if the road to riches and fame WAS through astrology and fortune telling, you know that I would go for it in a minute."

Mike and Donna broke into hysterical laughter. Said Donna, "I can see it now! Randy on the stage at Carnegie Hall, playing his heart out with thousands of fans crooning and cheering him on vociferously!"

"Laugh all you want," said Randy. "But don't you worry about the idea of me being a famous singing star or a concert pianist. Why, I can't even keep my voice in the high registers for very long without tightening up my throat, and my runs and arpeggios on the piano are usually very erratic. No, I'll probably just go on the same way I am now—teaching a flat choir at Campolindo High and playing honky-tonk piano at that dinky pizza parlor in Lafayette."

Lila changed the conversation by asking, "What time is it, somebody?"

"About 2:30," said Mike.

"You know, I need a cold drink," said Randy. "We're coming up on Placerville in just a few miles. I think we'll stop there."

"Okay, sweetheart," said Lila.

They drove on in silence, and soon, the homes, stores, and motels of Placerville flashed by. This quaint and lovely town was situated in the very high part of the Mother Lode country, an area that had been so famous in the days of the California Gold Rush. Randy parked the car at an inviting motel called the Green Tea Inn. This motel featured rooms with double beds and color TV, a pool with a diving board, and a home-style coffee shop. Tall pine trees were interspersed among the old houses. The mountains towered high above the town to the east. The coffee shop was crowded with loggers, truck drivers, and vacationers returning home just like the Millers and Applebaums were. A plump blonde waitress led the four of them to a table near the window.

"Are you ready to order?" she asked.

"I think I'll just have a Busch beer," said Randy.

"The same for me please," said Donna.

"Give me a Coke, please," said Lila.

"And a cup of coffee for me, please," said Mike.

While they waited for their various drinks, they relaxed and made small talk.

"Well, Mike," said Randy. "Looks like the Oakland A's have it made again this year."

"Yeah, Randy, the California Angels aren't doing so hot."

"Well, the fact is, Michael, that the A's have outstanding pitchers this year like Rollie Fingers and Ken Holtzman."

"Yes, and they also have excellent sluggers like Reggie Jackson, Gene Tenace, and Joe Rudi."

"What do you think of their chances of winning the World Series again this year?"

"Not very good. The Baltimore Orioles have a very powerful team."

"Oh, come on Mike! I think the A's have a good chance. Look at how many times the New York Yankees won a World Series with the great players that they had such as Babe Ruth and Lou Gehrig."

"But there aren't any players with the A's that have hit nearly as many home runs as Babe Ruth—and Hank Aaron is a better hitter than anybody playing for Oakland."

Meanwhile, Lila and Donna were involved in girl talk, discussing such things as hair appointments, makeup, dresses, fancy coats, jewelry, and marital scandals they had heard about through gossip. Presently, the blonde waitress brought their various drinks. Between sips of beer, Coke, and coffee, they reminisced over their recent trip to South Lake Tahoe.

"Well, Randy, how does it feel to be thirty years old?" asked Donna.

"It's okay," replied Randy. "I still feel as young and chipper as ever."

"You realize of course," joked Donna, "that when you get to be twenty, it's all downhill—and according to a recent article in *Reader's Digest,* when you get to be eighteen, you lose 10,000 brain cells every single day!"

"Oooh," moaned Lila in mock dejection, "I guess I don't have any brains left!"

"I feel good being thirty and I basically had a good time at Tahoe," said Randy, "except that the lobster that we had Friday night was just terrible."

"And our room wasn't too hot," added Mike. "Only on the second floor with no view, and our toilet wouldn't flush."

"Well, our room was great," responded Randy. "We were on the tenth floor and had a beautiful view of Lake Tahoe and the surrounding mountains."

"Anyway," agreed Lila, "the red wine was great and I had my honey-bun all to myself!"

"We had a lot of fun," said Randy. "The chocolate birthday cake was delicious and that show on Friday night was fabulous."

Lila retorted, "Haw, haw! You fell asleep halfway through the show, and I had to wake you up to drive us back to the hotel!"

"Did not!"

"Did too!"

"Did not!"

"Did too!"

"Not!"

"Too!"

"Alright, break it up you two!" bantered Donna. "We don't need any broken arms in addition to our financial losses!"

Presently, the waitress came back with the bill.

"Two dollars and nineteen cents!" grumbled Randy. "That's robbery! Dang it, you can't get anything cheap these days."

"Oh, cool it!" said Lila. "At least you didn't get pick-pocketed like you did six years ago."

"Don't remind me. If I live to be 150, I'll never forget that event."

Randy paid the bill, and the four of them walked toward the car.

"Hey, I've got an idea," said Randy. "Let's have a look around this town before we head home."

"Yeah, good idea."

"Sure."

"Why not?"

The four of them climbed into the station wagon, and Randy started driving around the town while they all looked at the various buildings.

"Hey, that's a cute house there!"

"Look at that one with the funny pink shutters!"

"I sure wouldn't want to live in that dump over there!"

Eventually, they came to the edge of town where there was a large, two-story white house with a spacious flower garden in the front. The strange thing about this house was that all the shades on the windows were drawn. At the entrance of the walkway leading up to the front door was a large sign that read, "METAPHYSICAL EXPLORATION MEETINGS IN PROGRESS; VISITORS WELCOME!"

"This looks interesting!" said Lila. "Why don't we check it out?"

"Okay," said Randy. "Anything you say."

They walked through the front double doors into a reception office with a bulletin board on a side wall. This board had a list of different seminars: "INTRODUCTION TO WITCHCRAFT," room 101; "CRYSTALS AND LONGEVITY," room 103; "THE TRUTH ABOUT KARMA," room 106; "FACTS AND MYTHS ABOUT HERBS, POTIONS, AND FOLK MEDICINES," room 201; and "MEDITATION WORKSHOP," room 204.

"Let's go upstairs to that meditation class," said Lila. "We oughta' get a load of laughs there."

They walked up the red-carpeted staircase to the second floor and soon found room 204.

When they opened the door, a strange sight greeted them. There were nineteen people sitting in a circle with their legs crossed in the lotus position. The lights were very dim, and the curtains and shutters were drawn tightly shut so that no outside light could enter into the room. All of the people in the circle had their eyes closed and were chanting, "Ooooommmm! Ooooommmmm! Om, om, ooooommmmm!" In the center of the room was a table with a single bright candle burning on it. Standing behind the table was a pudgy old man wearing a white robe with a face full of wrinkles.

"Pay no attention to the man behind the curtain!" giggled Donna, softly. "The great and powerful Oz has spok—"

"Shhhh!" cautioned several people close to her.

They sat quietly in the circle for a few minutes. Presently, the pudgy old man spoke, saying, "I feel the presence of a disembodied person who has just entered this room!"

At that same instant, all four of the newcomers felt a sudden chill, and the hair on their heads stood straight up.

"I have a message for someone in this room!" said the pudgy old man. "Does anyone here have a deceased father named Tom Miller?"

Randy gasped. Why, that was *his* dad!

"Y-yes-s, I d-do!" stammered Randy. "How the heck did y-you know his n-name?"

"Your father's spirit is in this room right now and he is speaking to me." (Tears flowed from Randy's eyes; he was blown away.) "What's this? He is saying to me that he knows your toil as a choir director and pianist at a pizza parlor. He knows you lost a little money after winning a slight jackpot at Tahoe. He says your fortunes are about to take a huge leap for the better. Riches and fame are coming your way. Within four months, your name will be a household word. He also advises you to be extra careful on your way home as there is danger lurking."

Randy gazed at the pudgy man in utter amazement and exclaimed with tears, "I'm blown away! I just c-can't believe it! My dad and I were s-so close! (Sob.) He was s-such a k-kind man! (Sob.) He was involved in spiritualism most of his life. He w-worked in the p-post office! (Sob.) Even though he was a busy man, he st-still had a deeply spiritual s-side to him! (Sob.) He had a lot of visions and dreams during his life! Then he was k-killed in that terrible auto wreck in November 1971 when his c-car went over the embankment on Highway 24 near Walnut Creek! My dad was the k-kindest p-person I-I-I ever knew!" He took out a tissue and blew his nose.

He was stunned. *Me, a famous musician? I can't play the piano or guitar THAT well, and my voice has crummy tone quality. My throat gets tight every time I try to sing the high pitches! I teach my choirs at high school proper singing technique, yet I don't practice what I preach! How in the world did that old man know about my dad? It couldn't be! But suppose this is real? What if the spirit of a dead relative can really appear and communicate with you? Could it be possible that I, Randy Miller, am really destined to make it to the top in the music business? Will my dream of fame and fortune come true after all?*

Randy stirred himself from his reverie and asked, "S-sir. You're s-saying I'm going to be a famous star?"

"Your dad says so."

"Do you think I'll be performing at the Cow Palace?"

"Yes."

"Carnegie Hall?"

"Yep."

"Madison Square Garden?"

"Yes siree!"

Voices spoke up all over the room.

"Amazing!"

"Fantastic!"

"Incredible!"

"Cool, man!"

"Unbelievable!"

"Humbug." This last comment was from Mike Applebaum.

At this point, pudgy said, "I feel this disembodied spirit is leaving. He is gone."

Everyone in the room stirred and opened their eyes. Conversations began around the room as people began to prepare to leave or go to another seminar. The two couples greeted the old spiritualist after which they prepared to hit the road. Randy was very subdued and pensive as they walked down the red-carpeted stairway. As they trudged down the walkway outside the house, Randy tripped and almost fell on his face.

"Hon, do you want me to drive?" asked Lila.

"I'm okay. I can handle it."

They clambered into the car, and Randy started driving back through Placerville. He decided to take a scenic back road that would eventually lead to Lodi. As they rode along the beautiful winding road with gorgeous red cliffs and green trees, they mused over the red-letter experience they had just gone through.

"This is a day like I've never had before!" said Randy.

"Yes," agreed Lila, "we have seen wonderful things today."

"Folks, I would caution you about this crock," countered Mike. "You know I've been around for a while and have seen many things. You guys all know my involvement in magic. I've been practicing these illusions for sixteen years. I've studied the life story of one of the greatest magicians in modern history, Houdini. His escaping feats were remarkable, but there was nothing supernatural about them at all. He once thought that spiritualism was real but came to the point where he was disillusioned concerning it and realized it was only very clever trickery. Two years ago, I went to a magic seminar put on by Monty Slominski, probably the greatest illusionist living today. There are eight or more levels in sleight-of-hand magic. Monty gave a mind reading demonstration that seemed supernatural but was really no more than a bunch of shrewd tricks. After he did the mind reading exercise on a female subject, he retraced his performance step by step to show how everything he had done had a logical explanation. Now, that old geezer we met in that house back there is very impressive, but he is really nothing more than an extremely skillful trickster who has studied his art long and hard."

Mike Applebaum was an eleventh-grade American history teacher at Campolindo High School. He was a reserved and even-tempered man who rarely got emotional or angry. His political views were middle-of-the-road. (He had voted for LBJ in 1964 and Humphrey in 1968, but because of George McGovern's leftist views, he voted for Nixon in 1972.) He was of a skeptical cast of mind, needing hard, concrete evidence before he accepted anything as fact. He and Randy had been best friends since childhood.

Mike looked at Randy and said, "I'm going to prove to you, pal, that what we saw back there is nothing. Just wait a couple of months. When 1974 rolls around and you're still grinding away at Campolindo, teaching adolescents how to sing, you'll know—and this astrology craze; it's just a fad taken up by weak and emotionally unstable teenagers to give them an ego boost. It's a con game to hoodwink those boobs. And departed spirits of the dead? No such thing. Just look at Mary Todd Lincoln, the wife of Abraham Lincoln. She consorted with a spiritualist after the death of their son, Willie, and she ended up being committed to an insane asylum by Robert Todd Lincoln. This proves—"

"LOOK OUT!" shouted the two ladies. Out of nowhere, a red sports car was in their lane, rushing straight at them! In panic, Randy rammed the steering wheel to the left and slammed on the brakes. The brakes locked, the tires squealed in protest, and the station wagon fishtailed abruptly to the left. The two cars missed each other by less than an inch.

"TURKEY!" shouted Randy, hysterically. "YOU STUPID BLITHERING IDIOT!"

"Some people don't know how to drive at all!" gasped Lila, breathlessly.

"Probably spaced out on weed," quipped Mike.

"See there?" panted Randy. "There's your proof that what happened back there in Placerville is real."

"I still don't believe it, Randy," said Mike. "There are a lot of kooks in this world like that carrot-top slob, Eric Burns, living out there in Berkeley—and then there's my nephew, Brad, who was formerly strung out on drugs and alcohol and who has become a religious fanatic during the last seven months."

****

IT HAD BEEN A BAD DAY for Darryl Temple. He had been accosted by a cop around noon and fined twenty-five dollars for parking in a red zone area. He had spent some time in a bar in Lodi, drinking himself drunk, and had wound up getting into a fistfight with a fat, ungainly man. Because of this, he had been thrown out of the bar by the bartender. He had been speeding erratically on the curvy mountain highway when he had encountered the near wreck with the station wagon.

Darryl continued rocketing up the mountain road, passing cars on the blind curves, nearly crashing into a white Toyota, and barely missing a collision with a green Chevrolet. Presently, a policeman spotted the racing vehicle and took off in hot pursuit. The siren sounded, and the red sports car pulled off to the side of the road. The cop walked curtly over to the red car while Darryl rolled down his window.

"Sir, may I see your driver's license, please?"

"Drop dead, copper!"

"Don't get smart with me, punk! I oughta' run you in! Do you realize how fast you were going?"

Silence.

"I clocked you at seventy-five miles an hour. *Seventy-five miles an hour*—and on a curvy road where you coulda' caused a fatal car accident!"

Silence from the blonde-haired young man with sullen blue eyes.

"Hmmmm.......your breath smells like alcohol. Have you been drinking?"

"I ain't been drinkin' no booze, man!"

"I think you have. How much booze have you had, sir?"

"I ain't drunk no booze!"

"You haven't drunk anything, huh?" played Officer McDonald. "Maybe you've better come down to the station with me."

"I'm okay, man!" protested Darryl in a high, strident voice. "I'm okay, *I'm okay!*" A stream of cusswords came out of his mouth.

"You're okay," feigned Officer McDonald, "but you know? I think a nice ride in my squad car would do you good. You might need a little rest and relaxation and a nice cup of coffee to wake you up."

With this condescending speech, Officer McDonald grabbed the arms of Darryl Temple and escorted him rather forcibly to the black-and-white squad car.

2.

THE GIG

Randy and Lila's home was situated at 110 El Toyonal on the right side of a semi-forested road that wound up into the high hills towering above Orinda, California. It was a two-story house. The driveway sloped down to the house from the roadway. It was a reddish-brown, eight-room edifice with a red porch in the front, a little lawn and flower garden dotted with red roses and white lilies, and a garage that had no door leading into the rooms of the house; you had to walk outside of it to get to the front door. As you entered through the sand-colored double front doors, you would come into a small entryway with a stairway that led down to the bottom floor. Most of the rooms were on the top floor. The stairway had two landings, the second flight of eight stairs leading downward turning ninety degrees to the left.

The two downstairs rooms consisted of a large game room that doubled as the guest bedroom as well as a blue bathroom for the two Miller children. The game room had white concrete walls. The windows facing north had aqua curtains. This room was furnished with a pool table, a Ping-Pong table, and a double-sized bed covered with an aqua comforter. The concrete floor was covered with teal carpeting. A sliding glass door led out to a beautiful patio overlooking the picturesque view of parts of the suburban town of Orinda. On the west side of the room was a bar complete with a counter, stools, and a cupboard filled with bottles of ginger ale, 7-Up, wine, brandy, and vodka.

On the top floor was a spacious living room painted light green, all decked out with green carpeting and red sofas with an out-of-tune upright piano situated off to one side. This room also contained a stereo phonograph as well as the one TV set belonging to the Millers. There was a pink kitchen with a red-tiled floor with an enclosed space off to one side where the washing machine and the dryer were. Between the kitchen and the living room was the dining room, which was painted a cheerful light-yellow color, consisting of an ornate dining room table made out of oak as well as a brown cabinet. Off from these rooms was a hallway that led to the two bedrooms: the yellow master bedroom with its yellow master bathroom, and the pastel blue bedroom that housed the twin beds for the two Miller children, ten-year-old Jack, and eight-year-old Tommy Miller Junior.

Randy was sitting on the red sofa in the living room, watching the Oakland A's baseball game on TV. He thought back on the tumultuous weekend that he and Lila had experienced. He thought how good it was to be home again, relaxing after running around at Tahoe, seeing that show on Friday night when he had dozed off, playing lousy golf on Saturday morning when he had put three balls in the water and gotten into four sand traps, and then shoving all of those quarters into the slot machine on Saturday evening. On top of that was the adventure in Placerville with the aged medium. They had arrived home around 6:00, and Randy had given Barbara, the babysitter, the five dollars they owed her. Lila was in the kitchen fixing dinner.

He thought back to the family birthday celebration on Wednesday night, September 26. *Funny,* he thought to himself. *I have the same birthday as George Gershwin, probably the greatest serious composer in American history and a great popular songwriter and pianist to boot.* Lila had made for him a lovely lemon cake with chocolate frosting and lemon drops on top, while for a birthday present, she had given him an attractive blue tie. His son Jack had given him a bottle of *Trouble* after-shave lotion while Tommy had given him a sculpted man he had made in art class at school. *Sometimes, my children are real angels,* mused Randy, *but at other times, they could be real pills.*

The two boys came running into the living room at that very instant, yelling and jostling each other.

"Hey Dad!" yelled Jack. "I wanna' watch *Wonderful World of Disney* tonight! *The Computer Wore Tennis Shoes* is on and it's on channel—"

"Hey, wait a minute!" whined Tommy. "I don't wanna' watch that! I wanna' watch *The Brady Bunch!*"

"You do not!"

"I do too!"

"You do not!"

"I do too!"

"Not!"

"Too!"

"Not!"

"Well, it's my turn to watch *The Brady Bunch!*"

"Well, I wanna' watch *my* program!"

"You had the TV last week!"

"You wanna' fight about it?"

"I can lick you!"

"How would you like a bloody nose?"

"Just try it! I'll knock your block off!"

"KNOCK IT OFF, both of you!" snapped Randy. "I know two little boys who won't be able to sit down for a week if they don't cut it out! *I* have the TV tonight. There's a very exciting game on right now. The Oakland A's are playing the Cleveland Indians."

"Dad," whined Tommy. "Tell Jack to let me watch my program!"

"You mean *MY* program!" snarled Jack, insolently.

"ALL RIGHT!" roared Randy. "To your room, BOTH of you!"

22

"Yes Boss!" growled Jack, rudely.

Lila stormed angrily into the room and said, "One more smart aleck remark like that, Jack, and you'll find yourself going to bed without supper! Now, go to your room, *both* of you!"

The two boys scampered off to their room, and Lila came over to Randy and put a loving hand on his shoulder.

"Those kids can really be a nuisance sometimes," said Randy.

"I agree, sweet pea."

"I sure wish, dear, that we had enough money to afford two or even three television sets. Then I wouldn't have to listen to my boys whining and bellyaching every day, 'Lemme' watch this program,' or 'Lemme' watch that program!' 'I wanna' watch *The Flintstones!*' 'I wanna' watch *Bewitched!*' 'Wah, wah, wah!'"

"Well, Randy. Maybe you will someday. Maybe you will. Say, by the way, how about the two of us taking in a movie tomorrow night? *The Sting* is playing at the Orinda Movie Theater tomorrow evening at seven. I could call a babysitter for the kids, and we could have a nice little bite to eat beforehand at Lighteners."

"Yeah, sure."

The timer on the kitchen oven buzzed, letting Lila know that the chicken was ready.

"Tommy, come set the table please!" commanded Lila.

"Okay, Mom!" called Tommy from the kids' bedroom.

Dinner that night consisted of chicken, string beans, tossed green salad with Thousand Island dressing, Wonder Bread with butter, milk for the children, and red wine for Randy and Lila. Conversation was sparse that night; everyone was very tired.

"I think I'm going to turn in early tonight," yawned Randy.

"Me too," responded Lila. "I'm pooped! Eat your vegetables, Jack."

The telephone rang, and Randy rose from the table to answer it.

"Hello."

"Hi, Randy."

"Brian? Brian Manning?"

"Yes, that's me, Randy."

"Wow! It's been so long since I've talked to you! How the heck are you doing, buddy boy?"

"I'm doing fine, Randy."

"How's the wife?"

"She's slightly under the weather with a head cold."

"It sure is good to hear your voice after so long. What's up?"

"Well, Randy, it's like this. I have a favor to ask of you."

"Yeah, what is it?"

"Well, Randy, I'm in kind of a jam right now. I need a lead singer and guitar player to fill in for Wednesday night at a Shriners' meeting in Walnut

23

Creek on 330 California Street at the Masonic Temple. This gig will pay fifty dollars for each of the band members. My regular lead singer and guitar player, Herb Taylor, has been having problems with his voice for several weeks, and he is going in to have it checked on Wednesday. I'm sure he'll be fine. It's probably just a little laryngitis."

"Who's in the band, Brian?"

"Well, I sing the second part, Bart Anderson sings baritone, Keith Bryant is on rhythm guitar, George Newman plays piano, Fred Barnes plays bass guitar, and Mark Dole is our drummer. We've got a pretty tight band."

"What kind of songs will we be doing?"

"Songs sung by The Carpenters, Frank Sinatra, The Rolling Stones, The Beatles, Led Zeplin, Carole King, and a few songs that I wrote."

"I just don't know, Brian. You know how poor my singing voice is. You obviously remember that time seven years ago when I sang with your group for those two months at the Clover Club in Oakland and what a disaster that was. I couldn't nail the high pitches, and I kept messing up on the words. I'm a choir director, pal, not a lead singer."

"Hey, it's only for one night. You'll do fine. Just give it your best shot. Besides, you could use an extra fifty bucks, couldn't you?"

"Well yeah, Brian."

"There you go! Say, would you be able to meet me and the gang to rehearse tomorrow night and Tuesday night, say at 6:00 at my house?"

"I think I could probably hack that."

"Very good. I'll see you then."

"See ya'."

"Goodbye."

"Bye."

Randy hung up the phone and just stood there for a minute in deep thought.

Lila called out, "Who was that, darling?"

"Well, hon. Looks like our movie date for tomorrow night is off. You remember Brian Manning from several years back?"

"Yeah. Wasn't he that band leader you sang with for a few months?"

"Yeah. He was just on the phone, and he wants me to do a gig at a Shriners' get-together in Walnut Creek for fifty dollars. He wants to rehearse with the band tomorrow night and Tuesday night."

"Wow, this could be a big open door for you."

"Well, let's wait and see what happens. Number one: I'm a lousy singer. And number two: this is only a one-night stand."

Randy sat down and contemplated the upcoming gig. *Me, a lead singer? I can't even get up to Middle-C without tensing up my throat. I forget the words of songs so easily. My singing at the Clover Club seven years ago was so bad that Brian had to let me go after only two months! I hope I don't blow it again at this Wednesday night job. Oh well. It will be over quick enough! I wish I were just playing the piano; at least I can do a passable job there.*

****

IT WAS THREE O'CLOCK in the morning on Monday. Randy was not able to sleep. He tossed and turned on the queen-sized bed, worrying that he would wake Lila up. Instead of counting sheep, he tried remembering the names of famous composers and their songs. When that didn't work, he tried remembering baseball stats, but that didn't work either. Finally, he could stand it no longer. He quietly arose from the bed, tiptoed out into the dining room, and turned the light on. He grabbed some manuscript paper and took a pencil out of his pocket, hoping that maybe, just maybe, he would get an idea for a new tune. He sat down at the table—and all of a sudden, he became extremely dizzy! Randy thought to himself, *what's going on? I didn't have THAT much wine last night!*

The next thing he knew was that the pink light of dawn was filtering through the dining room window. Randy stirred and thought to himself, *I must have fallen asleep.* Then he looked down at the manuscript paper and gasped. There, right in front of him, was a completed song consisting of a melody, a set of lyrics, and a chord chart. The title on the top of the page read, "THE EVIL EYE." Randy felt a chill go throughout his whole body. He had never experienced anything like *this* before. Dumbfounded, he slipped back into his bathroom to shower and shave.

****

ERIC BURNS WAS DRIVING a school bus that Monday morning from Orinda to Campolindo High School in Rheem Valley. About fifty teenagers were riding the bus. The animated conversation among them covered such topics as varsity football, chemistry, the upcoming prom, who were the best teachers and who were the worst teachers at Campolindo, and the recent coup and assassination of the Socialist leader in Chile, Salvador Allende. Six feet tall and a little thin, Eric had brownish-red hair and fiery eyes that seemed to bore a hole right through you. He had a choleric and humorless personality, he was a political crusader whose ideology was far to the left, he had a tremendous hatred for President Nixon, and he was an atheist.

His dad, Art Burns, was a life insurance salesman who had never been rich but had been able to support his family with a fairly comfortable lifestyle. He was a fairly good dad albeit somewhat of a strict disciplinarian. Nevertheless, Eric had very little respect for him; he considered Art Burns to be far too materialistic and conservative. Jan, his mother, was a gentle and kindly lady who battled with health issues much of her life.

Eric Burns was thirty years old. He had been schoolmates with both Randy Miller and Mike Applebaum, both of them having a low opinion of him. Eric had once been an aspiring musician who had never attained anywhere near the skill of Randy Miller, let alone the ability of an accomplished virtuoso. When he was in junior high school, he had studied both violin and guitar. In the spring of 1958, while he was a freshman at Miramonte High School, Eric had entered a district music festival competition, playing a classical violin and piano piece by Vivaldi. Various adjudicators rated the contestants on their performance. Eric totally muffed his performance of the violin/piano duet, and the judge gave him a five, the lowest possible rating. In the first place, protocol called for the contestants to be dressed neatly, but he had been dressed very sloppily and his hair had been unkempt. The judge had taken him to task on that. Secondly, he had been way off rhythm from what the piano was playing; they had practiced the piece for only a half hour on the day before. Eric played a lot of wrong notes, his rhythms on the violin runs were extremely erratic, and his dynamics and expression were non-existent. Bitterly, he decided to quit the violin. He continued to practice the guitar; he loved the music of Chuck Berry, Janis Joplin, and Elvis Presley.

Eric's grades in school were on the low side of mediocre. He was not particularly a rowdy or mischievous student, but he was very pugnacious; one professor in high school remembered him as being very argumentative. It was during this time when his political views took a marked turn to the left. In his senior year in high school, he read Karl Marx's *Communist Manifesto* and was totally won over by it. He became more hardened after graduating from high school in 1961 and committing a year of service in India to the Peace Corps. He saw the squalor and hunger there and became more convinced than ever that capitalism was a horrible system of greed that neglected the poor and downtrodden of the world. During the Vietnam War, he protested bitterly against the U. S. involvement in that war and was totally on the side of the Viet Cong. He began to participate in American flag burning ceremonies. He spent a lot of time printing pro-communist tracts, which he would pass out to people. In addition to all of this, he was the leader of a small revolutionary group in Berkeley consisting of about twenty-five members called The Red Riding Rangers. They met once a week at Eric's apartment in Berkeley, planning ways on how to help in spreading the communist gospel around the USA.

Eric Burns was grouchy and sulky on this particular Monday morning. He hated this bus-driving job. The strain on his back was hard, the pay was low, and he felt that his boss, William Butcher, was a very draconian man. The noise level was really getting on his nerves today.

"Be quiet," he yelled, "or all of you are going to be walking to school!"

The chatter continued unabated.

"Shut up or I'm going to come back there and break some arms!"

26

Suddenly, Eric noticed that he was just about to run a red light. He slammed on the brakes, and a few people who were standing fell on their faces, one of them being a visually impaired boy near the front of the bus. Eric stopped less than a foot away from a blue Chevrolet. The teen with eye trouble had a bleeding lip. Protests rang throughout the bus.

"Sir," said the legally blind teenager, sheepishly. "You should really watch where you're going. There are a lot of people on this bus."

Eric looked at the youth and groaned, "Oh, terrific! Great! That's just great!" He then announced to the teens, "Don't worry about him. He's all right. Just relax. He's all right."

There were more protests from the student passengers on the bus.

"Boy, what a rude man!"

"I'm gonna kill him!"

"He oughta' be sued!"

"He should be horse-whipped!"

"That guy couldn't drive a kiddie tricycle!"

"I ain't ridin' this bus again in a million years!"

"The *nerve* of that guy, ignoring that poor blind boy!"

The light turned green, and Eric started moving the bus down Moraga Way again.

****

RANDY MILLER ARRIVED at Brian Manning's beautiful house in Pleasant Hill at about quarter to six on Monday evening. Other band members were also arriving. Brian's living room was large and well lighted with a beautiful baby grand piano near the large window. There were several beautiful impressionistic-style paintings on the wall. The room consisted of a blue sofa and gray carpeting. The golden rays of the evening sun could be seen filtering through the window. Occasional cars and bikes were passing by on the quiet lane.

Band members were lugging various pieces of equipment into the living room. Two people were hauling George Newman's Rhodes electric piano into the room and setting it up. Fred Barnes was setting up his bass guitar amp while Mark Dole was setting up his drum kit. The vocalists were setting up the PA system. Brian Manning had named the group, Sneezer.

"Guys. This is Randy Miller, our substitute lead singer and chief guitarist for Wednesday night," announced Brian to the group. "We're going to give him a try tonight."

Randy laughed nervously as he stood up to shake everyone's hand.

"Don't laugh at me if I blow it," he said to the group. "You know that I can barely carry a tune."

"Ah, no sweat man," said George Newman. "You're probably just as good as Herb is."

27

"Okay, everybody," said Brian. "I want to start off with 'The Age of Aquarius.' You got that, Randy?"

Randy nervously opened the Fake Book and found number 123.

"Yes, Brian," he gulped, clearing his throat. He looked at the lead sheet with the melody, lyrics, and chord chart written on it. He lifted up his guitar, preparing himself to sing that hit song from the musical, *Hair*.

"Okay, ready now?" asked Brian. "Here we go then! Ah one, ah two, ah one, two, three, four!"

Music flooded the living room. *D minor seventh, G dominant seventh, C major seventh, A minor seventh, D minor seventh, G dominant seventh, C major seventh, A minor seventh.* The sound of the electric piano, bass guitar, rhythm guitar, lead guitar, and drums flooded through the living room and house of Brian Manning. The three singers started belting out the lyrics of that famous song, which prophesized the coming New Age of Peace and Prosperity of the universe that was just around the corner, that golden age written in the stars and constellations of the cosmos.

A little way through the song, Brian waved his hand in the air to signal everyone to stop. "Hold it!" he cried. "Stop, STOP!"

The music disintegrated into a disorganized cacophony of dissonance and then finally died out.

"Dynamics!" barked Brian. "I need way more dynamics! The piano is too loud, the drums are too loud, and the guitars are too loud! You're drowning out the voices! Please bring the volume way down when the singers come in—and George! Don't rush the tempo at the beginning of the piece. You were getting ahead of the beat. Lay back."

They started the song again from scratch, and Brian called out over the music, "Much better!"

As they sang through the song the second time, Randy felt a new rush of energy and adrenaline flowing through him. His voice was clear, he nailed the high pitches, and his lead guitar licks were very accurate and smooth. At the end of the song, everybody looked around the room with joy and surprise.

"Boy, we did good!" exclaimed Mark Dole, the drummer.

"Yeah, we sure did!" agreed George from the piano.

"Wow!" exclaimed Brian. "That was pretty darn good, Randy! I never knew that you had it in you!"

"Thank you," said Randy. "I guess this is a good day for me. I can thank my lucky stars for that. Say, do you have any suggestions for me as far as my singing technique is concerned?"

"Just one thing," replied Brian. "I don't like your diphthongs you're forming on your words that have 'R's in them. They sound very twangy. Back off of them on words like 'Aquarius' and 'perfect.' Otherwise, your singing was very good."

They rehearsed "You've Got a Friend" after that and then went into the rock-and-roll song, "Stairway to Heaven." *A minor, G-sharp augmented, C major over G, D major over F-sharp, F major seventh, E minor seventh, G major over A, A minor.* The soft intro flowed through the room as the guitars strummed their mellow chords. Randy came in singing very softly and expressively. The dynamics of the song gradually built up to a paroxysm of screaming and loud distortion guitar riffs. Randy was amazed at his newfound singing ability; he was even able to nail the high C's in the stratosphere with ease and poise. When the song was finished, everyone in the group applauded.

"Where did you learn to sing so well?" exclaimed Brian.

"I don't know," mumbled Randy.

"I wonder why we didn't have Randy in the band a long time ago," said Fred Barnes, the bass player.

They rehearsed many other songs that night: hits performed by such stars as Elvis Presley, The Beatles, Frank Sinatra, The Rolling Stones, The Beach Boys, and a few songs Brian had written. Finally, Brian felt like they were ready for Wednesday night.

"You know," said Randy. "I came up with this new tune late, late last night. I got the music right here. What about the idea of giving it a whirl?"

"Well," said Brian, "I don't see any harm in it. Okay, let's see what you got."

Randy passed out the manuscript sheets to the group members of Sneezer. They looked with interest at the title: "THE EVIL EYE."

"Now, this is a very peppy and funky tune," announced Randy. "Please keep it rocking!"

The band started off the fast and loud rock-and-roll song that Randy had composed the night before: *E dominant seventh, A dominant seventh, B dominant seventh, E dominant seventh.* The intro was loud and boisterous. The singers came in with their vocal lines. The melody was very catchy and the lyrics were very interesting and up-to-date. The words talked about the evil eye being a protection against all sorts of bad luck and disasters. After two verses and choruses, Randy took off on a harsh and pounding distortion guitar solo. After that, the three vocalists came back in with the third verse and the repeat of the chorus. The melody had a very memorable 'hook' that most popular song hits have, that certain 'something' that distinguishes famous hit songs from unknown tunes, which end up being flops. When the final sustained E dominant seventh chord sounded, everyone in the room applauded.

"Wow!" said Brian. "That's a hot piece of music you wrote there, Randy!"

"Yeah, nice job!" echoed Fred Barnes.

A chorus of assents from the group followed.

"Yes, Randy," said Brian. "We'll do your tune on Wednesday."

Everybody tore down the band equipment and said their goodbyes. Randy felt exhilaration; he felt like he was on a 'high.'

****

LATER THAT NIGHT, Randy was again having trouble sleeping. He finally got up at 2:30 A. M. and sneaked off to the dining room where he took out his pencil and manuscript paper in the hopes that his creative juices would be able to flow again. Once again, the dizzy spell he had experienced the night before came over him. *Here we go again*, thought Randy. Again, he blacked out. When he came to, there, in front of him, was a completed song with melody, lyrics, and chord chart. The title at the top of the page read, "JUST LIKE CREAMY SILK," a slow, romantic love ballad. Daylight was shining through the dining room window. Randy glanced at his watch, which read 6:30 A. M. Well, he would try this song on the group, Sneezer, at the rehearsal tonight.

****

ONCE AGAIN, the rehearsal on Tuesday night went like clockwork, the rhythm section being very accurate and tight, the music being very expressive, and Randy singing and playing the guitar brilliantly. When Randy showed the group his new song, "Just like Creamy Silk," they were more than eager to give it a try. Randy decided to play the piano on this particular song, so George let him have his spot at the grand piano. Randy quietly counted off the piece, and music filled the Manning house: *G major, G diminished, A minor, G-sharp diminished, A minor seventh, A half-diminished, D dominant seventh;* the lush harmonies of the piano and acoustic guitar resounded through the living room. Once again, the melody was very catchy. But this time, it was slow, mellow, and poignant as opposed to the peppy melody in the song, "The Evil Eye." Once again, the members of Sneezer were won over by the original song, and once again, Brian promised that they would put that song into the repertoire for the gig on Wednesday night. Everyone looked with anticipation and excitement toward the upcoming performance at the Shriners' get-together.

****

ON WEDNESDAY AFTERNOON, October 3, Eric Burns parked his bus in the main bus yard where many other school buses were sitting. He was looking forward to getting back to his apartment flat near Telegraph Avenue in Berkeley to work on some more communist tracts to pass out to people. He had gone through another grueling day of driving those obnoxious, noisy teenagers, and he was looking forward to his version of 'peace and quiet.' He would stop by the office to change out of his bus uniform into his everyday sloppy clothes, hop into his ramshackle blue compact car, and mosey on home to Berkeley. He entered into the reception room.

"Mr. Burns," said the secretary. "Mr. Butcher, the boss, wants to see you."

"What now?" muttered Eric. Then in a louder voice, "Okay, I'm ready to see him."

"I'll tell Willie that you're here." She punched the intercom system to Mr. Butcher's office and said, "Mr. Burns is here to see you sir."

"Send him in," said a gruff and husky voice.

Eric walked into the office of William Butcher, an overweight, middle-aged man with salty red hair. His family background was heavily Irish, he was a Roman Catholic, and he was a hard worker. His office was very neat, everything being well organized on his desk and in the room. A large map of Contra Costa County hung on the wall. Mr. Butcher was a kindly, but no-nonsense type of man. He glared at Eric.

"Burns, come in here and have a seat," he said.

Eric plodded over to a black swivel chair and plopped down into the soft cushion.

"Burns, I want to talk to you," continued Mr. Butcher, an angry look on his face.

"What?" the communist murmured.

"I have a bone to pick with you, Burns."

"What about?" mumbled Eric.

"Last night, I got a call from Mr. Ben Goodwin, the father of one of the students who goes to Campolindo, whose name is Paul Goodwin. This boy, Paul, is considered to be legally blind. He has enough eyesight to be able to read and write with strong glasses and contact lenses, but he doesn't have enough vision to drive a car, nor will he ever."

A sick feeling began to rise up in the pit of Eric Burns' stomach.

"This kid, Paul Goodwin," continued the boss, "came home Monday evening with an unsightly gash on his lips."

Eric nodded his head.

"Ben Goodwin was extremely upset. He tried to call us on Monday night, but was unable to reach anybody. He finally got through last night. Any idea how Paul got that cut?"

"I have no idea," lied Eric.

William Butcher looked him squarely in the eye and said, "Paul told his dad that *you* were responsible for his bleeding lip. You were rude to the youngsters, you nearly ran a red light, you almost had a bus accident, you slammed on the brakes, causing several teens who were standing to fall, and to top it off, you sugarcoated that whole outrageous episode and didn't even apologize to those kids!"

"That's not true!" protested Eric. "The kids were being rowdy, the light changed to red when I was practically on top of the intersection so that I had to slam on the brakes very fast, and that blind boy exaggerated the whole story."

"Mr. Burns!" barked the boss. "Haven't you heard of something called a yellow light that gives you about four seconds of warning before it turns red?! Haven't you heard of that, or are you colorblind? Maybe you should get your eyes examined, and while they're at it, they should look into your brain! I sometimes wonder if your IQ is any higher than that of a baboon in Borneo! Your bus-driving job is a very serious business. You hold the safety of dozens of teenagers in your hands. If something goes wrong, the heavy load gets dumped on me. We're just lucky Mr. Goodwin didn't take legal action to sue us. Mr. Burns, did you ever read about that terrible bus accident that happened in New York State?"

"No."

"Well, the driver of that bus was not paying attention and crashed into an oncoming train. Five schoolchildren were killed, and most of the others were injured, some very seriously. There was one girl who had to have a limb amputated."

Eric was silent.

"Burns," said the boss. "I'm going to be watching you very closely. I'm docking your pay twenty-five dollars for this month—and if I ever hear about another incident like what happened on Monday, I'm giving you fair warning that your job here will be in great danger. You keep going the way you are now, and I'll not only fire you, but I will also write a fitness report that wouldn't qualify you to drive a little boy's red scooter down Grover Lane! Now, GET OUT OF HERE!"

Eric Burns sulkily left the office, hurriedly changed into his regular clothes, and headed for his blue car.

****

IT WAS ABOUT QUARTER PAST SEVEN in the evening of Wednesday, October 3, when Randy Miller and the other members of the band Sneezer arrived at the Masonic Temple on 330 California Street in Walnut Creek and started setting up the equipment. The entertainment was going to be on the stage in the front of the hall. Soon, the microphones, the Rhodes electric piano, the drum set of Mark Dole, the guitars, the bass, the amp, and the speakers were all set up and ready to go. The group had a quick sound check and then waited for the emcee to introduce them. At around twenty to eight, the Lodge members started to trickle into the hall.

Brian Manning was talking to the person in charge of the night's festivities while Randy nervously chewed on a ballpoint pen. *This isn't at all like directing my high school choirs at a Christmas concert or a spring concert,* thought Randy to himself. *There, I only directed, but here, I will be singing and playing lead guitar in front of 150 men, TONIGHT! Is there any way I can get out of this? Maybe I can bolt out through the front doors of the hall real fast before anyone can catch me. No, that won't work. I'll only make a fool of myself. Maybe I can quietly sneak out the back door. No, that wouldn't work either. Someone is sure to see me sneaking out—and besides, what will that do to the band?*

Randy looked out at the group of men. Most of them had bored looks on their faces. It would take something nearly as exciting as a trip to the moon to stir them. The ages of the men ranged from the early twenties on up into the seventies. The older men looked especially jaded due to old age and having experienced many things; to them, it was a case of 'been there, done that.'

"Well Jack, do you think there will be anything exciting on tonight's program?"

"I doubt it, Charlie. It will probably be another dull evening of long, boring speeches and second-rate entertainment."

"What do you think, Ed? Do you think the group tonight will be any good?"

"Not likely, Joe. It will probably be the same junk I've been hearing for the last two years!"

Randy felt as nervous as ever when the time drew near when they would start singing. His hands were shaking, his lips were parched and dry, and his throat was tight. He didn't know what he was doing, being on a stage like this in front of all these men. He was still wondering how he could get out of this. Maybe he could pretend he was sick and needed a doctor. Maybe—

"All set to go, Randy?" asked Brian, a big grin on his face as if he knew that everything was going to turn out great.

"Brian, I-I-I don't th-think I can m-make it," stuttered Randy. "Get somebody else!"

"Oh, don't worry, Randy. You'll do great. I know you will."

"But Brian, I (cough), I feel sick! I—"

The emcee for the night greeted the men in the room, went through some preliminary announcements, and then introduced the entertainment for the night.

"Fellow Lodge brothers," he said. "Our entertainment for tonight is Brian Manning and his singing group called—um, Sneezer?" His voice became high and doubtful.

"Yeah, Sneezer!" responded Brian, a little indignantly.

Brian came up to the microphone and started introducing the band members. He said, "We have a surprise for you tonight. Our lead singer for this evening is filling in for our regular lead singer and guitarist, Herb Taylor, who is battling a little bit of laryngitis. Tonight, we are proud to present to you RANDY MILLER!"

Polite applause filtered through the room along with low-level conversation.

"Sneezer? How could anyone come up with a stupid name like that?"

"Probably a group prone to colds and allergies!"

"Another lousy music group!"

Brian kicked things off with "The Age of Aquarius." As the first notes of Randy Miller rang through the hall, the ears of the men in the audience immediately perked up with interest; these musicians were *good!* The rhythm section was tight, the song arrangements were interesting, and the singers were in tune, rhythmically together, and expressive. Randy Miller felt a surge of energy flowing through his whole body, a high, a kick, a shot in the arm! His singing and guitar riffs were brilliant and dynamic. He had no problem nailing the high notes—even the high C's on "Stairway to Heaven." His singing style was loose yet knitted together well. He had a new style of singing that was uniquely Randy Miller. There was electricity in the room; the audience sat transfixed. When the first song was finished, enthusiastic applause with some cheers and whistles broke out, and Randy had to take two bows.

The rest of the night went smooth as silk. The band had three forty-five-minute sets with a half hour break after the second set for the leader of the Shriners to give a speech to the men there. Sneezer did songs sung by The Carpenters, Frank Sinatra, The Rolling Stones, Led Zeplin, The Beatles, Carole King, Elvis Presley, The Beach Boys, a few songs Brian Manning had written, and Randy's two pieces, "The Evil Eye," and "Just like Creamy Silk." These two original songs of Randy Miller were especially well received by the 150 men. At the end of these songs, Randy had to take bow after bow as the room reverberated with thunderous cheering.

A little after 11:00 P. M., men were coming up to Randy and congratulating him on his musical talent.

"You sang and played so beautifully tonight, Randy!" exclaimed Brian. "I wish we could keep you on. Unfortunately for you, Herb Taylor will be back in the band by Saturday night, all healed up from his laryngitis, his vocal cords as good as new, and able to sing as skillfully as ever."

3.

THE REVOLUTIONISTS

Eric Burns' spirits were high as he walked into his small four-room apartment in Berkeley on Friday, October 5. It was a beautiful evening with red cirrus clouds in the sky, making the sunset a picture of spectacular splendor, but he was not interested in that. Tonight would be the weekly meeting of his ragtag revolutionary group that he led, The Red Riding Rangers. This was the night when this group of twenty-five of his fellow comrades would gather in his flat to plan on how to do their part to spread communism all around the world.

The apartment flat where Eric lived in consisted of a medium-sized living room, a dimly lit kitchen, a bedroom, and a small, dirty bathroom. The apartment reeked of a stale, uneaten ham and cheese sandwich on a plate in the kitchen sink that had been sitting there for days. The paint was peeling off of the kitchen walls. The floor of the bedroom was littered with filthy clothes, cigarette butts, and communist literature. A portrait of Lenin hung on the wall above his bed. Several books were stacked haphazardly on a small table in the living room that included such works as Marx and Engel's *Communist Manifesto,* Thomas Paine's *The Age of Reason*, and a book by Norman Mailer. A totally tattered American flag was on the floor in one corner—he had ripped it apart to show his disrespect for the USA. There was no TV set or stereo player in the apartment, but he always had enough money to supply himself with food, clothing, cigarettes, wine, and beer.

Members of The Red Riding Rangers began to file into the living room at about quarter to seven. The ages of those men ranged anywhere from nineteen to thirty-five. Some of the men sported beards while others wore mustaches. Some of them were dressed sloppily. A few of them, though not many, had experimented with drugs. Most of them had been sexually promiscuous. All of them were committed to the far-left political views that Eric Burns espoused.

Two of the group members who were very close to Eric Burns were twenty-eight-year-old Ted Johnson and nineteen-year-old Scott Williams. Ted was short and stocky, being five feet, five inches tall with dark brown hair and brown eyes. He had a more reserved and passive personality than Eric did. He was very studious and well read, well organized, and a loyal follower of the more aggressive Eric Burns. He had read the works of Marx and Lenin in his freshman year in high school and had been totally won over to the communist cause.

Meanwhile, Scott Williams was five feet, eleven inches tall and very slender. African American in race, he had been raised in a rather poor neighborhood in Berkeley during his preteen and teenage years where he had lived in a run-down apartment complex. He had been forced to wear cast off clothing from the Salvation Army most of his life. He had been born in Birmingham, Alabama, and had spent the first ten years of his life there where he and his family had experienced much racial discrimination. He had graduated from Berkeley High School in 1972 and was presently working as a mechanic in a car repair garage. He had an easygoing temperament with a dry sense of humor. Scott had teamed up with Eric Burns after he had become very concerned about the problems in the slums of the U. S. and around the world as well as the race riots that had erupted in many U. S. cities after the Civil Rights Bill had been passed on July 2, 1964. He practically adored Eric Burns and was 100 percent behind his leftist cause. While the members of Eric's 'army' were arriving, Ted and Scott were having a friendly comrade-to-comrade jaw.

"Hey, Scott," asked Ted. "What do you think of this Watergate scandal?"

"I think dat' Nixon is a liar. He got a big mouth. Every time he speaks, de' stock market crashes. His mouth is so large dat' he can easily cram a fifty-ounce steak inside it wif'out cuttin' it and chew it up wif' one bite."

"Scott, do you think that Nixon knew about Watergate?"

"Oh, yes! In fact, Tricky Dick was pro'bly de' one who ordered de' break-in and been coverin' it up for more dan' a year. Hey man, a lot of people at de' top are turnin' away from him."

"But people like Chuck Colson are still on his side."

"Man, Chuck Colson got a slip'pry mouth. Ain't he de' one who vowed to run ovah' his grandmudder'? I think dat' we in de' Red Ridin' Rangers are destined to save de' poor ole' granny from dat' wolf, Charl' Colson."

Ted laughed and said, "Obviously, we have a lot of problems in the U. S. that underscore the bankruptcy of capitalism: the shaky U. S. dollar, the gas shortage, the weak stock market, inflation, air and water pollution, overpopulation, and all those greedy politicians and their scandals. All of them are dishonest crooks."

"Yeah man. All of dem' are corrupt. Soon, cap'lism will fall and comm'nism will rise to save de' day."

Eric stood up in front of the crowded living room, pounded his gavel against the table, and yelled, "Quiet! EVERYBODY SHUT UP! It's time to get started!"

Everyone became as quiet as a mouse. Eric Burns cleared his throat and began to speak at almost a whisper.

"Welcome, fellow comrades to this meeting of my group, The Red Riding Rangers. We have a lot of ground to cover tonight. We have very serious problems in the United States and around Mother Earth today. To begin with, air and water pollution is on the rise. Many lakes and rivers have become so dirty today that they have lost their blue color and have become an ugly brown hue and worse yet; the water in these lakes and rivers is undrinkable. Look at how polluted Clear Lake is. You see the problem—we are fast running out of drinkable water. In Los Angeles, the smog is so bad that the sky is an ugly brown color. On many days, the smog hurts the eyes of the people who live there. It is becoming a real health hazard. And what about the San Francisco Bay Area; are we squeaky clean? Nope! I remember the days about ten years ago when our air was nice and clean, but not anymore. In the last couple of years, there have been several days when the smog here has been so bad that the people in charge had to call a smog alert. Scientists are warning us that if we don't get on the ball and solve our pollution problems on Mother Earth, we may all be wearing oxygen masks by the year 2000—or worse yet, we may all be dead."

As he was delivering this harangue, he was gradually getting louder and louder.

"Furthermore," he continued, "Mother Earth is having serious financial trouble today. Inflation continues to get worse and worse in the U. S. and around the world. Shortages of food, gas, and electricity have occurred around our planet. Overpopulation has brought famine to many Third World countries and is threatening to bring mass starvation on Mother Earth, the only ship that we have to live on. Meanwhile, the rich get richer and the poor get poorer!

"Now I want to take a closer look at the U. S. economy for a minute. Inflation in the U. S. is now running at an annual rate of more than 6 percent; it was running at close to 9 percent a couple of months ago. The price of gas and food is especially bad. Scientists are warning us today that we are fast running out of many natural resources such as oil and natural gas. This summer, the U. S. was plagued with a shortage of beef. Since the end of 1968, the U. S. stock market has crashed precipitously. The Dow Jones Industrial Average is a poor reflector on how bad things really are there. Many stocks have lost close to 90 percent of their value. Meanwhile, the U. S. dollar continues to be shaky. All of this stuff shows us the weakness of capitalism and free enterprise."

At this point, Eric was speaking somewhat above normal conversational volume, and he continued to get louder and louder.

"Now, comrades," he continued. "We've nailed down the problems that face us today. So now, this brings us to the Big Question, which is, 'What is the cause of all of this?' Well, the answer is basically an *economic* one. The whole problem today is the greed among the capitalistic pigs in our world. For example, let's look at air and water pollution once again; did you know that the government of the United States has done nothing to fix these problems? While those imperialistic hustlers in Washington sit around on their duffs, playing golf, and living it up at their swank cocktail parties, innumerable species of fish are dying in our rivers and lakes.

"Comrades, let me tell you this! There isn't any inflation in the Soviet Union, Communist China, or Cuba—and as for the economies of these countries, they are growing at a faster clip than the economies of the West. As for the Communist Bloc countries, they feed their people. You won't find any food shortages in the Soviet Union, China, Cuba, Poland, or Hungary, whereas when you go to the Middle East, you see all of those poor Palestinian refugees who are living in squalid refugee camps, oppressed by those greedy Zionists in Israel who have stolen their land away from these poor people, yet they want more land, more land, *more land!* And furthermore, comrades, let me tell you this! The Communist Bloc is trying to do something about the Energy Crisis! Really, when you get right down to it, all of these problems are a sign of the decadence of the West. These problems are signs of the coming Glorious Revolution when communism will reign supreme!"

Many of the men shouted their approval. Eric's scintillating tirade was having a hypnotic effect over them.

"Right on!"

"Outta' sight!"

"Groovy man! Groovy!"

Eric continued his violent speech, yelling at the top of his lungs.

****

EARLIER THAT DAY, at around 4:00 in the afternoon, twelve other revolutionists of a different political slant were meeting at an apartment suite in another part of Berkeley. Hal Odell was a thin, muscular twenty-year-old youth who stood at a towering six feet, four inches tall. He had jet-black hair and handsome brown eyes. He was an extremely skilled basketball player; he had played on the Cal Berkeley basketball team during the previous season. He presently was in his third year at college. He had been a good student and a great basketball player in high school until the day a group of his friends had introduced him to marijuana. They promised him that he would be 'cool' if he tried the joint and have a wonderful 'trip' on the drug. Hal had given in, and one thing led to another. Soon, he was regularly smoking marijuana and he eventually went on to try LSD. At first, his new life was fun, but soon after that, life became a bummer for Hal: bad trips, plummeting grades in school, heated arguments with his parents. Finally, the day came in his senior year in high school when he hit rock bottom. He met a very nice and happy schoolmate in whom he was able to bare his soul to. This friend told Hal the secret of his happiness: he had a relationship with the Lord Jesus Christ. This friend invited Hal to his church, Berkeley Tabernacle Fellowship. Hal was desperate, and he willingly agreed to go. On that Sunday during the fall of 1970, the pastor preached a powerful message about the bondage of sin, mentioning among other things, the scourge of marijuana, LSD, speed, barbiturates, and heroin. He went into detail about the dire consequences of drug abuse: ruined lives, serious brain damage, broken relationships, and radical negative changes in personality. He climaxed his sermon by reading Revelation 1, the last part of verse 5 that says, "Unto Him that loved us and washed us from our sins in His own blood." He showed how Jesus could set people free. At the invitation time, Hal ran down the aisle, wanting to be free. The pastor led him in a prayer to receive Jesus into his heart. When Hal called on the name of the Lord, he felt a great burden lift from his body, and he felt clean and happy. He laughed heartily for the first time in months. He went home and told his folks about his drug addiction, apologized to them for his bad behavior and attitudes, and told them that he had accepted Jesus as his Lord and Savior. His folks enrolled him in a drug rehab program. He stayed clean and sober, and his grades rallied. Hal managed to squeak into Cal Berkeley on probation due to his much better grades during the last part of his senior year in high school, a good entrance exam, and the Lord. Before his bondage to drugs, he had planned on being a pro-basketball player, but now his ambitions were different. He was looking toward the idea of pastoring a church. He attended Berkeley Tabernacle Fellowship regularly, he was heavily involved in the ministry of Campus Crusade for Christ on the Cal Berkeley campus, and he was majoring in history and had a minor in journalism. He was the leader of this group of twelve 'revolutionists.'

One of the young men in the group was the nineteen-year-old 'religious fanatic,' Brad Applebaum, the son of Sid and Harriet Applebaum. Brad was in his second year at Cal Berkeley and was majoring in creative writing. He had been drinking 'moderately' since his freshman year in high school, but during his first month in college, he had started drinking much more as well as starting to use 'Uppers.' Things became very bad until that day in February 1973 when he had run into Hal Odell who had shared *The Four Spiritual Laws* with him. Brad had accepted Jesus in late February and had become clean and sober also.

Hal Odell started the group meeting with the eleven other 'revolutionists' by opening with prayer. After this, he said, "Turn to Acts 17 and look at the last part of verse 6 with me. Somebody read it please."

Brad volunteered and read, "'These that have turned the world upside down are come hither also.'"

Hal asked, "Somebody, what do you think this means?"

"Well," replied Brad in a loud voice. "I think it means that the disciples changed the whole fabric of society for the better by telling people about Jesus and that he was risen from the dead."

John Patterson, a soft-spoken man with blonde hair and thick glasses, spoke up, saying, "I think it was the love of the disciples that turned the world upside down."

"Very good," said Hal. "Both of you are right. Let me camp on Brad's point first. Many people think it's simply about getting folks saved, but notice: He says in Matthew 28: 18-20, 'Go ye and *teach* all nations.' You see, God's plan for turning the world upside down with the gospel is *multiplication,* not addition. Imagine with me for a minute that I'm the only Christian on Planet Earth. Let's say I'm a great soul winner. I win 10,000 to Christ every year. At this rate, in 1,000 years, I will have won ten million people to the Lord. At this rate, it will take me 460,000 years to reach the world for Christ. Now, let's imagine for a minute that instead of winning 10,000 people to Christ a year, I win only one, but I disciple that one person and he in turn goes out, leads one person to Christ, and disciples him. All of those converts lead one person to Christ a year and disciple them. At this rate, do you know how long it would take to reach all of the world's 4.6 billion people for the gospel?"

Most of the group scratched their heads in confusion while Phillip Scheer said, "Well.....um, in five years, you get thirty-two believers."

Suddenly, Bill Mitchell's face lighted up. He said, "I got it! In thirty-three years, the whole world could be won to Christ."

"Bingo!" exclaimed Hal. "We see in the book of Acts and in the Pauline epistles to Timothy the whole concept of discipleship. Now, I want to hone in on John's comment. Turn to First Corinthians 13, verses 4 to 7, and somebody read it please."

Dwayne Downing, a twenty-two-year-old young adult with curly red hair, volunteered. He read, "'Charity suffers long, and is kind; charity does not envy; charity does not parade itself, is not puffed up; does not behave unseemly, does not seek its own, is not provoked, thinks no evil; does not rejoice in iniquity, but rejoices in the truth; bears all things, believes all things, hopes all things, endures all things.'"[1]

"Gang," probed Hal. "What are some of the insights that you get from this passage?"

"Well," said Brad. "The part about love suffering long means to be hanging in there, no matter what. Even when the communist conspirators are throwing you in jail, torturing you, and even killing you."

"Mm-hm, yes," said Hal. "Indeed, it does mean to love those who persecute you."

"What I see in there," said Roger Bennett, "is being satisfied with what you have in life and rejoicing when somebody else gets good things instead of being envious of his good fortune."

"Very good!" exclaimed Hal. "So, someone tell me, in what ways do you think that this portion of Scripture might jibe with the character of God?"

Bob Hurst answered and said, "Well, it says in John 3:16 that, 'For God so loved the world that He gave His only Begotten Son that whosoever believeth in Him should not perish, but have everlasting life.'"

"Yeah," agreed Bill. "You know, you can also get a real good example of love as expressed in these verses by looking at Jesus. Now, Jesus was, of course, God in the flesh. Yet He humbled Himself and took all of that pain and punishment on Himself because He loved us so much."

"Excellent, Bill!" cried Hal, a radiant smile on his face. "Note how First Corinthians 13, the love chapter, lines up perfectly with the character of Jesus. Take patience, for example. Jesus never became impatient in His life for any reason, even though He had more trials than any of us will ever have. He was always kind, even to those who hated, scorned, and blasphemed Him. Jesus was never envious of anyone, even though He was often treated unfairly. Also, Jesus never bragged. Whenever He claimed to be God, He wasn't bragging, but He was only revealing His true identity. If He *didn't* claim to be God, He would be lying as well as dishonoring the Father. Now brothers, I think there are some very significant words in the love chapter. It says, 'Love does not seek its own.' Now watch this! Remember when Jesus was out in the wilderness for forty days and forty nights being tempted by Satan? Hey Roger, what was one of those temptations?"

"Well, I think the biggest temptation that Jesus had was when Satan offered Him all of the kingdoms of the world and all their glory if He would just fall down and worship Satan. Satan was saying essentially that Jesus could have all the money, fame, and women that He could want. It would be like being the biggest movie or rock-and-roll star imaginable! I imagine that Jesus would 'have it made in the shade' as they say today."

"So what did Jesus do?" prompted Hal. "Did He accept the devil's offer of fame and fortune?"

"Absolutely not!" declared Peter Thal. "He *refused* to take Satan's bait. Instead, He quoted Scripture, saying 'It is written.'"

"Why did He refuse to take all of this glory by bowing down to Satan?"

John replied, "Because He loved God and men so much that He wouldn't do anything that would conflict with His Father's will, not even to obtain pleasure for Himself by following Satan."

Hal prompted, "Somebody tell me what you think would have happened if Jesus had yielded to one of Satan's temptations."

Brad responded, "God's plans would had been thwarted, and there would have been nobody to pay the penalty for man's sin. Also, Jesus would have joined the slave market of Satan that includes all men. In other words, all men would be doomed to hell!"

"Right you are, Brad," said Hal. "Now, what happened because Jesus obeyed the will of God the Father instead of bowing down to Satan?"

Peter responded, "A way of salvation was opened up for the whole human race, and all men that get themselves under the cross of Christ are freed from sin, hell, and the clutches of that dirty rascal, Satan! As for Jesus, He endured a torturous death on a cross, but He rose again on the third day and is alive forever. Soon, He is coming again."

"Very good, Pete," said Hal.

The Christian 'revolutionists' in the Circle of Love continued their Bible study for a while longer after which they had a time of taking prayer requests.

"Please pray for my parents," said Brad. "They are very ungodly people. They don't believe in Christianity. They believe in evolution. They smoke, drink, gamble, and swear as well as being very worldly and materialistic."

"Please pray for my math exam coming up next week," said Bill. "Pray that God will give me wisdom so that I will do well on that test."

"I have a prayer request," said Dwayne. "Yesterday, I shared the *Four Spiritual Laws* with a guy on campus and he prayed to receive Christ. Praise the Lord for that. I just want prayer for follow up and his growth in the Lord."

Other guys in the group voiced their sundry prayer requests. Hal called on different people in the group to pray for the various prayer requests after which he closed out with a final prayer. After that, all of the 'revolutionists' hugged each other lovingly and spent a little time having a nice, friendly jaw. They then went to a coffee shop for a bite to eat and more fellowship.

****

ON THAT FRIDAY NIGHT, there was a birthday celebration at the home of Sid and Harriet Applebaum for Harriet. Brad, their son, was there, as well as his two younger sisters, Kimberly, aged eighteen, and Lisa, aged fifteen. Mike and Donna Applebaum were also there with their children, Michelle and Sharon. Also in attendance was Anthony Richardson, the brother of Harriet, and his wife, Mary.

Sid and Harriet lived in a beautiful house on a high hill overlooking the town of Moraga. The house was almost in Lafayette. Being of modern architecture, the floors were made of polished cedar wood and the walls were painted in beautiful pastel colors. You could see spectacular sunrises and sunsets from the high perch where Sid's house was.

Sid was a stockbroker for Reynolds and Co. He was a very hard worker, well-organized, fairly even-tempered, fun loving, a faithful and loving husband and dad, and in addition, had a dry and wry sense of humor. His wife Harriet had a very vivacious personality. She was loving, compassionate, outgoing, and friendly. She could easily fly off the handle but would get over her anger very quickly and not hold a grudge. Both Sid and Harriet were golfing aficionados; they were members of the Mira Vista Country Club, which towered high in the hills above El Cerrito. When the weather was good, they played there at least twice a week. In addition to her golf, Harriet loved bridge while Sid loved poker.

Anthony Richardson was a biologist who worked at a science lab in Walnut Creek. Being of a very intellectual cast of mind, he had a slow-burn type of personality that had a skeptical and sarcastic side to it. There were times when he tended to be grouchy. These traits turned many people off— he didn't have a great many close friends. On the other hand, Mary, his wife, had a very easygoing temperament; she was kind, giving, and very rarely got angry.

Presently, the chocolate birthday cake with chocolate frosting and many candles was ready, and everyone was called to the dining room to sing "Happy Birthday" in the key of F. The cake was a gorgeous affair decorated with the words, 'HAPPY BIRTHDAY' written with green frosting. After Harriet blew out the candles and everyone got a piece of cake, she then opened her various presents. As she opened each gift, she thanked the giver very heartily. After this pageantry, everyone sat around and joined in a nice chitchat.

"Well, Sid," said Mike Applebaum. "Looks like the market is doing better these days."

"Yeah, Mike. We may finally be out of the woods. We've had such a terrible market these last five years. The Dow made it over 970 today."

"What goes up must come down," philosophized Anthony, blandly. "In science and in business, everything runs in cycles."

"Sid," asked Mike. "Where do you think the market is going from here?"

"I'm very optimistic. I believe that by next summer, the Dow will be at 1,500."

"Hey, Mike and Donna," asked Mary. "How was your trip to Tahoe last weekend?"

"It was pretty good," said Mike. "We didn't win any money gambling, but we had a lot of fun."

"We had the weirdest experience in Placerville, though," said Donna. "We visited this big white house where there were all these New Age seminars. We went into the meditation room upstairs. There was this old man there who claimed that Randy's dad appeared to him and gave him a message about Randy's future. He said that Randy was going to be rich and famous, and he knew a lot about his past life, even though they had never met before. It was amazing!"

Brad Applebaum looked at the others with horror on his face and exclaimed, "People! Don't you realize how dangerous this type of thing is? If Randy plays around with the occult and isn't careful, he might end up demon-possessed!"

"Demon possession?" roared Sid, laughing hysterically. "Demons! DEMON POSSESSION? There is no such thing as demons, buddy boy! That's a bunch of baloney. Haw, haw, haw, haw, haw! Any boob that believes in demons ought to have his head examined."

"But demons *are* real. I read in one of my Christian books about several examples of people that ended up demon-possessed after fooling around with Ouija boards or crystal balls."

"Son," said Mike. "I've been around for a while and have seen many things. I've studied a lot of history, but I've never seen anything to make me believe in a personal red devil with horns and a tail that goes around prodding people with a pitchfork. Neither do I see any evidence of minions of demons.

I've done a lot of magical tricks. All magic has to do with a lot of sleight-of-hand. Everything in the universe has a logical explanation. I have found in my life that the best course is to go down the middle of the road. There are a lot of radical kooks in the world who go off the deep end. On one side are the John Birchers who see a communist conspirator under every rock and are afraid of both Bilderbergers and hamburgers, and on the other side are people like our friend, Eric Burns, who is a flaming Marxist radical who has no respect for our wonderful country of freedom and who foments rebellion against our government."

"But there *is* a communist plot," said Brad. "It consists of some of the Big Boys that want to rule the world. The Bible talks about that conspiracy in Jeremiah, chapter 11. One of the things that the conspirators have done is to promote the teaching of evolution as opposed to the fact that God created the universe in six 24-hour days."

"Hold it, Brad!" snapped Anthony in a crabby voice. "You don't know anything about this at all. Who are you to tell me about these myths?! You have no right to cram this nonsense down my throat! I have studied biology, geology, and chemistry for more than twenty years. You are only nineteen years old and not very smart at science. We scientists *know* the universe came into being through the Big Bang. We know through carbon-14 dating and uniformitarianism that the earth is 4.6 billion years old. We *know* as a *fact* that man evolved from the ape. That little book, the Bible, is a book full of fables like Jonah and the whale and Noah and his little rainstorm."

Brad, who was getting very red in the face, tried the best he could to suppress his anger. "That's not true!" he exclaimed. "The Bible *is* fact! God *did* make the world in six days! There *was* a worldwide Flood! Jesus *did* rise from the dead!"

"Brad, you're not making any sense at all," commented Sid, his dad. "What you're saying doesn't compute."

"You say Jesus rose from the dead," said Anthony, "yet you can't give me any evidence of that. Son, I've studied archeology and the facts concerning The Church of the Holy Sepulcher, the place traditionally thought to be the burial and resurrection site of Jesus. Yet the facts of archeology there don't match up with what the Bible describes as the site of the death and resurrection of Christ. How do you explain that?"

Brad nervously responded, "Well, um, in order to answer that question about the resurrection of Christ, I think I've better talk about the miracle of National Israel first. When Abraham was a hundred years old and Sarah ninety years old, God gave them that miracle baby that he had promised them many years earlier—that child of promise, Isaac. Isaac sired Jacob, and Jacob sired his twelve sons that became the twelve tribes of Israel. There was a great famine, and the Israelites ended up in Egypt where they became slaves for 400 years. They grew to be about two million people, but the Pharaoh oppressed them cruelly in hard labor. And, um, at this point, God raised up Moses who led Israel out of Egypt and into the Promised Land of—"

"Here we go again!" whispered Kimberly to Lisa. "He is like giving this long religious speech."

"Yeah," responded Lisa. "He *lectures* you! He's just like our grandpa!"

"Dude!" said Kimberly. "His rambling on and on is *bor-ing!*"

Brad continued talking. "God gave the Ten Commandments to Israel and warned them that if they disobeyed God, they would be punished severely. You can read about these blessings and curses in Deuteronomy 28. But note this: God promised them that there would come a day when He would restore and bless them forever and ever, prospering them far more than ever before. History underscores these debacles that happened to the Jewish people: first, the division of Judah and the ten northern tribes at the time of King Rehoboam; secondly, the captivity of the ten northern tribes by Assyria in 722 B. C.; and thirdly, the captivity of Judah by King Nebuchadnezzar of Babylon in 586 B. C. Some of the Jews returned to the Land between 538 and 515 B. C. under Zerubbabel where they eventually built the second temple in tumultuous times. Eventually, Jesus, who is their Messiah, came into the world. Yet most of them rejected Him, and He was crucified on that cross. Yet He rose again on that gorgeous Sunday morning. He warned the Jewish nation concerning the terrible days that lay ahead, saying that they would not see Him again until they would say, 'Blessed is He that comes in the name of the LORD.' He warned that not one stone of the temple would remain on another stone that would not be torn down. This was tragically fulfilled in A. D. 70 when the Roman general Titus besieged the city of Jerusalem, resulting in the burning down to the ground of Herod's temple. The country of Israel was no more. And, um, the next 1900 years is a sad history of persecution and rejection of the Jewish people as they were scattered into all the countries of the world. Events like the Crusades, the Pogroms, and the Holocaust under Adolph Hitler are a melancholy testimony to the world's hatred of the Jewish peo—"

"Now hold on, Brad," interrupted Mike. "The Crusades—did you know they were instigated by Christian people?"

"They weren't real Christians, Uncle Mike. They believed in salvation through works instead of the free grace of Jesus."

"And you didn't answer my question about the burial place of Jesus," said Anthony.

"Mike, honey," asked Donna, his wife. "What do you think about this Jesus?"

"I think he was a great teacher, but not God," responded Mike.

"I'm an atheist," declared Anthony. "Nobody can prove to me that God exists."

"I believe in a Supreme Being," said Sid, "but I don't think we can know who He is. There are so many religions in the world with everyone thinking that they are right, but how can we know who is right and who is wrong?"

"I believe in reincarnation," commented Mary. "There are books out there that have strong evidence concerning that."

Harriet lit up a cigarette and said, "I agree. I believe in reincarnation too. We have all experienced the feeling of Déjà vu, the feeling of 'I've been there and done that before, but I can't remember when in this life'—and something else—I had the weirdest dream sometime ago. I dreamed that I was on a covered wagon train going west to California from a Mid-western state. There were a lot of oxen, the pace was very slow, and I was very tired, yet I knew I had to keep moving, even though I didn't want to. Now how do you explain this except that I was on a wagon train in a previous life?"

"Mom," said Brad. "Reincarnation is wrong. The Bible says that there are only two destinies for you after you die—heaven or hell. The Bible also talks about an event called the Rapture when all of us who are saved will be taken up to heaven. Meanwhile, the Master Communist Conspiracy will take over the whole world, and there will be a Superman Dictator that will rule the world for a short time. The Bible says in First Thessalonians 4, verses 16 and 17, 'For the Lord Himself shall descend from heaven, with a shout, with the voice of the archangel, and with the trump of God, and the dead in Christ shall rise first: Then we which are alive and remain shall be caught up together with them in the clouds to meet the Lord in the air: and so shall we ever be with the Lord.' So, how about it, gang? Are you ready for the Rapture? Will you be in the company of the Bride? Or will you be left behind? You can be ready by repenting of your sins and receiving the Lord Jesus Christ as your Sav—"

"That's a bunch of garbage!" retorted Sid. "This is *your* point of view, but what about the viewpoints of the Buddhists? What about the viewpoints of the Hindus? Hey, what about Muhammad? Who is right? We don't know."

"You're not gonna convert me, Brad," added Lisa.

Brad was rendered speechless and sullenly withdrew away from the animated discussion into his bedroom to brood over the less-than-perfect birthday celebration.

4.

MORE OPEN DOORS

Randy woke up on Saturday morning at around 8:00 A. M. and lay there for a while, musing over the events of the previous week. Lila was lying beside him, still asleep. Jack and Tommy were in the living room watching cartoons on TV. A light rain was falling outside; it was going to be a gray day today.

The previous night at the pizza parlor had been very interesting, not so much because of the tips, but rather because of other events not directly related to his honky-tonk piano playing. He had performed especially well and had received a lot of money in tips, namely twenty-five dollars. He had started entertaining at 6:00 and had finished around 10:00. After that, he had sat around with some friends, socializing with them, eating pizza, and drinking beer. The three people he was sitting with were Sam, Donny, and Natalie. The conversation was about topics such as baseball, the upcoming football season, the Watergate Cover-up, and the high prices of food and gas.

"So, Donny," asked Sam. "What's your prognosis on the U. S. economy during the coming year?"

"I think that there'll be slow growth, but no recession. Inflation has been slowing down during the last couple of months."

"I'm kind of worried about the economic outlook," said Randy. "The dollar has been looking shaky, inflation has been bad, interest rates have risen, and the stock market has been just terrible most of the year."

"Well," volunteered Natalie, jokingly. "Maybe there's a way to find out about the future. Did you know that Jeane Dixon uses a crystal ball and an old deck of cards to predict the future? I brought along a crystal ball with me tonight just for laughs. Maybe we can take turns looking into it."

"What a bunch of bunk!" jeered Randy. "You really believe in that fiddle-faddle?"

"Well, Randy! Humor the fat old lady! It's only a game."

"Okay!" mocked Randy. "Everybody close your eyes so that I can sneak a peek in your wallets and purses in order to gain information about you guys so I can impress you with my mind reading skills."

Everyone in the room laughed. Sam was the first one to gaze into the crystal ball. All he saw was a blur. The other two then gazed into the crystal and also saw nothing.

"What's this?" parodied Randy, quoting a line from *The Wizard of Oz.* "I see a little farmhouse with a picket fence. There's a lady wearing a dark dress. Her face is careworn."

Everyone snickered, and the crystal ball was passed to Randy who immediately gazed into it, intending to join in the fun. At first, everything was hazy, but then, he began to see moving images in it. He gasped in surprise.

"What?" asked the others.

"Wow! I see moving images. Wait a minute—I see men with weapons of mass destruction! I see a barren landscape. It looks a little like the Mojave Desert, but the men are definitely not Americans. They are fighting each other! See?" Randy then passed the crystal ball to Donny who looked into it again.

"I don't see anything," he said. "All I see is a great big blur."

The crystal was then passed around to the other two people who glanced into it. Neither of them saw anything out of the ordinary.

"You must be seeing things, Randy," said Sam.

"I'm telling you, it was not my imagination! I really did see images in there."

"None of us saw anything," commented Natalie. "Maybe we're not blessed with that gift like Jeane Dixon is."

They handed the crystal back to Randy who looked into it again. At first, he could see only a blur, but then, images slowly started to take shape. This time, the picture was different. Randy saw what looked like a stage in a large concert hall filled to overflowing with cheering people. Randy gasped. This was *weird! Bizarre!*

"The p-picture has changed!" stammered Randy. "What is this, an LSD trip?!" He went on to describe what he was seeing, and the other three people gawked in wonder.

"Maybe the gift that Jeane Dixon had has rubbed off on you," quipped Natalie.

******

RANDY STIRRED HIMSELF from his reverie and thought about the day's agenda: eat a nice breakfast of bacon and scrambled eggs, watch the ball game on TV, and then, off to the pizza parlor for another night of honky-tonk entertainment. He would—

The telephone rang, and Randy stumbled out of bed and dragged himself in his pajamas toward the kitchen in order to answer it.

"Hello!"

"Hi, Randy! Brian Manning here."

"Yeah. What's up?"

"Well, we really have an emergency here, and I'm going to need you for our gig tonight. In fact, I'll probably be needing you for a bunch of gigs that are coming up. You remember Herb Taylor, our lead singer?"

"Well, yeah. He's the one who had the laryngitis and was going to see the doctor on Wednesday to get it treated."

"It's far worse than that, Randy. When he had it checked on Wednesday, Doctor Perez was very concerned about what he saw and advised him to be checked immediately into John Muir Hospital. They found cancer of the larynx, and he had surgery last night. The doctors removed his voice box."

"Oh, my word!" cried Randy. "That is absolutely terrible, Brian! What is the prognosis for Herb?"

"Well, they are hoping that they got it all. If it hasn't spread, he'll live, but if it comes back, they would give him up to two years to live. Either way, his singing days are over."

"Holy Toledo! Struck down in his prime! It's just too bad. Well, so where's the gig going to be tonight?"

"At the Claremont Hotel in Berkeley for a big dinner in the grand ballroom. We will start our first set at 7:00 P. M. and finish at 11:00 tonight. They're expecting about 500 people, and it's a formal dress-up affair. I want everybody at the hotel, set up, and all ready to rehearse at 5:00 sharp."

This time, Randy was excited over the chance to perform again, even though he had a pang of sadness over Herb Taylor's misfortune.

****

LATER ON THAT DAY, Randy was relaxing in front of the TV set, watching the ball game. He had spent some time that morning practicing his singing and felt he needed a break before the big performance tonight. Nevertheless, it was hard to focus on the game; his mind was on the opportunity to perform in front of hundreds of people tonight. Suddenly, the words, 'SPECIAL REPORT' appeared on the TV screen.

"Interruptions, interruptions!" grumbled Randy.

"We interrupt this program to bring you a special report. War has broken out in the Middle East. Here is International News Editor, Ernest Augustus with more details."

The TV screen showed a picture of soldiers fighting on a desert landscape that looked *exactly like the picture Randy had seen in the crystal ball last night!*

Ernest started his soundbite. "Ladies and gentlemen! Hours ago, war broke out in the Middle East. On this holiest of days on the Jewish calendar, Yom Kippur, Israel is being bombarded. Both Egypt and Syria have attacked Israeli forces on their own lands occupied by the Israelis since the 1967 Six Day War. Egyptian forces have marched into the Sinai Peninsula southwest of Israel, and Syrian forces have attacked on the Golan Heights east of the northern part of Israel. The Jewish state was caught napping—and because it's a high holy day for the Jews, they won't be able to fight back for a few days."

At this point, the picture changed to a close-up view of Jerusalem with its limestone buildings, the Dome of the Rock, and the Mount of Olives in the background.

"Lila! Lila!" cried Randy, excitedly.

"What is it dear?"

"Come here for a minute!"

"Can't right now. I'm busy."

"But honey, this is important!"

"All right," she said as she grumpily plodded into the room. "What's the big deal?"

"War just broke out in the Middle East! Those images that I saw on the TV just now are the exact images I saw in the crystal ball last night."

"Holy cow! That's incredible, dear. I *knew* that there was something funny going on this last week."

Both Randy and Lila were mute for a few moments as they stared at the images on the TV screen. Lila wondered anew at the strange events that had taken place over the last week. Little did she know, she would have much more cause to wonder at the events that would transpire in their lives in the weeks, months, and years that lay ahead. Things were looming that would have a very remarkable and unexpected climax.

****

AT 5:00 P. M., all the members of the group Sneezer were gathered at the big ballroom, all ready for a sound check and a quickie rehearsal before the big performance tonight. Randy's face was flushed with excitement. He was dressed in a natty outfit consisting of a light-blue dress coat, a navy-blue tie, a white dress shirt, and some black slacks. He was wearing well-polished black shoes. The rehearsal went smooth as oil. Randy had another of his songs to try out on the group entitled "The American Dream." Brian and the members of Sneezer liked that song just as they had liked the other two songs, which Randy had received through automatic writing.

At around 6:30, the grand ballroom began to fill up with people who were anticipating an evening of fun and relaxation. They were all sharply dressed—all the men wearing suits and ties, all the women decked out in dazzling dresses and evening gowns, many of which were studded with sparkling jewels. As 7:00 drew near, the ballroom became nearly full. People were deep in small talk. Harry Gates, a big-time popular music impresario, sat down in a seat near the front of the ballroom. He and disc jockey Hiram Quinn were there to scout out possible new talent—they didn't really expect to find any new music star tonight, but they were always keeping their eyes open, 'just in case.' Both men were exhausted and had very bored looks on their faces.

"Hey Hiram," asked Harry Gates. "Do you think we'll hear any real talent tonight?"

"Not likely, Harry," answered Hiram. "I think we'll just hear some more junk like we've been hearing for the last few months: singers who don't have it, rhythm sections that have lousy rhythm, boring songs, corny lyrics, and a dull name for a group."

"Well, I'll tell you one thing, Hiram! If I hear any more ragtime songs played by hack pianists who can't even go four bars without hitting a wrong note, or see any more of those dancing girls with their flimsy outfits, or hear any more of those sopranos that end up going a half step flat, I'm going to scream!"

"Well, Harry. What we need is an act with a gimmick. We need a strong, solid group that will look good on television and hit the young people right where they are. What we need is a singer who has a good image, somebody we can make a star out of."

"You never know, Hiram. We just might run into somebody like that any day now."

The emcee for the evening walked up to the podium, grabbed the microphone, and started speaking, saying, "Ladies and gentlemen, it's great to see you here tonight! I see you're all dressed very nicely. We have a fun evening in store for you and a real musical treat to whet your appetite for the roast pork, red wine, and sexy girls to dance with." (Hearty laughter from the crowd.) "The group of seven you see up on stage right now sing and play a wide variety of musical styles: easy listening, jazz, rhythm and blues, country, and both soft and hard rock-and-roll. Please join me in giving a warm welcome to Brian Manning and the group, SNEEZER!"

The audience clapped politely, and both of the music scouts groaned in exasperation. "Here we go again, Hiram! Another third-rate musical group!"

"Yeah. How they ever came up with a crummy name like Sneezer, I'll never know!"

Randy felt the rush of energy and excitement again. He was nervous yet sensed that he and the rest of the group were going to come through with flying colors tonight. The band started the first piece, "The Age of Aquarius," and Randy, Brian, and Bart started to sing their parts after an eight-bar band intro. Harry and Hiram's ears immediately perked up with interest; here was a group that really had potential, maybe even *star* potential.

"Wow!" whispered Harry. "This band is good!"

"Yeah, Harry. I think we may have found our diamond in the rough. With some polishing up, we might end up with a winner."

"You know, to me, the style of the three singers up there is slightly reminiscent of The Beach Boys, yet there is a unique twist to their sound."

The rest of the 500 people in the ballroom were equally intrigued by the excellent performance of the group. The trio's singing technique was fabulous, the rhythm section was tight and sensitive, and Randy's guitar solos were very well performed. The execution of his guitar riffs was very clean and sensitive. After each song, the audience heartily applauded. The crowd was particularly enamored over the three songs Randy had written. At the end of the evening, the audience gave the group a standing ovation, cheering and whistling franticly. The noisy outburst went on for five minutes, and the group of seven had to take bow after bow. After this, as the group was tearing down their equipment, people in the audience thronged the seven group members with praise and accolades.

"Man, you guys were great!"

"You really have a hot band there!"

"You guys really had it together tonight!"

"You were outta' sight!"

"Sir! I want to congratulate you on your singing and guitar playing!"

"I want to congratulate you on your original songs! You are a genius, sir, *a genius!"*

Presently, Harry Gates approached Brian and Randy and said, "Hi! Let me introduce myself. My name is Harry Gates. I'm a manager who has helped certain singing groups to rise to the top."

"Wow!" exclaimed Randy. "Aren't you the one that helped the group Seven in Heaven make it big?"

"The same one. Listen. I want to talk to you guys for a few minutes."

"Okay, shoot," responded Brian.

"First of all, your band has an excellent sound. It's fresh and unique, it's clean and accurate, and it's expressive! You guys are very accomplished singers, and you carried yourselves with a lot of poise tonight."

"Thank you!" responded Randy and Brian in unison.

"I am especially impressed with the original songs you folks did tonight. The tunes are very fresh and catchy, and they were very well performed. I think your group has potential to go places—maybe even to the big-time. I'll be in contact with you folks in the next several days to explore some fine-tuning ideas so that your band can become top-flight. One thing that is a possibility (now I don't want to get your hopes up too high), but the group, Sha-Na-Na, is going to be performing at the Concord Pavilion in two weeks on Saturday, October 20. I'm looking at the possibility of your band being the opening act. You would be performing for half an hour right before they come on."

"Wow!" exclaimed Randy. "That would really be fantastic! When will you know for sure?"

"Probably between Monday and Wednesday. If it works for you to open for Sha-Na-Na, we'll see where things go from there."

Randy was thrilled as he dictated his home and school phone numbers to Harry. *An opportunity to sing and play on the same program as a world-famous music group! This could be my stepping-stone to riches, fame, a new mansion, a swimming pool, a new grand piano, and all those other things that will bring me real happiness!* As Randy put away his electric guitar in its case and loaded it and the amp into his brown-and-blue station wagon, he felt high as a kite as he anticipated possible days of excitement and opportunities ahead.

****

SUNDAY MORNING was another gray and rainy day in Orinda, California. At 11:00 A. M., people were strolling into The United Church of the Valley, a medium-sized building situated on a hill overlooking that bedroom town. It was shaped like a triangle with the outside walls painted white and the roof paneled with wood painted light blue. The sanctuary could hold about 300 people. The shape of it was like this: the rear part of it was longer than the front while the sides ran in an angle that moved inward. The walls on the sides were mostly stained-glass windows that sloped upward and inward toward the ceiling. The church was interdenominational and liberal in its doctrines. Pastor Kevin Harmon was a dignified and friendly man who was thirty-eight years old and very fat. Randy Miller was the choir director there.

On that morning, the service started with prelude organ music performed by twenty-two-year-old Matthew Langley, a pretty good musician who especially enjoyed music from the baroque and early classical eras. Today, he played the second movement of the Mozart *Sonata Number 7 in C Major* for the prelude. Randy then rose and led the choir in a slow, ponderous 'call to worship' piece in D-flat major. The words went like this: "The Lord is in His holy temple, the Lord is in His holy temple, let all the earth keep quiet, let all the earth keep quiet—"

"WAAAHH, WAAHH, WAAHHH!" resounded throughout the sanctuary. A two-year-old toddler was screaming while his mother was trying to calm him down.

"Quiet, Bret! Be quiet now! We're in the house of God, so hush!"

"Waaah! WAAAH!"

The choir was wearing gorgeous and shiny purple robes. The singers consisted of thirty people ranging in age from seventeen to sixty-eight. They sat down for a few minutes while the church announcements were read, the Apostles' Creed was recited, and the responsorial readings were spoken. After that, the hand bell choir played a beautiful rendition of the hymn, "Take My Life and Let It Be." Then, Randy led the choir in a rather complicated arrangement of "O, For a Thousand Tongues." After this, one of the ladies in the choir sat down at the piano and hacked her way through Bach's "Jesus, Joy of Man's Desiring." She made some very noticeable mistakes, her playing was choppy, and the piece was taken at the tempo of a funeral dirge. The doxology was then sung, and Pastor Harmon made his way to the pulpit to deliver his sermon.

"Yesterday," he began, "a very pivotal and sad event happened in our world. War broke out in the Middle East. Egypt attacked Israeli forces in the Sinai Peninsula, and Syrian forces attacked on the Golan Heights. This needless warfare in our world underscores the hatred that exists among many people groups and is a deterrent to the goal we all long for: World Peace."

"Wah, wah, WAAAAHHH!" cried the little toddler.

"On one side of the conflict are the Jews in Israel who lust after more land for themselves at the expense of the poor Palestinians who are suffering horribly in those crowded, dirty refugee camps. On the other side are the Egyptians and Syrians, many of them being zealous Muslims who won't budge on their religious beliefs. When are we on Spaceship Earth going to learn how to live with one another in peace and harmony, no matter what our nationality, race, economic status, or religion? When are we on Spaceship Earth going to embrace the Universal Fatherhood of God and the Universal Brotherhood of Man, whether we're a Jew, Christian, Muslim, Buddhist, Hindu—or an atheist?"

"WAAAHHHH! AAAUUUGGH! WAAAAHHHHH!"

"We must learn to cooperate with each other. We, who are fortunate with riches here in the West, must learn to share our goods with the poor, starving people who are living in other underprivileged countries. Spaceship Earth faces a lot of perils today: the peril of starvation on Planet Earth, the peril of the limited supplies of vital natural resources on Planet Earth like oil and natural gas that we are quickly running out of, the peril of the population explosion, the peril of conflicting political ideologies, the peril of air and water pollution, the peril of the extinction of many species of fish, birds, and wild animals, and worst of all, the peril of the extinction of the whole human race through thermonuclear war."

"WAAAHHH! MOMMY! WAAAHHHH!" The piercing cries of the toddler stood in sharp contrast to the staid, semi-monotone preaching of Pastor Kevin Harmon.

"There's a kid's story that Dr. Seuss wrote with a great lesson for the world today. It's about a north-going Zax and a south-going Zax. One day, they run into each other. The north-going Zax said, 'I'm not budging because I always go north!' The other Zax said, 'I'm not budging to the right or to the left because I always go south.' So, neither one budged, and eventually, a highway was built right over them! Ladies and gentlemen, our plight in the world today is much like those obstinate Zax—a lot of people on Spaceship Earth just plain won't compromise their political or religious views for the good of mankind. A lot of people—"

"WAH! WAAAHHH! MOM-MY!"

"SHUT UP, BRET!"

The angry voice of the toddler's mother reverberated through the entire church and woke up the people who were dozing or daydreaming. Some people were indignant while others grew red in the face trying to suppress their laughter.

"What does that lady think she's doing?"

"Oh boy, what a mean mother!"

"This is outrageous—and in the temple of God!"

"No manners at all!"

"What she did shows no class!"

Pastor Kevin continued his dry, unemotional sermon on World Peace, quoting the story in the book of Luke about the rich young ruler who wouldn't give up all of his wealth, relating that passage of Scripture to conditions in the world today—the West had an overabundance of material goods while millions of children were starving in Africa. Nevertheless, only a few people were still able to concentrate on the pastor's message because of the distraction of the mother with her noisy two-year-old kid. Finally, the sermon was over, and Pastor Harmon gave the benediction.

"May the Lord bless you! May the Lord keep you! May the Lord shine His love upon you this week! The Lord be with you, the Lord who knows us better than we know ourselves! Go in peace and have one heck of a good week!"

Matthew Langley broke into the lively Bach *Fugue in F Minor*, playing it on the organ for the postlude as the people began to chat with each other and shake hands while they headed toward the narthex. Randy made a beeline for Pastor Kevin because he had some very pressing issues on his mind. The pastor was at one of the doors in the back of the sanctuary, greeting people, making comments on the early rains in the San Francisco Bay Area, and how well the Oakland A's had played that year while he was kissing little babies on their cheeks.

"Pastor, could I have a few minutes with you?"

"Well, yes. What's going on?"

Randy related his strange experiences of the last week: the trip to Lake Tahoe, the meeting with the pudgy old man in Placerville, the appearance of the departed spirit of his dad, the strange nighttime experiences when he had blacked out and then awakened to find completed new songs staring him right in the face, and finally, the two successful gigs: the one on Wednesday night, and the one last night.

"So, this is my story, Pastor," said Randy. "I don't know what to make of it. What do you think about all of this?"

"This is all very interesting—oh, hi there, Charlie!" said Pastor Kevin to an older white-haired man. "How's your barbershop in Berkeley doing these days?"

"Just fine, Pastor Kevin. Just fine! Great sermon!"

The pastor turned his attention back to Randy and said, "This is indeed interesting. I would like to discuss this with you in more depth when I have more time. Could you call my secretary to make an appointment with me for later on this week?"

"Well, Pastor, it will have to be sometime late in the afternoon. I'm the choral teacher at Campolindo High School, you know."

"I'm sure that won't be a problem. Give my secretary a call early tomorrow morning."

"Righto!"

And with that, Randy, Lila, and the two boys piled into the station wagon for the short ride home to eat lunch and watch TV.

****

ON THAT SAME MORNING, Hal Odell, Brad Applebaum, John Patterson, Peter Thal, and close to 500 other worshippers were sitting in the sanctuary at Berkeley Tabernacle Fellowship, avidly enjoying the choir, special offertory solo, and the preaching of Pastor David Maxwell. Berkeley Tabernacle Fellowship was a fairly large non-denominational church in the northern part of Berkeley near Shattuck Avenue. The outside of the building was built of stone painted a light-pink color. It was a two-story edifice with the sanctuary and the fellowship hall on the first floor and the Sunday school rooms on the second floor. The church had started out with a congregation of fifteen in 1952, but the membership had mushroomed to the place where it was today. The building was fairly new, having been built in 1969. The church was fundamentalist and very conservative in its Biblical and moral tenets. There was a large and skilled choir of 110 people led by an excellent minister of music, Cameron Lindsay. Pastor David Maxwell was a twenty-seven-year-old man with blonde hair and blue eyes. He was five feet, ten inches tall and was both slender and athletic. His preaching style was both dynamic and systematic, and he was concise and well informed on his subject matter. He was outspoken and uncompromising when it came to the doctrinal truths of the Bible.

On this morning, the choir started the service out by singing several songs that consisted of up to six-part vocal harmony. After that, a lady sang a solo piece composed by Ralph Carmichael. The song was well received by the congregation with many "amens." At this point, Pastor David walked on over to the pulpit to give his message for the day. He opened the Bible to Genesis, chapter 12.

He said, "'Now the LORD had said unto Abram, Get thee out of thy country, and from thy kindred, and from thy father's house, unto a land that I will show thee; And I will make of thee a great nation, and I will bless thee, and make thy name great, and thou shalt be a blessing; And I will bless them that bless thee, and curse them that curseth thee, and in thee shall all families of the earth be blessed.' Folks! This is the cornerstone Scripture that reveals God's eternal plan for National Israel—and these promises are unconditional and unbreakable. These words are totally relevant to the war in the Middle East that has just broken out."

The pastor gave a history of the birth of National Israel, their slavery in Egypt, their exodus into Israel, the giving of the Law, their breaking the Law, the terrible disasters that befell them during the centuries, and their miraculous preservation and restoration.

"The return of the Jews back to the Land began during the nineteenth century. By 1871, a few Jews lived in Israel, and by 1881, about 25,000 Jewish settlers resided there. In 1897, Theodore Herzl called the first Zionist congress together where the idea of bringing the Jews back to Palestine was formally stated. Then came the Balfour Declaration of November 2, 1917 that endorsed the plans of the Jews to settle back in the Land. By the way, if you're having trouble remembering the name of this declaration, I have the perfect solution for you. Imagine with me that there's a game between the Oakland A's and the Baltimore Orioles. The A's are up and the bases are loaded. Joe Rudi is at bat and Reggie Jackson is on third. There are two outs and the count is three balls and two strikes. The pitcher for the Orioles winds up and throws the ball high and outside. The umpire calls 'Ball four!' This means Reggie Jackson can walk home. In the same way, the Balfour Declaration said to the Jews, 'You can go home now!'"

Hearty laughter erupted from the congregation due to this wry analogy.

"Unfortunately, the British leaders were tempted by greed and imperialistic lust and reneged on their promises. The discovery of vast amounts of oil in several countries in the Middle East was too enticing. Nevertheless, by 1939, 400,000 Jews had managed to return to the Promised Land. Meanwhile, Hitler would soon murder about six million of them.

"Then came May 14, 1948, when the State of Israel was born. This new state was comprised of 650,000 Jews and many hundreds of thousands of Arabs. On May 15, 1948, Egypt, Jordan, Saudi Arabia, Lebanon, Iraq, and Syria launched a major massed attack against Israel to try to destroy the new nation. Israel could field an army of only 18,000 men against the huge, well equipped, and well-trained Arab armies. (Many of the men in Israel's piddly army didn't even have a weapon.) Nevertheless, the Israelis were miraculously victorious in that war, and by the time of the ceasefire on January 7, 1949, Israel had increased the size of her land from 5,000 square miles to 8,000 square miles, including much of the Negev. There's an interesting story concerning this war of how Mother Nature seemed to fight on the side of Israel. When the enemy approached Tel Aviv, swarms of bees from the groves east of the Jewish agricultural settlement of Petah Tikva attacked the Arab armies. Petah Tikva means 'Door of Hope.' My interpretation of this event is that God sent His angels to give some 'bee vitamins' to benefit the small army of Israel."

Hilarious laughter erupted again from the attentive congregation.

"I guess you folks don't need any more Geritol vitamin pills from Lawrence Welk! You are obviously wide awake this morning!" (More guffaws from the crowd.) "Going from the ridiculous to the sublime, sickness paralyzed Lebanese and Syrian forces in the area of Galilee, and Egyptian forces surrendered because they swore they were surrounded by a large army.

"In October 1956, the Israeli army easily overran the Gaza Strip. Then came the Six Day War on June 5, 1967, when Israeli jets destroyed the Egyptian air force and Israeli torpedo boats and commandos devastated most of Egypt's naval power. Arab forces and Nasser had been itching to wipe Israel off the map for a while, and Egypt had blockaded the Israeli port of Eilat on the Gulf of Aqaba. Finally, Israel felt it had no choice but to attack first. The war was an overwhelming victory for the Jews. Instead of decimating Israel, the Arabs suffered a great defeat. The United Nations initially had little interest in the war plans of the Israeli and Arab armies. But when Israel was routing the Arab armed forces, it called for an immediate cease-fire, something Israel refused to accede to. Communist Russia was supplying arms to the enemies of Israel, a decision that country would live to regret. Meanwhile, Israel occupied the city of Jerusalem for the first time in 1900 years. They also increased their land size from 8,000 square miles to 34,000 square miles and doubled their population. On the third day of the war, General Moshe Dayan walked up to the Wailing Wall in Old Jerusalem and declared to the world that 'The Jews have returned to their Holy of Holies, never to retreat again.'

"Along with these military victories during the last twenty-five years is the fantastic economic and agricultural growth going on in that country today. At this present time, Israel is discovering its boundless mineral resources—one of them being potash. This mineral is a potent fertilizer that could help stave off world famine. There is also enough steam trapped under the faults of Israel to supply a huge amount of electricity. Even now, Israel is becoming tremendously prosperous—all the more remarkable when you consider the fact that just one hundred years ago, it was a desolate desert waste. It is all the more mind-boggling when you consider all the attempts to wipe out the Jew that have transpired over the centuries. In addition to all of this, the Hebrew language has been miraculously restored during this century. No other language in history has ever died out and then been revived. Another uncanny thing is the huge increase in rainfall in Israel over the last century.

"I want to digress for a moment and read a passage from Zechariah 8: 23 that says, 'Thus saith the LORD of hosts; In those days it shall come to pass, that ten men shall take hold out of all languages of the nations, even shall take hold of the skirt of him that is a Jew, saying, We will go with you: for we have heard that God is with you.'

"Listen, folks! The fame of Harry Morgan, John Lennon, and Jim Palmer may fade away. Future famous celebrities will rise and fall. But according to this Scripture, there is coming a day when the Jews will be the famous stars of the world with Jesus being the biggest star of them all!

"So now, gang, how does all of this history apply to us today? I would submit to you that National Israel shall live and not die! How do I know this? Simply, by the Word of God that cannot lie! We can expect that God, who never sleeps or slumbers, will protect Israel in this war just like He has protected them in the past. Remember Gideon and his 300 men who defeated a Midianite army of 135,000 soldiers? God has saved Israel before and He will do it again!"

At this point, the pastor segued smoothly into an invitation time when one person received Christ. After that, Pastor David gave the benediction after which the pianist and organist played a duet of a lively arrangement of "Joyful, Joyful, We Adore Thee" for the postlude. Animated, friendly conversations broke out among the people as some of them lingered for a little time of fellowship. Some of them walked up to congratulate Pastor David on his excellent and well-researched message while others headed toward the foyer and the parking lot. Brad Applebaum headed toward the choir director, Cameron Lindsay, to say "Hi!"

"Boy, Mr. Lindsay, that sure was a great message, wasn't it? I really liked the part when Dave shared from Ezekiel 37 about the dry bones, you know, 'De' toe bone connected to de'—foot bone. De' foot bone connected to de'—leg bone. De' leg bone connected to de'—tummy bone. De' tummy bone connected to de'—throat bone. De' throat bone connected to de'—mouth bone. De' mouth bone connected to de'—nose bone. De' nose bone connected to de'—eye bone. De' eye bone connected to de'—brain bone. Now hear de' Word of de'—"

"Cool it, Brad," sighed Cameron in a tired and slightly disgusted voice. "That's not even close to being the right lyrics in that spiritual, you know."

A radiant young college girl was standing nearby. Pam Jackson was twenty years old, five feet, five inches tall, and had shoulder-length brown hair and sparkling hazel eyes that had a lovely glow in them. She had a friendly, bubbly, and vibrant personality, was very excited and zealous about the things of God, and she had a very musical laugh. She had known the Lord for four years, having been saved and healed from painful arthritis at a Kathryn Kuhlman crusade. She was in her third year at UC Berkeley and was majoring in vocal performance as well as studying applied piano. Brad Applebaum had a strong crush on Pam; her extreme outward beauty combined with her love for the Lord was very attractive to him.

"Hi, Pammypoo!" he said, reaching out to shake her hand. "It sure is a nice day, ain't it?"

"Hi, Brad," she replied, rather coolly.

"Boy, that sure was a good message today! Maybe I'll write a novel on end-time Bible prophecy someday. Hey Pammypoo. What are you doing Friday night? I wanna' take you out to dinner at the Square Rigger! Good ole'

Braddy, the baddy daddy, can give you a real hot time! How about it? C'mon! We'll paint the town red!"

"Brad," said Pam, coolly. "I'm not really interested in a romantic relationship with anybody right now. I consider you to be one of my friends—nothing else—and I don't like being called 'Pammypoo!' Please just call me Pam."

"Please, Pam! I really think that you are a foxy chick. I—"

"Look Brad! I told you I'm not interested—so lay off! Otherwise, I may have to belt you one!"

"Okay, okay! I'm sorry I called you 'Pammypoo!' I guess I'm just a no-good, stupid moron!"

Crestfallen and a little sullen, Brad walked away. Obviously, the idea of a romantic relationship with Pam was only a pipedream.

****

ERIC BURNS, Ted Johnson, and Scott Williams were meeting at a sleazy bar in Berkeley that afternoon, discussing plans for the upcoming Red Riding Rangers meetings as well as current world events.

"What do you think of the new war in the Middle East?" prodded Eric.

"Man, I don't think it's any big deal," said Scott. "It's jest' a little fightin' ovah' a piece of dinky dirt. In three months, de' world will have forgotten all about it."

"I disagree with Scott," countered Ted. "I believe this war is very important. We will probably see an Arab oil embargo, gas lines, a second Great Depression, and even starvation in America and around the world."

"I think you're right, Ted," said Eric. "And all of this will help to bring the Revolution here to usher in a Soviet America. This is a good thing; the blood bath must happen for the ultimate good of society. And besides that, it will also help to curb the population explosion in this world. This is also a big reason why *Roe-v.-Wade,* which the Supreme Court ruled on this year on January 22, is a good thing. Legalizing abortion is a good way to limit the size of families."

Ted asked, "So who do you think will win this war, Eric?"

"There's no doubt about the outcome, Ted. Israel doesn't stand a chance. Their army is small and inexperienced, they were attacked by huge armies while they were asleep at the wheel, and the Soviet Union has every intention to help the Arab Bloc countries."

"You know what is interesting to me, Eric, is how the Middle East has become the center of world attention in the last twenty-five years," said Ted. "For one thing, the U. S. is relying more and more on Middle East oil to fill up our gas tanks. We now have an energy crisis that is hitting America and the rest of the world. Gas stations across the board are shutting down while fuel prices are rising significantly. Oil wells in the U. S. aren't pumping nearly

60

enough oil, and there is not much exploration going on to try to find alternative sources of energy."

"The silver lining on that cloud is that this will help to curb air pollution," said Eric.

Ted continued his information blitz. "At any rate, while this deficit in our oil reserves worsens, we are relying more and more on the Middle East for our energy needs. In 1972, we imported 29 percent of our oil, much of it from Canada and Venezuela, but it is estimated that by 1980, we will have to import roughly 50 percent of our oil from the Middle East. Much of it will come from Saudi Arabia, estimated to hold about 30 percent of the world's oil reserves. This new war in the Middle East is a real danger to our oil supplies. Ronald Schiller's article in the January 1973 article of *Reader's Digest,* 'It's Time to Face the Energy Crunch,' warned that we face dire consequences if the Arab Bloc decides to cut off oil supplies to the West. Meanwhile, William Griffith wrote in the July 1973 *Reader's Digest* article, 'Crisis in Middle East Oil,' that there was a constant threat of the war we are seeing unravel before our very eyes. He pointed out the hostility between Israel and the Arab confederacy over the territories Israel conquered in the 1967 Six Day War, especially the conquest of the Golan Heights. Israel wants to hang onto those territories while the Arabs want them back. He said another threat is the anti-American sentiment among many Arabs. Even King Faisal of Saudi Arabia, for the most part a friend of America, doesn't like the U. S. support for Israel. Meanwhile, Quaddafi of Libya has used his money to finance Palestinian terrorism."

"This Arab terrorism is a very interesting thing, Ted," said Eric. "Let me talk about the radical Shi'ite Muslim Arabs for a moment. They are a little misguided in their worship of their false god, Allah, but they have many good points that we communists around the world can take a lesson from. They are fully committed to their cause, they have a sense in their actions that 'the end justifies the means' when they use violence and kill their 'infidel enemies' of Islam, and they have a righteous hatred of the Zionist cause just like we do here in the Red Riding Rangers. Many of the radical Palestinians also embrace communist doctrines. If the radical Muslims would learn that there is no God, they would be practically in agreement with what I espouse.

"On the other hand, we have those warmonging capitalistic pigs in Israel who are just like Lyndon B. Johnson who started the Vietnam War, and that tyrant, Nixon, who mercilessly attacked the Viet Cong with his ruthless bombing attack against Hanoi last December."

"Yeah, Nixon is a strange one," said Scott. "He don't know whetha' it's hot or cold. I hear he rams up de' air conditionin' to sixty-eight degrees while sittin' in front of a roarin' fire in de' ole' 'zecutive office. He ain't got no social skill."

"And he's wrecking this whole country with his support of Israel," said Ted. "The Arab Bloc isn't going to like this and will surely cut off our oil supplies. We have to realize that the Arab countries are growing exponentially in their financial clout. Saudi Arabia, for example, will hit the top spot in oil production within the next few years. When that happens, that desert land, with over five million people, will acquire tremendous wealth. Her oil reserves, about $4 billion today, will soar to $20 billion by 1980. Meanwhile, Saudi Arabia has $3.2 billion tucked away in foreign banks that will probably zoom to $30 billion by 1983. With more money flowing into its coffers than it can spend, that Arab country's leverage will be worldwide in scope. Saudi Arabia will then have the power to buy or sell major American companies at will. If the Arabs don't invest in the United States, our billions of dollars we pay to them for our oil will play havoc with our balance of payments. Moreover, with this new wealth, the Arabs will be in a position to suddenly dump billions of dollars into the international money markets, possibly wrecking the standing of the U. S. dollar."

"Those super-rich Arabs need to be corralled and contained," declared Eric. "The day must soon come when we will have a Communist Middle East."

Scott asked, "So you think Israel is doomed even dough' dey've' won a couple of wars in de' past?"

"Lucky flukes!" opined Eric. "They have to hit a brick wall sometime, and some of them think that 'Gawd Almighty' will help them. They're DEAD WRONG! I know that all religion, whether Christianity, Judaism, Buddhism, or whatever, is a big hunk of junk! It is concocted by mankind so that they can have false comfort in a fairy tale afterlife that doesn't even exist. People buy that phony baloney so that they won't have to face the reality that when you die, that's it! It's nothingness forever and ever. What this means is that the only hope for the world is communism. Heaven and hell? —They are right here on earth! Heaven is communism, and hell is living out in the cold ice of Siberia; sick, covered with sores, and starving to death!"

Eric lit up a cigarette and continued, "I'm going to say it again; this war can only help the communist cause. It will wreck the economy in the U. S. and Europe, and in the ensuing chaos, we communists will take over the world. Even now, things are on the brink of collapse! Marriages are falling apart, adultery and premarital sex are on the rise, and the divorce rate is sky high. *This is a very good thing.* Our communist leaders have always said that a good way to take over a country is to go to the young people, get them interested in trivial things, sports and sex, and bang, the next thing you know, you got them!"

Eric took a sip of brandy as Scott changed the subject, saying, "You know, Eric, your speech was great on Friday night, but I think dat' it was too long. You rambled on and on and your topics became disjointed. You need to cut it by half."

"What do you know, Scott? I have a lot of intelligence, and you are just a little hick garage worker with not much brains. I think I had good reason to get a little carried away. Sometimes, the truth of communism needs to be drummed into people's ears."

****

ON MONDAY MORNING, Randy was teaching the a cappella choir, practicing a baroque piece of music entitled "Sanctus." Ray Palmer was whispering something to his friend, Greg Darrow.

"You've better cut it out, Palmer," ordered Randy, "or there's gonna be trouble—in River City!"

They resumed rehearsing the anthem, Randy stopping them at various times to give the choir or certain individuals some bits of constructive criticism, things like, "You're flat, sopranos!" or, "Why so tight, Todd? Loosen up your throat and just yawn into the sound."

Ray and Greg resumed their conversation.

"All right, Palmer! I'm warning you for the last time! If you don't stop talking, I'm gonna have to order you to go outside!"

Soon, the two culprits started whispering again, and Randy ordered them to leave the room.

The telephone in the inner cubicle rang, and Randy excused himself for a couple of minutes.

"Hello?"

"Hello, Randy! Harry Gates here!"

"Yeah, what's up?" asked Randy, roller coaster type excitement leaping up on the inside of his gut.

"I've got good news for you. Your band is invited to open for the group, Sha-Na-Na, on Saturday, the 20th. You guys will be on at 4:30 for a half hour before the main act comes on. Hopefully, the weather will be nice at the Concord Pavilion so that we will be able to have a large crowd. There will be a first-rate sound system for you guys so you don't have to bring anything except your musical instruments. You'll need to be at the Pavilion at about 9:00 A. M. to get everything relating to the sound and musical selections sorted. You, Brian, and I need to get together to hash out some things concerning your group. Would it be possible to meet me in my office, say, at 10:00 on Wednesday morning?"

"Well, Harry, I teach choir during the day. I'll try to get a substitute for that day so that I can make it. I'll get back to you as soon as I can."

"Good. Call me as soon as possible. My number is (415)-458-9666. I'm very excited about the possibilities here."

"Me too, Harry! Goodbye now!"

"Goodbye!"

Randy went back into the rehearsal, but he had a lot of trouble concentrating on the choir; his mind was on the upcoming chance to open up a concert for a famous rock-and-roll group.

****

LATER ON THAT DAY, Randy was sitting in the office of Pastor Kevin Harmon, describing to him the details that had transpired in his life during the last ten days. He had gotten his appointment with the pastor for 5:00 on Monday afternoon. The wall was covered with yellow-white wallpaper.

"So, Pastor Kevin," concluded Randy. "This is where things stand right now. What do you make of all of this? Are these experiences for real or am I losing my marbles?"

"This is all very interesting," responded the pastor. "God works in mysterious ways. There have been experiences throughout the history of mankind that don't seem to have any logical explanation. Sometimes, people have had encounters with silhouettes that claimed to be a dead mother, father, uncle, or aunt, and the messages these beings gave ended up coming true. There are people who have had encounters with UFOs that cannot be scientifically explained. There are occurrences right and left around the world of ESP and telepathy. Dr. Rhine, the director of the Parapsychology Laboratory, has done some very fascinating and convincing studies in these areas."

"So what do you think I should do about it, Pastor?"

"Randy, I would go for it. I think God has given you a gift encompassing not just music, but also some latent supernatural powers that reside deep inside of you. My suggestion is that you get involved with this group of men who can help unleash the full potential of your powers and help you to go places. These men are part of a group called The Royal Order of the Blue Knights. I'll give you the number of the person who can help to connect you to these people."

"Is this the same as the Royal Order of Water Buffaloes in *The Flintstones?*"

"Pretty similar."

"So you think that this 'club' could help me go far in the music racket?"

"Randy. If you play your cards right, I believe you will end up being another Elvis Presley—or another Chuck Berry!"

****

AT 10:00 ON WEDNESDAY MORNING, Randy Miller, Brian Manning, and Hiram Quinn were sitting in the plush, yellow-green office of music impresario Harry Gates. It was located on Shattuck Avenue in the middle of downtown Berkeley. Automobile traffic and honking horns could be heard dimly in the background. Harry Gates was a very fastidious man. He was sharply dressed in a black suit with a red tie, his office was immaculately clean, and his desk was very neat and well organized. The office was very bright and cheery.

"First of all," began Harry, "I want to again congratulate you people in the band for a great show on Saturday night. You have a great and unique sound. Randy, your singing and guitar playing were outstanding, and your original songs were also terrific. The audience was enthralled with you guys."

"Thank you," responded Randy, meekly.

"I think there are real possibilities of you guys going places," continued Harry. "But there are some areas that will have to be fine-tuned, some of them even before the Concord Pavilion concert. One thing that has to change right away is the name of your group. 'Sneezer' is simply not going to cut the mustard. Let's brainstorm this area right now and see what we can come up with."

They thought for a few minutes until Randy finally suggested, "Maybe we could call our group 'Clouds of Silver.' That would work a lot better than 'Sneezer' would."

"Well, that's better, but still not catchy enough."

"Maybe 'Music Universal?'" queried Brian.

"Naw, not quite."

"How about 'Universal Mind?'" asked Randy.

"Well, now you're in the ballpark. Let's play around with this."

Randy mused, "Well, um, 'Musical Universal Mind,' —um, 'Mindset Musical,' —um, 'The Musical Mindset,' —Wait! I've got it! How about 'The Universal Mindset?' BINGO!"

"Zowie!" exclaimed Harry. "That's it! That's what will grab today's crowd! I like it! The name has zing, the name has life, and the name is up-to-date! We'll use it!"

The other people assented vocally to the name change.

"The second thing," continued Harry, "is that we're going to have to come up with stylish and uniform outfits for your group. Your suits that you guys wore on Saturday night were very natty and classy, but they were disjointed and old-school."

The group hashed out some ideas for a little while until Hiram Quinn asked, "I've got an idea. How about black suits, gray dress shirts, and yellow ties?"

"Yeah, Hiram. I like it! I like it!" exclaimed Harry. "We'll get to work on that in the next couple of weeks. My other goals will be to refine the stage presence of your group as well as working toward the goal of having all original songs in your group. Do you guys think you can come up with some hot original music in the next several weeks?"

"Well, I hope so," said Randy. "I'll give it my best shot."

"We'll give it the old college try," agreed Brian.

"If you can come up with some more hot, original music, it will really help you to get into the big-time. We're looking at concert tours all over the

United States and Great Britain at huge concert halls and stadiums, LP recordings, and spots on radio and TV broadcasts."

****

"THIS IS NBC NEWS coming to you tonight! Here is news anchor, Chad Baer, with top stories from around the world!"

"Good evening!" said Chad Baer over the TV screens of America. "On the national scene tonight, Vice President Spiro Agnew announced his resignation today due to accusations of dishonesty and criminal activity. Agnew has been accused of accepting bribes as well as falsifying his federal tax returns. Agnew has pleaded *nolo contendere* to the second charge. His replacement for vice president—"

Mike Applebaum was relaxing in front of the TV set on Wednesday evening after a hard day of teaching history at Campolindo High School. A couple of his students, Ray Palmer and Greg Darrow, were missing from his fifth period U. S. history class—they were in trouble with the principal because of an act of terrorism during the lunch period. A large crowd of students were eating lunch in the multi-purpose room and chattering away just like they did on any normal day, when suddenly, there was a shout at one of the exit doors.

"EVERYBODY, STAY WHERE YOU ARE! WE GOT ALL THE DOORS COVERED! WE ARE THE NAUGHTY KNIGHTS OF THE BLACK BARON, AND WE ARE HERE TO BOTHER YOU, YOU FREAKS!"

The next thing everyone knew, a terrible stench permeated the whole multi-purpose room as well as some harmless, but uncomfortable wisps of smoke. Ray Palmer, Greg Darrow, and two other high school troublemakers had detonated a very smelly stink bomb! Coughs and cries of "EEEEEEWWWWWW!" reverberated through the cafeteria as many students expressed their discomfort at the sudden fumes and stench.

"Haw, haw, haw!" exclaimed Ray. "We have a serious gas shortage in our world today, and we four students have just solved it! There's enough gas in this room to fill up every car in the U. S.!"

Groans erupted from the student body while the other three terrorists were bowled over with laughter.

Mike couldn't help chuckling over the whole incident. He had some trouble teaching his fifth period history class. It was hard trying to concentrate on things like Manifest Destiny or the U. S.-Mexican war of the 1840s because of the humorous trick of the pranksters. The phone rang, and Mike sauntered over to the kitchen to answer it.

"Hello."

"Hi, Mike. This is Randy. I've got great news! It looks like I'm on my way to Easy Street! Guess what! I'm going to be opening for the rock group, Sha-Na-Na, a week from Saturday at the Concord Pavilion! Isn't that great?"

"That's wonderful, Randy. I'm glad for you. I have some advice, though. 'Don't count your chickens before they hatch.' This might be a big open door or it might amount to nothing at all. I would say, keep it cool and steady."

"I'll try, Mike, but it's hard to keep from being excited about this opportunity."

They talked for a while about various things: choir, U. S. history, the Watergate Cover-up, the Agnew scandal, and the war in the Middle East. Eventually they hung up, and Mike went back to watching the NBC news.

****

ON FRIDAY, October 12, the twelve Christian 'revolutionists' were gathered together for another Bible study led by Hal Odell. The topic today had to do with Pastor David Maxwell's sermon of last Sunday.

"So, tell me, guys," prodded Hal. "What is your take on Genesis, chapter 12, concerning God's promises to Abraham to bless the world through him and his descendants?"

"Well," volunteered Brad. "Abraham went into Israel in faith and obedience to God's call, a land that was then occupied by heathen nations. At the age of one hundred, his barren wife, Sarah, bore him a son named Isaac. Isaac went on to marry Rebekah who bore him Jacob. One of Jacob's sons, Joseph, had a couple of prophetic dreams when he was a teenager. Jacob gave Joseph a coat of many colors because Joseph was Jacob's favorite son. Joseph's brothers were very envious of him and sold him to a caravan that was on its way to Egypt. Joseph landed in the house of Potiphar who was an officer of the Pharaoh and captain of the guard. The Lord was with Joseph in Egypt—he was faithful in everything that he did, and the Lord blessed the house of Potiphar. The time came when Potiphar's wife tried to entice Joseph to have sex with her, and when he resisted temptation she accused him of trying to rape her. This landed Joseph in jail. After this, Pharaoh had two dreams that Joseph correctly interpreted as referring to seven years of prosperity that would be followed by seven years of horrible famine. At this point, Joseph was exalted to be the ruler over Egypt, second only to Pharaoh himself. Joseph was in charge of storing away food to be used during the coming bad years. In the second year of this dearth, Joseph and his brothers met each other again in Egypt."

"You know," said John Patterson. "I cry every time I read this account in the Bible. It is such a beautiful story of reconciliation."

"It seems to me," added Bill Mitchell, "that from what Pastor David said last Sunday, this whole account of Joseph and his brothers has a prophetic parallel, which will be fulfilled in the future, relating to the Jews, and even to the nations."

"Right you are, Bill!" exclaimed Hal.

"This is all so rich!" said Brad. "I just wish that my parents could understand the Bible for themselves instead of spending all that time reading their horoscopes!"

****

THE NEXT TEN DAYS were very eventful for the U. S. and the world. On October 11, Syria suffered defeat in the Golan Heights. On October 12, Nixon announced his plan of 'Operation Nickel Grass,' an airlift of arms and supplies to Israel after the USSR had sent arms to Syria and Egypt. On the 16th, there were victories for Israel in Egypt as well as OPEC deciding to raise oil prices by 70 percent to $5.11 a barrel, the beginning of the Arab Oil Embargo on the 17th, Nixon's call for $2.2 billion in aid for Israel on the 19th, and Libya's response in cutting off all shipments of oil to the U. S., and Saudi Arabia and all the other Arab countries following suit on the 20th. Israel was experiencing surprising success in the Yom Kippur War. They had an army no larger than 300,000 with every man mustered against the combined armies of more than 1,200,000 troops from fourteen enemy nations. Yet, they were giving a beating to these much larger armies. Eric Burns was raving over the victories of the "Jewish capitalistic pigs!"

Meanwhile, Randy and the erstwhile Sneezer group continued to perform at different venues. There was the gig at the Masonic Lodge in Vallejo on Friday, October 12; the Blue Moon Night Club in San Francisco on Saturday, the 13th; a party on Treasure Island on Sunday, the 14th; the Black Ace Night Club on the 17th; and a dinner party and dance in San Francisco on Friday, the 19th. Everywhere that The Universal Mindset performed at was a great success. Randy had received two new songs in his trance states. One of them was entitled, "The Devil's Dilemma."

5.

ONWARD AND UPWARD

Saturday, October 20, was a mostly sunny day with temperatures peaking in the high sixties. It promised to be a perfect day for the concert at the Concord Pavilion. All of the members of The Universal Mindset as well as the famous rock band, Sha-Na-Na, were at the Pavilion at 9:00 A. M. sharp. The roadies for Sha-Na-Na were busy hauling speakers and monitors to the stage and the soundboard to an area about two thirds of the way toward the back of the Pavilion. Meanwhile, the members of The Universal Mindset were busy setting up the electric Rhodes piano, the guitars and bass guitar, and Mark Dole's drum kit.

By noon, everything was set up, and the vocalists and instrumentalists began to test their microphones and levels of all of the instruments. Various commands of the singers and sound technician reverberated through the concert venue.

"Check! Check, check! One, two, three, check! Bring mike 1 down in volume! Check, check! Bring mike 2 up a scotch!" High feedback rings. "OW! Mike 4 is way too loud! Check, check, checkmate! I'm not getting anything on mike 6! Check the patch cord, please!"

Finally, the sound levels were close enough to ideal for the group, Sha-Na-Na, to do a sound check. They practiced several hard rock songs, making adjustments as they went. The singers belted out their parts, the drums clanged, the bass guitar boomed out its low-pitched notes, the piano banged out its rock-and-roll eighth note triads in the medium-high registers, and the electric guitars screamed out their distortion solos. It took a while for everything to come together, but they finally tweaked everything to their satisfaction, and the group, The Universal Mindset, was able to do their sound check at about 3:30 P. M. Things went fairly smoothly, and at about four, the fans of Sha-Na-Na were able to start trickling into the Pavilion. Harry Gates had a last-minute debriefing with the members of The Universal Mindset to discuss the schedule of songs for their half hour set.

"Now," he began. "Here's the scoop, gang. I would like you to open the program with Randy's tune, 'The Evil Eye.' After that, you'll do 'The Age of Aquarius.' Next on the agenda will be 'Just like Creamy Silk' by Randy. After that, 'The Devil's Dilemma.' Following that, I think a good song would be your song, Brian, 'Blue Love.' Next will be 'The American Dream' by Randy followed by the tune 'Sensual Sue.' A good song to finish things off would be 'Stairway to Heaven.' You all got it?"

"Sure thing, Boss," replied Randy.

"Well then, let's go out there and give 'em heck!"

The sky was mostly clear with some high cirrus clouds floating overhead. The golden sunlight illuminated the grassy eastern part of the Pavilion while the western part was cloaked in shadow. Various conversations could be heard by the entering crowds of people. Many of them were teenagers with their autograph books at the ready, waiting eagerly to see the group Sha-Na-Na perform. Some adults with their children were also present who were eagerly anticipating tonight's performance.

"Boy, this is gonna be a great concert!"

"Sha-Na-Na is my favorite group!"

"I like Elvis Presley better. Elvis is my idol!"

"Yeah, he's outta sight, man!"

"I like 'Blue Eyes' better."

"Oh, come on, Henry. Frank Sinatra is a square!"

Randy and the rest of the group were off to the side of the stage, gearing up for the evening's performance. Said he, "I feel a little nervous tonight."

"Don't worry," responded Brian. "You'll knock them dead."

Just then, a tall man walked over to Harry and asked, "You got everything organized here?"

"Oh sure, Mr. Green. Boy, wait 'til you hear this group perform!"

"What do they call themselves?"

"The Universal Mindset."

The emcee for the evening's festivities approached the main microphone. Yappy Yellowfield was a rock-and-roll DJ for the Bay Area radio station KROK. He was known for cracking corny jokes and for his sarcastic humor. Many people were turned off to him even though they loved the hard rock music on FM station KROK. He had long black hair that went down well below his shoulders, mischievous green eyes, and a potbelly. He was dressed in patched-up blue jeans with a light-pink shirt. He looked just like a perfect example of a 1970s hippie.

He started announcing the evening's schedule saying, "Hello out there all you hipsters in rock-and-roll land! We have a real treat for you tonight! In just a few minutes, Sha-Na-Na is going to blast this tiny little field and this hick town of Concord down to the ground. They'll probably cause a 9.8 earthquake, but if they do, it won't be my fault, haw, haw, haw!"

At this point, Yappy Yellowfield made some imitation bird sounds with his mike and continued, "Now before we get going with these world-famous rock stars, I have a few announcements I need to make. First off, if you should happen to get cold in this outdoor venue, we will be selling hot dogs in the back—and also hot toddies—and I'm not talking about little boys named

Toddy! Tweet, tweet, tweet! By the way, just kidding about the hot toddies! Only hot dogs will be sold!"

At this point, Yappy made a loud snorting sound that brought some laughter and some groans from the crowd.

"Another announcement: we have an eight-year-old boy here who is lost and separated from his mama and papa. If anyone has a kid named Billy Gaylark, please come up to the front gate. The kid is lost, and he sure doesn't look gay to me like the name Gaylark implies. Neither does he look like a bird."

He again made the high bird sound, and the Pavilion filled up with some low groans, some booing, and some murmuring.

"Oh no! Another one of that announcer's worn-out jokes!"

"I can't *stand* him! Not only is he not funny, but he is also downright rude!"

"He sure is insulting!"

"I'd sure hate to be that poor little boy!"

"Ladies and jellybeans!" continued Yappy Yellowfield. "Before we bring you this evening's main attraction, we have a little pre-glow musical act for you! These cats call themselves The Universal Sedimentary Mind."

"The Universal Mindset!" cried Brian savagely. "Get it right, you jerk!"

"Oh, 'scuse me, The Universal Mindset, led by Brian Canning and sponsored by manager Harry Dates! Well, I don't know about you rock-and-roll freaks, but I wonder what kind of girls he's been dating lately! Do they have a lot of hair on their heads?"

"One more stupid joke like that," muttered Harry, "and I'll pop him one right in the nose!"

"Hey, sir!" yelled George Newman, the piano player. "The name is Gates, not Dates!"

"Oh, sorry! Well, anyway," (birdcall), "the name is Gates. And over here, we have Randy Killer, the lead singer and guitarist for the group. Randy Killer, huh? Well, I hope he doesn't kill anybody!" (Birdcall.)

"I'm gonna kill *him* if he doesn't cut out the corn!" muttered Lila, who was seated in the front row.

"He must be hard of hearing," commented Donna Applebaum to Lila.

"Mr. Yellowfield!" fumed Harry. "The name is Miller—not Killer, okay?"

"Oops, I done it again! The name is Randy Miller!" (Polite applause.) "Another singer is Bart Anderson!" (Polite applause.) "Obviously Bart rides the BART trains a whole lot!" (Birdcalls that brought more groans from the crowd.) "On piano, we have George Blueman; on rhythm guitar, we have Keys Bryant, tweet, tweet! On bass, there is Freddy Barnyard; and on drums, Mark Mole!"

"Dole, not Mole!" muttered Mark.

71

There was more polite applause and tittering as Yappy continued his spiel. "May I have your attention, please? Attention please! There is a car out in the parking lot with its lights on and its motor running. The car is a 1969 turquoise Mustang with the license plate SDA665. Please turn your lights and motor off. We have a gas shortage in our country today, and I'm sure all of you hippies would suffer severe *gas*tric pains if too much fuel was wasted!"

More boos from the crowd while Yappy did another birdcall.

Lila fumed, "SHUT UP! Save your cutting and crummy jokes for your rinky-tink radio station!"

Mercifully, the program finally began with "The Evil Eye." Right from the first E dominant seventh chord, the crowd was riveted with fascination on the seven people up on the stage. The tune was an instant hit. At the end of the song, wild cheering and screaming broke out with the intensity of cheering that would happen only at a ball game or an Elvis concert. "Yay!" yelled Lila, joining in with the enthusiastic outburst. All the songs were performed flawlessly and were extremely well received by the crowd. By the end of their set, there was a five-minute standing ovation for The Universal Mindset, and the group had to take bow after bow. Randy Miller was a smash hit! Randy walked triumphantly back to where Lila, Jack, Tommy, Mike, and Donna were sitting while Yappy Yellowfield started to bring on the main stars for tonight, Sha-Na-Na.

"Sweetheart, you were wonderful!" gushed Lila.

"Your music was beautiful," agreed Donna.

"Yeah, Dad, you sure were swell," agreed Tommy.

"Thank you," said Randy.

The Sha-Na-Na set went well with a fair amount of cheering after their famous songs. They did songs from their repertoire including hits like "Rock-and-Roll is here to Stay." They also did their usual talking between some of their pieces that went over well with the crowd. At 7:00, the show was finally over, and both groups were called to the stage to receive their final rounds of applause. After that, the two groups made themselves available for any autograph seekers who might come their way. Of course, there were oodles of autograph seekers for Sha-Na-Na, but the surprising thing was that the musicians in The Universal Mindset were also thronged with fans. Randy Miller had a whole bunch of people surrounding him.

"Randy, you were great!"

"You sure write hot songs!"

"Oh, Randy, you're my idol!"

"Sign my notebook, please! Sign my notebook so that when you are famous, I can say, 'I knew him when'—"

"Hey, Randy, you sure are sexy!"

The majority of the fans surrounding Randy were beautiful girls. Lila felt a twinge of jealousy and apprehension rising up within her gut. She was thinking how there might be some real disadvantages to great musical success.

72

A little later, Harry Gates was having a little close-the-loop conference with the band. "You guys were terrific tonight!" he said. "Absolutely terrific! Great singing, Randy—and you other two guys! Great guitar playing, Randy and Keith. Great job on the piano, George—and you too, Randy on 'Just like Creamy Silk.' Great bass playing, Fred, and great job on the drums, Mark! Sha-Na-Na has nothing on you guys. You were a huge hit tonight. I believe there will be big things ahead of us. I had a radio announcer who was very interested in playing your songs, Randy."

"Far out!" responded Randy.

"I'll be in touch with all of you in the days to come concerning upcoming possibilities. We also still need to smooth over some things here and there to make us top notch. Anyway, great job once again. You guys have a wonderful weekend! Relax, go out and celebrate, and take it easy tomorrow! Watch the baseball game. Do whatever. See you later!"

With that, everybody packed up their gear and got ready to leave the Pavilion for home—or their favorite bar.

****

ON SUNDAY MORNING, October 21, the Miller family was getting ready to go to church as they usually did. Randy would be directing the choir again while Lila and the two boys would be sitting in the pews. Many of these Sunday mornings were orchestrated by petty arguments between Randy and Lila and/or arguments between Lila and one of the boys. Every Sunday, Lila would get miffed, and this Sunday was no exception. A common problem concerned the appearance of the children.

"Jack, go comb your hair!" ordered Lila.

"Do I have to, Mom?" whined Jack.

"Yes! Do as you're told. Go comb your hair NOW!"

"Okay, okay!" mumbled Jack. He dragged himself into the bathroom, took his hairbrush out of the drawer, wetted it down with water, and started brushing his hair, grumbling about what a big deal his mom made over such a stupid thing. Presently, Lila came into the bathroom to inspect her son's hair.

"Oh, Jack!" moaned Lila in exasperation. "How many times do I have to tell you to comb it right?! It looks terrible!"

"I think it looks all right," protested Jack sullenly.

"No, Jack. It doesn't look all right. You plastered down your hair again. You used too much water on it."

"I think it's stupid!"

"Don't argue with me, Jack!" exclaimed Lila angrily. "Act your age!" She took the brush and redid his hair until it was brushed the right way with the part done properly and neatly.

Jack was sullen that morning while they were driving to church; his pride was deeply hurt. At church, the choir sang a bunch of their usual pieces including the popular song, "They Will Know We Are Christians by Our Love," and the communion song, "Let Us Break Bread Together on Our Knees." Pastor Kevin preached almost the identical sermon from two weeks ago. Same people, same type of music, similar sermon, same liturgy there Sunday after Sunday.

****

MEANWHILE, the service at Berkeley Tabernacle Fellowship was lively and very interesting as it usually was. Pastor David preached a message on the sin of worry, using a number of passages from the book of Philippians as his text. One of the things he pointed out was the fact that about 95 percent of the things people worry about never come to pass. Once again, the music was very elaborate and well performed. At the end of the service, many of the people in the congregation lingered around for a while to discuss spiritual things.

"Hi, Pam," said Brad. "How are you doing?"

"I'm fine, thank you. Did you have a good week, Brad?"

"Yeah, in some ways. Friday night at Campus Crusade was great, and I've been reading a great book on angels this week. On the negative side, I tried to witness to my parents, and they stubbornly refuse to hear about the truth of the Bible and Christianity. They just don't want to hear about spiritual things, and I've been suffering a lot of persecution for the sake of the gospel."

"Well, just hang in there, Brad. They will be won over, not by your arguments, but by showing them the love of Jesus by the way you live."

"Well, I'll try, but it's very hard. I worry about my parents and two younger sisters all the time."

"You remember Pastor's Scripture in Philippians 4 about being careful for nothing? It tells us not to worry about anything, but rather, to pray about everything. Worry is sin, hallelujah! But we can have the surpassing peace that comes from the Holy Spirit, praise you, Jesus! Just pray and trust in the Lord and he will bring them in! You are very precious to the Lord, and He cares about every detail of your life! Look at me! He healed me from very painful arthritis."

"Thank you so much, Pam. You're a real encouragement to me."

"And you're a real encouragement to me, too."

****

LATER ON THAT AFTERNOON, Brad was talking on the phone with Hal Odell, relating some of the experiences he had gone through during the last several weeks. Brad was sitting on a black-cushioned chair in the downstairs

TV room. Sid and Harriet were out at Mira Vista Country Club, finishing up a golf game with two other people who had a tee-off time of 10:30 A. M.

"So," Brad was saying. "They were arguing to me about evolution on Friday night two weeks ago. I know that the Bible is right, but I don't know how to answer my relatives. They seem to be a lot smarter than me on these issues."

"Well, Brad," said Hal. "There's an area of study in Christianity called 'apologetics.' This word doesn't mean what it sounds like because there is no need to apologize for the gospel; there is very abundant evidence for the truthfulness of Scripture. One of the books I recommend that you try to get and read is the book by Richard Schiller entitled *The Evidence for Creationism*. Let me just give you a few facts against evolution to help get you started.

"To begin with, there are two irrefutable laws in physics, the First and Second Laws of Thermodynamics. The first law is called 'The Law of Conservation of Energy,' and it says that energy can neither be created nor destroyed. The Bible confirms this fact in two ways: one, the Bible points out that God rested from all His creation work on the seventh day so that energy is not now being created; and two, the writer of the book of Hebrews said that Jesus Christ is upholding everything by the word of His power, showing that energy is not being destroyed. The Second Law of Thermodynamics says that natural processes, when left to themselves, are going from a state of order to a state of disorder. This is why an apple will rot, a watch will wind down, and a washing machine will eventually break.

"Some of the other inconsistencies in evolution involve these facts: many teachers and evolutionary scientists won't tell you that when they try to figure out whether certain bones belong to a man, an ape, or something in between, they often have only a few bones to work with, leaving the rest as speculation. An example of this is the Piltdown Man. This discovery of an ancestral form of man took place in 1912, and was, for a long time considered the greatest proof of evolution and the theory that man descended from the ape. The 'evidence' consisted of nine pieces of a skull and most of one side of the lower jaw with the second and first molar teeth still in place. But as better tests were developed, scientists found out that the jaw and the teeth did not belong to the cranium and that they were of an age a good deal later than the skull. The teeth had been ground down by hand. In order to match the skull, the teeth and the jaw had been stained with chromate. As it turned out, they found that the jaw was that of a modern ape, and the discovery of Piltdown man was called a hoax in 1953.

"Another thing against evolution is the fact that there are so many missing links in the fossil record. These include gaps between different kinds of animals and especially between the ape and man. Also, if man has really been around for a million years or more with even a conservative rate of population growth, there would be trillions upon trillions of fossils on the earth. The whole thing just does not jell mathematically. Also, the geologic evidence strongly points to water, water everywhere, a worldwide Flood that destroyed almost all life on Earth. The fossil record says so—if these fossils had been there millions of years with no flood, they would have decomposed or been eaten by scavengers."

"Yeah, thank you Hal! I will try to buy that book as soon as I can."

At this point, the garage door opened, and there was the sound of Sid and Harriet's car coming into the garage. Then, there was the sound of the car doors opening and shutting and the voices of Brad's parents.

Harriet: "I don't know what my problem was today! I shanked the ball on my tee shot on number seven and sliced the ball on my iron shot on hole eight. I shot into the water on twelve and fourteen."

Sid: "Honey, you need to learn to just relax. You swung too fast on some of those holes—and you need to remember to keep your head down and follow through on the shot."

Harriet: "I keep trying, dear, but I still keep messing up!"

Sid: "Relax! It's all a matter of rhythm and smoothness. Your swing was too jerky. Just relax, swing smoothly, and follow all the way through the swing—and don't forget to keep your head down while you swing and keep your eye on the ball."

The door to the TV room opened up, and Harriet walked into the room while Brad was talking on the phone. He was saying to Hal, "Man, I'll tell you! It was a real dogfight on that Friday night when my dad and Uncle Anthony were ribbing me about my belief in creationism. My mom and Aunt Mary were giving me the business about reincarnation. They just don't understand the things of God at all. They are godless people. Please pray for their salvation. I've really gone through some persecution for the sake of the gospel, but I know that it's not really me that they are coming against, but the Christ in me that my parents are coming against."

"Don't worry, Brad. I will continue to pray for your folks. I love you!"

"I love you too!"

"Goodbye Brad!"

"Goodbye!"

Brad hung up the phone, and his mother turned to glare at him with eyes of fire that would have melted the coldest iceberg at the North Pole.

"Brad. I heard your conversation to your Christian friend on the phone just now," said Harriet angrily, "and you were very disrespectful to your dad and me! I don't appreciate the way you just *badmouthed* us! It shows no class at all the way you called us ungodly people! I want you to know that we have been good Christians for a longer period than you've been alive—and we do a dern' good job of feeding you, clothing you, and providing a good education for you at Cal Berkeley and all the thanks we get is this slander against us from you!"

"I'm sorry, Mom," mumbled Brad, "but I just want to see you and Dad accept Jesus as your personal Savior."

"I've known Jesus for a long time!" said Harriet in a low, savage voice.

All of the rest of that afternoon, Brad brooded over the events of that day and the past few weeks. *Yeah, this is more persecution I'm going through. Jesus said that if anyone came to Him and did not hate his mother, father, wife, sons, daughters—and even his own life, he couldn't be His disciple.*

****

MEANWHILE, Mike and Donna Applebaum spent that Sunday relaxing with their two daughters and watching the final Oakland A's' World Series game against the New York Mets on TV. Mike had been sure the A's didn't have a chance to win another World Series, especially after the fifth game of the series when the Oakland A's had gone behind 2-3. They had won the sixth game yesterday to stay alive, and today was the crucial game. Mike mused over all the internal conflicts that seemed to be a blight on the swinging A's team: Charles O. Finley's attempt to 'fire' second baseman Mike Andrews after game two, the resentment of manager Dick Williams toward Charles Finley, and the infighting among the A's themselves.

The first two innings were uneventful with no score on either side. Then came the third inning. As Bert Campaneris hit a two-run homer, Donna and the two girls yelled out, "YEAH, WAY TO GO BABY! YOU'RE DOING IT! YAY!" Reggie Jackson then brought in another two runs in the third and also hit a one-run homer in the fifth to make the score 5-0, A's. The Met's came back with one run in the sixth and another in the ninth, but Bert Campaneris caught a pop fly by Garrett in the ninth to pocket another World Series for the A's. Pitcher Ken Holtzman had won the game, and relief pitcher Darold Knowles had secured the save. Jon Matlack was the losing New York pitcher. When Campaneris caught that pop fly ball, the whole Applebaum family went ape, even the stoic and staid Mike Applebaum.

****

IN THE ENSUING DAYS, Randy and Lila Miller also went ape with happiness. The Saturday night concert had been a huge success. The songs, "The Evil Eye" and, "Just like Creamy Silk," were on their way to being published, and a recording session in late November at Tower Records in Berkeley was being planned for The Universal Mindset. Besides all of this, the group had a plethora of bookings at wedding receptions, nightclubs, and Lodge meetings. Meanwhile, Randy continued to experience the phenomenon of automatic writing of new songs with lyrics, blacking out and then waking up with the new piece right in front of him. The group's repertoire of original music was getting larger and larger. During the regular gigs, the band continued to do a lot of standard and well-known songs along with the original music. The gigs were in towns like Orinda, San Carlos, El Cerrito, San Francisco, Oakland, Fremont, San Jose, and even as far away as Stockton and Sacramento. Everywhere the group went turned out to be a smashing success.

Randy was no longer playing the piano at the Lafayette pizza parlor because he was making much more money in other places. The day came early in November when his song, "The Evil Eye," was introduced on radio station KROK and became an instant hit just like Frank Sinatra's rendition of "Strangers in the Night" had about seven years earlier. Indeed, Randy Miller was getting closer to becoming nationally famous.

6.

SPIRITUAL VITAMINS

Pam Jackson was sitting with eleven other Christian college girls in her apartment complex in Oakland on Saturday morning, November 3. (Even though she was a student at Cal Berkeley, her parents thought Oakland would be a safer place for her to live than Berkeley would because of all the unrest in Berkeley.) Among the girls were such Campus Crusader friends as Debbie Thatcher, Cristy Hunt, and her best friend who she had led to Christ a year-and-a-half ago, Laura Wilkerson. The soft, brown rug in Pam's living room was spotlessly clean. Two tan-colored sofas were situated on the floor. A bookshelf was situated against one wall with many Christian books by such authors as Billy Graham, Hal Lindsey, Kathryn Kuhlman, C. S. Lewis, Gordon Lindsay, and many other well-known Christian authors. Bright sunlight illuminated the cheery living room, matching the joyful, bouncy spirits of the twelve girls.

The conversation was very animated and cheerful. They laughed and giggled a whole lot and talked about teachers at Cal Berkeley, hairdos, makeup, funny incidents with family members, and gossip over some of the college boys.

"Hey Pam," asked Debbie. "What do you think of that guy, Brad Applebaum? He seems to have the hots for you."

"Well, honestly, he is a little weird. To begin with, he dresses sort of sloppily and also talks rather funny. I told him off a couple of weeks ago when he tried to get fresh with me."

All the other girls burst into prolonged and hearty laughter.

"Isn't he a pretty new believer?" asked Cristy Hunt.

"Yeah, I believe he accepted Christ earlier this year. I can tell that even though he is a bit different, he truly loves the Lord. It is *obvious*. He is very zealous in his witnessing about Christ to other people all around campus. He just needs some work on his social skills."

All the girls burst into a fresh paroxysm of giggles.

Said Laura Wilkerson, "I think Hal Odell is a dream! He is so tall, handsome, considerate, and spiritual! His knowledge of the Bible is boundless!"

"So when is the wedding day going to be?!" bantered Debbie.

"As the Lord leads," replied Laura.

At this point, the group delved into the Scriptures, starting things off with a word of prayer. After that, they spent an hour mining out the boundless treasures in Ephesians 3. The whole group was encouraged as Pam read these wonderful words of Paul that said, "'For this cause, I bow my knees unto the Father of our Lord Jesus Christ, of whom the whole family in heaven and earth is named, that He would grant you according to the riches of His glory, to be strengthened with might by His Spirit in the inner man; that Christ may dwell in your hearts by faith; that ye, being rooted and grounded in love, may be able to comprehend with all saints what is the breadth, and length, and depth, and height; and to know the love of Christ, which passeth knowledge, that ye might be filled with all the fullness of God.'" Pam excitedly commented, "Isn't that rich? Hallelujah, hallelujah, sweetest, most precious and lovely Jesus! We have a huge reservoir of treasures of the love of God right inside of us through the Holy Spirit, thank you Jesus!"

The rest of the girls responded with excitement. They continued the Bible study, Pam prodding them with questions over the meaning of various verses, and different people responding with their insights. Finally, the Bible study was over, and Pam asked if there were prayer requests. There were different things offered up: people that some of the girls had witnessed to, family issues, upcoming college exams, the problems in the U. S. such as the Arab Oil Embargo and Watergate. Pam assigned various people to pray for different issues, and then the time of intercession began.

"Father God," started Debbie. "I thank You so much for this sweet time of fellowship as well as the chance to dig deeply into Your Word. I just pray for Jessica, the girl that Paula witnessed to on Wednesday. Please open her heart to accept Jesus as her Lord and Savior! I bind Satan from blinding her mind. In the name of Jesus, amen."

"Precious Heavenly Father," continued Laura. "We pray for You to open up people to the gospel on this dark, dark campus here in Berkeley. This city has been such a hotbed of revolution, rebellion, and violence during the last eight years. Please soften hearts to receive Jesus."

"And I pray for Heidi's science exam on Monday," said Cristy, softly, "that You would give her wisdom to pass the test with flying colors."

Different people in the group prayed over the sundry issues that had been brought to the floor while the rest of the group assented with comments like, "Amen!" "Hallelujah!" and "Praise You Jesus!"

Finally, Pam finished off by, "Oh, precious Lord! You are so wonderful and mega-lovely! I love You so much! I adore You! I give my whole life and heart to You! I pray for Your angelic protection and the precious Blood of Jesus to be over all of these precious sisters in Christ. Please meet all of their needs. I pray also for our wonderful country of the United States of America. We are living in dangerous times today with the gas crisis and the shaky economy. Please give our president supernatural wisdom on how to handle the tough issues in this land." (At this point, Pam started to weep with tears of love and compassion.) "Lord, President Nixon has such a hard job and big burden on his shoulders. This Watergate scandal has no simple answers. Please show Your love to him and bring godly people into his life to show him the way. I pray all of this in the wonderful name of Jesus, amen!"

Everybody echoed their "amens," and the girls started chatting and giggling once again. After that, Pam and Laura walked together towards Pam's white compact car to go to Denny's and have a nice brunch together.

****

ERIC BURNS was having another powwow meeting with Ted Johnson and Scott Williams. They were sitting together at a booth at Denny's, discussing the upcoming meetings of the Red Riding Rangers, what was going on in the various American Leftist movements today, and the current affairs in America and the world.

"I can't *believe,*" Eric was saying to the other two conspirators, "that Israel was so victorious during this last Yom Kippur War. It makes absolutely no sense to me at all."

"Yeah," responded Ted. "Their armies were so vastly outnumbered. They should have been decimated."

"Their luck must eventually run out," continued Eric, "and when it does, those greedy Zionists will go down forever and ever! At any rate, we now have an Arab Oil Embargo that is already beginning to devastate the economy in the U. S. The second Great Depression has already started. The Dow Jones Industrial Average peaked at not too much under 1,000 eight days ago and has been crashing all of this week. The coming gas shortage will help to cut down on air pollution."

Ted changed the subject by saying, "I read in the entertainment section of the *Contra Costa Times* about a rock singer named Randy Miller opening up for Sha-Na-Na a couple of weeks ago and being a smash hit. Is that possibly the same Randy Miller you went to high school with?"

"I think it is, Ted. I'll have to fix that greedy pig!" said Eric. He was only half-way joking; Eric felt some genuine envy against Randy Miller because he was experiencing some real success while Eric hadn't gotten very far in his life at all. Deep down inside his soul, he coveted the wealth that super-rich people had that he didn't have, and he longed to have some of their luxuries. He lit up a cigarette as he mused over these things.

The three of them finished their discussion and said their goodbyes after which Eric paid the bill for his meal only, leaving no tip whatsoever. He then headed toward the front door. Two beautiful college girls were just outside the door as Eric was exiting the restaurant. There was a radiant glow on their faces and in their eyes, and Pam was humming the melody to "The Old Rugged Cross" in the key of E-flat. The girl who was humming had beautiful brown hair and sparkling hazel eyes that radiated love. The other girl had gorgeous blonde hair with lovely blue eyes.

The brown-haired girl looked at Eric and said in a very nice and winsome voice, "Hello, sir! Let me introduce myself to you. My name is Pam Jackson, and I'm part of a group called Campus Crusade for Christ. Do you have a minute or two to talk to us?"

"No I don't!" fumed Eric in a rude voice. "I'm very busy right now!"

"Yeah, but this is very important! We want to tell you that we love you and that God loves you and has a wonderful plan for your li—"

"Get out of here! I don't want you cramming that religious trash down my throat! You have some nerve, butting into the private business of a total stranger!"

Laura responded gently, "But all we want is for you to know the love of Jesus. He died on a cross for—"

Eric took the name of the Lord in vain and then hissed, "Enough! If you don't scram out of here right now, both of you are going to wish you had!" More blasphemies came out of the mouth of Eric Burns as the two lovely ladies said, "Goodbye," and, "have a lovely day, sir," and walked quietly away.

Eric stood there fuming for a few minutes and muttered to himself, "Rude, impudent girls! How dare they encroach on the private life of a man they've never met?"

The communist crusader angrily clambered into his ramshackle car, slammed the car door shut, and drove back toward his apartment flat.

****

BRAD APPLEBAUM'S MINOR WAS MUSIC. He was an amateur flutist. On the first Monday in November, he was sitting in a master class, where different instrumentalists were performing their classical pieces, which they had learned for Professor Frank Douglas. On that particular early afternoon, he was not paying very much attention to the performers but was chewing gum loudly and reading a novel on end-time Bible prophecy by author Charlie Laughlin called *The Rise of Brother Bart, the Beast.* While the other students were playing musical works by Bach, Beethoven, Schubert, Chopin, and Scriabin, Brad was engrossed in the world of the Great Tribulation with its heroes fleeing famine, torture, imprisonment, and death by beheading.

Eventually, the master class was over, and Brad prepared to go to his weekly flute lesson.

Frank Douglas was a stodgy, humorless middle-aged man who was glued onto classical music only. He didn't like jazz, folk, or rock music at all. He was onto Brad's profession of Christianity because Brad was very outspoken about his faith. Frank Douglas was a Roman Catholic who went to mass regularly, prayed to the Blessed Virgin, and believed in all of the doctrines of the Catholic Church.

"I've been working hard on the second movement of the Poulenc *Flute and Piano Sonata* this week," said Brad. "Are you all ready to go, Professor?"

The learned music teacher glowered at Brad and then said, "Before we start on your lesson today, Brad, I want to talk to you."

"Yeah, what about?"

"I am very disappointed in you, Brad! *Extremely* disappointed! You claim to be a good Christian, *but the way you acted in master class today totally discredits that profession.* You were extremely rude. First off, you were chewing gum. Second off, you were reading a book, which shows you weren't paying any attention to the student performers. To sum up, you were downright disrespectful and *dishonored my students!"*

Brad felt his face get hot and red, and his heart sank down into his feet. He said in a low voice, "I'm so sorry, Mr. Douglas! I'll never, *never* do it again. I never wanted to be a discredit to my Lord!"

"I accept your apology," said Frank in a formal voice.

The lesson then proceeded with the professor giving some praises that were overshadowed by the criticisms of things like wrong notes, erratic rhythms, and dynamic changes, Frank commenting that Brad's dynamics were in need of vitamins. The lesson didn't go too well that day; Brad had trouble concentrating on the music because of the chewing out he had just received.

Later on that afternoon, Brad found a lonely grassy area on the campus where he spent some time pouring out his heart before God.

"Lord," he prayed. "I'm just a no good, stupid, rotten person. I blew it today! I never wanted to discredit Christ. Please forgive my great sin according to First John 1:9 that says, 'If we confess our sins, He is faithful and just to forgive us our sins and cleanse us from all unrighteousness.' I want to lead many people to Christ!"

He continued his prayer with a few tears that ran down his face.

****

TUESDAY MORNING, NOVEMBER 6, was a rainy day in the Bay Area. The skies were very dark, and the hills were already turning green. Kimberly Applebaum was carpooling with some friends to DVC Junior College in Pleasant Hill, California, talking, giggling, and cussing it up. They were riding in a small Buick, and the car radio was playing background rock music on station KROK. Kimberly was in her first year at DVC, and she was majoring in applied business.

"The dance on Saturday night was like totally a drag," said Kimberly. "The guy I hung out with was no fun at all! Don got smashed and threw up in the car on the way home. I'm never going out with him again!"

"I had a terrific time," said Linda. "Craig was a really fun guy. He had a great sense of humor, he knew how to dance, and he was so romantic! He's a brainy guy, too!"

"Old zitface Biff was sure a clumsy oaf!" said Suzanne. "He couldn't dance to save his life. He didn't know any of the steps, and he tripped, fell, and pulled me down with him. We were both lying down on that dance floor, and everybody was laughing their heads off at us. I was never so embarrassed in my whole life. Then he like wanted to race his sports car up to Grizzly Peak at three o'clock in the morning."

The girls tittered again while a hit song was playing on the radio about friends who had joy and fun and seasons in the sun but were now dying. When the song ended, the DJ spent a moment to announce the next song.

"Well, that song was called 'Seasons in the Sun.' This is Happy Yappy here playing you all the hit songs! It's a gray day today, but Happy Yappy hopes to turn this gray day into a gay day for you today! (Birdcall.) This next song is a new song by Randy Miller and is called 'The Evil Eye.' I hope none of you long haired guys will give any of your girlfriends an evil eye, (tweet, tweet)!"

"Wow, Randy Miller!" exclaimed Kimberly. "That's the best friend of my uncle! Isn't that exciting?"

Suzanne responded irrelevantly, "Dude! That worn-out radio DJ calls himself 'Happy Yappy.' He really should be called 'Drippy, Lippy, Mouth-trappy, Flappy, Scrappy Yappy!'"

The other two girls went into stitches with laughter. The Randy Miller song played, and the three girls were immediately captivated by the catchy tune and lyrics. After the song was finished, the news came on with headlines about the Energy Crisis, the Watergate Scandal, and among other things, another dead and dismembered body of a girl raped and killed by some unknown serial rapist in the town of Lodi.

"This is the tenth body found in that vicinity of the Central Valley this year. Other bodies have been found in Stockton, Modesto, Manteca, Tracy, and Turlock over the last two years. Police officers and investigators are mystified as to who may have done these dastardly, outrageous deeds."

****

ON WEDNESDAY NIGHT, Brad was eating dinner with his parents, Sid and Harriet, and with his sisters, Kimberly and Lisa. Conversation was about topics such as school, bridge (it had been too rainy for golf), Lisa's slumber party of last weekend, and contemporary news in the world.

Sid was saying, "It was another terrible day on Wall Street. The market really took a beating. Powell especially lost a whole lot of money on 'RCA.' The way things are going, we may have to sell the house."

84

"I think it's that Arab Oil Embargo that is hurting stocks," said Harriet, his wife. "People are worried about the economy and the availability of gasoline and electricity."

"I think that it is a sign that Jesus is about to come," said Brad, "and that the Seven-Year Tribulation is about to start."

"The seven-year itch, huh?" replied Sid.

"Yeah, soon we who have received Christ will be raptured up to escape the Tribulation. Praise the Lord!"

"Pass the ammunition!" laughed Sid. "This is *your* religious view, Brad, but there are other religions in the world that see things differently than you see them. What about Buddhists, Hindus, and Moslems?"

"None of these religions teach salvation by grace alone. They all teach you that you have to work your way to God." (Brad was getting red in the face.) "All the believers in those false religions will *go to hell!*"

"Whoa!" protested Harriet, taking another sip of her white wine. "There are a whole lot of good people in the world who don't believe the way you do. Remember Carrie? She was the kindest and most loving person I ever knew! Are you saying that God would send her to hell?"

"If she didn't know Jesus, YES!" exclaimed Brad.

"Kid, you're not making any sense at all," said Sid. "There are millions of people in this world who have never heard about Christianity. What about people in Africa—or the rice paddies in China? Brad, my boy, I think you are just going through a phase right now, just a phase. In a few months, you'll get over it."

"No, this knowledge of Jesus will last forever!" exclaimed Brad, angrily. "You're wrong, Dad, *you're wrong!*"

****

DARRYL TEMPLE WAS A JANITOR at Lodi High School, cleaning up toilets, sinks, walls, and floors in the bathrooms, as well as mopping and vacuuming all the floors in the classrooms and the multi-purpose room. Most of the students looked down on him—they considered him to be dumb, socially boorish, and weird. Students would joke among themselves saying, "Tem*po*, Tem*po!*" His uniform was wrinkled, his hair was unkempt, and he had bad breath. He lived in a small, dingy four-room apartment in downtown Lodi. He had only an eleventh-grade high school education. He was not very literate in reading, English, spelling, or math.

On this Thursday in mid-November, he sat across from his boss, Andy Hester, in a light-blue office. Once again, Darryl was in hot water. He waited anxiously for the axe to fall.

"Temple!" roared Andy. "You are the biggest dingbat I've ever hired! You are also a clumsy and lazy bum!"

"What did I do now?" whined Darryl.

"You did it again! You messed up! I found two of the toilets in the bathrooms clogged up and dirty. One classroom was absolutely *filthy!* There was spilled apple juice on one part of the floor in the cafeteria. Obviously, you've been goldbricking again. I warn you, you've better shape up or ship out! If you keep fooling around like this, you'll be out on your ear! Now get back to work!"

"Okay, okay," said Darryl as he headed toward the classroom with the vacuum cleaner and mop. He started to clean up the room, but about three quarters of the way through, his enthusiasm began to fizzle out, and so he stopped his work to rest for a little bit. He had snuck in a bottle of hard liquor. He took it out of his duffle bag, unscrewed the lid, and started to drink its contents. Soon, he began to feel the 'buzz' and started to waddle around the room like a fat duck and talk to himself.

"I am the president of the United States'h! I have the solution to all the problems'h of the world! I have lots'h and lots'h of gas to solve the gas'h shortage! I prom—"

"Temple, you got gas in your brain!" roared Andy. "Now quit goofing off and GET WITH IT!" (Mr. Hester had quietly snuck into the room while Darryl was giving his drunken speech.)

Darryl spun around absolutely stunned. "Yes'h sir!" he stammered. "Anything you s-s-say!"

Darryl resumed his work in the classroom, scrubbing, scrubbing, scrubbing. Soon, he put the mop down and said, "Well, that's'h good. I'm all done, Boss'h. There ain't no more dirt."

"Oh, yes there is!" roared the boss. "THERE! OVER THERE! See the gunk here? Now quit fooling around and get busy!"

Darryl picked up the mop, put it into the bucket—and knocked over the bucket, spilling soapy water on the floor.

"TEMPLE, YOU KNOTHEAD!" roared the boss. "Quick! Get some more cleaner to clean up this mess and finish your job in this classroom! You know, you act like you've been drinking."

"I ain't been drinking nothin', sir."

"Well, I think you have. I'm telling you, Temple, if you keep messing up, you'll be waxing your way to the unemployment office!"

****

ON FRIDAY, NOVEMBER 16, Brad was sitting in Professor James Corrigan's public speaking class, listening to other students give their speeches, and preparing to recite his own speech he had prepared on "America, A Christian Nation." After each speech, Professor Corrigan gave praise and/or constructive criticism to each of the speakers on areas such as poise, delivery, grammar, structure, and content. The other students also had a chance to interact and put in their input concerning the value of each speech. Some parts of these speeches deserve to be heard again.

A girl named Jody Flores arose to give her speech on "God's Plan for National Israel." She said, "God is restoring Israel again. A hundred years ago, Israel was a desert waste, but today, the desert is blooming just like God said it would.

"I want to talk for a moment about a couple of misconceptions concerning Israel. One false teaching says that the Church is Israel at this present time. This tenet is called 'Replacement Theology,' the view that either through the sins of Israel or through God's eternal sovereign purpose, the Church has replaced Israel as far as being in the place of God's favor. No, my friend, when God says Israel, He means Israel, and when God says the Church, He means the Church. Sad to say, even most of the godly ministers in the last centuries believed this off-base view. Nevertheless, there were a minority of preachers who understood God's literal promises for the restoration of Israel long before the events of 1948. Hal Lindsey documents some of those preachers in his excellent book, *The Late, Great Planet Earth*. For example, there was Increase Mather, one of the godliest and well-respected Puritan preachers in New England. He wrote a book that was published in 1669 where he demonstrated from his study of the Bible that the Jews would return to the land of Israel prior to their spiritual conversion and the second coming of Christ. Another example is the great English Bible scholar James Grant who in 1866 wrote these words: 'The personal coming of Christ, to establish His millennial reign on earth, will not take place until the Jews are restored to their own land, and the enemies of Christ and the Jews has gathered together their armies from all parts of the world, and have commenced the seize of Jerusalem.........now the return of the Jews to the Holy Land, and the mustering and marshalling of these mighty armies, with a view to capturing Jerusalem, must require a considerable time yet.' In addition, here is a little-known fact: Saint Francis of Assisi believed there would be a literal thousand-year reign of Christ on the earth.

"Another misconception we hear a lot of people saying today is the myth that the Jews stole the Land from the Palestinians. Let me clear this up right now. First of all, the facts of history show that in the last century, there were forty-three Jewish communities in Israel, *but no sign of Arabs!* Both Mark Twain and W. M. Thompson document this fact. Secondly, the majority of Arabs have been supportive of the Jews coming back to the Land. It is a minority of radical Palestinians who have made this big stink concerning Israel. Thirdly, while it is true that many Palestinians have suffered great squalor and hardship, the blame for this does not rest upon Israel, but on the *Arab* countries. These countries have way more than enough land for the Palestinians to settle in, yet *where is their helping hand?* They aren't interested in helping them out but want fuel to put on the fire of their grievances. Lastly, the facts show that the Israeli government has treated

Palestinians and other non-Jewish settlers who dwell in the Land relatively well. It is a fact that the Arab settlers who migrated to Israel during this century did so because they saw the prosperity of the Jews and wanted these opportunities for themselves."

There was a mixture of praise and criticism heaped on this speech. The consensus was that it was very well organized and presented, but there was disagreement about the allegations Jody Flores made about Israel. Professor Corrigan did not believe that God had a plan for National Israel.

Ken Clark now walked to the front to present his speech on the topic of "Agnosticism: The Only Solution to the Religious Nemesis."

"Fundamentalists miss the whole point of what the mission of Jesus really was, putting their emphasis like they do on the supposed miracles and resurrection of Jesus. There's a word entombed within the word 'fundamentalist' that describes those people very well: the word, 'mental.' We need to disregard the fabled miracles of Jesus and just look at His lofty teachings, things like 'Love your enemies,' 'Give to the poor,' and 'Turn the other cheek.'"

This speech received quite a bit of praise, but Doctor Corrigan did not agree with Ken's ideas about Jesus.

The next speaker was Hal Odell, who spoke on "Tomorrow: An Uncertain Mist."

"Most of us make plans for our lives, certain that we'll be around tomorrow, next month, next year, and twenty years from now. But how can we be sure these plans will pan out? We can't! Every day, people's lives are dramatically changed—and even taken away from them, because of some unexpected emergency.

"Many of you may have heard of the disastrous plane crash of the *Fairchild* last year in Argentina in the middle of the Andes Mountains on October 13. There were forty-five passengers on that plane, most of them rugby football players who were flying to Santiago to play against the Chilean national rugby team, seeking to cover themselves with fame and glory. None of them had a clue about the coming plane crash that would kill thirteen of the *Fairchild*'s passengers right away. During the next seventy days, another sixteen of them would die, and the survivors would have to eat the flesh of their dead companions in order to survive in that inhospitable desert with no vegetation whatsoever up there at 11,500 feet above sea level. On December 12, two of them, Roberto Canessa and Nando Parrado, set out through the mountains on foot to try to get back to civilization. They were successful, and on December 22 and 23, 1972, helicopters were flown to the crash site in order to rescue the remaining fourteen survivors.

"Some of you may have heard about a new upcoming rock star named Randy Miller and his recent hit, 'The Evil Eye.' Things are going well for him now, but even for him, there is no guarantee of tomorrow. How do we know he won't be involved in a fatal auto wreck—or even a plane crash—on his way to a rock concert?"

This speech received a standing ovation, and the professor had hardly any criticism to give the budding toastmaster.

Peter Thal now came forward to speak on "Nicotine: The Great Scourge."

"Many people wrongly think we have totally abolished slavery today, but unfortunately, there is still an insidious and deadly type of slavery in the land today. Yes, the Negro has been set free from his bondage to the cruel, inhumane slave owner, but there are still millions of slaves who are addicted to cigarettes, and the slave owners are those no-good, money-grubbing tobacco companies that make those cancersticks with brands like 'Winston,' 'Salem,' and 'Lucky Strike!' We need to rise up and get rid of those crooks and hooligans who are poisoning the health of those millions of victims who die every year of heart disease, emphysema, and lung cancer! The commercial for Winston says, 'Winston Tastes Good like a Cigarette Should,' but it really oughta' say 'Winston Tastes Bad like a Cancerstick Always Had.'" Peter's eyes flashed with fire as he yelled out, "LET'S GET RID OF THOSE CONNIVING NICOTINE GANGSTERS!"

The consensus on this speech was that it was well presented, but that he needed to cool his temper a little.

Brad's turn came to speak, and he walked to the front of the class to deliver his speech. He had a slight stammering problem and sometimes slurred his words. He had a bad habit of saying 'fer' instead of 'for.' He often looked at the ceiling instead of the students.

"Our country was once a great country, and, um, we had great Christian men that gave us this country of freedom. But you know—we are losing those freedoms today. When America was founded on freedom, the people relied on God and Jesus Christ, not the government. George Washington was a Christian. John Adams and Thomas Jefferson were Christians. Most of our Founding Fathers were Christians. And, um, in the good old days, we used to have great revivals under great heroes like George Whitefield, Spurgeon, Wesley, Charles G. Finney, and Dwight L. Moody.

"But today, times have changed. America have gone down the drain. We don't have a revival today like in, um, the good old days. We are losing our freedoms and are no longer a Christian nation because of a communist conspiracy consisting of the Big Boys, the men that are part of the CFR and the International Bankers that are trying to take over this God-blessed country and, um, you know, make America a dictatorship. And our morals are really bad today. Sexual immorality is all over the place, people are playing around with astrology, Ouija boards, and fortune telling, putting themselves in great danger of becoming demon-possessed. And the lie of evolution taught by the communists is everywhere. The worst thing is that people are trying to work their way to God through such things as, um, 'Go to church!' and, um, 'Be good!' and, um, 'Keep the Ten Commandments!' and 'Follow the Golden Rule!' instead of believing in the free grace of Jesus and Him dying on the cross as most of our Founding Fathers did, you know."

At the end of the speech, Professor Corrigan rose from his seat to face the bumbling orator.

"Brad," he said. "You turn people off! You focus on the negative things in this country too much, your speech was often disjointed, and many of your claims were not factual. For example, you said, 'America was founded on Christianity.' That is wrong. The correct thing for you to say would have been, 'America was founded on Christian principles.' Also, you painted a rosy picture of America in the past and a dreary and horrid picture of our country today. First off, what about things like slavery, the mistreatment of the American Indians, and the sins in the Wild West? Moreover, you mention people in the past like Finney and Moody. Well what about people like Billy Graham today? And lastly, the end of your talk would have a tendency to encourage people to backslide. I'm sure that was not your intention, but that's the way it came across."

The professor went on to criticize Brad on his organization, grammar, and stage presence. Some of the other students followed with their feedback. Brad sat down feeling dejected, miffed, and that once again, he was suffering persecution for righteousness sake.

****

ON FRIDAY NIGHT, Randy Miller was performing with the group at the Municipal Auditorium in Sacramento. Everybody in the band was dog-tired—they had gotten up at 4:30 A. M. and had performed at two high schools. They were performing the song, "The Evil Eye," when suddenly Mark Dole lost his grip on his drumsticks, which went flying through the air, falling at the feet of George Newman. George reached down with his left hand and threw the sticks back toward Mark. Randy and the other two singers burst into uncontrollable laughter and couldn't properly stay on pitch or enunciate their words during the rest of that song.

When the last chord sounded, Randy announced, "Well, that piece was 'The Feeble Fly'—I mean 'The Freeble Fry'—'scuse me?! Wh-what's wong' with my voice?! Forget it! We are The University Mendsit—I mean The Demented—The Dementia Universal—WHAT?!! Why can't I speak?" Randy's face turned beet-red, and he motioned for the band to start the next song.

****

ON THAT SAME FRIDAY NIGHT, Brad was at the weekly meeting of the Berkeley branch of Campus Crusade for Christ in an upstairs Sunday school room at Berkeley Tabernacle Fellowship. He eagerly looked forward to this weekly meeting and was there whenever he didn't have another commitment like a family birthday party he had to be at. Usually, about forty male and female students attended these meetings. It would start at 7:00 P. M. and go until about 9:30. The students were loving, friendly, and bright-faced, and there was a sweet spirit in the room. The evening would start out with singing, led by a guitar player named Charlie Paulson, followed by testimonies of different people who often talked about leading this or that person to Christ. Brad often felt envious of these people because although he tried to witness a lot, he hadn't really seen anyone come to Christ. After this would be announcements and prayer requests followed by a time of corporate prayer. Next, Chris Lincoln, the leader of the Berkeley Branch of Campus Crusade for Christ, would give an extended teaching. Brad loved the way Chris spoke; he was articulate, had a great knowledge of the Bible, and presented his teachings in an interesting and down-to-earth manner. There was much fun and laughter mixed in with the deeply spiritual teaching, and the meetings by no means had any sense of being super-religious or somber. The songs were a mixture of popular country songs interspersed with some contemporary Christian choruses. One song that was particularly memorable to Brad was, "I Am the Resurrection and the Life" in E minor. On this particular night after the meeting, the usual time of conversation between the young Christians there commenced. Instead of the light, worldly conversations, which were common at the end of many church services in the U. S., here, the talk was often about the things of the Lord.

Brad sauntered over to where a newcomer was talking to some other Campus Crusaders about his gifts of the Holy Spirit. He was obviously a charismatic Christian.

"The Lord has given me the gift of prophecy," he was saying to some of the bystanders. "I also have the gift of the discerning of spirits. There have been times when I have discerned the presence of angels or demons. I have discerned at times whether a person is a real Christian or a phony."

Brad said, "Hello, my name is Brad. What is your name?"

"My name is Roy Gomez."

"Pleased to meet you," said Brad. "I'm sure that you can discern whether or not I'm a true believer." Brad felt half-certain that he was a fake believer; he was well aware of his sins and that he was standing in the presence of a godly man.

"The Lord is showing me that you just need to spend more time in prayer and in reading and studying your Bible," said Roy. "You are a young Christian, and when the Lord cleans up your life, you will be effective in the purpose He has called you to." Roy looked into the eyes of Brad and continued, "I feel *honored* to be in your presence! The Lord has great plans for your life and is going to use you in a mighty way!"

This was a real encouragement to Brad who had undergone much criticism for his faults as a baby Christian and had seriously began to wonder where he really was with the Lord.

****

THE NEXT MORNING, Brad was engrossed in reading the biography of evangelist D. L. Moody in a Christian book he had checked out of the church library the previous Sunday. He read about how Moody started out as a shoe salesman and accepted Christ when he was a teenager. He read about his evangelistic work over the following years until the terrible fire in Chicago on October 8, 1871, when both Farwell Hall and Illinois Street Church were destroyed. These were places where Moody preached and ministered regularly. Moody's house was also burned down in the great fire of Chicago that devastated the city, and the family was only able to save a few of their belongings, including a portrait of the evangelist. Concurrently, Moody experienced a great hunger for the power of the Holy Spirit due to three holy women—three intercessory prayer warriors who sat in the front row at his meetings. One day, they said to the evangelist, "We are praying that the Lord will baptize you in the Holy Spirit." A Battle Royal raged in the preacher's heart over the ensuing weeks after the Great Fire to surrender to the will of God or not. Finally, he surrendered. One day, in New York City, Moody was baptized in the Holy Spirit and experienced such a baptism of love from the Divine Presence that he exclaimed, "God, take this power away from me lest I be consumed!" The great physical fire in Chicago had been followed by the great spiritual fire in the evangelist's soul. After this, he added no new doctrines in his sermons, yet hundreds, and then thousands received Christ at his crusades. During the 1870s, 80s, and 90s, he ministered extensively in America and Great Britain, leading many thousands to salvation through Jesus. Ira Sankey, who worked alongside of him in music, was very instrumental in shaping the landscape of nineteenth century Christian music. Brad read how D. L. Moody died on December 22, 1899, of fatty degeneration of the heart, and how he had said, "If this is death, it's not bad at all, it's *sweet!!*" He had described how he had been beyond the gates of death to the very portals of heaven. He also exclaimed in rapture that he saw the faces of Dwight and Irene who were two grandchildren who had died within the last year.

Brad had never heard the Baptism in the Holy Spirit explained the way it was in the biography he was reading because the church he went to didn't teach it as a work of God subsequent to salvation. Instead, they taught that you were always baptized in the Holy Spirit when you were saved. Brad wanted to be a victorious Christian and lead many people to Christ, and the biography whetted his appetite for more of the Holy Spirit's power in his life.

****

ON SATURDAY AFTERNOON, the members of The Universal Mindset were sitting in Brian Manning's living room, rehashing the train wreck of the previous evening.

"Well, last night was mega-blooper number one!" announced Brian.

"I don't know what happened to me," replied Randy. "I just couldn't stop laughing!"

"Yeah," said Bart. "Those drumsticks just went whizzing through the air, and we all just died laughing through the rest of the concert!"

"My sides are still hurtin'!" remarked Keith.

****

ON SUNDAY MORNING, Pastor David Maxwell preached a sermon on the grace of God, using as his text Romans 8 that says, "For there is therefore now no condemnation for those who are in Christ Jesus, who walk not after the flesh, but after the Spirit." After the service, Brad made a beeline for Pam Jackson in order to ask some serious questions.

"Hello, Pam."

"Hello, Brad. How are you doing today?"

"I'm all right. Hey, I have a serious question for you. Do you have a few minutes to rap?"

"Yeah sure, Brad. What's up?"

"Well, I was wondering, what do you think of the Baptism with the Holy Spirit? Dave says that we received the Holy Spirit when we got saved, yet I was reading about D. L. Moody yesterday about how he got baptized in the Holy Spirit many years after he got saved."

"Well, Brad, let's have a seat over here because it's going to take a little time to explain everything to you about this wonderful experience."

Brad and Pam sat down together on a pew toward the back of the sanctuary, and Pam began to describe this great experience of the filling of the Holy Spirit.

"First of all, Brad," she said. "It's important to know that when you got saved, the Holy Spirit came to live inside of you. According to Scripture, we were baptized by the Holy Spirit into the body of Christ when we were saved. The Bible points out in a couple of places that we were sealed by the Holy Spirit unto the day of redemption. The Scriptures point out that no one can say that 'Jesus is Lord' and really mean it except by the Holy Spirit. The Word of God also points out that if a person doesn't have the Holy Spirit, then he doesn't belong to Jesus at all. This means the person is not even saved.

"Now, it's one thing to have the Holy Spirit residing inside of you, but it's another thing altogether to operate in the Baptism of the Holy Ghost, to have His power flowing through you like a river. In all the Gospels, we see

John the Baptist promising that Jesus would baptize with the Holy Ghost and with fire. We see that promise fulfilled in the Upper Room when the 120 disciples were together and the mighty rushing wind came into the room, and there appeared to them, as it were, tongues of fire resting on each of them. The book of Acts says they were all filled with the Holy Spirit and began to speak in other tongues as the Spirit gave utterance. They praised God in their new languages, they were filled with new joy, and they had power like they had never experienced before. Their demeanor was such that some people accused them of being drunk.

"Jesus said they would receive power when the Holy Spirit came upon them, and they would be His witnesses in Jerusalem, in Judea, in Samaria, and even to the most remote parts of the earth. There are two Greek words for 'power.' The word used here is 'dunamis,' the word where we get our modern word 'dynamite' from. How were the disciples able to speak in languages they had never learned before? Through the Holy Spirit! How were they able to perform miracles and healing of the sick and casting out demons? Through the Holy Spirit! How were they able to go throughout the world and preach the gospel? Through the Holy Spirit! How was Peter, who had denied Jesus three times on the night before His crucifixion, transformed into a man who boldly shared Christ, even in the midst of great opposition and was eventually crucified upside down because he felt he wasn't worthy to be crucified right side up? Through the Holy Spirit! How have multitudes of the early Christians and saints throughout the ages been able to bear up under intense persecution, unspeakable tortures, and gruesome deaths without denying Jesus and even with a smile on their lips and a song in their hearts? Through the Holy Spirit! Thank you, Jesus, precious, lovely Jesus! Ooohhh, I love you Jesus, you are so worthy! Hallelujah, hallelujah, hallelujah! Oh, glory to God!

"Now Brad. What does all this have to do with us today? A whole lot! This same experience and power is available for every single born-again Christian today. Four years ago, I not only suffered excruciating pain from arthritis, but had deep darkness and despair within my soul. Then I heard about a lady named Kathryn Kuhlman. I went to a crusade of hers, and my first impression of her was, 'What kind of wacko mental case is this? She's a phony show-off and a crazy nut!' Kathryn started the service by saying, 'Hello there, have you been waiting for me?' really elongating the syllables in a very weird and ridiculous manner. I was turned off until a very quiet time in her service when people all around me started falling backwards. At first, I thought, 'Oh no, not more of this foolishness!' But the next thing I knew, there I was laying on the floor, and I couldn't get up if there had been a life-threatening fire in the place. She taught about sin, heaven, hell, and salvation through the Blood of Jesus. I felt like I was the worst sinner in the whole world, and when she gave the invitation to accept Christ, down to the front I went! The Lord saved me that day, and it was only while we were on the way home that I realized I didn't have any arthritic pain at all and that I had total mobility in my joints! (Oh, You are so wonderful, precious Jesus, and I love You so much! JESUS, JESUS, SWEET PRECIOUS JESUS!) I also knew my sins were gone and that I was saved! A few days later, I went to a Pentecostal church in Concord named Glad Tidings International Fellowship. That night, the pastor preached about the Baptism in the Holy Spirit, and when he gave the invitation, down to the altar I went again. Pastor Jeremy prayed over me, and there came such a joy and peace over me like I had never experienced before, and I immediately began to speak in a tongue that I had never known before. The syllables were right there in my brain, and I also had a new sense of the excellency and majesty of Jesus! (Hallelujah, thank you marvelous, outstanding Jesus!) My life has been full of victory ever since that day!

"If you want, Brad, you can come with me to that wonderful church in Concord tonight. The name of that church is Glad Tidings International Fellowship, and the service starts at 7:00 P. M."

"Yeah, I think that I would be interested, Pam. I'm not very happy with my Christian life right now. I try to witness and can't seem to lead anybody to Christ, I have problems getting victory over the besetting sins in my life, and I keep putting my foot into my mouth."

"Well, being full of the Holy Ghost is the answer. It's interesting to read the testimonies of people who have experienced this wonderful infilling of the Holy Spirit. Have you ever heard of Nicky Cruz?"

"No, who the heck is he?"

"Well, he was a gang leader of the Mau Mau's in New York City. He was a really bad kid who had a whole lot of turmoil in his life. Then, one day, he ran into a preacher named Dave Wilkerson. David said to Nicky, 'Jesus loves you, Nicky.' These words haunted Nicky, and he resisted for several days. But the time soon came when Nicky Cruz was at a crusade with a whole bunch of people who were in gangs. Nicky received Christ into his heart that night and found peace and joy he had never experienced before as well as freedom from the blood-curdling nightmares that had plagued his life for years. Sometime later, when he was going to Bible College in California, he received the Baptism in the Holy Spirit one night, and his life was dramatically changed. I have a book that talks about his life that you can borrow if you like."

"Yeah, sure. You know how much I love to read."

Brad mused over the idea of checking out this new church with Pam. He had gone to services in a number of churches and fellowships within the Bay Area because he wanted to be where the Christians were. He would be able to meet some new saints there, and maybe he would get more of the Holy Spirit tonight.

****

JACK AND TOMMY MILLER were sitting in the game room on Sunday evening, their eyes glued to the screen of the new color TV set Randy had just bought with some of the extra money he had made over the preceding weeks. They were engrossed in the Walt Disney movie, *The Horse in the Flannel Suit*. Meanwhile, Randy was watching the football game on the upstairs TV set in the living room. He thought about how wonderful it would be now that the amount of squabbling over who would watch what show would be greatly cut down, although not totally eliminated. *Yes, money maybe isn't everything, but it can buy a lot of happiness.*

****

THAT EVENING AT AROUND 6:30 P. M., Brad Applebaum was driving his compact car through the streets of Concord with Pam Jackson sitting beside him and calling out directions to Glad Tidings International Fellowship.

"Turn right, Brad, on Clayton Boulevard," Pam was directing. "That street is coming up after the next block."

Brad made the turn, and Pam continued to call out directions.

"Okay, Brad, we're going to keep on this road for a couple of miles until we see a big white building to the right. That is the sanctuary of Glad Tidings. It's a good thing we got an early start because the church is usually packed and the parking lot fills up very fast."

"Pam, is this church fundamentalist and theologically sound?"

"Oh, yes, hallelujah! Pastor Norris preaches that the Bible is the inerrant Word of God, that Jesus is God in the flesh, that He died on the cross for our sins, that He rose again bodily on the third day, and is coming for His Bride very, very soon, thank You, Jesus!"

They were soon standing in the newly built sanctuary of Glad Tidings International Fellowship with Pam introducing Brad to many of her Christian friends. The outside of the building was paneled with wood painted a spotlessly snow-white color. A grassy lawn and a flower garden beautified the front of the church. The inside of the sanctuary had wooden walls painted a bright white color. The floor was covered with sky-blue carpeting, and the pews were an attractive light-blue hue. The pulpit was a lightweight transparent fiberglass piece of furniture that exuded freedom from parsimonious stodginess. On the left side of the room was a beautiful and perfectly tuned Chickering grand piano with great key action and tone quality. On the other side was a large drum set that was of a lovely silver hue. No organ was in the sanctuary. Instead, the worship band consisted of a piano player, a drummer, a bass player, and two acoustic guitar players. The singers consisted of three males and three females who wore casual clothes at the Sunday worship services. A great sense of peace and serenity permeated the sanctuary.

"Well hi, Karen!" Pam exclaimed. "Praise God! It's such a fantastic day today! How are you, Karen?"

"I'm blessed, Pam! Hey, did you hear that my sister is engaged to be married next summer to Ricky?"

"OH, KAREN, THAT'S SO FANTASTIC! Glory to God! When's the wedding going to be?"

"Saturday, July 6. They're planning an outside reception at Week's Park in Hayward. It's going to be a really beautiful wedding."

"I'm so happy for them! Hey Karen, I'd like you to meet my friend, Brad Applebaum from Moraga. He's known the Lord for almost a year."

"Praise the Lord! Hi, Brad. I'm Karen Thompson. Nice to meet you!"

"Hello. Good to meet you Karen."

At 7:00, the evening service started with announcements, followed by the worship band leading the congregation in several contemporary Christian choruses. Although the style was not rock, it was upbeat and a far cry from the solemn music so common in many churches. Among the songs was "It Took a Miracle," "I Believe in Miracles," and "The Comforter Has Come." Brad noticed how the band would linger on one chorus for a long period of time as compared to most churches he had been at rushing from one hymn or song to the next one. He also noticed how there were spontaneous outbursts of worship and praise from the congregation members with phrases like "Glory to God!" "Thank You Jesus!" "Hallelujah!" and "I worship You, precious Jesus!" This was a new experience for Brad who felt deep inside of him that perhaps the people in this church were a bit emotional, maybe even off their rails a little bit. He was used to the staid worship in his home church in Berkeley with its systematic preaching of sound Biblical doctrine. He was a little unnerved as he remembered hearing from Hal Odell and other Christian friends to be wary of false doctrines as well as careful concerning the pitfall of emotionalism and religious fanaticism. He thought to himself, *I'm not going to get involved in any religious conniptions.*

Presently, Pastor Jeremy Norris walked to the fiberglass pulpit to start his sermon. He always opened things up with a joke; he believed that laughter was a healing gift from the Lord and often quoted Proverbs 17, verse 22, which says, "A merry heart doeth good like a medicine."

He started out by saying, "Oral Roberts was conducting a tent meeting in Little Rock, Arkansas one evening. After the meeting, there was a long line of people waiting to be healed of various ailments from the anointing of the Holy Spirit working through the evangelist. An elderly man approached Mr. Roberts and said, 'I need some help.' 'What can I do for you?' asked the evangelist. 'Well sir,' said the man, 'I need prayer for my hearing.' So, Oral Roberts laid his hands on the man's ears and prayed, 'Oh, Lord, we pray for this man's ears right now in the name of Jesus Christ of Nazareth! I REBUKE thee, thou spirit of deafness in the name of Jesus, COME OUT OF HIM! May you be able to hear perfectly right now in the name of Jesus, amen!' After praying, Oral Roberts asked the man, 'So how is your hearing now?' 'I don't know,' answered the man. 'My hearing isn't until next Friday morning at 8:00 A. M.'" (The whole congregation of 400 people responded with a loud roar of laughter.)

"Turn with me to John, chapter 14," continued the pastor, "and I'm really going to be concentrating on verses 16 to 18 and also looking at verse 21. It says, 'And I will pray the Father, and He shall give you another Comforter, that He may abide with you for ever; Even the Spirit of truth; whom the world cannot receive, because it seeth Him not, neither knoweth Him; but ye know Him; for He dwelleth with you, and shall be in you. I will not leave you comfortless, I will come to you.' Verse 21 says, 'He that hath my commandments, and keepeth them, he it is that loveth Me: and he that loveth Me shall be loved of My Father, and I will love him, and will manifest Myself to him.' The promises for us in these verses are absolutely awesome and mind-boggling! We have the power of the third person of the Trinity living right inside of us to make us more than conquerors over anything that might come our way in life."

Pastor Jeremy talked about his own experience of being baptized in the Holy Spirit. He shared from the four Gospels what John the Baptist had said on the subject. He then shared from Acts, chapter 2, about how Peter had led 3,000 people to Christ on the day of Pentecost. He also talked about what the Greek word for 'Comforter' really meant: the beautiful sounding word, 'Paraclete.' He explained that it meant 'Comforter, Helper, Counselor, Advocate, Strengthener, Intercessor, and Stand-by.' He then said he believed it was a normal and common experience for those who had been baptized in the Holy Spirit to speak in an unknown tongue. He said it would help in opening up a new dimension of worship in one's personal life, in finding victory over besetting sins, and in effectively fulfilling the Great Commission. He finished out his sermon by explaining how one could receive the Baptism in the Holy Spirit; it was a gift that couldn't be earned, but could only be simply received, and an important key was total surrender to the Lordship of Jesus Christ.

The piano player began to underscore very softly in the key of C as Pastor Jeremy said, "We're going to sing 'I Surrender All.' If any of you want the Baptism in the Holy Spirit, come forward, and our prayer counselors are here to stand with you in prayer. Also, I know the majority of you love the Lord, but I feel in my spirit there are some phony 'Christians' here tonight who are faking it, but don't really know Him. If you were to die tonight, you would go straight to hell. It's time for you to quit playing games and get serious with the Lord. If that describes you, come on down to the altar and give your life to Christ tonight. The Lord will welcome you and wash you clean by the precious Blood of Jesus!"

The worship band started to sing these words:

"All to Jesus, I surrender,
All to Him I freely give:
I will ever love and trust Him,
In His presence daily live.

I surrender all!
I surrender all!
All to Thee my blessed Savior,
*I surrender all!"*₁

Brad walked down to the front of the church. He had issues in his life with sins common among men and felt convicted of the inconsistencies in his Christian life.

"Lord, fill me with Your Holy Spirit," he prayed. "Forgive me of my habitual sins that I keep falling into, and also, save my parents."

Brad felt like his prayer was unclean and didn't have much personality in it, but all of a sudden, he felt a great cleansing charge throughout His whole being and a great load lift off from him. He heard unfamiliar syllables in his brain while a counselor kneeling by him urged him to let it go and speak it out. Brad began to speak those syllables that on the surface seemed like gibberish. He felt joy and really understood what the Word of God meant when it called the Holy Spirit the Comforter. *He was indeed a comforter!* Brad also had a new sense of the Majesty and Excellency of Jesus Christ and began to speak out in English, words of worship.

"Praise You, Jesus! Hallelujah, hallelujah! Thank You, beautiful Jesus for Your beautiful Holy Spirit!"

Brad laughed in response to the great joy and freedom he now felt within his being. He then poured out more words of worship to his Lord. He now understood the spontaneous outbursts of praise and worship in that congregation. It wasn't mindless emotionalism, and even if it was, Brad wouldn't trade it off for anything because he was free! Even if the entire world would accuse him of being mentally retarded, he would be *happily* mentally retarded because of the joy in his heart.

Brad continued to praise God in English and in his new tongue. He was having a ball with the Lord and really having a Holy Ghost party. *This is really living! I could stay here forever! I never want to leave this place of communion with Jesus!* Eventually, there was a tap on Brad's arm.

"Brad! *Brad!* It's time to go."

It was Pam who was trying to get his attention.

"This is so wonderful! Praise You, beautiful, beautiful, wonderful Jesus! I want to stay here forever! I feel like I can fly!

'I coulda' danced all night,
I coulda' danced all night

And still have begged for more!
I coulda' spread my wings
And done a thousand things
I've never done before!
I'll never know what made it so exciting,
Why all at once my heart took flight,
I only know when Jesus filled me with His joy,
I coulda' danced, danced, danced all night!'

"Oh, Jesus, You are so lovely!" sang Brad.

Pam was very familiar with Brad's experience, having been filled with the Holy Spirit herself. It was interesting how everyone was different in his or her response to the Baptism. She had never seen a person receiving the Holy Spirit respond by singing that smash hit tune from Lowe and Lerner's *My Fair Lady* with the spiritualized variations of the lyrics, which Brad had sung.

Everyone is unique in his or her personality. The Lord really has a sense of humor!

"Brad, I know how happy you are. I think it's great and am thrilled for you, but we have to get going. It's after ten o'clock."

"Holy hot dog, after ten o'clock? It feels like I've been here only three minutes."

"Well. It's really after ten, and we need to hit the road. You look drunk. Do you want me to drive?"

"No, Pam, I can drive! I got the joy of the Lord! I adore You, sweetest Jesus!" Brad staggered around the room, obviously drunk in the Holy Spirit.

"Brad, I really think I should drive. You're too drunk on the Lord right now to handle it."

"Okay, Pam, whatever you say."

They climbed into Brad's car, and Pam fumbled around, trying to find the accelerator and the brakes. They started heading toward the Orinda BART station where Pam had parked her car. Hopefully, Brad would come in for a landing before then so that he would be able to drop off Pam and be sober enough to drive himself back to Moraga. As Pam was driving, Brad continued his drunken worship of the Lord by singing:

"The Comforter has come, the Comforter has come!
The Holy Ghost from heav'n, the Father's promise giv'n:
O spread the tidings 'round wherever man is found—
*The Comforter has come!"*₂

Brad knew that his life would never be the same again; he was *free!*

7.

THE WORMS IN THE BIG APPLE

At 10:00 A. M. on Monday, November 26, Randy Miller, Brian Manning, and Hiram Quinn were sitting once again in the plush, yellow-green office of manager Harry Gates for another brainstorming powwow concerning the future of the group, The Universal Mindset. It was a very tense and nerve-racking session for Randy as he was sitting in front of the great kingmaker of the American pop music industry. He knew Harry Gates had the power to make or break the image of famous singing stars, and that there were many details, which had to be taken care of on the bumpy road to the rainbow treasure trove of Fame and Fortune. Brian Manning was fairly nervous and excited himself while the brain of Hiram Quinn was working on a whole lot of ideas and details.

"Let's get started, guys," said Harry. "All of you have a seat."

All the men sat down in the plush seats around the big brown desk of impresario Harry Gates.

"First of all, you guys are doing a great job. The concert at the Pavilion last month was a huge success. You guys were stellar. We're still getting feedback on how good the performance was and words of praise on the original tunes. Randy, your song, 'The Evil Eye,' is already a big hit on radio station KROK and is beginning to be played on other radio stations around the country.

"To continue, I have big plans for you guys. We have the recording session at Tower Records here in town coming up in two days. This should really help to get publicity for us around the country. If all goes well, we are looking at a smash hit LP. I have some big venues for you that I'm looking at. I'm trying to get you booked in for a full concert at the Cow Palace around Christmas time. After that, we're trying to book a three-month tour around the country, beginning at the start of January that will include Carnegie Hall around January 15. Our goal is to perform in such cities as Washington D. C., Cleveland, Chicago, Seattle, Birmingham, Denver, and Las Vegas. If we play our cards right, you will be tremendously rich and famous within the next several weeks.

"To be able to reach these goals, we're going to have to fine-tune several things. One of these has to do with getting a gimmick for the group. Randy, we've got to work on getting a catchier stage name for you; the name, Randy Miller, just doesn't quite cut the mustard."

"Nothing wrong that I can see with my name," said Randy.

"Well, your name is nice, but it just doesn't quite have the oomph we need for a pop group that will catch the fancy of the masses. Let's try out some ideas of how to improve on this."

"Well, let me see," said Randy. "How about 'Red Randy?'"

"Nah," said Brian. "Too corny!"

"It's just too hokey," said Hiram. "We need something with a little more pizzazz."

"Wait a minute, how about 'Randy the Remarkable?'"

"No, sorry!" said Harry. "That won't do it either."

"Well, there's got to be *something!*" said Randy.

"How about, 'Rock-and-Roll Randy,' or 'Randy, the Wild Rock-and-Roller?'" asked Brian.

"Nope," said Harry. "It doesn't have enough originality and sparkle."

They tried a bunch of other titles like 'Roadmaster Randy' and 'Marvelous Miller' with no affirmation from the producers.

Harry finally asked, "What's your middle name, Randy?"

"Joshua. But I don't particularly like the idea of using my middle name as the one that the public remembers me by."

"Well, you're going to have to be open to doing it," said Hiram, "if you want to be a smash hit in this racket."

Randy was not too happy about it, but said, "Well, okay, if we have to, we have to. How about 'Jolly Joshua?'"

"Nah," said Harry. "Not catchy enough."

"Maybe, 'Jazzy Joshua?'"

"A little better," said Hiram, "but not quite there yet. Maybe if we just use 'Josh' instead of 'Joshua' to begin with."

Harry thought for a few moments. Then he suddenly snapped his fingers in excited inspiration. "I got it, I got it! How about— 'Jitterbug Josh?' I think that is where the gimmick is!"

"Yeah, I like it, I like it!" exclaimed Hiram.

"Good idea," said Brian. "I think that will sell."

"Well, okay," said Randy. "If you really think that will do the trick, I'll buy that."

"Good, good!" exclaimed Harry. "We're all agreed on that, then. Now, we've got to work on the movements of you on stage, that is, stage presence and personality projection. The outfits we ordered and had tailored for you guys look really snazzy. The yellow ties really blend in well with the black suits and gray shirts, but we need to take some time, Josh, to work on your movements on stage and your small talk between songs to make you and the members of Universal Mindset really hip. Remember this: image is everything!"

Over the next four hours, they practiced on Randy's presentation and expression as well as helping to come up with some movements during his songs.

"Say these lines from your gut, using a vivacious radio emcee voice," he was told.

The movements on stage they came up with included among other things, a kind of twitching movement with his whole body on the fast tunes, and a sensuous smoother movement on the ballads such as "Just like Creamy Silk." The two producers were finally satisfied with the gimmick they had come up with.

****

"BURNS, you are a great big troublemaker and I've a good mind to skin you alive!"

Once again, Eric Burns was sitting in the office of his boss, William Butcher, on the last Tuesday of November. He was seated on the soft-cushioned, black swivel chair in front of Mr. Butcher's dull-colored light-green desk with its maps neatly piled on it. A cup full of pens was right in front of the boss.

"I didn't do anything wrong, Boss," whined Eric in a low voice. "Honest! I swear it."

"Well, the report I got today says otherwise, Burns! Yesterday, you threw a fit on the bus in the afternoon when you were transporting the teenagers to their homes."

"THAT'S A LIE!" exclaimed Eric. "I didn't lose my temper or hit anybody."

"Well, let me enumerate your wrongs that I heard from several people. You yelled at the youths to shut up. Then you stopped the bus for fifteen minutes and went into a big screaming tirade. You used horrible language that would make the most profane sailor blush—and to cap it off, you greatly insulted the students, calling them things like 'fatheaded mental retards,' and 'dirty, stinking, rotten swine.' Burns, this is TOTALLY UNACCEPTABLE AND UNCALLED FOR in a school bus-driver!"

"Well, I don't know where you get your information from," sniveled Eric. "It's all a big exaggeration."

"From three people? I don't think so, Charlie Brown! Burns, I want you to apologize to the whole bus tomorrow. I'm docking your pay thirty dollars for this month—and I warn you, just one more goof up or infraction, and you can kiss your ever-loving bus-driving job goodbye! Do you understand?"

"Yes, Mr. Butcher."

"Dismissed!"

Eric left the office in a great rage, feeling both embarrassed at himself and angry with his mega-strict boss. He muttered to himself, "I hate my life! That Mr. Butcher! He gets all the good things and sits around all day in the lap of luxury, while guys like me have to break our necks transporting those rotten kids to school and back. Oh well! Comes the day of a Soviet America when greed will be no more and the government will take care of everybody."

****

DURING THE ENSUING WEEKS, things were really going well for Randy and the group, The Universal Mindset. The recording session at Tower Records on November 28 went as smooth as silk. The recording studio was HUGE. There was the recording booth where the engineer, Jon Stevens, had his mixing board, his 24-track Tascam reel-to-reel tape recorder, and his two-track stereo tape recorder. Outside of the booth was the main room with a Steinway grand piano, a big drum kit, and many microphones on mike stands. The recording session took three days—November 28, 29, and 30. The first day was taken up with the rhythm section recording the songs that were going on the album, Randy playing guitar, and filling in on piano on a few songs. The second day was devoted to the singers recording their parts on the songs, while the third day was devoted to mix-down of the project. There were ten songs on the album, all of them being original songs by Randy or Brian. Harry Gates was the executive producer of the project who sat in the sound booth, giving the word whether to accept the take or do part or all of the song over. All the band members were there to perform their parts: George Newman on piano, Keith Bryant on rhythm guitar, Mark Dole on drums, Fred Barnes on bass, and Bart Anderson, Brian Manning, and Randy Miller (alias 'Jitterbug Josh') being the three male singers.

On Friday night, Brian Manning threw a big party at his lovely house in Pleasant Hill to listen to the mixed-down project on his record player. The entire band along with their wives and kids sat in the large, bright living room facing west. The girls were sitting on the blue sofa while the men sat on the floor. As the record played, the band members voiced out proud boasts of admiration for their project. At this moment, they were listening to the final mix-down of "The Evil Eye."

"Wow!" exclaimed Bart. "Listen to those overtones!"

"And I really like the way Jon panned all the singers and instruments— and that reverb setting really hits the spot," added Fred.

"I sure did a good job on my guitar solo!" crowed Randy. "That distortion and those slides really added a lot to my tune!"

"Boy, I love those vocal harmonies!" gloated Brian. "We're really on our way to Easy Street."

"And the rhythm section is sure tight!" exclaimed Mark Dole. "We really got a hot band."

The group continued to exult as they listened to the master cut of the album while sipping their cans of beer and munching on Lay's Potato Chips.

****

BRAD APPLEBAUM was a very happy person for days on end after that fateful Sunday night when he had received the Baptism in the Holy Spirit. He had a new sense of the reality of Jesus and His love. Before that experience, there had been times when he had doubted the reality of the bodily resurrection of Jesus, due to all the anti-Christian teaching at UC Berkeley, but no more. He had a new joy and peace, which he had never experienced before, which came directly from the Holy Spirit. The first two nights after that church service, he hadn't been able to sleep at all because of the great joy flowing through him; he had spent the nights praising the Lord and speaking in tongues. He laughed a lot during the days that followed, which he had not done very much of in the preceding years. His grades began to improve, and his self-confidence and poise soared. He sensed a new power in his prayer life as well as his attempts to witness to people about Christ. During a speech class a couple of weeks after his new-found experience with being filled by the Holy Spirit, Brad gave a speech on the resurrection of Christ, which was much improved over his previous attempts at public speaking. Professor James Corrigan was very impressed and didn't have much criticism to give Brad. Professor Corrigan was himself a Christian, even though there were some differences of opinion between Brad and himself on some minor issues. Of course, the students who were atheistic or agnostic in the class still found some ways to criticize him on his speech.

Later that day, Brad was again meeting with his Christian 'revolutionary' friends for their weekly Bible study with Hal Odell presiding over the get-together. Today, the study was on being filled with the Holy Spirit by faith, confessing and receiving forgiveness of sins, praying for the Lord to fill you with the Holy Spirit, and then believing that you were filled with the Holy Spirit not by relying on feelings, but relying on the sure promises in God's Word. After the study, there was the usual time set aside for prayer requests.

"I had another rough time with my parents last night," said Brad. "We were arguing about how old the earth is, life on other planets, and UFOs. My dad and mom think that the earth is 4.6 billion years old, while I know that it is only 6,000 years old as is the case with the age of the universe. They argue that there is life on other planets and that there are UFOs visiting the earth right now that are beings from another planet while I know that these UFOs are demons. My parents just have no knowledge of God at all and are great sinners. Please pray for them."

"Well, one thing you might want to be careful of, Brad," said Hal. "Watch out that you don't get side-tracked and run off on a tangent. When you witness to people, try to keep it simple and centered on the main issues of sin, heaven, hell, and the death and resurrection of Jesus to save them from their sins through His free gift. Also, it's important to witness to them by the way you live and by your love and respect for them."

"But they do so many things wrong, besides being so materialistic and earthly minded rather than heavenly minded."

"It doesn't matter, Brad. They are still your mom and dad and will be won over by your love, rather than you nagging them or trying to push the gospel on them. Coming on as a 'Mr. Know-it-all' never wins anyone to Christ."

"Well, they need information from the Word of God, and they've got to know the truth."

Brad was a youth who was resistant and somewhat stubborn against the idea of change and was sensitive and touchy when he received constructive criticism. He had experienced some wonderful things from the Lord and was sure he knew more about spiritual things than most people did.

****

THINGS WERE BUMPING RIGHT ALONG for 'Jitterbug Josh' and the group, Universal Mindset. Harry Gates was able to book the Cow Palace for the band to do a full concert on Saturday evening, December 22. Publicity was getting around fast because of Randy's new hit single, "The Evil Eye," that had already soared to number 7 on the rock-and-roll hit parade, and 20th on the pop charts. Harry was also having success in booking concerts on the planned cross-country tour slated for the early part of 1974, including an upcoming concert at Carnegie Hall scheduled for the evening of January 19. The band members were eagerly looking forward to the big Cow Palace performance. Randy was writing out chord chart arrangements for some popular Christmas carols like "Jingle Bells," "White Christmas," and "Winter Wonderland," and Scot Coates, a famous orchestral arranger, was blitzing out some quickie arrangements for an auxiliary orchestra and choir that would be sweetening up the sound of Randy's band.

****

ON SATURDAY AFTERNOON, Brad was practicing his flute part on Claude Bolling's *Suite for Flute and Piano,* a crossover classical/jazz suite, which had just recently been published. He had coaxed Professor Frank Douglas into letting him learn that suite, even though the professor hated any music that had even a hint of jazz in it. The composition was a very beautiful and tough piece of music to learn, and Brad was practicing lines he was having trouble with over and over again. The flute parts were loud, and the rest of the family's nerves were getting frayed.

Finally, Harriet walked into the living room to put a stop to it. "Brad, BRAD!"

"What, Mom?" asked Brad as he stopped playing his flute in the middle of a phrase.

"You've been playing the same thing over and over again, and your father and I are getting sick and tired of it! Would you please play something else?"

"But Mom, I got to practice this piece for my professor at school. I want to do good. No way I'm going to stop this practice until I get it perfect."

"Don't argue with me Brad! Do as you're told! We've been listening to the same flute part for more than an hour!" stormed Harriet.

"Okay, okay," mumbled Brad in a grumpy voice, his pride badly hurt.

He went back to practicing his flute part, honing in on another part of the suite. A little later, Harriet came back into the living room again saying, "All right, Brad! That's enough. No more practice for this afternoon. We've had it!"

"Oh, come on, Mom, you're not being a bit fair! You're not thinking of me and my needs! You don't care about my music or the things of the Lord! All you and Dad care about is money, golf, bridge, and poker! You—"

"Brad, I told you! I'm your mom, and you are to do as I tell you without griping about it! GROW UP! You are nineteen years old, not a two-year-old who sucks his thumb!"

Brad began to walk heavily and angrily out of the living room toward his bedroom when Harriet called out to him again.

"Brad, you come back here and get your stuff out of my living room!"

"Right, Mom," growled Brad as he waddled back into the living room, mumbling to himself, "this idea of keeping this living room squeaky clean is *stupid!*"

"And quit acting like a little baby who needs diapers. When I tell you to do something, you should do it without whining, without making a big scene over it, and without that big pout on your face. And you need to learn something that is lacking in your life right now, *CONSIDERATION OF OTHERS!*"

Brad snappily picked up his music book and flute, packed the flute in its protective case, and trudged dejectedly towards his bedroom.

****

OVER THE NEXT FEW DAYS, Brad felt as if the Lord had withdrawn Himself from him. He read the Bible and prayed a lot but had no joy in his life. When he tried to witness, he stammered over his words and couldn't get any inspiration of ideas to say to people. When he read the Bible, he had trouble understanding the passages he would peruse. His creative juices just wouldn't flow when he would try to write a short story or some poetry. On Tuesday night, he kneeled in his bedroom to spend some time in prayer. He started praying like this:

"Lord, thank You for this day—and I thank You that Jesus died on the cross for my sins. I thank You for Your beautiful Holy Spirit. I've been feeling depressed lately, and I pray for You to fill me with Your Holy Spirit again. Please fill me with the joy of the Lord and take this depression away from me. Right now, I pray for the salvation of my mom and dad. They don't understand the things of God at all. They have no knowledge of the Bible or spiritual things, let alone the wonderful experience that I've gotten of being baptized with the Holy Spirit with the evidence of speaking in other tongues. They believe in evolution, UFOs, and reincarnation. They are very godless people. They smoke, drink, and gamble. They—"

Honor thy father and thy mother that thy days may be long upon the land which the LORD thy God giveth thee.

Brad was startled; "Lord, is that You or only my imagination?"

Yes, Brad, it is I, the Great I AM. You need to honor and respect your father and your mother.

"But Lord, they don't know or love You at all! They are not Christians."

It doesn't matter, Brad! My Word doesn't say, 'Honor thy father and thy mother only if they're God-fearing people.' It says, 'Honor thy father and thy mother,' period. Many of My servants have made shipwreck of their lives simply because of their disrespect for their mother and father.

"Lord, what does it mean, then, when You said that if anyone comes after You and does not hate his father and mother—and even his own life, he cannot be Your disciple?"

Brad, it simply means your love for Me should be so great that it makes your love for your parents look like hatred in comparison. You are to put Me first in everything. You are not to compromise your walk with Me or your convictions in any way in order to be like your parents—or to gain acceptance with the world. But you need to honor, love, obey, and respect your parents—And Brad. I want you to read Acts 16:31.

Brad opened his Bible to the verse in Acts that said, "Believe on the Lord Jesus Christ and thou shalt be saved and thy house."

He fell to his knees, tears running down his face, and cried out, "Forgive me, Lord! Please wash me with Your precious Blood!" He spent a lot of time pouring his heart out to the Lord, confessing his sins of gossiping against his parents, as well as his attitudes he had often had when they had asked him to do something he didn't like. After a while, he climbed into his double-sized bed in his light yellow-painted room on the northwest side of the house and fell into a peaceful sleep.

The next evening, Sid and Harriet were in the living room upstairs, talking about how the stock market had done that day. November had been a terrible month for Wall Street because of the Arab Oil Embargo and the threat of bad inflation and serious gas shortages. While they were conversing, Brad walked into the room.

"Mom! Dad!" said Brad in a low and contrite voice.

"What is it, son?" asked Sid.

"Um—I want to apologize for something."

"What about, son?" queried Sid.

"The Lord told me last night that I've not been honoring you the way I should. I've been gossiping against you and badmouthing you to my friends, and I'm very, very sorry for that. I've also had a bad attitude during the times that you told me to do something I didn't want to do, like the time last Saturday afternoon when I wouldn't quit playing those tedious flute parts over and over again. I want to say, from here on out, what you say, goes. You know that I just want to see you get saved and washed in the Blood of the Lamb."

"Oh, thank you, Brad! You're quite a guy!" exclaimed Harriet. "Apology accepted!"

"Yes, thank you," said Sid. "You are forgiven."

Harriet rose up from her soft-cushioned, white swivel chair and gave Brad a great big body hug. "I love you, son!"

"I love you too, Mom and Dad."

As Brad walked back into his bedroom to do his homework for college, the parents changed their conversation from business matters to the recent conversation with their son.

Said Harriet, "Wow! Brad is really into his religion big-time! He's really radical about it, but I must say, I really like and appreciate what he says 'the Lord' told him to say to us."

"Yeah, it really shows a lot of class."

"I think religion is doing a lot of good for him. It's making him happy. We have three pretty wonderful children! We are very lucky parents."

"Uh huh. I think you're right, I think you're right."

****

DECEMBER 22 FINALLY ARRIVED with cloudy weather, but with sunshine in 'Jitterbug Josh's' soul. The band arrived at the Cow Palace early in the morning to set up the equipment and do a sound check. They also practiced with the orchestra and choir. Everything came together without any major problems, and the time for the big concert finally arrived. It was a full house, and the performance was well-nigh perfect. The audience responded with ovation after ovation. At the end of the concert, the budding music star was thronged with autograph seekers who were totally enamored with his music. Randy's ears were ringing with the cries of adulation and admiration, especially from the pretty teenage girls who encircled him.

"Hey, Jitterbug Josh, can I have your autograph?"

"You're hip, man! You're cool!"

"You're the greatest, Jitterbug Josh!"

"You're my idol! I like the way you move your body on stage!"

"You're a hot cat! You really know how to sing those songs!"

"You're the best singer and guitar player in the whole world!"

"Sign my forehead, please," said a man who was in his early twenties. "Yeah, that's cool, right on man! Hey everybody, look at me! Jitterbug Josh just signed my forehead! I'll never wash my face again!"

Finally, Randy and the band members were able to get out of there around 11:00 P. M.

Late that night, the band members and their families were having a big celebration at the Top of the Town restaurant on the fifty-second floor of the Bank of America building in San Francisco. Everybody was in a lighthearted mood, and Randy was gulping down glass after glass of Champagne, getting more and more buzzed by the minute.

"The orchestra and choir sure sounded great tonight!" exulted Bart Anderson.

"Yeah, those harmonies were gorgeous," commented George Newman, "and my piano playing was great, too!"

"And did you see the people thronging me, tonight?" asked Randy. "They really like me and my singing and guitar playing!"

They continued to live it up until 2:30 in the morning when they began to break it up and prepare to drive home. Randy staggered toward the elevator, loudly singing the refrain to "Just like Creamy Silk," slurring the words and changing the 'S's into 'SH's. While they were in the elevator, Randy teetered and fell against the back wall.

"Ooohh, are you all right?" asked an elderly man in a concerned voice.

"He's okay," assured Lila to the kindly stranger. "He's just had a tiny bit too much to drink. Honey, I think you should let me drive."

"No, I'm okay, I can drive."

Lila responded lovingly and gently, "I really think you should let me do the honors."

Randy was finally convinced by the persistent coaxing of his lovely wife and agreed to let her drive home.

The rest of that night was tough for both of them. Lila had a dickens of a time helping him out of the car and into bed. Neither of them got a wink of sleep that night. Randy groaned and raved in his drunken state and threw up several times on his pillow. Lila had a very disgusting mess to clean up the next morning.

****

MEANWHILE, IN A SLEAZY BAR in Lodi, California, Darryl Temple was drinking himself drunk and getting rowdier by the minute. Louie, the bartender, had just gotten to the point where he couldn't take it anymore.

"Gimme' anodder' whiskey, please'h, I'm thirsty!" whined Darryl to the bartender.

"No, I think you've had enough for one night. You've already had six large glasses."

110

"If you don' gimme' anodder' drink, I'm gonna get real angry! You rotten bartenders do a crummy job in this'h town! Your cruelty is matched only by your stupidity!"

"All right, sir! That's the last straw!" yelled Louie. "Git' your stinkin' body out of here before I call the cops!"

"Who you callin' stinkin'?" protested Darryl loudly, throwing his glass across the room where it shattered into smithereens on the floor. Protests rang out from the bar patrons.

"Okay, you little punk kid!" snarled Louie, grabbing Darryl by the ear. "I'm gonna throw you outta' this place! You've been nothing but a great big troublemaker tonight, and I'm gonna hafta' bounce you outta' here!"

"NO, you ain't!" barked Darryl. He started punching Louie in the face. Louie slapped Darryl's mouth hard and knocked him down. Bewildered and dazed, Darryl got back on his feet and swung a hard haymaker to the right eye of Louie. Louie winced in pain and staggered to the telephone while some of the patrons headed toward Darryl to try to restrain him. Darryl lashed out at them with all his might, and a free-for-all broke out in the bar, Darryl swinging wildly at all his attackers, throwing whiskey glasses across the room, knocking over chairs and tables, and breaking the window that looked out onto the street. The crowd was finally able to subdue Darryl, and soon, the sound of police sirens could be heard in the distance, getting closer and closer. In short order, four policemen entered the bar and handcuffed Darryl Temple.

"Oh, it's you again huh?!" exclaimed one of the officers. "Okay, cowboy, the nice horsy ride is over! We're going to round you up and lasso you in!"

Another of the cops was reading Darryl his constitutional rights.

"You have the right to remain silent, you have the right to an attorney of law, if you cannot afford an attorney, the state will gladly supply—"

Darryl looked up at the police officers with a dazed look on his face. Through blurry and bloodshot eyes, he espied the right eye of Louie the bartender rapidly turning a dark purple color. His lip was bleeding, his nose was battered, and the handcuffs were cutting very sharply into his wrists, but in his drunken state, Darryl felt hardly any pain at all. He had a dim recollection of several nights when he had been confined in a jail cell in Jackson.

A little later, the rowdy youth was sitting in a hard chair at the police station while the judge was enumerating the wrongs he had committed that night.

"Public drunkenness, disturbing the peace, breaking a window, damage to chairs and tables at the bar, assaulting the bartender and patrons, etcetera. This is going to cost you some time shut up in jail, Temple!"

The warden led the drunk Darryl Temple to his dank prison cell in the local jailhouse in Jackson, California.

****

DECEMBER 30, 1973 was a cold, sunshiny day in the Bay Area. Brad, Pam, and about 500 other people attended the service at Berkeley Tabernacle Fellowship on that morning. Today, Pastor David Maxwell preached another sermon on the crisis in the Middle East and related it to end-time Bible prophecy.

"America and much of the world is teetering on the verge of a depression due to the Arab Oil Embargo," he said, "and many experts have started to recommend a pro-Arab policy in order to save our skins, but I do not share their viewpoint at all. We need to bless the Jew. Bless National Israel. Bless and curse not! I want to take a closer look at that Scripture in Genesis 12 concerning blessing and cursing Abraham and his descendants. In the original Hebrew, the two occurrences of the word 'bless' are the same, but 'curse' and 'curseth' are two different Hebrew words. 'I will curse them' literally means, 'I will cause calamity, trouble, and harm to them,' while 'that curseth thee' means, 'that despises thee, that makes light of thee, that looks with disdain upon thee.' This is *heavy!* This means, if you dishonor the Jewish people in any way, you are in big-time hot water with God. Just look at history: Egypt, Babylon, Nazi Germany, and the Arab Bloc in the last three Middle East wars—all of them have experienced God's judgment—and it will continue to be that way in the future. There is coming a time very soon when Russia and many other countries will try to attack Israel and experience God's wrath for touching the Apple of His eyes. You can read about it in Ezekiel, chapters 38 and 39. Later on, all the nations of the world are going to come against Israel at Armageddon, and God will pour out His wrath upon them. Read about it in Zechariah and in the book of Revelation, chapter 19. In contrast to that, I would submit to you that the reason we have prospered so much as a nation here in America is due to the fact that we have stood by National Israel and been a safe haven for the Jewish people over the centuries. However, if we ever turn against National Israel, WATCH OUT! Our blessed country will fall so fast, it will make your hair curl! The bottom line here is this: do you have Jewish friends and neighbors? Love them. Be a friend to them. Yes, share the gospel with them, but don't do it in an arrogant way. They have been trodden underfoot and they need love more than words.

"Secondly, pray for the Jews and National Israel. Psalm 122 tells us to 'Pray for the peace of Jerusalem; they shall prosper that love thee.' Pray God's blessings and prosperity on them. Pray that many of them will come to know Jesus their Messiah. Most Jews continue to reject Jesus as Messiah, and I believe there are two reasons for this. Number one: the Bible tells us in Romans, chapters 9, 10, and 11 that a partial blindness has fallen upon most of them until the fullness of the Gentiles has come in. But the day is coming soon when the Holy Spirit will be poured out on them, and multitudes upon multitudes of Jews will come to saving faith in Jesus. Number two: too many professing Christians throughout the ages have had the false belief that God has rejected the Jews forever, even killing and torturing multitudes of them. This has helped to embitter their hearts against Christians.

"Lastly: Jesus is coming very, very soon to rapture His Church, and we need to be ready! As the organ plays softly, please make sure of your salvation today. Don't delay!"

The choir, which was clad in their beautiful blue robes, walked on up to the risers and started singing "Just as I Am." Two people came forward to make decisions for Christ.

****

IT WAS NOW EARLY in the year 1974, and the nationwide tour of The Universal Mindset was well under way. They started out with a big concert on Friday, January 4, at the Oakland Arena, a place that could hold close to 7,000 people. The place was packed, and the concert was a huge success. On the next day, the band started their national tour using two vans. Their first stop was Lake Tahoe at the Saharan Inn. After that, they performed in Reno, Las Vegas, Denver, Kansas City, St. Louis, Chicago, Cleveland, Pittsburgh, and finally, New York City where they had their big booking at Carnegie Hall on Saturday evening, January 19. Every place where they performed at was a huge success with full to overflowing houses and rave reviews. The attendance at the concerts ranged anywhere from 650 to 10,000 people, the average being around 3,000.

Life had changed radically for 'Jitterbug Josh,' Lila, and their two young boys. Gone were the quiet evenings with the family watching TV or playing Monopoly together. Gone were the nights out at a nice restaurant like Petars or the Casa Orinda for Randy and Lila. Also gone were the friendly golf games at Mira Vista Country Club for Randy. Even before his big trip, Randy's growing fame was taking away much of his free time. When he arrived at his eight-room house in the afternoons, there were often autograph seekers or magazine and newspaper reporters seeking an audience with the budding new celebrity. Randy had recently turned in his resignation as the choral teacher of Campolindo High School due to his newfound career as a rock-and-roll star. Jack and Tommy were now the envy of all their classmates at school, as everybody in the student body now knew who they were because of their famous papa.

Now, Randy was sitting on the stage at Carnegie Hall itself, the Granddaddy of concert halls in the USA. He looked around at the very large auditorium with its 3,000 light-green colored, padded seats. The stage had a wooden floor and a beautiful Steinway grand piano while the walls were a quasi-white color. Brightly lit lamps added luster to the stage. Mark Dole had a drum kit with the letters, 'JJ' printed on the bass drum, the letters standing for 'Jitterbug Josh.' The amber music stands for the bass and guitar players also had the initials 'JJ' printed on them. Randy mused with great pride at where he was right now. *This is the big day for me! I've actually arrived at Carnegie Hall and am making my debut here tonight! How cool is that?! I'm now right up there with the big boys like George Gershwin, Leonard Bernstein, Benny Goodman, Frank Sinatra—and Elvis!*

The group rehearsed their program, and in short order was all ready to go. The doors opened at 7:15 for the crowd to take their seats, and the whole band met for a short pep talk by manager Harry Gates and group leader Brian Manning in the Green Room.

"Well, gang, this is our big day!" started Brian. "We've come a long way and are actually nationally famous! Who would have thought last September that we would be a big-name group by the time the New Year rolled in? We were just a little ragtag group called Sneezer at the time. Who would have guessed that our lead singer, Herb Taylor, would come down with cancer of the larynx? (Well, I guess it was possible to see it coming since Herbie smoked so many cigarettes.) Nevertheless, who could have guessed that Randy over here would come on board with us to sub at a one-night-stand and end up writing a couple of tunes for us that would become such smash hits? Who could have guessed he would also prove to be such a marvelous lead singer and guitar player? Who could have guessed that we would open for Sha-Na-Na at the Concord Pavilion in October and then cut a smash hit album, perform at the Cow Palace, and also perform at the Oakland Arena? And lookie here; we are actually at Carnegie Hall! Many times, fate has a way of doing some funny twists; look at all the musicians who became famous overnight. We can really thank our lucky stars that the gods of the music world decided to give us a good turn. So, since this is our big day, I want us to go out there and give it all we got with that good old Universal Mindset spirit! Are you with me?"

"Yeah!" exclaimed everybody enthusiastically.

Harry Gates now took the floor to give his short pep talk saying, "Are you all nervous tonight? It's a good and normal thing to be nervous. If you were not nervous, but sitting on your duffs, cracking jokes, fooling around, and bantering each other, that's the time I would start to worry. You know, the human body has a natural way of preparing for danger through the fabulous gift of something called 'Adrenaline.' Our cavemen ancestors hundreds of thousands of years ago experienced this adrenaline when they encountered a wild and dangerous animal like a lion or tiger. Today in America, we usually don't have to worry about fighting off a wild beast, but there are times in each of our lives when the body is called on to give us that boost, that certain 'oomph,' that certain 'shot in the arm.' It can be that big shot business tycoon who has to lead a very important business meeting. It can be a great actor like Burt Lancaster starring in a pivotal movie with a chance of winning an Oscar in Hollywood. Or it can be people like us who are budding rock stars performing right here at Carnegie Hall. Bottom line: all of us need that special something called 'Adrenaline.'

"So now, what should you do about this nervousness? This is what you do: relax, take some deep breaths, and go out there and give 'em heck! Get everything else out of your mind like the football game between the New York Jets and the Oakland Raiders—or the argument you may have had with your wife earlier today and concentrate completely on this important concert. And lastly, the most important thing is not to think about the audience at all and what they are thinking of your singing and playing, but to concentrate solely on the music itself. I know you guys are going to take this city by storm and be dynamite tonight. I am very proud of you and you are all winners! Now, let's go out there and BREAK A LEG!"

The band members in the Green Room cheered and made several comments of approval.

Presently, the stage manager knocked on the door and exclaimed, "Okay, Jitterbug Josh! You're on!"

The members of The Universal Mindset walked out to the stage of Carnegie Hall to be greeted by a full house and a colossal standing ovation. The band then kicked into their opening number, "The Evil Eye," with the roars from the crowd erupting anew. After that, they did the slow ballad written by Randy, "Just like Creamy Silk." The whole concert thereafter consisted of pieces, written either by Randy in his trance states or songs written by Brian. Some of the songs included pieces like "Hollywood Honeymoon," "Blue Love," "The American Dream," "Sensual Sue," "It Happened on Highway 5," "Lullaby of the Las Vegas Lovers," and "A Young Astrologer's Vision." Everything went off without a hitch, and the crowd was very enthusiastic in their cheering after each number. As in many other concerts, the band had the opportunity of taking bow after bow at the end of the concert as the people frantically cheered the celebrities.

Then there were the autograph seekers who thronged the music group as well as the various newspaper and magazine reporters itching for information of the possible future plans of 'Jitterbug Josh.' Lila and the two boys were waiting at the back of the auditorium when Randy was finally finished dealing with all of his many fans.

"Let's hurry it up, Randy," said Lila. "Me and the boys are worn out."

"I'm almost ready to go, dear. We still have that big celebration party at the Elegant Chateau Restaurant."

"You go without us," sighed Lila. "We're just too pooped to join in the festivities."

"But aren't you proud of me?" asked Randy. "You know that this was my big night, and you saw for yourself how much the crowd loved me. Obviously, they know how great I am and can appreciate real talent when they hear it."

"Yes," responded Lila coolly. "You sang and played very brilliantly tonight. Come on, Jack and Tommy. Let's get going!"

Randy and the rest of the band celebrated at the Elegant Chateau Restaurant without Lila or his two sons. Overall, he felt very happy and excited over the wonderful events of the evening, yet there was something missing; there was a void, an emptiness in his heart that he couldn't put his finger on. He felt a nagging and vague depression at the sides of his heart that he couldn't figure out. *I must be more tired than I realize. We HAVE been going at a breakneck pace during these past several weeks. I should be flying high as a kite because of my triumph tonight, and yet, I feel jaded, tired, lethargic. What's the matter with me?*

The band members were exulting over the great success of the evening, eating their New York steak and lobster dinners, and swilling down their glasses of white Chablis and red Claret. Randy joined in with them on their eating, drinking, and bragging.

"Well, we were a smash tonight!" crowed Brian.

"Yeah, I did a great job on the piano," boasted George. "My chops were really in the pocket today!"

"Yeah," said Randy. "I was a big sensation here at Carnegie Hall! Did you hear all the cheering and compliments that I got from the audience? Maybe I am the greatest singer, songwriter, and guitar player in the world! Don't you guys think I'm great?"

"Oh boy, here we go again!" mumbled Fred Barnes to himself. "Old Jitterbug Josh's head is getting bigger and bigger."

"I propose a toast to the great concert I did tonight," said Randy, "and even greater success in the years ahead for me and you guys in the Universal Mindset!"

"A toast!" echoed the other group members as they clinked their wine glasses together. Randy rammed his glass against the glass of George Newman too hard and broke his glass, spilling wine all over the table.

****

LATE THAT NIGHT, Randy walked into his presidential suite room at the Waldorf Astoria Hotel where he and Lila were staying. Lila was still up, working on a crossword puzzle at the table. The two boys were asleep in the adjoining bedroom.

"Hi you honey!" said Randy.

"Hello," said Lila in a subdued and unenthusiastic voice.

"What's the matter, dear? This is my big night. My great talent has brought me the desire of my heart, fame and fortune. We have two TV sets at home, we're staying at the swankiest hotel in New York City, and I have millions of fans who adore me."

"I'll tell you 'what the matter' is," snapped Lila. "I feel that I don't have the same husband that I've had just a few months ago! I don't even know who you are anymore!"

"You're not making any sense at all, Lila. Of course I'm the same old man that I always was."

"The same old man? Oh yeah, sure, sure! You've changed, Randy. It used to be that we had time together as a couple and as a family. Even with the busy schedule you had as a choir director at Campolindo and at the United Church of the Valley, we still had times when we would go out to dinner or go see a movie. We had times when we would go bowling at Rheem Valley Bowl or go miniature golfing in Concord or play a nice parlor game like Monopoly or Sorry. Now we don't have any time together."

"But I have my career. I got to make the money that we need to support you and the boys and make you happy. I also have contracts to fulfill. After all, I thought that you approved the idea of me becoming rich and famous."

"But I had no idea that it was going to be like this! There's no time for ourselves. It's things like 'this gig at that nightclub' or 'this Lodge meeting' or 'the big concert tour.' I'm getting sick and tired of it! And besides, I'm sick and tired of not spending time with my best friend, Donna Applebaum!"

"Well, this is the way things have to be—so get over it and quit your bellyaching!"

"Don't you talk to me in that mean tone of voice, Randy Miller! I'm also sick and tired of being treated like a piece of dirt! I've had it! I'm sick of cleaning up your vomit off of your pillow after a drunken night of celebrating after one of your 'Big Concerts!' I'm sick of listening to your sarcastic, cutting remarks! I'm sick of you being called by that idiotstick, imbecile name of Jitterbug Josh instead of just plain old Randy Miller! And, most of all, I'm sick of hearing you talk about 'my wonderful musical talent' and 'how great I am!' You know what, Jitterbug Josh? You're nothing but a great big conceited old brat!"

"And you are an ungrateful ingrate," retorted Randy. "I thought that this twist in my career would make you happy. I thought that you would enjoy having all that extra money. I thought that you would be happy with your new fancy coat. I thought that you would have a ball out here in the Big Apple at this luxurious hotel, eating the best food, drinking the best wines, and staying in the loveliest hotel in the whole world. That's why I brought you and the kids out here. I thought that you would be thrilled to see me perform at Carnegie Hall, *at Carnegie Hall!* I thought that you would go 'gaga' over my big night and lavish me with praise. But what do I get? A lot of nagging and whining! All I can ask is, do you want some cheese with your whine?!"

"That was a corny and sarcastic joke!" lashed out Lila. "That's exactly what I mean by your sarcastic and cutting remarks—and no, I'm not at all happy being out here in New York City, especially when I have to watch all of those beautiful girls asking for your autograph and making googoo eyes at you! I feel like I'm being shared with other girls and wonder at times if you have things going on with any of them!"

"Lila, that is a stinking, low-down thing to accuse me of, and it is all a great big pack of lies! I've never had anything going on with any other woman except you. I can see that you are livid with jealousy and greener than the hundred-dollar bills in my wallet."

"JEALOUS, huh? Of course I'm jealous! What do you expect from me since you're never home and always surrounded by newspaper reporters, magazine writers, and teen idol worshippers? I've had it up to here! Why the way things are going, I think maybe I should drop the whole thing and just go ahead and get a divorce!"

"OKAY, OKAY! I'VE HAD ENOUGH OF YOU!" stormed Randy. "I'm going down to the bar and cool off a little with a few beers! Maybe tomorrow, you'll be in a better mood."

The music star stormed out of the room, slamming the door behind him, his pride deeply wounded, his spirits dejected, and hoping that maybe a couple of beers would numb the pain and emptiness deep within his soul.

8.

EXCURSION INTO THE SPIRIT WORLD

"**J**itterbug Josh and The Universal Mindset Band Boffo at Carnegie Hall," read the front-page article in *Variety* on Sunday, January 20, 1974. Mike Applebaum was sitting in his living room, reading the article about his best friend in that magazine and musing over the events of the last four months. *This is unbelievable! One encounter with that ridiculous spiritualist in Placerville and bam, Randy Miller is a famous rock star! This doesn't make any sense to me at all. This is an incredible fluke, a flash in the pan, a case of lightning striking the same place twice, an event like a 100-degree day in Antarctica!* Donna was sitting beside him, reading *Better Housekeeping,* while Michelle and Sharon were watching *The Waltons* on TV in the game room.

"You know, Mike," said Donna. "It seems like ages since we've even seen the Millers, let alone had an evening together with them."

"Yeah honey, things just aren't the same as they were only a few months ago. Randy doesn't seem to be his old self."

"You too, huh? Oh Mike, he's changed! He used to be a nice guy, but now, he's become very snobbish—and I sure miss Lila and the two boys!"

"Yeah, yeah. Randy does seem to be very unapproachable these days. He seems to think he is higher up than everyone else, and he is always surrounded by fans and the press."

"He *intimidates* me, Mike! The few times I've seen him in the last few months, I've felt like I've had to walk on eggshells. It's not the good old buddy-buddy relationship that we used to have."

"Lord Acton said it so clearly and succinctly, dear, when he said, 'Power corrupts and absolute power corrupts absolutely.'"

"But honey, do you really think that everybody who becomes rich and famous ends up being corrupted and conceited?"

"Oh, I don't know; there seems to be a few people who continue to be nice and friendly, who don't get the big head, who aren't affected by the trappings of fame and fortune."

"Name a few."

"Well, er—the great golfer Bobby Jones, for example, and also Bob Hope—and then there's Governor Ronald Reagan. I remember when we saw him at that Lion's Club meeting in 1966 when he was running for governor— he was very friendly and approachable, and I was very impressed with his grasp of the issues, his poise and demeanor, and his oratorical abilities, even though I think he's slightly too far to the right."

"But everyone else seems to become proud, vain, and conceited. I can name a whole lot of famous musicians, Mike, who have become too high and mighty to fit into their britches."

At that moment, their two daughters, ten-year-old Michelle and nine-year-old Sharon, came scampering into the room, giggling and making small talk. They were very friendly girls who were well behaved as well as excellent students.

"Hey Mom and Dad!" announced Sharon. "I've got to show you this watercolor painting of the seacoast that I did at school! Do you like it?"

"Why, that's a lovely picture!" exclaimed Donna. "You did a beautiful job, Sharon!"

"Yeah, that's pretty good," said Mike. "Keep it up."

"Thanks, Dad!"

The sky was darkening outside of their medium-sized, Spanish-style house on the east side of Moraga Road. It had been a fairly rainy January, but it had cleared up nicely on that Sunday, and the forecast for the coming week promised to bring fair and somewhat warmer weather for the San Francisco Bay Area.

****

"WHY, THAT'S A LOVELY POEM you wrote, Brad!"

"Thank you, Pam!"

It had been another wonderful night at Glad Tidings International Fellowship with uplifting and boisterous singing, heartfelt worship, and excellent preaching from Pastor Jeremy Norris. Tonight, he had preached on the imminent coming of the Lord for His Bride, relating the message to the current events happening in the world. He urged everybody in the congregation to make sure that their hearts were right before God because no one knew exactly when Jesus was coming back for His people. The worship band had sung a very contemporary Christian song for the invitation written by Christian artist Larry Norman called "I Wish We'd All Been Ready." Ever since that fateful night when Brad had received the Baptism in the Holy Spirit, he had made a habit of coming to Glad Tidings every Sunday night with Pam and was seriously thinking of making this new church his regular church home. He had written the poem he had just shown to Pam shortly after that fateful Sunday night in November 1973. The poem read like this:

> Like a bright landscape of glistening snow
> The Holy Ghost set my heart aglow,
> On that clear and star-studded wonderful night
> My soul He filled with matchless delight!

120

A forlorn vagabond lost in sin
On a vicious downward tailspin,
Was I 'til Jesus became my Boss
Giving me liberty at the Cross.

What freedom from fear, unrest, and strife!
What purpose I now have in my life!
My desire is to the whole world tell
How Jesus saved me from the jaws of hell.

The sweet Comforter has quenched my thirst
With love, joy, and peace, I feel I could burst!
With beautiful Jesus I will soon abide
As part of His spotless glorious Bride!

"Wow, Brad Applebaum!" exclaimed Pam. "I'm impressed! I didn't think you had it in you!"

"Thank you, Pam," said Brad. "It was from my heart."

"I could tell, Brad. I could tell."

While they were talking, Karen Thompson sidled up to them and asked, "Are either of you two interested in going for coffee with some of the gang at Denny's?"

"Yeah, I think I could hack it if it is okay with Pam, here," replied Brad.

"It's okay with me as long as we don't stay out too late. I have to get up early tomorrow morning."

****

TEN COLLEGE STUDENTS from Glad Tidings decided to have coffee and fellowship at Denny's. Brad was seated next to Walt Pickering, an English major at Diablo Valley Junior College. Pam and Karen were sitting across the table from them. Some of the other churchgoers included Stan Post, Nathan Reed, Julie Lopez, and Ellen Lovejoy. Conversation was animated and joyful, and much of the talk was about spiritual things. Stan and Nathan were involved in a friendly doctrinal discussion concerning whether the doctrine of Eternal Security was true or false, while some of the girls were talking about a man in Southern California who had experienced a dream about the Rapture a few years ago, describing how it would feel to be raptured up, and conversely, what it would be like to be one of those hapless people who were left behind. The talk eventually digressed into various students' attempts to lead other students to Christ on the DVC campus. The conversation among the men eventually centered on the unrelated topic of the current pro-basketball scene, although even there, the things of the Lord found their way into the conversation as some of the guys mentioned the names of a few pro-basketball players who were Christians.

"Hey Karen," said Pam. "Did you know that Brad over here is quite a poet?"

"No, I didn't."

"Well he showed me a poem he wrote a number of weeks ago, and it is absolutely *beautiful!*"

"Oh, really. Is it about the wonders of nature?"

"Well, it has a little of that in it, but it's mostly about his testimony of becoming saved and getting intimate with the Holy Spirit. Hey Brad, do you think you would mind showing the group your masterpiece?"

"Well, uh—I guess—well it's just a little poem, it's not much really," said Brad bashfully. "Well, okay, I guess it couldn't hurt."

Brad passed the piece of paper with his poem on it around the table for all the students to read. The title read, "A Heart Aglow."

"Wow!" exclaimed Karen. "This is really a beautiful poem!"

"Yeah, it shows a lot of spiritual depth," agreed Julie.

"Nice job, Brad," said Stan. "Very well written indeed."

"You did a pretty blooming good job, buddy boy," said Walt, the English major. "You have a lot of potential. With practice, I think you have the ability to become a really good writer."

"You know," said Pam. "I would really like to see somebody set this poem to music. It could definitely go places if somebody writes a great melody for it."

****

LATER THAT NIGHT, Brad was driving Pam back to Orinda BART where she had parked her car in order to be able to carpool to Concord and back. She would drive her car the rest of the way back to her apartment in Oakland, while Brad would drive his compact back to his parents' home in Moraga. This had been their routine ever since Brad had started going to those Sunday night services at Glad Tidings. When they got to the BART station, Brad prepared to say his goodbye.

"Brad," said Pam. "I want to throw an idea at you and see what you think."

"What is it?"

"I've been thinking about the idea of starting up an intercessory prayer group early in the morning that would run Monday through Friday. I already talked to Hal Odell, Laura Wilkerson, Cristy Hunt, and Debbie Thatcher, and all of them are very up about the idea. What do you think, Brad? Do you think you would be open to participating in this prayer gathering?"

"I would be very excited about it!" exclaimed Brad. "I think it's a great idea!"

Just to be in an environment where he could pray and praise the Lord Jesus with abandon turned him on, and besides, he liked every moment that was spent in the presence of Pam.

"Where and when will the prayer gatherings be?" he asked.

"From 6:00 A. M. to 7:00 A. M. at my apartment in Oakland."

"I'm going to have to figure out the logistics of all of this. Give me a few days in order for me to talk to my folks about it."

****

MEANWHILE, the tour was continuing for 'Jitterbug Josh' and The Universal Mindset. Randy had done the best he could to reconcile with his wife on the morning after the big Carnegie Hall performance, and Lila promised not to walk out on him—at least for a while. They went on to Washington, D. C. where they performed at Kennedy Center. They continued their trek down the Eastern Seaboard, doing sold-out, ticketed concerts in Norfolk, Winston-Salem, Atlanta, and Miami Beach. One of their most successful concerts was at the University of Florida Auditorium in Gainesville, Florida, on January 28, even though the concert hall was one of their smaller venues, seating only 843 people. The schedule was extremely grueling, and Randy was getting more and more worn down. Often, he would have to get up at 5:00 A. M. and couldn't get to bed until midnight. There were at least two concerts a day with the performing, the sound checks, and the signing of thousands of autographs every day, seven days a week. On a few nights, Randy was not able to fall asleep, but would get up and fall into one of his familiar trances with the pen and paper in front of him, waking up drenched with cold sweat, feeling drained of vitality, with a completed new song right in front of him. One of those new songs was called "Dragon Diamond," while on another occasion the new song was dubbed "For the Love of Leviathan."

On February 3, the group had an evening concert at Robinson Center Music Hall in Little Rock, Arkansas. The hall had a seating capacity of 2,609, and the place was full to overflowing. Randy and the group did their usual program of original songs, and the concert seemed to be going just like a charm with the crowd yelling out their vociferous cries of approval after each song. They started performing Randy's new song, "For the Love of Leviathan," and everything seemed to be going just fine. Suddenly, from the front row, there was an eruption of blood-curdling screams as the faces of a teenage boy and a teenage girl became distorted with abject torment and terror. At first, the bystanders thought it was just some more frenzied cheering until they saw the terrorized faces and twitching bodies of the two teenagers and heard their desperate cries.

"HELP! HELP! HELP!! OH, PLEASE! NO, NO, NOOOOOO!!"

"SOMEBODY HELP ME! OH, MAKE IT STOP! I'M DYING, *DYING!!*"

Some of the people around them tried to encourage them by making consoling comments. "Calm down! Calm down! Everything's gonna be all right."

"Easy now, you'll be okay."

"What's the trouble?"

"Let's get these two out into the lobby where we can attend to them better."

A group of about ten people helped the struggling, raving teenagers toward the lobby, and the emcee for the evening walked onto the stage, motioned for the band to hold the music for a few minutes, and grabbed the house microphone.

"Ladies and gentlemen!" he announced. "May I have your attention, please? Attention, please! We seem to have a little emergency here with a couple of teenagers. Just stay calm. Everything is under control. The ambulance is on its way. I don't know what the problem is, but as soon as we know, we'll give you the scoop. It might be a drug overdose or even a heart attack. We're going to take a break for a few minutes after which we hope to be able to resume the concert."

Subdued talking broke forth throughout the stunned audience.

"What's going on?"

"This is *weird!* I've never seen anything like *this* happen at a concert before!"

"This is really bizarre, man! This is a bummer!"

"I hope those two are going to be okay!"

Out in the lobby, there was an almost hysterical commotion; the faces of the two teenagers were turning blue, and they had already lost consciousness.

"These kids are dying! Does anybody around here know how to do CPR?"

"No, not me man!"

"Nor me!"

"Nope!"

"RATS!"

Screaming, shrieking sirens could be heard in the distance, coming closer and closer. Soon, the lobby doors crashed open and several paramedics rushed in.

"ONE SIDE, EVERYONE! GIVE US ROOM! GET CPR GOING QUICK, *QUICK!!* ON THE DOUBLE!"

The paramedics got to work on the two teenagers, giving them mouth-to-mouth respiration, CPR, and shots of adrenaline. They kept barking out desperate orders.

124

"Hit it, NOW! Go, GO, GO!! NOOO!! WE'RE LOSING THEM!! WATCH OUT! *WATCH OUT!!* OH, NOOOO!! We've lost them! They're gone!"

Cries of dismay broke out from the bystanders in the lobby. There was no pulse, heart activity, or brain activity on the two youngsters. They were dead.

Back in the auditorium, the announcer came back to the mike and somberly announced the sad and mysterious death of the two teenagers and the cancellation of the rest of the concert.

****

THE NEXT DAY, the members of the group were sitting in Brian Manning's hotel room at the Holiday Inn in Little Rock, brooding over the surreal events of the previous evening. A snow flurry was going on outside, a rarity for Arkansas. The ground was covered with white, and the air was very chilly. Most of the time, the area surrounding the city was a luscious green color, dotted as it was with those beautiful little pine trees. The room was crowded with the group members, some of whom were seated on the floor. Most of them were clothed in bell-bottoms, and Randy was needing a shave.

"Anybody know the situation on those two teenagers who died," asked Bart, "that is, what the cause of death was?"

"I don't know," said Brian. "Nobody has told me anything yet."

"I'll bet you is was a drug overdose," said Mark.

"Or a heart attack," said Bart.

"I don't think so," commented Fred, skeptically. "Two heart attacks at the same time with the people that suffered them standing next to each other, IMPOSSIBLE!"

At that moment, the telephone rang, and Brian Manning answered it.

"Hello!..........oh, hi, Harry! What's up?.........What?...The coroner's report?.........So what was the cause of death, Harry, drugs, alcohol?......*WHAT?!*.......Would you please repeat that slowly?......I can't believe it! Oh, what a tragedy, what a terrible thing to happen to those unlucky youths!.....Have their parents been notified?......Okay, Harry......Okay, Harry, I'll let everybody in the group know.....So long, now."

Brian hung up the phone and looked at the group, his face a tableau of bewilderment mixed with despondency.

"What's cooking?" asked Randy.

"Yeah, what's the news?" asked George Newman. "Was it an overdose of drugs?"

"Or maybe it was alcohol," commented Bart Anderson.

Brian looked intently at all of the group members and said, "You all are going to find this hard to believe, and I have real problems believing this myself. But they got the coroner's report on what the cause of death for those two teenagers was, and get this: *they can't find anything whatsoever to cause their deaths;* there was no sign of heart attack, no sign of stroke, no evidence of drugs or alcohol, nor was there any sign of infection or injury."

"But this makes absolutely no sense at all!" protested Fred. "There's *got* to be *something* that would have caused their deaths, at least drugs or something."

"Must be some rare and mysterious disease," speculated Keith. "You know how they haven't figured out what causes infant crib death."

"Well anyway," said Brian. "It's a macabre and tragic biological fluke that may never have an explanation. Hopefully, this is the last time that we'll see something like *this* happen." His tone brightened up as he continued, "Okay, everybody! Let's get all our gear loaded into the two vans and hit the road. It's about a six-hour drive to our venue in Oklahoma City, and we need to be there no later than 3:00 P. M."

Everybody in the group dejectedly headed toward their hotel rooms to pack and get ready to check out of the hotel and load up the two vans for the trip west.

****

"YOU want to do *what?"*

"Dad, I want to be a part of this prayer group that meets in Oakland on weekday mornings."

Sid, Harriet, Brad, Kimberly, and Lisa were having a conference over the use of their cars in order to save energy.

"Well, where will this group meet?" asked Sid.

"At Pam Jackson's pad."

"Pam Jackson, who's she?"

"She is this fabulous Christian girl that goes to Cal Berkeley. She's a wonderful soprano singer and a fairly good piano player. She's involved with Campus Crusade, and she also is the one that I've been carpooling with the last couple of months to go to that wonderful church in Concord where I received the gift of tongues."

"And what time will it meet at?"

"6:00 A. M. to 7:00 A. M."

"Hmm," said Sid. "This is a rather thorny problem, kid. All of us are going to have to cut down on the use of our cars. You and Kimberly don't have jobs yet, the stock market is not doing too hot, and the energy crisis is hurting all of us."

"We're not going to starve to death," said Harriet, "but we will have to cut down. No big vacations to Hawaii, no trips to Disneyland, and not too many nights out."

Sid added, "We pay a lot of money for Kimberly to use gasoline for her car to go to her proms, girlfriends' parties, and dates with boys. We also pay

126

a lot of gas money for your trips to school, Campus Crusade, church on Sunday morning, and church on Sunday night. I think this early morning prayer meeting is going to be a little bit too much, my boy."

"I could take BART, Dad, and walk from the station to Pam's apartment."

"I don't like the idea of you walking the streets at that time of night," said Harriet.

"Yeah, that part of Oakland is not safe," added Sid. "A lot of creeps out there."

"Honey," countered Harriet. "Maybe this prayer group *does* have value. Brad is very happy in his newfound religion and it certainly can't do any harm. Maybe we can figure out a way to get around these financial and energy hurdles."

"Maybe I can find a part-time job at McDonalds or something," said Brad. "It's really about time for me to start learning how to shift for myself and be independent, anyway."

"Well, give your father and me a little time to hash this all out," said Harriet. "Maybe we can work something out."

"Thank you!" exclaimed Brad, hugging his mom and dad.

****

THE CONCERT IN OKLAHOMA CITY started out to be another successful show for 'Jitterbug Josh' and the group. They opened with "The Evil Eye." The next piece was "Blue Love." After that, they did "The American Dream" followed by "Just like Creamy Silk." The next piece was "Dragon Diamond." Then came, "For the Love of Leviathan......."

While they were performing this tune, blood-curdling screams reverberated throughout the auditorium. This time, the victim was a tall young man in his twenties. A group of people gathered around him as his face turned white, and then blue. The concert was halted, the man was carried out into the lobby, and the paramedics were called. As was the case on the previous evening, they tried to revive him with no success. Soon, he was dead. The next day, the coroner's report came in concerning the cause of death: they could find no logical explanation whatsoever.

That afternoon, after the sound check of the group, Brian Manning had another little powwow with the band members concerning the events of the last two nights.

"Okay, gang," he started out. "Listen up, everybody! I'm sure you all are wondering why I called you together for this meeting."

Everybody looked at Brian with quizzical expressions mixed with a slight bit of foreboding.

"I have somewhat bad news to share with you."

"What?" asked everyone.

"Well, here's the deal. We have been doing really well with our concert tour. The response and turnout have been out of this world. People everywhere adore our group, and our album has been selling like hotcakes— but," Brian cleared his throat because of some unexpected hoarseness in his voice. "We have a little problem. It seems we've had a little bump in our smooth boat ride during the last few days, a little pest that has invaded paradise. Three youths have died with no logical explanation at all. On top of that, we are subject to this Arab Oil Embargo. As you can see, this has affected our country more than just a little bit. You all know firsthand about the gas shortages. We see and experience it daily in the long gas lines at every filling station and the sky-high cost of filling up our tanks in our vans. It has also forced us to get up earlier in the morning than we would otherwise have to. Harry and Hiram have been discussing the situation with me over the last two days, and they both feel that it would be best to cut the tour short and head back to the Bay Area quickly. Originally, we were going to do an uninterrupted tour until April, but that was before things became as hairy as they are now. So this is the new plan: we'll do the concert here in Denver tonight. Then we'll drive a straight shot back to San Francisco, getting there by Thursday evening."

Everyone in the group looked at Brian with stunned surprise mixed with dismay.

"That's bad," said George, "and we were really going good!"

"What does this mean?" gasped Mark.

"Does that mean that our band is folding for good?" asked Fred.

"Not at all," replied Brian. "You see, this is only a temporary situation related to the death of those three youths and the gas shortage. Once things get stabilized and the Oil Embargo is lifted, we'll be able to get right back into the swing of things. We have a great group, the songs are popular, our band is tight, and we have a very unique sound. Overall, we are doing very well. Once the air clears pertaining to the death of those youngsters and we have abundant oil supplies again, we'll be able to resume our concert tour."

"That is, if the Oil Embargo ever ends," countered Fred Barnes pessimistically.

"Don't worry, Fred," said Keith Bryant. "The Arab Oil Embargo will end eventually, and we'll have the gas supplies we need again."

Brian changed the subject by probing, "I'd like to get your input on this situation concerning the deaths of those youths. Do any of you have any ideas?"

"You're sure they can't find any cause of death whatsoever?" asked Fred. "Not even drug overdose?"

"No, Fred," said Brian. "They can find nothing. The coroners are absolutely mystified."

"There is one thing," commented Mark. "Both times that these incidents have happened have been while we were performing Randy's new piece, 'For the Love of Leviathan.'"

"Bah, there's nothing to that!" protested Randy. "It's got to be nothing more than a coincidence!"

"Yeah, but every time we do that piece," said Bart, "I get a bad feeling that comes over me. I get a cold chill, and my hair stands up on my head. I feel suddenly scared."

"The same thing happens to me," said Fred.

"Oh, baloney!" exclaimed Randy.

"But look at the facts, Randy," said Brian. "Three people die unexpectedly during the same tune on two different nights—and I've felt the same bad vibes that Bart and Fred here are talking about. I really think we should put 'For the Love of Leviathan' on the shelf, at least for a while. There seems to be a jinx on that song."

"You're not making any sense at all, Brian!" cried Randy. "That piece is, I think, one of the best songs that I ever wrote. The melody is hauntingly beautiful, the harmonies are unusual, I like the key I wrote it in, namely G minor, and the lyrics are very unique. The song is so good that I can hardly believe I wrote it."

"Maybe the problem is in the lyrics," volunteered Mark. "All that talk about that deadly and invincible sea monster."

"Rubbish!" protested Randy. "The lyrics are talking about a mythological sea monster that is like a dragon breathing out fire and smoke, likening it to the famous crocodile that slew Captain Hook in *Peter Pan.* What harm could possibly come from that?"

"But three people are *dead!*" countered Fred.

"I have another idea," suggested George, "and I want you all to hear me out for a minute as I put in my two cents worth."

All the members of The Universal Mindset fixed their eyes intently on George Newman as he spoke his mind.

"Suppose," he continued, "just supposing that the music has something to do with these deaths. Now before you write me off as a superstitious nutcase, let me fill you in on a little bit of musical history. This phenomenon of the last few days is really nothing new but has happened on a few other occasions in musical history. Let me cite just one example. Peter Tchaikovsky was one of the most beloved serious composers in the Romantic Era of classical music. He wrote beautiful masterpieces like *The 1812 Overture, The Nutcracker Suite Ballet, Sleeping Beauty,* and two piano concertos. He wrote six symphonies. The sixth symphony includes a movement known as the *Pathetique.* This movement of the symphony is very controversial because of the macabre events surrounding it. When it was first introduced, a number of people died in conjunction to its performance, and Tchaikovsky himself died of cholera nine days after its premier. It is a fact that neither the famous conductors, Toscanini or Walter Damrosch, would dare to perform this movement of the symphony. Also, there have been a few other instances throughout musical history that are like this."

"George, you aren't making any sense, either," protested Randy. "Listen! I have heard that *Pathetique* movement of *Tchaikovsky's Sixth* and think it is an incredibly beautiful piece of music—and way ahead of its time in its complex harmonies, for example, those rich B minor chord voicings with the G-sharps and C-sharps added in. Look at me! I've listened to *Tchaikovsky's Sixth* a number of times and I'm still alive and kicking! All that stuff is just a bunch of old wives' tales!"

"Well, I think we're still going to put 'For the Love of Leviathan' aside for the time being," said Brian. "We'll see what happens tonight."

"Oh, okay," said Randy bitterly. "Go ahead; nix and deep-six the piece."

The show went on without the Leviathan song that evening, and the concert went off without a hitch; there were no terrorized youths, no mysterious deaths, and 'Jitterbug Josh' with his music was a smash hit.

****

"YOU RIDING with me?"

It was 4:15 A. M., and Brad stirred sleepily, groaned, and staggered out of bed. Brad and his parents had come to a makeshift solution to the problem of getting Brad to the morning prayer meeting that all three of them hoped would work out. Sid's office was in downtown Oakland on the corner of Broadway and 16th street. Brad would get up violently early in the morning, shower, shave, and eat a quickie breakfast. He would ride with his dad to his office and then catch BART at the 19th street station, riding the train to the Lake Merritt station. He would then walk the half-mile distance to Pam's apartment complex. Both Sid and Harriet were still worried over Brad walking the cold streets in the dark.

The two of them climbed into Sid's green Plymouth with Sid turning the radio on to station KCBS and Brad putting the front seat to as close to a reclining position as possible so that he could rest on the trip to Oakland. Everything went just fine until Brad got off of BART at the Lake Merritt station and tried to find Pam's apartment—he got lost and couldn't find the address. He walked down one street, then another, then another. It was still dark, it was getting later and later, and Brad's legs were beginning to get tired.

"Well Lord, I guess You're trying to teach me patience, which is one of the fruits of the Spirit. I guess this is a little tribulation to help me become more Christ-like." At first, Brad felt a bit like a spiritual hero, but as time went by and he still couldn't find the apartment building, he first became concerned, then aggravated, and then downright boiling mad. He prayed loudly, "LORD, PLEASE HELP ME FIND PAM'S APARTMENT IN TIME TO MAKE THE PRAYER MEETING! *LORD!*"

Six o'clock came, and Brad still hadn't found the place. Then quarter after six, six thirty, quarter to seven. Brad was having a big fit because of his frustration and worry. Finally, at ten minutes to seven, he found the right street, the right building, and finally, the right apartment suite where Pam lived. He knocked on the door, and Laura Wilkerson let him in. Five people were in the room praying fervently, and Brad felt a little spiritually embarrassed because of his tardiness and the emotional carnage in his soul that had come about because of his anger.

"I'm sorry that I'm late," he said in a low voice, his head hanging down in shame. "I just couldn't find the darn place."

"Hey, don't worry about it," said Laura.

"Yeah, don't sweat it," said Pam. "It's all good."

They finished their prayer time. It was still dark outside because in the year of 1973-74, the clocks were not turned back due to the Energy Crisis. They soon finished the prayer time, the six people spent a little time talking to each other, and then they dispersed with Brad walking back to BART to ride the train to Berkeley in order to get off at the station closest to Cal Berkeley. After school, he would get back on BART, get off at the Lafayette station, and then catch an AC/transit bus to Moraga that would put him a quarter of a mile away from where he lived.

****

"I STILL DON'T LIKE IT, Brian! I think it's a great song."

The famous rock group was driving back to California, traveling through the beautiful Rocky Mountains west of Denver. Gorgeous evergreen trees mixed in with snow flashed by. During summer, you would be able to see the pinkish-red rock formations that were unique to that part of the country. They were driving near the famous ski resort, Vail, Colorado. Randy was sitting next to Brian who was driving one of the vans.

"Well, Randy," he said. "You witnessed the deaths of those youths during those two nights and then how everything went as smooth as silk last night when we didn't do your new song."

"Well, it still doesn't make any sense to me," said Randy. "Brian, when we get to the next stop for a cold drink, I want to have a talk, just the two of us."

"Yeah, sure, Randy. What about?"

"Well, it's a secret—and I hope you won't laugh or think that I'm a nutcase."

"Don't worry, Randy. I promise to hear you out and not make fun of you."

They made a lunch stop at Grand Junction, Colorado, and the two of them walked away from the rest of the group to a lonely place outside of the restaurant.

"Now," said Brian. "Tell me what's on your mind."

"Well, Brian, there is an unknown thing I haven't told you about concerning my smash hit songs."

Randy related the whole story of his rise to fame that had happened since last September, including the strange trance states he had often experienced late at night, and the songs that had come from those experiences. When he had finished his narrative, he looked bashfully at Brian.

"Well, that's the scoop, Brian. I hope you won't write me off as a mentally deranged fruitcase from California."

Brian gazed at Randy with a very serious look on his face and said, "Hmm. This is a very interesting story you've been telling me. Very interesting indeed. There seems to be some spiritual entities outside the normal world around us that affect each of our lives. You can call it angels, spirit beings, silhouettes, a divine Force, whatever. I have seen some things in my life that are impossible to explain logically. There was the time in November 1964, when I was living in Los Angeles. One night, I had a dream that my sister, Patricia, had just been killed. In this dream, I was at her funeral looking at her dead body in her casket. Two hours after I woke up the next morning, I got an emergency call from my mom in New York City telling me she had just been killed in a bicycle accident. There is no logical explanation for that. And then, there is the case of Abraham Lincoln's famous dream that he had just days before he was assassinated by John Wilkes Booth at Ford's Theater. In the dream, he heard all of this weeping going on and was mystified until he came to one room where he saw a casket. He asked one of the bystanders, 'Who's the dead person in the casket?' and was told that the president had died, shot by an assassin's bullet. How can this be explained except that there is a spiritual world out there we know very little about?"

Brian looked intently at the singing star and said, "Randy. I'm going to suggest that we get in contact with somebody I know who is tied in deeply to some of these spiritual mysteries. She is a psychiatrist who lives in the town of Weed, California. Her name is Isis Butterfield. Would you be interested in taking a trip up there to check her out?"

"Yes, I would, Brian. This sounds very interesting. Thank you for not laughing at me."

****

"PSST! BRAD! Wake up, wake up!"

Brad had dozed off at the early morning prayer meeting at Pam Jackson's apartment and had been snoring loudly. Pam was tapping him on the shoulder.

"Dad, let me sleep five minutes more," mumbled Brad as he stirred and then realized where he was. The other five intercessors broke into hysterical and hearty laughter.

"Well, hallelujah!" exclaimed Pam. "The Lord has a sense of humor. The Bible says that the joy of the Lord is our strength!"

"Well, I guess I'm just like the apostle Peter," quipped Brad. "Jesus had to ask him why he couldn't even tarry one hour in prayer."

More laughter from the intercessors.

Brad had experienced no more trouble with finding Pam's apartment and had been making the 6:00 A. M. meetings on time.

****

"YOU ARE GETTING 'shleepy, 'shleepy! Just relax. Breathe deeply. Breathe 'shlowly. Let the tensions of this stressful 'world float away. Relax. Breathe deeply, deeply, *deeply!* You are floating deeply into your inner self, your higher self, the real you! That's it! Go deeper 'shtill*! Go even deeper 'shtill!"*

It was February 12, 1974, and the majestic mountains and landscape surrounding the small town of Weed, California, were covered with a thick covering of frosty white snow. Randy was at the split-level home of Psychiatrist Isis Butterfield in a room with the shades drawn. It was illuminated by a single solitary candle. The house was an eight-room log cabin building with wooden floors. Isis Butterfield was a believer in the ecology movement. A member of the Sierra Club, she believed in having her house to be in as much harmony with the natural surroundings as possible. Isis Butterfield was a medium-built woman in her late forties with blonde hair that was turning halfway gray. She was Swedish in background and had a heavily European accent.

Brian and Randy had left the Bay Area early that morning to drive up to Weed where Isis had her house that doubled as her consultation office. She had started out the session by having Randy take an oral personality profile test; she was a believer in the four-temperament theory dating back a couple thousand years. Isis explained that the four temperaments were sanguine (the warm and friendly 'life of the party' temperament), choleric (the crusader and 'let's get with it' temperament), melancholy (the sensitive, artistic, perfectionist temperament), and phlegmatic (the easy-going, 'never get upset' nice guy temperament that would perfectly fit the personality of the fairy tale figure 'Rip Van Winkle' who fell asleep for twenty years in the Catskill Mountains). Isis diagnosed Randy as being mainly melancholy with his secondary temperament being sanguine. After the personality test, Isis started the hypnotism part of the session.

Randy felt the outside world melt away as Isis was giving out her hypnotic suggestions to him. The next thing Randy knew, he felt his spirit leaving his body just as if his body were a pair of pants and a shirt he was taking off. Randy gasped. This was *weird!* In front of him was his inert body lying on the salmon-colored sofa while the real Randy Miller was observing everything in his cloudlike spiritual body. He tried to grasp the hand of Isis but could not make contact. He tried to grab the desk but could get no firm hold on it. Then he tried to make contact with Brian with no success. But wonders of wonders, he floated right *through* the body of Brian! Randy gasped with unbelief. He then tried to float through the walls of the log cabin to the outside street *with success!* He stared with unbelief at the snow-covered houses of Weed. The next thing he knew, he felt a tap on his shoulder and turned to see a very familiar spirit entity, *Thomas Miller Senior, his deceased daddy!*

"Come with me, son!" he said in a very serious and formal voice. "I must show you many things concerning the mysteries of the spirit world and what really happens after death."

"Oh, Dad, Dad! It's really you! I've missed you so much since your car accident that killed you in 1971! Now I get to see your face!"

Randy reached out with his spirit arms to hug his dad when Tom abruptly stopped him and grabbed his spiritual wrists with an iron grip that sent sharp pains shooting down into his forearms.

"Knock it off, Randy!" he said brutally. "We don't have time for that nonsense, but we have a lot that needs to be accomplished in a very short time!"

Thomas Miller Senior softened up his voice and continued his talk, saying, "Of course, you remember how I was killed when my car went off that embankment on that rainy Sunday on November 29, 1971. My spirit immediately left my body that was contorted and crushed beyond recognition, and I am now free to roam around the world and commune with all the myriads of deceased spirits who are gradually evolving to a higher and higher state. People wonder what's on the other side. Well, the truth is like this: Normally, when a person dies, his or her spirit leaves his or her body and is able to roam around for a season as a disembodied spirit. After approximately six years, that spirit will be reincarnated as a new human being, and the quality of his life will be determined by how well he has lived in the previous life. If the person has done good deeds, he will be reincarnated as a rich and popular person who will have a lot of comfort in his life. However, if the person has been a bad criminal, he will be reincarnated as a poor person with the cards stacked against him. If the person has been really especially good, he has the chance of becoming one of the highly evolved Ascended Masters. Some of the esoteric religions of the world have taught these truths while many other people remain in the darkness of ignorance and superstition. Sometimes in the spirit world, it is possible to go back in time. This is what we're going to do for you right now. You are to be taken back into a tiny snapshot of your last life to be able to relate to people back on Earth the truth about the afterlife."

Tom waved his spirit arms and shouted, "BEHOLD!" The next thing Randy knew, he was rushing rapidly through a tunnel of blurry, indistinguishable images—and then, the fog cleared as things became solid again. He found himself dressed up in a natty outfit and sitting on an elegant concert stage with a large orchestra. The auditorium was huge, yet not as big as Carnegie Hall. The seating capacity was approximately 1,300, and the concert hall was well-nigh packed to capacity. He was sitting at a beautiful Chickering grand piano. The conductor raised his baton and started the next piece on the program: the famous clarinet glissando at the beginning of the *Rhapsody in Blue*! Randy was flabbergasted. The glissando was played in a much freer and drunken way than Randy had heard it in concerts or on famous recordings. The piece proceeded along, and he came in at the piano entrance and played through the whole piece flawlessly and brilliantly. Randy played the big cadenza part differently than he had remembered it on the standard recordings—it was freer and more brilliant. Finally, the end of the fifteen-minute piece arrived with the B-flat fortissimo finale 'stinger' being played by the whole band.

As the reverberation of the last chord died out, there was almost two seconds of dead silence—and then total pandemonium as the house that was now absolutely full broke out in wild and frantic cheering. Paul Whiteman and Randy—alias 'Jitterbug Josh,' and the reincarnated George Gershwin—had to take bow after bow. As the huge standing ovation died away, Randy heard a voice in the distance calling out, "Randy! Randy! 'Vake up! 'Vake up!" The voice was getting nearer and nearer, Randy felt himself rushing through the blurry tunnel again, and the next thing he knew, he was lying on the salmon-colored sofa in Isis Butterfield's darkened consultation room. Randy stirred and groaned. He could hardly move; his body was numb all over. This scared him for a moment, but then he noticed that the numbness was receding very slowly and he calmed down. He shivered violently. He felt very cold, and it was *not* because of the freezing temperature outside. The log cabin was very well insulated against the cold with a very efficient gas heating system.

"'Vow!" exclaimed Isis. "That 'vas quite an experience! I heard everything that you 'vere saying; your conversation 'vith your deceased dad, and your brilliant performance of the *Rhapsody in Blue* at that big concert hall. How do you feel?"

"I feel weak," slurred Randy.

"Don't 'vorry about it," said Isis. "Take it easy for a 'vhile. Your normal bodily functions 'vill totally return to you in just a little bit. Returning to your body from a trip of astral projection has a lot of temporary side-affects."

Randy continued to lay on the sofa as his strength slowly returned. After some minutes, he was able to prop himself up to a sitting position. After some more time elapsed, he was finally able to stand up on his feet, tottering like a drunken sailor. Finally, he was able to walk fairly normally, even though he still felt very cold and sluggish. He paid Isis Butterfield the consultation fee he owed her and walked out the door in order for Brian and Randy to start their long five-hour drive back to the East Bay.

"That was quite an experience, wasn't it?" queried Brian as they started to drive south down the mountain toward Redding.

"Yeah, I guess so," he responded lukewarmly.

Randy pondered the experience he had gone through today. Yes, it had been a red-letter experience. *I now know for sure what happens after you die. Some exciting years roaming around as a free spirit, going wherever I dern' please. That's cool—and to be able to fly—and think of it; I was actually the great George Gershwin in my previous life!* Yet, Randy had a mixture of despondency and disappointment, too. For one thing, he had read about how painful it was for a baby to be born into this world—far more painful for the baby than for the mother. Another thing that depressed him was the change he saw in his dad. Randy remembered that while he was on Earth, Thomas Miller Senior had been caring, gentle, unselfish, kind, giving, and very rarely given over to anger. In his spiritual body though, his dad was cold, abrupt, terse, and plastic. He was more intelligent than he had been on Earth, yet he lacked something that Randy couldn't put his finger on right away. What was it? Humanity? Humor? Friendliness? Warmth? Congeniality? All of a sudden, the realization of the thing that the spiritualized Thomas Miller Senior lacked hit Randy like a ton of bricks. Thomas Miller Senior lacked the quality of *LOVE!!*

9.

THE MYSTERIOUS MANSION

On a partly cloudy Saturday in late February, Randy, Lila, and the two boys drove down Sleepy Hollow Road in Orinda, looking for a bigger house to live in. Over the last week, they had looked at several different homes in Lafayette, Moraga, and Orinda, but hadn't found anything that was to Randy's liking. This road they traveled on was a side avenue, branching off to the right from the Dam Road, leading northwest to El Sobrante and Richmond. Sleepy Hollow Road was two lanes wide and semi-forested. It continued for about four miles until it came to a dead end not very far from the Lafayette town limits. At the beginning of this road, you could see part of the Orinda Golf Course on your right. As you continued traveling on it, you would pass other side roads, and the traffic would get lighter and lighter.

The Miller family traveled a long way down it, eventually coming to a huge three-story house. The outside of the house was painted a light-green color. There was a huge lawn in front with a large water fountain, a beautiful flower garden, and a large oak tree with its branches spreading a long way out from its trunk, offering a lot of shade from the hot sun during summertime. Leading up to the huge front double-doors was a brick walkway with six brick steps leading up to the front porch. Randy thought it was the most beautiful and majestic house he had ever seen.

The four family members walked inside. They found themselves standing in a spacious entryway with a stairway right in front of them, clothed with blood-red carpeting that gradually spiraled ninety degrees to the left leading up to the second floor. To the right of the entryway was a large dining room with the floor covered with cedar wood and the walls tinted light brown. To the right of the dining room was a large kitchen, totally snow-white in color, floor and walls. To the left of the entryway was a huge living room with walls painted a light-green color while the floor was covered with gray carpeting. The living room had large windows facing out toward the north. A large fireplace was on the opposite side of the room from where the entryway was situated. Adjacent to the living room on the other side of the house was a small bowling alley with one lane and an automatic pinsetter. Next to that was a game room with brown carpeting and walls covered with tan wallpaper. Randy planned to put a slot machine in this room. Next to that and adjacent to the kitchen was a large ballroom with a checkered floor of red-and-black squares. A door from the kitchen led out to the big garage and laundry alcove.

On the second floor was a long hallway that traversed the whole length of the house right down the middle. Three rooms were on each side of the hallway. On one side was a huge master bedroom with a gigantic bathroom as well as a room suited to be a library while on the other side were two other bedrooms and one bathroom. The walls in the master bedroom were painted a bright yellowish-green color, and there were blood-red curtains that covered the large window. In contrast to the loud colors in the master bedroom, the other rooms on this floor were painted in cheery pastel colors.

Another semi-spiral staircase led up to the top floor where another hallway split the house right down the middle. Up here were two more bedrooms and a bathroom on one side painted in pastel colors—one of these bedrooms was light bluish-green while the other was a light-pink hue. On the other side of the hall was another bedroom, a room with brown carpeting and bright yellow painted walls that would work perfectly for Randy's music room, and finally, a semi-alfresco room that would work perfectly as a semi patio/playroom. The side facing outward had one continuous window covering the whole side from wall to wall with the bottom being about four feet above the floor. There was a wall running along the bottom part. The elongated window curved up toward the top to make a long skylight. A bluish-green patio rug covered the floor of this room.

As they walked out the sliding glass door that went all the way down to the floor and led out from the kitchen into the backyard of the mansion, Randy saw more things to make him fall in love with this house. There was a large patio made of redwood planks with steps leading down into a large lawn with several pine trees, and beside that, a large Olympic-sized swimming pool with a white-and-aqua diving board at one end. A fountain flowed down some rugged dark bluish-gray rocks located near the diving board.

Jack and Tommy scampered joyously all over the mansion, trying to beat each other in their adjectives of the good qualities of this house.

"Look at that beautiful pool!" exclaimed Tommy. "That thing is *huge!*"

"And just think, Tommy, my own bowling alley. Now I don't have to go to Rheem Valley to bowl anymore but can bowl anytime I want! Fantastic!"

"Marvelous!" responded Tommy.

"It's just excellent!"

"More than excellent! It's *outstanding!*"

"It's *mega*-outstanding!"

"It's mega-outstanding, fabulous, terrific, tremendous, wonderful, and marvelous to the max!"

Meanwhile, Randy and Lila were wandering around the mansion, surveying every nook and cranny. Presently, Randy said, "Honey, I think this is the house for us! I like everything about this place."

Lila looked back at Randy with apprehension in her eyes and responded, "This is indeed a gorgeous home, and yet—something doesn't feel right about this place. I don't know. I just can't put my finger on it, but for some reason, I have a bad feeling about this house."

"Oh, my love, that's just a bunch of bushwa! This house is absolutely perfect in every way. It has everything I could ever want. I'm surprised that you even have any doubts about this place, having the optimistic sanguine and choleric temperament that you do."

"Honey, you've become obsessed with these temperaments ever since you got back from Weed eleven days ago. This is practically all I ever hear about anymore. I really could care less about whether my temperament is penguin, collie, or that temperament having something to do with the American flag."

"It's *sanguine,* not penguin," corrected Randy, "and it's *choleric,* not collie, and it's *phlegmatic,* not flag."

"Well, I still don't feel good about moving into this house—and to be honest with you, I am really quite happy living in our cozy little eight-room castle on El Toyonal. Why must we even think about moving anyway?"

"Lila, you keep forgetting that things have changed; I am now that famous star, 'Jitterbug Josh.' I have a new social standard to project to the world, to my public. Remember this, honey: *image is everything.* And besides, this beautiful house has a lot of luxuries my other little dinky home on 110 El Toyonal just doesn't have: things like my own bowling alley, the swimming pool that I can have somebody build the ten-foot-high slide I've been wanting for a long time, and the beautiful room on the third floor that will work perfectly as my own music room where I can eventually put a grand piano in as well as my desk to write my future song hits on. These are the things that will give all of us that true and elusive happiness we all long for."

"All of these things are very nice, but there's something fishy about this whole place—I just feel cold on the inside of me."

"Lila, Lila! There's nothing to worry about. Everything is going to be all right. I think we'll all be very happy here. There's lots of room for us and the kids plus extra room for the many guests we can invite over."

Lila shrugged her shoulders in resignation, sighed, and said, "Whatever! You're the boss. I just hope that you're right and I'm wrong."

****

OVER THE NEXT FEW WEEKS, the Miller family was very busy getting ready to move into the bigger and roomier house. They had put their home on El Toyonal on the market. Randy was rather worried about the prospects of getting a buyer because of the sluggish housing market and the sky-high interest rates. He was fortunate that he had a wonderful real estate couple who had their small office at the very northwest edge of Orinda Village on the Dam Road. Their names were Matthew and Victoria Lott, and they were very efficient and wise. Because of their excellent sales ability and business acumen, a family was interested in buying the eight-room house after it had been on the market for only two weeks. The family was a husband and wife who had one child. The man worked as a used car salesman in Berkeley, while the wife was a second-grade school teacher at Emerson Elementary School in Berkeley. By the middle of March, the whole Miller family had moved into the big three-story house on Sleepy Hollow Road with the two boys being very excited and happy, Randy having a heart full of pride, and Lila being happy at all the luxuries in this new mansion, yet still being bothered by a nagging fear and worry that gnawed at the corner of her heart like a worm nibbling slowly at a rosy, luscious peach.

****

DARRYL TEMPLE was in the light-blue boy's bathroom at Lodi High School. He was supposed to be cleaning the bathroom that morning, yet at the moment, he was not doing anything productive. Instead, he was sitting down on the floor, a row of several empty beer cans beside him and a half-full can in front of him. Presently, he was singing off-key at the top of his lungs. The sound reverberated through the bathroom and out into the hall where there were many student lockers. He was singing an old folk song.

"Oh, my darlin', oh, my darlin', oh, my darlin' Clementine! She is gone and lost for—"

"Temple."

The voice was ominously soft.

Darryl Temple swung around with total shock and fear to face the angry face of his boss, Andy Hester. Said he in panic, "Sir, I'll get back to work r-r-right away, B-B-Boss'h!"

"Forget it, Temple. This is the last straw. You've been nothing but trouble ever since I hired you. You're sloppy, you're a lazy bum, and now I see the evidence that you've been drinking again. You slur your words, I can smell the alcohol in your breath, and here are all these beer cans right in front of me."

"I ain't slurrin' my words'h, Boss'h. You're just like my mean third-grade teacher who used to pick on me all the time and was a dictator just like Mussolini was. (Oh, my darlin', oh, my darlin', oh, my darlin' Clemen—")

"Yes, you *are* slurring your words, Temple. I've had it up to here! The fun and games is over. Temple, come and pick up your check here tomorrow morning; you are fired. You can put the vacuum cleaner, the soap, and the mop back where they belong."

"You're not being fair to me! I don't make enough money to buy a TV set, a new car, or even a pool table!" groveled Darryl, half whining and half snarling. "Go fly a kite! I've been workin' and I ain't no drunk! I need the work! I need money! That'sh' right. I need money. *I need money!*"

"Yes, you *are* drunk!" roared Andy. "I can't put up with a person who won't do his job! We have enough economic troubles in our country as it is! Prices are zooming up and the gas lines at the service stations around the USA are worse than ever. I need responsible and reliable people who won't shirk their work. You obviously are not one of these people! You would be a drag on any employer's business. So, with all of that, GOODBYE MR. TEMPLE! GET YOUR STUFF TOGETHER AND GET THE HECK OUT OF HERE!"

Darryl lunged toward Andy and hit him lightly on the left cheek. Andy slapped Darryl rather smartly on the mouth. Darryl retaliated by punching Andy very hard in the stomach. Andy grabbed his arms and pushed him against the wall. A tussle developed between the two of them. Darryl slipped and fell upon his back while Andy held onto his shoulders with an iron grip.

"GET OUT, Temple! I want you outta' here this very instant, and I never, never want to see your face around here again!" said the boss in a soft and threatening voice.

"Okay, okay," murmured Darryl in a sluggish, yet angry voice as he staggered back onto his feet. "I don't care to have this'h stupid job, anyway. All you do is yell, scream, and bark at me and find fault with every little nitpickin' thing that I do. As'h far as'h I'm concerned, you can go jump off a cliff!"

Darryl started to walk unsteadily toward the exit—

"Pick up those beer cans and throw them away, you idiotstick!"

"Yes'h sir!" said Darryl.

He picked up the cans, threw them into the garbage can, took the name of the Lord in vain, gave one final dirty look at Andy Hester, and got out of there. As he left, he was singing off-key the song, "Oh, my darlin', oh, my darlin', oh, my darlin' Clemetine."

****

ON FRIDAY EVENING, March 29, Eric Burns and the Red Riding Rangers had one of their usual weekly meetings at the flat of the flamboyant Marxist revolutionist. The conversations among the young men were animated with Ted and Scott having a hearty chat about all the terrible crimes of President Nixon, both of them being convinced that the president had ordered the Watergate break in.

At precisely 7:00, Eric stood up in front of the crowded living room, pounded his gavel against the table, and yelled, "Quiet!"

The low rumble of conversation continued unabated.

"I WANT QUIET!!" screamed Eric, pounding the table even harder, accidentally knocking over a glass half-filled with beer onto the floor, staining the rug yellow with the alcoholic beverage. There were several gasps and whispers from the group members. A few of them went and got a rag to try to clean up the spill. As they worked, Eric went into his usual tirade, attacking capitalism, starting at a whisper, growing louder and louder, and finally screaming at the top of his lungs. The men in the room sat transfixed as the young Marxist reached the climax of his message.

"Speaking of decadence, you should take a close look at the churches today and then realize how many people wind up in mental institutions. The suicide rate in the world is higher than ever before. Anyway, Karl Marx said that religion is the opium of the people. We will eventually win over all Jews, Christians, Buddhists, Hindus, and all other religions in the world because WE WORK HARDER!"

Eric paused in his speech for effect and glanced toward his bedroom where the portrait of Lenin hung. His eyes took on a strange and eerie look, as a matter of fact, a *demonic* look.

"At any rate, this is our dilemma. So then, what is the solution? I'll tell you what the solution is! *BURN EVERYTHING DOWN AND START ALL OVER AGAIN!!* BURN DOWN AMERICA! BURN DOWN WALL STREET! GET RID OF THAT TWO-LIPPED SLOB, PRESIDENT NIXON! USHER IN THE GLORIOUS REVOLUTION! REDISTRIBUTE THE WEALTH OF THE RICH TO THE POOR! *KILL!! MURDER!!* DO ANYTHING YOU HAVE TO DO! THE END JUSTIFIES THE MEANS! *KILL THE JEWS!! KILL THE CHRIST—*"

CRASH! A half-filled beer bottle totally shattered the living room window. In his excitement, Eric had thrown the bottle toward the window. Men jumped off the floor in surprise and gasped. Some of them started shoving against each other, aggravated conversation breaking out among them.

"What the devil is going on?"

"The window's broken!"

"Quit pushing me!"

"I'm not pushing you!"

"Git' out of the way!"

"LOOK OUT! LOOK OUT! There's glass all over the place!"

They pushed and shoved their way out the front door, moved away from the dangerous shards of glass, and then they started hitting and punching each other as a free-for-all fistfight broke out among them. The noise aroused a large, frisky German shepherd dog that came bounding toward the men, barking with all her might.

"Ruff, ruff, rrrrrr-ruff, ruff, ruff!"

"SHUT UP YOU STUPID DOG!" shouted Eric as he ran on the porch outside. He tripped and fell on his back, and the German shepherd dog jumped all over him.

"Get off of me!" shouted Eric, angrily. "Go home, you mangy mutt!" Cusswords flowed out of his mouth. He rose to his feet and gave the frisky dog a very hard kick. The German shepherd pet yelped in pain.

"Perky!" called out a female voice. "Perky! PER-KEE! Come on home to mama!"

The lady came over to where Eric and the gang were gathered and gasped, "What the—"

She saw the huge mess: glass all over the place, the rowdy, restless men, the raving, cussing man with beer all over his clothes, and poor Perky whimpering in pain from the merciless kick of Eric Burns.

"You—bad—people!" the woman cried. "What are you doing, making all this trouble? Commere' poor Perky! Did that bad man hurt you?"

Gertrude, the landlord, stormed out of her apartment with white-hot coals burning in her eyes.

"WHAT'S GOING ON HERE?!" she shouted.

Gertrude surveyed the scene of bedlam, after which she looked straight at Eric and said, "How in heaven's green pastures did this happen?"

Eric looked blankly at her and said not a single word.

"Well, sir, that broken window is gonna cost you thirty bucks! I want you to clean up this dangerous mess RIGHT NOW—and any more of this hanky-panky and you'll be living in a cardboard box out in the streets!"

Gertrude walked back to her apartment, and many of the Red Riding Rangers got ready to go home. About five of them were now disillusioned after the unnerving events of this night, and they started conversing with each other.

"That does it! I quit!"

"Yeah, there's something fishy about this hotheaded guy and his kinky little group."

"Capitalism is evil and socialism is the answer, but that dude is going about it in the wrong way."

"He's going too far."

The rest of the group members were still on the side of Eric Burns although some of them were a little lukewarm. Among those twenty were Ted Johnson and Scott Williams.

A middle-aged couple walked out of their apartment, approached Eric, and accosted him.

"Hmmmmm, what happened to you?" asked the middle-aged man.

"Nothing," growled Eric. "Just shut up and get back into your apartment!"

"Well," said the middle-aged man. "I would like to know who all of those men were who just ran out of your apartment, trampling down each other and making a big spectacle of themselves."

"None of your business!" snarled Eric.

"Sir?" queried the woman. "I just want to know what's going on here."

"Nothing, madam. Nothing at all."

"Well, the broken window for one thing—and what about all the screaming and waving of your arms that you were doing? Why you looked like a wild animal, certainly way wilder than that cute little dog."

"What was he yelling?" asked the middle-aged man.

"Oh, I don't know," wearily sighed the woman. "Bah! It sounded like he was talking about redistributing the Jews and killing Wall Street and revolutionizing President Nixon." She looked into Eric's living room and commented, "Looks like you need to get your window fixed, and that living room is sure a mess. You need to keep your place a lot neater, sir."

"Listen!" snapped Eric. "Just go to bed and leave me alone. I've got work to do."

And with that, Eric stomped back into his filthy quarters in order to get a broom and a wastepaper basket to clean up the dangerous shards of broken glass.

Late that night, the middle-aged couple, who had witnessed all of the chaos that had happened at the Red Riding Rangers' meeting, was getting ready for bed. They rehashed the events of this weird evening.

"That was quite something," said the woman.

"Yeah, quite a rowdy group."

"Every Friday night, those men gather for those meetings, and that man rambles on, cramming his political views down those men's throats."

"Yeah, they've been around for a while, but I've never witnessed anything like what we saw tonight."

"That man is a strange one. Do you think he is dangerous?"

"Bah! I don't think there's anything to worry about. I'm sure that man will never hurt anybody."

****

RANDY MILLER was in the master bedroom of his new mansion on Sleepy Hollow Road. He was sitting on the bed he and Lila shared. Suddenly, through the window appeared several human-like creatures dressed in gaudy clothing. They didn't have to open the window to get in; they just floated through the glass as if the barrier didn't even exist. One of these beings was nine feet tall and wearing an outfit checkered with loud and harsh red and yellowish-green squares. He had a mean looking face covered with warts and had a pointed chin. His head was covered with a fiery-orange cape. The other two creatures were much smaller; one was three feet tall while the other was two feet tall. One of them wore an outfit with white, red, and green squares on it while the other was decked out in an outfit with blue, red, green, orange, white, and black triangles on them. The three of them were jabbering in a language that Randy had never heard before. Then the big apparition grabbed Randy and dragged him over to the window.

"Aha, aha!" he said in a low, sinister voice. "Take a last look at your beautiful mansion, Jitterbug Josh! You're a bad boy; we're going to throw you away!"

The other two beings cackled with harsh, grating laughter that sent chills through the whole body of the famous music star. The big man pushed Randy to the window and made him look out. Then he dragged him to a room on the other side of the hallway and made him look out that window. After that, he dragged poor Randy back to the master bedroom window and made him look out one more time. All this time, Randy was wildly flailing his arms and legs, trying to get free of these mean beings to no avail. He was crying out in stark terror.

"What's going on?! What are you guys doing?! Put me down! Put me down! Let me alone! Lila, Lila, oh Lila! Where are you? Come and help me! Help, HELP, *HELP!!* OH, NO! NOOOO!! NO!"

A hole in the floor of the master bedroom appeared out of nowhere. The nine-foot-tall man threw Randy headfirst into that bottomless pit. Total blackness surrounded him. He was falling, falling, falling. He would keep on falling forever and ever. Randy screamed in terror. The beautiful outside world had disappeared, everything was black, his head hurt, and he was scared spitless. He felt a great sense of loneliness and isolation. He shivered with cold and fear.

"Randy, wake up! Wake up, Randy dear!" The voice seemed to be coming from a long way away but was getting closer and closer. Randy then felt like he was traveling upward through a foggy tunnel, and then—his eyes opened to look at the worried face of Lila lying beside him. He gasped with surprise. The master bedroom was dark. It was nighttime. He was still only halfway conscious and much disoriented.

"What the—" he gurgled in a bewildered voice.

"You were having a nightmare, honey. You were really screaming and hollering. Are you okay?"

"No," said Randy, his face mirroring great fear. "I feel like I'm going to die! That was the worst dream I've ever had in my whole lifetime!"

Lila turned on the bedside lamp, and they both blinked in the blinding light. She looked worriedly at Randy's face, which was a picture of stark terror. Randy was breathing rapidly and heavily, and his pajamas were wet with sweat.

"Oh, honey, I'm really worried about you!" said Lila. "Are you sure you're going to be all right?"

"Yeah, I guess so. I'm beginning to feel a little calmer."

"Is there anything I can do for you—maybe go get you a warm glass of milk?"

"No, Lila dear!" exclaimed Randy with a tremor in his voice. "All I want is for you to just hold me! Hold me, dear!"

He looked like a terrified nine-year-old boy running to his mother in order for her to comfort him. Lila took hold of her scared husband and just held him in a loving, comforting, motherly embrace.

10.

TROUBLE FOR ERIC BURNS

The orange-yellow school bus came to a screeching halt at the side of Moraga Road, and the furious driver turned to face the fifty teenage students chattering away. It was a rainy Monday on that April Fools day with dark gray skies, slippery roads, and the windows on the bus splotched with big raindrops that were slowly slithering and sliding down toward the tires. The youths had been conversing on many different topics. Some people were talking about the long gas lines that were still continuing to this day even though the Arab Oil Embargo had been lifted in March. Another group of three teens had been joking about the gap in the Watergate tapes. One of the teens had parodied President Nixon, saying that the gap in the tapes was where Nixon had said, "I knew about Watergate all along and ordered the break in," to the response of uncontrollable laughter from the bystanders. Other students had been talking about varsity baseball while others were talking about the upcoming student body elections at Campolindo. Finally, a group of students were slated to compete in the school talent show scheduled at 10:00 A. M. today. In this last bunch were students involving two different groups that would be competing against each other. One was a hard rock-and-roll group who would sing a song by the Rolling Stones while the other performers involved several boys and girls who would be doing a couple of more mellow jazz songs. As the angry man faced the students, the conversations subsided to a low murmur of questions over what this was all about.

"YOU NASTY BROOD OF FILTHY PIGS!" screamed Eric Burns at the top of his lungs. "I'VE HAD ENOUGH OF YOUR OUTRAGEOUS FOOLERY! I'VE TOLD YOU AND TOLD YOU AND TOLD YOU TO KEEP THE NOISE DOWN, BUT YOU JACKASSES JUST NEVER LISTEN! I DRIVE YOU FAITHFULLY TO SCHOOL AND BACK HOME EVERY DAY! —AND WHAT THANKS DO I GET? YOU AND THAT CAPITALISTIC, SNOBBISH SCUM THAT YOU ALL COME FROM HAVE FAR LESS BRAINS THAN THE *STUPIDEST SLITHERING SLIMEY SLUG THAT EXISTS ON THE PLANET OF MOTHER EARTH!!"* A stream of profanity from the mouth of Eric Burns followed this outburst. He continued his harangue, complaining about how tough his bus-driving job was and how little pay he got. Then, he climaxed it all by yelling, *"I OUGHT TO TAKE A GUN AND SHOOT ALL OF YOU RATS DEAD!!"*

"Smart aleck blowhard!" mumbled a boy sitting close to the back of the bus.

"QUIET, YOU LITTLE TWERPY TURKEY!" yelled Eric. He followed this up with a stream of more obscenities and blasphemies, picked up a tenth-grade geometry textbook on one of the front-row seats, and threw it toward the back of the bus. The book smashed into the face of a petite freshman girl with brown hair. She immediately burst into loud weeping while gasps and low-level conversation broke out through the whole bus. Eric immediately left his seat and rushed back to where the crying girl was. He was afraid that this incident would cost him his job.

"Sorry," he said, "I didn't mean to hit you. It was an accident. Are you okay, honey?"

"NOOOO!" moaned the brown-haired girl in rage. "Just leave me alone! I'm gonna tell my folks what a horrible man you are!"

The low murmuring continued in the bus; the students were intimidated by the antics of Eric Burns. He looked her over, saw that there was really no physical harm that had come to the petite freshman girl, and headed back toward the front of the bus. He revved the engine and started rolling again toward Campolindo High School.

****

BRAD WAS ELATED and praising the Lord. He had just landed his first job, a part-time worker at Jack-In-The-Box in El Sobrante. He would be working there from five to nine P. M. on Monday through Thursday of each week. This would be his first step on the road to independence and financial security. True, this job was not the love of his life, yet it was a beginning—and after all, a person had to start his career somewhere. The big thing was that now he would be able to fill his gas tank on his own for his trips to school, Berkeley Tabernacle Fellowship, Glad Tidings International Fellowship, and the early morning prayer meetings at Pam Jackson's apartment.

"Hey, Mom and Dad!" exulted Brad. "Isn't it great about this new job that I have? I can help supply some of my own money now and take a little of the financial burden off of you!"

"Yeah, Brad, that's great," responded Harriet. "I'm proud of you, son!"

"Yeah, you did good, buddy boy," said Sid.

****

"COME IN HERE and have a seat, Burns."

Eric limped into the neat, well-organized office of William Butcher, his boss. Eric was both apprehensive and resentful; he could guess what the meeting was going to be about. He would probably get a chewing out over the events that had happened on the school bus yesterday morning. As it turned out, his hunch was absolutely correct.

"Burns, you been throwing more temper tantrums?"

"Temper tantrums, sir?"

"You heard me, Burns. I just got another complaint last night from a distraught parent of a freshman girl that you threw a book at. She cried for two hours."

"Sir, it was an accident."

Mr. Butcher ignored the denial and continued, "Moreover, you screamed at the teenagers at the top of your lungs, you intimidated them, you used extremely foul and abusive language once again, and to top it off, you threatened their lives. Besides all this, you made the kids late for school."

Eric just sat there speechless, shaking in his boots while the seconds ticked off with neither of the two saying a word. The boss's eyes were boring into the eyes of Eric. Eric turned his gaze downward and hung his head in shame. Finally, Mr. Butcher spoke in a calm, yet determined voice.

"Burns. You have just crossed the line. You have passed the point of no return, and we can no longer put up with your actions. You are a disgrace and even a danger to the students of Campolindo High. You are rude, obnoxious, and lacking in self-control. Besides all of this, you are undependable. I really don't know what's got into you, but you obviously need some serious help. I strongly advise you to look up a good psychiatrist who will be able to help you with anger management. As things stand right now, you have some real serious emotional problems, Burns—and I'm not going to put up with it anymore. As of right now, I am firing you. You can turn in your uniform and pick up your check here tomorrow morning."

"You're *firing* me? That's not fair!"

"Yes, it is fair, Burns. You got some real problems in your life right now, and the only hope I see for you is to turn to God."

"There is no God, fatso! I've put up with that tissue of lies from my hypocritical parents who are a bunch of money-grubbing, capitalistic pigs for most of my life. Now I see the truth behind all of those professing Christians who don't practice what they preach!"

Mr. Butcher shook his head in resignation and looked at Eric with pity. "I don't know, Burns. I just don't know. I have nothing more to say. I feel sorry for you. I really do. Goodbye, Eric Burns. I wish you the best of luck. I really do."

With that, Eric breathed a final four-letter word and dragged himself slowly out of the office of William Butcher, muttering bitter complaints under his breath.

"I hate that crummy boss, Mr. Butcher! I hate that snobbish, greedy, capitalistic ingrate! That big fat pig! Look at him, big swanky office, big fancy car, nice mansion in Orinda! He's just like all the other greedy, money-grubbing hucksters in our world today, hypocrites like Billy Graham—and that lying crook, President Nixon! Capitalism has caused this whole mess, all the air pollution, all the water pollution, and the poverty that is my own. All those big shots get all the money and I've got nothing. When the communist revolution comes to America, he and all the rest of them will go down!"

Eric thought of his former girlfriend, Adrienne Quigley. He had asked her to marry him at one time, but she had turned him down. Eric thought it was because of his poverty, but that had nothing to do with it. The real reason was that Adrienne found Eric to be rude, argumentative, opinionated, conceited, sloppy, and socially backward. All in all, she considered him to be a creep, neither was she very friendly toward his leftist political views. Eric bitterly thought about the last conversation between the two of them before their breakup.

"I love you," Adrienne had said, "but I cannot live with you. I need a man who is unselfish, considerate, fun to be with, and a guy who knows how to tickle a lady pink. I'm afraid that I find all of these qualities lacking in you, love."

"You're just saying that because of my poverty," whined Eric.

"No, dear. That's not it at all. It's because you don't know much about women. And you need to be neater and more organized."

"You're just like my washed-out, decrepit, and sorry old woman that brought me into this world! All right! Be that way! Get out of my life and don't show your face around here anymore! I've got work to do."

So had ended the tumultuous relationship of Eric Burns and Adrienne Quigley.

****

"I'VE GOT A GUN! Stick 'em up! Open up that safe and gimme' $25,000. *HURRY UP!!* DON'T MOVE TOWARD THAT PHONE OR *I'LL KILL YOU!!* If you do as I tell you, you won't get hurt!"

The black-haired young man sporting a beard and wearing dark glasses that covered his eyes was pointing a gun at the tellers inside the Wells Fargo Bank. The tellers, who were scared out of their wits, quickly scrambled to come up with the $25,000 and handed it to the young man who quickly rammed the money into a brown attaché case and ran at full speed out of the bank. One of the tellers quickly ran to a phone and called the police.

"Officer! This is an emergency! Please come quickly! The Wells Fargo Bank here in Stockton has just been robbed!"

"Can you describe the suspect, please?"

"A thin white male with black hair and dark shades. He was probably in his twenties and was about six feet tall. He was sporting a beard. He was armed with a loaded gun."

"Okay, hang tight! We'll be right there."

The black-haired bank robber ran at full speed down a side street away from the bank. Police sirens began to be heard in the distance. Two blocks away from the Wells Fargo Bank, the young bank robber ducked into a parking garage, sprinted up the stairs to the second floor, and climbed into his red sports car. He then quickly hid the attaché case and the gun under an old green blanket in the back seat, removed his dark glasses to reveal blue eyes, removed his false beard, and then removed his wig to reveal a shock of curly blonde hair. He quickly stuffed the items into the glove compartment, started the motor, and drove onto the street. He headed toward highway 99 for the ten-minute drive to his apartment suite in Lodi. As he drove down the freeway, he gloated over his successful bank robbery. *I did it! I am now $25,000 richer. That will hold me for a while. It was all too easy. Those pretty female bank tellers were so compliant.*

Soon, he was driving on the back streets in the town of Lodi. He turned right on Camino Del Diamante, the street where his apartment complex was on. He carefully parked the car in his parking space and slowly got out, making sure there were no cops around. Nobody was in sight. He walked up to his run-down suite of four rooms in the one-story apartment building. He unlocked the door to his apartment and walked in. Then, he walked back to the red sports car to very carefully and quietly bring his attaché case with the stolen money into his suite. The coast was clear. He slowly and silently took hold of the case, shut the door very quietly, and started walking toward his front door. He was planning to hide the attaché case in his bedroom closet. Nobody would have a clue. Over the ensuing weeks, he would spend the $25,000 bit by bit. He would—

"FREEZE! POLICE!"

Darryl Temple whirled around in shock and terror to face four policemen aiming revolvers at him.

"Search warrant!" said the leader tersely. He snatched the brown attaché case out of the hand of Darryl Temple and opened it up. He looked at the hundred-dollar and thousand-dollar bills that were inside and counted them up.

"Yeah, it fits," he announced to the others. "Exactly $25,000!"

One of the other officers opened the front passenger door to the red sports car and started to search its interior. In short order, he retrieved the false beard, the black wig, the gun, and the dark glasses.

"Yeah, it fits the description of the armed bank robber."

The lead police officer slapped handcuffs on the wrists of Darryl Temple and started to read his rights he had as a criminal suspect on his way to jail. "Search the apartment!" he commanded.

The two idle officers headed into the seedy four-room flat of Darryl Temple. The place was totally filthy and cluttered with clothes, empty wine and beer bottles, and pornographic girlie magazines. The officers gagged in disgust.

"Ugh! What's that horrible smell?!" asked one of them. "Smells like somebody died!"

"Let's check the back yard."

They opened the sliding glass door to a small patio area that had nothing but bare ground. The smell was especially bad out here.

"Search the area under the ground!" commanded one of the policemen.

"I'll get a shovel," said the other one.

Very soon, they were hacking away at the dirt, shoveling, shoveling, shoveling. By and by, one of the officers encountered something different from the normal dirt. In a few moments, they found out what this thing was that was buried under the ground. The two officers gasped in horror and disgust.

****

"THIS IS KTVU, CHANNEL 2, bringing you the top stories from across the northern part of the state. A gruesome discovery was uncovered today in Lodi that would turn the stomach of even the most stalwart, stouthearted detective. It all started when an armed young man wearing dark glasses, a false beard, and a wig robbed a Wells Fargo Bank in Stockton of $25,000. Undercover cops traced his steps to 334 Camino Del Diamante where he lived in a one-bedroom apartment. When the cops searched the backyard, they discovered the dismembered bodies of two murdered teenage girls. Temple is under arrest in the county jail, being held without bail. This is not the first time that bank robber/murderer Darryl Temple has been arrested. Previously, he has spent several nights in jail with charges of speeding, drunkenness, starting fistfights, and damage to public property. The discovery of these two bodies raises a lot of questions: is it possible that this murderer and bank robber might also be related to the mysterious, gruesome killings and rapes of a number of teenage women over the last couple of years in towns surrounding Lodi? Without a doubt, this crime rivals—and perhaps even surpasses the terrible saga of the recent Patty Hearst kidnapping."

The millions of Californian TV viewers watched this report, some with horror, and others with apathy. There were so many other scandals and gruesome stories in the news today. Big deal! Who cares!

****

ART AND JAN BURNS were watching the news on KTVU that evening, horrified at this new and gross double-murder. Their son, Eric Burns, was sitting in a chair, watching the news right along with them.

"Terrible!" exclaimed Art with indignation. "They oughta' kill that dirty, rotten, no-good crook. The electric chair is too good for him! They should just take a seventy-five-foot-long rope and hang him from the tallest redwood tree here in California!"

"The poor teenage girls!" moaned Jan. "My heart goes out for them! I don't think my stomach can take any more of this news."

"If the government was controlling everything, we wouldn't have these terrible things going on," said Eric. "Communist countries don't have problems like this."

"That is absolutely and totally wrong, son, and you are out of your cotton-picking head!" exclaimed Art. "Over the decades, there have been many millions of murders performed in communist countries by the communists themselves. Look at how many people Stalin sent to Siberian prison camps and how many of them he murdered, not to mention all the people that he deliberately starved to death during his planned famine. At the end of World War II, the Soviet Union occupied Austria, raping many women, both preteen and elderly. The communist invaders razed the land and dismantled whole factories. They sawed down many fruit orchards, and what they couldn't cut down, they burned. They brought desolation to a country that had already suffered brutally under the Nazi regime of Adolph Hitler. And then there's all the Christians who have been murdered in Communist China—and what about Fidel Castro's butchery in Cuba?"

"Dad, those figures are grossly exaggerated—and besides, sometimes, a blood bath is needed for the good of mankind. Also, there will need to be a planned great whittling down of Mother Earth's population because of the population explosion. Dad, you are just so stupid that you just don't dig it!"

"I think you are being unfair and disrespectful to your dad," said Jan, "and I think he is right concerning the communist danger in the world today. He has been a hard worker and a good father to you. He's also a smart man who has studied a lot of world history. On the other hand, your father and I are very worried about you, Eric. In the first place, you dress like a slob and your apartment is absolutely filthy. Far worse than this, you have a real struggle keeping a job—and I think a lot of it is because you can't seem to control your rage. And those political groups that you are a crusader with? It really gives me the willies! Son, I can remember the good old days when you were a happy-go-lucky kid who went to Sunday school, sang in the kid's choir, and loved the Lord Jesus. But ever since your time in high school, I've noticed a change in you. You're just not the friendly, fun-loving boy you used to be. Why don't you just come back to Jesus? He can give you happiness."

"JUMP OFF THE GOLDEN GATE BRIDGE, MOM! I've been around for a long time and have seen the hypocrisy of you, my old man, and the church group that you hang around with. You claim to be good Christians, yet your lives don't conform at all with the message you preach!"

"How have we failed to walk the talk?" asked Jan, gently.

"Well, for one thing, you live in this big luxurious house and are concerned only about your material things while all of those people in countries like India are starving to death. I've read the whole Bible through. What about where Jesus said to the rich man to sell everything he had and give to the poor?"

"Well, the communist leaders have not really given to the poor, either," said Art. "In Russia, China, and Cuba, the leaders live in great opulence while 99 percent of the people are practically dirt poor—and they don't have any freedom of speech, travel, or job choice. And in India, there is the caste system where there are a tiny minority at the top who have it real good and the rest of the masses who live in abject poverty—even to the verge of starvation— and the root of the problem is the Hindu religion that teaches reincarnation and the Law of Karma. Because of this, the poor people in that country really don't have a chance to get ahead. By contrast, our wonderful country of America was founded on Christian principles and the premise that anybody can get ahead with hard work and clean, honest living. The economic standard of living here in America is much better because of the wonderful free enterprise system we have. Besides all this, our American government does give a lot of financial aid to foreign countries."

"Drop dead, Dad!"

"Mother Teresa has done much more for the poor than Marxism ever has—and the Bible never commanded everybody to sell everything they owned and give it all to the poor. The Bible is not against having a lot of wealth, only the worship of it. The rich man that Jesus asked to sell all he had was a person who worshipped money as an idol. There were men like Abraham, Isaac, Job, and Joseph who were enormously wealthy and yet walked with God. And then there was Zacchaeus who said that he would give only half of his goods away, and Jesus accepted him as a truly repentant believer."

"Which proves the Bible has many contradictions in it!"

"No, son, it has no contradictions in it."

"Eric, your father and I do regularly give. We give our tithes and offerings to the church faithfully. In addition to that, we give to people who show up soliciting for funds on the outside of Safeway—groups like Teen Challenge or people raising money for homeless shelters. We also give to missionaries in Africa and Hong Kong from time to time. Another thing to realize is that none of us who call ourselves Christians are perfect—just forgiven."

"Oh, yeah, sure Mom! I've heard that tripe more than a million times."

Jan walked into the kitchen to check on how the steaks were coming along. Art looked out the living room window overlooking the city of Oakland spread out before them hundreds of feet below. The bay was a beautiful blue color with a stripe of yellow fire that was the reflection of the late afternoon sun shining off of it. Eric was totally disinterested in the beautiful panoramic view spread out before him; his mind was fixated on his own political agendas. Art and Jan lived in a beautiful nine-room house high in the Oakland hills. Eric was eating dinner with his folks that evening.

******

AFTER ERIC HAD LEFT his parents' home that night to drive back to his apartment, Art and Jan had a long, serious talk about their radical, fiery son.

"I don't want to give any financial help to a son who is going to waste it all on worthless radical causes and be a traitor to our country!" said Art.

"But honey, Eric needs our help. He's out of a job, and he isn't going to have enough money to feed his face and pay the rent."

"He's a disgrace to our family. He is a communist, he's disrespectful to us, he is unfriendly and rude, and I don't like it. On top of that, he dresses like a slob and his apartment is a filthy pigpen. And yuck! That terrible smell of nicotine and alcohol in his flat! How can you *stand* to be around that smell?"

"Maybe we should invite him to move in with us for a while."

"Honey, there are several problems with that. Number one, he has refused to live with us. He hates the things that we stand for. Number two, when he was with us in the past, he didn't lift one finger to help with household chores. And number three, he had those friends come in my house who were no-good slobs and creeps with their dirty long hair and unshaven beards. You remember what a dickens of a time we had with that group?"

"Well still, dear, he is our son—and I think we should give him some financial aid."

"Well, okay. Fifty dollars a week. That's all I'm gonna do—and I hope he shapes up and gets a good steady job soon. And he better not be spending any of that money on cancersticks, booze, or worst of all, his renegade political activities!"

****

ERIC WAS BROODING over his loss of the bus-driving job with a churning stomach. He had lost his big source of income, the money for his food, rent, cigarettes, booze, and Marxist activities. He had to find an answer to his problem, but he was stumped. What to do, what to do? He was driving his car home. A ballad was playing on the radio, an intense and romantic song sung by a men's trio. The song came to an end, and then, there was the voice of the DJ, Yappy Yellowfield.

"Well, you lip-kissing loverboys and romantic, ravished rock-and-rollers out there in wedding cake land! That was 'Just like Creamy Silk,' sung by Jitterbug Josh and the Universal Mindset. I hope all you hipsters have a creamy and dreamy day today. That song sung by your own Randy Miller is real boss, man! It's not just another of those vanilla pieces, (tweet, tweet)!"

An idea hit the brain of Eric Burns like a ton of bricks. *RANDY MILLER! I know that guy! There's the solution to my whole problem! I can kill two birds with one stone. I can audition for his music group and play guitar with them, making a ton of money and solving all my financial difficulties. And moreover, I can use the tool of music to spread the communist revolution around America and the world.*

11.

THE EASTER SERMON

Sunday morning, April 14, 1974, was warm and pleasant with bright sunshine in the Bay Area. 'Jitterbug Josh' and The Universal Mindset performed at an Easter sunrise service at The United Church of the Valley in Orinda. The service was outside of the church in a large picnic area. Everybody in the group was extremely tired. They were performing the piece, "Say Yay for Yoga," when suddenly, Keith Bryant started screaming and whacking his guitar with a songbook. A large bumblebee was buzzing around him, threatening to sting him.

WHUMP! WHUMP! WHUMP! "SHOO! Curse you, you rotten bumble! GIT'!"

They finished the song, and Randy started to introduce the next song as the whole group tried to stifle their laughter.

"Well, that song was entitled 'Play Gay for Yoga'—I mean, 'Spray Hay for Yogi'—OH, BOY! I done it again!"

That incident was mega-blooper number two!

****

MEANWHILE, the sanctuary at Berkeley Tabernacle Fellowship was completely packed this Easter morning with standing room only. Brad Applebaum was there, of course. He was sitting with his Christian friends who were in the Friday afternoon Bible study led by Hal Odell. John Patterson was there sitting by Hal Odell. On the other side of the tall frame of Hal Odell was Laura Wilkerson who was madly infatuated with Hal. Peter Thal was there as was Bob Hurst, Bill Mitchell, and Dwayne Downing. They were in animated conversation about school, the beginning of baseball season, and the recent Masters Golf Tournament.

Some visitors were also present that morning who sat near the rear of the church. Eric Burns had decided to bring his closest confidants from the Red Riding Rangers to the service, not to be fed spiritually, but that he could give them concrete evidence of the falsity of Christianity and the lying hypocrisy of all churchgoers. Ted Johnson was sitting with him, as was Scott Williams. These three were also involved in animated conversation.

"Well, the gas shortage has eased for now," said Ted, "but the economy is looking pretty hairy at this present time. People are very fearful about what may come down the pike. The housing industry is going kaput, and the auto industry is taking a terrible beating. It looks good for the coming Revolution."

"And Nixon continues to lie," said Scott. "And what a dirty mouth he got. All dat' cussin' and obscene talk. I'm sure dat' gap in de' tapes got not only his order to break into de' Dem'cratic headquarters, but language dat' would make a twenty-foot pile of mud mixed in wif' cow poopoo seem like a clean, 'maculate house in compar'son. And dat' criminal, James 'Cord! 'Dere's hardly any good pol'ticians today. I like Ron Reagan, dough.' He's a real comm'nist. Y'know, he shares his jellybeans fairly to everyone on his gov'ment staff." (Laughter from Ted, but not from Eric.) "And what a sense of humor he got."

"Scott, you have the brains of a two-year-old ape!" exclaimed Eric. "Reagan is nearly as far away from being a communist as he possibly could be. He is a right-wing fanatic and a capitalistic pig!"

Presently, the large choir led by Minister of Music, Cameron Lindsay, walked on to the risers and started singing their call to worship song, glorifying the fact of the resurrection of Christ. Several musical numbers were sung by the choir as well as a special piano solo performed by a twenty-year-old man. The piece he played was called, "He Lives!" The young man did a pretty good job on the tough piano arrangement with its copious assortment of scales and arpeggios. After about twenty minutes of worship music, Pastor David Maxwell walked joyfully up to the pulpit to deliver his sermon to the congregation on this Easter morning.

He cleared his throat and shouted, "He is risen!"

The audience responded, "He is risen!"

"He is risen!" shouted the pastor again.

"He is risen indeed!" responded most of the people in the audience, minus the three Red Riding Rangers.

"Turn with me in your Bibles to First Corinthians, chapter 15. I'm going to be all over this chapter, but I especially want to be concentrating on the first eight verses. Are you there yet? Very good! It says, 'Moreover, brethren, I declare unto you the gospel which I preached unto you, which also you have received, and wherein ye stand; by which also ye are saved, if you keep in memory what I preached unto you, unless ye have believed in vain. For I delivered unto you first of all that which I also received; how that Christ died for our sins according to the scriptures; and that He was buried, and that He rose again the third day according to the scriptures: and that He was seen of Cephas, then of the twelve. After that, He was seen of above five hundred brethren at once; of whom the greater part remain unto this present, but some are fallen asleep. After that, He was seen of James; then of all the apostles. And last of all He was seen of me also, as of one born out of due time.'

"Gang, I would submit to you that the bodily resurrection of Christ is of primary importance and is essential to believe in for you and me to be saved. Paul says in these latter verses of First Corinthians 15 that if Jesus didn't rise from the dead, then there is no hope, you are still in your sins, and you might as well just live it up because there is nothing good to look forward to after you die.

"When approaching this question about the resurrection of Christ, we must first ask ourselves, 'Did Jesus Christ of Nazareth even exist?' The historical evidence is so super-abundant for Jesus being a real historical figure, it would take months for me to present all the evidence. Unfortunately, I don't have the time, so I'm going to have to give you the *Reader's Digest Condensed* version." (Hearty laughter from the congregation.) "The bottom line is that the non-Christian historians who lived not too long after the time of Jesus attest to the fact that He was a real historical man and not a myth. One of these historians was Cornelius Tacitus who was the governor of Asia during the early second century A. D. Others included Pliny the Younger, Lucian of Samosata, and Flavius Josephus. Bringing us more up-to-date, the outstanding historian, F. F. Bruce wrote, 'The historicity of Christ is as axiomatic as the historicity of Julius Caesar.' No, my friend; Jesus was NOT a myth."

Eric Burns, Ted Johnson, and Scott Williams began to whisper to each other.

"That preacher up there is not going to convert me," said Ted.

"That numb-skull up there thinks that this Jesus is the Son of Gawd,'" sneered Eric. "But in reality, He is nothing but a big fat imposter, and that Christian garbage that hypocrite is preaching about up there is nothing but a huge and smelly tissue of lies!"

"Well, all I knowed'," whispered Scott, "is dat' every preacha' dat' I come across is very mean. When I was nine and we was livin' in Al'bama, me and my folks went into a little diner one night. De' owner of de' café was also a preacha' at a little church in Birm'ham. When we entered, he was singin' 'Amazin' Grace.' When he saw us, he got real mad and said, 'Git' outta' here, you black scum! You don't belong in dis' joint!' Dat' white preacha' really hurt my ma and pa and me."

"Another proof that Jesus really existed," continued the pastor, "is the fame his name has in many parts of the world. Think about it! Randy Miller is a recent famous name in the rock music field. He has blitzed his way to the top with hits like 'The Evil Eye.' But just like many famous people of history—Alexander the Great, Julius Caesar, and Nebuchadnezzar, his name will eventually fade—but, according to Philippians 2, the name of Jesus will always be above every name known in heaven and on Earth. A learned historian has pointed out that Jesus wrote no books, but more books have been written about Him than any other person in history. Jesus never wrote a song, but more songs have been written about him than any other person in history."

"You know, Renee," whispered a middle-aged man to his wife. "I saw Randy Miller on TV recently, and he looked kinda' pale to me."

"Yes, dear. I've been keeping up with him during the last few months, and every time I see him, he looks more and more jaded."

"I remember how he looked back in January when he was on *The Tonight Show.* He had more spunk and personality than he did on the recent TV show I saw."

Pastor Maxwell was continuing his sermon, saying, "Now that we have established the fact that Jesus was really a historical figure, our second question we need to ask is, 'How reliable are the New Testament accounts about the life of Christ?' Liberal scholars tell us they are not very reliable at all, but let's take a quick look at this. William Ramsay was a brilliant English scholar who traveled to Asia Minor during the nineteenth century with the goal to prove that the book of Luke and the book of Acts were both terribly inaccurate in their historical claims. He was amazed to find that, on the contrary, the archeological evidence verified the accuracy of these books, and consequently, he accepted Christ as his Lord and Savior. William F. Albright was one of the world's most brilliant and outstanding archeologists. He stated that the books in the New Testament were written no later than between the years of 50 and 75 A. D., and because of this, it was next to impossible for any significant corruption to creep into the texts of the New Testament, not even in the words themselves. Many other outstanding scholars have supplied us with superabundant evidence that the New Testament is a highly trustworthy account of the history of Jesus of Nazareth and his disciples.

"Now we come to the question of whether the resurrection of Christ really happened and whether it was a bodily resurrection or just a spiritual resurrection. Many liberal scholars will tell you today that the resurrection of Christ was only a spiritual resurrection or even just a good thought. Jehovah's Witnesses also believe the resurrection of Christ was only spiritual, but what is the real story? I'm going to read a few verses from Luke, chapter 24 that say this: 'And as they thus spake, Jesus Himself stood in the midst of them, and saith unto them, Peace be unto you. But they were terrified and affrighted, and supposed that they had seen a spirit. And He said unto them, Why are ye troubled? And why do thoughts arise in your hearts? Behold my hands and my feet, that it is I myself: handle me, and see; for a spirit hath not flesh and bones, as you see Me have. And when He had thus spoken, He shewed them His hands and His feet.' There's also a Scripture in Ephesians, chapter 5 that says, 'For we are members of His body, of His flesh, and of His bones.' Bottom line: The Bible says the resurrection of Christ was a bodily resurrection, not a spiritual resurrection.

"The Bible claims unequivocally that the resurrection really happened, but what are the pros and cons concerning it? Throughout history, some scholars have come up with five different theories to try to deny the resurrection of Jesus. Let's take a look at each of these theories. First, there is

160

the oldest theory the enemies of Christ tried to spread. This theory was backed up with a lot of hush money. (Does that remind you of anything going on in our government during the 1970s?) This theory says that the disciples of Jesus sneaked into the tomb at night and stole the body of Jesus. Right away, several holes totally discredit this theory. For one thing, the tomb was heavily guarded by Roman soldiers. Now, mind you, the Roman soldiers were extremely disciplined, and the Roman army was very, very strict. There were very, very tough penalties for any Roman soldier to fall asleep while he was on guard duty. Another problem with this theft theory is the size and weight of the stone covering the entrance of the cave. It would be impossible for the disciples to move the stone away and steal the body of Jesus. The third problem with the theft theory is this: if the disciples stole the body, all the Jews would have to do is recover the body and say to the world, 'Here's the body of Jesus!' Yet they never were able to do that because they couldn't find the body."

(Eric was beginning to get uncomfortable with the way this sermon was going and began to fidget in his chair. Meanwhile, Scott was becoming interested in what was being said.)

"The second theory says the Jews *themselves* stole the body of Jesus, but again, where is the dead body? There's an old song from *My Fair Lady* entitled 'Show Me.' This is what I would say to all skeptics today: 'show me!'"

Brad winked at Pam and whispered, "That's the song that Eliza Doolittle sang to Freddie, the man on the street!"

"Cut it out, Brad!" whispered Pam as her face turned beet-red.

"The third theory says the disciples went to the wrong tomb. Once again, the problem here is, 'Show me the right tomb with the dead body of Jesus in it.' Besides all this, the disciples were not stupid people.

"The fourth theory is called the Swoon Theory. This theory says Jesus didn't really die, but only fainted. There are many problems with this theory. First of all, we need to take a look at what people who were crucified really went through. The Scriptures are clear that Jesus was scourged before He even went to the cross. The scourging was done with an instrument called a flagellum, which was a whip of leather thongs with pieces of metal or bone attached. The scourging of criminals at that time would make hamburger out of anyone's body who went through that cruel punishment. Many people died from the scourging alone. And as for the crucifixion itself, it was the worst form of punishment that had been invented at that time. It was reserved for the worst criminals. No Roman citizen was allowed to be crucified. The mortality rate of crucified people was 100 percent, and the torture of the procedure was *extremely* horrendous. Crucified people were forced to carry the cross to their place of execution. They would stagger under the weight of the cross. When they got to the execution spot, they would be lifted up on a stake, their hands and feet would have nails driven through them to attach them to the post, and the condemned people would slowly suffocate. The

161

Bible also records that the two criminals who were crucified on each side of Jesus had their legs broken so that they would die before the Sabbath started. The Bible records that when they came to Jesus to break His legs, there was no need to do it because He was already dead. In addition to all of this, His side was pierced with a spear and water and blood came out. Physicians know today that the cause of this is a broken heart. Now, someone might ask, 'Would being in a tomb for three days revive a swooned person?' Nope! Even if the person wasn't dead, the tomb would not revive, but *kill* him. On top of this, can you imagine a person revived from a dead faint trying to break out of a tomb sealed with a large and heavy stone with strong Roman guards keeping watch over the tomb? Come on, people! Give me a break! The bottom line is this: Jesus was *stone dead* so we can put that theory to rest." (Laughter from the congregation.)

"The last theory says the disciples were only having hallucinations, but this idea also has unsolvable problems. We know one person can have hallucinations. There is an outside chance that two people can have the same hallucination. But *more than 500 people?* There is no way! Bottom line: Jesus is indeed risen from the dead. Hallelujah!

"Now," continued Pastor David Maxwell. "There is a question concerning exactly where the tomb of Jesus really is. The traditional site is considered to be the Church of the Holy Sepulcher, but many problems exist with this site actually being the place of the tomb. It doesn't fit in with the facts of archeology. For one thing, the Bible makes it clear that Jesus was crucified outside the city, yet the Church of the Holy Sepulcher is inside the old city. However, there is a probable solution to this problem. In late July and early August of 1972, I had the privilege of going on a tour to Israel. On Wednesday, August 2, our tour had a chance to visit a very interesting and lovely site. This place is known as the Garden Tomb. We were there for an hour and a half. Our guide gave us a history of this place. After that, we went into one of the little chapels there, took communion, and sang a few hymns and worship choruses. First of all, on the subjective level, this site is an incredibly lovely and peaceful place with gorgeous flowers and trees. Also, there is an incredible sense of peace and of the Lord's presence there. I felt the Lord whisper to me there that this was the site where He was crucified and rose again from the dead. I sensed the Lord saying to me that He lives, and because He lives, I shall live also."

Hal looked at Laura and whispered, "I wish I coulda' been there. I coulda' brought you back a lovely bouquet."

"Oh, Hal! You're so sweet!"

"Now, the question is what is the history of this Garden Tomb? Well, this archeological site was discovered in the year 1867. The facts about this site and what the Bible says about the death and resurrection of Jesus have very, very striking similarities. To begin with, this site was in Roman days like what we would call a freeway today. The gospels point out that there were

162

many people passing by the place where Jesus was crucified who were mocking Him and wagging their heads at Him. In addition to this, the Bible calls the place where Jesus was crucified 'Golgotha.' This word in the Aramaic language means 'the place of the skull.' Now, there are two interesting facts about the Garden Tomb. One, there are a lot of bones at this site; and two, the rock formation looks like a skull. Also, many executions took place at this site. It is also a fact that this site was visited by many Christians in the first couple of centuries after the crucifixion of Christ.

"Continuing on, the New Testament points out that early on that Sunday morning, the angel appeared on the right side of the tomb. The interesting thing about this is that in most Jewish tombs, the place where the dead body was laid was to the left, but in this Garden Tomb, the place where the body of Jesus was happened to be to the right. Another piece of evidence is the fact that about ten people at one time can fit in what we would call the 'narthex' of this tomb, yet most Jewish tombs in those days could only fit about three people in the 'narthex.' This shows us the owner of this tomb had to be a rich man. Isn't it interesting how the gospels say the tomb where Jesus was buried in was owned by a rich man named Joseph? Also, geologic evidence shows us there was earthquake activity that happened right there at that very time of the crucifixion and resurrection of Jesus. Lastly, there is no body in the tomb. Bottom line: the evidence points to the fact that Jesus is risen. He is risen indeed!

"Besides the historical evidence of the resurrection, there is much subjective and contemporary evidence proving the fact of the resurrection. One is the many changed lives—people delivered from drugs, alcohol, and immorality through the 'Higher Power', which we know is the presence of the Holy Spirit living in believers. Also, consider the millions upon millions of martyred believers throughout history who died as heroes rather than deny Jesus. Consider the Apostle Peter, the Apostle Paul, the martyrs of the Middle Ages, and the people who have suffered horrible persecution for the sake of the gospel in Communist Russia, Communist China, Cuba, Hungary, Romania, and Poland." (Eric growled angrily and bit his lip as Pastor Dave said this phrase.) "There is another subjective proof that the triune God of the Bible is the true God and it is this: the way people cuss and swear. Think about it for a moment! 'Buddha damn!' This phrase just doesn't make it!" (The congregation burst into uncontrollable laughter.) "No, my friend. When people swear, what names do they use? *They use the names of God and Jesus Christ!*"

"Hm," mumbled a man sitting right next to Eric. "Pretty convincing evidence."

"Enough!" whispered Eric savagely to that man. "Keep your stupid, no-good views to yourself!"

Eric sat there fuming and thought to himself, *how dare for him to force his religious views on me! He is a total mental retard just like all the other religious fanatics in this world! That fairytale Jesus is nothing but a pack of lies! They try to foist their religious views on guys like me! Soon, we communists will crush them!*

He squirmed restlessly in his pew and thought of his childhood. He had attended Sunday school at First Baptist Church in Walnut Creek when he was nine years old. He had sung in the kid's choir and heard the story about the love of Jesus for each and every person. He remembered one song the kid's choir had sung during the Christmas Eve service in 1952. It was called "Praise ye the Lord." He had believed in God and the salvation story in those days. His parents, Art and Jan, were professing Christians who had invited the Lord into their lives during their puberty years. His religious views had soured in high school when his science teachers espoused evolution, and he totally stopped believing in God when he read the communist materials of Marx, Engels, and Lenin. *I know better,* he thought to himself. *Those days of my childhood were the days when I was a fool. I was dumb then, but now, I am a lot smarter and totally enlightened.*

Pastor Maxwell wrapped up his sermon by saying, "So, the conclusion to this matter is, what does the resurrection have to do with us today? Everything in the world! The Bible makes it clear that all of us who have called on the name of the Lord will be resurrected in incorruptible bodies that cannot die anymore when Jesus returns again. Now some of you may be asking, 'How can there possibly be a resurrection and what would our new body be like?' Well, guess what! Some of the unbelieving Corinthians were asking the same question. There's a verse in the middle of chapter 15 of First Corinthians that says this: 'But some man will say, how are the dead raised up? And with what body do they come? Thou fool.' Now I would like to update this 1611 King James Version translation of this verse to my own 1974 rendering: 'But somebody will say, how are the dead raised up? And with what kind of body do they receive? You boob! Can't you guys dig the fact of the resurrection of the body?'" (Hearty laughter from the congregation.) "Paul goes on to describe the differences between the different planets and stars and likens it to the resurrection body. He compares the physical, mortal, weak, corrupt physical body to the spiritual, immortal, strong, perfect, resurrection body of believers. He goes on at the end of the chapter to say that not everyone is going to die physically, but some believers will merely go through a glorious transformation at the Rapture of the Church. I'm excited! When Jesus comes back for His Church, all the dead believers in the world will come out of their graves, and cremated bodies of believers will be put back together again by the mighty power of God. Then, a minute later, all the living believers will go flying through the air to meet Jesus at a certain gathering place in the skies. Then we will go flying through the universe and galaxies to a marvelous place that will give a new definition to the word, 'beautiful.' There, we will celebrate the Wedding Feast of the Lamb while the Antichrist takes over the whole world for a short time. Then, Jesus and all of us will return with Him riding on white horses to reign with Him for a thousand years while He reigns from Jerusalem.

"This brings us to the key question: who do you say that Jesus is and what will you do with Him? Do you think He is a great teacher, but not God? This position is not tenable. The noted author C. S. Lewis said you can call Him either a liar, a raving lunatic, or just who He claimed to be—God in the flesh who came and died on a bloody cross and rose bodily from the dead—but you can't call Him just a good teacher. It logically doesn't work. Now, what are you going to do with Jesus of Nazareth? You can either continue to reject Him and make fun of Him. But if you keep doing that my friend, you will eventually die and spend eternity in a real and horrible hell with literal flames, weeping, and gnashing of teeth. Or you can come to Him, realizing you are a sinner who has offended a holy God, repent of your sins, call on the name of the Lord Jesus, and receive the free gift of salvation. The choice is yours! I urge you not to delay. But as the piano and organ play softly, come on down to the altar and make your peace with God."

Eric Burns felt a Presence, a Power that he didn't understand. He felt miserable; he felt he should go down to the altar and make things right with God, but he ignored these feelings and brushed them off as nothing more than psychological brainwashing and hypnotism. Ted and Scott felt the same Presence.

"I-I-I th-think I really s-should go down and ask J-Jesus into my life," said Scott.

"That is the stupidest thing I've heard in my whole life!" exclaimed Eric in a loud whisper. "That guy up there is a great big knuckle-head! Are you being brainwashed concerning this imposter who is dead? That harebrained preacher up there is saying a whole lot of tripe! It's all a con game and a great big tissue of lies!"

"B-but I-I r-really feel somethin'. Maybe he's speakin' de' truth. Maybe......."

"I'll fix you good if you go down there, you big block of black trash! Pay no attention to that sorry money-grubbing hypocrite up there and his infantile fairy tales! Just stick with me. *I* have the answers!"

One person came down to the altar to accept Jesus. The service finished with a rousing choir anthem followed by the postlude. Animated conversations started up as people stood up and started walking toward the narthex.

"Wow, what a great service!" exclaimed Peter Thal.

"Yeah, Pastor Dave sure gave a wonderful message today!" agreed Hal Odell.

"I'm excited!" exclaimed Brad. "I learned something today that I never knew before. You know, Uncle Anthony told me last fall that there were inconsistencies between the traditional site of the tomb of Jesus and archeology, and I didn't know how to answer him. But now I know the truth and will be able to convince him that he is wrong. I now have some real ammunition to be able to nail to the cross some agnostic and atheistic theories!"

Debbie Thatcher walked up to the group and said, "You're all invited to an Easter picnic at my mom and dad's house. We're going to have barbecued hamburgers, hot dogs, chips, and soft drinks. Anyone want to come?"

Happy affirmative answers came from several of the Christian young adults.

Meanwhile, Eric, Ted, and Scott were walking out of the sanctuary, deep in conversation about the Easter service.

"Dat' preacha' dude makes a lot of sense," Scott was saying. "He knowed' de' Bible very good and is very convincin'. He knowed' a lot of his'try."

"He's an old windbag full of hot air!" mocked Eric. "He said some of the most stupid, brainless, off-the-wall garbage that I've heard in my whole life! All that bushwa about bodies being put back together and rising again. Why that's *impossible!* And then the outrageous story of all the good guys flying through the air to a place of happiness! What a piece of trash! Imagine, flying through the air like Mary Poppins or Peter Pan! Snow White is a better fairy tale than that! And the whole idea of coming back from outer space on white horses. Where do these clowns get their ideas? Don't they know that no human beings or animals can survive for even a minute in outer space without a rocket and space suit? There's no oxygen out there, and the temperatures are either way too hot or way too cold to support human life!"

"Yeah," said Ted, "you make a lot of sense, Eric. Christianity is indeed a fraud, and all we have to rely on is our own brains and wits to get us through life."

"Yeah, I suppose you guys are right," said Scott. "I guess dat' preacha' is all mixed up. Only comm'nism can save de' day."

All three of them had spoken their assent against the message of the preacher. And yet, deep down in their hearts was a vague and nagging fear that the preacher might be right after all.

12.

THE FIGHT AT MILLS COLLEGE

About sixteen Christian youths showed up at the Easter barbecue at Mr. and Mrs. Thatcher's large two-story house high in the hills overlooking the city of Berkeley. The middle-aged couple was very gregarious and polite. They both loved the Lord and had a very gentle spirit about them. Their house had a very large back yard with a grassy picnic area, a pool, and a volleyball court. Many flowering shrubs beautified the sides of this peaceful lawn. A group of verdant trees offered areas of shade from the bright sunshine. A large wooden table covered with a checkered red-and-white tablecloth was situated on one side of the lawn.

Mary Thatcher and her daughter, Debbie, were carrying out the food, drinks, paper plates, and disposable utensils to the back yard while Peter Thal and Dwayne Downing were helping Mr. Roger Thatcher to barbecue the hamburgers and hot dogs. The other people were chattering away in joyful conversations. Presently, Roger Thatcher stepped to the front of the happy youths and called everyone to attention.

"Well, folks! This is a beautiful day today! This is the day that the Lord has made, and we will rejoice and be glad in it. Did you all enjoy the church service today and Pastor's message?"

The whole group broke into spontaneous clapping with shouts of hearty assent.

"Yes, it was a magnificent and accurate sermon today, and we have the best church and the best pastor in the whole wide world! Let's give it up for PASTOR DAVID MAXWELL!" (Cheering and hearty applause.) "Well, anyway, I don't think there was any snoring going on this morning!" (Hearty laughter.) "At any rate, we got fed a wonderful spiritual meal this morning and now, we're all going to enjoy a delicious physical meal together! Let's bow for the blessing over the food. Father God, we thank You for the wonderful service this morning and for this bountiful harvest of food that we are about to receive now. We just pray that You will bless this food for our bodies and use it to nourish us now and bless the fellowship around the table. In Jesus' precious name, amen!"

Everybody lined up with the ladies going first to get their hamburgers, hot dogs, potato chips, Frito's Corn Chips, Cokes, 7-Ups, and Kool-Aid. Everyone enjoyed the food greatly, and there was much laughter, joy, and deep fellowship around the table. After the meal, most of the young adults participated in a rollicking volleyball game. Both Hal and Debbie were experts at volleyball. Their serves were very well executed and hard for the other team to answer. They were also able to hit a lot of balls that were coming at them and spike it to the other side. On the other hand, Brad and Pam were both pushovers at this game, but they enjoyed themselves and were bowled over with paroxysms of laughter. Both Pam and Brad kept on missing the balls that came their way. When it was Pam's turn to serve, she totally muffed it and crashed the ball right into the middle of the net. When it was Brad's turn to serve, he executed two spectacular serves, which the other side couldn't answer for two points, but then muffed the third serve. Brad's team lost by the lopsided score of 21-8.

After the volleyball game, the young people gathered in various groups in order to "shoot the breeze" and tell funny jokes and stories to each other. They ate the delicious hard-boiled dyed Easter eggs the Thatchers had supplied in abundance. Hal and Laura were paired off in a corner, talking about basketball, the history of Germany under Adolph Hitler and the Third Reich, and different events that happened in the Bible.

"You know, Laura," Hal was saying. "It really is interesting how much alike King Saul of Israel and Adolph Hitler were: they were both skilled military leaders, they were both demon-possessed, and they were both mass murderers."

"Isn't that sad?" replied Laura.

"Another similarity is that they both committed suicide, King Saul by falling on his sword, and Hitler by shooting himself. They both had close companions who also committed suicide: Saul's armor bearer, and Hitler's brand-new wife."

"But I'll bet you a million bucks that Adolph Hitler wouldn't have been a very good basketball player."

"But King Saul woulda'. He woulda' been the star player for the Lakers if he had been living today. The Bible says he was head and shoulders taller than all the other people in Israel. Why he woulda' shot perfect layup shots, swishing them right through the middle of the hoop."

"I'm sure that Goliath would have been even better. He was taller than King Saul, you know. But King David would have been the best basketball player of them all."

"I don't think so, sweet Laura. It is true that he was a mighty man of God, a tremendous military leader, and a great musician, but I feel he woulda' been a fabulous baseball star rather than a basketball star. Why with the way he killed Goliath with a sling and a stone, he woulda' walked circles around Babe Ruth and Hank Aaron."

"Oh, Hal, I love you! You are so smart. You never cease to amaze me with your knowledge of the Bible and world history."

Meanwhile, Brad Applebaum, Cristy Hunt, Bob Hurst, Dwayne Downing, Peter Thal, and Pam Jackson were sitting together on a corner of the grassy lawn, making conversation over different issues and laughing their heads off.

Bob Hurst asked, "What do you think about that new famous pop music star, Jitterbug Josh?"

"I *know* him!" exclaimed Brad. "He's Randy Miller. He's the best friend of my close relatives, Uncle Mike and Aunt Donna."

"He's the one who wrote the new smash hit, 'The Evil Eye,'" commented Dwayne. "He also wrote 'Say Yay for Yoga' and 'Dragon Diamond'."

"The only song of his that I remotely like at all is 'The American Dream'," said Cristy.

"He rocketed to the top amazingly fast," commented Bob. "At the end of last summer, nobody knew who Randy Miller was."

"This light-speed rise to the top is *demonic!*" declared Brad indignantly. "Randy Miller is involved in the occult. Early last October, I tried to warn my family members about the danger of sorcery and the dark road that Randy Miller was traveling down, but nobody would listen to me."

"There's a bizarre story that happened a few weeks ago relating to Jitterbug Josh," said Dwayne. "Did any of you hear about those three youths who died mysteriously during a couple of his concerts? It was weird, man! Nobody was able to figure out what caused their deaths."

"Some people speculated that it was related to a new song that Randy wrote," commented Brad. "This new song was performed for two nights, and each night that it was performed, there were those mysterious deaths. Then, when the band decided to cut the song from the program, the deaths stopped."

"I remember reading about that," said Peter. "It was something about loving Levis or blue jeans or something like that."

"Nobody would happen to know what the lyrics to that song were, would they?" asked Pam.

"Wait a minute!" said Brad. "I think I have a copy of those lyrics in my car. Would you like me to go and see if I can find them and bring them right back?"

"Yeah, sure."

"It couldn't hurt."

"Why not."

Brad ran to his car and returned shortly thereafter with a piece of paper having the lyrics to that controversial song typed on it. He handed it to Peter Thal who began reading it out loud, his voice getting louder, more incredulous, and more disgusted as he spoke.

" 'Lay your head on the great sea dragon,
Holding in his hand a bottomless flagon,
Out of the mouth of this invincible crocodile,
Gushes poisonous vengeance, hatred, and bile,
Concerning this crooked and scaly snake,

Of his matchless power make no mistake.'

"*WHAT?!!*

"*'Leviathan, Leviathan, his jaws lead to Hades,*
To the dark and desolate land of shadies.'

"This is the *stupidest,* the most *dreadful,* the most *terrible,* the most *infantile,* and the most depressing poem that I have seen in my whole life!" Peter shook his head and said in a low voice of disdain, "No, no, *noooo!*"

"No wonder those youths died," commented Dwayne. "A dreary song like that would bring anybody's spirits down to the dumps."

"I don't want to hear any more about that song," said Cristy. "I feel like I'm going to be sick."

"I *told* you," declared Brad, "that Randy Miller is getting his power from demonic spirits. His rise to fame and fortune has been too quick, too meteoric, too inexplicable to have a natural explanation. Anytime people start dabbling in things like astrology, black magic, witchcraft, spiritualism, fortune telling, and sorcery, they are courting big-time trouble."

"Guys!" said Pam. "Let's not focus so much on these dark things. One of my favorite songs is from *The Sound of Music* and is called 'These Are a Few of my Favorite Things.' There's a lot of truth in this song. You know, Philippians, chapter 4, verse 8 says, 'Finally, brethren, whatsoever things are true, whatsoever things are honest, whatsoever things are just, whatsoever things are pure, whatsoever things are lovely, whatsoever things are of good report; if there be any virtue, and if there be any praise, think on these things.' You know, my grandparents live in Knoxville, Tennessee. My favorite flower in the whole world is the magnolia. I think they are so gorgeous and awe-inspiring when they come out in the spring. Another of my favorite things is the rugged, beautiful seacoast of Northern California. Those waves crashing upon the surf are so peaceful and the air smells so good and refreshing. Another of my favorite things is a nice tall glass of Martinelli's Sparkling Cider with its exquisite taste. Another of my favorite things is a concert of truly *good* music. Listening to the music of Bach, Mendelssohn, Grieg, or Rachmaninoff does a lot more for me than being at a Jitterbug Josh concert ever will. I also like the jazz music of Dave Brubeck, Bill Evans, and Oscar Peterson. But you know what my favorite thing in the whole world is? It's Jesus, the lover of my soul, the most beautiful One, the sweet rose of Sharon, Wonderful, Counselor, Everlasting Father, the Prince of Peace, the Bright and Morning Star, the Alpha and Omega, my loving Bridegroom! Oh, hallelujah, hallelujah, HALLELUJAH! You are so worthy and awesome, precious Jesus! Thank You Jesus for Your precious Holy Spirit, my Comforter and Friend!"

Brad joined in the praise and worship, his countenance glowing with the joy of the Lord. Pam soon started to guffaw, letting out uncontrollable belly laughs that shook her whole frame.

"And we have lift-off!" quipped Brad.

The bystanders broke into hearty laughter, Brad joining in freely.

****

RANDY AND THE GROUP were still doing concerts regularly, even though they were doing them only in California and Nevada for the time being. They were continuing to have great success at their concerts, and Randy was raking in the dough. Every night that The Universal Mindset performed, 'Jitterbug Josh' was thronged with autograph seekers. The group album was selling astronautically. "The Evil Eye," "Say Yay for Yoga," and "Dragon Diamond" were getting a whole lot of airplay on radio stations across the USA. "Sensual Sue," "Hoodwinked Hustler," "Just like Creamy Silk," and "The American Dream" were not as popular on the radio rock stations but were still having moderate success and getting some airplay on the American radio stations. Adding to Randy's success was the fact that there were some arrangers who did some arrangements for easy listening orchestras of "The Evil Eye," "Just like Creamy Silk," "The American Dream," and "Dragon Diamond." The Universal Mindset did concerts in towns like Fresno, Stockton, Sacramento, Redding, Eureka, Carmel, and Las Vegas.

While things couldn't have been better on the outside, things were not so hot on the inside. 'Jitterbug Josh' continued to have a feeling of emptiness and dissatisfaction with life. The blood-curdling nightmares of being thrown down a bottomless tube by infernal beings were a recurring routine, with Randy waking up haggard and drenched with cold sweat. Randy and Lila were getting more and more drained, both physically and in their marriage. The big three-story house on Sleepy Hollow Road had initially given him happiness and great excitement, but the novelty had worn off very quickly. 'Jitterbug Josh' had a lot of trouble keeping up with the fast pace of a life of a celebrity, so to keep him going, he had started using amphetamines. The problem with this was even though the diet pills helped to keep him awake, he couldn't come in for a landing to get the sleep he needed. As it was, 'Jitterbug Josh' was afraid to go to sleep these days because of the horrible nightmares.

He remembered the spiritual experience he had gone through in the town of Weed in February and couldn't wait to have another consultation session with Psychiatrist Isis Butterfield. Brian had given a number of books to Randy written by Taylor Caldwell and Jesse Stearn that fascinated him. He was amazed to find out that Taylor Caldwell had also had an encounter with a spiritualist right before her writing career took off. She had experienced the phenomenon of automatic writing while writing her books just like Randy was experiencing in writing his music. Also, he saw eye-to-eye on Taylor Caldwell's ultra-conservative political views. She warned against the great danger of socialism and communism, and preached a message of hard work, individualism, honesty, and clean living.

****

"BRAD. Aunt Mary has generously bought tickets for the whole extended family to go see Jitterbug Josh at Mills College on Friday night."

Brad steeled himself up with a very pious look on his face as he stared at his mom. The Applebaum family was eating dinner at the dining room table on Monday, April 15.

"Mom, I really don't want to go see that occultic artist. I would rather go to the Crusade meeting."

Harriet looked at her son with vague disappointment. "Well, it's your life, Brad. You do what you want. But don't you think you're taking your religion a little bit too seriously?"

"You know, Brad," said Sid. "I think I agree with your mom. Aunt Mary paid big money to get us those tickets."

Brad looked red-faced at his parents and said, "Oh, all right! I'll go! I'll pray during the whole blasted concert and prove to you guys that Jitterbug Josh is getting his musical inspiration from demons!"

"You're not making any sense, kid," responded Sid.

****

IT WAS A BEAUTIFUL SUNSHINY EVENING in the Bay Area on Friday, April 19. Spring seemed to be finally in the air with the temperatures warming up. The concert auditorium at Mills College was filling up with hundreds of fans of 'Jitterbug Josh' and the Universal Mindset. Sid and Harriet Applebaum were there with their three children, Brad, Kimberly, and Lisa. Mike and Donna Applebaum were there with their children, Michelle and Sharon. Of course, Lila, Jack, and Tommy were there as were Anthony and Mary Richardson. Eric Burns had put Ted Johnson in charge of the Red Riding Rangers meeting so that he could come to the concert to audition as a guitar player and singer for the group.

At exactly 7:00 P. M., the concert kicked off with the smash hit song, "The Evil Eye." Other Randy Miller and Brian Manning songs followed. As was the case with many other concerts, this one was well received. 'Jitterbug Josh' was extremely 'wired' tonight—the amphetamines had affected his nervous system, making him a bundle of frenetic nervous energy. He gyrated, twitched, and turned on stage with abandon and great jerkiness, and he talked between the songs with great rapidity and a very strident voice. The audience cheered him on with great enthusiasm as they usually did. At the end of the concert, the crowd descended on him, asking for autographs.

All the Richardsons and Applebaums enjoyed the Jitterbug Josh concert immensely—that is, everybody except Brad Applebaum. As the concert wore on, his spirit became more and more restless. Finally, he could stand it no longer. "'Scuse me," he whispered to his family members, "I need to get out!" They gave him room to move out of his seat and into the aisle. Once there, he headed quickly toward the lobby and out into the fresh air. When he got outside, he immediately started praying passionately.

"Oh, God!" he moaned. "Please help! HELP! This is TERRIBLE what is going on in there! The occult is being glorified, and besides that, Randy Miller is being worshipped as an idol! PLEASE intervene! Make Yourself known to these people in there! There are many idols in this nation, but You are the true and living God! And Lord, please save Randy Miller somehow! PLEASE show him how much You love him! In the beautiful name of Jesus, amen!" Tears were running down his face as he prayed.

Eric waited at the tail end of the long line for a chance to be able to speak to Randy. Finally, he was facing the great singing star.

"Hey, Jitterbug Josh, can I talk to you for a few minutes?" asked Eric.

"What is it? I'm in a hurry—so make it quick."

"Do you remember me—from Miramonte High School years ago? I used to play guitar and for a while was playing violin."

Randy looked at Eric with impatience and said, "Yes, I remember you. What's on your mind?"

"I want to audition as a singer and guitar player for your group. I have a lot of talent musically, and I think that we can use music to affect the whole world for good. We can get rid of poverty, the overpopulation problem, air and water pollution, and greedy rich people who don't care at all about the poor and downtrodden. We can destroy capitalism and help usher in socialism where the government can meet all of our needs. We can—"

"Stop right there! You're barking up the wrong tree. It's you communists who are the real problem in this world today. You guys fool around all day and go around trying to destroy our wonderful country by treason and subversion. You dodge the draft and even root for the Viet Cong, making yourselves traitors to this country of the USA. Our land is built on our Founding Fathers—people like George Washington, Thomas Jefferson, and Benjamin Franklin who were true patriots and built this country on God, honest and clean living, and hard work. Yet you guys with your long hair, dirty beards, and violent demonstrations want to destroy this God-blessed country of America."

"What does that mean, then? Aren't you even going to give me a chance to audition for your group?"

Randy looked at Eric with a patronizing glance and said, "No, Eric. I don't have time to audition you. Our group is doing just fine with the seven members we have. I have heard your guitar playing and singing and am not impressed. I've seen you around Miramonte High School years ago. You were disorganized, disorderly, and sloppy at that time—and I see from the way you're dressed today in your sloppy outfit and your uncombed hair that you haven't changed a bit. Your lackadaisical attitude is matched only by your stupidity."

Eric lashed back with a stream of horrible blasphemies and obscenities after which he continued, "Look who's talking! Who do you think you are, you sorry basket case? You think you're so great, but your supposed talent is just a sham! You sit up on that stage, pretending that you're so great, while really, you're just a big fat humbug! You live in luxury, ripping off people, living like a king, taking it easy all day! You are a dirty, rotten, horrible, smelly, stinking capitalistic pig and a pea-brained little fathead! You put on your show and espouse your greedy and wicked tenets to millions of people you—"

"Watch it, buddy!" interjected Randy. "You're getting me really angry! Just go away and let me alone." Randy's face was getting redder and his countenance darker as Eric continued his slanderous barrage of cutting remarks.

"You are not just an amoeba who mooches off the public but also a total mentally retarded idiot who has booboo where most people's brains are. You......."

WHACK! Randy's fists slammed forcibly and brutally into Eric's face. Eric fought back but was no match for Randy Miller. SLAP! POW! WHACK, WHACK, *WHACK!* Eric began to totter and slide to the floor. A host of bystanders bustled their way to the scene of action, making heated comments and trying to break up the fight.

"WHAT'S GOING ON THERE?!"

"WHAT ARE YOU DOIN', JITTERBUG JOSH?!"

"Com'n, break it up, BREAK IT UP!"

Several men grabbed the arms of Randy and wrestled him to the floor. Eric was lying on the floor, unconscious, with his face covered with bruises.

"Looks like he's badly hurt!"

"Somebody, call the police!"

"What's going on here?"

"WHAT?! It's JITTERBUG JOSH who assaulted that poor man! I don't believe it! I DON'T BELIEVE IT!"

"Somebody, get a doctor!"

Several strong men pinned Randy to the floor. In short order, the police entered the room and placed 'Jitterbug Josh' under arrest. Meanwhile, Eric began to regain consciousness and mumble incoherently. There were some cuts and bruises on his face, and he had two black eyes. Presently, he was taken to the emergency room at Oakland General Hospital where he was kept overnight and given a full and thorough checkup, the doctors being especially concerned about the possibility of a concussion. There was no concussion, though. By the time he was in the ambulance, he had regained full consciousness.

By the time morning had arrived, the diagnostic checkup of Eric Burns was complete. He had some painful cuts, bruises, and two black eyes, but no serious or deep injuries. He was released from the hospital with instructions on how to take care of his wounds and bruises. He was not badly hurt physically, but he was extremely mad at Randy Miller, and his heart was full of bitterness and resentment.

"I'm going to fix that rotten, no-good snob!" he muttered to himself. "I will never, NEVER forgive him for what he did to me! He's going to pay for this! *He's going to pay for this!!*"

13.

THE EVIL AGENDA

"I'm sure surprised at Randy Miller! I never thought that he had a mean streak in his whole body!" Donna was saying.

It was a sunshiny Saturday afternoon. Mike and Donna were having iced tea out on the backyard veranda on the day following the Mills College concert. When the fight had happened last night between Randy and Eric, they had already left the auditorium. Donna had heard about it when she had gotten home from Lila who phoned her and explained everything that had transpired: Randy hitting Eric and knocking him unconscious, the ambulance coming to take Eric to the hospital, and Randy being arrested and thrown into jail.

"He sure has changed, hasn't he?" said Mike. "I remember the good old days when he was friendly, fun-loving, and relatively calm and cool. Now he is not only hard to approach, but he seems to be restless and hyper. Did you notice any difference in his singing last night?"

"Yeah, I did, sweetheart. I don't know how to describe it. It's like he is trying to prove himself and is inwardly afraid that he is going to be a flop. He is obviously stressed out."

"You said it. To me, it's like he has all this nervous energy and can't slow down and relax. I've begun to wonder if he is *on* something."

"I don't know, Michael. But there is one thing; there's something strange about Randy. I can't put my finger on it, but his eyes—there's something there that gives me the creeps."

"Well anyway, there was that assault last night. Like I always say, 'The proof is in the pudding.' Whatever he's into, it's not really benefiting him. On the contrary, it seems to be doing him harm."

The couple looked toward the grassy backyard where their daughter, Michelle, was practicing her ballet steps.

"How's that, Mom and Dad?" she called out.

"Real good, honey!" replied Donna, appreciatively. "Keep it up!"

****

"THIS IS KTVU, CHANNEL 2 news on this Saturday evening. Top stories from around Northern California. Tonight, the story continues to get darker and darker concerning bank robber/serial rapist/murderer Darryl Temple. Evidence of his involvement in the murder of many young women in the Northern San Joaquin Valley is becoming more incriminating all the time.

The fingerprints on a couple more of the murdered girls were shown today to conclusively match the fingerprints of Darryl Temple. Temple is presently being held without bail at San Quentin Prison, pending his trial slated to begin in September. If found guilty of these multiple murders, Temple will probably spend the rest of his life behind bars.

"In other news, the famous singer and guitarist, Randy Miller, popularly known as 'Jitterbug Josh,' was released from jail today. He assaulted and beat up a young man named Eric Burns last night after his performance at Mills College with The Universal Mindset. In recent months, the name of Randy Miller has become a household word, due to several hit songs he has written as well as his legendary singing and guitar playing skills. Meanwhile, Eric Burns was released from Oakland General Hospital today with only minor injuries. The question remains: what was the motive prompting Jitterbug Josh to lash out at Eric Burns? This reporter doesn't have a clue to that one."

Art and Jan Burns were sitting in front of the television set, indignant against Randy Miller, glad that their son was all right, but still vaguely worried about him.

"That jerk should have been locked up for at least a month!" declared Art, angrily. "The nerve of that fat old geezer, picking on our poor son for no reason at all!"

"I don't understand why he did it," said Jan. "It doesn't make any sense at all."

****

THE EARLY MORNING PRAYER MEETING on Monday, April 22, was especially glorious. The presence of the Holy Spirit was very sweet, and the six intercessors were wide-awake. Hal Odell and Laura Wilkerson were cuddled close together, holding hands. The other four people in the room were Pam Jackson, Cristy Hunt, Heidi Knudsen, and Brad Applebaum. They all took turns praying in English, and those who had a prayer language spent some time speaking in tongues as well as praying in English. They prayed for the campus of Cal Berkeley, for the city of Berkeley itself, for the state of California, for America, and for the world that people would call on the name of Jesus and be saved. Brad prayed for the nation of Israel that God would prosper the Jews there and protect them from the enemy nations surrounding them. Heidi prayed for the Body of Christ around the world to be built up and strengthened. Pam prayed for the political and economic scene in America as well as things pertaining to the Watergate Cover-up. Hal prayed for the professional football, basketball, and baseball players who were Christians that they would be strong witnesses for the Lord to those who were unsaved. The group also spent some time just worshipping the Lord. They also sang several hymns and worship choruses. Pam's golden-brown cat, whose name

177

was Goldfinger, was lying on her lap and purring quietly. Seven o'clock arrived, Pam said the final 'amen,' and the small talk began.

"WOW!" exclaimed Brad, happily. "This was a fabulous morning! Praise You, beautiful Jesus!"

"Glory to God!" echoed Laura.

"Praise the Lord," agreed Hal, who was still holding her hand.

"What a wonderful morning of spiritual refreshing!" exulted Brad, joyfully. "This is sure a lot better than last Friday night was!"

"Tell us about it," said Heidi. "Where were you?"

"Well, I went and attended a Jitterbug Josh concert with my whole family at Mills College. It was awful! I sat there for a while, listening to those songs, and Randy wildly going all over the stage. Randy Miller is a great performer, but I sensed that something was terribly wrong. I don't know how to put it in words, but there was an evil presence there. I began to feel really *cold* even with the pleasant spring temperatures outside. I couldn't stay in there any longer, so I excused myself, walked outside, and started interceding in prayer for Randy Miller."

Pam listened to every word with complete attentiveness and said, "Brad, you have a true gift of discernment. I sense that the Holy Spirit was speaking strongly to your heart on Friday night at the concert. I feel very strongly that we need to pray for Randy Miller and the people in that band. There is an evil agenda behind that band and it's not Randy Miller himself, but the power working behind him and the people in the group. I'm fixing to pray right now. Let's bow our heads! Father, I pray right now for Randy Miller and the group, The Universal Mindset. I pray You will open their eyes to the truth of the gospel. I thank You that You loved the whole world so that You sent Jesus Your Son to bring salvation to the world. I pray right now that You open the eyes of Randy Miller to Your love so that he might be delivered out of the kingdom of darkness and brought into Your marvelous kingdom of light. Let him go, Lord! *Oh, Lord, let Him go!* Set him free from the chains of Satan binding Him. I pray You will gloriously save his soul and wash him in the Blood of the Lamb. Send Your angels to order Randy Miller's steps to make it easy for him to find the Savior." Tears of intercession were running down her face as she prayed, "Get him, Lord! Oh, Lord, get him, get him, *get him!* Give him a vision of the cross. In the beautiful name of Jesus, amen."

As Pam prayed, some of the other people in the room were quietly praying in tongues, (foreign languages they had never learned, but were given to them sovereignty by the Holy Spirit). Suddenly, Laura Wilkerson started praying rather loudly in a foreign tongue. About fifteen seconds after she finished her utterance, Pam began to voice the interpretation in English for the group.

"My little children, I love you so much! Pray without ceasing! Pray, pray, pray! My glory rests upon those who rise early in the morning to pray and seek my face. Let your supplications, prayers, intercessions, and giving of thanks be made for all men, for kings and for all that are in authority that ye may lead a quiet and peaceable life in all godliness and honesty. Have I not said in My Word that I desire that no one would perish, but that all would come to repentance? But many people will not be able to be saved from the clutches of Satan except for someone who will stand for their salvation through intercessory prayer. Was not My wrath against the Israelites in the wilderness turned away many times because of the intercessory prayers of My servant Moses? Yea, I would say to you My beloved children, pray, pray, pray! Pray without ceasing! Pray for the salvation of men's souls, and I will move by My Spirit to woo and draw them to Myself."

Most of the people in the group heartily said, "Amen," but Hal Odell was somewhat dubious concerning that utterance.

"Do your spirits witness to this word?" asked Pam.

"Yes!"

"Good word!"

"It's right on line with the Scriptures!"

"But is this gift for today?" asked Hal. "I don't know. I've always heard that many of these gifts passed away and were no longer needed when the canon of Scripture was completed at the end of the first century."

"But that word was 100 percent in agreement with God's written Word," protested Brad to Hal. "As a matter of fact, much of that interpretation of that tongue was actually *quoting* the Word of God."

"And I have a green light in my spirit concerning that word," concurred Cristy.

"Well, it certainly *sounds* good," said Hal, "but I would just be careful and cautious. That's all I want to say. I think we're better off being too cautious about these things than finding ourselves being led off the deep end by Satan."

"I understand your logic, Hal," said Pam, "and you being a stickler for the Word of God is commendable. But I think that we are on safe ground here. Certainly, we need to be praying for the salvation of men's souls. This will also help us as we tell people about Jesus and His love."

Goldfinger the cat let out a loud "meow," and all six of the prayer warriors broke out into hearty guffaws. Pam gently stroked the soft fur of Goldfinger and said, "Nice kitty! Nice kitty! You love your mommy, don't you? Mommy loves you too, Goldfinger!"

This episode lightened up the mood of all six of them as they started making small talk about classes at school, basketball, and a recent funny incident with Heidi's Dalmatian dog. One by one, they left Pam's apartment and walked out into the light rain to get ready to go to school.

****

ON TUESDAY EVENING, Jack and Tommy were eating dinner with Lila their mom. As usual these days, Randy was not home but out playing at another concert. Lila angrily took the lasagna dinner out of the oven and ladled the delicious contents onto her plate and the kids' plates. She greatly missed the good old days when the whole family had been together. Now, she hardly had a husband anymore. They were eating supper in the snow-white kitchen. She sat down wearily at the kitchen table and started eating her lasagna and drinking her Merlot.

"Mom," said Jack.

"What dear?" asked Lila.

"You know how I get to watch *Marcus Welby M. D.* at ten o'clock every Tuesday night?"

"Yes, son."

"Well, I wonder if it would be okay for me to stay up on Thursday night this week as well. They're going to show the second part of tonight's episode as a special feature. Marcus Welby is going to appear on the ten o'clock show, *Court Marshall, Counselor at Law.*"

Lila burst into laughter and said, "Jack, dear, the name of the show is **_Owen_** *Marshall, Counselor at Law,* but your title was a good title. And yes, you may stay up that night and watch that program."

"Thank you, Mom!"

This was an oasis in a desert—a precious moment of laughter. These days, those moments of laughter were few and far between for Lila Miller.

****

"COME ON IN, you guys. Close the door and have a seat."

It was an overcast Thursday morning on April 25, 1974. Randy Miller, Brian Manning, and Hiram Quinn walked nervously into the plush, yellow-green office of the pop music impresario, Harry Gates for another debriefing. The tension in the air was so thick, you could cut it with a knife. The three men took a seat in the large and softly cushioned black armchairs surrounding the neat and well-organized desk of pop music manager Harry Gates.

"Let's begin this meeting," said Harry Gates. "We have a couple of important things to cover today.

"First of all, I have good news for you guys. There have been no more mysterious deaths at our concerts, and the long gas lines have disappeared. What this means is that we're going to be able to start up our road trip once again, beginning in late June and continuing until about the middle of August. This tour will include a big Fourth of July concert at Madison Square Garden. We are also planning a weeklong tour of Great Britain in late July. There'll be spots on national TV, an appearance for President Nixon at the White House, and a five-day cruise to the Bahamas. This will mean more publicity and bigger bucks for us."

The other three people in the room smiled nervously and nodded their heads.

"Overall," continued Harry, "things have been going well. For the most part, the concerts have been off the charts, record sales have gone through the ceiling, and our songs that have been played on the radio stations across the U. S. have continued to be huge hits.

"Now," continued Harry in a more serious tone of voice. "What this means for you guys is that you're going to have to measure up to an even higher standard of musical excellence, you're going to have to project the very best and attractive image to your public, and you're going to have to be on top of things, both on and off the stage. Can I count on you to rise to the occasion and get your act together?"

"Oh, yes," replied Brian. "You can count on Randy and me."

"Y-yes," said Randy nervously. "I'll do good."

Harry looked intently into the eyes of Randy and asked, "A whole lot depends on you coming through and doing good, Jitterbug Josh. Are you *sure* you have it in you to produce?"

Randy felt hot anger gushing through him as he answered, "Why wouldn't I be able to wow the crowds with my great talent? I've done real good so far, haven't I?"

"Well, Randy, we've seen some problems with you as of late," said Brian. "You don't seem to have the same self-assurance and poise you did only a few months ago. I've noticed some concentration problems on stage (for example, forgetting the words on that one part of 'Blue Love' on Friday night) —and then there's the incident of the fistfight at Mills College."

"Yes, Harry and I are very concerned about that," said Hiram.

"Honest!" said Randy. "That redheaded turkey made me do it. He provoked me by his extremely insulting and cutting remarks. I really didn't mean for that assault to happen or for him to have to go to the hospital."

Harry kept his gaze firmly on Randy as he said, "Well, we can't afford to have a repeat of this incident. The cost to all of us is too high. *Behave yourself, Jitterbug Josh.*"

"I'll behave. I promise I'll behave. I swear it! I promise! No more booboos on stage, and no more knock-down fights."

"Okay then," said Harry in a dubious tone of voice. "We'll hold you to your word. Don't disappoint us."

****

"MR. APPLEBAUM, come in here and have a seat."

Charlie May was a short fat man with gray hair and a tense and serious demeanor about him. Brad sat down in front of his boss at the Jack-in-the-Box hamburger stand in El Sobrante, wondering what the boss was going to say to him. He didn't see the blow coming.

"Brad," the boss started out. "How are things going in your life?"

"Quite well, thank you! Praise the Lord! I just got my report cards for third quarter at Cal, and my grades were excellent. I got 'A's in journalism, American history, creative writing, English, and applied flute. I got a 'B' in sociology and astronomy. My family is doing great."

"Well, that's wonderful, Brad. Okay, let's get down to business. As you know, your four-week trial here at Jack-in-the-Box is completed. We have watched your performance over this time period, and I am sorry to say that we are going to have to let you go."

Brad's face fell with surprise and despondency as he said, "But *why?* I've done the best that I could do at this job. I know I've made mistakes, but I can learn and become an efficient worker here."

"Brad," said Charlie, sympathetically. "I know you have tried your very best. I have no complaints about your hard work and punctuality. But you just don't have it in you to do this type of job. You never were able to get into the swing of things as far as remembering the various orders that were given to you by the customers. Nor were you ever able to master the art of flipping and cooking the food orders or getting the orders to the customers at the fast rate of speed demanded by this company."

"Oh, no, NOOOO!" groaned Brad, nearly in tears. "I really thought that this job would work out. But now I see that I'm a great big failure. I'm just a no-good, stupid blockhead."

"Ah, don't take it so hard," consoled Charlie. "*Everybody* has times of failure in their lives. I'm going to give you some advice I imagine you won't take because of your dejection and that is, 'Don't let it get to you or get down on yourself.' I'm sure that with a positive attitude and perseverance, you'll find the line of work you will do just great at."

"Well, I guess I'll be going now," said Brad in a low, mournful voice.

"Okay, Mr. Applebaum. Goodbye and good luck to you. You can come by in the morning and pick up your last check."

****

"WHAT do you say, kid?"

"Dad (sob), I'm just a no-good, rotten, stupid idiot!"

"What happened, son?" asked Harriet, gently.

"I got fired from my job today."

"Don't sweat it, Brad. You tried your best and that's all that counts," said Sid. "I'm proud of you, son."

Said Harriet, "I want to encourage you with something, Brad. There's a line in the movie, *The Sound of Music,* which goes like this: 'When the Lord closes a door, somewhere He opens a window.' Just hang in there, and somewhere, somehow, you'll make a success of your life."

"I hope so!" said Brad. "I sure hope so!"

****

IT WAS 11:00 P. M. on Friday night, April 26. Seven men were sitting in a dim, secluded booth at Eric Burns' favorite bar in Berkeley—that familiar sleazy bar that Eric, Ted, and Scott had met at for planning sessions from time to time. Tonight was to be a very hush-hush meeting of these seven select Red Riding Rangers members to discuss a special evil agenda that Eric Burns had in mind for the future. Besides the three core members, there was Felix McDowell, Tony Fitch, Francis Zeeb, and Nick Weems.

Felix was a twenty-two-year-old pimply young man with long unkempt blonde hair and blue eyes. He was five feet, eight inches tall. He was a regular user of marijuana and speed and had taken several trips on LSD. He was a high school dropout who had trouble keeping a regular job.

Tony was twenty-six years old. He was short and fat with brown hair and green eyes. He had spent some time in jail for income tax fraud and was presently working as a landscaper.

Francis was the oldest member of The Red Riding Rangers. Thirty-six years of age, he was six feet tall, having jet-black hair with brown eyes. His job was selling guns and firearms to people. He had once been a Jehovah's Witness before converting to the Marxist cause.

Nick was twenty-nine years old. He was five feet, ten inches tall and had strawberry blonde hair with green eyes. Like Felix, he also had trouble keeping a steady job. He was a slow talker with a slight speech impediment and was not very intelligent.

The seven sat around the table, smoking cigarettes and downing whiskey and brandy until Eric called the secret meeting together.

"Now, let's get down to business," said Eric in a dead-serious tone of voice. "I've called you here because you comrades are the best. I completely trust you to be able to listen carefully, to be able to follow and obey orders to the nth degree, and to keep your mouths tightly shut.

"Now, here's the situation as it stands right now. You all know about that money-grubbing, fascist pig, Randy Miller, also known as Jitterbug Josh. He's a dude who rose very quickly from obscurity to being a household word in our accursed country of America today. I have known him since the days that we were in school together. He has always been a holier-than-thou snob. In the last year since his rise to the top, he has become much worse. He is an evil capitalistic freak who is loaded with filthy wealth, greedy, patronizing, conceited, vainglorious, and hot-tempered. I was going to audition for his group last week after I had unfairly lost my bus-driving job, but he was mean and wouldn't even give me a chance. He snubbed me off! I also found out that he is a right-wing fanatic. We know that free enterprise is a lie, and that Marx, Lenin, and Stalin were heroes all along. And to top things off, he knocked me unconscious for no reason at all, and I had to spend a night in the hospital with injuries that included two black eyes. I could have been killed! So you see the problem? Obviously, this calls for some big-time revenge against this outrage!"

"So what's the gig?" asked Felix.

"Yeah, what do you have in mind?" asked Francis.

"We have to fix that pop music monopolist for good. My plan is for us to go to a Jitterbug Josh concert sometime in the future, let's say sometime in late August. We'll get tickets well in advance. Some of us will have seats near the front of the concert hall while others of us will have seats near the back. When a good moment comes, you people in the back will start a fire. As the people are distracted, we who are in the front will rush onto the stage and grab Randy Miller, drag him out through a side entrance, tie him up with ropes, and spirit him away in a getaway vehicle that Scott will provide."

"You gonna *kidnap* Jitterbug Josh?" queried Tony, incredulously.

"How the heck can it possibly be pulled off and work?" asked Nick.

"Scott over here works in a car-repair garage. He'll have a truck all ready to go, close to the side entrance of the auditorium. We'll stuff Randy Miller into the truck, bind him up with ropes and gag him, and hightail it out of there. I'll have some communist associates that I'm in cohorts with in Newport Beach down in Southern California help me out in keeping Jitterbug Josh captive and quiet."

"So what's the catch to all of this?" asked Francis.

"We'll send a ransom note to Lila Miller, the wife of the music star demanding two million dollars or the life of Jitterbug Josh. If she produces, we will let the music star go free. If all goes well, each of you will get a cut of the dough. After we get the loot, we'll hightail it down to Caracas, Venezuela, where I have some secret communist allies who will protect us."

"Sounds like a crazy plan to me," said Scott. "Suppose de' plan don't work? We could all land in jail!"

"It'll work!" declared Eric. "Listen. This is only a very rough outline of the plan. We have several months to work on it, to practice and rehearse it thoroughly, and to fine-tune all the little intricate nitty-gritty details. We're not going to strike until we're ready."

"One thing that worries me," said Nick. "What 'bout those guys in the back setting the fire? How are they going to keep from getting caught?"

"We'll have to work on that detail," said Eric. "We'll brainstorm that area as we make our plans in the weeks to come."

"Don't worry, guys," said Ted Johnson to the other group members. "Eric is a very intelligent man, and I am a great strategist and planner. Between the two of us, we'll figure everything out down to a tee."

"One thing," said Eric, "is that everyone will have to move very quickly and at just the right moment. We'll need a getaway vehicle very close to the front entrance of the concert hall for the arsonists to make their escape as fast as they can. Don't worry. Somehow, someway, we'll make this caper work!"

All the faces of the seven conspirators were flushed with restless excitement at the prospect of pulling off this foolhardy, daring caper. Would it work? It would take perfect timing, execution, and planning with no mishaps for it to succeed.

14.

THE SUMMER OF '74

Saturday, May 4, was the birthday of Sid Applebaum. On that afternoon, there was a big celebration at the Sid and Harriet Applebaum residence in the high hills of Moraga. Of course, everyone in the immediate family was there. Also present were Mike and Donna Applebaum with their two daughters, Michelle and Sharon, as well as Anthony and Mary Richardson. Brad stayed in his room, working on his homework until all the partiers arrived. Balloons were up all over the place, and a sign with yellow letters was placed on the outside door with the words, 'Happy Birthday, Sid!' written on it. It promised to be a lively afternoon.

"What do you say, kid?" said Sid as Mike and Donna with their kids entered the Applebaum castle.

"Happy birthday, Sid!" exclaimed the couple together. "How does it feel to be a year older?"

"Okay," said Sid, stoically.

"What do you think of the market these days?" asked Mike.

"We're hanging in there," said Sid.

"And how's your golf game been lately?" asked Donna.

"Terrible! I shot an 88 this morning at Mira Vista. I got a double bogey on four, five, seven, and twelve and triple bogeys on fifteen, seventeen, and eighteen. I also missed a lot of short gimme putts. I did birdie three, nine, and eleven."

"You have some things go right and some things go wrong," philosophized Anthony. "It always works out that way. It's the Law of Averages."

Meanwhile, Mike was asking the children of Sid and Harriet how each of them was doing.

"Just great!" said Kimberly.

"I'm doing fine," said Lisa.

"I'm not doing so well," said Brad.

"What's the matter, Brad?" asked Mike.

"I'm a great big failure. I just can't do anything right."

"He got fired from his job at Jack-in-the-Box," explained Harriet, "and he is very crestfallen over it."

"Brad," soothed Mike. "Let me give you some advice, son, and tell you a true story that happened in history that should encourage you and cheer you up. I know you know all about this story because you are an extremely smart young man. Anyway, this man failed at a business when he was young. In the 1830s, his beloved fiancée died of an illness. Shortly after that, he had a nervous breakdown. The first time he ran for a seat in the Illinois legislature, he lost. He served only one term as a congressman and was not able to get re-elected. In 1856, he failed to become vice president of the United States. Then in 1858, he lost his campaign bid against Stephen A. Douglas in the race for the U. S. senate. Of course, you would know who this guy is, Brad, being as intelligent as you are."

"Abraham Lincoln, the sixteenth president of the United States and the best president that our country ever had."

"Right you are, Brad. I *knew* you would know the answer to that one. I agree that Old Abe was the best president we ever had. You know what I like about him?"

"What would that be?"

"He was a moderate. He went down the middle-of-the-road. There were politicians at that time who were either way on one side or the other. On one side were people like William Lloyd Garrison who were staunch, flaming abolitionists who wanted an end to slavery right now, no matter what. And then you had people on the other side like William L. Yancey, a 'fire-eater,' who were pro-slavery and supported secession from the Union. Brad, my point of this story is this: don't get discouraged. Just hang in there, keep your chin up, and keep it cool and level. You're going to make it."

"Yeah, I guess so."

"I *know* so."

Meanwhile, Sid and Anthony were in conversation, talking about the biology lab in Walnut Creek.

"So what's new, kid?" asked Sid.

"Well, the lab is trudging along slowly. We've been doing some in-depth experiments with different kinds of animals to test their intelligence so we can get a better picture of how evolution happened."

"Sounds very interesting."

"We've found that the chimpanzees are pretty smart, the pigs aren't all that dumb, but the geese are downright stupid. We have an idea how simple organisms slowly evolved up to fish. Then it's interesting to try to figure out the puzzle of the jump from fish to amphibians. We know that there is an extinct order of fish known as rhipidistians with features that are like early amphibians. And then there is the extinct coelacanth that existed about seventy million years ago. Then there's the jump from amphibians to reptiles. This is a complicated thing to figure out, and paleontologists are still trying to find the intermediaries here. It is very problematic. Then we have the jump from reptiles to mammals. Scientists are studying the intermediary therapsids. We also have the other connection stemming from reptiles to birds. Then we have the colossal jump from the ape to human beings. The study of our outdated and antiquated organs we don't need any more like the appendix and the tonsils is very good evidence of man evolving from the ape. The documentation—"

"May I say something?" asked Brad, meekly.

"You probably have a lot of religious old-school nonsense, but go ahead," said Anthony in a voice showing condescension and disdain.

"The Bible says in First Corinthians, chapter 1, verses 18 to 21, 'For the preaching of the cross is to them that perish foolishness; but unto us which are saved it is the power of God. For it is written, I will destroy the wisdom of the wise, and will bring to nothing the understanding of the prudent. Where is the wise? where is the scribe? where is the disputer of this world? Hath not God made foolish the wisdom of this world? For after that in the wisdom of God the world by wisdom knew not God, it pleased God by the foolishness of preaching to save them that believe.' And then verses 25 to 29 says this: 'Because the foolishness of God is wiser than men; and the weakness of God is stronger than men. For ye see your calling, brethren, how that not many wise men after the flesh, not many mighty, not many noble are called: But God hath chosen the foolish things of the world to confound the wise; and God hath chosen the weak things of the world to confound the things which are mighty; And base things of the world, and things which are despised, hath God chosen, yea, and things which are not, to bring to naught things that are: that no flesh should glory in His presence.'"

"That doesn't make any sense to me at all," said Sid.

"What the devil does any of that have to do with biology?" asked Anthony. "This is the silliest piece of tripe I've ever heard! What does this have to do with evolution?"

"Everything in the world. I'll admit that I'm not very smart at science, especially not biology, geology, and chemistry, but the Word of God is powerful on its own."

"You're right about the first part of your statement," retorted Anthony. "You're very stupid when it comes to science—and your archaic book there is......."

"WHAT?!" exclaimed Donna and Mary together.

"What is it?" asked the others in unison.

"It feels like somebody just entered this room," said Mary.

"Why it seems that *Randy Miller* is in this room!" exclaimed Donna.

"Impossible," said Mike. "He's off concertizing or rehearsing with his band somewhere."

"Well, there's a way to find out," said Sid. "RANDY! RANDY! ARE YOU ANYWHERE IN THIS ROOM OR HOUSE?"

"RANDY!" called out Donna and Mary together. "HEY JITTERBUG JOSH, ARE YOU ANYWHERE AROUND HERE?"

There was no answer.

"You see there?" said Sid. "There's nobody here."

"It's your imagination!" mocked Anthony. "You've been drinking too much beer and watching too many episodes of *The Twilight Zone* on TV."

"But I *feel* his presence!" exclaimed Mary.

"Maybe he sneaked in and is hiding somewhere," commented Donna. "Maybe he wanted to surprise us by crashing the party."

"Impossible," declared Sid.

"Hey, Jitterbug Josh, can you hear us?" called out Donna and Mary again.

No appearance of the form of Randy Miller or audible response.

The whole group was baffled.

****

ON THAT SAME SATURDAY, Randy had driven up to Weed for another session with Isis Butterfield. Most of the snow had melted, and the trees were a gorgeous green color. He had enjoyed the drive as he had passed by Shasta Lake and then wound up through the red cliffs of the mountains on Highway 5. When he arrived at the log cabin house of Isis Butterfield, they had started right into the session with Randy being hypnotized and his spirit leaving his body. He floated around the room for a moment, looking at his inert body lying on the salmon-colored sofa after which he floated outside. He found out that he could fly at great speed to anywhere he wanted to go. An idea cropped up in his mind: he could fly south above the mountains surrounding Mount Shasta and enjoy the beautiful scenery. This he did. Then another idea crossed his brain; he could fly all the way back to Orinda and Moraga. He picked up speed and was amazed at how fast he could travel—it seemed like almost at the speed of thought. Soon, he was peering down at the movie theater in downtown Orinda with the Wells Fargo Bank next to it and the drugstore across the street. Then Randy thought to himself, *Maybe I can sneak over to Sid's birthday party where I'm sure Mike and Donna must be. Wouldn't it be fun to look at everything going on and not be seen or heard by them as I spy on them?* It seemed like practically one second later that he was indeed standing in Sid and Harriet's house, looking down at the birthday party. Everybody was in animated conversation. Anthony was showing off his scientific knowledge while Brad quoted the Scriptures from First Corinthians. These verses were new to Randy, and he felt an ominous unrest in his spirit as the Scripture cut right into his musical and intellectual pride. He found that he could read the thoughts of everyone in the room. He heard the ridicule of Anthony against what Brad had read from the Bible yet read some conflicting thoughts from the arrogant scientist; he was scared that maybe the Bible was right, and if it was, he was in real hot water with God. Then came the exclamations from the ladies who claimed they felt the presence of Randy in the room. After about three minutes of this, Randy decided to leave the house in order to explore other places. Once outside, he started to fly south, when he encountered the all too familiar spiritual silhouette of Thomas Miller, Senior. Randy rushed up to the cloudlike form of his daddy but was cut short by the deceased spirit's terse response. This lack of love and affection greatly dismayed and frustrated Randy as he thought, *Does everyone that dies lose their warm personalities and end up being plastic like my spiritualized dad?*

"Quit trying to grab onto me! We have a lot to do and a short time to do it in."

"But Dad, I miss you! I wish you were the kindly man that I grew up knowing and loving."

SLAP! The contact on the face of Randy Miller was painful. His dad had a very strong and vise-like grip on Randy's spiritual wrists. The hands of Thomas were cold and clammy, and Randy winced in fear and pain.

"Now pay attention, son! We are going much further back in time on this session. Today, we are going to go back about 3,000 years and reveal to you a little bit of a previous life you had."

Suddenly, Randy found himself in an old and luxurious palace in a land he had never been in before. He was wearing a soft robe and had a crown on his head. The city he was in was on a high hill, and there was much limestone surrounding the whole city. One of the people in the great hall, obviously a general in an army of that time, walked forward to speak to him.

"King David," he said. "Your son, Absalom, is wishing to see your face and speak with you."

"Joab," Randy found himself saying. "I do not wish to see the face of that murderer—that son of mine who killed my son Amnon!" Randy felt mixed emotions of anger, sadness, and longing as he spoke these words. *So, I was actually the great King David of Israel in a former life as well as being the great George Gershwin later on! Wow!*

At this point, Randy heard the familiar faraway voice of Isis Butterfield calling for him to wake up. He felt his spirit returning to his body and went through the same routine as last time, coming back to his body and his strength gradually being restored to him.

******

"BURNS, I've had it up to here with you!" Gertrude, the landlord of the apartment complex where Eric lived, had an angry look on her face. "You have three days to get your stuff out of your apartment and get moved out!"

"You're not *evicting* me, are you?"

"Yes, I am!"

"But why?"

"I've had numerous complaints about you from fellow tenants—yelling, screaming, horrible swearing, and violence. There were also reports of you threatening people's lives."

"You can't do that, Gertrude! I don't have any place to go! You see the problem here? Where would I live?"

"That's your problem, Burns! You shoulda' thought of that beforehand."

Eric growled as he walked away and said, "You dirty, rotten fascist pig! I'll get you for this!"

****

"BRAD APPLEBAUM? Mr. Oliver Crane here! It's nice to meet you!"

Brad was sitting beside this boss who worked at Living Waters Christian Bookstore on Broadway Avenue in the center of downtown Oakland. He was applying for a new job. This opportunity looked like a real godsend to Brad who was sitting in front of the congenial man. Mr. Crane handed him the aptitude test, which he started working on. It didn't take long for him to finish the test. He handed it back to Oliver who started to peruse the answers Brad had written down.

"Hm, very good," said Mr. Crane. "I see that you are more intelligent than most people. You did especially well on the English and math parts of the test."

"What would I be doing if I get the job?" asked Brad.

"Among other things, you would be helping out with sales of the books, records, and songbooks in this store. I need someone who is intelligent, likeable, and dependable. I think there's a good chance that I'm going to hire you. I'll let you know in about two days."

Two days later, Oliver Crane called Brad up to let him know he had gotten the job. Brad was thrilled; he would be working part-time at the Christian bookstore on the late afternoon shifts from Monday to Thursday each week. Besides the money and the nice boss, he would be surrounded with a treasure trove of Christian books as well as having the joy of listening to the beautiful background music of the various Christian artists playing over the record player in the store.

****

ALAN SCHMIDT was one of the young men in the Red Riding Rangers. When he heard that Eric Burns had been evicted from his apartment, he graciously took him into his pad, which was located two miles north of where Eric had lived and promised to help him out financially until he could get back on his feet. Alan had a beautiful wife named Carmen who inflamed the lustful desires of Eric the first time he set his eyes on her. She had blonde hair, soft skin, and lustrous blue eyes. She also had a very vivacious and outgoing personality.

****

IT HAD BEEN ANOTHER GLORIOUS MORNING at the intercessory prayer meeting at Pam's apartment. There were seven people in attendance this morning, and the presence of the Holy Spirit was very thick. 7:00 rolled around all too quickly, and the prayer warriors began to say goodbye and leave one by one. Brad walked over to where Pam was standing because he wanted to talk to her for a moment.

"Well, Pam, I'll see you later. I just want to ask you one question real quick." Brad felt his face getting flushed and red and felt a lump forming in his throat.

"What is it, Brad?"

He just stood there for a couple of moments, trying to drum up the courage to say what was on his mind. Finally, he opened his mouth and started stumbling over his words. "Um, well it's like th-this. Um, uhh—dah, dahhhh! How c-can I s-say it in the right way. Um, well, I-I guess."

"Come on, Brad, spit it out."

"Well, um, I-I guess—oh, boy! Well, I want to—I want to, um, well, it would kinda' really be nice to get an ice cream cone at Baskin R-Robbins today—um, if you're g-g-game. I'll pay for it."

Pam smiled sweetly and said, "Why yes, Brad. It would be lovely to have an ice cream cone with you at Baskin Robbins. I would love it."

"What 'ya say we meet at four?"

"That would be wonderful, Brad."

Brad had been absolutely sure that Pam would shove him off like she had last fall, and he was pleasantly surprised at her warm, enthusiastic response to his request.

****

LATE THAT AFTERNOON after the classes at Cal Berkeley, the two of them met at Brad's small car for the little ice cream date. (Lately, Brad was allowed to drive his car to school and back home because of his new job, and also, because the gas shortage had eased.) Brad walked over to the passenger side of the compact and opened the door for Pam to climb in. After she was seated, he shut the door, climbed into the car, and started driving toward the ice cream shop.

Soon, the two of them were inside Baskin Robbins, ordering their ice cream cones. Brad ordered a double-decker cone of orange and lime sherbet in a sugar cone. Pam ordered a single scoop of Rocky Road ice cream in a regular cone. Brad paid the bill for the two of them, took hold of the two ice cream cones, and led Pam to a small table that could seat two. As he approached the table to sit down, he stumbled and dropped the Rocky Road ice cream cone right on the white-and-blue blouse of Pam Jackson. You never saw a face more crimson with embarrassment than the face of Brad at that moment. He reached for a napkin to try to help clean up the mess. *I've done it now,* he thought to himself. *This is the end of this friendship! I'm such a clumsy oaf!*

"I'm so sorry, Pam! Lemme' help you here," said Brad as he reached down with the napkin to wipe the mess off of her.

Pam looked at Brad with eyes of fire that would melt the biggest iceberg in Greenland and said, "I can take care of myself well enough, thank you very much!"

"But really, Pam, I wanna' help."

"BRAD APPLEBAUM, YOU CLUMSY CLOD, YOU LET ME ALONE! I can clean myself up without your help!"

"Is there a restroom?"

"Yes, over there."

She ran over to the restroom to try to clean the mess off of her blouse. Meanwhile, Brad walked up to the counter to order another Rocky Road ice cream cone for Pam, which he paid for. He sat back at the little table, anxiously waiting for Pam to come out of the bathroom. By and by, she came out and headed straight for Brad, her blouse cleaner, but still soiled with the stain from the ice cream cone.

"I see you weren't able to completely clean up that mess I made."

"No I wasn't," said Pam in a voice that was still a bit cross. "I'm going to have to put this through the wash to get this outfit totally clean."

"Well, I blew it big-time and I imagine this might be the last time you hang out with a dummy like me 'cept at church and prayer meeting, but for whatever it's worth, here's another ice cream cone."

They ate their goodies without much conversation after which they headed back toward Brad's car. They were both self-conscious over who might be looking at Pam's dirtied-up blouse. Finally, they were safely seated in the car, and Brad started the motor. All at once, Pam saw the funny side of the whole episode and started giggling softly, then started laughing more loudly, and finally was bowled over with a great big fit of belly laughing that went on and on. Brad thought that she had the most musical laugh he had ever heard in his whole life. He soon joined Pam with loud guffaws that rocked the whole car. They were nearly back at the Cal campus before the laughter subsided. When Brad parked the car close to where Pam had her car, he opened his front door and walked over to the passenger-side door to open it for her.

"Well here you are, Pam. I'll see ya' tomorrow."

"I had a good time this afternoon, Brad, ice cream spill and all! Thank you so much for being so thoughtful and considerate!" Pam gave Brad a quick hug and a hearty kiss on the cheek. "See you bright and early at prayer tomorrow."

With that, she walked toward her car, leaving Brad with a warm feeling of happiness in his soul. Over the next several weeks, there would be more outings for the two of them at Baskin Robbins with Brad paying for their ice cream cones. But never again did he have the mishap of spilling ice cream on the clothes of Pam Jackson.

****

IT WAS A SATURDAY AFTERNOON in early June of 1974, and Mike and Donna were visiting the Millers at Randy's huge mansion on Sleepy Hollow Road. It had been months since these best of friends had spent truly quality time together. It was a moderately warm day, and Jack, Tommy, Michelle, and Sharon were swimming in the Millers' pool, having a ball as they dived off the diving board and slid down the ten-foot-high yellow slide Randy had installed. Lila and Donna were in the large green living room, sipping tall glasses of lemonade and talking about girlie things. Randy and Mike were in the brown game room, sipping Busch beers and having their own man-to-man talk.

"So," Mike was saying, "it looks like you're doing real well. The dough is rolling in, and you have millions of fans who love your music."

Randy was tense and trying to put on a front as he responded to Mike's comments. "Yeah, things are going real good for me. We had to cut our nation-wide tour short because of the death of the three youths last winter, but we're resuming it at the end of this month. My concerts have been going real good here in Northern California this spring, my singing and guitar playing have been great, I have all these fans who love me and know what real talent is, and my album sales have been better than ever. This summer, I'm going to be performing at Madison Square Garden as well as in front of President Nixon at the White House. We're also doing a tour in Great Britain. And this new house here—don't you think it's great? You saw for yourself how beautiful that new Steinway grand sounds in the music room up on the third floor."

"Yeah, it's quite the pad you got there. I'm glad for you."

"Yeah, Mike my boy, I got it made. I couldn't be happier."

"Well, tell me what else is going on—how's your heart these days?"

Randy felt somewhat intimidated—he felt like his private space was being invaded as he said, "Well, for one thing, I know that there is life after death, and I now know what the other side is like." He then described his consultation sessions with Isis Butterfield during the last few months and his out-of-body experiences, his encounters with his dad, and his previous lives. He also shared about how similar the experiences of Taylor Caldwell were to his own.

Mike looked at Randy with concern and skepticism and then started a rather long refutation of the music star's experiences. "Randy, I would be cautious over jumping to conclusions concerning these experiences you have had. In the first place, your out-of-the-body trips you claim to have had are

194

nothing new or novel. There is much esoteric literature in history that talks about these same types of experiences. For example, there is *The Tibetan Book of the Dead*, which claims that the spirits of dead people hang around in a Hades-like area for three days before the separation of body and soul is complete. The ancient Chinese meditated to achieve astral projection. Out-of-the-body testimonies are engraved on some seventeenth century Chinese wooden tablets. Many cultures of the past also mention the spirit body: Hindu, Buddhist, Egyptian, Roman, Indian, Greek, and British.

"As far as reincarnation is concerned, several religions preach this doctrine. The Hindus in India believe strongly in reincarnation. They believe if you're bad in this life, you might come back as a cow, a dog, a rat—or even an itsy-bitsy fly. That's the main reason for the caste system there and why they are vegetarians and also why they are so uptight about killing any type of animal—that nasty gnat might have been somebody's grandpappy in a previous life. And then you have Helena Blavasky who around a hundred years ago founded the religion of Theosophy, which teaches karma and the doctrine of the Ascended Masters.

"Now the evidence for your experiences and the experiences of Taylor Caldwell being authentic is weak—and I'll tell you why: you say you were King David at one time and George Gershwin at a later time. The first problem here is that the Law of Probabilities rules strongly against it. Even for a person to be a famous historical figure just one time is very, very unlikely. But *two times?* It's really just impossible. This is something I've noticed in the claims of pop occultists who have claimed this person or that person had found out through hypnotic regression that he or she was a reincarnation of a certain individual. It seems it's always some notorious character of the past. I think there's something phony about all of this."

Randy responded, "Well, maybe I was a really good person being those dudes."

"I don't think that argument will work, Randy. George Gershwin was not *that* good or charitable of a man, even though he was a great musician. I read that he was a very conceited man—and King David? He was not a very good man at all. Remember: he committed adultery with Bathsheba and murdered her husband. At least the Hindus are more credible—they don't claim the lopsided number of supposed previous lives of rich and famous people.

"I don't know, Randy. I'm kind of worried about you."

"I'm really doing good!" denied Randy. "There's nothing to worry about."

"No, Randy. I know things seem really rosy on the outside, but 'All that glitters isn't gold.' I've seen a change in you over the last year. You seem to be hyper and out to prove yourself to everybody in the world. It feels to me that you are like a man sitting on top of a stack of bricks a hundred stories high and afraid that at any moment, it might topple and send you plummeting to the hard ground below. And these weird stories you've told me coupled with the glazed look in your eyes makes me wonder if you're on some kind of drug."

"I'm not taking any drug!" denied Randy hotly. "That's a bunch of baloney! Don't worry about me, Mike. I'm doing fine, just fine."

But deep inside, he felt anything but fine. He felt empty, depressed, and frightened. He was scared spitless that at any moment, his beautiful world might cave in on him.

****

"BRAD, you're doing a good job."

It was the end of another day at the Living Waters Christian Bookstore, and Oliver Crane was having another debriefing with his new employee. Brad had been scared of being a failure once again and breathed a deep sigh of relief.

"Thank you, Boss! I was so afraid that I was going to blow it again."

"Brad, let me give you some words of wisdom that will help you in your life. You are a young man loaded with potential. To begin with, you are an extremely intelligent man. Much more important than that, you love the Lord. You are also in love with God's Word and are studying it diligently. You are a hard worker and are picking up the knowledge of your job here at a satisfactory rate of speed. You are neatly dressed and groomed. But I see one area that can hold you back from reaching your full potential and that is the 'I'm afraid I'm going to fail' attitude you've been wearing like a cloak."

"But I've had so many failures in my life. How do I know that I'm going to succeed at anything?"

"Son, if you confess failure, you'll wind up being a failure. But if you confess the promises in God's Word, He'll put you over the top every time."

"Confessing God's Word? Isn't that sort of like positive thinking?"

"Not exactly. Positive thinking is simply looking on the bright side of things, no matter what. A person can have good thoughts and say them all day but be a very godless person and even fail to get a fraction of the results he is seeking for and positively confessing. On the other hand, God's Word has many marvelous promises for obedient believers who are walking in His will to the best of their ability. For them, God's unchangeable promises will always work. For example, there is the promise in the book of Philippians that says, 'I can do all things through Christ which strengtheneth me.' Repeat that back to me, Brad."

"I can do all things through Christ which strengtheneth me," responded Brad weakly. "I don't know if that has any effect, though."

"Brad. It *does* have an effect. The Bible is the absolute truth and will always work for those who accept its promises with faith. The book of

Proverbs points out that death and life are in the power of the tongue and those that love it will eat the fruit thereof. Now, how did you get saved?"

"By asking Jesus to come into my life and be my Boss."

"Right! God says in Romans 10 that if you confess with your mouth the Lord Jesus and believe in your heart that God raised Him from the dead, you will be saved. You see how important our words are? God has a lot to say in His Word concerning the tongue."

"So, you're saying that my words have a huge impact on the course of my life?"

"Brad, let me tell you a true story about a lady who I know personally. This girl is named Teresa Perkins and lives down in Visalia. She was mentally retarded due to brain damage that she suffered as an infant through an accident. She had an IQ of only 60. But one day, she was brought to a meeting where a Pentecostal evangelist was preaching the gospel. She immediately received Christ and thereafter regularly attended his meetings. She didn't know how to read or write, but she paid every bit of attention to the Bible verses that were being shared and started repeating those promises out loud continuously, for example, the 'I can do all things through Christ' promise. As time went on, there was a marked change in her whole personality and demeanor and even in her intelligence. People began to notice a glow in her face. She learned how to read and write. She became very outgoing, friendly, and happy. Now, twelve years after she accepted Christ, know where she is today?"

"I wouldn't have the smoggiest idea, Mr. Crane."

"She's an accomplished writer who has gotten several of her books published including a Christian novel with the title *Renewed like an Eagle*. She is also a great Bible teacher who speaks at many conferences in places like Fresno, Hanford, Bakersfield, and Visalia. This is a wonderful example of what God can do for a person who takes Him at His word."

Brad responded, "So that means that I can go very, very far in being a success by holding on tightly to the promises in this Book."

"Absolutely. There is one thing you have to realize, though. This is not just a motivational concept on how to be a success in this life. The really important things have to do with eternity: whether we'll experience the delights and raptures of heaven or the extreme tortures and agonies of hell, and also how much of an eternal reward we will have when we get to heaven. All true success on earth has to do mainly with our spiritual intimacy with Jesus, our usefulness in the Kingdom of God, and the treasures we lay up in heaven."

All of this was new and exciting to Brad. He decided right there and then that he was going to dig deeper into the Scriptures and claim every promise he could find there.

****

SUMMER WAS NOW IN FULL SWING; it was somewhat cooler than average in the San Francisco Bay Area that year. 'Jitterbug Josh' and the Universal Mindset started their tour at the end of June. They started out by traveling up the west coast of the U. S. and then turning east and going through the northern states on their way to the big concert at Madison Square Garden. They performed in Redding, Portland, Seattle, Spokane, Helena, Bismarck, Minneapolis, Detroit, Erie, and Albany before finally driving into the Big Apple for the big Fourth of July concert. Randy loved the scenery in the Pacific Northwest; everything was so green and mountainous in Oregon, Washington, Idaho, and Western Montana. He did not care for the treeless farmland in states like North Dakota, though. Even though the concerts were well attended and filled with enthusiastic crowds, Randy was not very happy. He continued to feel the deep void in his heart, and he often had to fight hard to keep from bursting into fits of protracted weeping during his concerts and while signing autographs. Moreover, the recurring horrible nightmares were continuing. On top of that, he was continuing to take his amphetamines in order to try to stay on top of his rigorous concert schedule, and to be able to crash, he was continuing to take his 'Blue Heavens' barbiturates. He was beginning to be addicted to those pills, and it was taking a toll on his physical and mental health. Lila was miserable also as she dwelt in their huge new three-story mansion. Randy was gone during those summer weeks, and a chilliness seemed to reside in that beautiful house, making it seem almost like a huge cemetery.

Meanwhile, Brad was growing in his walk with the Lord. He took very seriously the sage spiritual advice of his boss in Oakland and looked for Scriptures with promises that grabbed his heart and began to quote them out loud. The school semester was finished, and he had the summer off. Oliver Crane decided to let Brad work at the bookstore five days a week with eight-hour shifts that summer. The early morning prayer group at Pam's apartment continued, and Brad brought his Bible confession ideas into the prayer format. Pam was immediately gung-ho over it and incorporated it into the end of each morning. A typical group confession responsorial would go something like this: "This is a good day! This is a great day! This is a fantastic day! This is the day that the Lord has made, and I will rejoice and be glad in it! I am washed in the Blood of the Lamb! I am counted as righteous because of His sacrifice on the cross! I have the mind of Christ! I am an overcomer! I can do all things through Christ which strengtheneth me! I am the head and not the tail! I am above and not beneath! Greater is He that is in me than he that is in the world! This is a good day! This is a great day! This is a fantastic day! Hallelujah! Thank You, beautiful Jesus!"

****

THE FOURTH OF JULY was a spectacular day in the Bay Area. Kimberly and Lisa had plans to spend the day with their close girlfriends. Sid and Harriet had a golf game planned at Mira Vista Country Club, and they had asked Brad if he was interested in coming with them to caddie for them. He said "yes." On a sudden impulse, he asked Pam if she would be interested in coming with them and she willingly agreed. Brad's parents were happy to have her along so he gave her directions on how to get to the golf course: go to El Cerrito and drive up to the very top of Cutting Boulevard. At 11:00 A. M., all of them were standing in the pro shop, ready to tee off at 11:10. They would be walking instead of renting a golf cart, and Brad would be carrying the rather heavy golf bags of his parents on his shoulders.

Sid and Harriet started their round of golf with Brad and Pam walking right beside them. Brad knew little about what club to offer his parents for each shot. Sid commented, "Brad would be considered to be a Class D caddie." Sid was hitting some nice shots, but Harriet was having a lot of trouble with her game today. She drove her tee shot on the second hole way out of bounds. On the fourth hole, she drove her tee shot into the bushes with an unplayable lie and had to take a drop. On the sixth hole, she hit a tree with her tee shot that was only forty yards away. Three times, she landed in the water and also hit her ball into the sand trap on four different holes. Sid birdied the sixth, seventh, and fourteenth holes.

When they got to the seventh hole, Sid and Harriet offered to let the youths have a crack at hitting a few shots. Pam teed off first and managed to hit her first shot 125 yards. Sid and Harriet complimented her, saying she did a pretty good job at hitting the ball. Then Brad put a ball on the tee and positioned himself to tee off. He arched the driver far back and swung with all his might. He lost his rhythm, tripped, fell on his back, and totally missed the ball. Pam burst into uncontrollable laughter, gushing out her usual musical guffaws.

"Brad, you're tensing up too much," said Sid. "The key is to relax, keep your eye on the ball, and realize that the club is just an extension of your arm."

Brad got up on his feet and prepared to have another try at it. This time, he didn't fall down, but he still missed the ball.

"Keep your head down, Brad," said Harriet.

"Yeah, keep your eye on the ball," said Sid.

On the third try, Brad sliced the ball, sending it ten yards away to the right.

"Well, you hit it," said Harriet. "That's a start, anyway."

Brad had one more try at his tee shot, actually hitting the ball straight and fifty yards away. His mom and dad complimented him, saying the shot was much better, but that obviously, Brad was no Gary Player, who had won the Masters' tournament in Augusta, Georgia that spring. The youths had several other chances to hit tee shots and iron shots on a few of the succeeding holes. Pam made some pretty good shots, but most of Brad's attempts were futile. He hit one beautiful 7-iron shot on the sixteenth hole. They also had some tries at putting. Here again, Pam was far superior to Brad who usually putted much too hard. Finally, the round of golf was completed, and the foursome walked wearily, but happily into the clubhouse for drinks. Sid and Harriet ordered cocktails, Brad ordered a Shirley Temple, and Pam ordered a glass of iced tea. Sid walked into the game room to play a little poker with some of his buddies who happened to be there that day.

"Hey Pam," said Brad. "Would you be interested in watching the fireworks with me tonight? There's going to be a great fireworks show in downtown Moraga from nine to ten this evening."

"Well, I don't know. It's a long way from Oakland to Moraga, and we have to get up early tomorrow."

"Well, I'll give you gas money. I'm sure that Mom and Dad are going to watch the fireworks with us tonight."

"Brad, honey," said Harriet. "I think I'm too tired to watch the show this evening. I'm sure your dad will come with you to watch the show, though."

"How about it, Pam?"

"Well, um—okay. We'll have to make plans for dinner, thank You Jesus!"

"I'll tell you what," said Harriet. "The two of you can come over to our house in Moraga, and we'll fix you grilled cheese sandwiches and a plate of raw veggies. After that, Pam can drive herself back to Oakland. How does that sound?"

"I think that's great," said Brad.

"It will work, hallelujah!" chorused Pam.

****

AT 9:00 THAT EVENING, Sid, Brad, and Pam were sitting in a parking lot in downtown Moraga with the top of the Applebaum's aqua 1970 Mustang rolled up, all ready to see the fireworks. Soon, the streetlights were turned off, and the colorful pyrotechnic display began with the loud booms and the spreading out circles in the sky of multi-colored fireworks: blue mixed with white, blue alone, pink, red, white and green, purple and pink, blue and orange as well as other color combinations. All three of them were enjoying the show tremendously.

"Pam, tell me a little more about yourself," said Brad.

"Well, Brad, I was born in Pensacola, Florida, on July 27, 1953. My parents are named Phil and Sarah Jackson. I have two brothers, twenty-three-year-old Caleb and eighteen-year-old Doug. When I was fourteen, we moved from Pensacola over here to Stockton where my ma and pa have a nice house on 2844 Inglewood Street in Lincoln Village in the northern part of Stockton."

"Tell me about Pepsicola. I always wanted to travel all around the United States."

Pam burst into laughter and exclaimed, "Oh, Brad! It's *Pensacola,* not 'Pepsicola!' Anyway, it's absolutely gorgeous. There are forests of incredibly beautiful evergreen trees around that whole area growing on a landscape of red clay. The city is right on the Gulf Coast. The beaches there have this incredibly bright white sand, and the water is usually warm and very pleasant to swim in. There is a bay you can cross to get to another lovely beach at a place called Fort Walton. However, my favorite beach was about a two-hour drive east of Pensacola in a tourist town called Panama City. The water is so breathtaking in its beauty there with its hues of navy blue, aqua, turquoise, purple, and green. We used to go there every summer for a vacation. Every Christmas, Thanksgiving, and Easter, we would drive up to Knoxville, Tennessee, to visit my grandparents, Marcus and Sharon Jackson. The drive was so beautiful going through those forests in Alabama and then encountering those rocky hills that start a little bit south of Birmingham and continue all the way up to Knoxville. My grandparents live in this old, majestic two-story house out in the woods with this lovely garden full of flower beds and a large tree right in the middle of it."

"It sounds like my kind of house, Pam. I've never cared for the big city, but love homes that are in the mountains or on a beach out in the middle of nowhere."

"I'm not crazy about big cities in general, either, but there's one city I really like, and that's Chattanooga, Tennessee. The hills and trees are so gorgeous there, that city is very clean, and the people are really friendly there. Tell me about where you were born."

"I was born in Sacramento on January 7, 1954, at an apartment complex on 355 Cedar Avenue. When I was two years old, we moved to a five-room light-green house near the bottom of the hill on Cutting Boulevard in El Cerrito. We lived there for two years until the fall of 1958 when my parents found this nice eight-room house in the hills of Lafayette. We lived there until the spring of 1968 when we found our present lovely thirteen-room home in Moraga where we presently live."

The fireworks came to an exciting climax with a barrage of spectacular, spellbinding colors, moving in rapid progression. After that, the streetlights were turned back on, and Sid turned on the motor for the short drive back to the Applebaum castle. The youths climbed out of the car, and Pam prepared to get into her car to drive back home to Oakland.

"Drive carefully, kid," said Sid to Pam.

"See ya', tomorrow, Pam," said Brad. "Drive carefully."

Pam came over to Brad, gave him a kiss on the cheek, and said, "I had a wonderful time today, Brad. Thank you for everything."

"You're very welcome, Pam."

Pam clambered into her car and started her motor. She had a warm feeling about the whole day. It was more than just the fresh air, the fun on the golf course, and the fabulous display of fireworks; more and more, she was feeling a real sense of kinship with Brad Applebaum. *This boy has really matured in the last six months and is becoming more and more spiritual. His grooming is also much better. I'm really starting to like this guy.*

****

THAT SAME DAY, Randy Miller and the band performed their Fourth of July concert at Madison Square Garden. The concert was a huge success with wild cheering and frantic autograph seekers thronging him. They then traveled west, doing concerts in Charleston, Nashville, Little Rock, Dallas, Amarillo, Albuquerque, and Flagstaff. On July 13, Randy did a joint concert with Elvis and Frank Sinatra in Las Vegas, Nevada. The group stayed at the Dunes Hotel. It was 1:00 A. M. before Randy finally returned to his plush Presidential Suite quarters there. He was dog-tired. But more than that, he was very depressed. All the things that should have brought him joy were just not cutting the mustard. *Why do I feel so downcast? I have everything a man could want, and yet, I feel so empty!* Randy tried to jack up his spirits, but he just wasn't able to do it. Soon, a flood of tears was flowing down his face.

"What's the use!" he sobbed out loud. "What is my life really all about? My life is empty! I'm known by that insane and loveless name, 'Jitterbug Josh!' There's no real fulfillment in this whole rat-race of image, fame, money, and screaming autograph seekers!"

Randy rose up off his luxurious king-sized bed and paced aimlessly around the room. He looked out the window toward the neon lights of Las Vegas spread out below him, sparkling like myriads of glittering diamonds. *How easy it would be to open this window and just jump out headfirst to the street below—but what good would that do? I would just have to go through another painful birth experience in about six short years or so, and besides, it would bring great pain to my wife and kids.*

He walked over to a drawer next to his bed and apathetically opened it up. Inside was a Gideon Bible, which he mechanically took out and randomly opened it up to a page somewhere in the middle. Staring right back at him was the name of a beginning of a book: Ecclesiastes.

Randy started to read from the very beginning of this book.

"The words of the preacher, son of David, king of Jerusalem."

Randy gasped; why, *he* had been King David in a previous reincarnation according to his hypnosis experience at the hands of Psychiatrist Isis Butterfield!

He read on. "Vanities of vanities, saith the Preacher, vanities of vanities; all is vanity. What profit hath a man of all his labour which he taketh under the sun?"

Randy was blown away with these words; *how did this writer of that book pinpoint so accurately the present feelings in his heart?*

He continued to read. Verse 9 of the first chapter said this: "The thing that hath been, it is that which shall be; and that which is done is that which shall be done: and there is no new thing under the sun."

Randy had a flashback to that late September day last year when he was driving back home from Tahoe and had thought to himself, 'The more things change, the more they stay the same.' *Oh, the incredible wisdom of the writer of this book!*

He read some more. Chapter 2 really jumped out at him. "I said in mine heart, Go to now, I will prove thee with mirth, therefore enjoy pleasure: and, behold, this also is vanity." The beginning of verse 3 said, "I sought in mine heart to give myself unto wine," while verses 4 to 6 said, "I made me great works; I builded me houses; I planted me vineyards: I made me gardens and orchards, and I planted trees in them of all kind of fruits: I made me pools of water, to water therewith the wood that bringeth forth trees:"

Randy had another flashback to a scene in May 1973 when Mike Applebaum had shown him a very depressing little movie that had been shown in some freshman English classes at Campolindo. In this movie, there had been a man swimming through a number of swimming pools that were close together. The first swimming pool or two had been very pleasant with beautiful and sexy ladies serving him delicious drinks, but as he swam on, things began to turn sour. When he came to the last pool, the water was dried up, there were claps of thunder in the background, everyone he met was unfriendly and against him, his wife was divorcing him, and his kids despised him. The movie ended on a very low point with somber background music, with the man weeping and wailing loudly with great anguish.

Verses 7 to 11 of that chapter said this: "I got me servants and maidens, and had servants born in my house; also I had great possessions of great and small cattle above all that were in Jerusalem before me: I gathered me also silver and gold, and the peculiar treasure of kings and of the provinces: I gat me men singers and women singers, and the delights of the sons of men, as musical instruments, and that of all sorts. So I was great, and increased more than all that were before me in Jerusalem: also my wisdom remained with me. And whatsoever mine eyes desired I kept not from them, I withheld not my heart from any joy; for my heart rejoiced in all my labour: and this was my portion of all my labour. Then I looked on all the works that my hands had wrought, and on the labour that I had laboured to do: and, behold, all was vanity and vexation of spirit, and there was no profit under the sun."

Randy continued reading through that whole book of the Bible. The last two verses said this: "Let us hear the conclusion of the whole matter: Fear God and keep His commandments: for this is the whole duty of man. For God shall bring every work into judgment, with every secret thing, whether it be good, or whether it be evil."

He now turned the pages of the Gideon Bible to a random place many pages ahead and found himself reading the words of Jesus in Matthew, chapter 6, where Jesus advised the people not to lay treasures for themselves on Earth where moth and rust would corrupt and thieves would break in and steal, but to lay up treasure in heaven where there was no moth or rust to corrupt and where there was no thief to break in and steal. Jesus said that where your treasure is, there your heart will be also. This was all new to Randy who had been the choir director at the United Church of the Valley in Orinda and had heard many a sermon by Pastor Kevin Harmon but had never heard anything like this before. So, was there really a heaven? Reading these Scriptures was like having an ice-cold bucket of water thrown on his head on a hot and sultry summer day. In the days and weeks that followed, this experience would fade away out of his mind due to the busy concert schedule, the alcohol, and the drugs. But there was no doubt that for the moment, reading the Bible had made a strong impact on him.

****

IT WAS THE END of a long day in the middle of July, and Brad was getting ready to call it a night at the Christian bookstore. The last customer had been looking for a book on the Four Temperaments by Christian author, Tim LaHaye. Oliver Crane was in the process of locking up the store.

"Brad, before you go, I want to talk to you for a minute."

Brad's heart raced with nervousness as he responded, "Yeah, Boss. What is it?"

"Well, first of all, you're doing a fine job and I'm proud of you. Now the second thing I want to talk to you is about a proposition that I have for you."

"Yeah?"

"Brad. You are a very smart young man. I've also noticed that you've been growing spiritually in these weeks since I've known you as well as growing in the knowledge of the Word. This summer, I'm scheduled to do some preaching at a recovery center here in Oakland for people who are coming off drugs and alcohol. I've been looking for several people who could give their testimony and encourage these people to give their lives to Christ. Would you be interested in joining me on several of these crusades and giving your testimony?"

"Me, sir? What nights are we talking about here?"

"The meetings are on Monday night from eight to ten. You would be giving a five-minute testimony about what the Lord has done in your life. Sometime, I might even have you do a little preaching."

"Yeah, Boss, I sure would be interested in that."

Brad mused excitedly over this opportunity; just to do something that he loved: public speaking—and preaching the gospel to boot.

****

204

DURING THAT SUMMER, the Friday night meetings of the Red Riding Rangers were continuing at the home of Ted Johnson since Eric had recently been evicted from his apartment complex. During the daytime, he was sitting around in Alan Schmidt's apartment, smoking cigarettes, and writing Marxist literature. Alan worked at the CO-OP food store in Berkeley during the daytime while Carmen, his wife, stayed home most of the day. Eric had a tough time trying to keep from thinking about getting into the sack with her. The day came in early July when only the two of them were in the flat and Eric made a pass at her. She was totally appalled and told him off. She left the apartment immediately. Eric didn't give up, though. Day by day, he continued to try to seduce her. Little by little, the resolve of Carmen Schmidt began to weaken. Eric was a very handsome man, and his intelligence and forceful personality greatly fascinated her. The day finally came when she allowed him to hold hands, then to embrace her. After that came the necking and then the kissing.

Eric and the six other conspirators continued to meet each Friday night at the sleazy bar in Berkeley after the Red Riding Ranger meetings to plan the kidnapping of 'Jitterbug Josh'. Eric was looking at the possibility of doing it sometime in late August when The Universal Mindset would be doing a concert somewhere in the Bay Area. He figured out that they would have to spend some time beforehand studying the layout of the concert hall, all the exits, and all the escape routes from the theater. He figured that they would have a much better chance of success if the theater didn't have windows, and if they could execute the arson and kidnapping during a second when the light technician was making the stage dark for a second in the midst of changing the lighting. He figured that the kidnappers would have to sit together in the very front of the hall, as close to the singing star as possible, and that the arsonists would have to sit in the very back, as close to the doors leading to the lobby as possible. To be able to capture Randy Miller and escape out of the venue before the cops could catch and arrest them was of prime importance.

****

ON MONDAY MORNING, July 22, the group of intercessors had finished up another prayer meeting at Pam's place. It had been another wonderful meeting, and everyone was saying goodbye to each other. Brad approached Pam to ask her a question.

"Hey Pam."

"What, Brad?"

"Are you doing anything tonight?"

"No. Why?"

"Well, there's a meeting that my boss is involved in at a storefront recovery center for drug addicts and alcoholics tonight at 8:00. Mr. Crane has me scheduled to give my testimony. I was wondering if you'd like to come to the meeting and see me in action and hear some real hot preaching from Mr. Crane."

"Why yes, Brad. I think it's a lovely idea. Where is the meeting going to be?"

"At the Freedom Rehab Center on 62 Frederic Street in West Oakland. I really think that I should come and pick you up. That part of Oakland is a rough area with a lot of crime and drug trafficking."

"Okay, Brad. What time should I be ready to go?"

"I'd say about 7:30. Be out in front of your apartment building by then."

****

AT 7:45 THAT EVENING, the two of them were walking into the run-down storefront building, which was the meeting place of the Freedom Rehab Center. It was a very small room with a wooden floor and bare chairs with no cushions on them. The place was packed with about forty people, all of them on a recovery program from their drug and alcohol problems. In the front of the room was a chalkboard with a summary of *The Twelve Steps* written on it. Pam now knew how wise Brad had been in suggesting that he pick her up instead of her coming to the recovery center by herself. The street was crawling with shady-looking characters who looked like they could snatch her purse away from her—or worse. The meeting started with some announcements from Mario Consuelo, the leader of the recovery center. There followed two upbeat worship songs led by a young man who sang and played acoustic guitar. After that, there were the testimonies. Brad was the third person to speak. He walked up to the small wooden podium, put the microphone to his mouth, and started speaking. A wave of nervousness overtook him, and he breathed a silent prayer for supernatural wisdom from the Lord.

"Hello! (Ahem)! M-my name is Cr—I mean Brad Applebaum, and um, I'm twenty years old. I, um—oh boy, how do I start this? And you know, I used to be an atheistic reincarnationist, if you can believe there is such a thing. Well, you know, I just completed my sophomore year in college, and um, my major is cr-creative writing. I also am s-studying fl-flute.

"Well, um, m-my life was empty. Even though Moses was a lot like me because h-he had a lot of t-talent, but you know, my life w-was empty. When I was a freshman in high school, I had my first t-taste of red wine, and um, I started drinking more after that. At first, I thought it was cool because it numbed the emptiness in my life so I started to dr-drink a lot more heavier in my first college year, and um, I started using amphetamines at the same time. Man, it was a drag. Many nights, I would get s-sick and throw up, and you know, there were the terrible nightmares. I really thought that I was suffering dain bramage, 'scuse me, I mean brain damage. Things really went downhill

206

until February of 1973 when I met this real tall guy named Hal Odell who is a great b-basketball pl-player. He showed me love like I'd never experienced before and shared the *Four Spiritual Laws* with me. He explained to me about the love of God, heaven, hell, and Jesus dying on the cross to take my punishment. He explained to me that keeping the law of God perfectly was like trying to swim from San Francisco to Hawaii, which is totally impossible, and um, that's why we need Jesus to save us. I accepted Christ into my heart as my Boss and Savior on February 27 of last year, and you know, he took the dr-drugs a-and alcohol away from me. Last fall, I had a wonderful experience when God baptized me in the Holy Spirit at a beautiful Pentecostal church in Concord. The Lord filled me with His love, joy, and peace. I started speaking in a new language that I had never learned before, I had a new love for Jesus, and I felt a warmth come into me, starting at my feet, and radiating through my whole body. I have fulfillment in my life, and I know I'm going to heaven when I die. Praise the Lord and thank you very much."

Brad sat down by Pam and whispered to her, "I think that's the worst job at speaking in public that I've ever done."

"No, Brad, you did great."

"I was nervous and stumbled over my words."

"But you spoke from your heart, and the anointing of the Holy Spirit was very thick as you gave your testimony."

Oliver Crane then took the pulpit and gave a passionate sermon on the dangers of drugs and alcohol, pointing out that Jesus could set all of them free. At the invitation time, three people came down to the altar to receive Christ. Mario Consuelo closed down the meeting with a couple of announcements after which everyone rose from their seats and started chatting with each other. Oliver and Mario walked over to Brad to speak to him.

Said Mario, "Young man, I want to comment on your testimony tonight."

"Mr. Consuelo, I want to apologize. I totally muffed it tonight. I stuttered and couldn't get a good flow going."

"Well, you did stumble a little bit over your words, but you spoke from your heart and really ministered to these men. The Spirit was all over you as you spoke."

"Really?" said Brad incredulously.

"Yeah, really," said Oliver. "Everybody gets nervous the first time they speak."

A man in the group walked up to Mario and excitedly started speaking to him in Spanish. Tears were running down his face while the mouth of Mario opened wide in amazement and joy. Mario spoke very fluent Spanish and understood every word that the Spanish guy was saying. "Gloria a Dios!" he exclaimed. He then turned to Brad and said, "Young man, I want to just let you know how much your testimony ministered to this young man here. He has been deaf in his right ear since birth, but he told me that as you were

207

speaking, he felt a warmth go all over that ear, and now he can hear perfectly out of it."

"Thank You, beautiful Jesus!" exclaimed Brad.

"Wow!" echoed Oliver.

"Isn't God awesome?!" exclaimed Pam.

Soon, the two young adults clambered into Brad's little car, and he cranked the engine on in order to drive Pam home. Soon, they arrived at Pam's apartment building and they said their goodbyes.

"Pam."

"Yeah, Brad?"

"I understand that your birthday is on this coming Saturday. I w-was w-w-wondering wh-what you're doing that day."

"Well, I plan to drive to my mom and pop's home in Stockton on Saturday and spend the night with them. They're fixing to throw a little birthday party for me and take me out to dinner at the Elegant Bib. I'll go to church with them on Sunday morning at First Assembly. We'll have lunch together after which I'll drive back here to my apartment on late Sunday afternoon."

"Well, I was wondering, Pam. Would you—would you be at all interested—I mean, um, I want to—I want to, well, I just would like to do a little celebration of your birthday on Friday night. Are you game at all?"

"What would you have in mind?"

"I can't tell you. I want to keep it a surprise."

"Well, Brad. I think I better pray about it first. Could I let you know tomorrow or Wednesday at morning prayer?"

"No problem, Pam. I want the Lord's will, and I want to do everything in an upright and holy manner."

That night, Pam prayed over this situation. She was coming to like Brad more and more but wanted the mind of the Lord on this matter. As she prayed, she sensed a great peace from the Holy Spirit and a green light to go for it. The next morning after prayer, she walked up to Brad to talk to him.

"Brad!"

"Yeah?"

"The celebration get-together for Friday night is a go! You're on!"

"Praise the Lord!" exclaimed Brad as he looked at her with a mischievous twinkle in his eyes.

****

AT PRECISELY 4:30 ON FRIDAY AFTERNOON, Brad picked Pam up at her apartment suite. He was neatly dressed in a suit consisting of a natty sky-blue sports coat and a black pair of slacks. He had a white dress shirt on with a sharp-looking navy-blue tie and was wearing cologne. Pam was wearing a bright yellow dress and was wearing perfume. Brad opened the front passenger door for her and shut it again when she was seated and buckled in. He then buckled himself into the driver's seat and started heading toward the freeway entrance.

"Happy birthday, Pam!"

"Thank you, Brad. Say, tell me, where are you taking me?"

Brad glanced for a split second at her with a mischievous grin on his face and said, "I'm not telling you yet. I want it to be a complete surprise. I hope that you will like my surprise—I think you will."

He headed toward the Bay Bridge and drove across it, paying the fare at the tollbooth. He continued driving all the way through San Francisco until they came to the Pacific Ocean. He then turned south and drove until they came to a lovely restaurant overlooking the Pacific Ocean called The Blue Damsel Restaurant. He parked the car, opened her car door, and escorted her into the cute and dainty eatery.

"Why Brad, it's lovely! Praise You sweet Jesus!"

"I figured you'd like it."

They walked up to the front desk, and Brad said, "I have a reservation for two for 5:30. It's this lady's birthday tomorrow."

"Oh yes," said the handsome young man. "Right this way." He led them to a table right by the window overlooking the ocean. Background piano music floated toward the two of them from a bar pianist who was plunking out light jazz standards consisting of songs like "Satin Doll," "All the Things You Are," and "Yesterday." Already, Pam was enjoying herself to the nth degree.

"Brad, I need to go use the lady's room for a minute. Please excuse me."

"You go right ahead."

Pam went to the restroom to 'powder her nose.' When she returned to the dinner table, she was blown away by the sight that was on the table between her utensils. There, right in front of her, was a gift wrapped in pink tissue paper with yellow ribbon with a card on top. Beside the present was a bouquet of magnolia flowers.

She gasped with surprise and elation. "BRAD! HOW DID YOU KNOW? OH, THEY'RE SO BEAUTIFUL! THANK YOU, *THANK YOU!!*" She looked at Brad with radiant eyes of love and gratitude that bespoke volumes more than a thousand words could ever have done.

Presently, the waitress came over to their table and asked, "Would you like anything to drink? We have wine, champagne, or beer."

"Well, we would like a couple of non-alcoholic drinks," said Brad. "What do you got?"

"Well, there's coffee, milk, Coke, 7-Up, iced tea, Shirley Temple—or we do have Martinelli's Sparkling Cider."

"Wow!" exclaimed Pam. "Martinelli's Sparkling Cider! That's the drink for me!"

"And I will have a Shirley Temple, please," said Brad.

They happily sipped their drinks while they stared at the view of the beautiful ocean.

"Hey, Brad. Look at those surfing aficionados out there!"

"Yeah, that's quite something. It takes a lot of skill to be able to surf well. Me—I have about as much skill at it as I do at volleyball and golf."

Pam broke out into spirited guffaws of her musical laughter that was such a familiar trait of her personality.

"Oh Brad, you have such a great sense of humor! You bring such joy and laughter into my life."

"Yeah, thank you Pam. At any rate, I do better at sailing. Our family used to go out on the bay to Tiburon on our twenty-nine-foot-long sailboat. And then, two years ago, we had our vacation in the San Juan Islands for a week. I remember taking control of the boat and turning the sails into the wind. You know, now that I look back at it, it makes me think of letting go and letting the Holy Spirit take control of our lives. Just like the wind leads the sailboat if we let it, the Holy Spirit will lead my life in a beautiful way if I just let Him do it. Come to think of it, the Holy Spirit is likened to a wind in the book of John. In both cases, although you can't see them, they do have a tremendous effect."

Pam was bowled over with the wisdom coming from the mouth of Brad Applebaum. They looked out the window at a man who was windsurfing. The waitress returned to the table and asked for the dinner orders of the couple. Brad ordered a New York steak, medium rare, while Pam ordered lamb chops. The dinner orders came very quickly and were absolutely delicious. They talked about different things over dinner: school, Campus Crusade for Christ, their families, close chums they each had, and sundry experiences that each of them had gone through as they were growing up.

"So, Pam, how did the wedding go on the 6th with Karen Thompson's sister?"

"You mean between Ricky and Wendy? Oh Brad, it was absolutely beautiful. The wedding took place at Castro Valley Presbyterian Church. There were a lot of people and the ceremony was great. The lady pianist did a good job. The reception was at Week's Park in Hayward in a nice grassy area. There was plenty of good food and drinks, and most of the people there were Christians. There was a nice string quartet that provided the background music. During the wedding, I sang the song 'We've Only Just Begun.' The people really loved that selection."

"Oh, it sounds delightful."

The two of them finished their food, and the waitress came to take their plates away.

"You know, I was curious," said Pam. "The name 'Blue Damsel Restaurant' is very fascinating. I was wondering how you folks came up with that name."

"I'll be glad to answer that question. This restaurant used to be a house owned by a rich couple. When the lady died, the husband swore that the dead woman's spirit was appearing to him in the house. Sometime after he died, this house was converted into the restaurant where you are eating at today."

"I see," said Pam.

As the waitress left, Brad said, "Obviously, that supposed 'Blue Damsel' was really a demonic spirit masquerading as the man's dead wife. This world is crawling with demons out to deceive the populace."

"And there are also a multitude of angels to help us out."

"Oh yes, Pam. You know that the Bible says that the good angels outnumber the demons two to one. I've had more than one experience where I should have been killed but escaped by the skin of my teeth."

"Me too, Brad. Tell me about those experiences."

"Well, the first time was when I was three years old, when we were living at the small green starter house on Cutting Boulevard. I was a lot like *Curious George* as a toddler. At any rate, I was playing one afternoon out in the back yard. On an impulse, I decided to climb the wall fifteen feet up to my parents' bedroom. I got up to the windowsill of their room and suddenly became afraid that I wouldn't be able to get down again. Meanwhile, my folks were wondering where I was. My mom finally found me on the trellis. She called my dad who came down to the yard to try to catch me. I didn't know whether to come through the window or try to climb back down. I finally decided to climb back down and, with some help from my dad, I made it to the bottom of the wall, unharmed. I firmly believe that if it hadn't been for my guardian angel, I might have been very easily paralyzed—or worse.

"The second time was a couple of years ago when some friends of mine were driving me home from a drinking party in El Cerrito. We were driving on the Dam Road, and Charlie, who was driving the vehicle, was going ninety miles an hour. Suddenly, there was a car coming straight at us, and I was sure that we were going to have a head-on collision. I have no logical explanation how we missed that car or how I got home safely. It had to be my angel."

"My narrow escape was like this, Brad. When I was thirteen, I was involved in a student vocal recital in the mountains to the east of Knoxville. The building was an old ramshackle house with an unsafe electrical system in the basement. While we were doing the concert, this huge electrical storm broke out, and a tornado touched down only six feet away from where the house was. The lightening flashed, the thunder crashed, and the rain fell down in huge torrents. It literally seemed like Noah's Flood. We were told that the house would have a fiery explosion any minute, but a lot of the people prayed. How we were spared, I'll never know except there must have been a great big angel protecting us."

"That's fantastic, Pam!"

They looked tenderly into each other's eyes as Brad related still another incident.

"Pam, do you remember that incident in March of last year when I came into Berkeley Tabernacle Fellowship real late with my gray suit, white dress shirt, and red tie totally drenched and soaking wet?"

Pam laughed and said, "I'll never forget that! It was the first time I ever saw you, and my impression of you was not very good. I thought to myself, 'Oh brother, what a backward slob that guy is!' I remember the funny looks on many faces in the church as they saw your wrinkled, dripping outfit."

"Well, there's a story behind that, Pam. I had just gotten saved a couple of weeks before that Sunday. Well anyway, I wanted to ride my ten-speed bicycle all the way from my home in Moraga to Berkeley Tabernacle. It was cloudy that morning, and my parents were dubious about me doing that bike ride, but I prevailed. You know how much I love riding my bike and looking at the beautiful scenery on those hilly roads. Well anyway, I rode to Orinda and then climbed up El Toyonal. I then rode along the highway that goes past Grizzly Peak and then zigzags through the skyline above Berkeley. As I turned on a straight and steep road that led down to Berkeley, the skies opened up and it began to pour. As I was coasting down that very steep road, I grabbed my brakes hard—and both of my brake cables snapped and I was at the mercy of the steep and slippery street that had a lot of intersections. I must have been traveling at least thirty miles an hour and maybe even faster, and there was no way for me to stop! I prayed very hard and was sure that I was a goner. At any second, I could have run into a car at one of those intersections or taken a nasty fall on my bike. How I got to the bottom of that steep incline safely and was able to stop that bike, I'll never know! My guardian angel must have been protecting me even though I was a total idiotic nitwit that day who had done that foolhardy stunt."

"Yeah," said Pam. "I also remember how the Thatchers very kindly bailed you out that day. They drove you and your bike back to Moraga that afternoon."

At this point, Pam opened her birthday card and gasped with more delight. In front of her was a hand-made card with a drawing of yellow, red, pink, and purple flowers and a poem composed by Brad that went like this:

Beautiful mountains and magnolia flowers,
Spellbinding sunsets and spring thunder showers,
Trumpets and woodwinds and orchestra strings,
These are a few of my favorite things!
Hamburger, hot dog, and marshmallow roasts,
Spectacular, rugged, and stunning seacoasts,
The joy and the laughter your company brings,
These are a few of my favorite things!
Your gorgeous and radiant bright hazel eyes,
That glitter and glow just like free fireflies!
Your beauty that makes my heart mount up with wings,

These are a few of my favorite things!
When my grades fall or my car stalls,
When I'm feeling blue,
I simply look at your beautiful face
And then I just want to be with you!

HAPPY BIRTHDAY, PAM!

Once again, Pam was rendered speechless; *how could this guy be so very, very thoughtful?!* A whole lot of imagination and creativity went into making that lovely and romantic card! She felt exquisite exhilaration and ecstasy as the magic of this evening continued to get sweeter and sweeter; the *Sleeping Beauty* fairytale was surely tawdry and hollow compared to the wondrous unfolding of this whole evening. She felt that this Prince Charming sitting by her at the table was a hundred times more marvelous than any fairytale prince could ever be, and she felt like the most beloved and beautiful princess in the whole world!!! She opened her present to find two records: Oscar Peterson's *Night Train* jazz album, and a recording of some vocal pieces by Schubert.

Pam leaned over, gave Brad a loving hug, and exclaimed, "Oh, Brad! Thank you! THANK YOU! This is too lovely for words and these records are *exactly* what I've wanted for a long, long time! Your poem is so wonderful! How could you be so *considerate?!*"

The waitress reappeared with a dish of Rocky Road ice cream and a beautiful chocolate cake with chocolate frosting on it, and Brad, as well as the waitress, sang 'Happy Birthday' to Pam. This was another wonderful surprise for Pam who thought that there couldn't be anything else that could make this celebration any better, but she was wrong. They rose from the table while Brad paid the bill for the two of them and left a handsome tip after which they walked outside. The two of them spent a little bit of time, drinking in the lovely sights and sounds of the beach and breathing in the fresh, invigorating aromas of the sea.

After about ten minutes, Brad turned to Pam and said, "We've got to get moving."

"What's the hurry?"

"We have another place to go to before I take you home."

"Where, Brad?"

"I can't tell you; it's a surprise," said Brad, giving her a mischievous grin.

Pam felt roller coaster excitement rise up in her tummy; she had already experienced a number of delightful surprises from Brad. They climbed into the car, and Brad started driving back toward downtown San Francisco. He parked the car near the city hall, helped Pam out, and brandished a couple of tickets that were for the evening concert at the San Francisco Opera House. He led her into the huge concert hall and up to the top balcony situated about forty feet or so higher than the concert stage. Tonight, the San Francisco Symphony Orchestra would be doing a program of classical music, featuring on some of the concert works, piano virtuoso, Tomas Vasari. Pam gave a sigh of joy—this night was *too much!*

The concert started with Franck's *Symphony in D minor* with its opening of slow and soft string passages. The romantic piece continued, playing with and elaborating on the melodies that had been introduced toward the beginning of the first movement. The second movement featured that most well-known melody of Franck's career in B-flat minor.

The second work was Tchaikovsky's *Romeo and Juliet,* another piece that started slowly, but built up to paroxysms of fast and loud passages in the parts of the piece that painted a picture of the feuding going on between the two families. When the famous love melody in D-flat major sounded, Pam put her mouth up to Brad's right ear and whispered, "Romeo, Romeo, where forth art thou?" Brad burst into hearty, but soft laughter.

Tomas Vasari now came to the Steinway grand piano and performed Bach's *Italian Concerto.* The first movement in F major was joyful and fairly peppy, the second movement in D minor was slow and rather somber, and the third movement in F major was happy, playful, and very upbeat. After this, there was a fifteen-minute intermission followed by the second half of the concert.

At this point, the great concert pianist and the orchestra both appeared on the stage to perform Rachmaninoff's famous *Second Piano Concerto in C minor.* The couple continued to bask in the beautiful chromatic harmonies wafting to them from the piano and orchestra. The first few bars of the concerto started up rather slowly but were immediately followed by many passages played at a faster tempo with a copious number of *extremely* difficult piano runs and arpeggios, which Tomas Vasari played brilliantly. The second movement in E major was hauntingly beautiful. It brought tears to Brad's eyes with its passionate passages that started off in E major, wandered to various other keys, and finished off in E major with a finish to that movement that seemed to say, "All is well and peaceful. I can't complain; I am satisfied with life." The third movement in C minor was the fastest in tempo and the most difficult. It featured probably one of Rachmaninoff's most famous melodies he had written in his whole lifetime. It was first played in B-flat Major. The second time it sounded, it was in D-flat major. The concerto finished with the finale in C major, featuring that famous melody yet again.

The next piece was Debussy's *Three Nocturnes for Orchestra.* This was an incredibly gorgeous suite with very colorful and expressive passages of half-diminished chords, fully diminished chords, augmented chords, dominant seventh, dominant ninth, major, and minor chords. The first movement in B minor was slow and pensive. It made Brad think of a beautiful sunset at the top of Mount Rainier. The second movement in 6/8 time was very lively. The third movement featured a choir that accompanied the orchestra singing some incredibly beautiful harmonies. Pam thought the third nocturne was so beautiful, she wondered if maybe this was how the music in paradise sounded like.

The last number on the program was Grieg's *Piano Concerto in A Minor.* Both Brad and Pam loved this masterpiece with its beautiful harmonies. The first movement was in A minor, having a strange and winsome pathos to it. It was filled with the famous melodies of Grieg, chromatic and pleasant harmonies, and plenty of difficult scales, arpeggios, and runs in the piano part. The second movement was slow, peaceful, and very, very beautiful. It was in D-flat major and made Brad imagine a gorgeously clear day on the beautiful seacoast of Norway. Tears flowed down his face as he listened to this movement.

"Brad, what's the matter?" asked Pam, soothingly.

"Nothing, Pam. These are tears of joy. This second movement is so incredibly *beautiful!"*

The last movement was back in A minor. It was fast and stormy and had the toughest pianistic hurdles, which Tomas Vasari scaled with brilliance and seemingly ease. In the middle of this movement was a mega-peaceful and slow section in F major that again made Brad weep profusely because of the incredible beauty of the piano, string, and flute lines. The concerto finished happily and majestically in A major. As the last fortissimo note sounded, loud and hearty applause burst forth with many shouts of "Encore, encore!" The standing ovation lasted for five minutes.

The couple walked out of the Opera House toward Brad's car. The two of them headed back across the Bay Bridge toward Oakland and Pam's apartment suite. Brad parked the car and reached over to give Pam a goodnight hug.

"Happy birthday, Pam!" he exclaimed.

"Brad Applebaum! Thank you so much for a mega, mega fantastic evening! I have no words to express the magic that filled this whole night!"

"Sleep good. Have a wonderful celebration with your folks tomorrow and Sunday. See ya' Monday at prayer. Hey, listen. Before you go, would you like to have a few moments of prayer?"

"Love to!"

They took a few moments to exchange prayer requests. Brad prayed first. After that, Pam spent a few moments praying for salvation of some of her friends, praying for Brad's needs, and thanking the Lord for the magically wonderful evening they had had. After the "In the beautiful name of Jesus, amen," Brad leaned over to give her a goodnight kiss on the cheek. She kissed him back on the cheek—and then she pulled his face toward hers, pressed her lips toward his, and gave him a passionate kiss on the mouth. He returned the kiss tentatively, but then the volcano blew its top and they were kissing each other passionately. A few moments later, they broke away, both of them surprised and dazed. Pam felt like she could hardly breathe. Brad shakily opened up his door and walked to Pam's side to open up her car door. He felt like a little boy riding the Big Dipper Roller Coaster on the Santa Cruz boardwalk for the first time. He helped Pam out, said a final "goodnight," and kissed her on the left cheek, then the right cheek, the right eye, the left eye, and the top of her head with its glowing brown hair.

Pam walked back into her apartment suite in a daze; this day had been incredibly wonderful. She thought back on the movie, *Mary Poppins,* with the magical scene where Bert, Mary Poppins, Michael, and Jane Banks had taken a magical trip into fairyland through one of Bert's street drawings. That had been a lovely adventure, but surely, that would have been dull compared to the extraordinary things of this whole afternoon and evening. *Brad Applebaum, what a guy!* She had liked Brad for months now, and that friendship between the two of them had been steadily growing. But now, she no longer just liked Brad Applebaum. What she felt in her heart for him tonight was *deep and passionate love!!*

15.

THE LAST CHANCE

Monday morning, July 29, was another glorious morning of intercessory prayer at Pam's apartment. The number of people there had risen to seven. The prayer that morning was especially focused on the mess going on in Washington D. C. concerning the Watergate scandal. It looked more and more like Nixon would be driven out of office. A lot of prayer was going up concerning the shaky economy—there was something going on called 'stagflation'—double-digit inflation accompanied by an economic downturn. The most fervent prayers were for a great big revival in the U. S. and around the world.

After the prayer meeting, Debbie, Cristy, Heidi, and Laura went with Pam for coffee at Denny's for some fellowship and a girl-to-girl talk. All the girls noticed something different about Pam this morning; she was usually vibrant and upbeat, but she had an unusual glow on her countenance today. She was extremely happy, vivacious, and animated in her demeanor. She laughed even more than usual and hummed some famous hymns and worship choruses. They walked into the restaurant, and the waitress led them to a table.

"Hey girls," said Laura. "I bought a beautiful new pink dress on Friday. I can't wait to try it out on you ladies."

"Can't wait to see it," responded Heidi.

"Pink is nice, but it can't compare to a beautiful white wedding gown," said Pam.

"Yeah," said Laura. "For me, it would be very nice, especially if I were wearing it and had a big diamond ring on my finger and was walking down the aisle toward Hal Odell!"

All the other girls broke into hearty belly laughs. Pam guffawed the loudest, started praising the Lord, and then began to sing the words to "I Could Have Danced All Night."

"I say, you're certainly in a good mood this morning!" declared Laura. "What have you been eating this weekend?"

"It must be an overdose of Rocky Road ice cream!" declared Debbie, while all the other girls chortled uncontrollably.

"She's *on* something," said Heidi.

"I am?" feigned Pam. "Yes, I am addicted to this new drug—and I never want to be freed from it! This new drug is called 'Romeo and Juliet', and it has no hangover effects or bad trips!"

"Well anyway," commented Laura, "she *does* look different today. Her face is as shiny as the yellow lights on a Christmas tree, and she has the cheesiest smirk that was ever seen on this side of the Mississippi River."

The other girls chortled with all their might yet again with Pam joining in with her musical laugh.

"She kinda' looks like someone in love," said Cristy.

"Well I wonder who Loverboy is," remarked Debbie. "Does his name start with a 'B'?"

"No comment!" said Pam in a singsong tone of voice. "What y'all don't know won't hurt you. I take the fifth! I use my constitutional right to remain silent!"

All the other girls were sure that it had to be a love issue. Pam didn't really care what they said or thought.

****

THAT NIGHT, Brad was at the Freedom Rehab Center in West Oakland once again, and tonight, he was actually assigned to give a fifteen-minute sermon. He chose as his topic, "Pornography: A Destructive Lifestyle." He spoke with more confidence and poise this time than he had the last time he spoke there.

A summary of his sermon went like this: "Today, we hear a whole lot about sex in places like television, the news media, and Hollywood movies. Back in the sixties, we had something called 'The Sexual Revolution' that basically said, 'if it feels good, do it.' This is a radical step away from the Victorian Era, that time when many considered sex to be dirty, only fit for procreation. In reality, this 'Sexual Revolution' is really not new; neither does it bring true freedom. The Bible takes a middle course between these two extremes of Victorian Asceticism and the hedonism of the playboy society of today. I like the analogy that compares sex to fire; both can be very wonderful, but if allowed to run uncontrolled, can be very destructive. I like the statement that Billy Graham said when he declared, 'Sex can either be a wonderful servant or a terrible master.' The Bible declares throughout its pages that sex is good and wholesome, but *only* in the confines of marriage. We have many perversions today of this wonderful gift from God, one of the worst being the sin of pornography.

"Some of you may have heard about an infamous and contemporary criminal named Darryl Temple. This man is an extremely brutal and wicked person. He has been positively linked to the horrendous murder and rape of a number of young women in the towns surrounding his hometown of Lodi, California. His trial is slated to begin in a few weeks. What many people don't realize is this: when the police searched Mr. Temple's apartment the day he robbed a bank in Stockton, they found his apartment strewn with pornographic magazines and books. This fact speaks volumes to all of us today that we've better pay close attention to.

"There are two things about smut that are especially bad. The first thing is that you cannot have the true bonding on a spiritual level with porn that you can have when two people are married. The second thing is the fact that pornography is extremely addictive, just like heroin and cocaine are. After the first kick, people find themselves receiving diminishing returns from their addiction, and they have to experiment with more and more of their drug or porn to get the same high. Obviously, this is exactly what happened in the case of Darryl Temple and what is the result today? A totally wasted life that holds no future for that sinful man."

Brad went on to read passages from the Bible that talked about sex including Proverbs, chapters 5 and 7 as well as First Corinthians, chapter 7. He wrapped up his sermon by giving a call to the people in the room to receive Jesus, saying, "You may be involved in a little sin like gossip or a big, *big* sin like the crimes that Darryl Temple has committed. But the solution is always the same: repent, admit your sin, and throw yourselves on the mercy of Jesus and His cross to receive salvation and pardon from your iniquities."

There were many 'amens' said during his message, and when the invitation was given, three people came forward to accept Christ. At the end of the meeting, Oliver Crane came up to Brad, gave him a great big bear hug, and said, "I'm so proud of you, Brad!"

****

THAT WHOLE SUMMER OF 1974 was a tumultuous time for the United States and the world in many ways, all the way from shaky economies and high inflation to a political situation in the U. S. that was on very shaky ground. In June 1974, the House Judiciary Committee voted out three articles of impeachment against President Nixon. The Republican members of the committee voted overwhelmingly in favor of impeaching Nixon. But the thing that really put the nail in the coffin was when the U. S. Supreme Court unanimously ruled in *U. S. v. Nixon* that the president had to turn over his White House tapes. The tape dubbed 'The Smoking Gun' was quickly singled out from the others. It showed how Nixon knew about Watergate from the very beginning, and that he had tried to get the CIA to push the FBI to call off the investigation for the sake of 'national security.' This was the straw that broke the camel's back, and at noon on August 9, Nixon became the first president in U. S. history to resign from his elected post. Gerald Ford was sworn in as the new president. He chose as his new vice president Nelson Rockefeller. He soon alienated many Americans by pardoning Nixon from all crimes and misdeeds.

Meanwhile, the famous pop star was not able to do his planned performance before the president during that summer because of the stormy political events happening in Washington, D. C. Meanwhile, the official trial of Darryl Temple was slated to begin in early September.

****

DARRYL TEMPLE was a very forlorn and unhappy person these days. Locked up in one of the most famous maximum-security prisons in the U. S. was a total drag for him as it would be for anyone. He was cooped up and confined to a small space. He was told when he could eat, sleep, and go to the bathroom. Being held in solitary confinement, he couldn't get his kicks from liquor or any other thing he had been acquainted with that used to give him a 'high.'

One night in early August, Darryl became so depressed and upset that he totally blew a fuse. Fierce anger exploded out of him, and there was nobody to vent his rage on, so he started screaming, cursing God, and banging his head very hard against the concrete wall of his cell. Wes Marlow, the guard assigned to Darryl, immediately burst into the cell and cried, "WHOA, WHOA, DARRYL! STOP IT! You're going to HURT yourself!" He tackled the young criminal, and a giant wrestling match ensued. Wes had a tough time trying to subdue Darryl, but the guard was strong and muscular enough to finally knock him to the floor and sustain a firm hold on him. Darryl's face was badly bruised and he had a very black eye. Wes then saw to it that Darryl got the proper medical attention and, later on, had a talk with the uncontrollable young rapist. Wes was a firm, yet kindly guard who truly cared about that tormented man.

"Darryl," said Wes. "I've watched you over these weeks here in prison. I've seen your fierceness and rudeness of manner. I know that the other prisoners have a very low opinion of you. I've also seen the newspaper reports about your murders, rapes, thefts, and violence."

"So what, you sorry old man!" growled Darryl in a low and sullen voice.

"Darryl. I can see that you are a greatly troubled man. Obviously, you've been deeply hurt. I don't know the whole story, but I sense that you've been rejected your whole life by just about everybody. I'm sure you have not been brought up in a loving environment at all. You've had a rough time at it and have led a life of brutality, theft, and drunkenness—bottom line: a life of sin."

"Yeah, yeah, yeah!" snarled Darryl, savagely. "I know all about it. A preacher told me in jail some weeks ago that I'm a bad sinner goin' to hell! I've heard all this tripe, 'You're gonna burn in hell if you don't get your act together and clean up your life.' I've heard it all before!"

"Darryl, let me tell you something. You're a sinner and I'm a sinner. *Everyone* in this world is a sinner. Obviously, you've been considered to be nothing but garbage by most people, but I want you to know that I love you and Jesus Christ of Nazareth loves you!"

"SHUT YOUR FACE! If you give me anymore of this religious crap, I'm gonna get my hands on you and smash your brains into little pieces of mush!"

"Darryl. You can smash my brains into little pieces of mush right now. You can kill me, but that won't stop me from loving you. And Darryl—Jesus loves you! He was nailed on a cross two thousand years ago and suffered unimaginable tortures and still, He cried out, 'Father, forgive them, for they know not what they do!' He wants to give you hope and peace. He—"

"SHUT UP ABOUT JESUS, YOU SORRY LITTLE WIMP! Your little Jesus is a sissy and a mollycoddle just like you are! You're a chicken, and if you don't let me alone, I'm gonna clip those chicken wings right off of you and split your skull right open and let those yellow brains flow and gush out to this jail floor!"

"Okay, Darryl, but remember, Jesus still loves you and cares about you."

"LEAVE ME ALONE, YOU FECKLESS PIECE OF SCUM!"

Darryl stood there, his head spinning, his world undone. He had tried to put up a brave front, he had tried to bully his way through life, but he now felt like he had been stripped of all his weapons. Over and over in his head rang the words, "Jesus loves you, Jesus loves you, Jesus loves you!"

"Bah, I don't want anything to do with that little girlie sissy of a Savior!" growled Darryl in a low voice.

****

DURING THOSE WEEKS in August, the love between Brad and Pam continued to grow and blossom. They saw much of each other, and when they were apart, both of them missed each other a whole bunch. Brad continued to work hard at his job at the Christian bookstore in Oakland, but sometimes, it was all he could do to keep his mind on his work and off of the beautiful, spiritual Pam Jackson. Brad did his job faithfully, and there were times outside of his work schedule when he would browse through the treasure trove of Christian literature in that bookstore. He was like a kid in a candy store as he surveyed books on biographies of famous saints of the past like Charles G. Finney, George Whitefield, Billy Sunday, John Wesley, and Hudson Taylor. There were books on end-time Bible prophecy, the dangers of the cults and the occult, the person and ministry of the Holy Spirit, marriage, great heroes of the Bible, economic issues from a Biblical point of view, and systematic studies on different books of the Bible. One thing Brad was very interested in were the books which claimed that many of the Founding Fathers of America were Christians and God had a plan for the USA. Those times Brad and Pam had together were very happy: nights out at some restaurant or coffee shop, times spent swimming at the Park Pool in Orinda, miniature golf in Concord, and ice cream dates where Brad enjoyed his sherbet while Pam enjoyed her cones of Rocky Road ice cream. A big highlight for the couple was when they spent an evening sitting on the grass together at the Concord Pavilion, listening to the jazz music of George Shearing, Dave Brubeck, Tony Bennett, and Bill Evans on Saturday, August 17. They sat together on that cool and lovely evening, holding hands, and drinking in the beautiful jazz piano solos of George Shearing on songs like, "You've Got a Friend" and "Sweet and Low Down." Afterwards, Brad drove Pam back to their rendezvous at Orinda BART. She didn't get out of the car right away. Instead, the two of them spent some moments talking to each other about the evening.

"Brad, thank you so much for another lovely evening. You are quite a guy!"

"You're so welcome, Pam. I'm glad you enjoyed the concert."

"I did, Brad. I loved the way George Shearing played those piano solos with such calmness. The way that group plays is so cool and soothing. I don't know how George does it, being blind like he is. I have 20/20 vision and I'm nothing but a hack when it comes to my piano playing. I also love the way Tony Bennett sang 'I Left My Heart in San Francisco.' He has such a pure voice."

"What I liked, Pam, was the way that Dave Brubeck played 'Blue Rondo a la Turk.' I really loved 'Strange Meadow Lark' with those beautiful arpeggios on the piano at the beginning of that ballad. I didn't like 'Take Five' too much, though. Too monotonous!"

"Yeah, that piece is more of a drum-driven work. Otherwise, the evening was great. But you know what the best part of the night was?"

"What was it, Pam?"

Pam leaned over to kiss Brad and said, "The best part of the evening was *the company!*"

She kissed him tenderly on the mouth and he kissed back. After a few moments, they broke apart and spent the next few minutes taking turns praying for each other and for the needs of California, the U. S., and the world. After a short while, Brad closed out the prayer time with, "In the lovely name of Jesus, amen!" They sat quietly in the car for another moment and then Pam spoke.

"Brad, I have something to say to you tonight."

"What is it, Pam?"

"Brad, I praise the Lord so much for you. You have no idea how much the Lord is using you to impact the lives of many, many people—and how much the Lord has used you to impact my life. You are such an inspiration and encouragement to me. You have grown spiritually by leaps and bounds in these last nine months! You're no longer the insecure, immature, and sloppy person I remember last year. You are a wonderful guy to be around and I love you so much, Brad Applebaum!"

"And Pam," responded Brad. "I love you so much, too! I was attracted to you the first day I saw you—and it's not just your physical beauty. Yeah, you are the most beautiful girl on the outside that I've ever seen. Your skin is soft and smooth, your brown hair is so attractive, and your hazel eyes have such a sparkle to them that would make the brightest incandescent light bulb seem like the embers of a dying fire in comparison." (Hearty and musical laughter from Pam.) "But much more than that, your exuberant love for the Lord is what really turns me on. The way you unashamedly worship Jesus, the way you tell others about the Lord in a very excited, yet loving manner that is not at all pushy or holier-than-thou, your infectious joy that is obviously from the Holy Spirit, and your laugh. I have never, never met a girl in my whole life that has such a musical laugh like you do—or laughs so much." Brad looked straight into Pam's eyes and said, "I really want to—I, um, want to—well, what I mean is."

"Yes, Brad?"

"Well, I really would like to marry you—um, well. Would you think of being mine?"

"With all my heart, Brad. I've felt for a while that the Lord was drawing us together for a purpose."

The two of them came together for some more hugging and kissing. When they broke apart, Pam spoke again.

"Brad, my love. I want to tell you when I first had a clue about our relationship."

"When was that, honey?"

"Well, do you remember that day last fall at Tabernacle Fellowship after Pastor David gave his sermon on the Mid East war that had just broke out? You came up to me and asked me out—called me 'Pammypoo' and said that we would paint the town red."

Brad remembered that day very well.

"I was very turned off by you. I snubbed you that day and was thinking to myself what a weird and boorish guy you were. Suddenly, the Lord spoke to my heart in a still-small voice and said, 'Pam, My daughter, this man who just talked to you is going to be your future husband.' When I heard that, I was stunned and didn't want to believe it. Then I was angry. But as time went on, I began to ponder what the Lord had said to me. Now today, I'm glad and thankful that the Lord is choosing the two of us to be together!"

Brad was bowled over at this revelation. He thought for a minute and then said, "So when do you think the wedding day should be?"

"Well honestly, Brad, I really don't want to wait very long."

"What do you think about sometime near Christmas?"

"I think that would be a lovely time, Brad. Of course, we'll need to talk to each of our folks."

They kissed and hugged each other once again, said goodbye one last time, and separated to drive happily back to their respective places of abode.

****

IF IT HAD BEEN A COLD WINTER DAY in December, one might have dubbed that conference between Brad and his folks a 'fireside chat.' As it was, the three of them were sitting on their beautiful patio located right outside the living room on a warm and sunny evening late in August. Sid and Harriet were sipping martinis while Brad was enjoying a tall, delicious glass of 7-Up 'on the rocks.' From the living room stereo phonograph floated the beautiful lush sounds of Nat King Cole and George Shearing who were singing and playing songs such as "Pick Yourself Up" and "I've Got it Bad."

"So you want to *marry* Pam Jackson on Saturday, December 28?" Sid was asking his son.

"Yes, Dad. I am totally in love with her. She is the most gorgeous and spiritual girl that I've met in my whole life—and the neat thing about it is that she is in love with me too."

"So tell me, what does this kid do for a living?" asked Sid.

"She's not working at any job yet, Dad. She's a full-time student at Cal Berkeley, majoring in music and studying voice and applied piano."

"Brad my boy," said Sid. "The decision to marry is a major step in one's life not to be taken lightly. There is a lot more to it than the gushy feelings of romance and excitement. Marriage is a commitment that takes a lot of hard work to make it successful. For one thing, you have to be in a position to support and take care of your wife financially as well as the babies that will probably come along. You also have to be living in your own place. Right now, you are still living under our roof. Also, you have to realize that even the happiest marriages in the world, like the marriage your mom and I have for example, are not perfect. There will be arguments and disagreements that will come along that you will have to work through with your mate."

"One thing that has really helped us to survive and thrive in our marriage," said Harriet, "is that we have learned to laugh a lot."

"Brad," said his dad. "My suggestion is that you don't rush this thing. If I were you, I would wait a few years before you take this giant plunge into this huge ocean. I think you need to be established in your creative writing career you are working toward. You need to be making the money to take excellent care of your wife."

"But I am making some money now, Dad."

"Yes, you've gotten off to a good start, and Mom and I are proud of you, but you are not established yet in your full-time career."

"And your dad and I feel that you and Pam still have some growing up to do before you can handle that great commitment of a marriage. As you know, your dad and I got married when I was twenty-three and he was twenty. If we had to do it all over again, I think we would have waited until I was about twenty-six. You are only twenty years old, and that is really too young an age to get married at."

The song wafting to them from inside was the popular tune, "Unforgettable." Brad was feeling his face becoming red and hot as tears began to trickle down his face.

"Brad," said Harriet in a gentler voice. "I think it's wonderful concerning the relationship that you and Pam have. Believe me; I am thrilled for the two of you. You have a lot in common. Both of you have the same tastes in music, you both love good literature, and you both have a love for religion. I think it's great the way you do things together and the way you care for each other. I'm not saying 'no' to the idea of marriage between the two of you, but rather just simply 'wait.' Your dad and I only want the best for the two of you."

"Pam is a nice kid," said Sid, "but there is something about her that kinda' bothers me a little. She comes across to me as a slightly flighty and very flamboyant person that doesn't quite have her feet on the ground. I hear her saying every two minutes things like, 'hallelujah!' 'praise the Lord!' and 'thank You, beautiful Jesus!' It just seems a little weird to me."

"Dad, she loves Jesus and is a Pentecostal just like I am. It's the Holy Spirit that gives us that joy."

"Well, you kids have to be able to shift for yourselves. Didn't God say, 'The Lord helps those who help themselves?'"

"It was Ben Franklin that actually said that, Dad."

"Well, religion in and of itself isn't going to help you make it in this world—and Pam Jackson seems to be just a little bit off her rails. I just don't want to see you get yourself into trouble."

"But honey. Brad and Pam have the right to choose the religion they like the best," countered Harriet. "Obviously, Brad and Pam are very happy with their Christianity."

"All I'm saying, dear, is I want Brad to be happy in his marriage and well able to take care of his wife. I'm just saying 'don't rush,' and 'take it slow.' I only want the best for our son."

"I agree with your dad. We are not saying 'no,' but only 'wait.' Believe me, we love you very, very much and only want the very best for you."

"This is a hard thing for me!" wept Brad.

"I know it is," said Harriet, sympathetically, "but believe me, it's for your own good and happiness."

****

"THIS IS KTVU, CHANNEL 2, bringing you the top stories from all across the northern part of the state. Here is news anchor, Kathy Estritch, with today's top stories."

A picture appeared on the TV screen with the pretty face of the polished lady anchor who started her scripted lines.

"Thank you, Duane. In the news today, rapist and murderer Darryl Temple has been diagnosed by the San Quentin doctors as having terminal liver cancer. The prognosis is very dim for the young criminal whose trial is slated to begin in early September. The most optimistic prognosis for Temple is six months, and it's possible that he may be dead by the middle of October. Besides the cancer, Temple also has cirrhosis of the liver. It is common knowledge that Darryl Temple had a drinking problem before it was found that he was a serial rapist and murderer. He previously has had several run-ins with the cops because of drunkenness. Darryl was involved in a robbery of $25,000 from a Wells Fargo Bank in Stockton when undercover cops tracked him to his small apartment in Lodi and found the two bodies hidden in his back yard."

It was August 23, and Randy Miller was spending a rare evening in front of the TV set in the master bedroom of his new mansion. The cross-country tour was over, the last concert having occurred at the Hollywood Bowl on August 15. He was dog-tired from the long and harrowing tour, the drugs, the alcohol, and the recurring nightmares. Along with the tiredness was the relentless depression that seemed to dog his every waking moment. At the end of July, they had spent a week in Great Britain, performing in such places as London and Dover to very enthusiastic capacity crowds. Tomorrow, he and The Universal Mindset members would be leaving early to do a concert down in San Luis Obispo. On Sunday, they would be performing in Santa Cruz. On Monday night, the group would be performing at the main concert auditorium at UC Berkeley. His energy was flagging, and he needed some rest time. But even when he had a little time for rest, he just couldn't seem to unwind.

"Randy."

"Uh huh, Lila?"

"How do you like my beautiful new red dress?"

"I'm busy. I'm trying to rest and watch the news."

Lila raised her voice in agitation and protested, "You never pay attention to me anymore! You don't seem to care about me or the kids anymore! I thought that maybe when you got home from your big tour around the country, we would get back to a semblance of normalcy, but it hasn't happened! Things have not improved; instead, they've just gotten worse!"

"LOOK, LILA!" yelled Randy. "I DON'T NEED ANY OF THIS BULL FROM YOU! I'M REAL TIRED AND I'M TRYING TO GET A LITTLE RELAXATION HERE! I'M GETTING SICK AND TIRED OF YOUR STUPID NAGGING AND PESTERING ME ALL THE TIME! GIVE ME A LITTLE SPACE, YOU BATTLE AXE!"

"BATTLE AXE, HUH?! Well, maybe I should leave you alone! Maybe I should just go home to my mother and take the kids with me!" cried Lila, as tears of grief and anger flowed down her face.

"I didn't mean exactly that, Lila."

"Well, I'm nearly at the point where I can't take it anymore! This last year has been 'The Year of Hell' for me, Randy Miller!" Lila gave out a loud sob and continued, "Most of the time, you're gone on one of your 'Big Concert Tours.' And when you are around me, it's impossible to be happy. You yell and scream at me, you pay no attention to me, half the time you're drunk, you keep me awake with your terrible nightmares, and maybe you're on some drugs. I don't know."

"I'm not on any drugs, dear."

"Well, *something's* wrong and I don't know what it is! You used to be a lot of fun to be around. You used to have a wonderful sparkle in your eyes, but these days, the twinkle is gone! In place of that is the glazed look in your eyes! I don't seem to have the same good old Randy Miller, anymore!" She grabbed the arms of Randy, looked desperately into his eyes, and yelled, "RANDY MILLER, *WHERE ARE YOU?!!*"

Randy shoved her away from him and yelled, "I'M RIGHT HERE, LILA! WHAT'S THE MATTER WITH YOU, ARE YOU *BLIND?!!*"

"I'm outta' here!" muttered Lila, savagely, as she ran out of their bedroom, slamming the door behind her. She ran down the stairs, sobbing and wailing loudly, slammed the front door behind her, jumped into her car, and zoomed down Sleepy Hollow Road at a reckless pace.

****

ON THAT SAME NIGHT, Eric Burns presided over the weekly meeting of the communistic revolutionary group, The Red Riding Rangers. After the meeting, the group of conspirators, who were planning the kidnapping of Randy Miller, met at their favorite haunt—the sleazy bar in Berkeley.

"Okay, gang," he said in a soft voice. "Monday night is the big night! Jitterbug Josh is going to be performing at the main auditorium at UC Berkeley. We perform our kidnapping caper in the middle of the program that night. Ted and I have studied the layout of the whole area. The plan is to arrive there at 4:00 P. M., three hours before the concert begins. I've looked at all the escape routes and exits. Ted, fill the group in on where everyone will be sitting."

"All right, listen up, everybody!" said Ted Johnson. "Here's the layout. Felix, Tony, and Nick, you guys will be seated clear in the back of the auditorium. Felix, you be the one to set the diversionary fire. You other two guys are to help him out by making a big ruckus to divert attention from the front. When this happens, Frank, Eric, Scott, and I will rush onto the stage, grab Jitterbug Josh, and take him captive to our getaway truck that Scott over here is supplying us with from the repair garage where he is working at. You all got it?"

"Yeah!"

"I guess so!"

"You guys will have to pull this caper off to a tee or all of us will be sunk!" declared Eric. "We can't have any cracks! There's an old saying that goes like this: 'Loose lips sink ships!' Are you all up for this job?"

"Yeah!"

"Sure!"

"We can do it!"

"Well, all right then," said Eric. "We all better be hair-sharp and come through!"

Between cigarettes, whisky, and brandy, the seven of them fine-tuned the plan and worked on strategy over the next hour. After that, Eric and the rest of the gang paid for their drinks without leaving any tip and drove to their respective homes.

****

THE SUNDAY EVENING CONCERT of 'Jitterbug Josh' at the Municipal Auditorium in Santa Cruz was going well. The house was packed with a cheering crowd of mostly teenagers. Randy seemed to have his usual nervous energy that was lately a trademark of his singing career. They were about 70 percent of the way through the performance, and the band was playing the well-known Randy Miller song, "Say Yay for Yoga." Suddenly, the famous pop star toppled forward, his guitar flying from his hands onto the floor. The audience thought at first that this was a flamboyant bit of choreography until the rest of the band stopped singing that number and Brian Manning rushed over to try to revive 'Jitterbug Josh.'

"Randy! Randy! Randy! RANDY! WAKE UP!" Running over to the mike, he called out, "Somebody help us up here, please! We need medical attention! Jitterbug Josh has just collapsed! Somebody, call an ambulance!"

Soon, the sounds of sirens could be heard in the distance, getting closer and closer. The paramedics arrived at the concert venue, put the unconscious pop star on a stretcher, and rushed him to the hospital. After a thorough examination, the diagnosis was established: a mild drug overdose. He would be kept there for a few days until he could be detoxed and receive his strength back. This would be a scandal on the career of the famous pop star, similar to the early years of Johnny Cash, who also had been a one-time addict to prescription drugs.

Eric Burns and the other six conspirators met at precisely 4:00 P. M. on Monday outside the concert hall at Cal Berkeley. They had their getaway vehicles and supplies that they would need for the kidnapping in the middle of the concert tonight. At 6:00, they started walking toward the main auditorium to take their seats at their prearranged places. As they approached the doors, Eric gave a gasp of shock and dismay.

"What?! Those rotten turkeys!"

On the door was a sign that read, "Universal Mindset Concert Cancelled Due to Illness of Jitterbug Josh."

"What do we do now, Boss?" asked Felix McDowell.

"Let's go home," said Eric, glumly. "I'll be in touch with you guys about Plan B."

****

LABOR DAY WAS SUNNY AND WARM. Roger and Mary Thatcher hosted a barbecue for the Christian youth of Berkeley Tabernacle Fellowship. The youngsters had a wonderful time that day, gorging themselves on hamburgers and hotdogs, chugging down cans of Coke and 7-Up, swimming in the beautiful pool, and playing touch football and tennis. Some of the young adults there included Debbie Thatcher, Hal Odell, Laura Wilkerson, Bob Hurst, Dwayne Downing, Peter Thal, Cristy Hunt, John Patterson, Roger Bennett, Phillip Scheer, Bob Mitchell—and Brad and Pam. Pam had noticed that Brad had become more distant for some reason during the last couple of weeks at those early morning prayer meetings, but she couldn't figure out why. Also, they hadn't had any other dates since the evening of that conversation between Brad and his parents.

While everyone else was swimming, playing their different games, or talking in small groups, Brad sidled slowly and tentatively up to Pam.

"Hi," he said.

"Hi, Brad. I've missed you something awful!"

"I've missed you too, even though we see each other at those morning prayer sessions."

"It's not the same thing as being alone with you, Brad!"

"Come on over here to a quiet place where we can have a little talk together."

The two of them walked over to a secluded nook in the garden under a large oak tree, Brad walking very slowly and listlessly. The two of them sat down, and Pam noticed that Brad had his head hanging down a little bit.

"What's the matter, Brad? You don't seem to have the same zing lately that you usually have."

Brad was silent for a couple of minutes as he was trying to figure out the best way to begin this serious conversation. Finally, he spoke.

"Boy, where can I begin? Well, um, Pam, the first thing I want to say is that you are a fantastic girl and I love you." (This intro didn't give any reassurance to Pam.) "I think that you are a fabulous girl. I think that your love for the Lord knows no bounds. I think that the times we spend together are wonderful beyond description. When I'm with you, I feel like I can take on any challenge. I feel like I can fly just like Peter Pan. I feel like I could do a whole concert of classical music at Carnegie Hall and play everything perfectly. I feel that I could write the most inspiring bestseller novel that would be read by millions. I feel like I'm on top of the world." Brad paused before he continued his speech. "And because of all this, it makes it tougher for me to say the things that I feel I need to say." Brad cleared his throat and continued, "As you know, we talked about getting married around Christmas time of this year."

Pam steeled herself for the blow her feminine instincts told her was coming and hoped the news from her beau wouldn't be all that bad as she asked, "So what's the deal?"

"Well, um, Pam. I, um, talked to my mom and dad a couple of weeks ago about the wedding, and um, they strongly advised me against it. They said that we are too young and immature to think about that right now. As hard as it is for me to swallow, I have to admit that what they say makes a lot of sense."

Hot tears started to run down Pam's cheeks as she asked, "Does this mean the wedding is off for good?"

"I hope not, dear. My feelings are still very strong for you, and my mom didn't say 'no,' but only 'wait.' The thing that's so hard for me is that they think I really shouldn't get married until I'm twenty-five. That's a long time away, and for all we know, the Rapture may have occurred before I reach that age. Another thing that worries me is the sky-high divorce rate today. I have a cousin that married a flaming radical hippie when she was seventeen years old. It was a horrible marriage, and two years later, they got a divorce. Sometimes, I question whether our feelings are real or if I'm just falling in love with 'Love.' I'm afraid of taking a step too quickly and then waking up five years later and finding out what a huge mistake I made."

"So what are you saying, Brad?"

"This is what I think we should do. As tough as it is for me, I think we should back off on our relationship and see what happens. We should give it time and see where things are a couple of years down the line. If this is really love, it will endure, but if the flames die out, then what we were experiencing was not really love, but only infatuation. Also, there's the financial problem; right now, I'm not in a position to properly take care of you and support you financially, especially if a baby comes along—and I'm not able to give you a beautiful diamond engagement ring. I don't really have a full-time job, and I'm still in school. Believe me: I'm not saying 'no' to this marriage, but simply that I can't do it right now. I hope to God that we do get married because I really can't picture myself with any other girl except you."

"I understand the situation," said Pam through her tears. "I talked to my mom and dad, and they also feel that we should wait a bit. They are both wonderful Christians and they are thrilled about our relationship, but they feel the age of twenty is a little early for marriage."

"I'm glad your folks are Christians. Sad to say, my dad has some real reservations about your personality. He has a problem with all of this 'praise the Lord' and 'glory to God' that comes out of our mouths. He seems to think that you are flighty and weird. I know where he is coming from because before I got the Holy Spirit, I had the same feelings deep inside about the Pentecostals."

"Well, unfortunately, there's another problem. It turns out that my dad is having a job transfer, and that we are fixing to move to Nashville, Tennessee in January 1975. I'm going to have to go with them and transfer from Cal Berkeley and finish my college education in Tennessee."

This was an unexpected blow; it felt just like an arrow had penetrated Brad's heart. It was now *his* turn to feel the hot tears gushing down his face.

"Oh my word!" he moaned. "Oh my, my, my!" He thought for a moment and then lamented, "And I'm stuck here in the Bay Area. I'm only going to be a junior at Cal Berkeley this fall, which means at least two more years of school."

"I'll miss you so much!" wept Pam.

Brad put his arms around Pam in a passionate and affectionate body-hug and kissed her on the cheek. She kissed back—and then both of them exploded into a few moments of passionate smooches on the lips. *They were back in fairyland!* A thunderbolt shot down the spine of Pam Jackson and she could hardly breathe.

"See there?!" commented Brad. "It seems this always happens with us, doesn't it?" He kissed her again and said, "I love you, Pam! I love you! *I love you!*"

They gave each other a final squeeze and then broke apart, both of them feeling disconsolate and dejected. Both of them thought about what a drag it was that they were going to have to wait for an eternity to get married—if they would even be able to get married at all.

****

IN THE FOLLOWING WEEKS, Brad and Pam backed off on their romantic relationship, even though it was very tough for them, especially at the Sunday church services at Berkeley Tabernacle Fellowship and Glad Tidings International Fellowship as well as the prayer meetings at Pam's apartment and the Friday night Campus Crusade for Christ meetings. Brad continued to work hard on his creative writing as well as working at his job at the Living Waters Christian Bookstore. He also did some more preaching at the Freedom Rehab Center in West Oakland.

Meanwhile, 'Jitterbug Josh' and his band did a concert tour through the western states starting at Bakersfield. They then performed at Victorville. They went on to Las Vegas, Nevada; Phoenix, Arizona; Colorado Springs, Denver, Cheyenne, Wyoming; Butte, Montana; Boise, Idaho; Spokane, Washington; and Portland, Oregon. They did a concert in Salem, Oregon, and then traveled down highway 101 along the beautiful redwoods in Northern California, performing in Crescent City, Eureka, and Ukiah. They returned to the Bay Area on October 23 where they would be doing several concerts over the next few weeks.

Eric Burns was still living with Alan and Carmen Schmidt because he still hadn't been able to land a steady job. Carmen experienced morning sickness during that October and went to the doctor for a check-up where it was found that she was pregnant. However, the baby was not Alan's. Eric knew he was the father, and he demanded that Carmen have an abortion. She reluctantly went through with it on a cold morning in mid-October while Alan was at work at the CO-OP store. It was going to be hard for her to hide this secret because from that day onward, there was a pall over her countenance that was nearly impossible to hide. She felt an almost unbearable load of guilt and depression that seemed like it would choke her at any minute. Eric was disappointed at the delay of his revenge kidnapping plot against 'Jitterbug Josh,' but bided his time, waiting for just the right moment for the seven of them to make their move.

****

ON THE NIGHT OF OCTOBER 25, Eric called the other six conspirators to one of his special meetings at the sleazy bar in Berkeley after the regular meeting of the Red Riding Rangers. They smoked, drank, and conspired as usual.

"Hopefully, I now have the night when we will do the deed," said Eric to the others. "On November 7, The Universal Mindset will be doing a concert at San Francisco State University. That night will be the perfect time to bag that greedy, capitalistic pig!"

They talked and schemed for several hours, planning the time of arrival at the concert hall, strategizing on how they would kidnap the pop star, and nailing down the days when they would drive to the college to survey the escape routes around the college auditorium. They broke up the clandestine meeting at three o'clock in the morning.

The next day, Art and Jan called up Eric to invite him to lunch at Love's Restaurant. Eric agreed, and at 12:30 P. M., on the last Saturday of October, the three of them were sitting at that nice restaurant, enjoying a hearty lunch. The food was great there, but Eric was hardly enjoying it at all because of his resentment toward his folks.

"Eric," began Jan. "Your father and I are very worried about you."

"What's it to you, woman?"

"Well, for one thing, you still don't have a regular job," said Art. "You don't have your own place of abode but are mooching off a couple that I'm sure are having enough trouble taking care of their own financial needs."

"And the thing that concerns us the most," said Jan, "is how you're not walking with Christ anymore. I'm saying this in all gentleness and love, you've backslid from the love of Jesus and have turned 180 degrees to your communist ideals, but it's not too late to turn back to Christ. He loves you and will take you back."

"Shut up, Mother! You don't understand how things are in the real world!"

"Okay, son. Okay," said Jan, gently. "I know you don't believe in Christ anymore. But would you do me this tiny little favor? Would you go to a Bible-believing church just one more time?"

"Okay, Mom! Just to get you and the old man off my back, I'll do one better than that! Tomorrow night, there's a church service in Concord at a place called Glad Tidings International Fellowship. They claim to have miracles and healings. I'll not only go there, but I'll bring along my two closest friends in that little group of mine that you think is so terrible. I'll prove to them and to you through this that their Bible is a tissue of lies, their Jesus an imposter, and their miracles totally phony."

****

THE NEXT EVENING, Eric picked up Ted Johnson and Scott Williams in his little blue ramshackle car, and the three of them started driving toward Concord and the Pentecostal church. The three of them carried on a lively conversation in the car as they drove up highway 24 toward Concord.

"Well, the economy is sure going haywire right now," commented Ted. "Inflation is running at more than 12 percent, and the Gross National Product is falling."

"And Ford is sure a dumbbell as well as a capitalistic pig!" declared Eric. "I understand that LBJ said about him that he is too dumb to walk and chew gum at the same time."

Scott responded, "Actually, I understand dat' Johnson was a lot more risqué in what he really said. He was referrin' to Ford not bein' able to pass gas and chew gum at de' same time!"

Ted giggled and said, "Yeah, nor can he solve the gas shortage in this world."

"That whole idea of 'WIN-whip inflation now' is a crock!" declared Eric. "There's no way it will succeed. And Jerry Ford's idea of balancing the national budget by next year, it will totally fail."

"Dem' Dem'crats are gonna beat de' 'Publicans to mush," said Scott. "Jest' wait 'til a week from next Tuesday."

Soon, the three of them arrived at the snow-white building known as Glad Tidings International Fellowship. The parking lot was already almost full, and Eric was fortunate to be able to find a place to park. They walked into the modern sanctuary with its lovely sky-blue carpeting and blue seats. All three of them sensed the Presence that had been at Berkeley Tabernacle Fellowship last Easter—only it was stronger here. They also noticed that there was a great amount of genuine love here like they had never seen at any other church or gathering. People were hugging each other and involved in friendly conversations. It was crystal clear that they really cared about each other. Scott noticed there were a lot of African American people mixed in with the whites. There were also some Oriental, Mexican, and American Indian people. A number of folks came up to them to say "Hi."

233

"Well, hello you three! I don't think we've ever seen you here before," said an elderly lady, giving each of them a warm hug. "My name is Laurie and this is my husband, Ray."

"Hi, my name is Scott Williams!"

"My name is Ted Johnson."

"Eric Burns here."

Other people came up and introduced themselves to the three conspirators in a warm and friendly manner as well. Meanwhile, Brad and Pam were also talking to their friends, people like Karen Thompson for one. Presently, the worship singers and band started their musical numbers. This was also different to the three communists from anything they had seen before. This band lingered on one song before going to the next one, and the people responded with boisterous and heartfelt worship, saying things like, "Hallelujah!" and "Glory to God!"

"Batty!" whispered Eric. "Totally batty!"

"These people are total nutcases," agreed Ted.

Pastor Jeremy Norris then walked up to the pulpit while the piano player continued to underscore softly and sensitively. He said, "Folks. I feel the Spirit telling me there are some people in here who need healing in their bodies. Right now, I'm going to ask anybody who needs a touch from God to line up here at the front, and the elders of the church and I will pray for you."

About twelve people responded, and the pastor and elders started to pray for those people, quoting Isaiah, chapter 53, a passage promising physical healing. The first woman in the line suddenly fell backwards onto the floor and started to praise the Lord Jesus in a loud voice.

"What kind of game is this?" mocked Eric.

Shortly after that, another lady in the line exclaimed, "My back! There's no more pain! Oh, hallelujah, sweet Jesus! Thank you, Jesus!"

The three conspirators noticed a middle-aged man in the line whose left eye was badly crossed. All three of them were stunned as they saw it straighten up. But the most undeniable miracle they saw concerned a young girl with a withered arm. Suddenly, as Pastor Jeremy prayed for her, fresh new flesh grew on the arm, and it was as healthy as the other one. A fresh outburst of praise broke out in the congregation after this huge miracle. This wonderful time of prayer went on for about a half hour after which the pastor called the people to order and started preaching his sermon for the night. As was his custom, Pastor Jeremy started off with his idea of an 'ice-breaker,' a funny joke that he could use to segue into the sermon.

"There were once two Christian men who were golfing buddies. At least twice a week, they would get together on the links for a nice friendly round of golf. There was only one problem, though. They had a little theological disagreement and it was concerning whether or not there was golf in heaven. Tom Smith believed there was golf in heaven while Charlie Jones believed otherwise. They argued and argued over it until one day they came to a decision. 'I'll tell you what, Tom,' said Charlie. 'Whoever dies first among us can ask St. Peter for permission to appear to the other one and let you or me know whether or not there really are golf courses in heaven.' 'That sounds like a good idea!' responded Tom. They shook hands on it and immediately stopped arguing about this point.

"Two years later, Tom died of a heart attack. Two nights after he had passed away, Charlie was suddenly awakened by a voice saying, 'Charlie, *Charlie!*' 'Who's there?' 'Charlie, this is Tom speaking.' Charlie looked around the bedroom and saw the spirit form of his best friend. Charlie's wife was sleeping right next to him. The spiritualized Tom continued, 'Charlie. I was able to get permission from St. Peter to appear to you and let you know a little about heaven. Charlie, I have some good news and some bad news for you. What do you want first?' 'Well,' said Charlie, 'I guess I want the good news.' 'Well, Charlie, there *are* golf courses in heaven. They are incredibly beautiful like you wouldn't believe, and my golf game is really fantastic. My driving, chipping, and putting are so spectacular up here because I have the mind of Christ. I got a hole-in-one on number seven, fourteen, and sixteen today.' Charlie responded, 'Well that's great news, Tom. So now tell me, what's the bad news?' Tom softened up his voice as he said, 'Well, Charlie, it's like this: you and I are fixing to tee off together tomorrow night at 6:25 P. M.'"

The whole congregation broke out into boisterous guffaws after which Pastor Jeremy got into the meat of his sermon. "Open your Bibles to Acts, chapter 2, please! I'm going to start reading right at verse 1, and I'm going to be preaching about the events that happened right on through chapter 5 of that book because I believe it has tremendous relevance for all of us today. It says this: 'And when the day of Pentecost was fully come, they were all with one accord in one place. And suddenly there came a sound from heaven as of a rushing mighty wind, and it filled all the house where they were sitting. And there appeared unto them cloven tongues like as of fire, and it sat upon each of them. And they were all filled with the Holy Ghost, and began to speak with other tongues, as the Spirit gave them utterance.' Folks, this was the awesome event that birthed the New Testament church and brought a revolution of love that turned the world of that day upside down."

Pastor Norris preached about the fact that that particular day of Pentecost was actually a feast of the Lord, and that many Jews had traveled from a long way away to celebrate this feast. On the Hebrew calendar, it was also the date when Moses had given the Ten Commandments to the Jews at Mount Sinai. He said some people were there who were bewildered while others mocked the disciples and accused them of being drunk. Peter then stood up and gave a sermon, saying that they were not drunk, but what they were witnessing was the beginning of a fulfillment of Bible prophecy concerning the coming of the Holy Spirit. He then explained how the crux of Peter's sermon was that Jesus is risen from the dead and the crowd needed to repent—turn 180 degrees away from their course of hate, murder, and brutality and surrender totally to Jesus. "This is what God requires of each of us today," declared Pastor Jeremy.

Eric was sneering at the sermon, yet he was quaking in fear; *there was that Presence again!*

The pastor talked about 3,000 people receiving Christ that day, and then talked about the lame man who got healed at the Temple through the ministry of Peter and John. "I want to clear up one misconception," he said, "and that is the Scripture which says, 'Silver and gold have I none.' Many people think Peter was poor and was telling the man that he didn't have any money to give him, but the literal translation of that verse reads like this: 'It is not my purpose to give you silver or gold, but such as I have, I give thee.'"

He continued his sermon with the healing of the lame man, Peter's second sermon that again centered on the resurrection of Christ, the apostles being thrown into jail for a night, 5,000 more people receiving Christ, the leaders of the Jews demanding that the apostles preach no more in the name of Jesus, the intrepid response of the apostles, and their subsequent prayer meeting where the Holy Spirit was poured out on them in a fresh way, giving them renewed boldness to preach the gospel.

Said Pastor Jeremy, "The first century Christians had great fortitude even in the midst of tremendous persecution. You couldn't shut them up concerning Jesus. How many of us in America today have even a fraction of that boldness to tell people about Jesus? Not too many, I'm afraid! In Islamic and communist countries today, Christians are called on daily to suffer great persecution for the sake of the gospel: imprisonment, unspeakable torture, and even violent deaths." (Eric growled savagely at this statement.) "Yet they undergo these trials courageously and gladly because of the hope of heaven and the joy of the Holy Spirit within their hearts.

"Now, I want to draw your attention in these passages which talk about the fact that many of these early Christians sold all that they had and laid the proceeds at the apostles' feet who then distributed the proceeds to the people as anyone had need. I want to point out the fact that this was *not* communism. We have to understand that at that time, many Jews who received Christ were put out of the Jewish community and had their means of support cut off so they needed this type of help. Understand, also, that this was voluntary giving from members of the church who were subjects of a theocracy, the Kingdom of God, with Jesus as its head. It was *not* a human governmental thing. Communism in the world today simply does not work. In fact, the history of the last fifty-seven years is a strong witness to the cruelty and savagery in communist countries, for example, the Gulags of Josef Stalin where millions of innocent people were brutally enslaved and murdered, and the horrible torture of Christians going on right now in Communist China. We need to understand that Jesus gives life, not death! It was actually people like the Sadducees who were more like communists. That is why they were sad, you see!" (Hearty laughter from the congregation in which both Eric and Ted abstained from.)

"Now, I want to draw your attention to chapter 5 and the tragic death of Ananias and Sapphira. The account tells about how this couple sold some property, brought only a *part* of the proceeds to Peter, and told a lie, claiming that this was the full price of the land. Peter discerned their deception immediately by the power of the Holy Spirit and told them they had lied to the Holy Spirit and had put the Holy Spirit to the test. First, Ananias dropped dead, and three hours later, his wife Sapphira likewise fell down dead. *Folks! This is dead serious stuff!* We need to realize that sins against the Holy Spirit are a big deal with God. Peter pointed out to this couple that they had not lied against man, but against God—"

At that moment, the countenance of Pastor Jeremy Norris became gravely serious, and a holy hush came over the whole congregation. He said, *"I WANT EVERYBODY IN THIS ROOM TO BE VERY, VERY STILL RIGHT NOW AND I WANT EVERY EYE CLOSED IN THIS ROOM!!* EVERYBODY LISTEN!! *A cliff of fathomless blackness!!* I see in my spirit a cliff of fathomless blackness that somebody in this room is about to go over—it may be more than one person here tonight. I don't know what it means, but I sense the Spirit of God saying that there is someone in this room who needs to get right with God *right now* and return to Christ! I feel the Holy Spirit saying that this is your last chance. *If you don't surrender to the Lord right now, you are going to go over that cliff into the blackest darkness forever and ever!!* If you give your life to Christ tonight, you'll never go into that darkness."

Loud wailing broke out all over the room as many people cried out to the Lord for forgiveness. Brad groaned and cried out loudly in spiritual agony.

"Are you all right, Brad?" asked Pam.

"Nooo, Pam. I feel TERRIBLE! I think I'm lost! Maybe I better go forward to pray to receive Christ! Maybe my former prayers were not sincere enough!"

"But Brad, I've seen your walk with the Lord. I think that what we need to do is intercede for whoever the people are in this room who are in mortal danger. I think you're feeling a burden for some people who are lost tonight. Let's pray together!"

All three of the conspirators were shaking with great terror; the conviction of the Holy Spirit was very heavy upon them. Eric had a sudden flashback of the events in his life, starting from his teenage years. He remembered the strict moral guidelines of his mom and dad, how they frowned on things like smoking, drinking, and premarital sex. He had held a grudge against them, feeling that their values kept him from having fun. He then remembered his science teachers in high school who had taught evolution. This had been the solution! Those moral taboos were outdated and only restricted a person from giving in to those natural urges. He had started to be promiscuous with girls in high school followed by nights of debauchery with Adrienne Quigley before they had broken up. Lately, there had been the tryst with Carmen Schmidt and the secret abortion he had pushed her to have. His latest lover was Ted Johnson. He remembered reading and believing in Marx and Engels' *Communist Manifesto*. When he was twenty-three years old, he had bought *Age of Reason* by Thomas Paine with its anti-Christian tenets he had taken a liking to, even though he didn't believe in Paine's Deism. On top of that, there was all the smoking and drinking he had been involved in. Worst of all was his pride, profanity, and kidnapping plot.

Scott likewise felt the conviction of the Holy Spirit. He felt a great urge to go forward and surrender his life to Christ, but he hesitated. He had been strongly indoctrinated in communism and questioned in his mind whether this experience was real or only irrational emotionalism. Besides that, he was scared about what would happen to him if he did accept Christ. Also, there was the promised money from the kidnapping plot.

Eric and Ted sat there for a few moments as the piano underscored, wavering over whether to come forward or not. Tears began to flow down the face of Eric Burns, but suddenly, he brushed them aside and hardened his heart like steel while Ted just sat there forlornly with his head down. Eric wanted to discount what he had felt in his heart; he was very proud, and the pleasures of sin beckoned to him. He started to say the most horrible blasphemies imaginable and then capped it off with, "I don't want this filthy Jesus! Leave me alone!" The Presence that he had felt subsided, and Pastor Jeremy closed down the invitation time by saying, "All right, everyone. I'm going to lead us in a closing prayer."

Scott heard the horrible blasphemies and was appalled. *Okay, that does it! I WILL go down front and accept Jesus!* Looking intently at Eric, he stuttered, "I-I th-think I need to go down to de' front and 'cept Christ!"

The communist leader grabbed the arms of Scott firmly and softly spoke in a threatening voice, saying, "If you go down there, I'm going to kill you, you fat little pig! This whole thing is nothing but a dirty tissue of lies!"

"Okay, Eric," mumbled Scott. "If y-you s-say so."

Ted continued to sit there, his face a tableau of utter dejection.

Brad and Pam opened their eyes and glanced around the sanctuary. Suddenly, Pam gave a start.

"Brad! *Brad!*" she whispered excitedly.

"What is it?"

"That guy over there; I've seen him before!"

"Really? When?"

"Last fall. Laura and I tried to witness to him, and he got really angry with us and didn't want to listen. I'm fixing to pray for him right now."

Pam bowed her head and started to pray for that redheaded guy in tongues when suddenly, she heard a still-small voice.

Don't pray for him!

"What?" she asked softly. "That can't be You, Lord."

It is I, Pam. Don't pray for him!
"But why, Lord?"
Because he has committed the sin unto death.

She had read that Scripture in First John, chapter 5 a number of times and didn't know if it referred to physical or spiritual death. She sat there bewildered and dejected and brooded over the events of this whole tumultuous night.

****

ERIC DROVE THE OTHER TWO CONFIDANTS of his back toward Berkeley. He did drive a little bit more carefully than usual tonight because of the nagging prophecy of the Cliff of Blackness, but he pushed the thought away with all his might. It might refer to a car accident, but he would fix it. After all, car accidents happen every day, don't they? The other two men were very quiet and downcast, especially Scott. He felt very shaky and scared. He had wanted to go down to the front, but he hadn't done it! He looked anxiously out the window as they drove toward Berkeley on highway 24. Anytime when there was a steep drop off the freeway embankment, he shuddered with abject terror, expecting any minute that the terrible killer car accident—or massive earthquake would happen, killing all three of them. But it was not destined that the three of them were to die that night. They all made it safely to their places of abode.

****

SCOTT WILLIAMS spent a sleepless Sunday night. The sense of terror continued unabated in his soul. He tossed and turned. His heartbeat was racing at an alarming rate, threatening to split his head wide open, and cold sweat covered his whole body, soaking his pajamas. Over and over in his mind, the words of Pastor Jeremy played like a broken record, "A cliff of fathomless blackness, a cliff of fathomless blackness, a cliff of fathomless blackness! This is your last chance!" Could Scott have done anything about coming down the aisle? He had felt such a strong desire to do just that, but he had turned chicken and hesitated! *I should have gone forward the very instant that Pastor gave that warning, but I hesitated a little too long! And then, Eric grabbed my arms and bullied me! Surely, I could have ignored his intimidation and gone down to the front. Even during the time when the pastor was winding things down, I still could have gone down to the front of that church to accept Christ, but I didn't do it!* An overwhelming sense of guilt, panic, despair, and despondency flowed into Scott's soul. Along with this was the memory of those horrible blasphemies Eric had uttered. It made him sick to his stomach. The nausea was so great, he felt like he was going to die at any minute. Finally, a thought entered his mind that gave him the slightest sliver of hope, easing his depression only a tiny bit. *Well I could call this Pastor Jeremy on the phone tomorrow and try to get an appointment with him. I could bare my soul to him concerning everything, including the communist group I'm involved with and the kidnapping plot on November 7. It probably won't do any good, but it's my only hope.*

****

ON MONDAY, OCTOBER 28, Brad started writing an essay during his free time. He had always been interested in the history of World War II and how it had changed the world. Last night, a thought had entered into his mind: why not do an essay on how things in the world would have turned out if there hadn't been the intercessory prayer warriors who had prayed during the war. He found a secluded grassy area on the Cal Berkeley campus, opened up his notebook, and started writing.

One of the most beloved American Christmas movies is "It's a Wonderful Life," starring Jimmy Stewart. In this movie, George Bailey meets his angel after a suicide attempt and experiences an incredible adventure. George tells Clarence, the angel, that he wished he had never been born. Clarence then arranges for George to see what would have happened if he had never been born and the revelation is mind-boggling. This brings up a very important question: what would the world be like today if none of the prayer warriors who lived during World War II had been born? Let's explore a possible scenario here.

It is late May of 1940. Czechoslovakia, Austria, Poland, Denmark, Norway, and Holland were in Hitler's mitt. Italy was under the thumb of the fascist dictator, Mussolini. France was about to fall to the Nazis and the British armies had their backs against the wall at Dunkirk. What happens then is absolutely terrible. Instead of halting his attack, Adolph Hitler presses on and the whole British army is decimated in early June; most of them are either killed or taken prisoner. For all practical purposes, Winston Churchill and Great Britain don't have an army anymore.

France falls to the Nazis in short order and England hangs in there for some months, but is finally defeated around Christmas of 1940. Hitler then concentrates his war aims against Greece, Turkey, and all of the continent of Africa, winning victories against all of these countries and conquering them, continuing to slaughter myriads of Jews in whatever countries they live in.

*In real history, Adolph Hitler attacked Stalin and the Soviet Union on June 22, 1941 against the advice of some of his counselors, but in this scenario, Adolph Hitler does **not** turn against the Soviet Union and Stalin's services. This has dire consequences against the Free World*

240

as Hitler now has the resources of Stalin's huge Soviet armies at his disposal to help him in his conquest of the world and the extermination of the Jewish race. When Hitler had attacked the Soviet Union in real life, it looked like Russia was doomed to fall to the Nazis—and it came very close to doing exactly that, but history shows us that attacking the Soviet Union was Hitler's greatest military blunder as Stalin's forces managed to hold out and ended up helping the Allies to beat Adolph Hitler.

On December 7, 1941, Japan attacks Pearl Harbor, just like what really happened in history. Germany also declares war against America. But the difference in this fictional scenario is that both Japan and Nazi Germany are successful in their war against the United States. America puts up a gallant fight, but they are just too weak to stand against these mighty armies. By October of 1943, the U. S. surrenders to Japan, and by March of 1944, our wonderful country has ceded to the Axis Powers. Fifty million Americans lose their lives in this catastrophic scenario because Japan attacks the western states while Germany and Soviet forces attack the eastern states.

So now, let's explore what the world might look like after this scenario. Indeed, things are very, very dark at the beginning of 1945. Hitler, Stalin, Mussolini, and Hirohito get together for a summit in Berlin meeting to discuss how the conquered territories are going to be divided up. The summit is known as AWFUL, (Axis World Federated Union of the Liberation). The results of the meeting of these tyrants goes like this: North and South America are split up between the Japanese and the Nazi powers. The western states in the U. S., British Columbia in Canada, Ecuador, Peru, and Chile all become vassals of Yamamoto and the Japanese empire. For these people, it's not so absolutely terrible. They are weak, economically, but the Japanese pretty much leave these territories to themselves. It's much, much worse, though, for the rest of the United States that is east of the Rocky Mountain States as well as for all of Central America and the rest of South America. Here, the Nazis have absolute control and there is horrible death, imprisonment, torture, and slavery. Hitler also has dominion over most of the rest of Canada while Communist Russia has control over the Northwest Territories, Iceland, and Greenland. Japan has control over most of Asia including countries like Singapore, Hong Kong, the Philippines, Indonesia, Australia, and New Zealand. This is the part of the world that is the most desirable because it has a little more freedom than is the case elsewhere.[1]

Josef Stalin has control over China, Finland, the Middle East, and a few of the northern countries in Africa while Hitler has sway over the rest of Africa. For the people in this part of the world that are under Stalin's thumb, conditions are indeed horrible. Millions of Jews,

241

Christians, and other 'undesirables' are either killed or imprisoned in Stalin's famous gulags, (slave prison camps), where they are cruelly brutalized. Many people die horrible deaths in these gulags. Millions more starve to death because of the planned famine initiated by Stalin in these countries.

By 1962, almost all of the Jewish people in the world have been eradicated; there are only about 200,000 of them left. There is no State of Israel in the Holy Land, most of the Christian population in the world is gone—killed or imprisoned by the Nazis and the communists. Meanwhile, the world economies are in shambles and a spirit of fear stalks the whole planet. There is no freedom of speech, freedom of religion, freedom to choose your own occupation and prosper, and freedom from fear. These Four Freedoms that Franklin D. Roosevelt talked about in a speech are nowhere to be found. Instead, the world in this scenario looks a lot like conditions in George Orwell's novel, "1984", with its squalor, fear, thought-police, and hopelessness.

I hope you can see by this frightening scenario how important intercessory prayer really is. We live in a world where unseen forces are duking it out continually. Angels and demons are involved in a worldwide rumble for the souls of men and the redemption of nations. A lot depends on us Christians to be able to hear the voice of the Lord and to stand in prayer for men and nations. During World War II, we had prayer warriors like Rees Howells who helped to confound and turn back the evil agendas of the demonic realm by their prayers. Also, there is a little-known fact that is often glossed over by modern historians and it is this: George Washington was not only a devout Christian, but a mighty prayer warrior. I firmly believe that it was the prayers of this wonderful man that were instrumental in America winning the Revolutionary War and becoming the 'Land of the Free and the Home of the Brave.'

The sad fact is this: when the Rapture of the church takes place and the restraining power of the Holy Spirit and the prayers of the saints are taken away, the earth will actually experience a scenario that is far worse than the one I have just pictured. This is known as the Great Tribulation. So let us press on in helping the Kingdom of God to be established on earth. Let our prayer be, "Thy kingdom come, Thy will be done on earth as it is in heaven." And let us look up with hope and joy for our redemption draweth nigh.

Brad glanced up at the grassy retreat with a very sober look on his face as he pondered the things he had just written. The sky was a hazy blue color, and the sun was turning into a bright orange ball of fire because of all the smog in the air on that day. Brad would plan to show what he had written to Pam at the morning prayer session tomorrow to get her input on it.

****

"HELLO, Pastor Jeremy here! What can I do for you?"

Scott Williams was speechless for a moment, afraid of rejection, afraid he was on a wild goose chase. He had been able to reach the pastor on the phone by first talking to the friendly secretary of Glad Tidings International Fellowship. He finally was able to stutter out some words in a low, mournful voice.

"I-I-I-I g-got a problem, pastah'! I'm in real trouble and I wonder if I-I-I c-can see you right away."

Pastor Jeremy Norris felt a genuine love and compassion for this obviously troubled youth on the phone as he said, "No problem is too big for our Lord. We serve a great God. I'd be more than glad to meet with you. I have an hour free tomorrow at 11:00 A. M. Would you like to come see me then?"

"Y-yes, I-I-I-I w-would!" blurted Scott.

"Do you know where our church is located?"

"Oh yes! I w-was dere' on Sunday n-night."

"Very good, Scott. I look forward to talking with you tomorrow. See you then. Goodbye, now!"

"Bye'!"

Scott stood there for a minute as a slight trace of color began to return to his face. The phone rang and he answered it.

"Scott, my fellow comrade!"

Oh no! It's Eric Burns! I have no desire to talk to him right now!

"Yeah, what is it?" mumbled Scott, tepidly.

"We have a special meeting tomorrow afternoon at the bar in Berkeley to plan our kidnapping of Jitterbug Josh on November 7. Can you be there at 3:00?"

"Yeah, I guess so," murmured Scott, unenthusiastically.

"Okay then! All seven of us will be there. I got the whole layout of San Francisco U mapped out, and the plan should go like clockwork. We have some communist contacts down in L. A. who have promised to help us out. I'm even trying to enlist the help of a communist movie star, but he is kind of on the fence right now. So I'll see you then."

"See you. Goodbye!"

Scott hung up the phone, thoughts racing through his mind anew. He had no desire anymore to be a part of this kidnapping plot. He had lived in poverty all of his life, and his ancestors had suffered terribly as slaves and then later on, as second-rate citizens in the segregated state of Alabama. When he was ten, his family had moved from Birmingham to the more liberal California in the hopes of escaping some of the racial prejudice still rampant in the Deep South. Initially, communism had seemed to be the answer, and Eric Burns had appeared to be a wonderful and dynamic leader with all of his intelligence and charisma. But over the last few months, Scott was seeing more and more, the shortcomings, even the *raw evil and hypocrisy* in the soul of Eric Burns, and it made him want to throw up. What to do, what to do? He was in too deep. If he continued with Eric Burns in the caper, there was sure to be horrible trouble, but if he got out now, the future still looked dark and dreary for him. If he exposed the kidnapping plan he was involved in, he would still have to go to jail—and what might Eric do? *Either way, I lose,* thought Scott glumly.

****

IT WAS NIGHTTIME, and the sanctuary was packed at Glad Tidings International Fellowship. The seven people on the platform were all dressed in their black suits with their bright yellow ties and gray dress shirts. Randy Miller was the center of attention as he was belting out his vocal phrases on the songs he was singing and as his fingers flew across the fretboard of his electric guitar. A handsome man was pounding out rock-and-roll riffs on the grand piano. The audience was very appreciative. Pam noticed the three guys she had seen on Sunday night, one of them being the man the Lord had told her not to pray for. She was feeling a vague sense of apprehension and ominous foreboding.

Suddenly, a spark of fire flew out of the eyes of the hardhearted man, shooting like an arrow straight toward Randy Miller. The famous star's body immediately burst into flames that spread to the other members of the Universal Mindset. There were screams from the pop music group and the audience as the flames and smoke quickly raced toward the concertgoers. Pam wanted to run and escape from the sanctuary, but her legs felt like lead and she could hardly move. The flames were getting closer and closer—

Pam screamed and bolted up in her bed, sweat making her pajamas stick to her body. Her heart threatened to jump out of her chest and choke her. Tears ran down her face. She immediately arose from her bed and knelt on the floor. Her cat, Goldfinger, snuggled up beside her in a comforting way and meowed with sympathy.

"OH, GOD!" she prayed passionately, "WHAT DOES THIS MEAN? Please show me what I need to do and how I need to pray!"

****

EARLY THE NEXT MORNING, the seven prayer warriors were at Pam Jackson's apartment for their daily time of corporate intercession. They prayed concerning the usual needs and worshipped the Lord. After that, Pam told the group about the horrid nightmare she had experienced the previous night. She explained that since she had found Christ and been filled with the Holy Spirit, nightmares were very, very rare; most of her dreams were very pleasant, encouraging, and refreshing. Everybody in the room could see that she was visibly shaken. Her face was drawn and pale, and her eyes had dark circles around them.

"I just can't shake off the impression that something is very, very wrong," she said. "Does anyone in this room have any input concerning this dream?"

"Maybe death is hanging over the rock star's head," volunteered Brad. "Maybe there is some sort of conspiracy to get rid of him."

"That's my thought, too," said Laura.

"But what can we do about it?" asked Debbie.

"I don't know," said Pam. "Let me think on it for a minute." She prayed silently and thought deeply for a moment and then said, "I have an idea I want to throw out to y'all. I really think there is something urgent here that calls for some immediate action. What if we have an all-night prayer vigil—and I mean *quick?* I'm talking about like *tonight!"*

"Well, I don't think we should get too emotional about this or jump to conclusions too fast," cautioned Hal. "It was only a dream that might have been caused by too much pizza."

"I didn't have any pizza last night. I had fried chicken and green vegetables."

Everyone in the room broke out into hysterical laughter. This was a welcome breath of fresh air that temporarily broke the tension in the room.

"Hal, sweetheart," responded Laura. "I agree with Pam that there is a real need for some deep intercession here. You remember how God in the Bible often warned his people through dreams, for example, Pharaoh in Egypt before the seven-year famine, Nebuchadnezzar at the time of Daniel, and Joseph at the birth of Jesus?"

"I agree with Laura and Pam," said Brad. "Remember. I know this guy, Randy Miller—and I feel that things are very urgent."

Nods and voices of approval followed this comment from most of the other young adults.

"Okay," said Pam. "How many of you would be willing to meet here tonight to go deeply into prayer?"

Almost everyone in the room voiced their approval to the plan, and Hal finally agreed reluctantly.

"Good enough," said Pam. "Now, does anyone have any praise reports before we go our separate ways?"

"Yes, I do!" said Hal. "Yesterday, I witnessed to this guy who I come to find out is a real baseball buff. I told him about the career of Billy Sunday who started out playing baseball professionally. In 1883, Billy started playing for the White Stockings. He wasn't such a hot hitter, but he could sure run fast. In one season, he stole seventy-one bases while in another season, he stole eighty-four. In 1887, he had a religious experience and soon accepted Christ. I told the guy how Billy Sunday quit baseball and became a famous and flamboyant evangelist, preaching against drinking, and leading multitudes of people to Christ. I was able to lead that man to Christ."

"Praise the Lord!" exclaimed the rest of the group.

"Please pray for that guy. His name is Derek."

Everyone said their 'goodbyes' and headed out toward their cars. Tonight would be a sleepless night for all of them.

****

"COME ON IN, Scott!" said a friendly voice from inside the cheery office of Pastor Jeremy Norris.

Scott Williams walked into the office. Light-yellow wallpaper covered the walls, and the floor was clothed with yellow-brown carpeting. A large wooden desk served the pastor in writing down notes for his preparation of his sermons. On one side was a large bookshelf full of Christian literature, several English translations of the Bible, and a few commentaries. Scott looked into the compassionate face of the pastor. Scott was truly scared, but a little bit encouraged by the warmth of this man of God. He knew if anyone could help him, it would be this man.

"So, Scott Williams, I presume?" said Pastor Jeremy, rising from his seat to shake the hand of the wavering communist. "It's so good to meet you! Have a seat, have a seat!"

Scott sat down in the green swivel chair facing the pastor, and the two of them spent a few minutes in small talk on things like the history and present job of Scott, how Pastor Jeremy had become involved with Glad Tidings International Fellowship, and the recent World Series, which the Oakland A's had won for the third consecutive year.

"I was happily surprised that Oakland won again this year," said the pastor.

"Yeah man! De' A's were slippin' durin' de' last part of de' season. Dey' choked sev'ral games."

"But they came back, didn't they? First, they whipped the Baltimore Orioles in the playoffs, and after that, they nailed that third World Series against the Los Angeles Dodgers in five games."

"Yeah, Rollie Fingers clinched de' series in de' fifth game."

They talked for a few more minutes until the pastor finally tried to get to the bottom of Scott's need by saying, "I can see that you didn't come here to just shoot the breeze. So, tell me, Scott, what's on your mind?"

"Well, I-I-I!"

Scott was having a lot of trouble getting started. He felt the room spinning. He just sat there speechlessly for a moment.

"Don't be afraid, Scott! No matter what you've done or how big the burden you're carrying, I love you and Jesus loves you!"

Haltingly at first, Scott finally began to speak. Yet as he got into the meat of his story, he gained more courage and the words flowed with a lot of freedom and ease. He told about how his ancestors were greatly oppressed slaves and how his parents had suffered much racial prejudice in Alabama. He related the story of how he was brought out to California by his parents when he was ten—it was a tough trip, and they barely had enough money to move into that run-down flat in Berkeley. He told the pastor about his years of growing up in poverty, having little to eat, and having to wear cast-off clothes. He was now doing somewhat better financially at his present job at the garage.

He then told about how he had read about those horrible murders of the three men in the South by the Ku Klux Klan in 1964: Michael Schwerner, Andrew Goodman, and James Cheney. These were Civil Rights martyrs. Scott had also read about all the race riots in many U. S. cities during the late 1960s as well as the murder of Martin Luther King. Coupled with his concern with world poverty and the population explosion, all of this had drawn Scott to the charismatic Eric Burns and his communist doctrines.

Scott related to the pastor how he had practically adored Eric Burns at first, but how he had experienced more and more misgivings over the ensuing months as he had watched the actions and lifestyle of the flamboyant communist. He told Pastor Jeremy about the Easter service at Berkeley Tabernacle Fellowship, and how he had really felt something there. He had wanted to go down to the front, but Eric Burns had ridiculed him.

Now came the hardest part as he related the kidnapping plot against 'Jitterbug Josh' on November 7, and how he was responsible to supply the getaway vehicle to transport the famous singing star down to the Los Angeles area, and the planned ransom note to Lila Miller demanding two million dollars. (He explained how the prospect of receiving a cut of the money had been a real incentive and temptation that had kept him in on the kidnapping plot.) He finished off by rehashing the pastor's dire prophecy of Sunday night and how it had haunted him ever since.

"So," he concluded, "dat's de' whole sad story! I don't know what to do! I don't even know if dere's hope for me! I coulda' come down and 'cepted Christ on Sunday night and I jest' didn't do it! I hes'tated 'cuz of Eric Burns and also 'cuz of de' promise of de' kidnappin' loot. Even when you closed de' service down, I coulda' still come down and 'cepted Christ, but I chickened out and jest' didn't do it!"

Pastor Jeremy looked at Scott very intently and said, "First of all, I want to encourage you on something. It's not too late for you to give your life to Christ. You have not gone too far for the grace of God to reach you. If you had, you wouldn't be so worried and upset concerning that possibility. What I would advise you to do, then, is to repent and accept Christ right now. When is the next planning meeting of your gang to plan that kidnapping?"

"Today at 3:00."

"First off, I would call the leader of this gang and cancel. I would say to him that you can't be involved in this conspiracy anymore. Secondly, I would advise you to turn yourself in and tell the police about this plot."

"But I'm afeard', Pastah'! I'll haf'ta go to jail—and worse yet, Eric will kill me! Besides, I don't see any udder' solution besides comm'nism dat' can solve de' tough problems in de' world."

"You would go to jail, anyway—or worse. But if you turn yourself in—turn state's evidence, you'll get protection from the police. And the problems of the world like poverty and racial prejudice, Jesus has the answer to all of them. He commands us to love one another. And besides all of this, He is coming back to Earth soon. *He's* the one who will right all the wrongs on 'Mother Earth.' And Scott—something you didn't know is that Martin Luther King was a Christian as well as a staunch anti-communist."

Scott gasped with amazement when the pastor used the term 'Mother Earth;' how the heck could he know the peculiar phraseology of Eric Burns?

The pastor then went on to explain that virtually *none* of the Founding Fathers of America were pro-slavery; the Constitution, as they had written it, was meant to hold slavery in check and to prevent its spread. He talked about how during Reconstruction, a number of former slaves became congressmen who were all Republicans. He explained that in the year 1876, the progress of Civil Rights was greatly pushed back because of the racial prejudice of many, many Southern Democrats, some of them being involved with the Ku Klux Klan. It wouldn't be until 1964 when Civil Rights would advance again. He finally elaborated on how Christianity, which was anti-communist, was a very big part of African American history, both before and after slavery. He talked about the heroic ex-slave, Frederick Douglass, who was a strong voice against the Jim Crow laws and an outspoken proponent for equal rights for all Americans. He wrapped it up with a call for Scott to make a decision.

"The choice is yours, Scott! You can turn away from Christ and keep this heavy load on you—or you can repent and receive Christ into your life right now, no matter what the consequences. Come on, do it! You know you want to!"

Scott's face showed fear as he struggled with what decision to make. Finally, he softly said, "Okay, Pastah'. I'm ready."

The two of them knelt on the office rug, and both of them prayed. The pastor sensed that there were memories in Scott's mind greatly troubling him, so he prayed for the Holy Spirit to go deep into Scott's mind and heal those memories.

"Lawd' Jesus," Scott prayed. "Please come into my life. Forgive my sins and lead me in de' right way." As Scott prayed, he felt the terrible burden gradually lift off his body, and suddenly, he saw a very bright, yet soothing light flow into him. As he finished his prayer, his face now mirrored joy where before, it had mirrored fear.

****

"ERIC BURNS here!"

"Hello, Eric. I got news. I ain't gonna be able to come to de' meetin' dis' afternoon."

"WHAT?!!"

"Well, two reason. I can't give you help in dis' kidnappin' plot no more. I'm not givin' you a gitaway' car no more."

"HAVE YOU FLIPPED YOUR LID?!!" screamed Eric through the phone mouthpiece, nearly puncturing the eardrum of Scott Williams. "Why, Scott my comrade, WHY?!"

"'Cuz I 'cepted Christ de' Lawd' today and can't support your comm'nist cause no more. You can git' your own car to kidnap Jitterbug Josh. I want no part of it."

"YOU DIRTY, ROTTEN, TWO-TIMING TRAITOR!! THAT IS THE MOST STUPID AND INSANE THING THAT I'VE HEARD IN MY WHOLE LIFE!" A stream of profanities followed after which he continued, "If you don't take that yellow-bellied, liver-gizzard decision back, I will KILL YOU!! YOU HEAR ME?!! YOU ONE-TOED AMOEBA!!"

"I can't take it back, Comrade Eric. I have more peace and joy dan' I've evah' had in my life!"

Eric spoke in a low, threatening voice as he said, "I warn you, you filthy fathead! This is not the end. I'm going to come over and make the blood flow out of your body just like Red Claret! Consider yourself warned!"

****

THE SIX COMMUNIST CONSPIRATORS gathered at the sleazy bar in Berkeley. Felix McDowell had just taken a trip on acid the night before, and his eyes had a glazed look in them. His words were also slurred today. Francis Zeeb was in a grouchy mood on this afternoon. Nick Weems came up to Francis, slapped him on the back, and said, "How's it going, Loverboy? Have you found any blue-eyed foxy chicks to chase after this week?"

"Get your grimy hands off of me and get away from here, you jerk!" growled Francis, savagely.

Eric had a fierce look on his face as they all gathered at a secluded table for their clandestine meeting. Everyone could feel tension in the air that was threatening to explode into something like a nuclear war. They all ordered their favorite alcoholic beverages and smoked some cigarettes. Presently, Eric Burns cleared his throat and spoke in a low, ominous voice.

"Comrades of my Red Riding Rangers. We have an unexpected problem that has arisen today. I know that you are the cream of the crop. You guys are my loyal followers that will do everything I tell you to do. But it seems that every worthy organization has its share of traitors and turncoats—and I've discovered a traitor and turncoat today." Everyone looked inquisitively at Eric as he said, "The person that has turned against us is that rotter, Scott Williams! He has become a disgrace to my communist gods, Lenin, Trotsky, and Stalin, and given his affections to that dead liar, Jesus Christ. And because of this defection, we don't have a large truck to spirit Jitterbug Josh away in. Moreover, I suspect that Williams, our renegade comrade, is bound to rat against us to the fuzz. This will foil our kidnapping plan of November 7."

Eric looked around at the other five men and continued his talk. There was a lot of fire in his eyes.

"I have a new plan!" he said. "I want you to listen carefully, all of you. We are not going to San Francisco U on the seventh. That idea will no longer work. We need to get radical and act *fast!* Here's the new plan." He paused for a few seconds and then continued, "We are going to make our move on Thursday night—on Halloween!"

"While people are out trick-or-treating?" slurred Felix.

"How's it going to be, Boss?" asked the fat, green-eyed Tony Fitch.

"Well, Jitterbug Josh and his group are going to be doing a charity concert at Rheem Valley Theater on Thursday night. This concert is a benefit to raise money for cancer research in the hope of finding a cure for that disease. I understand their former lead singer and guitar player of The Universal Mindset just died of cancer that had spread to the brain. This theater is practically across the street from the bowling alley. We are going to attend this concert—we're going to get there nice and early so that we can have our pick of any seats we want. Felix, you'll still be in charge of the diversionary fire or explosion in the back, but I have a new plan for our sniveling music star."

"And what would that be?" asked Nick.

"Yeah, what?" asked Felix.

"We're not going to kidnap Jitterbug Josh—we're going to *kill* him!"

The other five men gasped. They sat there for a moment, their faces blanched, their mouths gaping wide open.

"Yes, we're going to kill that capitalistic pig. Francis, be sure to supply us with the guns and weapons that we'll need. Ted, you'll be the one to shoot the singing star—and anyone else in the band that you want to shoot dead. I'll be supervising everything up in the front seat next to Ted. Felix, you do your stuff in the back. And after we make our break from that theater, I have plans for our slippery-mouthed traitor. Ted, you and I are going to have to shut that traitor up for good. We're going to have to put him on ice. We'll escape the theater and take care of Scott after we kill the music pig and the others in the theater. The diversionary explosives of Felix will help us escape."

"But suppose the whole building burns down?" asked Felix.

"As far as I'm concerned," said Eric, "you can burn down that whole theater for all I care! You can kill everyone in that building! ***Good riddance to them!!***"

****

IT WAS HAPPENING AGAIN. Randy was in his bedroom, and those grotesque beings came flying through the window into the master bedroom. They were wearing their gaudy and multi-colored outfits. The nine-foot-tall being with the checkered red and yellow-green outfit grabbed the music star in a python-like grip and dragged him to the window. His wart-covered face was a picture of total evil.

"Aha, aha, aha, aha! You are going to die!"

"You are lost, little pig! You are lost!"

"We got you now!"

They threw him down the tube in the floor, and he screamed in terror. Randy was falling, falling, falling through the darkness forever and ever. There was the darkness, the clammy cold, the loneliness.

"Randy! Randy! Randy! Randy! Wake up!"

It was the sweet and welcome voice of his wife, Lila. As had happened many times before in the last several months, Randy felt himself rushing upwards. He opened blurry eyes to see the haggard form of his wife—but the three evil beings were also in the room. Randy gasped with terror and called out, "Lila! Help! Do something! Can't you see these specters?"

"No, I can't see anything," said Lila in a frightened voice, "but I sure *feel* something that gives me the creeps!"

"THAT DOES IT!!" yelled Randy. "STAY BACK!! I'm getting my gun!"

Randy rushed to his dresser and pulled out a handgun as Lila looked on in terror. He fired off shot after shot, running through the rooms in the mansion, chasing those malevolent beings that only his eyes could see.

"Stop it, STOP IT!!" yelled Lila.

The two boys were crying as they watched the commotion with terror. There were several broken windows, several chairs overturned, debris on the floors of some of the rooms, a drawer in the kitchen crashed to the floor. Randy staggered and fell to the floor in the living room. The handgun slipped out of his hands. Police sirens blared in the distance, getting closer and closer. The door was busted open, and four policemen entered the Mansion of Chaos. They encountered a crying mother, two weeping boys, and a dazed, scared music star lying on the floor of the living room.

"ALL RIGHT, HOLD IT, EVERYBODY!" called out one of the officers. They grabbed Randy and subdued him.

"They were here!" he blubbered. "I saw them! They were out to get me! Didn't you see those mean men that were out to get me?"

"Boy, oh boy," said one of the policemen. "This guy is *paranoid!*"

"Is he spaced out on drugs?" asked another.

"Calm down! Everything's gonna be all right!" said a third.

The next few minutes were spent in questions about what all the commotion was about. There had been calls by several concerned neighbors who had heard the gunfire and screaming and were worried that somebody in the mansion might have been wounded or even murdered. The cops asked if the famous music star had been taking any drugs tonight.

"Please don't send him to jail!" pleaded Lila, desperately. "My husband didn't hurt anybody. He was only having a terrible nightmare."

By and by, the Miller family calmed down, and the policemen said, "All right, we'll let it go this time, but watch yourself! Next time something like this happens, it's the slammer for you, Jitterbug Josh!"

When the cops had left, Lila turned to Randy and said, "I'm done, Jitterbug Josh! I can't take it anymore! I'm leaving!"

"And just what does that mean?" asked Randy in a tired, jaded voice.

"It means just this: I'm getting a divorce. It's for real this time. I can't take it anymore. I've put up with these nightmares, the long, drawn-out absences, the drugs and alcohol, the drastic change in your personality—and now this rampage tonight. It's the last straw, Jitterbug Josh. I'm outta' here. I love you and long for the good old Randy Miller, but I don't see any way out. So........ goodbye!"

A look of great dejection raced across the face of the famous pop star as Lila left the haunted mansion and drove off into the night in her fancy Lamborghini.

16.

THE PRAYER VIGIL

On that same Tuesday night, the group of intercessors met at Pam Jackson's apartment for their emergency night of corporate prayer. Brad, Debbie, and Laura supplied a liberal amount of coffee, tea, apple juice, and milk. Most of the prayer group had been fasting from any food or juices that whole day, and tonight, they would be indulging in drinks only. One by one, they arrived at the apartment at around 8:45 P. M. Their mood was subdued, and conversation was sparse.

At promptly 9:00, Pam started the vigil by leading the group in some worship choruses. They started by singing some fast choruses, and gradually segued into some slow and meditative worship songs. Between some of the songs were times of singing in tongues. This went on until 10:30. At that point, various people in the group started praying for different things.

They prayed for Glad Tidings International Fellowship and the ministry of Pastor Jeremy Norris. They prayed for the blessing and protection of the Lord on everybody in that congregation. They then prayed for America. They prayed for President Ford, the economy in the U. S. and around the world, they prayed for a solution to the Energy Crisis, and they prayed for the Lord's blessing and protection on National Israel. They then prayed for the fulfilling of the Great Commission around the world so that as many people as possible could be saved. Pam and Laura prayed that the preaching of the gospel would be attended by signs, wonders, and gifts of healing. Hal and Debbie prayed that God would send His light to pierce the darkness in the Islamic nations of the world. They then prayed for those people who were held captive in the grip of communism. Brad prayed for strength for the Christians who were suffering horrible persecution under Leonid Brezhnev in the Soviet Union. Hal prayed for the persecuted Christians in China, Cuba, Hungary, and Czechoslovakia. Brad prayed for the blessing of the Lord on a talented anti-communist writer from the Soviet Union named Aleksandr Solzhenitsyn, who had won the Nobel Prize for Literature in 1970. After that, Pam felt led to pray for the other two strangers whom she had seen at Glad Tidings on Sunday night. During this time, they were praying sometimes in English, and at other times in tongues.

They then prayed for the salvation and deliverance of those people in America and in the world who were involved in the occult: those who were involved in astrology, fortune telling, the study of Ouija boards, magical charms and transmutations, witchcraft, sorcery, drugs and alcohol, spiritualism and spiritism, and automatic writing. At this point, there came a very heavy burden of prayer on the group, especially on Pam. She started praying for the music stars in America and Great Britain, but especially for Randy Miller and the other members of The Universal Mindset. It was now about 3:00 A. M., and Pam began to groan loudly in agony; she was feeling a very heavy load on her soul. The others felt the load and also started crying out. (It was right around this time that Randy Miller was having his nightmare and his 'bad trip' with those mysterious, malignant beings that set off his shooting spree into the air.) Finally, the burden began to lift somewhat, and Pam and the others began to quiet down.

They then prayed for the millions of people trapped in Buddhism and Hinduism around the world that the Lord would shine His light to those in deep darkness and save many of them. After that, they prayed for the people who were caught up in adultery, fornication, homosexuality, and gambling. By the time they finished praying over these things, it was almost 6:00 A. M. Pam closed out the meeting with a couple more worship songs and then said the final "amen."

Everyone stirred, and Brad turned to face them all with a very serious look on his face. In a tentative voice, he said, "This is a crazy notion, and I don't know why I have this thought, but I feel that we need to go attend the Jitterbug Josh charity concert at the Rheem Valley Movie Theater tomorrow night. I don't know why I'm even thinking it because I don't even like the music of that friend of Uncle Mike, but—I don't know. Something tells me that we're needed there."

"I feel the same way," said Pam.

"Me too," chimed in Laura.

"It makes no sense to me," said Hal. "I'm sure it'll be a nice concert, but I really don't see the connection here."

"Well, I just feel we're needed there," said Pam. "I feel there will be trouble for us, but that the Lord is calling us there for some purpose."

"Okay, then," said Brad. "I don't have a clue why I'm doing this, and I'll probably live to regret it, but—let's do it! We're all going to the Josh concert tomorrow night, and we're going to get there early so that we can get front row seats."

****

AT 4:00 P. M. ON HALLOWEEN, all the members of The Universal Mindset were gathered at the Rheem Valley Theater, all set up and ready for their sound check. George Newman had his Rhodes electric piano set up; he would only be playing on it tonight since there was no grand piano in that theater. Mark Dole had his classy drum set situated on the left side of the stage with the letters, 'JJ' printed on the kick drum. Fred Barnes had his bass guitar set up while Keith Bryant had his rhythm guitar set up. Randy Miller had his electric guitar set up as well as his singing microphone. The other two singers,

Brian Manning and Bart Anderson, were standing beside him with their microphones. Observing them and sitting in the front seats was the manager Harry Gates and the disc jockey Hiram Quinn. Randy looked haggard and sad this evening. The amphetamines, barbiturates, alcohol, nightmares, strange occultic experiences, and upcoming divorce were taking their toll on him.

"Check, check, check!" could be heard throughout the theater as the vocalists tested their mikes. "One, two, three, check, check, CHECK! Bring mike 1 down slightly, please! Check, check, one, two, three, check, CHECK! I need more volume on mike 3!"

The piano was tested after which the bass, guitars, and drums were tested. When the balance was close to being desirable, the group started singing their main sound check piece, "The Evil Eye." They went through that song several times until the sound levels and effects of the vocals and instruments were satisfactory. After that, Randy Miller raised his hand to ask a favor.

"You know," he said. "I really would like to have one more crack at 'For the Love of Leviathan.' I think it's a great piece, and we've never done it since last winter."

There were dubious looks on the faces of some of the other band members.

"I don't know," said Mark Dole. "I've always had a bad feeling about that piece."

"Do you think that it will flow okay in the program tonight?" asked Fred Barnes.

"I hope nobody dies tonight!" commented Keith Bryant.

"Ah, come on you guys!" protested Randy. "You are all too superstitious. Let's have some fun. After all, it *is* Halloween."

"Yeah," said Brian Manning, "I think it will be okay. It won't hurt to do it just one more time."

"Okay, then," said Randy. "Let's rehearse through that number."

They played and sang that piece a few times in order to get it tight, musically, and then broke away from the stage for a little relaxation before the start of the concert. Some of the band members started to walk across the street to the Rheem Valley bowling alley.

"Hey, Jitterbug Josh. Hiram and I would like to see you for a few minutes," said Harry Gates. "We want to talk to you."

"Okay," murmured Randy in a tired and scared voice. The famous pop star had a bad feeling about this whole day. Something just didn't feel right. The three of them walked into the Green Room and sat down on the comfortable sofas.

"Jitterbug Josh," began Harry. "We are not very happy over your performances as of late. You're just not consistent and accurate anymore. What's the problem?"

"I don't see where I've really been messing up."

"Well, let me go over the last few weeks and enumerate some of the things that Brian and I have noticed. We all know about the drug overdose you had not that long ago, but there are quite a few other incidents that are just way below par and unacceptable. First, there was the concert in Las Vegas, Nevada, where your voice cracked on the high notes all the way through the concert. Then in Cheyenne, Wyoming, you forgot the words on 'Say Yay for Yoga,' and 'Karma Charma.' In Seattle, Washington, you were strung out and draggy, and we had to practically pull you onto the stage. We started the concert forty-five minutes late. Then there was the recent time in Ukiah where you threw a fit right on stage. Jitterbug Josh, *this is unacceptable!*"

Hiram added, "And besides all this, you just don't have the same bouncy personality anymore. You always look depressed and glum these days, and you talk to people in a monotone voice that has no energy whatsoever. What's the matter with you? Harry and I are very worried about you!"

"Because of these things," said Harry, "the popularity of The Universal Mindset has gone into a major nosedive as of late: album sales are way down, attendance has begun to fall at our concerts, and the financial situation has plummeted—and we're not going to have this going on."

"Well, there's a recession on," said Randy, weakly.

"That has little to do with it," said Harry. "If you perform good, things will go well. My suggestion to you is to shape up."

"Oh, I'll shape up," said Randy, lamely.

"Okay then," said Harry. "I want to see some action to back up your words! Your future is on the line, Jitterbug Josh!"

All three of them rose from the sofas and headed toward the dressing room to change into their concert outfits.

****

"YOU SAY you've been part of a secret communist revolutionary group and a kidnapping plot against Jitterbug Josh planned for November 7 at San Francisco U?"

Officer Riley was looking intently at Scott Williams as he queried the shaking erstwhile communist revolutionist. Scott was at the Berkeley police station, standing in front of the tall and sharply uniformed police officer. He was scared and tongue-tied. He was worried about the possible punishment he would have to undergo, but far more fearful of the fiery Eric Burns.

"I-I-I, well, um, yes-s s-sir! We been plannin' to git' Jitterbug Josh for sev'ral months now. I thought dat' comm'nism was de' answer and dat' Eric Burns was a wonderful guy, but ovah' de' last year, I come to see de' evil in dat' man."

"So what happened to make you change your mind?"

256

"Well, off'cer, it all started last March when we had dis' Friday night meetin' with de' Red Ridin' Rangers. Eric gave his usual long speech and went on gittin' louder and louder. He started ramblin' on about killin' de' Jews and de' Christians. He was really carryin' on about it and really hollerin' about it. Dere' was a scene in de' group. He abused a poor little German shepherd dog. Dat's' when I had my first misgivin'. Den' he got fired from a bus job last spring. After dat' he got throwed' outta' his 'partment 'cuz of his suspicious and rowdy doins'."

"And why was that?" asked the kindly policeman.

"'Cuz of all de' ruckus in de' flat. All de' screamin', yellin', and cussin' dat' he was doin' as well as de' vi'lence. He moved into de' flat of Alan and Carmen. Last April, he got beat up by Jitterbug Josh and spent a night in de' hospital."

"I remember that," said the policeman.

"Anyway, it was shortly after dat' when we planned de' kidnappin' for de' first time. We had dese' meetin's at de' bar here in town. We were gonna do de' caper some weeks ago when Jitterbug Josh was slated to do a concert here in town at UC Berkeley, but it didn't work 'cuz de' concert was cancelled 'cuz of de' sickness of de' music star. We didn't give up, dough', and de' latest plan is for de' 7th. I saw somethin' weird goin' on between Ted and Eric dat' really disturbed me in de' last sev'ral weeks. It seemed like dey' were queer and sweet on each udder'. It made me sick.

"The final straw was Sunday night at de' church service in Concord. I saw things in Eric and Ted dat' really turned me off. I went to see Pastah' Jeremy and 'cepted de' Lawd' Jesus into my heart. I feel relief now and am glad dat' I tole' you all dis' even if I hafta' go to jail. Off'cer, please do somethin' about dis' plot! Please protect me! Don't let dem' kidnap de' star on de' 7th."

"Don't worry, Scott. We'll get right on it."

"Please help me, off'cer! I need your protection! Dat' Eric Burns is mega-dangerous, and I mean *mega, mega* dangerous!"

"Don't worry, Scott. We'll take care of it. We're going to need the names and addresses of these hoodlums if you can."

"I'll do de' best I can."

Scott racked his brain, trying to supply all the addresses of the conspirators he could. He had no trouble with Eric's or Ted's addresses.

"Okay, Scott, we'll put out a bulletin alert for the arrest of all of these hooligans right away."

The clock on the wall of the police station read 8:05 on Halloween night.

****

AT 6:15 P. M., the doors opened at Rheem Valley Theater, and people started to walk in and take their seats in order to see the concert of The Universal

Mindset. Both Brad and Pam were very early comers. So were Eric, Ted, Felix, Tony, Francis, and Nick. The outside of the theater was adorned with the elaborate marquee, a fancy sign in lights reading, 'JITTERBUG JOSH AND THE UNIVERSAL MINDSET IN CONCERT, 7 P. M., THURSDAY, OCT. 31.' A ticket booth in front of the entryway stood out from the main doors leading into the movie theater. It was unmanned tonight since this was going to be a free, non-ticketed charity concert. The outside of the theater was painted in several different attractive colors; the lower part was painted a light aqua color while up higher, the walls were a pastel yellow color. Eric, Ted, and Francis took their seats in the very front row right next to each other. Brad and Pam sat down in the second row directly behind the three conspirators. Pam immediately recognized Eric and Ted and promptly started praying softly right there in her seat. Felix, Tony, and Nick sat in seats, close to the rear of the theater. Hal Odell, Laura Wilkerson, Debbie Thatcher, and Cristy Hunt sat in seats located about halfway back. By 7:00, the house was 80 percent full. It would almost be a full house tonight.

The emcee for the evening walked onto the stage to introduce the famous group. He said, "Ladies and gentlemen! It's the night for trick or treating, and we don't have any tricks for you tonight. But we do have a wonderful treat for you! We at the great Rheem Valley Movie Theater are proud and happy to present to you the world-famous singing group, JITTERBUG JOSH AND THE UNIVERSAL MINDSET! Please join me in giving a warm welcome to them!"

The audience burst into enthusiastic applause, and Randy Miller and the other members of the famous pop group walked out toward the stage. Randy was scared tonight. He experienced a premonition; something felt very, very wrong, and he felt like there was a bogey man that was near, threatening, all ready to jump out with his fangs and gobble him up. He felt like he should run out of the building and forget all about the concert, but he shrugged off the premonition with great effort. *I really must be going nuts! I guess Harry is right about me. All those drugs are making me paranoid. I want to get out of here fast, but if I did, I would be the laughingstock of Moraga, and Harry and Hiram would drop me like a hot potato! I've gotta' buck up, grin, and bear it! Think, Randy, think! Concentrate!* Randy forced himself out into the middle of the stage, and the concert started with the peppy Randy Miller smash hit, "The Evil Eye."

E dominant seventh, A dominant seventh, B dominant seventh, E dominant seventh. Randy and the other two male singers started belting out the memorable, catchy melody of that very rambunctious rock tune. Randy's fingers flew across the fretboard of his electric distortion guitar as he played his harsh pounding guitar solo. The piece received wild applause and cheers from the audience.

The next piece was "Just like Creamy Silk." *G major, G diminished, A minor, G-sharp diminished, A minor seventh, A half-diminished, D dominant*

258

seventh. The lush harmonies and sensual melodies of that romantic ballad filled the auditorium, and most of the audience was captivated just like they would have been if they had been at an Elvis concert. Very loud screaming came mostly from the teenage girls who were in the audience—it was very close to rock star worship. At the end of that song, wild cheering broke out that was almost deafening.

Pam felt a strong sense of foreboding as did Brad to a slightly less pronounced extent. The other Christians in the prayer group also felt somewhat uneasy. The ones in the middle of the room began to pray in tongues.

"Psst, Brad!" whispered Pam in a barely audible voice. "I feel we need to pray! Pray very, very quietly!"

Both of them began to pray almost silently as the music continued. When the wild cheering after "Just like Creamy Silk" had died down, Randy began to give a little speech, working like a beaver to hide his depression and fear.

"Hello, everybody out there!" (Wild cheering from the audience.) "Oh boy, it's sure good to be here tonight! I hope all you hipsters and hippies have a rock rolling, rip-roaring, rowdy good time tonight on this day of celebrating Halloween. Even as I speak, millions of kids here in the good old USA are knocking on doors and filling their bags with all kinds of goodies: Life Savers, Nestle Crunch Bars, Milky Ways, Snickers, packs of gum, and all other kinds of delicious sweets. There's enough candy around to make the mouth of Willy Wonka water!" (Laughter from the audience followed by more cheers and whistles.) "At any rate, the sad fact is that there are millions of people in our world tonight who are not so happy—and it's because of a green-eyed scourge, a silent killer that sneaks up on multitudes of people and bites them. This scourge is known as the Grim Reaper, Cancer. Less than two weeks ago, Cancer claimed the life of a man who used to be the lead vocalist as well as the chief guitarist for this group. A little over a year ago, that talented musician, Herb Taylor, was diagnosed with cancer of the larynx. The doctors did the best they knew how. They removed his voice box, but seven months later, a malignant growth was found in his brain. Herb Taylor fought hard and suffered intensely, but twelve days ago, he lost his battle against that malicious foe, Cancer.

"Our agenda here tonight is to raise money to try to find a cure for this great scourge. We need your help. Your $1, $5, $10, $25, $50, and $100 donations will go a long way into research to try to find a cure for this Great Scourge of mankind. Please be generous in your giving. I don't know why things like leukemia, Hodgkin's disease, melanoma, and glioblastoma strike so many people. I do know that the Law of Karma has something to do with it. Each of us has a long and arduous path as we go through many cycles of death and rebirth into new bodies as the eons roll by—reincarnation. It's a long trip that man has to take as he gradually ascends on his evolutionary journey, but it is our hope that the day will come soon that cancer finds itself on the ash heap of history, just like smallpox and polio. Thank you!"

There was enthusiastic applause, and the band started their next piece, "The American Dream." There followed, "Say Yay for Yoga," "Karma Charma," "Blue Love," "Hoodwinked Hustler," and "The Devil's Dilemma." Then came the song, "For the Love of Leviathan."

The song started with its haunting opening with the piecing distortion guitar solo from Randy. Then the rest of the band came in with the slow and hard rock opening featuring very sophisticated harmonies that were foreign to practically all the rock-and-roll music of that day. *G minor with A and E added in, C minor with D and A added in, C-sharp diminished, D augmented with a C added in, E-flat dominant seventh, C-sharp diminished, D augmented, D dominant seventh.* Randy started singing the lyrics.

> *"Lay your head on the great sea dragon,*
> *Holding in his hand a bottomless flagon,*
> *Out of the mouth of this invincible crocodile,*
> *Gushes poisonous vengeance, hatred, and bile,*
> *Concerning this crooked and scaly snake,*
> *Of his matchless power make no mistake……."*

Pam prayed like she had never prayed before.

> *"…….Leviathan, Leviathan, his jaws lead to Hades,*
> *To the dark and desolate land of shadies—"*

A glass 7-Up bottle went soaring from one side of the back of the auditorium to the other with a jet stream of smoke following it. The projectile slammed into the face of an elderly lady, knocking her unconscious. This 7-Up bottle was filled with an amber liquid, and a dirty rag clogged its neck.

It was a dangerous and smoldering Molotov cocktail!

There were shouts and even screams from the back of the movie theater as the low-grade flame smoldered and burned through the rag around the neck of the bottle. Any minute, it would explode.

A medium-sized man with brown hair who had seen Felix throwing the Molotov cocktail yelled, "What are you doing, you creep?!"

Felix lunged at him and started punching him. Tony and Nick also started hitting people that were around them, and promptly, a full-fledged melee erupted! The woman was being trampled on by the ruffians as well as being burned by the cocktail.

"Somebody stop those dirty ratfinks!"

"That thing's gonna go off in a minute!"

"Everybody out!"

"Let's get moving, everybody! Let's get moving! Everybody out of the theater!" People stood up and frantically began moving toward the lobby.

"Stay calm, everybody," yelled a burly man. "Don't panic. Keep cool everyone!"

Brad saw the short, stocky man with dark brown hair in front of him aiming a gun toward the stage. The stocky man pulled the trigger, and the bullet smashed into the skull of Brian Manning, ending his life instantly. He then aimed his gun toward Randy Miller, and Brad bravely grabbed him to try desperately to save more lives from being lost. His attempt worked. The gun fired some more bullets, but Ted Johnson's aim was off. The first bullet hit Randy in the upper right side of his chest, very close to his shoulder. Randy screamed in pain. He felt a sharp pain in his shoulder. Then he felt a horrible pain right in the middle of his chest—a very severe squeezing type of pain radiating up through his arms. He felt as if a truck had run over him. Another bullet hit George Newman in the arm while yet another smashed into the left leg of Bart Anderson.

Brad kept desperately wrestling against the stocky man and was successful in that he knocked him to the floor. Ted rose to his feet, and Eric Burns immediately grabbed a hold of Brad, brandished a sharp, glittering switchblade, and said in a low savage voice, "You move just one muscle, sucker, and you're a dead man!"

Brad prayed like he had never prayed before, and Eric heard it.

"You quit praying to that dirty imposter Jesus, you hear?! Renounce Jesus right now or I'll slit your throat!"

"I can't renounce Him! He is my mega-wonderful and lovely Savior who rose from the dead."

SLASH! The knife swathed a deep gash in the upper part of Brad's arm, and Eric prepared to finish him off, when he was startled and frightened by the sight of a huge man dressed in a black uniform holding a glittering and polished sword. *Where in blue blazes did that man come from?* He had to be more than eight feet tall and had a fierce countenance on his face. Eric dropped the switchblade in terror and ran toward the back entrance behind the stage. He rushed through the door and ran up the eight steps leading to the back driveway. He turned right and jumped into his blue ramshackle car parked at the side of the building. He turned the ignition key, revved the engine, and started driving toward the street.

Meanwhile, three strong men had muscled Ted Johnson to the floor, their heights being between five feet, eleven inches and six feet, four inches.

"All right, you perverted creep!" cried one of them. "That's the end of the line for you! The party's over!"

"Somebody needs to help the people on stage!" yelled Hal. "They're badly hurt!"

"Everybody out of the auditorium, *now!*"

"Call the ambulance!"

"Somebody call the cops! Don't let those stinking, no-good murderers get away!"

Pam and Brad headed toward the stage. Brad felt a burning pain in his upper arm, and he was beginning to feel weak. He was losing a lot of blood. The people who were unhurt in the band were helping the injured ones out through the back door. They carried the badly injured 'Jitterbug Josh' out unto the back alley where they laid him on the ground. Pam helped Brad up the eight steps where he staggered and sat down next to the hurt singing star.

"Is there anything I can do for you?" gasped Brad to Randy.

"Ohh!" groaned Randy. "Oohh! Ouch! Please do something for the pain!" he weakly gasped as he wept profusely.

Brad reached into his pocket and pulled out a bottle of Bayer Aspirin. He stumbled and weakly managed to put three of them into the mouth of the anguished pop star. He prayed fervently for wisdom, and a thought came to him. "Just relax, Josh! Take it easy now, everything's gonna be all right. God loves you very, very much. You are very special to Him. Just relax now! Breathe deeply, *deeply!* Take *deep* breaths!"

Even though it was tough for Randy, he forced himself to take deep breaths. This kept him from passing out.

"We need help over here!" yelled Pam. "We need tourniquets to stop the bleeding!"

Several people supplied coats, which they applied to the victims to staunch the bleeding of Randy Miller and Brad Applebaum. Ambulance and police sirens could be heard in the distance, getting closer and closer. Pam knelt down beside the terrorized singing star and prayed fervently and compassionately for him.

"Oh, Heavenly Father!" she cried out, tears running down her face. "Please show Yourself to this tormented man! Show Josh how much You love Him! Please comfort him through Your Holy Spirit. Please let him know about the surpassing love of Jesus on the cross for him that knows no limit! Pour Your soothing balm and oil of Your Holy Spirit on his fevered spirit." While Hal was pushing down tightly on Randy's chest with his makeshift tourniquet to try to dam up the blood flow from the gunshot wound, Pam gently and lovingly stroked his head and sang,

> *"'The love of God is greater far,*
> *Than tongue or pen can ever tell.*
> *It goes beyond the highest star,*
> *And reaches to the lowest hell.*
> *The guilty pair, bowed down with care,*
> *God gave His Son to win:*
> *His erring child He reconciled*
> *And pardoned from his sin.*

O love of God, how rich and pure!
How measureless and strong!
It shall forever more endure,
The saints and angels' song!'"[1]

Tears streamed down Randy Miller's face. He had never experienced anything like this in his whole life. The love flowing through that beautiful young woman was so comforting! Her loving hand on his face, her heartfelt prayer, the beautiful song! Her voice was sweet and musical, but it wasn't so much her musical talent that touched Randy Miller; it was something he just couldn't put his finger on. She was touching something deep inside him, which all of those out-of-the-body experiences just never had. She began to sing another song entitled, "Oh Love That Will Not Let Me Go!" At this point, Randy totally lost it and bawled like a little baby, taking deep and slow breaths.

Brad slipped two more aspirin tablets into the mouth of the singing star after which he lost consciousness. Pam, who had been running on the strength of the Lord and adrenaline, finally succumbed to the terror deeply submerged in her heart. She started crying out with convulsive sobbing and then went into shock.

More and more people were filling up that back alley. Presently, the ambulances arrived, and the injured people were speedily loaded into the vehicles. They would be quickly rushed to John Muir Hospital in Walnut Creek. For Randy Miller and Brad Applebaum, the situation was especially urgent.

"Out of the way, people!" cried the paramedics. "Give us some room here! Make way!"

"There's an old lady still inside the theater who's badly hurt!" shouted a bystander.

The front of the theater was filled with stunned and shaken concertgoers. Two fire trucks stopped at the movie house, and firemen rushed into the theater, which was now almost deserted. They found the old woman who was very close to death. She was unconscious, and the smoldering flame from the Molotov cocktail had burned her very severely. Miraculously, the projectile had not exploded. The firemen took care of the Molotov cocktail and started working on trying to save the life of that aged woman. Meanwhile, Ted Johnson was pinned to the ground by the three muscular men. Four policemen were soon there to take over and read the litany of constitutional rights to him. "You are under arrest because of suspicion of first-degree murder! You have the right to remain silent........."

****

263

FELIX McDowell rushed out of the lobby into the sidewalk right after the gunfire that killed Brian Manning. He ran toward his red sports car and jumped into it. He drove erratically, almost running into a group of people who had escaped from the theater. He turned left and started zooming at a reckless pace up Rheem Valley Road toward Orinda, his tires screaming, his vehicle swerving from one side of the two-lane highway to the other. Cars were forced to veer wildly just to escape a serious accident. There was one time when his wheels actually left the ground for a second because of his great speed. It was only two minutes before a cop spotted him and pulled him to the side of the road.

"All right, punk kid!" yelled the cop. "The joyride's all over! Let me see your license!"

"Get lost, you dirty copper! I didn't do nothing wrong!"

But the cop smelled the telltale odor from the Molotov cocktail and quickly slapped handcuffs on his wrist. Felix fought with all his might, yelled, and cussed at the officer, but it was of no avail. It would be off to jail for him.

****

TONY FITCH ran out of the building right after Felix did. Some people had seen his involvement in helping Felix with the diversionary explosion attempt. There were cries from some of the people who were outside. They accused him of being one of the terrorists. With that, Tony took off running as fast as he could, but he was not fast enough to be able to escape the prying crowd. He was too short, too fat, and out of shape. It wasn't very long before several athletic men were able to catch up with him and pin him to the ground. Tony looked up at them with his devious, shifty, and catlike eyes and protested, "Why are you guys picking on an innocent bystander like me?"

They answered, "We saw what you were doing! There are a whole lot of reliable witnesses—so fess up, you jerk!"

****

NICK WEEMS ran out of the lobby at the same time as Tony. He headed toward his shiny navy-blue Volkswagen, running very erratically. He reached his car but was having trouble finding his keys. He fumbled and fumbled with his hands, feeling around in his pockets, searching for those keys. He finally found them, lifted them out of his pocket—and promptly dropped them to the pavement! He cussed loudly and stooped down to pick them up. He put a key in the car door. It was the wrong one! He tried another. That was wrong, too! He tried a third that was the right one, but he just couldn't seem to force it into the keyhole. In frustration, he took the name of the Lord in vain and pounded the hood of the car with his fists with all his might.

"There's another one of those dirty hoodlums!" shouted someone, pointing straight at him. "Let's git' him!"

People started running toward him and roughhoused him to the ground.

"Leave me alone!" shouted Nick. "Let me go! I didn't do nothing, man! I've got my rights! I demand to see a lawyer! I'll sue you for every red cent you got!"

"Shut up, you little twerp! We know you were involved in this plot! We saw what you did!"

****

FRANCIS ZEEB ran out of the backstage door right after Eric did. He jumped into his light-green Chevrolet parked on the other side of the building from where Eric had parked. He gunned the motor and zoomed out of the alley. He headed toward the shopping center alley. He turned right on Rheem Valley Road, zoomed through a gas station at the corner of Rheem Valley Road, side-swiped a white Ford, and screeched to the right on Moraga Road. The guy who owned the car yelled, "You ding-a-ling dummy!" as he surveyed the dent in his car. Francis raced down Moraga Road at a dizzying speed. Police cars with their sirens blaring were closing in on him.

****

ERIC BURNS heard the sirens too. While Francis continued racing down Moraga Road, Eric turned right on Corliss Drive, his tires squealing in a very menacing way. He raced up the residential winding street that led sharply uphill for a while. Modern ranch-style homes were on both sides of the street. Many kids were out trick-or-treating. The road crested at an intersection and then went sharply downhill. No cops were following Eric at this time; they had stayed on Moraga Road in their pursuit of Francis Zeeb. Eric didn't realize that the road he was on was a dead-end street until he was about a hundred yards away from the end of it. He panicked, turned his car around very fast, and sideswiped a brown Cadillac, breaking the windows on that car and splattering the glass on the road. He almost hit a couple of trick-or-treaters who screamed in terror and barely got out of the way of the crazy driver in time. He sped back up the hill and turned left on Hardie Drive, barely avoiding a head-on collision with a car going the other way. This street sloped sharply downward to a busy road known as Moraga Way. Eric was very familiar with this road because of his former bus-driving job. He turned left on that road that still had a lot of traffic on it at this time of night. He had to slow down and flow with the traffic. A side street was coming up on the right called St. Andrews Drive. He turned on to it to avoid the traffic, and also because he knew there was a fire station ahead and on the right on Moraga Way; he wanted to stay as far away from it as he could. He went a block down St. Andrews Drive, turned left on Country Club Drive, raced a few blocks down that street, and then turned right on Canyon Road. This enabled him to miss the police roadblock that had been set up at the junction where Moraga Way ended and Moraga Road became Canyon Road. Francis was not so fortunate but drove right into the police trap. There was no way out. The police surrounded him and immediately arrested that communist criminal.

Eric zoomed up Canyon Road, a winding and scenic back road that zigzagged through many groves of redwood trees. He was traveling at about seventy miles an hour. His tires squealed in protest at a deafening volume, more than once, he narrowly missed crashing into an oncoming vehicle, and a half dozen times, his ramshackle car almost went off the road. A driver of a blue Toyota had to swerve wildly to avoid a head-on collision with the communist revolutionary and winded up crashing into a hillside, badly damaging the car. Eric zoomed past car after car on the curvy road, jumping over the line into the left lane of oncoming traffic.

Eric had a plan. He was going to drive straight to Scott William's apartment in Berkeley and kill him. "That useful idiot has double-crossed me!" he muttered to himself. "This is treason! I'm going to make his death a slow and painful one!"

He finally came to Skyline Boulevard and turned right on that winding road with its spectacular views of Berkeley, Oakland, and San Francisco. Houses were on both sides of this boulevard. He soon came to a fork in the road. A police blockade already blocked the road that forked left and was rapidly blocking the road that wound to the right. Eric swerved heavily to the right and off the boulevard, his tires screaming, his car fishtailing. He barely made it through the blockade. Several black-and-white squad cars took off in hot pursuit of the fleeing communist. The road continued to wind around with hard-to-negotiate and treacherous hairpin turns. He was getting higher and higher in altitude. There were no more houses up here. Soon, he approached Fish Ranch Road. The route to the right led down to highway 24 that went east to Orinda. To the left, the road led down to Berkeley. *Oh no, there was a roadblock here, too!* It was hopeless! Eric made a sharp U-turn and started zooming back the other way, barely missing ramming into the oncoming police cars. It was all over, finished, checkmate!

Eric, just run your car off that cliff there! Eric gasped in amazement; the voice was the sweetest voice he had ever heard. *It's hopeless! Why don't you end it all this instant? There, there! That's it! There you go! Just end your life right now!* Despair filled the heart of Eric Burns. He drove on for a moment, unsure of himself over which decision he would make. Would he turn himself in or end his life right now? Suddenly, as the cops looked on in astonishment and horror, Eric rammed the steering wheel of his car sharply to the right and ran his car straight over the chasm that yawned for a distance of 200 feet below the road. The blue car seemed to float in midair for a couple of seconds, and then it plummeted, turning over and over again. The vehicle was smashed to an unrecognizable deathtrap on some sharp jagged rocks sticking out of the embankment below.

As the car hit the ground and was crushed into a mishmash of sharp and twisted metal, Eric felt intense pain for a split fraction of a second—and then the pain abruptly stopped. However, the great load of depression and despair was still there. He looked around with shock. He was standing outside of the unrecognizable wreck that had been his car. He looked down at the many thousands of lights in the cities below that sparkled like myriads upon myriads of diamonds against the backdrop of the nighttime sky. Eric then looked back into the mutilated car. He saw a crushed body spewing forth a copious amount of blood, the face distorted with terror, the limbs of that torso mangled. *Now who in blue blazes could that guy be? I was the only one in that car.* Then all of a sudden, a revelation hit the brain of Eric Burns like a huge tsunami, and he screamed in amazement and terror. The mangled body he was looking at was *his own* body and he was separated from it. *But this just can't be! What is this? Am I having one of those weird nightmares we all experience from time to time? I know it can't be an LSD trip since I never dropped acid in my entire life.*

Less than thirty seconds had elapsed since the crash. That was all the time Eric had to muse over his situation because suddenly, there were four monsters standing before him. Two of them were about nine feet tall. The other two of them were the height of an average grownup man in America. All of these man-like creatures were wearing gaudy, loud-colored outfits and had capes on their heads. They had warty faces and pointed chins, and all four of them had the most exceedingly mean, cruel, and malevolent expressions on their faces imaginable. The terror Eric experienced at that moment was too horrible for words.

"Who are you guys?" asked Eric. "What are you doing here? Is this some Halloween joke or something?"

They all laughed hideously and gloated at him, their eyes full of the most unnerving malice and hate. They took turns speaking in low, gravelly, and ugly voices. One of them screamed out an unnerving hard rock song and danced in a very obscene manner.

"Aha, aha, aha, aha, you fool! We told you to end it all, and you listened to us! You committed suicide by driving your car right over that cliff! We got you, and we're going to drag you down to the realms of gross darkness and pain!"

"And you listened to us to abandon God and follow the path of atheism and communism! Haw, haw, haw! It worked, and we're going to throw you away forever!"

All four of them cursed and blasphemed God with the most horrid language. One of the tall apparitions was holding a heavy load of glittering chains, which all four of them began to wind around the spirit body of Eric

Burns. He screamed in abject horror, but it was of no avail. The being with the chains smacked Eric with great force on his spiritualized face. The pain would had made him faint if he had been in his earthly body. The chains were also cutting into his spirit body, bringing about intense torment. That tall apparition had on an outfit decorated with many triangles, squares, and circles in many Rubik Cube-like colors: blues, greens, whites, black, oranges, and reds. The beings grabbed the spirit body of Eric Burns and knocked him to the ground. Then they jerked him upright again. Then they threw him to the ground and dragged him along the rocky terrain. This they did numerous times as they cackled with their hideous and blood-curdling laughter. Eric screamed with all the strength he had; no Halloween nightmare had ever been in the same ballpark as this!

Finally, the leader of the four commanded, "Enough of this foolery! Let's get rid of this suicidal piece of garbage!"

"Yeah, yeah, yeah!" the others sing-songed in a hard rock musical type tone.

Eric could hear the background traffic in the distance as well as the anguished and grieved comments of the police officers floating down to him from about 200 feet above. The malignant beings dragged the terrorized Eric Burns to a gaping hole that appeared in the ground and threw him down into the yawning maelstrom. The lights and sounds from above disappeared as he fell at breakneck speed into the horrid vortex below. As he fell, the oppressive darkness and depression went from bad to worse. Down, down, down the tube he plummeted, getting more and more scared every moment. Eric was sure that things couldn't get any worse, but they did.

The abject terror, despondency, and hopelessness continued to increase with ever widening intensity, and the heavy chains were cutting into his spirit body, causing him unbearable agony. Darker and darker and darker it became—a darkness that was stifling and oppressive beyond description. The air was extremely hard to breathe down here, and Eric was feeling weaker and weaker every second. He noticed that he was stark naked. The freefall seemed like it would go on forever. Finally, he saw the faintest flickering light in the distance, getting closer and closer. The sides of the pit became illuminated just enough for him to see humongous snakes, spiders, rats, and other grotesque creatures hanging on the walls. Soon, Eric could hear the faraway sounds of the most terrible and hideous screams of torture that grew louder and louder every second. Oh, no! These horrific screams came from *human beings!* Finally, the source of the dim and flickering light became visible. A huge wall of raging fire loomed straight ahead of him, and he was rapidly rushing toward it. *It was the Ultimate Horror!!* As he plunged in, unbelievable pain surged through him.

******

"ON THE DOUBLE! Move, people, MOVE! Let's get these folks into Emergency right away! There's no time to spare!"

The ambulances had just arrived at John Muir Hospital in Walnut Creek on Ignacio Valley Road. They carried the patients Randy Miller, Brad Applebaum, George Newman, and Bart Anderson. One of the ambulances also carried the woman who had been badly hurt by being trampled on by the crowd as well as being burned by the smoldering Molotov cocktail. Her name was Helen Parker. She was very close to death. So were Randy Miller and Brad Applebaum. The doctors found out what type of blood these people had and ordered immediate blood transfusions. For Randy and Brad, the transfusions came barely in the nick of time. Only a few more minutes and they would have bled to death.

****

"MRS. MILLER?"

"Yes, who is it?"

"This is John Muir Hospital in Walnut Creek, and we're calling because there was a terrorist attack at the Jitterbug Josh concert tonight. A couple of people got killed, and there are several people who were injured."

Lila felt like *she* had been shot in the heart as she asked anxiously, "Randy Miller! Randy Miller! Is he all right?"

"Well, he is alive right now. He is one of the people who got hurt. Evidently, he was shot two times; once in the upper right-hand side of his chest, and once around the area of his heart."

"OH, NOOO!" wailed Lila. "NO, NO, *NOOO!*"

"Can you get over to the hospital right away?"

"Oh, yes! I'll be right over!"

She slammed down the phone that was in the kitchen of the three-story mansion and called out in a weeping voice, "Jack! Tommy! JACK! TOMMY! GET DOWN HERE QUICKLY! THIS IS AN EMERGENCY!"

"WHAT?" squealed the boys in apprehension and dismay.

"WE'RE GOING TO THE HOSPITAL RIGHT NOW! DADDY'S BEEN HURT!"

All three of them clambered into the Lamborghini, and Lila started driving to the hospital as fast as she could, tears flowing down her face as well as the faces of the two boys.

****

BRAD WOKE UP to find himself in a hospital room with the upper part of his arm all bandaged up. Standing beside him was the whole Applebaum family, their faces a tableau of concern mixed with some relief. He was in

269

quite a bit of pain from the knife wound and still groggy from the pain medication and passing out.

"Oh, Brad, my son, my son!" exclaimed Harriet. "I'm so thankful you're alive and that you are going to make it!" She kissed him lovingly on his cheeks and said, "Oh, my precious, precious beloved son! I love you so much! I'm thankful we didn't lose you! You don't know how close to death you came!"

"Well, what do you say, kid?" asked Sid. "I'm so glad you made it through! You are one heck of a lucky person! You know that, don't you?"

"Yeah, Dad," said Brad with a weak smile on his face. "I praise the Lord that His protection was on me the whole time."

"Anything you say, son," said Sid.

Brad's sisters, Kimberly and Lisa, were there and filled him in on everything that was going on in their lives: school, the latest prom, Lisa's slumber party of last weekend. Presently, Pam came into the room and made a beeline for her wounded beau.

"Oh Brad, Brad!" she exclaimed, kissing him on his cheeks. "I'm so thankful that you're going to be all right! Oh, thank You, beautiful, beautiful Jesus!"

"Anything you say, kid," said Sid.

"Oh, Mr. and Mrs. Applebaum!" said Pam. "You don't know what a real hero Brad was at that concert tonight! He risked his own life trying to save the members of the Universal Mindset from being killed by those no-good terrorists, and he might have indeed been successful in his attempt."

"Does anybody know how Randy Miller is doing?" asked Brad.

"Well, he was hurt pretty bad," responded Pam. "He was shot in the upper chest and evidently, a bullet must have grazed his heart. You remember how he had tremendous chest pains similar to those a person would experience who was having a heart attack?"

"Yeah, I gave him two more Bayer Aspirin tablets right before I passed out. He had a total of five tablets that I gave him."

"Yeah, we're really going to have to pray for him, big-time," said Pam.

"Hey, Pam. Do you have any idea how the other band members fared?" asked Brad.

"Well, I know that Brian Manning, one of the singers, is dead. That first bullet that fat creep shot off went right through his skull and ended his life immediately. As far as I know, though, most of the other band members are going to be okay."

"And what about the theater, Pam?" asked Brad. "Did it burn to the ground?"

"Well, strangely, it didn't. The old lady that the cocktail hit was badly hurt, but for some uncanny reason, the cocktail didn't explode. Brad, I really believe it was the power of our prayers that saved a lot of lives. I'm so proud of you and I love you so much!"

"And your dad and I are so proud of you, too!" echoed Harriet. "You are quite a guy! We have a great family, and we are both very proud of all three of our children."

"Oh, Mr. and Mrs. Applebaum!" said Pam. "It was incredible! Brad was praying and wrestling against that fat gunman. And then that redheaded jerk grabbed him and threatened to kill him if he wouldn't renounce Jesus. But Brad was firm in his confession of Jesus. And he was going to do anything it would take to try to save lives, even if he had to die in the process! And then that creep plunged that switchblade into him. I was sure, then, that Brad was a goner, but then for some inexplicable reason, that man with the knife dropped the weapon and ran toward the back exit."

"There was this huge and muscular man right next to us that appeared out of nowhere," explained Brad. "He had to be between eight and nine feet tall. He was wearing a black uniform with golden buttons on it and had a glistening sword in his right hand. He had a kindly, yet stern face, and he had the most piercing eyes that I've ever seen on anybody. The redhead got real scared and hightailed it out of there as fast as he could. The next moment, that huge dude was nowhere to be found. He looked like a professional basketball player or something."

Pam's eyes grew big with wonder as she said, "Why, there was no such person like that there! There was just you, the fat crook, and the carrot-top reprobate!" Then a thought suddenly hit her like a ton of bricks and she exclaimed, "WELL, HALLELUJAH AND GLORY TO GOD! PRAISE YOU, MEGA-LOVELY JESUS! That had to be a guardian angel that you saw, Brad!"

****

"HELLO, MRS. MILLER. My name is Doctor Martin Perez."

This doctor had a kindly face that reflected a great amount of wisdom, brown eyes, and a shock of white hair. His grandparents on both sides had come from Mexico, and he had been born in Calexico, very close to the Mexican border in the very southern part of California.

"So, please tell me, Doc!" exclaimed Lila anxiously. "What's the prognosis for my husband? Is there any hope for him?"

"Well, here's the story," said the doctor with a somber look on his face. "There was only one bullet that hit your husband. The doctors removed it from the upper part of his chest. Your husband was very, very lucky that he didn't die on the way to the hospital. He had lost a whole lot of blood. In and of itself, the gunshot wound, once we removed the bullet and gave him the blood transfusion, was not a life-threatening thing. However, the doctors found that Randy has had a massive heart attack tonight. Your husband is a very young man for something like this to happen to, and we all thought at

271

first that a bullet had entered his heart. But when we checked him out thoroughly at triage, there was no bullet to be found."

Lila gasped with unbelief and dismay. "You're sure, Doc, that it was a heart attack?"

"Yes, Mrs. Miller, we're absolutely sure. Let me ask you a question if I may, and I hope you won't get mad at me for asking this, but—has your husband been taking any drugs?"

Lila's face turned white as a ghost as she responded at barely a whisper, "Yes!"

"What kind of drugs?"

"Uppers and downers."

"You mean amphetamines and barbiturates?"

"Yes." Then in a defensive voice, she said, "My husband is a very busy man. He felt like he needed something to keep him on top in his fast-moving career! So, is there any hope?"

"Well," said Doctor Martin, tentatively, "I don't know yet. We're going to have to wait and see. Heart attack patients either get better or they get worse and die. There's no middle ground. Your husband's heart attack was a massive one. It's a good thing he didn't pass out before we got him here. If he had, he would have already been dead. Even if he pulls through, he's going to have to drastically change his lifestyle. No more uppers or downers. He'll have to change his diet radically—and he'll have to avoid the huge amount of stress he's been under. Evidently, it was the trauma of the gunshot wound that set off the heart attack. What I advise you to do is to pray that he gets better."

"Doctor Perez, may we see him?"

"Yes, you can go in and see him for five minutes. He's in ICU, and only immediate family members are allowed to see him. His condition is serious, and on top of that, there is the matter of the terrorist attack that brought him here in the first place. The cops are not absolutely sure they've apprehended all of the terrorists and are not taking any chances. Come along now."

Doctor Martin Perez led Lila, Jack, and Tommy down the hallway to the Intensive Care Unit. Small cubicles all around this area housed the various seriously sick or injured patients. The doctor led them to a side cubicle where 'Jitterbug Josh' was lying in a bed. He was hooked up to a heart monitor that looked like a TV screen and had squiggly lines running across it, signifying that his heart was still functioning and that he was still alive. There was a constant rhythm of *beep, beep, beep* sounding on and off from the machine signifying that he was still kicking. An oxygen tube was stuck up his nose, running into the side of the wall, while an intravenous feeding tube provided needed nutrients to the famous singing star.

Lila approached the wan form of her husband and said, "Hello dear! I've brought your two sons to visit you."

"Hello," responded Randy, weakly.

"How are you feeling, honey?"

"It hurts!" groaned Randy. "Ow! It hurts so bad!"

"I know, dear!" said Lila, consolingly. "I know it hurts. I'm so sorry this had to happen!"

The talk was subdued in that room as Lila filled Randy in about how things were going at home, and the two boys told him about school and football. Pretty soon, their five minutes were up. Doctor Perez informed them that they would be able to visit the patient for five minutes out of each hour. The Miller family would be staying at the hospital all night long.

****

PAM, DEBBIE, CRISTY, LAURA, AND HAL were all standing outside of the hospital that night. Pam had a very serious look on her face, and she asked all the other prayer warriors to huddle in very close.

"Here's the scoop," she said. "I want everybody to listen up. I feel a very, very heavy burden for Jitterbug Josh. I have no explanation why I feel this burden. I'm not into either rock star worship or famous pop musicians; I generally could care less about them. But—I just feel the Lord impressing me big-time that we need to pray for this guy—and I mean *deep, deep* intercession. The latest word about Jitterbug Josh is that he's suffered a big-time heart attack and his life is hanging in the balance. I feel, first of all, that the five of us need to get together tonight for corporate prayer for the whole night. Are you all with me?"

"Yes."

"Sure thing."

"Whatever."

"The second thing," continued Pam, "is that we need to alert as many people as possible to pray for that man. We need to get a prayer chain going. I'm sure thankful that Pastor Norris's day off is Wednesday and not Friday. I intend to call him up first thing tomorrow morning and solicit his prayers and also urge him to get as many people praying for him as possible. I'm also going to try to get a hold of Pastor David Maxwell at Berkeley Tabernacle Fellowship tomorrow. I praise the Lord Jesus Christ that Brad is going to be okay, but obviously, he will not be able to join us. He is out of commission tonight because of his stab wound. However, we owe a whole lot to him for his prayer support and heroism tonight. I am so proud of Brad Applebaum! Aren't you?"

There was a universal round of assents from the other young adults; they were also proud of Brad and his courageous stand for the Lord tonight. All five of them started heading toward Pam's apartment for the all-night prayer meeting.

****

BEFORE THE HALLOWEEN NIGHT WAS OVER, the whole nation was made aware of the terrorist attack at the movie theater in Moraga, the injury and death of several people, and the heart attack and attempted assassination of 'Jitterbug Josh.' It would be a little later before the whole country was made aware of the spectacular suicide of the suspected communist terrorist, Eric Burns.

During that whole night and throughout Friday, multitudes flocked to John Muir Hospital to try to see their famous singing idol but were denied entrance to the cubicle of 'Jitterbug Josh' because of the tight restrictions limiting the visitors to immediate family members only as well as one clergyman. They were very disappointed and upset about that and left the hospital fuming. The next day, Pam was able to reach Pastor Jeremy Norris on the phone, and he promised to join in the prayers for 'Jitterbug Josh.' He also started a prayer chain going at Glad Tidings International Fellowship. Other groups of people across the country from all denominations also started praying for the music icon on that All Saints Day. From many a Catholic church could be heard the words from the Rosary, "Hail Mary, full of grace, blessed art thou and the fruit of thy womb, Jesus. Holy Mary, Mother of God, pray for us sinners now and at the hour of our death." From Protestant churches, more spontaneous prayers for the salvation of the music star burst forth. Meanwhile, Yappy Yellowfield announced the injury and heart attack of 'Jitterbug Josh' with a great deal of insensitivity and sarcastic humor.

****

EARLY ON FRIDAY MORNING, Mike and Donna Applebaum came to the hospital to try to comfort Lila who was dog-tired and full of grief. She was in no state of mind to be able to drive herself and the boys home, so Donna offered to drive them back to Orinda in Lila's car and then take a cab home. She willingly agreed, and when they got back to the Sleepy Hollow mansion, she didn't even go upstairs to her room. She walked into the green living room, plopped down onto the soft red sofa, and instantly fell into a fitful sleep.

It was a couple of hours later when the jangling sound of the phone brought her wide-awake. She rose unsteadily to her feet and trotted nervously to the phone.

"Hello."

"Hello, is this Mrs. Miller?"

"Yes, it is."

"Mrs. Miller, you've better get to the hospital fast. Your husband is getting worse. A few minutes ago, his heart monitor stopped, and we almost lost him. We were able to get it going again, but he is in bad shape. It looks like only a matter of hours before the end comes."

"Um, um, um, hours?"

"Yes, Mrs. Miller. I'm sorry."

Lila hung up the phone, her head spinning, tears running down her face. This couldn't be happening! How could it be that something, which had seemed to start out so good, had turned into this nightmare? She got dizzy and felt like she was going to faint at any minute. Suddenly, she started crying out and cursing God in her state of hopelessness and grief.

"GOD, WHY?! WHY ARE YOU DOING THIS TO ME?! WHAT HAVE I DONE TO DESERVE THIS?! ARE YOU SOME KIND OF IDIOT? YOUR HAND HAS BEEN HEAVY ON ME AND YOU HAVE CAUSED THIS TERRIBLE DISASTER IN MY LIFE!!" She ranted and raved against the Lord with some more blasphemies—

Lila, Lila! Why are you blaspheming My name? It is hard for you to kick against the goads!

The voice that spoke these words was exceedingly compassionate and loving.

Lila stopped and looked around the room with a start. Nobody was there! She was sure she was going crazy with grief and said, "WH-WH-WHAT?"

It is I who you have blasphemed. Peace, be still! I'm not the author of these calamities. I love you, Lila! I desire the very best for you and your family.

"Is th-that r-r-really You, God?"

Yes, Lila.

"What do You want me to do, Lord?"

Call out on My name! Seek My face and repent! I have the answer to all your needs.

Lila fell to her knees sobbing and cried out, "I'm sorry, Lord! Please forgive me! Please help me! I'm at the end of my rope, and I need You to show me what to do!"

Lila had grown up with practically no knowledge of God whatsoever. The God that Pastor Kevin Harmon preached from the pulpit of United Church of the Valley was a very vague and faraway God who was never really involved in the personal lives of people. Her parents had taught her nothing about God or the Bible. The only real input she had ever gotten about the Lord was from her strange grandmother in Newport News, Virginia, whom she had seen only a couple of times when she was a young girl.

Wait a minute! Grandma Brenda! Maybe she was the answer to this whole hopeless mess! She had not kept in contact with her grandma during her adult years because her parents had been estranged from Grandma Brenda and had discouraged Lila from keeping in contact with her because of her 'weird' religious views. She had heard that her grandmother spent a lot of time in prayer. She also remembered the stories of her grandma preaching in many venues throughout the state of Virginia some years ago when she was a younger woman. This was certainly odd since almost every other preacher whom she had heard about was a man—well there was the controversial Kathryn Kuhlman of whom Lila knew practically nothing about. The most unbelievable stories about Grandma Brenda were the anecdotes about people who had experienced miraculous healings through her ministry. There had even been reports of people being raised from the dead. Lila had always shrugged off those stories out of hand as being a bunch of hooey, but now, she was desperate. She was ready to try anything. She started heading back toward the phone and the phonebook. She was fortunate in that she had kept the address and telephone number of Grandma Brenda Gardiner in her address book. She found the number, dialed, and prayed desperately and fervently that Grandma Brenda would answer the phone. She did.

After two rings, a kindly and elderly lady's voice came over the receiver saying, "Hello!"

"Hello! Is this Grandma Brenda?"

"Yes, it is. Your voice kinda' sounds familiar. Do I know you?"

"Yes. I'm your granddaughter Lila that you've not seen since I was a kid, and I need your help desperately. I don't know if you can do anything, but I think you're my only hope. My husband, Randy, is dying of a massive heart attack."

"Oh, my goodness! How did it happen?"

Lila told the whole sad story of the last year including the terrorist attack of last night.

"I'm so sorry!" exclaimed the compassionate grandma, bursting into tears. Lila sensed the genuine love of her grandma as the two of them cried together for a few moments.

Finally, Grandma Brenda said, "I had no idea! You know, I don't watch television or pay attention to the news. I have been praying for you and your family for years. Is there any way I can help you out, my precious child?"

"Yes, Grandma. Is there any way I can bring you out here to California to come into the intensive care unit at John Muir Hospital to pray for my husband? They're only letting immediate family members and one clergyman in, and I need a big-time miracle. I just can't let my husband die like this! He's too young! I know it's a long shot, but I want to bring you out here. I don't care if I have to spend a million bucks! I've heard stories about you healing people and even raising them from the dead."

"Lila, my darling grandchild. Grandma Brenda cannot heal anybody or raise them from the dead, but we have a mighty God who can. And yes, I'd be more than happy to come out to the west coast and pray for Randy. And let me encourage you with something: it's *never* too late for God to act on our behalf. Our God is greater than any problem that we'll ever have to face. Remember: Lazarus was dead for *four days* before Jesus brought him back to life."

"Okay then, Grandma. I'm going to bring you out here on the very first flight I can get you on, and price is absolutely no object."

They spent the next few minutes organizing all the details of how to bring Grandma Brenda out to the San Francisco Bay Area. After they hung up, Lila called the Oakland Airport and got a reservation for a flight from Norfolk, Virginia to Oakland in order to bring Grandma Brenda out to California. She was able to book a seat on Delta Airlines on a flight going out of Norfolk at 4:30 P. M., Eastern Standard Time and landing in Oakland International Airport at 6:40 P. M., Pacific Standard Time.

Lila's phone conversation with her grandma greatly encouraged her. Grandma Brenda was so upbeat! Now, at least, Lila had a little hope that had entered into her heart, even if it was only a tiny ray.

****

GRANDMA BRENDA started praying right away after she hung up the phone. She spent some time praying for Randy, sometimes in English, and sometimes in tongues. She would have little time to pack; she would only be packing the bare necessities. She got the call from the airport to inform her about the time her flight would be leaving Norfolk for Oakland and what time she needed to be at the airport. She wouldn't have much time to get there, and to top it off, she was an elderly lady in her eighties. She picked up her small carry-on bag and her purse, hobbled outside the door of her apartment, shut the front door, and headed toward her car.

She would do the best she could to get to the airport on time. She searched in her purse for her keys—and couldn't find them! Surely, they must be in her pockets. She felt around in her pockets but couldn't find them! "Oh, dear!" she mumbled to herself. "Those keys gotta' be around somewhere!" She fumbled around in her pockets and purse once again, and also searched inside her carry-on bag. No keys! This was serious stuff because she was under a lot of time pressure.

Grandma Brenda lived in a very nice senior village. Her house had six rooms in it. The senior village was a gated community, featuring such things as a restaurant, a multi-purpose community center, an eighteen-hole golf course, a swimming pool, and a tennis court. Grandma Brenda hobbled toward the home of a neighbor she knew and prayed that someone would be home. Fortunately, an elderly gentleman answered the door.

"What can I do for you, Brenda?"

"I need your help real quick, Vick. My granddaughter's husband is dying, and I'm fixing to go see him. I got a plane to catch, and I think I left my car keys inside my house. Could I please use your phone to call security so that they can come and open up my house? I'm in a hurry!"

"Sure, Brenda! The phone's right over there in the kitchen."

Grandma Brenda took hold of the phone and dialed the number of Security. In short order, the security man was there to open up her home with the security keys. She thanked him and started looking through the house, but she was not able to find the keys. She looked and looked. Twenty minutes went by, and she was getting more and more worried. Finally, in desperation, she cried out, "JESUS! Please help me find those keys! You said in Your Word that I have the mind of Christ!" She looked throughout the house a little more. Then suddenly, a thought came into her brain. It was the Scripture in the book of Revelation talking about the fact that Jesus was dead and is now alive forever and has the keys of death and hell. Her Bible study commentary on the book of Revelation on top of her piano! *But I've already looked all around the living room, including the top of that keyboard!* However, that Scripture just wouldn't go away. She finally decided to look in her living room just one more time. There was her Revelation commentary book sitting right on top of the piano, but no keys. She let out a little yelp and decided to pick the book off that piano of eighty-eight black-and-white keys and look under it, even though she was sure the keys would not be there. She stooped over the top of the piano, picked the book up—and *voila!* There were her keys! They were hidden all this time under the commentary.

"Thank You, Jesus!" she exclaimed as she walked slowly toward her blue Toyota, clambered in, and started the engine. This was not the end of her trials and tribulations, though, as she missed a turn on the way to the airport, got a little bit lost, and had to do some backtracking. When she finally arrived at the airport, it was 4:25 P. M. She parked her car and headed as fast as her aged body would let her toward the Delta ticket counter. She sensed in her spirit that she had missed the plane and she was right. As she was standing with dismay at the ticket counter, she asked the ticket agent what her options were.

"Well, Mrs. Gardiner, the next flight we can get you on leaves this airport at 11:15 tonight, and will get you into Oakland International at 1:35 A. M."

"There isn't any way you can get me on an earlier flight? My granddaughter's husband is dying, and I need to be there as fast as I can!"

"Nope! This is the best we can do."

Grandma Brenda knew that the situation was more desperate than ever. Not being able to find her keys and getting lost on the way to the airport was going to get her to the hospital to pray for 'Jitterbug Josh' more than seven hours later than if she had made that 4:30 flight. By the time she got there, it might very well be too late! Grandma Brenda prayed like she had never prayed before.

****

AFTER LILA HAD TALKED TO GRANDMA BRENDA and made arrangements to fly her out to the west coast to come and see her dying husband, she hopped into her car for the drive back to John Muir Hospital. She turned on the car radio that was set to FM station KROK. The hit song, "The Evil Eye," was playing. After that rock song finished, the infamous radio DJ came on the air to do his usual spiel of sarcastic humor and corny jokes.

"Hello there, all you hipsters, LSD tripsters, alcohol sipsters, and 'The Twist' flipsters! This is Happy Yappy Yellowfield coming to you on FM radio station K. R. O. K., K-ROK, the radio station that brings you all the greatest hits in the whole world. That piece was called 'The Evil Eye,' and we've had a number of evil eyes shot between Jitterbug Josh and Eric Burns in the last few months! It was last April when the dying pop star knocked Eric Burns out and spent a night in jail. And then last night, we had a really hot time in good ol' Moraga. It started at the Jitterbug Josh charity concert when some guy threw a 'hot' 7-Up bottle across the back of the theater while there were seven up on stage. (Birdcalls.) Well, all you rambling rock-and-rollers, there ain't gonna be seven up on that stage no more! (Tweet, tweet, tweet.) The 7-Up bottle was a Molotov cocktail that hit a woman in the back of the theater. I don't like my cocktails hot like that—I like them cool and on the rock-and-rollers! How do you like that cool joke?

"Anyway, shots were fired onto the stage, and the concert turned out to be a befuddle muddle of a puddle of bloodle. (Wild birdcalls.) Singer Brian Manning was killed immediately, and three of the other musicians were hurt. The Universal Mindset just hasn't had any good luck in the last two years. A year ago, their lead vocalist and guitar player, Herb Taylor, got cancer, and now their new famous lead guitar player and singer, Jitterbug Josh, is surely going to die from his massive heart attack he just had. (Tweet, tweet, tweet.) Tough luck, Josh! May you rest in peace!"

Lila slammed her right fist on the dashboard furiously and yelled, "YOU JABBERING JACKASS OF A JERK!! WHY DON'T YOU JUST SHUT UP AND GET OFF YOUR ANILE IDIOTSTICK RADIO STATION FOR GOOD?!"

Suddenly, an oncoming car came by as she made a turn, and Lila barely missed having a head-on collision. She pulled to the side of the road for a couple of moments as a fresh paroxysm of weeping overtook her. Eventually, she started on her way again. How she ever made it to the hospital in one piece she would never know, as she was halfway in shock. She was also fearful as she drove there that her husband might had already cashed in his chips.

When she arrived at John Muir, she made a beeline for the ICU area and met Doctor Perez there.

"How is he?" she asked the doctor.

"Well, he's still hanging right in there, but barely. As you heard, he had a very, very close shave today, and it looks very dim."

"So what's the story here, Doc?"

"Well, it's like this, Mrs. Miller. Your husband has had what is known as an acute inferior myocardial infarction. What this means is that the main artery leading from the back of the heart muscle has had an infarction."

"And what's an infarction?"

"The best way that I could simplify it for you is to make you think of what happens when one of your car tires has a blowout. This is what has happened to that main artery. Because of this, the blood flow to the heart has stopped, and the heart muscle has started to form scar tissue. What we've been doing is giving your husband stimulants to keep the remaining part of his heart beating and to keep the blood flowing. We're doing everything we can to keep him alive for as long as possible."

They walked into the Intensive Care Unit cubicle where Randy Miller was lying, still hooked up to all the life-saving machines and tubes. He looked much paler than he had last night. It was clear that hope was indeed dim.

"Hi, honey," said Lila.

"Hi," said Randy, very weakly.

"How are you holding out?"

Randy groaned weakly and responded, "I feel terrible!"

"I know, honey! I know! Just hang in there."

"When they gave me that shot of adrenaline to stop me from fibrillating, it hurt like hell. The pain was so bad that I was sure I was going to die. Then they gave me morphine to help the pain, but that made me go crazy. I saw these weird hallucinations. I saw this whole army of phonographs marching around the room with these gaudy-colored records on them. Some of the records and turntables were round while others were triangular in shape. I don't think I ever want another shot of morphine in my whole life."

"I know, dear! It's real hard!"

At that moment, one of the nurses walked in and said, "Mr. Miller, there's another visitor who would like to see you. Would it be okay with you if I let him come in?"

"Who is it?" asked Randy.

"It's a clergyman named Pastor Jeremy Norris. He was contacted by some girl named Pam Jackson. He would like to come in and pray for you. Would that be okay?"

"Yes, by all means!" exclaimed Lila.

Randy nodded his head with all the vigor his weak body could muster up. He well remembered the encounter with that lovely praying girl outside the theater.

Immediately, a young robust man walked into the cubicle. He had a very friendly grin on his face and was dressed semi-casually in navy-blue slacks with a bright aqua shirt. Randy had never seen a pastor like this in his whole life. This guy had an attractive glow about him.

"Well, hello there!" he said. "God bless you, Randy! My name is Pastor Jeremy Norris from Glad Tidings International Fellowship in Concord, and I would like to pray for you for a moment if I may."

"Yes, Pastor," said Randy, weakly, "I need prayer a whole lot."

The pastor laid his hand gently on the forehead of the dying patient and prayed, "Dear Heavenly Father. Thank You that nothing is impossible with You. You still do miracles and even raise people from the dead today. Lord, we are all sinners. But You loved the world so much that You sent Your beautiful Son, Jesus Christ into the world to die and take the punishment for everybody, including Randy, so that by believing on Him, he would not have to perish in a fiery hell forever, but have everlasting life in a perfect body; in a world without death, sickness, war, depression, crying, or pain. Father, Randy is very precious and special in Your sight. Lord, I know that with all the fame and fortune he has had, being dubbed as 'Jitterbug Josh' over this last year, he has never been shown what the real love that You have for him really is. Please reveal Your love to him. Father, he has committed great sins—things like getting involved in the occult as well as many other sins. But Lord, thank You so much that Your grace and mercy is infinite. Your sure Word has promised that 'Him that cometh to Me, I will in no wise cast out.'

"And Father. Your Son said 'I am the Resurrection and the Life. He that believeth on Me, though he were dead, yet shall he live.' Father, You have not changed nor will You ever. I'm asking You to do a miracle here. I thank You that all things are possible with You! You said if we asked anything in the name of Jesus, You would grant us our request. So, I'm holding You to Your Word. Holy Spirit, raise Randy Miller up to be a testimony to Your saving power. I thank You that You will. In the beautiful name of Jesus, amen and amen!"

"Okay," said the nurse. "Your time is up for now."

Lila and the pastor left the cubicle. Lila would be able to return and see her husband in about another hour or so. The positive, upbeat prayer of this pastor really gave her spirits a lift and gave her a bit of hope that maybe, just maybe, God would pull off a miracle and bring her husband back to health. The way this wonderful pastor carried himself was in stark contrast to that rude, insensitive, and sarcastic DJ, Yappy Yellowfield. She made a mental note that she was going to sue that slanderous man.

Randy felt like a thirsty man who had just been given a very refreshing and cold cup of water in the Sahara Desert. The same love that had permeated from that girl back there at the theater had also flowed through Pastor Norris. He began to muse about some things; was there really a place where a person wouldn't ever have to suffer pain again? Who was this Jesus, anyway, and how did he figure into the picture? Was there possibly a place called hell? In all the adulation Randy had gotten as a famous star, he had never felt love like he had from that praying girl or that praying pastor. Neither had he felt any love at all from his spiritualized dad when he had experienced his out-of-the-body trips. Randy really began to hope that somehow, reincarnation wasn't true after all.

Lila was pacing the floor in the lobby when an intern came to her and announced that she had a phone call. She rose up anxiously, and the intern led her to the phone.

"Hello?"

"Hello, Lila dear. This is Grandma Brenda."

"What's up, Grandma?"

"I'm afraid I have some bad news for you. I missed my flight, and the next one I can get on is at 11:15 tonight. It's going to get into Oakland at 1:35 tonight." *Oh, no! This was indeed bad news as time was of the essence!*

"Well, please don't cancel! I need you here, Grandma. We're going for broke!"

"Okay, Lila, I'm still gonna come—and I'm fixing to pray for your husband all the way to California. And Lila—don't lose hope! I know in my spirit that the Lord is fixing to do an awesome miracle that will bring many people into eternal life!"

****

AT 11:00 ON FRIDAY NIGHT, Sid, Harriet, Kimberly, and Lisa returned home after a strenuous day of visiting Brad. Everyone was bone-tired, and the two girls went straight to bed. Sid and Harriet spent a few moments rehashing the traumatic events of the last twenty-four hours.

"Honey," said Harriet. "We were sure lucky that we didn't lose our boy."

"Yeah. He coulda' been killed."

"Last night was a terrible night, but I'm just so thankful that we have our son back."

Tears flowed down the face of Harriet as Sid drew her close in a loving embrace, saying, "Oh, sweetie pie! I love you so much!"

"And vice versa, dear! The longer we're together, the more I appreciate you!"

They spent several moments hugging and kissing each other.

****

IT WAS 1:00 A. M. Lila was sitting outside the ICU area in a waiting area. Every hour, she had gone into Randy's cubicle for a couple of minutes to see her husband. He was still alive, but slowly fading. Suddenly, several doctors came running toward one of the cubicles.

"THE PATIENT'S HEART HAS STOPPED!" one of them exclaimed to the other.

Great terror went through the spine of Lila Miller. Was it her husband? No, thank God! The doctors were heading toward another cubicle. A few minutes later, one of the doctors walked slowly and somberly to a family consisting of an elderly man, a middle-aged couple, and three teenagers. He stood there for a moment before he finally broke the bad news that they all knew was coming.

"I'm sorry! Helen is gone! We tried everything we could to save her, but the injuries she received at the Rheem Valley Theater were just too serious."

Loud weeping broke out among the family members. They spent some time hugging each other.

Finally, the middle-aged man spoke.

"Well, anyway. Helen is happy now. No more pain from that terrible arthritis she suffered from during the last fifteen years of her life."

"Yes," agreed the wife. "She's at home with the Lord now."

"How many years was she in church again, Dad?" asked one of the teenage boys.

"About fifty-five years, son. She committed her life to the Lord when she was just a little child. She sang in the choir for forty years, and also was that wonderful Sunday school teacher for thirty of those years."

"What church did she go to?" asked Lila.

"Cornerstone Community Church in Pinole," replied the middle-aged dad. "We're all members there. It's a fundamentalist, Bible-believing church. We love it."

"Helen Parker, my mom, is the person who just died," said the middle-aged woman, tears still running down her face. "She was the most godly person that I ever knew. She was kind, generous, gracious, a faithful and hard worker, and a very able Bible teacher. She had a way of relating to children, and they loved her. She knew how to sew and cook real good and did a lot of community work. She was part of a corporate prayer group for several years and witnessed to a lot of people about Christ."

"I'm really sorry for your loss," said Lila, sadly. "My condolences to you."

"Well anyway, the Lord took her home," said the middle-aged man.

****

ABOUT A HALF HOUR LATER, Lila got another telephone call. She had enlisted Mike and Donna Applebaum to go pick up Grandma Brenda at Oakland International Airport. The phone call brought more bad news. Brenda's plane, Delta flight 774, was going to be more than an hour late in its arrival at the Oakland airport. Lila began to pray like she had never prayed before.

****

IT WAS ACTUALLY TEN TO FOUR in the morning when Delta flight 774 touched down on the Oakland runway. The plane took about ten minutes taxiing before it could unload its passengers at the deplaning gate. Grandma Brenda walked slowly off the plane and started the long trek toward the baggage claim area where hopefully, she would meet the couple who would be giving her a ride to Walnut Creek and the hospital. She was fortunate that they did find each other. The three of them headed straight for the Applebaum's car and headed for John Muir Hospital as fast as they could. There was no time to lose; any minute now and 'Jitterbug Josh' might be dead.

By the time they arrived at the hospital, the clock on the wall read twelve minutes to five. As they started to walk toward Randy's cubicle, a nurse accosted them.

"Who are you?" she asked.

"This is Brenda Gardiner, the grandmother of the wife of Randy Miller."

"She can't come in here. Only immediate family members are allowed to see that patient at this time."

"Well, *I'm* part of the immediate family," declared Grandma Brenda, militantly, "and I'm fixing to come in here whether you like it or not! My grandson in-law needs prayer."

"Well, you can't see the patient! He's very close to death."

The voice of Doctor Martin Perez floated out from the cubicle saying, "Ah, come on! Let her come in!"

"Um, uh—well, okay!"

Grandma Brenda hobbled slowly into Randy Miller's cubicle. As she entered the room, she could literally feel a spirit of death there. Randy was in a coma, and his face was sheet-white. She wasted no time in starting to intercede for him. The other people who were in the room could sense a strong Presence that flowed into the cubicle as the aged prayer warrior entered.

She prayed, "Dear Heavenly Father. You sent Your Son into the world not to condemn it, but to save it. All of us have sinned and fall short of the glory of God, but You sent Jesus into the world to shed His Blood to cleanse us of our sins and that we might have forgiveness of sins freely. Please show Randy Your unfathomable love—and please raise him up. You raised up several people from the dead in Bible days, and I've seen You resurrect several people from the dead myself."

She continued praying along these lines for several minutes, sometimes in English, and sometimes in a foreign language she had never learned. There was power in her prayer, there was an anointing of the Holy Spirit in her prayer, and there was an almost tangible sense of faith in her prayer that everybody could feel. Life and death were in a mighty struggle. Suddenly, Randy mouthed some unintelligible words, which no one in the room could understand. Right after that, the lines on the monitor went flat, and the steady beeping turned into a sustained and harsh buzzing noise, signifying that Randy Miller had clinically died. The doctors rushed into the room to revive him. They spent several minutes at that, but they were having no results. Grandma Brenda kept right on praying while Lila wept.

"Oh, my dear husband Randy! I'm so sorry. I never wanted this to happen to you, but only wanted the best for you! (Sob.) Please forgive me for all those mean things I've said to you in the last year. I love you, Randy Miller!"

The clock read 5:10 A. M., Saturday morning.

****

284

THE WORD QUICKLY SPREAD that 'Jitterbug Josh' had just died. Early risers on Saturday morning heard the news on radio stations like KCBS and KGO. What they also heard was that a far less known man, the infamous murderer and rapist Darryl Temple, had just passed away due to his liver cancer. Many people would mourn the famous singing star, but nobody mourned the death of Darryl Temple. Recently, a side story had surfaced to further besmirch the reputation of the bank robber/rapist/murderer. The bartender Louie Carroll, who had received the eye injury at the hands of Darryl Temple, was reported to be almost totally blind in his right eye due to a detached retina that was not treated early enough to restore much sight. Louie blamed the criminal for his blindness in that eye. Ironically, it was discovered that Darryl *himself* had a torn and detached retina in his right eye, which the doctors said looked very much like the type boxers receive. It obviously had occurred from his head-banging fit he had thrown in his cell in August. It had never been repaired because of the much more serious health condition with his liver. Art and Jan Burns bitterly mourned the death of their errant son. Jan commented tearfully that Eric had finally found the happiness in heaven that seemed to elude him on earth.

****

BACK IN THE HOSPITAL, the doctors were on the verge of disconnecting the life monitor and support systems of Randy Miller when they noticed a hiccup in the straight lines of the monitor. It went back to its straight lines of death for about ten seconds, and then there was another hiccup. Grandma Brenda redoubled her prayer effort.

"This is *weird!*" exclaimed one of the nurses.

One of the doctors, cardiologist Howard Clarvoe said, "Go ahead and unplug him!"

"Don't you *dare* unplug him!" protested Grandma Brenda, stubbornly. "I'm believing God for a miracle."

Doctor Clarvoe shot back, "He's been brain-dead for five minutes! Even if I could bring him back, he would be a vegetable for the rest of his life! Besides, there is no God!"

"You touch that machine," protested Lila, vehemently, "and I will personally kill you myself! That monitor stays attached to my husband, *you hear?!*"

"Doctor Clarvoe," said Martin Perez. "You let these ladies alone. I'm a devout Catholic who believes in and worships God and honors the Blessed Virgin. I have heard of many miracles that have happened relating to her appearances around the world in places like Fatima and Guadalupe."[2]

285

"All right, all right!" grumbled Doctor Clarvoe. "I'll give it an hour and a half. If there's no change by 6:40, the plug comes out and the body will be buried."

The periodic hiccups between the flat lines on the monitor continued, and Grandma Brenda continued praying very, very hard. At the beginning of the failure of the machine, everyone in the room had sensed *something* that had come into the room. Then it was gone. Ten minutes, twenty minutes, thirty minutes went by. The strange hiccups continued, and Grandma Brenda continued her prayer vigil. 6:00 came, then 6:10, 6:20, and 6:30. Time was running out! She started praying as if she were the great TV lawyer, Perry Mason. Tears of compassion and love were streaming from her eyes as she wept convulsively.

"Lord, let me bring my case to You! I will reason with You, and You *will* answer me! Your Word says that Jesus is the Resurrection and the Life, and that if I ask anything in the name of Jesus, You will grant my request. Lord, I'm not quitting until You give me my request! Remember: You will be dishonoring Your great name and Your Word if You don't raise Randy Miller up!"

She looked at the clock. It read 6:38. Only two minutes remained before the upstart and arrogant cardiologist would come in to unplug the machine for good!

17.

BEHIND THE CURTAIN

Everybody in the room on that late, late night thought Randy Miller was perfectly unconscious, but he was not. He could not speak and he could not move, but he was well aware of what was going on around him. When Grandma Brenda came into the room, he felt the same refreshing Presence he had felt when that college girl had prayed for him as well as that bright and cheerful young pastor. When Grandma Brenda was praying in tongues, Randy at first thought it was nothing but gibberish, but then, wonders of wonders, he could understand the meaning of all those foreign words. They revealed all his sins, his selfishness and pride, his lust for fame and money, and his involvement in the occult. But those foreign words also revealed how much God loved him, and the fact that if Randy was the only person in the world, Jesus would have still died on the cross just for him. Those words revealed that no sin he had ever committed was too great for Jesus to forgive; His love and mercy were without limit.

The dying celebrity contemplated his whole life. *Well, Randy Joshua Miller. You've run after fame and fortune with all the gusto you could muster, and where are you? A hopeless basket case lying on this bed about to die, and what good is all your adulation doing for you now? It all amounts to nothing! Jitterbug Josh, what a stupid and idiotic name! Randy Miller, you knothead! You deserve everything that came to you! Well, everybody can walk into this room right now and autograph this sorry old body of Jitterbug Josh, the world's biggest first-class stoop!* As that loving old woman continued her prayer, Randy decided to call out to this God he knew absolutely nothing about with all his might.

"God, help me! Jesus, help me! I've come to the end of my rope! Please show me the way! Come to my aid, sweet Jesus! I've nothing to bring You. Save me!"

Those were the unintelligible words that no one in the room could understand.

Suddenly, Randy noticed that his cardiac machine was making a very loud beeping sound. He felt himself shedding his mortal body like coming out of a pair of pants. *What's the story here? What a time to have another one of those out-of-the-body experiences—and Isis Butterfield isn't even here!* He

287

heard Lila weep and apologize for every unkind word she had said to him. Randy drank it up. If only he could grab a hold of his wife and bask in her embrace and comfort her, but he could make no physical contact with her nor with anything else in the room.

"Joshua Randall Miller!"

Randy turned around with a gasp and was blown away with the sight that met his spiritualized eyes. There, standing before him, was the most beautiful being he had ever seen in his whole life. This apparition looked like a man, but oh, how tall he was! Randy estimated that this being had to be around seven-and-a-half feet in height. He had a tremendously handsome face that glowed brightly and radiated a great deal of love, yet there was a serious demeanor about him as well. He had blonde hair, sparkling blue eyes, and no scars or defects on his body whatsoever. He wore an incredibly beautiful white robe, and there was a golden girdle encircling his waist. He was wearing very classy sandals on his feet. Randy Miller gaped. He had never sensed love like this during the times he had spent with his spiritualized dad.

"Joshua Randall Miller!" said the beautiful being once again. "Come! I am sent to you from Yahweh God the Almighty to show you many things that are behind the Curtain of Death and that pertain to the spiritual world."

It had always bothered Randy being called by the name, 'Jitterbug Josh,' but being called 'Joshua Randall Miller' didn't faze him. Somehow, it felt right. Randy then noticed another beautiful being who was standing beside the first spirit. He was a little bit shorter than the first being, about seven feet tall. They clasped the hands of Randy, and the three of them started flying out of the cubicle, out of the hospital, and into the cold night air. The streetlights sparkled like many diamonds below them. Randy could see the bright headlights of the cars traveling along Ignacio Valley Boulevard. They picked up speed, rose up higher and higher, and flew rapidly in a trajectory that ran south/southeast. Soon, the city of San Jose sparkled below them. They continued flying in a straight line. Highway 17 in the Santa Cruz Mountains was right below them with its traffic on both sides of the highway.

"So, tell me, who are you?" asked Randy. "Are you a couple of the Ascended Masters I've heard about?"

"No," answered the golden-haired being. "We are the messengers of Yahweh God who were created by Him a long, long time ago. We are His ministering spirits sent forth to minister for them who shall be heirs of salvation."

They soon started landing toward a house located high in the Santa Cruz Mountains. Randy noticed that all the shades were drawn on this edifice. The three of them flew right through the walls of the house into a dimly lighted living room. A candle was on the table, and several people were in the room, consisting of an old lady wearing a white robe and four other ordinary people who were obviously under her services. These four people were very sad, and their faces showed signs that they had been recently weeping. The two beings led Randy to a spot toward the back of the room and stationed themselves there.

The blonde being said to Randy, "Joshua Randall Miller, thou son of the earth, look, listen, and learn!"

The old lady was chanting with her eyes closed saying, "Om, om, oh yesssss! Ooommmmm!" Then suddenly, "I see a spirit entering this room! It's an old man with white hair!"

Randy looked and saw something that scared him spitless. It was his worst nightmare, *literally!* Into the room floated a man-like creature who was about six feet tall. He wore gaudy-colored clothing and had a hideous and cruel face full of hate, dotted with a number of warts. This creature was similar to what Randy had seen in his recurring nightmares. The creature spoke to the people in the room with an ugly and creaking low voice that sounded like a normal human voice to the physical people in the room.

"I see this spirit here!" declared the old white-robed woman. "Yes, I see him! He says his name is Dennis Royer and says that he's your dad. Does that sound right?"

"Oh, yes, YES!" exclaimed the others. "Speak to us, Dad! Speak to us! How is it on the other side?"

"I'm doing well, my children. I've been flying around, hobnobbing with a lot of my deceased family members and friends. This morning, I had a good time with Tim. We sat around, smoked some cigarettes, played some poker, and cussed it up. It was just like the good old days on the earth. You see that there is really no death, only change."

"Oh, Daddy, tell us more! Please tell us more!" exclaimed the relatives in the room.

"We are all on a long evolutionary train ride, striving for self-realization in order to make it to the place where we can become one of those lucky Ascended Masters. Our goal during our many lives is to get acquainted with our higher self."

"Wow!"

"That's awesome!"

"Groovy, man. Right on!"

"Please speak some more, Dad!"

"I'm sorry, but I gotta' run! Bye now!"

"I see that the spirit is leaving the room now!" chanted the lady in a slow, high, and eerie voice.

Randy heard that monster cackle out a most hideous laugh that made chills run through his whole spirit being. The monster then crowed, "Oh, how sweet revenge is! What a beautiful thing deception is—and they all fell for it! They are all a bunch of feeble-minded suckers!" He then took turns laughing and uttering the most horrible blasphemies and then continued, "That lame-brained filth of feckless folks will follow my deception right down into the dark depths of Hades!" And with that, the grotesque being let out a final horrible laugh and flew away.

"Let's get the heck outta' here!" exclaimed Randy. "Tell me, who was that horrible monster?"

The smaller angel replied, "He is one of the fallen angels who sided with Lucifer in his great rebellion against God Almighty. He is among those beings who were thrown out of heaven and now wander about the earth to deceive and destroy as many human beings as possible."

"You see, Joshua Randall," the other angel added. "One of the things that some of these fallen angels do to deceive men and lead them away from God is to masquerade and appear to people on Earth as a dead relative in order to lead them down the path to eternal destruction. Do you remember those two times earlier this year when you left your physical body and traveled around in your spirit for a time? You met a being who said he was your father. He looked and sounded just like your dad. He was *not* your dad but was one of those malevolent angels assigned with the commission to deceive you and lead you astray. Do you remember how he took you on a couple of trips back in time? That was also deception to lead you away from the truth concerning the spirit world and the things of eternity."

Randy was greatly relieved as well as astonished to hear all of this. He had always been disappointed and disillusioned about those excursions of soul-travel, especially regarding the lack of love he had felt from that apparition who had claimed to be his daddy.

The golden-haired angel said, "We are going to take a quick trip into the Second Heaven."

Boy, oh boy, thought Randy. *Going into one of the parts of heaven! I bet you this is going to be good!*

The three of them flew through an invisible wall, and Randy found himself in a huge place that was far from his definition of what heaven would be like. It was a vacuum, crammed-jammed with millions of beings of various sizes and shapes. The topmost group consisted of gigantic human-like creatures who were sitting on gorgeous thrones studded with many types of gems: diamonds, rubies, sapphires, topazes; you name it! A second group looked a lot like normal human beings. They were dressed in fancy suits and natty ties and were between five and six feet tall. A third group were beings who looked part human and part animal. There were smaller creatures who were ugly and extremely smelly; they ranged in height from only a few inches tall to about a foot-and-a-half tall. One thing Randy noticed was that all these grotesque beings were in contention with each other. He also noticed that the beings who were not sitting on the beautiful thrones were very envious of the ones who were. Randy felt a sensation not unlike very severe nausea; he was sure if he were still in his human body, he would have thrown up profusely by now.

"Wh-who are these horrible cr-creatures?" stammered Randy.

"These are the different ranks of the army of the Enemy," replied the blonde angel. "The various ranks of these evil spirits are given different assignments by Lucifer to destroy men's souls and to try to thwart the Kingdom of God from being established on Earth. The giants who sit on the great thrones have authority over the lower-ranked spirits. The spirits who look like sharply dressed businessmen are commissioned to destroy the economies of the world through the sin of greed. These higher spirits are using many super rich and powerful men as their pawns to bring about their evil plans on Earth. They are also working through various secret organizations and fraternities on Earth to bring about their sinister agendas. Soon, there will be an extremely abominable Superman who will rule the whole planet and deceive the whole world, whom the Lamb of God will destroy with the brightness of His coming. Other spirits' expertise is in the area of false religions that deny Christ, the Only Begotten Son of God. Among this third group are those spirits who lead people into forbidden things like fortune telling, astrology, spiritualism, and witchcraft. In this group of evil spirits are also those who seduce depressed men and women into committing suicide. There's another group of spirits whose specialty is murder and brutality. Then, finally, those filthy spirits you see here are commissioned to seduce mankind with all kinds of sex sins that are outside of marriage."

Randy was standing right beside an especially fetid-smelling spirit. He really *did* want to retch and asked, "And what does that spirit do, there?"

The blonde angel answered, "His expertise is in the area of promoting homosexuality. In these last of the last days, the Enemy is going to try to promote this lifestyle around the world and mislead people into thinking that it's okay."

The other angel added, "From time to time, Satan sends some of these spirits to Earth to fulfill a specific assignment of harm. Once their evil deed is done, they return here to the Second Heaven."

"I don't think I like this place very much!" exclaimed Randy.

"You're right," said the tall, blonde angel. "We don't like this place very much, either. The big thing that you feel here is this: there is no love here whatsoever."

The three of them flew out of the demonic void of inner space and back into the atmosphere overlooking San Jose. They flew down into the midst of the city, and Randy gasped with horror. Everywhere he looked, he could see myriads upon myriads of horrid creatures who were mingling with the human beings who were sitting, standing, driving, and walking about. The human beings were totally obvious and blinded to all these terrible creatures swarming all around them. The two messengers led Randy into a hospital in downtown San Jose. They flew into a cubicle in the ICU unit there. On the bed was a man who was in the process of dying and standing all around him were several of those malicious beings Randy was all too familiar with. They were tying heavy chains around him, and he was screaming out with abject terror, "OH, HELP!! *HELP!!* PLEASE LEAVE ME ALONE! OH, NO, NO, *NOOOOOOOO!!*" The apparitions were mocking him with the most hideous and horrible laughter. Just outside the cubicle were a few handsome and kindly beings who were dressed in white robes. Their faces were a picture of sadness and grief.

"What's going on?" asked Randy. "Why don't any of you good spirits do something to save that poor man from those horrible creatures?"

"The evil spirits have a legal right to the soul of that dying sinner," answered the tall, blonde angel, sadly. "He rejected the Savior and now must pay the penalty for his sinful choices, which is eternal separation from God."

As they watched sadly, the evil spirits completed their work of chaining up the man and pushed him down a bottomless and horribly black hole that appeared in the floor of the hospital room. The screams of that dead man were far, far more heart wrenching than any screams of terror Randy had ever heard while he was in his mortal body. He shuddered as he remembered all the recurring nightmares he had experienced since moving into his huge mansion.

"Thou son of the earth, look, listen and learn!" commanded the tall, blonde angel. "Every human being who is born on Earth has a special guardian angel assigned to them for their welfare and protection. God is love and desires that no one would perish, but that all would come to repentance. Even the worst sinners on Earth have a guardian angel. *Adolph Hitler* had a guardian angel. *Josef Stalin* had a guardian angel. However, every human being has a choice: they can either accept Christ and have eternal life or reject Christ and be lost forever and ever. We would love to be able to escort everybody to heaven, but when people die in their sins, those evil spirits have a legal right to do to them as they please, and we have no power to rescue them anymore. *Oh, if only men had a real grasp on the importance of the things of eternity!*" At this point, the angel's countenance took on a more cheerful look as he said, "Come! You have an appointment to see what God has prepared for those who love Him!"

And with that, the angels lovingly clasped the hands of Randy Miller, and the three of them flew swiftly out of the hospital room and high into the air. They flew due north. Higher and higher they zoomed. Randy could see the earth getting smaller and smaller behind him, and soon, the sun, brighter than he had ever seen it, shone out of the east. The stars were also far brighter than any stars he had ever seen on Earth, even at a deserted campground high in the mountains—and many, many more of them were visible. Randy looked down and could see the North Pole cloaked in blackness. They continued traveling upwards. Faster and faster they went. The earth quickly grew smaller and smaller. Soon, it was the size of a tennis ball, then the size of a marble, then the size of a tiny speck, and finally, it had disappeared altogether. A moment later, the rays of the sun were no brighter than a full moon, then they were no brighter than Venus, then it was just one of the millions upon millions of stars in the Milky Way Galaxy. They continued picking up speed.

Soon, the Milky Way was far behind them. Randy felt a sense of freedom, exhilaration, and excitement. He also noticed that his mind was suddenly clearer. None of those horrible spirits whom he had seen on Earth were present.

By and by, Randy could see a speck of light far ahead of him, brighter than all the other millions of stars in the cosmos that were swishing by at a dizzying speed. The light grew bigger and bigger and brighter and brighter until it seemed to cover the whole side of that part of the universe. The next moment, they were flying through an incredibly thick and delightful mist consisting of all the colors of the rainbow and even some colors Randy had never seen before.

There were reds, oranges, yellows, whites, greens, aquas, blues, indigos, purples, and pinks. The closest thing he could compare this with was when he had flown on an airplane and witnessed a sunrise beautified by the presence of many colorful and high clouds, except that this mist was infinitely more magnificent than that airplane scene. In a few moments, the mist cleared away, the three of them were standing on solid ground, and Randy was able to look at the landscape that greeted his eyes. What he saw totally blew him away.

The sights were far, far too beautiful for words. The landscape was covered with the softest and greenest grass Randy had ever seen and stood on. All around him, as far as the eye could see, were gorgeous trees loaded down with the most inviting and luscious fruits imaginable. Also, there were quite a few different types of fruit on the trees. Dotted everywhere along the countryside was a profusion of the most breathtaking flowers in all the colors of the rainbow: red roses, violets, bluebells, daisies, magnolias, heliotropes, lilies, lilacs, and many, many other types. Randy was totally flabbergasted and delighted. Over to the left was a crystal-clear river filled with sparkling water that murmured delightfully in the light breeze. At the bottom of this river could be seen multi-colored stones and gems. On both sides could be seen towering mountain peaks covered with beautiful forests of firs, pines, oaks, alders, aspens, and even tall redwoods. Nothing brown or dead existed in this whole lovely countryside. Randy looked up at the sky. It was a pure and awe-inspiring blue, far bluer than any sky he had ever seen on Earth. He noticed with surprise that there was no sun in that sky; the source of the great light permeating the whole place seemed to come from a city that glistened far in the distance. He noticed that there were no shadows. Randy tried to make a shadow and couldn't do it. He gasped with surprise.

"Thou son of the earth, look, listen, and learn!" said the golden-haired angel. "You see, Joshua, no darkness can exist here in the eternal Kingdom of Light. The Scriptures point out that Jesus is the light of the world, and in Him is no darkness at all."

Randy was sure if he had been here in his mortal body, he would have been blinded by the great light.

He noticed multitudes upon multitudes of lovely angelic creatures who were all over this place. Some of them had wings, and some of them didn't. He also noticed multitudes of people walking around with the happiest faces he had ever seen. They were clothed in extremely beautiful and glistening white robes. He also noticed other people who were clothed in beautiful white gowns that didn't match up to the beauty of the robes. These people were serene, but also dazed. They would walk up to the beautiful trees and rub the leaves on their eyes, which seemed to strengthen them. Randy looked at his body to see what he was wearing and noticed that he had on his 'Jitterbug Josh' concert outfit consisting of his black suit, gray dress shirt, and yellow tie.

The sounds Randy was hearing in this place were unlike anything he had ever heard in his whole lifetime. First, he noticed the music that seemed to come from all directions. It was so beautiful, he just stood there and gasped. No music he had ever heard on Earth could even begin to compare with this music. The best masterpieces of Beethoven, Mozart, Mendelssohn, Grieg, Debussy, Gershwin, and even J. S. Bach were like harsh and grating noise compared to this exquisite music. First off, it was perfectly in tune and altogether lovely and sweet to listen to. Secondly, none of it was sad. Rather, it was joyful and uplifting. Thirdly, none of it was harsh, pounding, or grating like some of the modern music on Earth, especially not like the dissonant, atonal music of serious composers like Schoenberg, or the hard rock-and-roll music that was so popular with the youth of this day and age. Along with the music was the caroling of the birds that were everywhere in those gorgeous trees, singing their melodies with a sweetness beyond description. On Earth, their songs had often seemed mournful; but here, their songs were joyful and praised the Lord. He could see the happy birds all around with their plumaged colors that were unlike anything he had ever seen on Earth. The trees and flowers were also praising and worshipping the Lord. Randy walked through a lovely bed of flowers and noticed how they went right through his cloudlike body, undisturbed. Randy was also overwhelmed by the smells in this marvelous place. They consisted of fragrant perfumes so sweet and wonderful that it made him feel drunk.

He noticed that all his senses were heightened up here. His eyesight was greatly improved, and he could hear very, very high pitches he had never been able to hear while he had been on Earth, even in his younger boyhood days when his hearing had been sharp and acute. (Over the years, he had suffered some hearing loss related to noise pollution.)

He also noticed a marvelous harmony existing between all the happy angels and human beings who dwelt here. There was no strife, no contention, no selfishness, no harsh or sarcastic words, and no obscene or blasphemous language from anyone. True praise and worship, which Randy could tell was heartfelt, was all over the place. "Hallelujah!" "Praise the Lord!" "Glory to God!" and "Worthy is the Lamb who was slain to receive glory, honor, and dominion!" was heard everywhere. Also, every being here radiated kindness, friendliness, winsomeness, and good will.

"You see, Joshua Randall," said the blonde angel, "the ruling principle of this place is love. Nobody here lives to please himself, but rather, to please the living God and others. Love is the law of the angels and of the redeemed saints. You will notice that the attitude of everyone here is, 'What can I do to serve you and make you happy?' Everyone here lives in unity with everyone else and with God."

At that moment, a very dignified and regal man walked toward Randy. He was very big with a large chest that looked like a barrel. He had the appearance of one who had lived for thousands of years, yet a great youthfulness and vigor clothed him. As lovely as the other saints appeared, it was no match for the loveliness gracing this man. Randy was so bowled over by this wonderful personage, he fell on his face and started worshipping him.

"Get up!" commanded the regal man. "I am a fellow servant here in this land of eternal bliss. Worship God!"

"Who are you?"

"I am Father Abraham. I am here to assist you in the knowledge of the eternal kingdom. You have a divine appointment here to be shown many things about the eternal happiness of the righteous."

Abraham then greeted a couple of newcomers who were clad in white robes. He offered them a drink from the crystal river, which they accepted. He filled several golden goblets with the clear water and gave it to the newcomers who started drinking from the goblets. Joy filled their faces, and they immediately started praising God with all their might.

"What's happening there?" asked Randy, curiously.

"They have just had a drink from the River of Living Water, flowing from the Throne Room in the midst of the Holy City you see in the distance. Those who drink that water can never get tired again. Neither can they ever die. This water energizes them and imparts spiritual vitality to them."

Suddenly, a magnificent chariot, driven by four angels, stopped beside them. Out jumped a radiant oriental lady dressed in a stunning white robe. She immediately fell to the ground and started worshipping God loudly with all her might in a Chinese dialect.

"PRAISE GOD!! PRAISE GOD!! PRAISE YOU, HEAVENLY FATHER!! THANK YOU, BEAUTIFUL, MARVELOUS, FABULOUS, FANTASTIC, MEGA-WONDERFUL JESUS!! OH, YESHUA, AWESOME LAMB OF GOD!! I WORSHIP YOU, INFINITELY SWEET HOLY SPIRIT!! THANK YOU, *THANK YOU!! OH, GLORY TO THE HIGHEST GOD FOREVER AND EVER!!*"

All the angels and saints who were standing around also fell down and worshipped God with loud praises and adoration.

"Who is this happy woman?" asked Randy.

The golden-haired angel responded, "She was a faithful Christian who served the Lord Jesus much of her life with her whole heart. She lived in Communist China and testified faithfully of the Lord Jesus under the most difficult circumstances. She led multitudes to Christ and was a prayer warrior. She suffered much persecution for the sake of Christ and finally was martyred by the communists. Therefore, her reward here is very great."

"Come, my faithful child!" said Abraham. "Welcome! Enter into your eternal reward! Eat from these fruit trees that bear twelve different types of fruit on them! Drink freely from the River of Living Water you see before you. All of heaven is before you, and the joys and glories of this place will unfold before you more and more as the endless ages of eternity roll by."

The intensely happy woman drank from the golden goblet Abraham gave her and rejoiced with even more gusto. She took off running at full speed toward the Holy City that glistened far in the distance.

At that moment, another chariot arrived, and a blonde-haired man with blue eyes stumbled out and fell to the ground, totally stunned and dazed. For several minutes, he could not even lift his eyes off the ground. The angels who had brought him here spoke to him gently with many comforting words. Finally, the man plucked up enough courage to speak in a faltering voice. He was dressed in a gown, not a robe.

"Oh, my God!" he exclaimed. "Am I really in heaven?!"

"My son," said Abraham. "You have safely arrived in the land of eternal happiness."

"B-b-but am I even worthy to be here?" asked the man in a totally bewildered voice. "I ain't worthy to be in this place that's too beautiful for words. I ain't worthy to eat these fabulous fruits from those trees!"

"You are worthy to eat those fruits because of the Blood of the Lamb," responded Abraham. "When you are prepared, you'll be able to appear before the Throne."

"But I was such a great sinner!" protested the man in the white gown. "I was the greatest sinner that ever walked the face of the whole earth!"

"But your sins have all been forgiven and washed away through Jesus, the great Redeemer," said the golden-haired angel.

All this time, Randy was staring intently at the newcomer. *I've seen that man somewhere before! I know I have—but where?* At that instant, Randy saw another man in a white gown walking toward them. When he arrived, one of the angels spoke to him saying, "Ben Simeon, assist this newcomer in the knowledge of the things pertaining to the paradisiacal kingdom. This newcomer, Darryl Allen Temple, has much to learn. He will have to start from the very beginning. He knows practically nothing of the spiritual graces of the Christian life."

Darryl?! DARRYL TEMPLE?! The infamous murderer and rapist? How could an evil criminal like him make it here?

Abraham could read the thoughts of Randy and answered them saying, "We are not saved by our good works or our own righteousness. The Scripture points out that 'Abraham believed God and it was counted unto him for righteousness.' Scripture also says, 'For by grace are ye saved through faith, and that not of yourselves; it is the gift of God. Not of works lest any man should boast.' This man, Darryl Temple, was a great sinner, but he called on the name of the Lord Jesus at the end of his life and was cleansed of all his sins by His Blood."

"Tell me, Father Abraham," asked Randy. "Who is that newcomer in the white gown that is leading Darryl away?"

"His name is Ben Simeon. He was the repentant thief on the cross who was crucified beside Jesus and repented at the last minute. You can read in the book of Luke how Jesus promised him that 'Today, thou shalt be with Me in paradise.' He is aptly qualified to assist this redeemed sinner from the earth in the ways of the Kingdom of God."

Suddenly, it dawned on Randy, and he cried out, "I know where I've seen that guy! He was the guy in the red sports car who almost hit me last year near Placerville!"

"That's right," said Abraham.

"Father Abraham, can you tell me more of the story concerning this man's life?"

"Certainly!" responded Abraham.

They sat down in the comfortable green grass, and Abraham started his narrative of this man's life.

"Darryl Allen Temple had a very rotten deck of cards dealt to him right from the very beginning of his life. He was born out of wedlock to an alcoholic father who soon abandoned his live-in girlfriend and the newly born child. This mother was a cocaine addict, and the living conditions were deplorable. He was soon taken away and placed in another very bad family situation with another drunken man who lived in great poverty.

"When Darryl was one-and-a-half years old, he fell headfirst into a basement. This enabled a demon to enter into him, and his spiritual troubles started in earnest. Meanwhile, the man who adopted him abused him severely: physically, verbally, and even sexually. The man beat Darryl a lot, he was often locked in a dark, dank closet, and he usually had far too little to eat and went hungry.

"When he was eight years old, he had his first baptism into pornography through a girlie magazine he stumbled upon one day. This escalated his fall into crime big-time, and one thing led to another. Besides all of this, he became an alcoholic. He could never get a high-paying job, and the work that he did get never lasted all that long; the alcohol addiction was a damper on that. He got arrested for misdemeanors related to the alcoholism several times and spent a few nights in jail. All that time, he was committing those terrible rapes and murders of those teenage prostitutes as he was goaded on by the demonic spirits that resided in him. The day finally came when he robbed that bank in Stockton, which led to him getting caught by the police. The cops found the two dead girls buried in his back yard, and he was immediately booked as a major, major felon. He was thrown into prison and was tried a few weeks ago and found guilty of one count of armed bank robbery, twenty-two counts of murder, and twenty-two counts of rape.

"Darryl never had any exposure to the gospel until that day at the maximum-security prison of San Quentin when Wes Marlow, a Christian guard, shared the love of God with him for the first time. Darryl was very antagonistic and hard during that first encounter and cursed that guard out. Nevertheless, Darryl couldn't shrug off what he had heard; a seed had been planted in him. It was soon after that day when terminal cancer of the liver was discovered in him. When Darryl first learned of it, he spent half a day cursing and railing against God due to this mind-shattering news. However, he calmed down after that, and his heart began to soften to the gospel. The next time that Wes the guard offered to tell Darryl about the love of God, Darryl let out a very grumpy, 'Oh, all right!' He muttered out some words of protest concerning religious fanatics, but then listened attentively to the compassionate guard.

"The third time Wes had a chance to talk with Darryl about Jesus, he was very open and receptive to the things the guard spoke. Wes talked about the joys of heaven, the horrors of hell, and the infinite love of God that could save even the worst of sinners. Darryl asked hungrily if God could really forgive even him, and Wes answered in the affirmative.

"The fourth time Wes spoke to Darryl was a week before he died of liver cancer. By this time, he was very, very sick and jaundiced. He was ready to receive Christ and asked the guard how he could be saved. The guard led him in the sinner's prayer and then spent several hours in a deliverance session to set Darryl free from the demons that had tormented him all his life. He cried like a baby and forgave all of those who had abused and hurt him. As you see, God forgave him of all his sins, and now he has begun to enjoy the eternal life that is up here."

"WOW, WHAT A STORY!" shouted Randy with great wonder and awe. "OH, HOW GREAT THE MERCY OF GOD IS!"

"Yes," responded Abraham. "The Blood of Jesus can cleanse even the dirtiest of sinners, but it is time for you to move on. Coming to us from yonder is a chariot to transport you to another part of paradise. You have an appointment with an old friend whom you knew on Earth who is now partaking of the blessed life here."

The beautiful chariot soon arrived, and Randy clambered eagerly into it. The vehicle seemed to be made of light and reminded him of a cable car that took people up to a scenic peak in the Rocky Mountains. The inside of the chariot was so luxurious that Randy gasped with rapture. It had crystal clear windows surrounding it. The floor was covered with soft carpeting of a gorgeous red hue with brilliant gold dust sprinkled on it. The seats were covered with very, very soft red cushions with silk trimming. As he stepped onto the carpet and sat down in the exquisite seats, comfort just reached out and grabbed him. The floor and the seats felt so *alive!*

The chariot started racing noiselessly toward the mountains that were in the distance. Randy had no idea how the vehicle was powered. Soon, they were traveling through the foothills, and then after that, the majestic mountain range towering for thousands upon thousands of feet into the clear and smog-free skies situated above paradise. The scenery that zoomed by was beautiful beyond description. Randy had taken a train trip from California on up to Washington when he was nineteen years old. The scenery between Klamath Falls and Eugene, Oregon had been the most spectacular he had seen in his whole life. He had enjoyed the mountain cliffs, verdant forests, lakes, and waterfalls immensely that he had seen on that trip, but the scenes on that train trip were a garbage dump compared to what he was seeing now. First of all, the mountains were far, far taller than any on Earth. The trees were greener and more gorgeous, by far, than any he had seen on Earth—and there were no dead or brown leaves anywhere. Neither were there any shadows. Multi-colored waterfalls whizzed by. Canyons flashed by that fell thousands of feet below to reveal the exquisite views of paradise spread out below them. These cliffs consisted of rocky formations that glistened in the most stunning and brightest colors: reds, blues, slate, oranges, yellows, whites, and pink. Neither Bryce Canyon in Utah nor the Grand Canyon in Arizona could begin to compare with this! They also crossed over many roaring streams and rivers. Randy also espied all sorts of animals: horses, deer, lions, tigers, dogs, cats, bears, rabbits—you name it!

The chariot finally began to slacken its speed as they approached an extremely spellbinding and beautiful blue lake. Along this body of water were many, many impressive resort cabins made of various types of wood: redwood, plywood, and oak, as well as many other kinds. They stopped at a large edifice made out of redwood, and the angels motioned for Randy to get out. They headed toward the front door of this lovely cabin, and one of the angels knocked on the door. As the resident of this house opened the door, Randy let out a shout of joy and wonder as he recognized a friend who had died of colon cancer three years ago.

"Randy Miller!" the friend cried out with surprise and joy, grabbing him in an affectionate bear hug, and covering his cheek with kiss after kiss. "What a pleasant surprise to see you in this most blessed land of Jesus, the precious Lamb of God!"

"Why, Wally Sanchez! It's so great to see you! What an extraordinary place this land is, and what a lovely cabin this is! You look so young and handsome!"

"Yes, praise the mighty name of Jesus! This is a blessed land, and I'm so thankful to God Almighty for bringing me to this marvelous place of eternal happiness! You are welcome to this vacation resort home of mine, my dear, dear friend! Allow me of having the pleasure of showing you around this house and surrounding garden area the Lord has so graciously given to me up here!"

"Love to, Wally!"

Wally Sanchez had been a close friend of Randy when he was living on Earth. They had been golfing buddies, playing many a round at Mira Vista Country Club. He and his wife, Jane (who was still alive on Earth) had been a very lovely couple. Wally had been a very kind, friendly, and generous man while he had lived on Earth. Randy had noticed some real differences in that man from the other members of Mira Vista Country Club whom he had known. For one thing, he never used blasphemous or obscene language. Neither was he involved in the petty gambling that took place in the game room of the club where many of the club members would play poker and other card games. Wally never either smoked or drank alcohol like most of the other members. On top of all this, he was an extremely patient and even-tempered man. Randy had seen him get angry only once in all the years he had known him. There was talk about Wally from the other club members, many of them who considered him to be weird.

Wally led Randy on a tour around the fancy log cabin that consisted of eight rooms. Filling the living room were two cream-colored sofas adjacent to each other, a little table between them, a TV set, and many other things that had been on Earth as well as some things Randy didn't recognize. There was a spacious family room with bluish-green carpeting on the floor and walls painted a cheery light-blue color. This room housed a large brown table made out of highly polished oak wood. On the wall were many family photographs. Many other lovely things were in this room as was the case for all the other rooms in this cottage. The kitchen was painted in an eye-pleasing salmon color. A large oak table was situated in the yellow dining room. Right next to the dining room was an attractive bluish-green game room with some of the games Randy had remembered while he had lived on Earth.

A gray, spiral stairway led up to the second floor where the other three rooms were. The bedroom had a large king-sized bed covered with a bright red bedspread. The library was full of books, including several Bibles. The walls were festooned with yellow, pink, and purple flowers. Alongside of that room was a large study overlooking the clear blue lake. All the windows of this very inviting vacation house had attractive curtains on them made of the most highly refined silks that were only seen in heaven.

Randy stared out of the large window in the study with a transfixed look on his face. The blue water of the lake was as smooth as glass. He could see many happy people who were on the water. Some were swimming, others were floating, others, still, were in boats, some of them with sails, and others without sails. Some people were jumping from high tree branches that hung over the water into the lake. Off in the distance was a curvy and fast waterslide that some people were sliding down and falling into the water with mighty splashes. Everywhere could be heard the happy and animated conversations, the sweet laughter, and the praises and worship of God from those people.

"You know, Wally," said Randy. "Something that I notice here is there is no bathroom with the toilet seats we used to have on Earth."

Wally guffawed heartily and said, "How could there be toilets here in heaven? There is no waste here! Everything that enters into this perfect land is clean and holy. Neither is there any sexual activity up here since we who have been redeemed by the Blood of Jesus are part of His holy Bride."

Suddenly, Randy noticed something that had escaped his attention until now: his spiritual body had no genitals on it.

"What an incredibly wonderful house this is!" exclaimed Randy.

"Yes, Randy, but this is not my main abode. This is only my vacation cabin out in the country. My main mansion of twenty-five rooms is in the Holy City. Our wonderful Redeemer is so gracious! He grants all of our desires and then some."

"I have no more breath in me! This is all too much!"

"Come with me, Randy. I have some more things outside I wanna' show you."

They walked down the winding staircase, through the kitchen, and then through a door leading outside that had a stained-glass window on it. Randy found himself in an exquisitely beautiful garden with a winding gray marble walkway. Along this path was a profusion of many different types of trees and flowers in all the colors of the rainbow. There was even a towering redwood tree. Here and there were placid and serene ponds with slate, pink, and red rocks at the bottom. Presently, they came out into a clearing, and yet again, Randy was blown away by what he saw.

There, right in front of them, was the most gargantuan golf course he had ever seen in his whole life. Besides its size, it was so beautiful, Randy just stood there and stared speechlessly, his mouth wide open in awe and wonder. He had watched the Masters' Golf Tournament on TV last spring, that big sporting event held yearly in Augusta, Georgia. He remembered how Gary Player had won the Green Jacket this year, and also, what a gorgeous golf course Augusta was with its array of pretty trees and beds of variegated flowers everywhere. But Augusta couldn't even begin to compare with the excellence of this course. At the beginning of this Links was a golden shed, which Wally entered and then came back outside with his bag of golf clubs, balls, and tees.

"Come, my friend," said Wally. "Let's play a couple of holes together."

"Sure thing, Wally!"

Wally teed off first, hitting a beautiful shot that went right down the middle of the fairway. Randy then hit his tee shot, which would have been outstanding for any pro on Earth, but which didn't travel nearly as far as

Wally's shot did. They both started walking down the fairway. Once again, Randy was amazed that no shadows could be seen anywhere.

"How long is this hole, Wally?"

"3,000 cubits, pal."

"Cubits?" responded Randy, dumbly. "What's a cubit?"

"Cubits are one of the heavenly measurements. A cubit is equal to half a yard. Therefore, this hole is about 1,500 yards long."

"Oh."

They presently came up to Randy's ball, which he hit with a 2-iron.

"Uh, oh! Looks like you're in trouble! You landed in the bunker."

Wally then came up to his ball and hit a beautiful shot with a 5-iron that landed right on the green. They then walked up to the sand trap where Randy had hit his errant second shot. Here was another wonderful surprise; Randy had never seen a sand trap like this on Earth. Instead of a brownish-white color, this sand shone in many different colors: gold, slate, salmon, blue, red, and purple. Like everything else here, it was incredibly breathtaking. Randy proceeded to make two shots with the sand wedge before he could get his ball out of the trap and onto the green. He then proceeded to two-putt the ball to get a double bogey. Wally proceeded to sink a long putt for a birdie.

They played one more hole together. The second hole was 4,264 cubits, (2,132 yards) long, and it was a five-par. On this hole, Randy missed his third shot to the right and landed in a beautiful water trap that had all kinds of gems at the bottom of the pond: gold, silver, diamonds, rubies, emeralds, sapphires, amethysts, and several others. Wally related one very special experience he had had on this golf course about a year ago, according to earthly time.

"I'll never forget the time when Jesus, the Son of God, actually played a round of golf with me here. It was so much fun! We were playing on this hole, and I sliced my third shot right into the water—and do you know what He did? He grabbed my head, said to me with His sweet and musical laugh, 'Wally Sanchez, you need to remember to keep your head down when you swing at the ball!' and He dunked me in that pond. We had a great big water fight right there! We laughed and laughed. We were both having a ball (pun intended). I'll tell you, my friend. I'll never forget that day throughout eternity.

"Then, on the seventh hole, I missed a short putt because my swing with the putter was timid. He said to me, 'Wally, you need to follow through with your shots. The goal that you're aiming at is the hole.' He then used that illustration of golf to relate it to truths about the Kingdom of God. He said, 'When I was on Earth, I preached the parable of the sower who dropped seed along the different types of soil. You will remember that there were four different types of soil representing four different types of people and their responses to the gospel. You remember the stony ground hearers? They were the ones who heard the Word and immediately received it with joy, but they had no root in themselves. When trials or persecution came along, they quickly fell away and were offended. *They didn't follow through!* Neither did the thorny ground hearers. They let the lust for material things, the pleasures of Earth, and the worries of the world below choke the Word, and they became unfruitful. But the good seed hearers who heard the Word from a good heart and hung in there did succeed in producing good fruit: some thirtyfold, some sixtyfold, and some a hundredfold. They *did* follow through!

"'Now the goal of this game is to go down the center of the fairway and get the ball into the hole. There's a spiritual lesson here, and it has to do with the fact that God has a purpose for all of His creation. God's perfect will is like that hole on the green, but men miss the target of God's will. This is what sin is: missing the mark of God's perfect will.'

"I had never in my life heard anybody who teaches and preaches the way Jesus Christ does. It made a big impact on my life even up here."

At this point, the chariot of light came swishing toward the two of them, and the blonde-headed angel walked out of it and said, "Joshua Randall! It is time for you to be moving on. You have an appointment to keep in the Holy City that lies over yonder."

The two of them climbed into the luxurious and mega-comfortable chariot after Randy had given Wally an affectionate hug and kiss. The vehicle then took off in a different direction than that from whence they had come. Their direction was ninety degrees to the right.

The scenery on this journey was just as spectacular as the journey coming to this Edenic lake had been. Numerous towering mountain passes with pine trees, firs, giant redwoods, oaks, aspens, beech, and many other types of trees whizzed by them. The rocky multi-colored cliffs were covered with spellbinding flowers of all kinds. Chasms and canyons rushed by that were thousands upon thousands of feet deep. They passed by many rivers, streams, and lakes. There were many, many waterfalls and gushing cataracts that flashed by. Eventually, the mountains became foothills, and the foothills subsided into the beautiful plains and orchards of paradise. Far ahead of them towered the City of Light, the central focal point of this Land of Delight.

As they got closer to the city, Randy began to feel weaker and weaker. The chariot stopped near a grove of lovely fruit trees, and the golden-haired angel got out of the chariot, walked over to one of the trees, picked some fruit off of it, walked back to the chariot, and handed it to Randy.

"Eat this!" he commanded. "It will strengthen you to be able to enter into the Holy City."

Randy obeyed. The fruit was copper-colored and very delicious and juicy. As they traveled along the lovely countryside, they made several other stops in order for Randy to eat some more of the strengthening fruit. They finally made it to one of the gates of the city. The sights that Randy now saw made everything else he had seen before pale in comparison.

The city standing before them towered high, high up into the heavenly sky. The wall was indescribably huge and was made out of jasper. Fathomless light shone forth from the whole city. The jasper wall rested on twelve huge foundations that had the appearance of a beautiful stairway, each having different sparkling gems and having the different names of the apostles written upon them. The first foundation had the name Peter, the second, Paul, the third, John, and the fourth, James. The jasper wall towered high above the topmost foundation. Randy was stunned by the beauty and magnificence of the beautiful gemstones that garnished the foundations. He especially was fond of the blue sapphire on the second foundation, the green emerald on the fourth foundation, and the purple amethyst on the twelfth foundation. They were standing by a gate made out of pearl with the name 'Judah' written on it.

"Explain all this incredible glory I now see!" exclaimed Randy to the angel.

"Right now, thou son of the earth, we are standing at one of the three gates on the north side of the Holy City. Where we are standing is the gate of Judah. All the gates are named after one of the twelve tribes of Israel. There are three other gates on the east side of the city, three on the south side, and three on the west side. The wall measures 144 cubits, in other words, seventy-two yards. This city is about 1,500 miles long, wide, and high. Let us go inside!"

As they went through the gate, Randy noticed the transparent golden street they were walking on as well as the breathtaking columns that towered above them. Gorgeous houses and stores were on each side of the street as well as the beautiful trees and flowers that were everywhere. There were thousands upon thousands of happy people clad in gorgeous white garments. Their faces shone with the glory of the light of Christ. Mingled with the joyful people were myriads upon myriads of angels.

Soon, they came to a humongous sand-colored building made out of exquisite marble and walked in. It was the biggest library Randy had ever seen. There was row upon row of bookshelves stacked with a huge array of cheerful-looking books. The walls of this library were paneled with the most highly refined woods and festooned with the most entrancing flowers in hues of yellow, pink, red, lavender, violet, and sky-blue.

"You mean there are books in heaven?" asked Randy.

"Yes, there are. Those who have served the Redeemer well on Earth and have the gift of writing continue to produce books that are published up here. Also, their works they wrote on Earth that edified people spiritually can also be found here in heaven. Moreover, there are books that have been written in heaven that have not come down to Earth yet because nobody has paid the price in order to be able to write them. You will notice that all the books up here glorify the Great Yahweh God. No pornographic, blasphemous, or obscene literature exists up here, but the books you see around you are very interesting to read as well as uplifting. They are not boring. There are also perfect translations of the Holy Scriptures here that are exactly the way God originally inspired them, even down to the very punctuation."

Randy spent some time browsing through the books, and indeed, there was a huge collection. There were all kinds of topics, and much of the literature did not have overtly religious titles. Many, many novels were stacked on the bookshelves, some of them having been written in previous centuries, and some of them being up-to-date fictional stories that had been written in the twentieth century. In one place, Randy saw a copy of John Bunyan's *Pilgrim's Progress* as well as a copy of Harriet Beecher Stowe's *Uncle Tom's Cabin*. A history section was there with literature that went back in time far beyond the creation of Planet Earth. Some books talked about the early history of heaven when Lucifer was the highest ranked angel in heaven as well as its worship leader. Other books talked about the ancient history of the perfect and incredibly beautiful earth during the time when dinosaurs roamed on it, the fall of Satan and how he messed up the earth, how that planet became a desolate waste, and finally, how God reconstructed it in six solar days and created Adam and Eve. Still other books related the history of early mankind before the worldwide Flood. The gamut of history books spanned all the way up to the present time and even into the future. There were also other areas of the library that were grouped under many different topics: biology, geology, astronomy, mathematics, physics, music, business and economics, heavenly affairs, biographies, the spiritual growth of the Christian, the Trinity, and future prophecy. One section of the library contained books pertaining to all kinds of sports and games: archery, golf, tennis, horseback riding, chess, backgammon, swimming, football, basketball, and baseball. Books on knitting and weaving were also there.

They soon walked out of the library onto the transparent golden street. The angel then led Randy into a music store filled with a huge plethora of published heavenly music. Randy was overjoyed at everything here that was far, far beyond his wildest dreams he had ever harbored on Earth.

"So there is music that is being published here as well?" asked Randy.

"Yes! There is also music up here that has never been brought down to Earth yet because nobody has paid the price to bring it down."

"Wow! This is too wonderful for words! If I had only known that this place existed, how differently I would have lived my life!"

18.

INTO THE PIT

Randy looked around the store at the thousands of songs, hymns, and classical compositions that had been published in heaven. There were orchestral pieces, choral arrangements, piano pieces, string quartets, brass quartets, woodwind quintets, and shofar quintets. The covers of these manuscripts were very attractive, and the parchment they were written on was very refined. Randy recognized the names and music of a few classical composers who had lived on Earth: Bach, Handel, and Mendelssohn, for example. Happy redeemed saints were walking in and out of the store, humming hymns and heavenly songs, happily conversing with each other, and praising the Lord.

"Note this," said the golden-haired angel. "Everyone who makes it to heaven will have a job to do according to each one's talents and faithfulness to the Lord. Work is good. Work existed before the Fall. There is no laziness here in heaven. The work that each person will do here is incredibly exhilarating and exciting. Different ranks of authority and stewardship exist here. Some saints continue to compose music here. Some are worship leaders in the various heavenly choirs and bands. Some are praisers who lead people in praising the Lord. Some are writers who expound on different topics. Some are involved in heavenly industrial arts while others are workers in heavenly agriculture. Some are bakers while others are great cooks. The saints who have been the most faithful and have overcome will sit on thrones with Jesus in the great Throne Room, reigning with Christ. They are especially blessed, and their responsibilities throughout the eternal ages will be very weighty and awesome."

After some time, the golden-haired angel led Randy back out into the golden street. He looked all around at the fantastic sights of heaven, its super-elaborate buildings, its trees, bushes, and flowers of surpassing splendor, its sparkling and gushing fountains, and all sorts of enchanting gems. Great numbers of happy people were walking this way or that or sitting down on luxurious benches or perfectly manicured lawns. Some of them were alone while others were in groups, 'shooting the breeze' or praising the Lord. Many, many children were present, also. Their ages ranged from ten all the way down to the toddler age. Many of them were playing beautiful pieces of music on golden harps. They had grownup people around them who were instructing them in the things pertaining to the Kingdom of God. Some of the angels were also attending to them.

"Note this," said the angel, "the Master said, 'Suffer little children and forbid them not, to come unto Me: for of such is the Kingdom of Heaven,' and also, 'Take heed that ye despise not one of these little ones: for I say unto you, that in heaven their angels do always behold the face of My Father which is in heaven.' These kids you see here all died before they could know the difference between right and wrong, and God has graciously applied the Blood of Jesus to their account."

Randy noticed the marvelous aromas permeating this place. He also was aware of the altogether delightful music coming from all directions, when something hit him like a ton of bricks: *He could actually hear colors in the different harmonies just like he could see different colors with his eyes!* The C major chords were a pure yellow color, the E major chords were snow-white, the augmented chords were navy-blue, the diminished chords were royal-purple, the half-diminished chords were sky-blue, the A-flat major chords were green with just a hint of blue in them, the G-flat chords were carrot-orange, and G major was blood-red. The major chords had an incandescent hue to them while the minor chords were fluorescent.

"This is amazing! The beautiful music actually has colors!"

"Yes, it does, Joshua Randall!"

Randy turned around to the speaker with a start of surprise and found himself facing a very regal and commanding personage. He was about five feet, nine inches tall with reddish hair and sported an auburn beard. He was wearing a crown on his head, signifying that he was a great king in this place. He was wearing an especially splendid white robe, elaborately decorated with rubies, diamonds, gold, and emerald gems.

"How did you know my name, sir?!" exclaimed Randy.

"Everybody knows each other in this place," answered the royal stranger.

"Who are you?"

"I am King David of Israel."

"Y-y-you are K-K-King David?"

Randy fell on his face in worship.

"On your feet, Joshua Randall! I am just a servant! The only one you worship here is the Triune God. I am assigned to show you around for a short time in this great city."

King David had a chariot, which he was driving, and he motioned to Randy to climb into the vehicle. The king started driving the chariot, rushing into the midst of the city, and the two of them chatted happily. Randy found out that this famous king of Israel had a very outgoing personality and a very friendly and animated demeanor. He laughed a lot, and his laugh made his whole body shake.

Said the king, "I hear you were quite a famous music star in your country of America during the last year."

"How did you know that about me, pray tell?"

"We are watching what is going on in the earth, and we are praying for the salvation of as many people as possible. When I was on Earth, I, too, was a musician. I played the harp for King Saul in order to minister to him after the Holy Spirit had left him and he had become demon-possessed. Many times, as I played the harp with my hand, the demonic spirit would leave King Saul and he would be better for a while until the demon would come back to torment him again. I often look for him in this marvelous land of bliss, hoping that someday, I will see his face. But alas! I greatly fear that he wound up going to the land of eternal gloom and darkness!"

"Are you the one who wrote the 23rd Psalm?"

"I am he."

"We used to sing an arrangement for choir called 'The New 23rd.' It had a contemporary beat to it."

They rode on for a little longer, and then stopped at the most magnificent street Randy had seen yet. The mansions here were huge and more splendid than any others he had seen before. The king led him to a gorgeous limestone and marble edifice. A humongous garden surrounded it, with a winding walkway bordered with flowers, trees, lawns, and flashing fountains that made the most pleasant sound. They entered a huge front door into a super-spacious entryway leading to a winding staircase carpeted with the most beautiful purple carpeting. King David then spent the next few minutes showing him around this grand castle. Randy found out that this was King David's own mansion. It consisted of thirty-five stupendous rooms. There was a huge ballroom, a dining room, a library, and a music room consisting of the most gorgeous grand piano Randy had ever seen, a huge harp, five large golden shofars, and many musical instruments he could not identify. These were just a few of the rooms in King David's heavenly palace. Randy remembered how when he was twelve years old, he had been a fan of the Land of Oz. He had read all fourteen of L. Frank Baum's books about that enchanting fairyland. He had been mesmerized by this fictional country and the fabled Emerald City, but that fairytale land was garbage compared to what he was seeing now.

The two of them walked out of King David's palace onto the awe-inspiring avenue.

"This is all too wonderful for me to take in!" gasped Randy. "Tell me, is this real? Am I here to stay for good?"

Suddenly, he felt a great sense of foreboding. Right after this, he felt a great suction that pulled him right out of that terrific land, and the next moment, he found himself hurtling through the regions of outer space at a dizzying rate of speed. He felt suddenly cold. He looked at his spiritual body and noticed he was suddenly stark naked; he no longer was wearing his 'Jitterbug Josh' outfit. The galaxies zoomed by at an inconceivable clip. Faster and faster he flew, sailing through the universe as if it were a small backyard. He felt a mixture of keen disappointment and apprehension. He thought to himself, *what's the story here? Am I going to have to climb back into my crummy broken up body of death? What a drag! No, God, no!*

He continued his faster than light speed plunge, and soon, a familiar and colorful speck appeared in the distance. It got bigger and bigger, and soon, he could see the outlines of the continents: Europe, Asia, and North America. He figured that soon enough, he would be looking down at California. He continued getting closer and closer to the earth, and the rays of the sun were getting brighter and brighter. All of a sudden, he noticed he was not heading toward California, but somewhere vastly to the southeast of that state. *What's the deal? It looks like I'm headed toward Florida. That makes no sense at all. I don't live in that state. Hey, wait a minute! Now, I'm somewhere over the Gulf Coast.* Randy guessed that he was still a hundred miles away from the earth—

Suddenly, he shot through an opening that appeared out of nowhere into a dark, frightening tunnel. It was just like those terrible nightmares and like the horrid scene he had witnessed in San Jose when that dying man had been pushed down that bottomless tube. He continued plummeting. It became darker and darker as well as more and more depressing. He could feel the darkness crushing his spirits. One of his fancies that terrorized him as a kid was the thought of a heavy house falling on him. This was much, much worse than that.

"HELP!" he cried out desperately. "SOMEBODY HELP ME PLEASE!!"

It did him no good. He continued to fall into the yawning black abyss, and the sense of oppression became worse and worse. He began to wonder, *Will this freefall ever end? Or will I keep falling forever and ever? Is this a bottomless pit?* A moment later, Randy experienced a new horror: two of those demonic monsters suddenly appeared and cruelly grabbed him in a vise-like embrace. They wouldn't let go of him, and they were laughing in a most hideous manner and uttering horrible blasphemies and taunts.

He continued falling and finally began to see a very dim light flickering far in the distance. He then noticed gigantic snakes, rats, and spiders hanging on the side of the wall of the tube. He began to notice an awfully fetid smell that grew in intensity that he was sure would have killed him if he had still been in his mortal body. The temperature began to skyrocket. First, it was uncomfortably warm, then it was stifling, then it was nearly unbearable. Strangely enough, he felt *cold* as well as hot. He heard horrible-beyond-description screams of torture in the distance, growing louder and louder. The next thing he knew, he saw a cavern ahead filled with a raging fire. As he got closer, he could see a countless number of cells housing totally pitiful beings who were being consumed by those terrible flames.

"HELP!! *HELP!!* PLEASE DON'T LET ME FALL INTO THIS PLACE OF TORTURE!!"

But he continued to get closer and closer to this cavern of fire, the grotesque beings dragging him along. He began to give up hope. *Why was I so stupid to get involved in the occult in the first place?! I HATE MYSELF!!*

He was now just a few feet away from that fiery cavern. He could now clearly see inside this awful place. The only colors here were a dull orange, brown, and black. The cavern went up into the expanse for miles, and there had to be millions upon millions of hapless people in this place of unspeakable woe.

Randy was sure there was no hope, but he gave it one more try. He knew practically nothing about this Jesus, but he would call out to Him, come what may.

"JESUS!! PLEASE SAVE ME!! I'M A GREAT SINNER, BUT PLEASE WASH ME IN YOUR PRECIOUS BLOOD!!"

Suddenly, the monsters let out a fierce cry of dismay and rage. Randy found himself standing right on the outside of the entrance of the huge fiery cavern. He was freed from the vise-like grip of those horrid demons. He turned around and almost fainted with joy and relief. There, standing right beside him, were those two kind-hearted angels. The golden-haired one spoke.

"Joshua Randall, thou son of the earth! Look, listen, and learn!"

19.

THE VALLEY OF TIME TRAVEL

Randy had never been to such a gruesome place in all his life as this inferno right in front of him. The only comfort he had right now was those two angels who were standing beside him. He wanted to turn his eyes as far away from that terrible scene as he could, but some mysterious power was causing him to look with fixed eyes upon this scene of matchless terror and torment. There were the millions of cells holding those miserable inmates. The horrible raging fires would totally consume their bodies until they were nothing but skeletons of blackened bones—and then, new skin would grow on these beings, and the process would start all over again. Randy could not stand the sight of the burning flesh nor the hideous screams of these tormented people that sounded forth.

"PLEASE!" he cried. "HOW LONG WILL THEY HAVE TO ENDURE THIS AWFUL SUFFERING?"

"Forever," said the blonde angel sadly. "These unfortunate multitudes in these realms of eternal night died in their sins and will have to appear before God to be judged for their sins and cast into the Lake of Fire forever."

"This is but one part of Hades that you're looking into," said the other angel. "This section here is the prison house for all those who were involved in idolatry, sorcery, or drug addiction. As you can see, it is a terrible, terrible place."

A voice floated over to Randy, which he immediately recognized with shock that sent a chill through his spine.

"HELP!! HELP!! JITTERBUG JOSH, THIS IS BRIAN MANNING HERE!! I CAN'T STAND THE PAIN OF THIS FIRE!! GET ME OUT!! *GET ME OUT!!*"

"I can't get you out! Oh, Brian, Brian, how absolutely sad! Isn't there anything that can be done for him?"

"Nothing," said the golden-haired angel. "Sadly, billions of people are suffering in these regions of night. The Scripture is so clear when it says, 'For the wages of sin is death.' Here in this dark domain are the fornicators, the sorcerers, the murderers, the alcoholics, thieves, homosexuals, liars, slanderers, the fearful, the unbelieving, and idolaters. All people who deliberately and successfully commit suicide who were not suffering from mental illness that impairs the reasoning abilities of the mind are also here. The man who planned your assassination is also here." (Randy shuddered when the angel spoke these next words.) "And Joshua Randall—if that man who instigated the assassination plot against you had actually been successful in having you shot dead right there in the theater just like your friend was over there in the flames, *you* would be spending eternity in this place of eternal misery. But come, it is time to move on."

Mercifully, the two angels led Randy away from that awful cavern through the black tube. They came to a side tube shortly, and the angels led him through this new route.

"We have one more place we need to visit down here," said the golden-haired angel.

Soon, they came to an area of hell where there were a lot of pits housing lost people who were burning in them and screaming out in torture. The angels stopped at one of them where an elderly lady was writhing and crying out in agony.

"I CAN'T STAND THE PAIN!! *LET ME OUT!! LET ME OUT!! WHY AM I HERE?* I ACCEPTED THE LORD WHEN I WAS BUT A LITTLE GIRL! I SANG IN THE CHOIR AT CORNERSTONE COMMUNITY CHURCH FOR FORTY YEARS AND WAS A SUNDAY SCHOOL TEACHER FOR THIRTY YEARS. I WAS GREAT WITH THE CHILDREN AND THEY LOVED ME! I PRAYED A LOT AND WITNESSED FAITHFULLY FOR OUR LORD TO A LOT OF PEOPLE! I DID A LOT OF GOOD WORKS INCLUDING A LOT OF WORK FOR THE COMMUNITY!"

"I can't help you now, Helen Parker!" declared the chief angel. "You died in your sins and judgment is set."

"So what's the story concerning this poor woman?" asked Randy in a low and depressed voice.

"Well," said the golden-haired angel. "Helen Parker over here did do all the good works she just mentioned. But her downfall is that she walked in unforgiveness for twenty years. When she was in her forties, a dishonest man took advantage of her husband and cheated him out of a large sum of money. She took an offense against him. Time and time again over the years, the Spirit urged her to forgive that man, but she stubbornly resisted and became more and more hard and bitter. That bitterness and unforgiveness was the thing that triggered her very painful arthritis she suffered from for the last fifteen years of her life."

"So it was bitterness that brought her here?"

"Yes! The Lord Jesus has made it clear that if you forgive men their trespasses against you, the Heavenly Father will also forgive your trespasses, but if you refuse to forgive men their trespasses against you, neither will the Heavenly Father forgive you. The Scriptures mean exactly what they say, and you MUST forgive everyone who hurts you in order to enter the heavenly kingdom."

The angels led Randy up another dark corridor leading them away from those horrible regions. The sense of depression and despondency gradually lifted, and the gross darkness lessened as well. They soon came to the top of the vortex, and Randy blinked in the newfound and welcome light. He could feel clothes covering his spiritual body; once again, he was wearing his 'Jitterbug Josh' outfit.

"Why did I have to go and see that horrible place?" asked Randy.

"The Lord needed to teach you a lesson about Hades," responded the golden-haired angel.

Randy took a good, thorough look around at his surroundings for the first time and gave a start of astonishment. He was not on the surface of the earth like he thought he would be, but in a large sort of valley clothed in twilight. There were periodic claps of thunder and flashes of lightning that turned the twilight into bright daylight for just a split second. Rocky, slate-colored walls were beside them with many doors carved into them with fancy signs printed on them. Some of the doors were very elaborately decked out with many beautiful jewels, while others were very plain and bare. Randy noticed that the chute they had emerged from was also a door—a very forbidding door with the words, 'ETERNAL DAMNATION' written on it.

"Where are we now?" asked Randy.

"We are, as it were, in a sort of time machine," said the blonde angel. "You probably know by now that time in heaven is not like time on Earth. Everybody on Earth knows about Einstein's Theory of Relativity. What we are about to do is actually take you on several trips of time travel. This is for your spiritual instruction on certain important aspects of prophetic truth about the person of Jesus and eternal things."

They started walking through this large valley, passing many doors that were carved into the side of the rugged, rocky mountainside. The ground they were standing on was solid stone. Randy noticed that the writing on the different doors they were passing was written in a language and even with script he had never seen before, yet surprisingly, he could understand everything the signs said. The first entryway they passed was decked out with many different types of beautiful flowers and read, 'The Garden of Eden.' They passed another door made out of gopher wood with the words, 'The Worldwide Flood' written on it. Another door said, 'THE REIGN OF KING DAVID OF ISRAEL.' This door had a plethora of valuable jewels on it as well as a large crown.

"The language that these signs are written in is Hebrew," said the golden-haired angel. "Hebrew was the language Yahweh used to call the heavens and earth into being, and it was the language that Adam, Eve, and all their descendants spoke up to the time of the Tower of Babel."

Soon, they stopped at a very plain door made out of roughly hewn wood. The sign said, 'The Cross.' The golden-haired angel lifted the latch and opened the door, and the three of them walked through the opening. Randy found himself in a place he didn't recognize at all.

He found himself standing in a large garden full of olive trees on a moonlit night. All around this place could be seen multitudes of tall, kind, and benevolent beings who were like the two angels who had been instructing him and leading him around to those various places. All these beings had somber and sad looks on their faces, and their heads were down. Straight ahead of them were four human beings dressed in garb that was totally unfamiliar to Randy. They were strong and burly men. Three of them looked like hard-working day laborers. The fourth one looked like an average human being except for this: there was something inexplicably different about his face. A loveliness clothed His face that Randy had never seen on any other person before. His face radiated indescribable meekness, gentleness, compassion, and benevolence. His eyes were wells of immeasurable and fathomless love that seemed to penetrate right through you. All four of their faces were etched with sadness, but the lovely Man's face looked sad to a much, much greater degree.

Suddenly, the Man of Loveliness spoke to the other three men in a voice full of pathos and said, "My soul is exceedingly sorrowful, even unto death. You guys stay here and watch with Me!"

He then walked some distance away from the other three men. Randy and the two angels followed the exceedingly lovely Man. Randy was very baffled by the surroundings, by the lack of modern conveniences like electricity, and by the strange things that were happening.

"Where am I?" he asked.

The golden-haired angel answered, saying, "We have taken a trip in time, more than 1,900 years backwards. We are in the city of Jerusalem in a place called the Garden of Gethsemane. You remember, Joshua Randall, when that deceiving spirit who masqueraded as your dad, took you on those deceptive trips backward in time? First, he made you think you were George Gershwin on February 12, 1924, debuting the Rhapsody in Blue at Aeolian Hall, and later on, King David, sitting on the throne of his palace in Jerusalem almost 3,000 years ago. Those experiences were clever illusions, but this trip is the real deal.

"That Man over yonder is the Christ, and the other three men over here are three of His disciples, Peter, James, and John. The time period we are in is the most important event that has happened in history. Thou son of the earth, look, listen, and learn!"

Randy looked around, and soon could hear the Man of Love crying out in agony, saying, "O, my Father, if it be possible, let this cup pass from Me: nevertheless, not as I will, but as Thou wilt!"

Soon, the heads of the other three men drooped forward, and loud snores reverberated through the grove of olive trees. Presently, the Man of Loveliness rose from His prone stance of prayer and walked heavily back to the other three men and tapped them on the shoulders to stir them awake.

"What is this, Peter?" He asked. "Could you guys not watch with Me one hour? Watch and pray so that you guys won't enter into temptation: the spirit indeed is willing, but the flesh is weak."

Randy then watched as the lovely Man walked away from them, knelt on the ground, and prayed again, crying out, "O my Father, if this cup may not pass away from Me, except I drink it, Thy will be done."

As He continued praying with great passion, the snores of the three other men again sounded forth. The Man of Loveliness eventually rose from prayer again and came back to observe the three snoozers.

"I don't understand this at all!" said Randy. "Why don't those people take notice of us?"

The golden-haired angel responded, "Because you aren't here in your mortal body, but in your spirit. It's just like when you were flying around outside your body in the twentieth century when mortal men couldn't see you and you couldn't make contact with the physical world."

They watched as the Man of Love went back to His spot of prayer and prayed the same words with even more intensity. Suddenly, Randy noticed a benevolent angel approach that Man and start to give Him strength and encouragement. It is impossible to describe exactly how this was done. The closest analogy that Randy could compare what the angel was doing for this Man would be the good fairies in the Walt Disney movie, *The Sleeping Beauty,* breathing their impartations of blessing into the baby Princess Aurora.

Suddenly, Randy cried out in dismay, "Look! Oh, my, my, MY! He's *bleeding!* It looks like great drops of blood are flowing down His body."

"Yes," said the second angel. "He is in great agony of soul!"

The time came when He slowly rose from His kneeling position, walked heavily toward the other three men, and said, "That's right! Go ahead! Sleep on now and take your rest: behold, the hour is at hand, and the Son of Man is betrayed into the hands of sinners. Rise, let us be going: behold, he is at hand that doth betray Me."

As Randy watched, he saw a great band of agitated men coming toward the lovely Man, being led by a tall, handsome man with reddish hair. His face mirrored a business-like, calculating personality. Alongside this group of people was a whole herd of those horrible monsters he had first seen in his nightmares back in his mortal body. They all had gloating looks of hatred on their countenances, and were, by turns, mocking, blaspheming, and laughing with hideous cackles. On top of the tall, redheaded, businesslike leader of the pack was the most imposing and horrible monster of them all. He towered in height above all the rest of them, had something like a malicious flame that issued from his mouth, and totally possessed the body of the redheaded man. A swarm of other hideous apparitions was right beside the huge fiery demon. The great company of men was carrying torches, lanterns, swords, and clubs.

The tall, redheaded man walked right up to the lovely Man, kissed him profusely with many smooches, and exclaimed, "Rabbi, Rabbi! Hail, Rabbi!"

It was obvious to Randy that the Man of Loveliness could read the mind of the redheaded man like a book when He answered, "Friend, why have you come? Judas, are you betraying the Son of Man with a kiss?" He then looked at the redheaded man with sadness and pity. It was obvious that He loved the devious, two-faced person named Judas.

He then turned to the multitude and asked, "Who do you guys seek?"

They answered, "Jesus of Nazareth."

"I am He."

When He said this, the whole crowd was thrown backward onto the ground.

Again, He asked, "Who do you guys seek?"

"Jesus of Nazareth."

"I told you before that I am He." He then pointed toward eleven men who were obviously His followers and said, "If therefore you folks seek Me, let these men over here go their way."

Randy then watched as those eleven followers of the lovely Man got into a heated conversation among themselves.

"That's downright low-down and dirty!"

"Those rotten, no-good turkeys!"

"Lord, shall we smite with the sword?"

At this point, a muscular man among the eleven followers, who obviously had natural leadership abilities, took out a sword and slashed at one of the antagonistic people in the crowd who was obviously a servant. He succeeded in cutting off his right ear. The man screamed in pain.

"Lookie there! He got Malchus, the servant of the high priest!"

The Man of Love turned sternly on the man with the sword and exclaimed, "That's enough, Peter! Put up your sword into the sheath: for all they that take up the sword shall perish by the sword! The cup which My Father hath given Me, shall I not drink it? Don't you know that if I wanted to, I could pray to My Father and He would have now given Me more than twelve legions of angels to rescue Me? But how then shall the Scriptures be fulfilled, that thus it must be?"

The Man of Love then touched with incredible gentleness the place on the cheek of Malchus where the ear had been shorn off. Randy then marveled as he saw the ear totally restored the way it had been before. A look of tremendous gratefulness came upon the countenance of Malchus. The eleven disciples then fled, and the crowd with torches and swords took the Man of Love captive and started leading Him away. Randy and the two angels followed the crowd. The Man of Love then spoke to the large crowd again.

"Have you guys come out against Me with swords and clubs to arrest Me just like you would if you were arresting a thief? Every day, I sat with you folks in the temple as I taught and you never laid a hand on Me, but this is your hour and the power of darkness. All this was done that the Scriptures of the prophets might be fulfilled."

"I don't get it!" exclaimed Randy. "That man is so kind and loving! There is a sweetness in his voice like I've never ever heard before—and did you see the way he healed that man's ear? What in blue blazes has he ever done to deserve this treatment from those dirty scoundrels?!"

"Thou son of the earth, look, listen, and learn!" responded the blonde angel. "Behold! He is the Lamb of God that taketh away the sin of the world."

Randy was still bewildered. That Person was a man, not a lamb. He knew very little about Jesus. Pastor Kevin at his church in Orinda had only given him a picture of Jesus Christ as the greatest teacher who had ever lived. He had heard the same idea from his teachers while he was in the fifth grade. He had led his choirs in many a song that talked about the Lamb, but it never made any sense to him. As they walked along, he mused over these things. He looked around him. They were climbing up a hill. Many buildings below them to the east glistened in the moonlight. Randy espied a large, beautiful building to the east, and beyond that, a large hill.

"What you are looking at is Herod's temple, and that hill you see beyond it is called The Mount of Olives," said the second angel.

When they had first entered this land through the door, they had been right at the bottom of that hill.

They soon walked into a courtyard and then into a room that was luxurious for that day and age. A man was in the room who was seated and dressed in a fancy robe.

"Who is that guy?" asked Randy to the blonde angel.

"He's Annas, the father in-law of the high priest, Caiaphas."

The man in the soft robe then asked Jesus, "So, tell me Jesus! What do You have to say about Yourself? Please inform me about Your disciples and fill me in on the doctrines You teach."

Jesus, the Man of Loveliness, responded to Annas, "I spoke openly to the world: I always taught in the synagogue, and in the temple, where the Jews always hang out in; I never said anything in secret. Why do you ask Me? Ask them which heard Me, what I have said unto them: behold, they know what I said—"

SLAP! "You dare to answer the high priest like that?!" shouted an officer who was standing by Jesus.

"If I have spoken evil, bear witness of the evil: but if well, why do you hit me?"

At this point, the officers led Jesus to Caiaphas. A quickie meeting of the Sanhedrin, an elitist Jewish group of seventy of the top leaders in Israel, had been called. Its purpose was to try this controversial figure of notoriety. They were assembled, and the proceedings began.

Caiaphas, the high priest, opened his mouth and began, "Fellow members of the Council! Men, brethren, and fathers! I have called you all together on this Passover night for a very important reason. We have a problem! It concerns this controversial man standing before us who has brought much upheaval in this most blessed land of Israel. Jesus, the

Nazarene, has brought much trouble to our land of Judea. We need to get to the bottom of this quickly. I need your input on this matter."

Different people came forward and offered many accusations against Jesus.

"He is a revolutionary who has been stirring up the people towards insubordination against our nation, all the way from this city on up to Bethsaida!"

"Rabbi. This fellow has repeatedly and brazenly broken the Sabbath by working on it. You remember how in the Law, there was that account of that man who was gathering wood on a Sabbath day who was stoned by the whole congregation?"

"Your Excellency. That man has constantly incited rebellion against Rome. He has told people not to pay taxes to Caesar."

"And that fellow once called Herod a lying, conniving fox! He is a menace both to our Jewish nation and to Rome! He should be stoned to death!"

And so, the damning testimonies went on, many of them contradicting each other in various points. Finally, two witnesses testified, each of them accusing Jesus of the same thing.

The first false witness alleged, "This fellow said, 'I am able to destroy the temple of God and to build it in three days.'"

The second man said, "We heard him say, 'I will destroy this temple that is made with hands, and within three days, I will build another made without hands.'"

"What Jesus *really* said," explained the blonde angel, "was, 'Destroy this temple, and in three days I will raise it up'—and He was talking about His body, not the building."

Caiaphas stood to his feet and asked, "Do you have nothing to say for yourself? What is it which these people witness against you?"

Jesus didn't say one word in reply.

"I adjure you by the living God that you tell us whether you are Christ, the Son of God."

"It is as you said. Nevertheless, I say to you folks, hereafter, you guys shall see the Son of Man sitting on the right hand of power and coming in the clouds of heaven."

The face of the high priest turned purple with rage as he tore his clothes and shouted, "He has blasphemed! What further need have we of witnesses! Behold now, you guys have heard the blasphemy! What do you all think?"

Shouts rang throughout the whole room.

"KILL HIM!"

"HE IS GUILTY OF DEATH!"

"AWAY WITH THAT BLASPHEMOUS REVOLUTIONIST!"

Then many of the people in that room began to abuse Jesus in many ways. Some of them spit on Him. Others beat Him up. Someone blindfolded

Him while others slapped Him hard with the palms of their hands, all the while mocking Him with lots of verbal abuse.

"Prophesy unto us, you that claims that you're Christ! Who hit you?"

"He can't see who hit him! Haw, haw, haw! This proves he's a false prophet!"

"He claims to be a king. Come on, guys, let's crown him!"

Hard slaps on the top of the head.

"He don't look like any king I've ever seen!"

"Aha, aha, aha!"

At this point, Randy had a flashback to the time about a year ago when he had become a Freemason. He had gone through the initiation into The Royal Order of the Blue Knights. It had been a real nightmare for him. The Lodge members had put a 'hoodwink' on him (that is to say, blindfolding him). Then they had taken turns slapping him, punching him, and kicking him all over his body. He ended up bruised all over and greatly frightened. When he returned home, Lila had commented on the fact that he looked as white as a ghost and asked what had happened. Of course, Randy refused to divulge anything because it was a Lodge secret.

Eventually, the men finished having their fun with Jesus, and Caiaphas said, "All right, you! It's down to the dungeon for you until the early morning!"

And with that, some of the men led Him out of the room.

Randy just stood there, his mouth wide open, his face etched with great dismay and unbelief. Said he, "This is *crazy!* What's gotten into those no-good crooks?!"

"This is nothing compared to what's coming," said the blonde angel. "Do you remember when you were in heaven and heard all of the rejoicing and beautiful music from the angels and saints? Do you remember seeing the incredible light, the lovely flowers, and the fantastic fruit trees?"

"How could I ever forget it?"

"Well, in this moment of history when the Son of God, the Messiah, is giving His life for the world, there is no singing going on in the realms of bliss. The flowers and trees seem to droop in sympathy for the Second Person of the Trinity, the birds in paradise have ceased their joyful heavenly songs of praise to God Almighty, and a strange twilight has clouded heaven in shadow. The price for the redemption of the world is very, very high."

"Tell me. What is your name?"

"My name is Mystery Revealer," said the blonde angel.

"And my name is Godly Discretion," said the smaller angel.

Several other things happened on that short night. One of those things, Randy would never forget. There was a time between the trials when he espied the man who had cut off the ear of Malchus standing in the courtyard. He and several other people were warming themselves in front of a fire on that cold night. Suddenly, one of the people there looked at him and said, "You are one of the disciples of Jesus, aren't you?"

"I don't know that man," he replied.

After a while, another person, who was related to Malchus, said, "Yeah, didn't I see you in the garden with Him?"

"I don't know what you're talking about. I swear it!" said Peter with an oath.

A little later, a third person said, "Yeah, you were with Him. I know. You are from Galilee and your accent gives you away."

"(BLANKETY-BLANK-BLANK)! I do not know that Man! I don't know what you guys are talking about, so just shut up! May God strike me dead with a lightning bolt from heaven if I'm lying to you—"

The crowing of a rooster interrupted his speech, and Jesus turned to look at the muscular man who immediately burst into loud weeping, turned, and trotted out of the courtyard.

Gray colors and then red colors began to form in the eastern skies above the Mount of Olives, signaling the advent of dawn. Jesus was led upstairs from his dungeon cell by a number of guards. Once again, He would appear before Caiaphas, the high priest of Israel. Jesus was covered with many bruises and had two black eyes. Many very important Jewish leaders were here. Once again, the proceedings began.

"So, Jesus, I'm going to ask You one more time. Are You the Christ? Tell us."

"If I tell you, you guys will not believe. And if I also ask you, you guys will not answer Me, nor let Me go. Hereafter, the Son of Man shall sit on the right hand of the power of God."

"Are You then the Son of God?" asked the crowd.

"It is as you say."

Shouts of anger reverberated through the hall.

"That does it!"

"What need do we have of any further witness?"

"We ourselves have heard it from His own mouth!"

"Tie His hands!"

"Let's take Him to Pontius Pilate!"

They all rose up and led Jesus to Pilate, Mystery Revealer and Godly Discretion leading Randy right alongside the crowd. They came to the residence of the governor, which was close to the temple, but all the Jews stayed outside. It was considered unkosher for them to enter a house with leaven in it during the time of Passover. Soon, Jesus was facing Pontius Pilate, the governor, who was dressed in a soft white-and-purple robe. He glanced at Jesus with a weary look on his face. He had to deal with a lot of problems—robbers, murderers, and insurrectionists. He then went outside to face the crowd of Jews.

"What's the trouble?" he asked. "What accusation do you guys bring against this Man?"

Many insults resounded through the room.

"If He were not a malefactor, we would not have delivered Him up to you!"

"He's been fobbing off His anarchic ideas to our nation and inciting rebellion!"

"Yeah, we found this fellow perverting our nation and forbidding to pay tribute to Caesar!"

"He says that He is Christ, a king!"

Pilate replied, "Get out of here! I don't want to get involved! You guys take Him and judge Him according to your own law!"

The crowd responded, "It is not lawful for us to put any man to death."

Godly Discretion nudged Randy and said, "Take note of this: they just lied. The Torah is full of commands to enforce the death penalty for such things as murder, adultery, homosexuality, and involvement in occultic practices like spiritualism, witchcraft, and black magic."

"Black magic?" asked Randy in a confused voice. "Are you talking about illusionists like Houdini? I have a close friend who is an expert at performing sleight-of-hand magic tricks."

"No, Joshua Randall," explained Mystery Revealer. "Illusion shows like what your friend, Mike Applebaum performs, are perfectly harmless—provided that people understand that they are just illusions. The black magic the Bible is talking about refers to supernatural feats performed by demons to entrap the people of the world. Right now, many sorcerers are burning in those cells of Hades, which you saw who once practiced those acts of black magic and spiritualism on Earth."

Randy had a terrible thought, which he was afraid to inquire about: *Is my dad, Thomas Miller, burning in one of those horrible cells in hell?*

Pilate then walked back into the room, looked at Jesus, and asked, "Are You the King of the Jews?"

"Are you asking Me this on your own initiative or did others tell you about this?"

"Am I a Jew? Your own nation and the chief priests have delivered You up to me. What have You done?"

"My kingdom is not of this world. If My kingdom were of this world, then My servants would fight that I should not be delivered to the Jews, but at this present time, My kingdom is not from hence."

"Are You a king then?"

"What you say is true," answered Jesus. "I am a king. To this end was I born, and for this cause, I came into the world that I should bear witness unto the truth. Everyone that is of the truth hears My voice."

"What is truth?" asked Pilate, who rose up, walked outside, looked intently at everybody, and declared, "There's nothing wrong with Him! I find no fault in this man. Nevertheless, you guys have a custom that I should release to you good people one accused person at the Passover. Therefore, do you want me to release unto you the king of the Jews?"

A flood of protests followed from the crowd.

"Not this Man, but Barabbas!"

"Crucify Jesus!"

"He stirs up the people, inciting rebellion among them!"

"Yeah, He's spoken against the priesthood and leaders of all Jewry, He's spoken against Jerusalem, He's spoken against the Law of Moses, He's blasphemed repeatedly, and He's even spoken against the Roman government!"

"And He's spread His poisonous teaching from His home area of Galilee all the way down to this place!"

Pontius Pilate gave a start of surprise and asked, "Galilee? Is He really from Galilee? Somebody please tell me!"

"I believe He is, Governor!"

"Anyone know what town He's from?"

"He used to live in Nazareth as a carpenter, and the last few years has spent a lot of time in towns like Chorazin, Bethsaida, and Capernaum."

"You know what?" said Pilate. "I think I'm going to send Him to Herod since He is under Herod's jurisdiction. It just so happens that he is also in Jerusalem today."

When Herod saw them bringing Jesus to be tried by him, he got very excited and exclaimed, "Jesus is coming here? Oh, joy! Oh, rapture! I've heard a lot of things about this Man! I've always wanted to see Him! Maybe I can get Him to do some type of spectacular miracle!"

Jesus was brought to Herod who began peppering Him with a lot of questions.

"I understand that You're Jesus the Nazarene. Is that true?"

Silence.

"I have heard numerous reports that You can do a lot of magic tricks. Is that true?"

Silence.

"I've been told that blind people have received their sight, the deaf hear, the lame walk, there are even reports of people rising again from the dead."

Silence.

Many cries broke out from the religious leaders.

"Na-na-na-na-na-na! That king of the Jews has no voice!"

"He won't say anything now!"

"Haw, haw, haw! He won't speak now because He's worn out His voice spreading His radical ideas to the masses!"

"He's nothing but a big fat imposter!"

Herod was becoming more and more irritated at the silence of Jesus. He exclaimed, "Aren't You even going to say one word? Come on, Jesus! Show us Your stuff! Do a great big miracle for me! Let's see You put on a great show!"

Silence.

"What's the matter with You? You don't talk, You don't show me any sign or wonder! Okay, then! If You won't give me a show, then I will! Come on, guys, let the games begin! This will be a Roman circus like has never been seen on Earth before!"

The whole crowd burst into a cascade of evil laughter, and Herod and his men arrayed Jesus in a gorgeous robe and continued to mock Him. Eventually, Herod said, "I can't make out anything concerning this 'king' either. Come on, let's go back to Pilate!"

So back to the governor's residence they went.

Here we go again, thought Pilate to himself.

He then called the crowd together and said, "Listen, people! We've already been through this once before! You guys have brought this Man unto me as one that perverts the people, and behold; I, having examined Him before you have found no fault in this Man concerning those things you folks accuse Him of. No, nor has Herod, for I sent you back to him; and lo, nothing worthy of death is done unto him. Therefore, I will chastise Him and let Him go."

But the multitude cried out, "Away with this Man and release unto us Barabbas!"

Pilate stood there, hating this moment of decision. He could see goodness in this Man and knew that He had been delivered up to him because of envy. On the other hand, he had the great masses of the people to think about. He was accountable directly to the Roman emperor himself. The Jews were very discontented under Roman rule, but they did have one 'ace in the hole.' If they thought a governor was unfair, they could write the Caesar himself who could 'fire' Pilate from the governorship. *I got to do something here! What to do, what to do?* As his mind whirled around and around, he saw a man running through the crowd and heading straight for him. When he had reached Pilate, he spoke in a breathless voice.

"Your Excellency, a message from your wife! She says it's urgent!"

"Speak!"

"Your wife says, 'Have nothing to do with that just Man for I have suffered many things in a dream this day because of Him.'"

Okay! There it is! He should do the right thing and let Him go free.

"Look, guys! Let's discuss this thing in a reasonable way and act like rational men. I really think that I should let this Jesus go free. He is—"

"CRUCIFY HIM!! *CRUCIFY HIM!!*"

"Why, what evil has He done? I have found no cause of death in Him: I will therefore chastise Him and let Him go."

"CRUCIFY HIM!! CRUCIFY HIM!! *CRUCIFY HIM!!*"

The shouts from the crowd were deafening. Randy looked out at the huge masses outside the governor's residence. Not only were there great masses of those people, but there were countless numbers of those horrible monsters interspersed among the human beings who were yelling at the top of their lungs and goading the people on in their insanity. He looked at the other accused criminal and experienced a moment of déjà vu. The face of the one called Barabbas was distorted with evil very much like the face of Eric Burns had been in the last several months of his life.

Godly Discretion, who could read the thoughts of Randy, answered them by saying, "That man, who you see over there, whose name is Barabbas, is a revolutionary, a robber, and a murderer. The crowd wants Pilate to release that murderer and put to death the Prince of Life."

At this point, Pilate took Jesus and scourged Him with a very sharp instrument. The soldiers put a crown of thorns on His head and mocked Him.

"Hail, King of the Jews!"

"We worship You, Thou King!"

"He is still king!"

The soldiers spit on Him and hit Him on the head with a reed that they snatched out of His right hand.

"Lookit' Him! He's all purple! He's the most perfect, purple, pontific person we've ever seen! His robe is purple, His back is purple, His face is purple, and His eyes are purple!"

"Haw, haw, haw, haw!"

Tears flowed down the spiritualized face of Randy. *How could these crazy people do this to that wonderful Man?!* His whole body was a piece of raw hamburger. Soon, Pilate returned and spoke to the crowd.

"Had enough? Behold, I bring Him forth to you, that you guys may know that I find no fault in Him."

Jesus came forth wearing the platted crown of thorns and the purple robe.

"Behold the Man!" declared Pilate. "Take a good, long look at Him! Are you happy? Are you satisfied? Don't you think He's suffered enough?"

"CRUCIFY HIM!! *CRUCIFY HIM!!*" screamed the chief priests and officers at the top of their lungs.

"You guys take Him and crucify Him yourselves, for I find no fault in Him!"

The Jews in the crowd cried out, saying, "We have a law, and by our law He ought to die, because He made Himself the Son of God!"

Sheer terror filled Pilate's face. *This is getting worse all the time! Now, what do I do?* He walked back into the judgment hall to speak to Jesus yet again.

"Where are You from?" he asked Jesus.

Silence.

"Aren't You going to say anything to me? Don't You know that I have power to crucify You and power to release You?"

"You could have no power at all against Me except it had been given to you from above. Therefore, he that delivered Me up to you has the greater sin."

Pilate walked back outside to the crowd and said, "I beg you to let me release that righteous Guy and to condemn Barabbas! It is obvious to me that……."

"If you let this Man go," cried the Jews, "you are not Caesar's friend! Whoever makes himself a king speaks against Caesar!"

Pilate went and got Jesus and sat down at the judgment seat at a place called the Pavement, a place with the Hebrew name, Gabbatha.

"Behold your king!" cried Pilate.

"AWAY WITH HIM! AWAY WITH HIM! *CRUCIFY HIM!!*"

"Shall I crucify your king?"

"WE HAVE NO KING BUT CAESAR!" yelled the chief priests.

As a riot was beginning to blaze forth in the crowd, Godly Discretion spoke to Randy, saying, "Note this: Their actions are inconsistent. Those people hate the Roman government, and yet, they've just sided with them against Jesus Christ, who is their Jewish Messiah."

Pilate slapped his sides with his hands in resignation and exclaimed, "Very well! *Very well!* Have it your way!" He took water, washed his hands before the multitude, and declared, "I am innocent of the blood of this just Person! You guys take care of it!"

The crowd screamed, *"HIS BLOOD BE ON US AND ON OUR CHILDREN!!"*

At this point, Pilate released the man with the face etched with evil and delivered Jesus up to be crucified. The soldiers took the purple robe off of Jesus and put His own clothes back on Him. They put the heavy cross upon Jesus and started leading Him through the city and toward the west. Oh, what a terrible, awful scene it was! Randy was half-sure that Jesus could have easily died just from the scourging by itself. The crowd followed Jesus, mocking Him every step of the way. There came a point where His physical strength totally gave out, and He stumbled and fell under the weight of that great cross. At this point, they forced a man to bear the cross of the staggering Jesus.

"The man you see there bearing the cross of Jesus is Simon of Cyrene," explained Mystery Revealer to Randy.

They continued on. Soon, the crowd was augmented by a company of women who were weeping and bewailing the fate of Jesus.

He turned to them and said, "Daughters of Jerusalem! Don't weep for Me, but weep for yourselves and for your children. For behold, the days are coming when they shall say, 'Blessed are the barren and the wombs that never bore and the breasts which never gave suck!' Then they shall begin to say to the mountains, 'Fall on us!' and to the hills, 'cover us!' For if they do these things in a green tree, what shall be done in the dry?"

"What Jesus is talking about," explained Mystery Revealer, "is the coming terrible captivity of the Jews in A. D. 70 when Titus burned the temple down to the ground. What He means by the green tree and the dry tree is this: if the Romans can do this to a just Man like Jesus, then how can those evil people expect to escape the fierce wrath of the Romans?"

Randy looked at Jesus and saw within that piece of raw meat, within that mutilated piece of hamburger that was beyond human recognition, the same matchless love, the same gentleness, mercy, and compassion he had seen right from the very beginning of his time trip to the first century.

It was approximately 9:00 in the morning. They continued trudging through Jerusalem until they were outside the city where they stopped at a place where the rock formations looked a lot like a skull. It was a place where many, many people were traveling past, and also a site where there were obviously a lot of executions by the Romans that took place. Here, they raised up the stake and nailed the hands and feet of Jesus to it with huge nails. A lot of blood was flowing from Him. Two other men with evil-looking faces were nailed to crosses and raised up on each side of Jesus. Randy suddenly gave a start of surprise; he recognized the man who was to the right of Jesus (left of Jesus from Randy's view).

"The man you see to your left of Jesus is Ben Simeon, the repentant thief on the cross," explained Mystery Revealer. "You saw him a while ago in heaven. He was the one who was assigned to assist Darryl Temple in the knowledge of the Christian graces. Where we are standing right now is named Golgotha in the Hebrew tongue. That word means 'the place of a skull,' and is commonly known as Calvary."

Randy watched the terrible scene with increasing sadness and depression as the sufferings of Jesus increased exponentially. To add to His torment of suffocation, thirst, and the bruises and wounds from the nails, the scourging, and the beatings were the constant insults coming His way from the chief priests of the Jews, the Roman soldiers, the two thieves beside Him, and multitudes of people who were passing by. The most horrible barbs echoed through that site.

"Haw, haw, haw! He claimed to be the Son of God and look where He is now!"

"King of the Jews, huh? Oh, yeah, sure, sure, sure! Some king!"

"I've seen some idiots in my lifetime, but that one there really takes the cake! Haw, haw, haw!"

"Oh boy, what a stupid boob He is!"

"He saved others, but He cannot save Himself!"

"If He is the King of Israel, let Him now come down from the cross and we will believe Him!"

"He trusted in God; let Him deliver Him now, if He will have Him; for He said, 'I am the Son of God.' Look at Him! He just lies there up on that stake!"

The thief on the cross to the right sneered, saying, "Aha, aha, aha! Na, na, na, na! If You're really the Son of God, save Yourself! Come down from that cross!"

"Yeah," agreed Ben Simeon from the left side, "save us! Well, I guess You can't save us after all! Looks like You're just a weak and wimpy King of the Jews! Humph! Some king You turned out to be! Here we are, sorry basket cases, dying on these sticks of wood!"

Jesus looked around at everyone with nothing but pity and the purest love as He prayed, "Father, forgive them, for they know not what they do!"

Randy was deeply moved by the unsearchable love and mercy of Jesus toward all those people who were deriding Him. He was sure if he were suffering 1/10,000th of the torment that Jesus was, he would have wanted to kill all those dirty rascals. Time passed by, slowly. Every minute seemed like an hour, and every hour seemed like a day. The abuse against Jesus continued.

Sometime during that morning, a messenger came running up to the crowd with some big news. "One of the disciples of Jesus committed suicide early this morning!"

"Who was it?" asked some of the people in the crowd.

"It was Judas Iscariot. He hanged himself in the Valley of Hinnom, he burst open in the middle, and all his bowels fell out."

"Note this, thou son of the earth," said Mystery Revealer. "The mysterious power and destructive forces of sin. Tragic stories of individuals have happened on the earth through the ages over and over again that are similar to the story of Judas Iscariot. There have been many times when a small seed of resentment and offense was planted in a person's life. The seed grew until it blossomed into full-grown hatred. Satan was able to use that hatred to goad that person into committing acts of betrayal and murder. The person didn't realize the high cost to his soul and conscience of his premeditated deeds until after he performed them. After the evil deed was done, he would feel an unbearable load of depression, guilt, and hopelessness; and Satan would send one of his lackeys to goad the unfortunate person into taking his own life. Tragically, too many times, the individual did indeed end his own life."

Said Godly Discretion, "Judas Iscariot was born in Kerioth, a town in the southeastern part of Judea. His parents were both ungodly people, who today, are in the dark realms that lie far, far under the earth. He did not have a good upbringing that trained him in the ways of the Lord, and this allowed his sinful nature to flourish.

"The time came, just a few years ago, when Judas Iscariot met the Master for the first time. Jesus knew from the very beginning that it was this disciple who should betray Him, but still, He loved Judas. Remember this: the nature of God is love, even toward those who are the worst of people. Those dark realms of woe you saw were created for the devil and the angels who followed him, *never for a man*. Jesus only wanted the best for that disciple and was hoping against hope that the good qualities in Judas would triumph over the evil qualities. Judas was an extremely smart man who had aptitude for math and a keen, business-inclined mind. He had great reasoning abilities and foresight. He was handsome with a fairly outgoing personality.

"Jesus accepted him and chose him to be one of the twelve disciples that were in the inner circle. When Jesus sent the twelve out to preach, heal the sick, and cast out demons, Judas also preached, healed the sick, and cast out demons. Jesus sent the disciples out two-by-two, and Judas was paired up with Simon the Zealot. Both Judas and Simon had the same political views, being staunch lovers of the nation of Israel with a strong hatred toward the oppressive Roman Empire. Both of them thought that Jesus would be the one to free Judea from the tyranny of Rome and set up an earthly messianic kingdom. But unlike Judas, Simon was attracted to the inner beauty of Christ and followed Him with a whole heart. Simon learned to accept even the hard sayings of Jesus without guile, but Judas never gave his all to Christ. His motivation for following Jesus was for personal advancement and position in the earthly kingdom he was sure Jesus was going to bring on Earth at that time.

"Judas had a predisposition toward covetousness and self-conceit. Jesus made him treasurer of the band of disciples, and this was a test for him. He started to steal from the purse that held the money for the needs of Jesus and His disciples. The first time he did it, his conscience strongly condemned him, but he kept on stealing, the pricks of his conscience getting weaker and weaker with each sin. Satan himself had a strong pull on him from the very beginning. Jesus saw this and tried many times to warn that wayward disciple against the pitfalls of avarice. Judas heard Jesus say many things like, 'Lay not up for yourselves treasures on Earth, but lay up for yourselves treasures in heaven,' and 'You cannot serve God and Mammon.' He was there when Jesus had confronted the rich young ruler to sell everything and come follow Him. The rich man had sadly turned away, and Jesus had said that it was easier for a camel to go through the eye of a needle than for a rich man to enter the Kingdom of Heaven. He was there to hear the parable of the rich fool who was not rich toward God. He had heard the account about poor Lazarus who died and was carried by the angels to Abraham's bosom while the rich man who had neglected him died and went to hell. He also heard Jesus predict His coming death and resurrection. He began to become more and more disillusioned as it began to dawn on him that maybe Jesus was not planning to overthrow Rome and establish His own earthly kingdom. The disillusionment grew into an offense, and the offense grew into hatred. About a year before the crucifixion, Jesus had said to the Twelve, 'Did I not choose you twelve, and one of you is a devil?'

"The last straw came a few days ago when Jesus was in Bethany with Lazarus, Martha, and Mary. Mary poured some very expensive spikenard ointment on the head and feet of Jesus, and the wonderful smell filled the whole house. Judas was incensed at this because a lot of the money he could have stolen was being taken away from him. He protested, 'Why was this ointment not sold for 300 pence and given to the poor?' The other eleven echoed their protests against the deed of the woman. Judas Iscariot was highly esteemed by the other disciples, and *nobody* except Jesus had a clue concerning the great evil residing in his heart. When Jesus defended Mary's actions, that was when Judas decided to betray Jesus. During the Last Supper, Jesus repeatedly warned Judas indirectly by saying that one of the twelve would betray Him, and that it would be mega, mega horrible for the one who betrayed Him; it would have been better for that one never to have been born. Still, none of the other disciples had a clue about Judas, not even when he left the room and Jesus had said to him, 'What thou doest, do quickly.' They all thought Jesus was commanding him to go get some food for the Passover or to give something to the poor. Judas was one who could lie with a straight face and totally hide his evil deeds. After Jesus gave Judas the honored piece of sop, that was when Satan himself completely possessed him. That is what you saw when you saw that huge monster inside Judas last night."

Mystery Revealer continued the narration, saying, "When Judas saw that Jesus was condemned, he felt the great, great load of guilt over what he had done. He repented himself but didn't truly repent to God. He tried to return the thirty pieces of silver and was ridiculed by the chief priests. Satan then moved him to commit suicide. He is now in a far, far worse part of hell than those terrible cells that you saw.

"The man who tried to murder you had a life with some similarities to the life of Judas Iscariot. He had some very good instruction about the Lord from his parents when he was a kid, but when he was a teenager, he turned away from the Lord and accepted the communist doctrine. His mom and dad were not perfect, but they were righteous in the sight of Jehovah God. They did the best job they could in raising their son who totally disrespected and disowned them. That man committed sexual immorality and fomented revolution against the U. S. government. After the fight you two had last spring, a seed of revenge was planted in his heart that blossomed into full-blown hatred, leading to a kidnapping plot, and then a murder plot against your group. Still, God loved him and tried to warn him by His Spirit more than once. The last warning came at a church four nights before the concert when the Spirit spoke through the pastor. But he spurned the warning, totally and irrevocably rejected Jesus Christ, and blasphemed the Holy Spirit. He then became totally demon-possessed. After he had done the deed at the concert and tried to escape, he felt the horrible load of guilt and despondency, and Satan led him to end his own life."

As Randy listened to this narrative, he continued to watch the proceedings of the crucifixion. He began to see a softening on the face of the thief on his left while the thief on his right continued to jeer and insult Jesus. One of the disciples whom Randy had seen last night was standing there.

Some women were also present who were weeping and bewailing the fate of Jesus. One of the women there was wearing a blue gown. Jesus looked at the woman wearing the blue gown and said to her, "Behold, your son." Then he looked at the burly disciple and said, "Behold, your mother."

"The woman in the blue gown is Mary, the mother of Jesus," explained Mystery Revealer. "And that man there is the Apostle John."

Jesus was given vinegar to drink mixed with gall, which Jesus tasted, but did not drink. An inscription had been put up around the crosses written in Latin, Hebrew, and Greek that read, 'THIS IS THE KING OF THE JEWS.'

Many of the chief priests protested to Pilate, saying, "Write not 'the king of the Jews' but that He said, 'I am king of the Jews.'"

Pilate responded, "What I have written, I have written, so shut up!"

During those hours, the soldiers took the garments of Jesus and divided them into four parts. They also took the coat of Jesus and said among themselves, "Let us not rend it, but cast lots for it, whose it will be."

The thief on the right side of Jesus continued mocking Him, saying, "If You are Christ, save Yourself and us!"

But Ben Simeon, the thief on the left side of Jesus from Randy's viewpoint, had undergone a change of heart. He had been impressed by the tremendous love and patience of Jesus. He retorted, "Don't you even fear God, seeing that you are under the same condemnation and we, indeed, justly, for we are receiving the due punishment for our deeds, but this Man hasn't done anything amiss." Then the thief said to Jesus in a pleading voice, "Lord, remember me when You come into Your kingdom."

Jesus answered Ben Simeon, saying, "Verily, I say unto thee, today shalt thou be with Me in paradise."

Oh, what comfort came over the soul of Ben Simeon! Suddenly, it almost seemed like the terribly intense pains of crucifixion were nothing; he had experienced sweet freedom in his spirit!

It was now noon, and Randy saw something happening that the mortal people around the crosses couldn't see. A fathomless augmentation of the sufferings of Jesus was taking place. In fact, it was immeasurably worse than any suffering that Randy had witnessed in hell. Randy cried out, "Oh no, NO, NOOO! WHY, GOD, WHY?! WHAT HAS HE DONE TO MERIT THIS TORTURE?!" At that same moment, it began to get dark. It became darker and darker until Randy couldn't even see his hand in front of him. The darkness was extremely oppressive, just like the darkness in Hades had been. It became too much for him to handle, and he fell into a dead faint.

When he regained consciousness, Jesus was crying out, *"ELI, ELI, LAMA SABACHTHANI?!"* which means, *"MY GOD, MY GOD, WHY HAST THOU FORSAKEN ME?!"*

At that moment, it began to get light again, and some of the people who were standing around called out, "This man is calling for Elijah."

As daylight returned, Jesus exclaimed, "I am thirsty!"

Some people ran and got a sponge, which they filled with vinegar, put it on a reed, and gave it to Jesus for Him to drink.

"Hold it!" they exclaimed. "Let Him alone! Let's see if Elijah will come to take Him down!"

Then Jesus cried out with a loud voice, *"IT IS FINISHED!! FATHER, INTO THY HANDS I COMMEND MY SPIRIT!!"*

Right then, Randy saw an incredibly beautiful Spirit form of the body of Jesus leaving Him. The dead body of Jesus was marred and mutilated beyond recognition—a great big hunk of meat. Still, there shone through His battered and bruised face and eyes the most indescribable countenance of love, mercy, and kindness. Randy felt so very, very tired. He could not move at all; the drama of the crucifixion had drained him of all energy.

Suddenly, the ground he was lying on began to shake. The earthquake got stronger and stronger, and rocks began to be torn apart. The veil of the temple was torn into two pieces from top to bottom. Then the centurion cried out, "Surely, this was a righteous Man."

Many people exclaimed, "Yes! Surely, this was the Son of God!"

Soon, a discussion broke out between some of the Jews concerning the three condemned men on the crosses.

"The Sabbath comes at sundown! We can't leave those three men up on those stakes!"

"Yeah, we better tell Pontius Pilate about this!"

"Okay, let's go!"

They came to the Roman governor and asked him, "Your Excellency, our Sabbath starts at sundown, and it is against the Jewish religion for us to do any work on that day. Would you PLEASE break the legs of the three men who are on the crosses before nightfall? Tomorrow is a *high* Sabbath for us, you know."

"Go ahead. Let the soldiers kill the condemned men!"

The soldiers broke the legs of the two thieves to hasten their deaths, but when they came to Jesus, they found that He was already dead. One of the soldiers pierced His side with a spear, though, and water and blood flowed out. Randy had never seen anything like this in his whole life.

****

THE NEXT THING HE KNEW, Randy was lying in the Valley of Time Travel with its twilight, lightning, and thunder. He was extremely weary and could not move. He was sure he would never recover. Nothing, absolutely nothing, not even being back in heaven, would ever be able to restore his strength.

"Why?" he asked the angels in a very weak voice. "Why did that Man go through such unspeakable agony? He was so good, pure, loving, merciful, and kind! It makes no sense to me!"

"Thou son of the earth," responded Mystery Revealer. "Look, listen, and learn! That Man is the Lamb of God that taketh away the sin of the world. The Scripture says, 'For God so loved the world that He gave His only begotten Son that whosoever believeth in Him should not perish but have everlasting life. For God sent not His Son into the world to condemn the world, but that the world through Him might be saved.' Scripture also says, 'Surely, He hath borne our sicknesses and carried our pains: yet we did esteem Him stricken, smitten of God, and afflicted. But He was wounded for our transgressions, He was bruised for our iniquities: the chastisement of our peace was upon Him; and with His stripes we are healed. All we like sheep have gone astray; we have turned everyone to his own way; and the LORD hath laid on Him the iniquity of us all.'[1] These promises are for all mankind. We angels cannot really grasp this wonderful mystery, but we jealously long to look into it. That Man you saw is the only sinless Man who has ever lived on Earth. He is God and has existed from all eternity. When Adam and Eve ate the forbidden fruit from the Tree of the Knowledge of Good and Evil, God already had a plan to save men, and that was to become a man Himself, live a perfect life, and bear the punishment of sin for the whole world. When you saw the great darkness that came over the land and the sufferings of Christ magnified to an indescribable extent, you were getting a tiny glimpse of God's wrath being poured out upon Jesus. God the Father turned His back on the Son and said, as it were, 'Depart into eternal damnation!' Scripture says, 'For He hath made Him to be sin for us, who knew no sin; that we might be made the righteousness of God in Him.' When that great darkness came over the land, God put the huge pile of the sin of all mankind upon Him: all idol worship, all selfishness and pride, all blasphemy, all Sabbath breaking, all disrespect against parents, all murder, all adultery, fornication, homosexuality, and lust, all lying, cheating, and stealing, all envy, and all sorcery. Every sin that man had committed and ever would commit. You also saw the Blood that Jesus shed. That Blood is holy, pure, and undefiled and has the power to cleanse all sin—even the worst and most hideous sin. His death has the power to save the world from that horrible place you saw and open up the unfathomable treasures in heaven, which you've only seen a tiny, tiny little bit of. But come! We must be moving on!"

"I can't move," said Randy, weakly. "I know I will never recover."

Mystery Revealer touched the forehead of Randy and said, "Be thou strengthened, Joshua Randall! Yea, be thou strengthened!"

Randy felt power flowing into his spiritual body. He rose unsteadily to his feet, tottering and wobbling like a reed in the wind. Right in front of him was a door plated with the most exceedingly beautiful gold and encrusted with all kinds of sparkling gems and gorgeous flowers. The sign on it read, 'THE RESURRECTION OF CHRIST.' The two angels took the hands of the mega-weary pop star, unlatched the door, and led him through the opening.

Randy found himself standing in front of a huge, rocky tomb with its opening blocked by a very large and heavy stone. It was nighttime, and many Roman soldiers were guarding the tomb. Randy was still very, very tired and had a hard time even standing on his feet.

But then, he looked above the tomb and the company of soldiers who guarded it and saw multitudes of other soldiers of a different type. These were beautiful beings who were clothed in shining garments and looked a lot like Mystery Revealer and Godly Discretion. As Randy continued to look toward the sky, he saw the same beautiful Spirit-Man he had witnessed leaving the battered body of Jesus on that execution stake. This Spirit was pure light. He flew over to the large tomb where Randy was standing. Two large angels of very high rank accompanied Him. As He hovered over the entrance to the tomb, He spoke these words:

"Death, thou shalt no longer have dominion over this body. This body shall arise to incorruption forever and ever more! All ye tissues, muscles, organs, and skin, be thou immortalized, and let life and light flow into you!"

And with that, the Spirit of Light entered into the large tomb and climbed into the mutilated body of Jesus, which immediately became energized with life, totally healed, and filled with vitality. However, the scars and holes from the nails in His hands and feet remained. Jesus, in His new resurrected body, walked right out of the grave clothes without disturbing them (they continued to be neatly folded up like a cocoon), and then walked right through the heavy stone that blocked the entrance to the tomb. Right after that, one of the angels rolled away the stone from the tomb, and there was a great earthquake. The guards felt the earthquake, saw the stone rolled away, saw the angel, and became terribly frightened. Their faces became white as chalk; they shook like a leaf and could hardly move at all. At the same moment, Randy felt strength and vitality flowing into his body, dispelling the weariness and lifting his spirits. He felt like he was twenty years old once again. The angel who had rolled away the stone sat down on it. Praises and shouts of joy erupted from the multitude of angels who surrounded the tomb.

"Jesus is risen, hallelujah!"

"He triumphs over death, hell, and the grave! Jesus is victorious! He shall reign forever and ever!"

"Glory to God! GLORY TO GOD!! *GLORY TO GOD IN THE HIGHEST!!* The power of sin is broken! The Blood of Christ brings reconciliation between God and man!"

"Jesus reigns forever and ever! Glory to God in the highest! Peace on Earth and good will among men!"

Songs of victory resounded through the area around the tomb from the mouths of the host of angels—songs too beautiful for words.

Soon, three women carrying sweet spices could be seen walking toward the empty tomb, their countenances cloaked in deep sadness.

"Who will roll away the stone so that we can anoint the body of Jesus?" Mary Magdalene was asking the others.

"I don't know," said the other Mary. "I don't see how even the three of us together can even begin to move that stone. It's so very, very heavy."

"And there are all those Roman guards," added Salome. "I don't know how we can possibly get past them!"

"But we've *got* to do *something!*" protested Mary Magdalene. "There's got to be a way! Remember, He cast seven demons out of me, and I am gloriously free today! I owe everything to Jesus!"

"Who are those women?" asked Randy.

"They are Mary Magdalene, Mary, who is the mother of James, and Salome," answered Mystery Revealer.

"They want to see the tomb and anoint the body of Jesus," said Godly Discretion.

As they came near to the tomb, they gasped with surprise and dismay, and Salome exclaimed, "LOOK! The stone is rolled away! What does this mean?"

"OH, NO!" cried Mary Magdalene. "THIS IS TERRIBLE, *TERRIBLE!* Somebody must have stolen the body! I've got to tell Peter and John."

"Mary, *wait!*" cried out the other Mary as Mary Magdalene took to her heels, running away from the tomb.

Some time passed, and the eastern sky that faced toward the Mount of Olives turned from gray to pink to orange. It promised to be a gorgeous Sunday morning. Soon, the man whom Randy had seen standing by Mother Mary was seen running toward the tomb. Behind him was the man with the outgoing personality, who had cut off the ear of Malchus, denied Jesus, and taken the name of the Lord in vain. The first man arrived at the tomb, stooped down, looked in, and saw the folded grave clothes, but didn't go in.

"Peter! Peter! Come in here for a minute! I think you need to see this!"

Peter walked into the place where the grave clothes were and exclaimed, "Wow! Can you beat that?! What's going on here? This is *weird!*"

John then walked into the inner tomb and took a good, long look at the empty and neatly folded cocoon of grave clothes that had housed the dead body of Jesus. He then said, "This is absolutely remarkable! *Remarkable!* Well, I guess Jesus must have really risen from the dead! There's no other way to explain it!"

"Come on, John! Let's go home!"

The two men walked off, and soon, Mary Magdalene returned to the tomb, weeping. She stood outside for a short time and then stooped down and looked into the tomb, still weeping. But, wait a minute! What was this? Two angels were there, dressed in the most glistening white robes. One was sitting at the head and the other at the foot of the place where the body of Jesus had lain.

One of them asked, "Woman, why are you weeping?"

She burst into a fresh paroxysm of grief and exclaimed, "Oowww! Because they have taken away my Lord, and I don't have a clue where they have laid Him!"

She turned around and saw Jesus but didn't realize that it was Jesus. She thought that He was the gardener.

"Woman, why are you weeping? Who are you seeking?" asked Jesus.

"Sir, if you have taken Him away, please tell me where you have laid Him, and I will take Him away."

Jesus then said to her, "Mary."

Mary's face lighted up with joy and recognition as she responded, "Teacher."

"Don't touch Me," said Jesus, "for I haven't ascended to My Father yet, but go to My brethren, and say unto them, 'I ascend unto My Father, and your Father; and to My God, and your God.'"

Mary Magdalene ran out of the tomb, a new spring in her step, a new glow in her face. Jesus also walked out of the tomb and started heading toward the north. Presently, Salome and the other Mary walked back into the tomb. They saw the two angels who were clothed in long, beautiful snow-white garments. Their countenances were like lightning. The women were scared out of their wits and bowed down low before them.

"Don't be afraid, ladies," said the angel who was on the right side, "for I know that you ladies seek Jesus who was crucified. He is not here; for He is risen, just as He said. Come, see the place where the Lord lay. But go your way; tell His disciples and Peter that He is going before you into Galilee: there you folks shall see Him, just as He said unto you."

The other angel said, "Why do you ladies look for the living among the dead? He is not here, but is risen: remember how He spoke to you when He was still in Galilee, saying, 'The Son of Man must be delivered into the hands of sinful men, and be crucified, and rise again on the third day.'"

At this, the women skipped out of the large tomb, leaping and shouting with joy. Randy was also joyful, wide-awake, and full of energy. He could hardly believe that Jesus, who had been so horribly mutilated, now lived in that absolutely perfect new body that could even go right through doors and walls as if they were nothing but thin air. The only signs of His crucifixion were the scars and holes in His hands and feet that were from the nails, and even *they* were beautiful. But above all, the greatest thing about Jesus was the measureless love and compassion that flowed from His whole being.[2]

The next moment, Randy found himself back in the Valley of Time Travel. The two angels walked straight ahead, and Randy kept up with them with a new bounce in his step. They passed many doors with different signs on them. Here is a list of some of them that they passed: 'NERO'S PERSECUTION OF CHRISTIANS,' 'THE SPANISH INQUISITION,' 'THE REFORMATION,' 'THE AMERICAN REVOLUTION AND GEORGE WASHINGTON'S VISION AT VALLEY FORGE,' and

'CHRISTIANS UNDER THE THIRD REICH.' They eventually came to a forbidding door with little red flames shooting out of it with a sign that read, 'Left Behind.'

Mystery Revealer then spoke to Randy in a serious voice, saying, "Joshua Randall. This will not be a very pleasant door for you to go through, but this is for your instruction. Jesus said that He is coming again, and no one knows the hour or the day. While He was on Earth, He repeatedly warned His disciples to be ready. When you walk through this door of the future, you will be cast in the role of a person who is not prepared for His coming to take His saints home. Your name will be the same as it is now, but you will be a different age and will not remember anything about your real life. Neither will you have any idea about what day, month, or year it is. When you return here, you will have a new understanding of the importance of being ready for the return of Christ." He waved his right hand toward the fiery door and shouted, "Thou son of the earth, look, listen, and learn!" He motioned to Randy who obediently walked through the forbidding door.

He found himself back in his mortal body, but he was now only fourteen years old instead of thirty-one. He was with four other teenage boys on a warm night in a graveyard in Pleasant Hill, California. He had no memories of his real life but had other memories of the life of the person he had been cast in the role of. He had an implanted memory of the church service on that particular morning and the sermon preached by Pastor Arnold Pittman at Pleasant Hill Pentecostal Church. Some of the things the pastor had said ran along these lines:

"Turn with me to the book of Matthew, chapter 24. I want to read a few verses from *The Message* translation. There's a verse in there that says, 'Look out for doomsday preachers.' Lately, there have been many people predicting the end of the world. What many people forget, though, is that we have had many people predicting the end of the world and the second coming of Christ for almost 2,000 years—and look, it still hasn't happened yet. Just one example is William Miller in 1844 who set a date for Christ's return. That date came and went, and Jesus didn't return, and from that misguided teaching was born the legalistic sect of the Seventh Day Adventists who teach against the doctrines of free grace that are found in the New Testament. What those date-setters and dreamy-eyed eschatology kooks forget is the fact that *most of the so-called end-time prophecies in Matthew 24 and the book of Revelation were fulfilled in A. D. 70 when Titus brought his armies against Jerusalem, burned down the temple, and killed many thousands of Jews while taking many others captive*. So relax! Don't stress out! There are many, many things that have to happen before Jesus comes back! For one thing, we have to take this world for Christ and establish the Kingdom of God on the earth. It's up to us to do it and present a beautiful present for Christ when He does come back. You know, there are some people who preach that God is restoring National Israel, and that the Jews must come back to the Land in order for

Jesus to be able to reign from the capital city of Jerusalem during some fabled earthly 'millennium.' Got news for you! *We* are Israel! God's not going to bless a race that is shaking their fists at Him!

"I want to refer you to another time period during the 1940s when the world was at war. Many people thought that it was the end of the world. But there was a great musical called *South Pacific* that was set during World War II that had a great song in it that bears listening to once again. It's called, 'Cockeyed Optimist.' Now today, we've just come through the Second Great Depression as well as the recent huge Muslim terrorist attack on America when once again, there were many doomsday prophets predicting Jesus would come at any moment. But look what's happening. The world economy is recovering beautifully. People are going back to work. We had gas shortages, but now, we have these new and wonderful alternative sources of energy that has eliminated our great dependence on foreign oil. All of Europe has now been rising up as the new world superpower with Rome becoming tremendously prosperous.

"So let's not get off on a tangent that Jesus will come at any moment. He *is* coming again, but no one knows the day or hour. *He may not come for another million years!* The important thing is to be about His business. Hi, little Chip! You're really growing by leaps and bounds. I hope that when you're my age, you'll be preaching the gospel in some good church, and I hope that when your sons and grandsons are my age, they also will be preaching the gospel in some church pulpit!"

Randy had also remembered the music before the preaching began; very hard rock-and-roll with a group consisting of four singers, three guitar players, a bass player, a loud drummer, and a percussionist. The lyrics of the songs had been very, very shallow, and his ears were still ringing from the 115-decibel level of the Christian rock worship band. Many people had been late in coming to the church service, and there were many people who got out of their seats during the service and walked into the foyer, returning to their seats a little later. Some even walked outside to smoke a cigarette.

Randy stirred himself from his reverie and said to the four other teenage boys, "Come on, guys! Let's do this thing."

"Boy, this is gonna be fun!" exulted sixteen-year-old Jeff Dyson.

"I feel like I'm Tom Sawyer, sneaking into the graveyard with Huck," commented Ken Winger.

"You're a little old to be Tom Sawyer," declared Lennie Muncher.

"Got your picks and shovels all ready?" asked Randy.

"I don't think we'll find anything valuable buried with the body," said Mitch Lee.

"Sure, we will," countered Jeff.

The five of them started digging. All of them had modern flashlights with a type of lighting that Randy just wasn't familiar with. He noticed that he and all the rest of them were dressed in black.

Ken lit up a cigarette and said, "What did you guys think of Pastor Arnold's sermon today?"

"Pretty good," said Mitch.

"I wasn't even paying attention," said Jeff. "I was texting my girlfriend the whole time."

Lennie said, "What he said makes more sense than what my weird grandmother used to say! She was always carrying on about how Jesus can come at any time. She was part of that laughing revival that took place some years ago. Now the government authorities have carted her off to one of those reprogramming camps."

"Yeah," said Mitch. "I know a lot of kooky hallelujah people who were expecting the end of the world who are now in one of those retraining institutions. Rumor has it that some of them have mysteriously died."

"I've been doing a lot of twittering," said Randy, "and have spent a lot of time on the Net. There's a lot of ludicrous stuff on there that's way out in left field! Those demented fanatics *deserve* to be in jail!"

As they kept on digging at the gravesite, Mitch asked, "So what do you think we'll find inside this grave that's valuable?"

"Oh, I don't know," said Randy. "Maybe a wedding ring or a diamond brace—*WHAT?*"

At that very moment, something very strange happened. The grave burst open, and out popped a shining and perfect body of a lady who had been dead—and she was not the only one. All over that graveyard, graves were opening up, and out of them were emerging jubilant and glowing people. They started praising the Lord and immediately started flying into the skies like the most beautiful and graceful eagles. It was not every grave that was disturbed, but perhaps only one fourth of them.

All five of the youths were terrified. They started screaming and running as fast as they could away from the graveyard.

"What's going on?!" exclaimed Ken.

"I'm scared!" cried Lennie.

They ran down a residential street. Suddenly, a car lurched aimlessly and crashed into a telephone pole.

"Come on guys," said Jeff. "Let's see if we can help that person. He must be hurt!"

They looked into the car and had another big surprise. A blue dress, some panties, a bra, a pair of black women's shoes, and a long pair of brown stockings was inside the vehicle—but no driver! Panic began to set in among all five of them. Mitch was especially upset as he cried out in the most heart-rending anguish, *"OH, NO! OH, NO, NO, NOOOO!! I'VE MISSED THE RAPTURE!! I'VE BEEN LEFT BEHIND!!"*

Fourteen-year-old Randy felt the most horrible despondency, fear, and loneliness imaginable. He also felt extremely cold on this warm, humid night as well as totally drained of energy. The next thing he knew, he was walking the streets of Pleasant Hill in this new World of Chaos. He looked at a newspaper announcing the red-letter headlines of the mysterious vanishings of many millions of people on the earth with every baby and little child being 'victims' in this disappearance. Strangely enough, he could not find the day, the month, or the year they were in anywhere on the paper—and he had no idea of what day, month, or year it was, either. The headlines did say that there had been the strangest and brightest UFOs ever seen that had appeared in the vicinity of the North Pole around the time of the vanishings. The blasphemies issuing from the mouths of the populace were unbelievable. Many churches were vandalized while other churches were filled with people crying out in anguish and pulling their hair out. Strangely, Randy saw absolutely no repentance from sin going on. Buildings all over the world were on fire or being looted. When the vanishings had happened, there were mysterious car wrecks and planes crashing all over the world with many of the driver's seats and cockpits missing their drivers or pilots—the clothes still being there. Murders, thefts, and unheard-of sexual immorality were everywhere. The noise on the earth was indescribable.

The next thing Randy knew was that a superman dictator had taken over the whole planet and had created a one-world government that was very similar to George Orwell's *1984*. People everywhere were being rounded up, sent on railroad boxcars, and transported to faraway places the superman had dictated was the place where they would live and work at. People had nothing but the barest necessities. Everybody was being herded into special clinics with machines that implanted a special tiny little computer chip into their bodies. When they came out of those clinics, their personalities were totally changed. They were like zombies with no emotion, their eyes had a glazed look in them, and they did everything the superman told them to do. Randy did not at all like the change that he saw take place in the people who took that computer chip implant.

He was walking down a street when the secret police spotted him. "There's another one! Get him!"

Randy ran as fast as he could, but he was no match for those policemen of the world. They soon caught him, herded him into their truck, and drove to one of the clinics. He yelled and struggled all the way there. The officers forced him into the clinic as Randy kicked and screamed.

"NO, NOOO!! I DON'T WANT TO RECEIVE THAT CHIP!! I DON'T WANT MY BRAIN TO BE FRIED!! LET ME ALONE! I DON'T WANT TO BE BRAINWASHED!!"

It was no good. They forced him onto a table, booted up the implant machine, and unbuttoned the shirt of Randy in order to inject the chip into him. The needle was getting closer, closer, *closer*—

Randy blinked with a sudden start. He was back in the Valley of Time Travel, and Mystery Revealer and Godly Discretion were standing over him. He was back to being thirty-one years old and was in his spirit body again.

339

The memories of his real life had also returned. What a relief it was to be out of that forbidding future world of those who will be left behind!!

20.

THE CIRCLE OF CELESTIAL CELEBRANTS

"That was a real wake-up call for you," said Mystery Revealer. "While He was on Earth, Jesus said, 'And take heed to yourselves, lest at any time your hearts be overcharged with surfeiting, and drunkenness, and cares of this life, and so that day come upon you unawares. For as a snare shall it come on all them that dwell on the face of the whole earth. Watch ye therefore, and pray always, that ye may be accounted worthy to escape all these things that shall come to pass, and to stand before the Son of Man.' You have just experienced, first-hand, what it will feel like to be left behind when Jesus comes to take His people to heaven. The despondency, coldness, and loneliness that you felt had to do with another prophetic Scripture that says, 'Now we beseech you, brethren, by the coming of our Lord Jesus Christ, and by our gathering together unto Him, That ye be not soon shaken in mind, or be troubled, neither by spirit, nor by word, nor by letter as from us, as that the day of the Lord is at hand. Let no man deceive you by any means: for that day shall not come, except there come a falling away first, and that man of sin be revealed, the son of perdition; who opposes and exalts himself above all that is called God, or that is worshipped; so that he as God sits in the temple of God, showing himself that he is God. Remember ye not, that, when I was yet with you, I told you these things? And now ye know what is withholding him that he might be revealed in his time. For the mystery of iniquity is already at work: only He who now is restraining will restrain, until He be taken out of the way. And then shall that Wicked be revealed, whom the Lord shall consume with the spirit of His mouth, and shall destroy with the brightness of His coming: Even him, whose coming is after the working of Satan with all power and signs and lying wonders, and with all deceivableness of unrighteousness in them that perish; because they received not the love of the truth, that they might be saved. And for this cause God shall send them strong delusion, that they should believe a lie: That they all might be damned who believed not the truth, but had pleasure in unrighteousness.'[1]

"The Restrainer is the Holy Spirit. He is the One who is restraining sin, comforting Christians, and holding back that Superman from being revealed on the earth. When the Holy Spirit descended on the day of Pentecost, the Church was born. When the great Catching Away of the Church takes place, there will be, as it were, a reversal of what happened at Pentecost, and the operation of the Holy Spirit during the time of Great Tribulation will be similar to the way it was during Old Testament times. The depression you felt was a great vacuum as the saints who were filled with the Holy Spirit were suddenly gone. You also saw the utter chaos that descended on the earth as sin and lawlessness rose to new heights. You saw how Pastor Pittman and millions of other professing 'Christians' were among those who were left behind and how they totally turned away from the Lord. You saw all the anguish of the multitudes without true repentance. You saw the rise of the Superman who ruled over the whole world and who created the granddaddy of totalitarian governments with his 666 computer chip implant. You finally saw how everyone who received the chip became like a zombie and became a passive pawn of that Superman. Only a few of those who are left behind at the Catching Away will be saved, and most of those saved people will be martyred by the Superman. But those martyred saints will have a glorious future of reigning with Christ. But come, thou son of the earth! We must go through another door—a door you will like."

They walked over to the door situated right next to the fiery 'Left Behind' door. This one was the most beautifully decorated door Randy had seen yet. It was covered with many, many different types of flowers. The middle of the door was covered with the most stunning wedding gown he had ever seen, decorated as it was with a profusion of the most dazzling gems. The sign at the top of the door read, 'THE MARRIAGE SUPPER OF THE LAMB!!' The two angels led Randy through this door.

Once again, he found himself as a mortal human being in Pleasant Hill. But this time, he was not in that graveyard, but in a living room filled with about twenty-five people who were praising the Lord with all their might. Their faces were a vision of heavenly joy, and they were singing lively worship choruses, speaking in tongues, and testifying about things the Lord had done in their lives: salvation and deliverance from drugs and alcohol, escape from the severe persecution going on all over the world, healings from all manner of diseases and handicaps, being supernaturally transported to another place just like Philip and Elijah had, and even people being raised from the dead.

A middle-aged lady named Angela was speaking, saying, "It was so uncanny! About 4:00 in the afternoon today, I just had this feeling that the Rapture has to be tonight! And then Cheryl called me up announcing she was going to have this 'Rapture party!' I really praise the Lord for that! GLORY TO GOD!"

A lady named Betty spoke up next. She said, "I had the same feeling! Moreover, there are all those signs around us that His coming must be near. There are already some people who have received that computer chip implant—and then there are those new snacks laced with brain-altering drugs—chemicals that make a person more passive. There's that new product put out by the New World Omega Corporation that is called, 'Daham Graham

Crackers.' As you know, there were a lot of complaints against the name because of how it sounds like a profane word. It—WHAT?! OH, *GLORY TO GOD!!"*

Everyone else in the room joined in the sudden outburst of praise. Randy heard an incredibly pure and beautiful-beyond-description trumpet blast. The next second, he saw everyone in the room lighting up like a Christmas tree. At the same time, he felt a marvelous surge of life and joy flood his whole being that eclipsed even the most joyful moments he had experienced on Earth many times over. Everyone was saying, "JESUS, JESUS, JESUS!! I LOVE YOU SO MUCH, MARVELOUS, WORTHY, AWESOME JESUS!" and Randy joined in the praises. They all started to rise. They went right through the roof and zoomed into the skies like the most exquisitely graceful swans. They headed in a northerly direction as other glorified saints joined them. They were soon gathered together, millions upon millions of saints at a central point many miles above the North Pole. A huge multitude of benevolent angels, too numerous to count, were there with appearances very much like orbs of fire. And then, Randy saw the most glorious Being of all—the same Man of Loveliness he had seen as He was getting crucified, and later on had beheld in His resurrected body on Earth. His appearance now was glorious and awe-inspiring beyond description. Adding to all the joy that people were feeling due to their new resurrection bodies was the great numbers of family reunions as they saw departed loved ones who were now resurrected. The regions of outer space above the North Pole resounded with praises to God, joyful cries of reunion, hugs, and many, many kisses. Everyone was clothed in the most gorgeous white garments. The angels were everywhere as they ministered to the saints and formed them into different companies. There was the most beautiful music sung by the angels mingling in with the exclamations of praise and reunions of loved ones.

"Glory to God in the highest!"

"The Lord omnipotent reigns forever and ever!"

"Mary! MARY! O, my love, Mary! What a pleasant surprise! We are now together again, and death will never part us again!"

"O, Bud! My dearest sweetheart Bud! I've got you back forever!"

"Praise God! It's our little Craig who died of leukemia two years ago! O, my son! My most precious, precious son!"

Finally, a voice resounded through the skies that overshadowed everyone else's voice, and a mighty hush arose as Jesus spoke. *"O, MY BRIDE! MY PRECIOUS, PRECIOUS BRIDE! MY BEAUTIFUL, BEAUTIFUL, PERFECT SPOTLESS PRINCESS!! I HAVE WAITED A LONG, LONG TIME FOR THIS DAY! IT HAS FINALLY COME, AND THE JOYS THAT LIE AHEAD OF YOU ARE INFINITELY BEYOND YOUR WILDEST, WILDEST DREAMS! YOU HAVE COME FORTH THROUGH FIRE AND ARE NOW TOTALLY PURE, HOLY, AND SPOTLESS!! REJOICE, MY BELOVED BRIDE!! YEA, REJOICE!! LET US CELEBRATE TOGETHER OUR*

SUPREME JOY FOREVER AND EVER!!! YOU HAVE NO IDEA OF THE FATHOMLESS TREASURES THAT AWAIT YOU IN GLORY!!! REJOICE, REJOICE, REJOICE!!!"

A deafening whoop of supreme and inexpressible joy erupted that resounded through the cosmos from the holy angels and resurrected saints. And with that, the Lord Jesus Christ led the angels and the Circle of Celestial Celebrants through the universe and into heaven itself.

The next thing Randy knew was that he was among the exquisitely lovely trees, grass lawns, and flowers of paradise. Numberless and beautifully decorated tables were arranged in perfectly neat rows. Millions upon millions of glorified people and angels were shouting joyfully, jumping, skipping about, singing, and playing beautiful and uplifting music on their golden harps, trumpets, and shofars. Some of the angels and saints were putting huge golden plates on those tables with the most inviting and varied foods that are only known in the cookbooks of heaven. There were also golden bottles of white wines, red wines, and various types of champagne as well as pitchers full of different types of beer.

"I don't understand!" exclaimed Randy to a saint who was standing to the left side of him. "You mean that there is beer and wine in heaven? You mean there's alcohol here?"

"Not alcohol," explained the saint. "Nothing impure can enter into this celestial world. Alcohol is something on Earth that has gone through corruption and is a counterfeit of Satan that tries to take the place of the new wine of the joy from the Holy Spirit. The wine and beer of the world below will lead to the destruction of men's bodies and souls, but the wine, beer, and champagne you see in this World of Light cannot hurt you. It can only enlighten you spiritually and enlarge your ability to enjoy eternal life."

Another saint standing to Randy's right added, "Did you not ever read in the Scriptures the prophetic passages that talked about this very day? Isaiah predicted, 'And in this mountain shall the LORD of hosts make unto all people a feast of fat things, a feast of wines on the lees, of the things full of marrow, of wines on the lees well refined. And He shall destroy on this mountain the face of the covering cast over all people, and the veil that is spread over all nations. He will swallow up death in victory; and the Lord GOD will wipe away tears from off all faces; and the rebuke of His people shall He take away from off all the people: for the LORD hath spoken it.' And remember how Jesus spoke to His disciples during the Last Supper and Passover in the Upper Room? He said, 'But I say unto you, I will not drink henceforth of this fruit of the vine, until that day when I drink it new with you in My Father's kingdom.' The fruit of the vine that the disciples drank in the Upper Room was not intoxicating alcohol, but sweet wine that was not totally unlike some of the grape juices that people drink down on Planet Earth. Neither was the wine Jesus produced from the water in Cana intoxicating."

Soon, Jesus appeared at the head of the great assembly, and everybody took a seat in that humongous, beautiful lawn. He gave the most majestic benediction; and then, the Great Party, the Wedding Feast of the Lamb, the Celebration to end all celebrations began. Randy had never ever seen such rejoicing as he now saw here, not even on his first trip into heaven. The next minute, however, he had a huge disappointment. He found himself back in the Valley of Time Travel with the two holy angels, Mystery Revealer and Godly Discretion.

"OH, RATS! I wish I could have stayed there forever!"

"You see, Joshua Randall," said Mystery Revealer. "That feast you saw is something that is soon to take place. Jesus often alluded to it while He was on Earth, and the apostle John witnessed it on the Isle of Patmos. It will be the Great Party when Jesus, the heavenly Bridegroom, will throw a big celebration with His Bride."

Godly Discretion added, "The Bride of Christ consists of people from every nation, language, class, and race. It consists of both the rich and the poor, both the good and the bad. Among the people in this heavenly Bride can be found those who were formerly adulterers, prostitutes, homosexuals, lesbians, sorcerers, idolaters, murderers, cheats, thieves, drug addicts, alcoholics, and materialistic and greedy people—but all of those have repented of their sins and been washed in the Blood of the Lamb before they left the earth. Many of those in the Bride are folks who would be considered good people by earthly standards, but they, too, had to repent and be washed in the Blood. All children and babies who died at a young age are also part of the Bride."

"Come, Joshua Randall," said Mystery Revealer. "We still have a couple of doors to walk through."

And with that, they walked a short distance until they came to a very lovely door with many palm branches on it that read, 'THE GREAT SHABBAT OF PLANET EARTH.' The three of them walked through that very pleasant door and found themselves in a very nice place indeed. Randy recognized the Mount of Olives and the architecture of limestone buildings that was a unique feature in the land of Israel. But there were a lot of marked differences between this setting and the setting he had seen belonging to the time of the crucifixion of Jesus. For one thing, the daylight was far brighter than normal daylight, and the sky was a far brighter and prettier blue than he had ever seen on Earth. There was not even a trace of smog in the air. Also, the buildings were far more beautiful and elaborate than any he had ever seen here before. Strangely, there were also some Spanish traits in the architecture here. Multitudes of happy people in ordinary bodies were going about their business. Randy didn't see even one person among them who was injured or handicapped in any way—there were no blind, deaf, crippled, or paralyzed people here. Also, none of those hideous beings whom Randy had seen in some of the places where he had been were there. A great sense of peace and contentment permeated the land.

As he looked east, Randy could see a huge wall encircling a beautiful temple. He also noticed that the Mount of Olives was no longer just one mountain but was now split into two parts: one half was to the north, and the other half was to the south with a valley between the peaks. Jerusalem was several thousand feet above the rest of Israel. He looked north and saw the lush, verdant farmlands that lay below. To the south and west were more lovely vistas with farmlands, orchards, brightly colored flowers, pools of water, and gorgeous forests. Far to the west, the Mediterranean Sea shone with the most brilliant blue color that Randy had ever seen on Earth. A beautiful river flowed from the temple all the way down to the western sea.

The angels led him to a vehicle, the likes of which Randy had never seen before. It was a circular vehicle, painted an attractive green color. Somehow, Randy knew how to operate this strange 'car.' All three of them climbed in, and Randy took his place at the driver's seat where he turned on the power. They immediately took off into the air, and Randy started flying due west. There was no noise from an internal engine, and neither was there any exhaust from the vehicle to pollute the air. Randy flew at an altitude of about 7,000 feet at a speed of about 2,000 miles per hour. Soon, the eastern part of the United States could be seen, and Randy landed the craft in a beautiful park that turned out to be the renovated Mall in the new Washington, D. C.

The three of them clambered out of the strange 'flying saucer,' and Randy was able to take a good, thorough look at the surroundings. It was nighttime, but it wasn't that dark. Instead of being black, the sky was a dark purple-blue color, similar to what it would look like on a dusky evening when it is only half-way dark. The streets were thronged with happy people who were obviously celebrating something. The buildings bespoke great prosperity to an extent that Randy had never seen in his own era of the 1970s.

Soon, an emcee walked up to the front of the Mall, picked up a microphone, and started speaking to the happy masses thronging the Mall.

"Ladies and gentlemen! Citizens of the United States and of the world under the benign government of our glorious Lord Jesus Christ! Tonight, we celebrate the Fourth of July with thanksgiving to our magnificent God who has raised up this wonderful land of America through our Founding Fathers hundreds of years ago. We are blessed because it happens to be the New Moon, enabling us to have an excellent view of the fireworks display that is on the agenda for tonight. But first, we have a musical treat for you, a concert that will be put on by The George Washington Symphony Orchestra and Choir."

Spirited cheering broke out among the huge crowd of people, and a huge orchestra and choir all decked out in stunning red, white, and blue outfits made their way to the front of the Mall. There were 2,000 singers; and the orchestra consisted of 300 violinists, 120 viola players, 80 cellists, 60 double bass players, 56 flautists, 45 oboe players, 39 clarinetists, 32 bassoonists, 77 trumpet players, 62 French horns, 76 trombonists, 30 tuba blowers, 5 percussionists, a pianist, and a synthesizer player. On the side were ten guitarists and twenty banjo players who were scheduled to perform a couple of pieces tonight. Randy gawked at the grandiose sight.

Everybody stood to their feet as "The Star-Spangled Banner" was played and sung followed by the national anthem of Israel. After that came the famous piece by John Phillip Sousa, "Stars and Stripes Forever." The piccolo player aced his high-pitched solo with no mistakes whatsoever, nailing those high A-flat notes. Irving Berlin's, "Give Me Your Tired, Your Poor" followed with the massed choir singing a cappella with eight-part vocal harmony. After that, fifty singers stepped out to do a special rendition of "This Land is Your Land" accompanied by the guitar and banjo players. This arrangement had a bluegrass feel to it. Next came "Statue of Liberty," performed by both the choir and the orchestra. There followed the most gorgeous rendition of Ferde Grofe's *Grand Canyon Suite* that Randy had ever heard. Following this was a beautiful and lush vocal and orchestral arrangement of "Jerusalem of Gold." The concert finished up with three blockbusters: "Battle Hymn of the Republic," "America the Beautiful," and Irving Berlin's "God Bless America." Randy was spellbound; he had never heard such beautiful music while he had been in his mortal body.

Now, there came a time when four different speakers rose to give their respective speeches. The angels explained to Randy that those speakers were resurrected saints while everybody in the huge crowd was mortal and unglorified. The first speech was from George Washington, a tall and dignified man with piercing eyes. He spoke about the blessings of Jesus Christ who was that Divine Providence that was instrumental in America being established and rising to its blessed position it had today in the Kingdom Age. Abraham Lincoln spoke next. Some of his words went along these lines: "Ten score and three years ago, our great Lord and Savior returned to this earth to save this planet from destruction and to set up His glorious reign upon Earth. We now live in a blessed time of freedom, that freedom which can only be found in Jesus Christ. We live in that time when there is indeed malice toward none, charity towards all, and where the faith that right makes might has now become sight." Lincoln put some of his famous jokes and anecdotes into his speech. He was very tall and skinny and still sported his black beard. Martin Luther King was the next speaker who expounded on the fact that his dream of equality for all people had come true and thanked God for this wonderful new world that was free of the oppression that had existed in the old and evil world. Ronald Reagan was the fourth speaker. He was relaxed and happy. He had not lost any of his good humor and wit; he filled his speech with funny jokes and stories. The speeches were attended by rousing and vociferous cheers from the huge audience.

Following this was a fireworks display to end all pyrotechnic shows that Randy had ever seen. The colors were stunning, and the show was prolonged. The last fifteen minutes was the best part. Not only were the fireworks the most spectacular at this time, but the orchestra played the famous piece by Tchaikovsky, *The 1812 Overture.* The beginning section with the huge string section playing their parts in E-flat major was stunning. The whole piece was performed with its exciting sections that alternated between the major chords and diminished chords interspersed with the slow and brooding interludes. The finale in E-flat major had an added twist. Not only did it feature the famous bells and cannons, but also 120 shofar blowers joined the orchestra with an effect that was altogether electric. Randy clapped and whooped with all his might. Oh, if only he had known what the future was going to bring for the USA and the world!

After that, he found himself once again in the Valley of Time Travel with its twilight, flashes of lightning, and claps of thunder. The two angels led him a short distance, passing several more doors, until they came to a very attractive golden door covered with variegated gems and beautiful flowers of many varieties. The sign on this door read, 'HEAVEN.' Right beside that supremely beautiful door was some Scripture that read, "Thus saith the LORD the King of Israel, and His Redeemer, the LORD of hosts; I am the first and I am the last; and beside Me there is no God. And who, as I, shall call, and shall declare it, and set it in order for Me, since I appointed the ancient people? And the things that are coming, and shall come, let them show unto them. I am Aleph and Tav, the Beginning and the Ending, saith the Lord, which is, and which was, and which is to come, the Almighty."[2]

Mystery Revealer said to Randy, "As you have seen, God Almighty has complete control over time. He knows the beginning from the end, and He has revealed it all in His Word. The time is coming when learned men on Earth will begin to fathom some of the deep mysteries in His Word that are irrefutable proofs that God did indeed breathe out every single word in the Scriptures. This is needed as more and more men will come up with theories to try to refute the Scriptures and the historical things it says. In so doing, they teach destructive heresies that lead men down the road to perdition.

"You have seen some of the things that have happened in the past as well as some of the things that will happen in the future. When you were in the time period of the Great Shabbat, you noticed how the sunlight was much brighter and the nighttime was not nearly as dark. This will literally happen during that future thousand-year period when Jesus will reign on Earth from the capital city of Jerusalem, which you were also in. The Scriptures say that the sun will be seven times brighter during those days. If there had been a full moon on the night of the Fourth of July celebration that you saw, it would have been as bright as your normal daylight hours on the earth as it presently exists in your time period of the 1970s. But come! We have one more door to go through."

The angels led Randy to the door leading into heaven. Randy was very happy about this as he thought that maybe he was going to stay there for good. As they walked through the door, he found himself in another part of paradise he had not seen before. He was in a grassy orchard full of those exquisitely marvelous fruit trees loaded down with the twelve different types of fruit that were only known in heaven. Flowering shrubbery was everywhere as well. The intoxicating smells were also back. Randy rejoiced, exclaiming, "All right! All right! Far out! Praise the Lord!"

Three people were seated on a marble bench of a bluish-gray color. Two of them Randy recognized, but the third person was a stranger to him.

"Who is that guy in the gown I've never seen before?" asked Randy.

"He is King Manasseh who once ruled over Judah," answered Godly Discretion. "He barely made it into the heavenly kingdom."

Randy smiled at the three men decked out in white gowns and said, "Good morning, Darryl Temple! Good morning, Ben Simeon! Good morning, Manasseh!"

"Good morning!" answered the three men in a friendly voice. "Welcome to this land of bliss!"

"Please tell me a little more about yourselves," said Randy.

"Certainly," responded Darryl, "your wish is our command! We'd be more than happy to tell you our individual stories."

Darryl Temple related his story first, of which Randy had heard a lot of already. "When Wes Marlow first shared about the love of Jesus to me in jail, I wanted to kill him. But I couldn't get his words out of my head, and I had never experienced love like what he showed me. And then there was the cancer. I began to question and wonder about the things of eternity. And then came that day when I accepted Christ and Wes cast those demons out of me! It was like a million pounds had been lifted off my back! Bless God, I felt happy and free for the first time in my life! And lookie here! I am actually living in this blessed land even though I ain't worthy!"

"I had the same feelings," said Ben Simeon. "When Jesus told me that I would be with Him in paradise on that same day when I was being crucified, I felt this huge burden lift off of me, and I was so happy, even though I was in all that pain from the crucifixion."

"I'm sure not worthy to be here!" exclaimed Manasseh. "I was once a king, but I'm not a king anymore. I am so very, very fortunate to even be in this place at all! I deserve nothing but eternal doom!"

"Me too," said Ben Simeon.

"Ditto," said Darryl.

"Well, my story is like this," said Manasseh. "I am the son of godly King Hezekiah who now has great honor here in the Kingdom of Heaven. I was twelve years old when I began to reign over Judah and was king for fifty-five years. I should have followed the example of my dad who was mightily blessed of God. The Lord gave him a big-time supernatural victory against the huge Assyrian army that came against Jerusalem, and also cured him from a terminal disease and added fifteen years unto his life. But, did I learn? NO! I was determined to go my own stubborn way! I rebuilt the high places that my daddy had torn down. I erected altars for the worship of Baalim, made groves, and worshipped and served all the host of heaven. I even went as far so as to build those altars of idolatry right there in the temple of God! I even made a carved image of an idol and put it right there in the house of God!

"I was also a mass murderer! To begin with, I burnt my children in the fire in the Valley of Hinnom to Molech. I also murdered a whole bunch of people in Judah! Why, I was just like Adolph Hitler!

"I was heavily involved in the occult as well. To begin with, I was into astrology." (Randy shuddered as he heard these words.) "I used enchantments and witchcraft. I also consulted a spiritualist that had a familiar spirit. I also consulted with wizards. Because of all my evil, the Lord decided that he was going to destroy Judah and take the Jews captive to Babylon. God had had enough.

"Again and again, the Lord sent prophets my way to warn me concerning my course of life. But, did I listen? Nope! I continued to go my own stubborn way. Finally, the captain of the armies of the king of Assyria captured me, bound me with fetters, and took me to Babylon. I was really in hot water! As I was going through all that tribulation, I finally came to my senses. I repented of my great, great sins, humbled myself tremendously before the Lord, prayed fervently, and sought His face—and, OH, THE FANTASTIC MERCY OF MY MIGHTY GOD! He *listened* to my prayer and delivered me out of that terrible jail. He let me come back to Jerusalem where I reigned as king for just a few more years. I made a 180-degree turnaround. I got rid of all of the idols and altars, repaired the altar of the Lord, sacrificed peace offerings and thanksgiving offerings on it, and commanded the people of Judah to serve the Lord only. Thank God that He was gracious to me in letting me be sent to that Babylonian prison so that I could escape going to the eternal prison!"

At that moment, a caravan of heavenly vehicles that Randy could only describe as a train appeared on the far horizon. It got closer and closer, and soon, it stopped in front of the four men. The driver at the front of the train of chariots leaped out, and Randy immediately recognized him by his reddish hair, the crown on his head, and his forceful personality. It was King David holding his beautiful heavenly harp. The train of chariots was filled with joyful men, women, boys, and girls. David strolled right over to the four men and said, "Good morning!"

"Good morning, King David!" they all responded.

"It's good to see you back here, Joshua Randall! Would you like to take a little trip into the foothills to join us in a picnic with the prophets of God?"

"I sure would, King David!"

The great king led him into a seat in the front chariot, and he hopped in joyfully and started driving down a lovely road, bordered by the splendid fruit trees and flowery shrubbery at a great rate of speed. The people in the chariot train were chatting with each other, laughing, singing the most exceedingly beautiful songs, and praising the Lord. When they came to the bottom of the foothills, the road became very curvy and winding, something that Randy had always loved. All those twists and turns added romance to any trip on Earth or heaven, and there were so many wonderful sights, he was overwhelmed and couldn't even begin to take it all in. As they rode along the vistas of trees, fountains, flowers, and cliffs, Randy and King David made small talk.

"Hey, King David. I notice that I can hear different colors in the harmonies of the beautiful music up here. I never had that ability on Earth, even though I did have perfect pitch."

"Well, I'll be very happy to tell you about that," said the king. "Most people on Earth don't even have perfect pitch."

"I know that."

"Far, far fewer people on Earth hear music in colors, but up here, it's a common thing. Remember: men on Earth are fallen and have lost many of the blessings that Adam and Eve had in the Garden of Eden. One of these things has to do with having an ear for music. Moreover, you have found out that you can hear frequencies up here you could never hear on Earth. What makes it worse for them in the twentieth century is all the noise pollution, especially the loud, harsh noise of hard rock-and-roll music. However, a few people on Earth can hear music in colors. Scientists down there will soon discover that sound and light are related to each other. And Joshua Randall—before Jesus returns to Earth, He is going to pour out an anointing of heavenly music on some of His servants that will bring great healing and blessing to multitudes of people. The reason He hasn't done it yet is because the musicians of Earth wouldn't be able to handle it today."

"And why is that, O great king?"

"Because of the egos musicians have. You have noticed that musicians in general are concerned about how great their talent is and are also caught up into the applause and acclaim of the great crowds. Many of them lust after fame and fortune and compare themselves with other musicians. If somebody can sing or play better than they can, they get envious. But if they are more skilled than most or all of their peers, then they get conceited and prideful."

"I'm afraid that I've been very guilty of all of the above."

"Just like most talented musicians on Planet Earth."

"O, King David. There's something that has been bothering me for a long time and it is this: I've seen so many tragedies happen to great musicians. Beethoven went totally deaf, Schubert died of painful venereal disease, Schumann damaged his piano-playing hands and went insane at the end of his life, Tchaikovsky was emotionally unstable as well as a homosexual, Hugo Wolf was afflicted with poverty and became insane at the end of his life, George Gershwin died of brain cancer before he was thirty-nine, and the list goes on and on. I just don't understand it."

"Well, Joshua Randall. A lot of the answer to that question lies in the fact that Satan hates both musicians and worship leaders. The reason for this is because he was the chief musician and worship leader of heaven until the day when he fell into pride and wanted to usurp God's throne and be God himself. The prophets Isaiah and Ezekiel have talked about that event in their holy Writings. Lucifer was able to entice one-third of the angels to follow him, and that's when he became Satan."

"I never knew that before."

"Yes, it is a terrible thing. When Lucifer fell into pride, a great gap developed in the worship within heaven. Jehovah God still misses the worship that issued from Lucifer before he fell into the first sin that ever happened in the universe."

"So, what's going to happen in the future, King David?"

"Well, Lucifer and the angels who followed him cannot be saved. God created the Lake of Fire for them on the second day of creation, and they will spend eternity there. Meanwhile, God is raising up an army of worshippers on Earth who will worship Him in spirit and in truth, and many of them will be accomplished singers and musicians."

"Wow! That's heavy!"

The chariot train slowed and soon stopped at a beautiful park in the foothills of the huge heavenly mountain range. This park was still thousands of feet above the paradisiacal plains that lay below. The park was festooned with a profusion of many different types of flowers in sky blue, violet, pink, red, and white colors. There were many picnic tables made out of redwood and plywood planks, loaded down with dishes of all sorts of fruit and heavenly veggies. Other chariots were arriving, and dignified and majestic men dressed in beautiful and elaborate white robes were leaping joyfully out of the cars. Randy had never seen anything like this before.

Abraham was there whom Randy had seen before. There was Moses who had a very dignified and sweet demeanor about him. He had frosty white hair, but he looked very, very young and had not even the slightest defect on his body. Next to him was standing the prophet Samuel who had piercing eyes and a very forceful personality. Isaiah was there. He had a very colorful personality, being a somewhat quiet man with a little side of his temperament that was outgoing. Jeremiah was a man of great compassion and love. Ezekiel had a somewhat more reserved personality than Jeremiah. Daniel was a man with tremendous wisdom. Randy could tell that he must have been an extremely brainy man while he had lived on Earth. Joseph had a very friendly, sweet, and winsome personality. Randy had the feeling that this man must have been a great political leader in the past, even though he knew nothing about his story as told in the Bible. Enoch was a man full of mega-tremendous joy.

Randy was impressed with the amount of hugging and kissing going on among them, and they all came up to him and gave him the most cordial greetings.

"Beloved friends!" announced King David. "I want to introduce to you a newcomer from the earth who is a fellow musician. His name is Joshua Randall!"

"Welcome, my friend!" exclaimed Jeremiah.

"Yeah, it's very lovely to see you, son of man!" echoed Ezekiel. "Shalom, shalom to you!"

"The honor is mine," chorused Joseph.

"I'm speechless, guys!" said Randy. "I don't even feel worthy to be in the company of such great men as you wonderful glorified people are! Please tell me your individual stories."

Moses started the ball rolling by telling them all about his life.

"I was born in Egypt and spent the first forty years of my life living in the lap of luxury. Then, one day, I killed an Egyptian who was smiting a Hebrew. When I found out that this deed was known among my fellow Hebrew brethren, I fled to the land of Midian for forty years where I met Jethro and married his daughter, Zipporah. Then, when I was eighty years old, God spoke to me out of a burning bush and commissioned me to deliver the Jews out of the land of Egypt. The Lord delivered my countrymen from the iron fist of Pharaoh through many judgments against the land of Egypt, and He led us through the Red Sea on dry ground while the Egyptians were drowned there. God gave the Law to me at Mount Sinai on two tablets of stone. He also gave me his statutes and precepts to pass on to the Jews, and really, these laws are a prescription for a happy life of health and wealth."

"Take two tablets, three times a day," Randy joked to himself, giggling a little.

"Anyway, one of the things the Lord spoke to me was this: 'And the soul that turneth after such as have familiar spirits, and have wizards, to go a-whoring after them, I will even set my face against that soul, and will cut him off from among his people.' This law is for the good of the people to protect them from the evil spirits who joined Lucifer in the Great Rebellion who are out to hurt men and destroy their souls."

"My story is very fascinating," said Samuel. "My parents, Elkanah and Hannah, were very godly people. I was an answer to the prayer of my mom as she asked the Lord to give her children. When I was just a little boy, my mom brought me to the house of the Lord at Shiloh to live and grow up with Eli, the high priest. Now the two sons of Eli, Hophni and Phinehas, were extremely wicked men who didn't have an intimate relationship with the Lord. They despised the offerings of the Lord through their greed and gluttony, and in so doing, they were blaspheming against God, for the sacrificial system of that day was a picture of what Jesus, the Lamb of God, would do for all mankind by dying on a cross. Besides all this, they were fornicators. Eli was a weak-willed and compromising priest who really didn't take action against his sons. He loved his food too much and was a very fat man when he died at the age of ninety-eight. One night, God spoke to me a dire prophecy concerning Eli and his family, and that was the beginning of my prophetic ministry.

"When I grew up, I became both a prophet and a judge to national Israel. The Lord didn't let anything that I said fall to the ground. I went on a circuit every year from Bethel to Gilgal to Mizpeh as I judged Israel. The time came when my sons became judges over Israel, but they were greedy and dishonest men who took bribes and perverted judgment. When the people of Israel saw this, they whined to me and asked for a king. I wasn't a happy camper and tried to warn them concerning what would happen to them if they had a king, but they wouldn't listen. God told me to go ahead and grant their request, but to warn them of what the consequences would be. Therefore, they got their wish.

"I loved Saul, their first king. He was the most handsome man I had ever seen. He was far taller than any other man in Israel and was an exceedingly skillful warrior. Initially, he had a lot of good qualities in him. He was very humble at the time he started his reign, he was kind, and he had the anointing of the Holy Spirit on his life. But soon, he began to become proud and arrogant. The time came when the Philistines were squeezing Israel right up to the wall. I had given Saul a message from the mouth of God to wait seven full days for me to come and sacrifice the burnt offering, but he didn't obey. He didn't trust God but took matters into his own hands and sacrificed the burnt offering himself. This was something that only a priest was allowed to do. When I arrived there and confronted him with his sin, he made excuses. I told him his kingdom wouldn't last, but that God had already picked out a man after His own heart to replace Saul. This was strike one.

"Strike two came when King Saul made his rash oath that whoever ate anything before sundown would die, even if it was his own son, Jonathan. (Jonathan ate some honey because he knew nothing about his dad's rash oath.) Saul did some other very bad things that day. Nevertheless, God didn't give up on him yet.

"Strike three happened when God told King Saul through me to utterly destroy the Amalekites, a totally evil and demonic nation. He was supposed to kill everything that pertained to that nation—men and animals, but he didn't obey the Lord completely. Remember this: *99 percent obedience and 1 percent disobedience is really total disobedience against the Lord.* King Saul spared King Agag and the best of the animals. When the Lord spoke to me about Saul being disobedient again, I cried out to Him all night long. I loved King Saul. I didn't want to see him fall but wanted him to be a success. It was with great anguish that I confronted him the next day. He made a lot of excuses once again. The root of his sin was greed, arrogance, and fear of what the people would think. I told him that rebellion was as the sin of witchcraft, and that stubbornness was as iniquity and idolatry. I told him that because of his disobedience, the Lord had rejected him from being king. But still, he was more concerned with his image with the people than he was with pleasing God. He badgered me to come with him to worship the Lord before the people.

"The Lord sent me to Jesse's house to anoint one of his sons as the new king of Israel. When I first saw Eliab, Jesse's oldest son, I was *sure* that he was the Lord's anointed; he was so tall and handsome. However, the Lord told me that Eliab was not the Lord's choice to be the new king. King David over here was the last one to appear before me and the last one Jesse would have ever expected to be made king. He wasn't even invited to the sacrifice but was out tending the sheep. When he appeared before me, the Lord told me that he was the one, and the Holy Spirit came mightily upon him. At that same time, the Lord took His Holy Spirit away from Saul and he became demon-possessed. David was sent to the house of Saul to play soothing music on his harp so that Saul could get temporary relief from the demon that overwhelmed him with such tormenting fear and depression. There was only one other time after that when the Holy Spirit came temporarily upon Saul. It was when he came to Ramah to try to kill David.

"Then a seed of envy and jealousy entered into the heart of Saul after David had killed Goliath and the women of Israel sang their songs that said, 'Saul has killed his thousands and David his tens of thousands.' This envy and jealousy blossomed into a garden of mega-poisonous fruit in the heart of Saul. He ended up trying to murder David again and again. Saul even murdered a whole lot of the Lord's priests.

"The day came when I died and was gathered to my fathers. My soul went down to Hades, which is in the center of the earth. Before Jesus went to the cross, two compartments were situated in Hades: a realm of comfort and peace for the righteous dead, and the place of great agony for the wicked who are still there today. I went to the compartment of rest and comfort. Remember: before the cross, almost nobody went directly to the Third Heaven except for a very few special people. Now when Jesus rose from the dead, he came into our compartment of Hades, got us, and took us up here to heaven. Oh, what a glorious day that was! One day, a few years after I died, a few angels came to me in Hades and led me to the spiritualistic witch in Endor to give a message of doom to Saul who was about to fight the Philistines the next day. He was in great trouble and had sought a prophetic word from God with no success. He was a man full of iniquity who did not seek God with a pure and honest heart. In the earlier years of his reign, he had purged the Land of mediums and spiritualists, but now, he was up against the wall. In desperation, he sought counsel from a familiar spirit. That witch of Endor was really surprised when a real human being was brought up from the dead. Usually, it was impersonating demons who appeared to her. I told Saul that he and his sons would die the next day, and that the Israeli army would be defeated by the Philistines. The next day, they did indeed die. Jonathan joined me in the realm of comfort and is here in heaven today, but Saul went to the realm of intense torment where he still is.

"Now, consulting with familiar spirits is like playing with fire. The demonic forces use spiritualism to hoodwink and enslave multitudes of people on Earth by their deception. People who have lost a loved one are often duped into bondage by those spirits who masquerade as their dead family members. There are very rare cases where a deceased person has appeared to a person on Earth, but only when it is the sovereign will of God as was the case when I appeared to King Saul. But again, a person must never, *never* consult spiritualistic mediums!

"One thing you should know concerning the time when the angels brought me up from Hades to prophesy doom to Saul; I appeared as an old man wearing a robe to the witch. But look at me now! Do I look old?"

"No!" exclaimed Randy. "You look so young and radiant!"

"Remember. When my spirit was brought up to talk to Saul, I had not been to this marvelous land yet, I had not eaten from the Tree of Life, and I had not drunk from the river of living water yet."

"This is a very interesting story!" exclaimed Randy.

The next one to speak was the prophet Isaiah. He talked about his ministry on Earth that started during the days of the reign of King Uzziah in Judah. His death came during the reign of wicked King Manasseh whom Randy had met a little earlier. One thing Isaiah talked about was who Leviathan *really* was.

"God, through His Holy Spirit, spoke these words to me to prophesy to Israel and to all the world, saying, 'In that day the LORD with His sure and great and strong sword shall punish Leviathan the piercing serpent, even Leviathan that crooked serpent; and He shall slay the dragon that is in the sea.'" (Randy gave a gasp of surprise when he heard these words.) "Many people on Earth, even believers, think that this is only a myth. But the truth is that Leviathan is real. He is a very strong demonic spirit who controls the seagates. When the LORD appeared to Job over here and spoke to him out of the whirlwind, He told him all about Leviathan and his great power. But praise God! The day is soon coming when God will deal with Leviathan as well as with all the other demons, and there will be a bright new future on Planet Earth."

Job now continued the narrative, saying, "Presently, Leviathan controls the oceans of the world. There are several funnels leading down to hell located at different parts of the oceans. One of them is in the Bermuda Triangle, located to the south of Florida." (Randy remembered that when he had fallen into that dark tube leading down to Hades, he had been right over the Gulf Coast.) "Also, there are many coastal cities in the world like San Francisco that have very oppressive demonic strongholds."

The apostle John now spoke, saying, "This witness is true. Jesus, the Light of the world, in whom there is no darkness at all, spoke to me about the sea in a negative way. Demonic strongholds exist over all the oceans of the world. Hell, as it now exists, is under the oceans. But praise Jesus! No sea controlled by demons will exist in the new heavens and earth the Lord will create. The Lord also showed me the coming destruction of the great Whore of Babylon. When this happens, all heaven will rejoice and shout, 'Hallelujah!'"

"I also saw the destruction of the last ungodly empire and the setting up of the eternal Kingdom of God on Earth," said Daniel. "Oh, that will be such a magnificent day when that happens! I was among the first of the captives who were taken to Babylon by King Nebuchadnezzar. The Lord blessed and promoted me in that land, and I had several high positions of leadership in the government. The Lord also used me as a prophet and showed me many things that were to happen in the future. For example, there was the time when Nebuchadnezzar had a dream about a huge statue that represented the great secular empires that were to arise in the future before Jesus, the large mountain that will smash those secular empires to smithereens, sets up the eternal Kingdom of God. The king was greatly disturbed by his dream, and the next morning called on his staff of magicians, astrologers, and sorcerers to interpret the dream for him. They couldn't do it. They said, 'Tell us the dream, and we will interpret it.' Finally, I told the king, 'Give me time, and I will tell you the dream you had.' I prayed hard, and the Lord showed me the king's dream about the huge statue and its interpretation. The supernatural power of God is infinitely greater than the supernatural power of Satan that works through astrologers, wizards, and sorcerers. Satan is a defeated foe and is *greatly afraid of every saint who has been washed in the Blood of Jesus!* We are more than conquerors through Christ who loved us with an eternal love! Jesus has conquered that hated enemy, death!"

Randy caught the anagram of death/hated and realized just how brainy and wise Daniel really was. Why that prophet would have aced even the toughest puzzles found in any crossword puzzle book in America today, and surely would have beaten every opponent on the game show, *Jeopardy*.

"You are welcome to join us in this picnic, Joshua Randall," said Jeremiah.

"Thank you!" exclaimed Randy.

No words can be penned on Earth to describe what those heavenly fruits and vegetables tasted like. Compared to those heavenly munchies, the sweetest grapes on Earth tasted like cardboard, the best peaches tasted like sawdust, and the most delicious cherries tasted like totally dry and moldy bread that had no savor whatsoever. There was the copper fruit he had sampled the last time he was here. Another looked similar to a very large apple. A third type was in clusters and looked like a pear. It tasted like frozen cream, only far, far more delicious than that. A fourth was shaped somewhat like a banana. During the feast, Randy continued to converse with the prophets who were sitting at the magnificent picnic table. He found out that Moses, Abraham, and Daniel were three of the twenty-four elders the book of Revelation talks about.

After the unforgettable repast, the prophets rose from the table and indulged in a very delightful romp around that huge recreational area. Some of the prophets played a hearty game of touch football. By this time, Jonathan, the son of Saul, had joined them in the park. David and Jonathan took off sprinting, chasing each other through the many, many winding pathways running through the delightful park. The whole recreation area was a huge maze with every variety of flora bordering the twisting and turning avenues. *If I had only known that there is a lot of fun in heaven,* thought Randy to himself. As a kid, he had harbored the Christo/platonic stereotype of heaven as a boring place where all a person did was sit around on a cloud all day, strumming a harp. The animated voices rang throughout the large park.

"YAHAAAAA! Come and catch me if you can, King David!"

"I'm gonna git' you, Jonathan!"

"You can't git' me! Go ahead and try! Run, run, as fast as you can! You can't catch me, I'm the Gingerbread Man!"

"Oh, yeah? We'll see about that!"

Laughter broke out among all the romping saints, and when they had finished all of their sports, they weren't a bit tired. They weren't even the least bit out of breath. They sat down in the totally-alive grass near a stunning bed of scarlet carnations and indulged in some more friendly conversation. After a while, King David rose up from the group and walked toward Randy.

"Come along, now. You have an appointment in the Holy City."

The two of them climbed into one of the chariots of light, and the king started driving down a delightful road, which twisted this way and that way down the high foothills toward the plains of heaven. Randy had not traveled on this road before. There were new spellbinding sights that could never be expressed on Earth concerning their beauty. One of the many points of great interest they passed was a lake filled with pleasure boats. A little later, Randy found himself traveling through a charming valley dotted with many lovely houses. Randy saw every type of animal that you could find in a zoo, all of them docile and peaceable, and every one of them seeming to praise the Lord in its own way. Some of them included kangaroos, elephants, zebras, and the most beautiful, regal horses. The huge and beautiful city could now be seen in the far distance, getting closer and closer. Soon, the chariot stopped at a gate that Randy had not seen before, and King David motioned for him to get out.

Randy was sure he could never get tired of looking at the entrancing sights, no matter how long he lived in this delightful place.

"The place where you are standing now is the gate of Joseph, which is one of the three gates on the east side of the city," explained King David. "Come! Let's go in."

They walked through that glittering, stupendous gate. There were the transparent golden streets with buildings that would make the mansion of Hearst's Castle seem like a Hooverville cardboard dwelling in comparison, inviting trees and flowers, statues, fountains of sparkling water, and the River of Living Water that was perhaps the width of the Jordan River in Israel. The streets were thronged with thousands upon thousands of angels and happy people who had the loveliest glow on their faces. And then—

There, straight ahead of them, was the most beautiful Person of them all. He was the One who Randy had seen in the Garden of Gethsemane, in Pilate's judgment hall, and on the cross being crucified and mutilated. He was the One who he had seen at the garden tomb after He had risen from the dead. He was the One who he had seen as the great and glorious Bridegroom at the Marriage Feast of the Lamb. Now, Randy Miller was seeing Him for real, face to face, and the experience was both wonderful and terrible beyond description. There were those eyes of love that were so exquisitely beautiful beyond description. They were wells of infinite knowledge, wisdom, power, and love. Also, He seemed to be pure and complete light. His hair was a brownish color, and His hands still had the holes from the nails, which were now shafts of the loveliest light. Randy immediately fell on his face and could hardly move. *Oh, the unpolluted purity of this Man!!* Randy was sure that he was undone. He thought to himself, *well, here I am a great big basket case and sinner who has lived selfishly and dabbled in the occult! What hope is there for a great big boob like myself?* He noticed that he was still wearing his 'Jitterbug Josh' concert outfit, which was absolutely filthy. At that moment, Jesus spoke to him in a very, very tender, compassionate voice.

"Joshua Randall Miller! Your sins are all forgiven! Go, wash yourself in the River!"

"Y-y-you want me to j-jump in the River, Jesus?"

"Yes."

Joshua, as he was now called, rose slowly to his feet and headed toward the River of Life. He hesitated at the edge for a moment, sure that the water would be icy cold. Then, gathering up all the courage he could muster, he plunged in.

The water was deliciously warm. There were beautiful multi-colored rocks at the bottom of the crystal-clear River. Strangely enough, he didn't run out of breath, no matter how long he stayed submerged below the surface. Another surprising thing was that he could hear everything outside the water—the beautiful music, the happy conversations, and the worship—just as clearly, as if he had been standing on the shore. The water looked so clear and unpolluted that Joshua Randall decided to have a drink. It proved to be the most refreshing and delicious draught he had ever tasted. Coke, 7-Up, orange juice, and milk were no match for this, let alone Merlot wine or Budlight beer. Presently, he emerged from the River and leaped back onto the shore.

There were now more surprises. First of all, he was not dripping at all, but totally dry. Secondly, he was no longer clothed in that filthy old 'Jitterbug Josh' outfit, but instead, found himself wearing a beautiful white robe. But the most wonderful thing of all was how *alive* he felt!! He felt a warmth that had come over him from the bottom of his feet radiating all the way up his spiritual body. *Oh, the vibrant energy he felt coursing through his whole being!!*

"Wow! I feel like I could fly just like Peter Pan!" He ran over to Jesus and fell down at His feet. "Thank You, Jesus! I love and adore You, beautiful Jesus!"

"Rise, My son."

Joshua Randall stood up on his feet.

"My son, your sins are forgiven thee. Now hear the Word of the Lord! 'And he shewed me Joshua the high priest standing before the angel of the LORD, and Satan standing at his right hand to resist him. And the LORD said unto Satan, the Lord rebuke thee, O Satan; even the LORD that hath chosen Jerusalem rebuke thee; is not this a brand plucked out of the fire? Now Joshua was clothed with filthy garments and stood before the angel. And he answered and spake unto those that stood before him, saying, Take away the filthy garments from him. And unto him he said, Behold, I have caused thine iniquity to pass from thee, and I will clothe thee with change of raiment. And I said, Let them set a fair mitre upon his head. So they set a fair mitre upon his head, and clothed him with garments. And the angel of the LORD stood by. And the angel of the LORD protested unto Joshua, saying, Thus saith the LORD of hosts; If thou wilt walk in My ways, and if thou wilt keep My charge, then thou shalt also judge My house, and shalt also keep My courts, and I will give thee places to walk among these that stand by.'

"Joshua Randall Miller, I have a job for you. You have seen just a tiny bit of the unspeakable glories and delights I have prepared for My children up here. You have also witnessed the horrible suffering of the lost in the dark regions below. You have seen a few important things that have happened in the past as well as a few things that will occur in the future. I am sending you back to Earth to testify to the world concerning the things you have seen. I want you to tell them there is life eternal after death and a very, very bright future for those who love My Father and Me. Tell them that hell is a real place that was created for Satan and the demons who followed him in his rebellion. *It was never created for even a single human being.* I desire everyone to be saved and to enjoy the unsearchable treasures I have created for My children, but they must make a choice to follow Me. I want you to tell them I am coming for My people very soon—I REALLY am coming—it's not a Peter Pan fairy tale—even some of My own people doubt that I'm coming again, but I *really* am coming.

"You have seen the great celebration that is coming. My Word calls it 'The Marriage Supper of the Lamb.' This will be the consummation of the Granddaddy of all weddings—the day when I, the Heavenly Bridegroom, marry My beloved Bride, the Church. This will be the Great Party, the Grand Celebration, when the Circle of Celestial Celebrants and I will have a wedding feast to end all wedding feasts. I want you to tell My people to make themselves ready for that glorious day, with their loins girded about, and their lights burning. I am coming for a holy and pure Bride without spot or wrinkle. I want you to tell them that the devil is coming to Earth very soon. He will clothe himself in the son of perdition who will rule over the whole earth for a short time and deceive many into eternal destruction. His coming will be attended by lying signs and wonders, and there will be great tribulation on Earth such as there has never been before, neither will ever be again. After that horrid time, I will return to the earth with My people and with the holy angels to rule over the whole world from the capital city of Jerusalem.

"I want you to tell the world how much I love them. I gave My life on the cross and went to hell so that they could have the free gift of eternal life. Tell them they cannot earn it. There's not one red cent they have to pay in order to receive a ticket into heaven. All they have to do is call on My name, surrender their lives to Me, and make Me their Lord. Also, tell them that the doctrine of reincarnation is a lie. There is only one life to live, and after that comes eternity spent either with Me or totally separated from Me."

Joshua Randall listened to these words with a mixture of bewilderment and disappointment. He didn't want to leave this land of bliss and go back to the crummy old earth.

"Lord, You mean I can't stay here? I don't ever want to go back."

"Yes, My son. You must. Many of My servants are praying for you—and I have a plan, a blueprint for your life that the Trinity mapped out for you even before We created the earth. You have to go back, but I will allow you to stay here just a little longer so that you can enjoy a concert that is about to begin here in the Holy City. David is going to conduct you to the venue where the concert is going to be."

"Please, Lord," said Joshua Randall. "There's just one other thing I don't understand. I've always been known as Randy, and yet I'm known as Joshua Randall up here. Why is that?"

"My son. Your mom, Wendy Miller, wanted you to be named Joshua Randall, and your dad reluctantly went along with that. However, when your mom was killed by that poisonous snakebite when you were but one-and-a-half years old, he decided to call you by the name you've always gone by—Randy Joshua. He was involved in spiritualism during the whole time he was married to Wendy, your mother. He didn't like the name Joshua. It was too Christian for his tastes. You see, Joshua, Satan doesn't play the game fairly—

he plays dirty. Your dad was on his turf, and because of this, he was subject to the evil curses the devil was able to cook up. That's why both Wendy and Thomas died at such premature ages."

"I see," said Joshua Randall, soberly.

"Please come, Joshua Randall," said King David. "It's nearly time for the concert."

The two of them climbed into the lovely chariot, and the king started driving through the dazzling and magnificent city. They passed by many, many awe-inspiring sights. In one of those places, thousands upon thousands of people were cheering an especially glorious saint whose countenance bespoke indescribable joy and ecstasy. He would have been considered to be a god if he appeared on Earth looking like this.

"Who is that guy, O king?" asked Joshua Randall.

"He is Sergei Stokonoff who lived in Communist Russia and was martyred by the KGB for his faithful testimony concerning Jesus. He had a bad hand dealt to him and was not known by many people on Earth at all. He had many generations of evil and godless ancestors who gave him a very warped sin nature, but he cried out to Jesus for a special amount of mercy and was washed in the Blood of the Lamb. He overcame all the wiles of the Enemy and finally overcame death itself. Now, he is one of the highest kings who gets to sit on a beautiful throne very close to Christ Himself.

"Remember this, Joshua Randall: Many people who were famous on Earth are not even known in heaven. Even many of God's servants, who were famous on Earth, but did not truly live up to their full potential, find themselves walking in obscurity up here. They end up being 'saved, so as through fire,' their works of wood, hay, and stubble being burned up. Many of those people are in the great crowd you see before you who are cheering that great saint on. James, the brother of Jesus, warned that not many people should become teachers because they will receive a stricter judgment."

They soon stopped at a very huge circular pavilion made of snow-white marble with gorgeous colonnades and overhanging arches on the outside. Thousands upon thousands of redeemed saints were walking into the concert hall, hugging each other, kissing each other, and lovingly greeting each other. Friendly conversations filled the huge stadium.

"Well, hi there, Mary! Bless God! How lovely to see you again!"

"Thank you, Christina! Glory to God! How are you?"

"I'm doing fantastic! You look so fabulous!"

"Good morning, Lori! Shalom, shalom to you!"

"Excuse me, Joshua," said King David. "I need to go get dressed for the concert."

"Okay, King David."

Joshua Randall found a seat midway between the front and the back of the auditorium. Many steps led down to where the elaborate concert stage was located. The seats were covered with soft and creamy scarlet cushions made out of high-class materials that were only known in heaven. Joshua Randall could look down from his perch and have an excellent view of the stage. Soon, the pinkish-red curtains opened up to reveal a stage floor constructed out of the finest woods that could only be found in heaven. A huge golden grand piano was on the stage that had to be at least fifteen feet long. A lovely golden harp was situated close to the piano as well as some instruments he could not identify. A very youthful emcee walked onto the stage to announce the first performer.

"Good morning and shalom, my beloved brothers and sisters," he started out. "Today, we have a real treat for you. We have a lot of talented musicians who are going to perform a variety of works for you that we are sure will uplift you. Please join me in giving a warm welcome to our first artist, J. S. Bach! Shalom and soli Deo gloria!"

Onto the stage walked a very dignified man with white hair, but full of youthful energy. He made a very graceful bow as the whole auditorium erupted into tumultuous applause. He sat down at the piano and dove into his famous *Italian Concerto in F major*. Bach's performance was flawless. He nailed the tough passages with ease, his rhythms were very smooth and concise, and there was tremendous dynamic contrast—anywhere from barely audible all the way up to so loud that if it had been performed on Earth at that volume, it would have been deafening. Moreover, the tone quality was sweet beyond description—far sweeter than anything that had ever been heard on Earth. Even Rachmaninoff, with his very pleasant tone quality on the piano, could not begin to approach the pleasurable sounds coming from the anointed hands of Bach. After his performance, the theater erupted into frantic cheering and cries of, "Soli Deo gloria!" (To God alone be all the glory!)

Next on the program was a group of redeemed American Indians from the Sioux tribe who performed a couple of songs that were their trademark. They had several large Indian drums that sounded absolutely beautiful as well as being very loud—far louder than a thunderclap on Earth. Their outfits were lovely and still had some of the aspects of their colorful qualities of their earthly clothing. Following this was an African choir with their only musical accompaniment being a couple of percussionists. The harmonies in their songs were in seven parts, extremely beautiful, and perfectly in tune.

Felix Mendelssohn now walked up to the piano and started his portion of the concert by playing his *Scherzo a Capriccio in F-sharp Minor*. Joshua Randall well remembered this composition. He had first heard it when he had been eighteen years old. It had been played in a Master Class by a girl with black hair whom he had developed a crush on. Her name was Peggy Brown. She had played the piece very well, but with extremely harsh tone quality. Mendelssohn played it absolutely beautifully. The piece was peppy with many staccato passages, which was a trademark of Mendelssohn's music. Next, he played his *Rondo Capriccioso* with its slow opening in E major followed by the fast and aggressive section in E minor with a great number of staccato passages. After this, a huge orchestra walked up onto the stage to perform his famous piece, *A Midsummer Night's Dream.* The gigantic orchestra was dressed in stunning black-and-white outfits. There were 500 violinists, 300 violists, 150 cellists, 96 double bass players, 95 flautists, 70 oboe players, 80 clarinetists, 60 bassoonists, 120 shofar blowers, 180 trumpeters, 110 French horn blowers, 120 trombonists, 200 harpists, 10 percussionists, and a celesta player. Never on earth had this composition been performed so beautifully.

King David now took his place at the harp and sang four of his psalms he had set to music. The first one was Psalm 23 followed by Psalm 33, Psalm 68, and Psalm 150. Of course, practically everyone knew the words to Psalm 23 that said, "The LORD is my Shepherd, I shall not want. He maketh me to lie down in green pastures—"

The last piece on the program was Handel's *Hallelujah Chorus* from *The Messiah.* Two thousand and six hundred singers walked onto the stage attired in the most gorgeous scarlet choir robes. Handel himself conducted the orchestra while Bach sat down at the piano to perform the keyboard part. The performance was so beautiful, Joshua Randall was rendered breathless. At the end of this piece, which was in D major, there was no applause. Instead, everybody—including Joshua Randall, broke out into loud praise and worship to God.

"Thank you, Lord! *Thank you!"*

"Glory to God in the highest!"

"Praise You, wonderful Jesus! You are the Prince of Peace, the Holy One of Israel, the One altogether lovely, the sweet Rose of Sharon!"

"Soli Deo gloria!"

Presently, King David walked up to Joshua Randall and said, "Well, how did you like it?"

"Oh, it was absolutely *wonderful!"* sighed Joshua Randall.

"I'm glad you had a great time! It's time for us to be moving on!"

Right next to the heavenly concert hall were two large golden buildings that were especially magnificent. The first building had many incredibly stupendous and lovely golden vials with the most wonderful fragrances that Joshua had smelled yet. It was so marvelous, he felt totally drunk. Right next to that building was another edifice filled with the most beautiful cloud. Inside this building were hundreds of especially happy and enraptured saints who were worshipping Jesus with all their might. Joshua's mental capacities were greatly increased up here, and he knew that 89 percent of the incredibly ecstatic people in this wonderful room were glorified women while 11 percent were glorified men. The Lord's presence was so strong in there that Joshua was not able to walk within thirty feet of this room. As it was, he felt very weak and had trouble standing.

"Explain these two wonderful buildings to me, O great king," said Joshua.

"That first building contains the golden vials of incense, which are the prayers of the saints on Earth. They will be opened during the Seven-Year Tribulation. You can read about it in Revelation 5, verse 8 and also Revelation 8, verses 3 and 4. That second building is a very unique place for special Christians who were great prayer intercessors on Earth and attained to levels of intimacy with the Lord such as few Christians on Earth ever reach. This is one of their favorite places to hang out in here in heaven. One of the people in there right now is Praying Hyde."

The king led Joshua Randall into the chariot, and he started driving it toward the gate of Simeon, one of the three gates on the southern edge of the Holy City. There were more breathtaking sights to see as they zoomed through the city and then out into the countryside, with its orchards of gorgeous trees, loaded down with the twelve kinds of heavenly fruit. The king eventually stopped the chariot in a grove of trees and flowers located far, far away from the Holy City that could be seen in the distance by looking back. As Joshua Randall exited the chariot, he saw two people who were walking straight toward him. They were wearing white gowns, not robes, and there was something familiar about them. He began to have a hunch, which grew into joyful recognition. With squeals of rapture, the three of them ran toward each other and were soon involved in a tight heavenly hug.

"Daddy! Mom!"

"Oh, my son! My son!"

"You've grown so big!" (These words were spoken by Joshua Randall's mom, Wendy Miller.)

After a few moments of emotional and loving embraces and kisses, the questions began.

"Dad! I'm so glad you made it here! At one time, I thought that deceiving demon I encountered on Earth was you. And then, when I saw hell and realized the truth about the occult being a trapdoor that led many people there, I was afraid that you were confined to hell forever. So—tell me, is this really you?"

"It's really me, my precious son."

"Tell me the story of how you were able to make it safely up here."

"Well, my son. Just two weeks before I died in that terrible car accident near Walnut Creek, I attended a Billy Graham crusade at the Oakland Arena. I remember that the place was packed. The music was very pretty that night, and Billy Graham preached a strong evangelistic message. He preached against all kinds of sin including the sins relating to dabbling in the occult. He scared the bejeebers out of me that night, and I felt the conviction of the Holy Spirit urging me to get right with God and not to put it off. Then Doctor Graham talked about what Jesus had done for the human race, giving up His life on the cross so that we could be freely forgiven of our sins through repentance and faith in Jesus. It was a tough choice and I almost didn't go forward, but I finally decided to go down front to pray the sinner's prayer.

The prayer counselors gave me some reading material to help me grow in my relationship with Christ. That night, I renounced spiritualism.

"However, the next week, I attended a meeting at my spiritualistic church with the intention of sharing Jesus with them. It didn't work very well. When I started to testify about how I had found the Lord, they got real angry, proclaimed dire curses against me, and threw me out. I was also a Lodge member in the Royal Order of the Blue Knights. I went to a Lodge meeting four days before my fatal car wreck and tried to share Christ with them, also. They didn't like that very much either and they threw me out. And then, four days later, I was killed and found myself in the outer courts of paradise, absolutely bewildered. A couple of very kind angels helped me to put those healing leaves from the Tree of Life on my body and also instructed me about spiritual things."

"I accepted the Lord when I was a young girl," said Wendy. "Unfortunately, I didn't make a whole lot of effort to grow spiritually in my walk with Christ. I felt a real check in my spirit when I was courting your dad, but I didn't listen to the still small voice inside of me and went ahead and married Tom anyway. Then, a year-and-a-half after I brought you into the world, I suffered that fatal bite from that snake up at Yosemite. When I first got here, I was dazed, much like your father was."

"Well, anyway. I'm so very, very happy to see you and Dad *for real!* I never felt any love from that demon who pretended to be my dad, but oh, *I sure feel a whole lot of love from the two of you!"*

"We love you so much, too, our son!" said both of the parents.

Suddenly, excited voices could be heard all around the vicinity where the three of them were standing.

"He's coming! *He's coming! HE's COMING!"*

Joshua Randall knew exactly what was going on. Jesus was coming their way. He walked up to the three of them and stopped right in front of Joshua Randall.

"My son," He said, "it is time for you to return to your physical body."

"But Lord! I don't want to return to that crummy old body of mine!"

"But you must! I have a holy commission for you."

"Lord, I've been away from my body for a long, long time. It must have been many days since I've left my body, and I'm sure that I must have already been buried or cremated."

"You've only been gone for slightly less than an hour-and-a-half. Remember that time in the spirit world is different than time on Earth."

"Yes, Lord."

"Now Joshua. I have a couple of important things I want you to do when you return to Earth. These are not optional, but important commands. First of all, I want you to destroy everything in your home that is occultic in any way. I want you to burn all your manuscripts of every song you received during those nighttime trance states. It was a demon who gave you those songs. From now on, you are to serve Me only. The second thing is this: never again will you perform with that group, The Universal Mindset. The agenda of that group was not from Me, but from the Enemy. You have seen how music can have an effect for good, and in these last days, I will pour out My anointed heavenly music on My choice servants when the time is right. But you have also seen how music can be an instrument of evil and death. King Nebuchadnezzar once used music as a tool to induce the people living in Babylon to worship a huge idol he had made. The third thing is this: some things you have seen are to be kept secret; you are not allowed to share them with anyone on Earth. One of those things is the fireworks show and the speeches of those four great American statesmen you saw in your vision of the Great Shabbat of Planet Earth."

Jesus mentioned a few other things that Joshua Randall was to keep totally secret. And then, Jesus finished by saying, "Joshua Randall!"

"Yes, Lord?"

"I love you!"

"I love You too, Jesus!"

"Be thou faithful to your ministry I am calling you to. When you have finished your course on Earth faithfully, you will return to this place and have a place of rulership with Me. And behold, I am with you always. I will never leave you or forsake you."

At this point, Jesus waved His right hand, and the strangest thing happened. It was like a large square window was opened right in front of Joshua Randall. On the left side, the right side, and the area below and above the window were the fantastic scenes of heaven, but within the window itself were the images of Planet Earth right in the town of Walnut Creek. When he had left the earth to come to heaven, it had still been dark, but now, it was clear daylight. The sun had just risen with its golden rays illuminating the city of Walnut Creek. To the southeast, Mount Diablo towered far above the metropolis, casting a gray-purple shadow. Ignacio Valley Boulevard was filled with the Saturday morning flow of cars, trucks, and motorcycles. John Muir Hospital towered above the countryside on the south side of that road. Strangely enough, Joshua Randall could see right through the roof of the hospital into the ICU cubicle where Grandma Brenda was praying over his inert body. He could hear every single word she was saying.

"Lord, let me bring my case to You! I will reason with You, and You *will* answer me! Your Word says that Jesus is the Resurrection and the Life, and that if I ask anything in the name of Jesus, You will grant my request. Lord, I'm not quitting until You give me my request! Remember: You will be dishonoring Your great name and Your Word if You don't raise Randy Miller up!"

At this point, Joshua Randall felt a great suction that pulled him right through the window and into the atmosphere that hovered above Ignacio Valley Boulevard. He glanced toward the west and saw some golden words reflected by the morning sunlight. They read, "Love not the world, neither the things that are in the world. If any man love the world, the love of the Father is not in him. For all that is in the world, the lust of the flesh, and the lust of the eyes, and the pride of life, is not of the Father, but is of the world. And the world passeth away, and the lust thereof: but he that doeth the will of God abideth for ever."

At this point, he started to float down toward the hospital.

****

THE ATMOSPHERE WAS DIM in the cubicle where the body of Joshua Randall lay. Grandma Brenda was continuing to pray. Footsteps could be heard coming toward the cubicle. Doctor Howard Clarvoe entered the room followed by Lila. The face of the grieving woman was a picture of great weariness and numbness.

"Well, that's it!" declared Doctor Clarvoe as the digital display on the clock changed from 6:39 to 6:40. "I'm going to unplug the machine. One side, Grandma!"

"But please, Doc!" said Grandma Brenda. "Couldn't we give it two more minutes?"

"No! I've given it more than enough time! That man is dead. It's time to bury the body. I—*WHAT?*"

The eyelids of 'Jitterbug Josh' fluttered, and at the same time, the heart monitor went into a normal rhythm of beeps, signaling that the heart of the famous singing star was beating again.

"Randy Joshua Miller!" Lila cried out as she rushed toward her husband and slipped to the floor right in front of him, her face a tableau of shock and pure joy. Tears were running down her face, but they were tears of gladness. She laughed and wept at the same time and cried, "Randy! Oh, Randy! *Randy!* My darling, *my darling!*"

"Lila," said the singing star in a weak, but happy voice.

"Praise God! Praise God!" shouted Grandma Brenda, joyfully. "Thank You, Jesus! *Thank You, Jesus!*"

"WHAT THE H—" Doctor Clarvoe just stood there with his mouth wide open, gawking in unbelief. "This can't be. This just cannot be!"

Doctor Martin Perez and a nurse came trotting toward the cubicle, strode in, and said, "What's going on here?"

Doctor Perez took one look at the face of Joshua Randall and exclaimed, "Why, look at that! His face is *glowing!!*"

"Yeah!" agreed the nurse. "It looks like a 100-watt light bulb. I just don't get it!"

"Mama Mia!" exclaimed Doctor Perez in bewilderment. *"MAMA MIMI!* Blessed be the Holy Mother!"

"All right, HOLD IT, EVERYBODY!" exclaimed Doctor Clarvoe. "Let's keep our feet on the ground! This man has been basically dead for a good hour-and-a-half. There is still not much hope for him. This whole thing is an impossible fluke! Even if he were to live, he'd be a useless vegetable for the rest of his life."

"Well, let's see about that," said Doctor Perez, walking toward the music star. "Hey, Jitterbug Josh. Speak to me. Can you say anything to me at all?"

Joshua Randall fluttered his eyes and said in a weak, yet audible voice, "You folks have no idea where I've been! I've seen the other side! Two angels took me to heaven where the joys and delights awaiting those who love Jesus have never been experienced on Earth. I've also looked into hell, which is way, way under the earth. The torture and pain of those people down there would make the most excruciating torture on Earth seem like a mere flu shot in comparison. The fires rage down there with mega, mega intense fury like you wouldn't believe."

"You see there?" exclaimed Doctor Clarvoe. "He's totally lost his marbles! His brain is totally fried because of the lack of oxygen. He's become a total religious fan—"

"Bunk!" protested Martin Perez. "A brainless vegetable wouldn't be able to say even one word, let alone putting the complex sentences we've just heard come out of the mouth of Jitterbug Josh here. What we're witnessing here, my friend, is a bona fide miracle."

"Well, just you wait, Martin! You'll see! All that bull about angels, heaven, and hell. Why, he's cracked up!"

But nobody in the room was listening to the skeptical, atheistic cardiologist. They were all amazed and full of joy over the revived singing star.

****

THIS TURN OF EVENTS mystified the major news networks, which had reported the 'death' of 'Jitterbug Josh.' By Saturday afternoon they were claiming that there had been an erroneous report from the doctors at John Muir Hospital. The new word was that 'Jitterbug Josh' was still alive but in very critical condition. The reporters claimed that the famous singing star would probably be only a vegetable for the rest of his life. A few days later, the prognosis was somewhat more optimistic. There was still a tight regulation concerning who could see the famous singing star, the visitor list being restricted to family members, relatives, and one clergyman.

****

ON TUESDAY, NOVEMBER 12, Joshua Randall was released from ICU and put into his own room in the hospital. His recovery was remarkable, and word of this colossal miracle had spread through the whole hospital. The restrictions on visitors were lessened some more. Now, close friends of the Miller family could visit the music star. One day, Pam Jackson and Brad Applebaum (who was recovering nicely from his stab wound) came into the room to visit the singing star. Lila, Jack, and Thomas Miller Junior were also there. The 'useless vegetable' was telling them about some of the things he had seen on the other side.

"Heaven is a real place. There are no words that can begin to convey just how incredibly wonderful it is. Many of the things we enjoy here on Earth are also in heaven, only many, many times more marvelous than they are here. And Brad—I owe you a whole lot of thanks for saving my life—and you too, Pam. I still shudder at the words Mystery Revealer, one of the angels who attended me, said to me at the entrance to the cells of Hades. He told me that if Eric Burns had succeeded in having me shot dead right there in the theater, I would have spent eternity in hell."

"We just felt such a burden to pray for you, Randy," said Pam. "I also think we owe a whole lot to Grandma Brenda. She is really a mega, mega big hero in my book."

"I think God should get all the glory," said Joshua Randall.

"Is Grandma Brenda still in the Bay Area?" asked Pam.

"Yes," answered Lila. "She is staying in one of the spare bedrooms in our house. She plans to go back to Virginia around the first of the month."

"Hey, Dad," said Tommy. "Guess what! I got an A- on my math test yesterday!"

"Good for you, Tommy!"

"And Dad," said Jack. "You know what? Yesterday at the school football game, I caught two passes and ran down to the end zone to make two touchdowns!"

"Good going, Jack! You know, when I was your age, I was a pushover at the game of football. When they picked players for the two teams, I was always the last one chosen."

"Hey, Jitterbug Josh," asked Brad. "What did Uncle Mike say when he found out that you practically came back from the dead?"

"He was very skeptical. He wouldn't believe the report until he came here today and talked to me face-to-face. Now he believes what the newspapers are saying: that some medic made a mistake in claiming that I was dead when I was never even in real danger of dying."

Brad responded, "Well, I guess we can just chalk him up as another 'Doubting Thomas.' I guess that's just his natural personality."

"A lot of people aren't buying the real story," said Lila. "But, you know what? I don't really care! I'm just so thankful to God that I have my honey-bun back from the dead—and I like the new Randy Joshua Miller far better than the old famous star, 'Jitterbug Josh!'"

****

THANKSGIVING AT THE MILLER MANSION that year was unlike any Thanksgiving Lila and Randy Miller/alias 'Jitterbug Josh'/Joshua Randall—the name he was now going by—had ever experienced. They were truly thankful people. Joshua Randall had truly come back to life from the dead and was recovering at a very fast rate of speed. In fact, some aspects of his health were better now than they had been in the days before that fateful Halloween night at the movie theater. The nightmares were gone as were the trance states where he had gotten his demon-inspired song hits. His addiction to amphetamines and barbiturates was also gone. In addition, there was no longer any alcohol in the house. He was also on a very strict diet in order to speed his recovery along. He was using a walker, and the family had set up a temporary bed for him downstairs until he could get enough strength to manage the stairs again. The house no longer had a feeling of being haunted or cold. Rather, a peace permeated the whole place. Joshua Randall had a new glow about him, coming from the Lord. Lila also had a relationship with the Lord, having completely surrendered to Him just a couple of days after Joshua Randall's big miracle.

On this Thanksgiving afternoon, there were a number of guests in the big Miller mansion. Mike and Donna Applebaum were there with their daughters, Michelle and Sharon. Brad was there with Sid, Harriet, Kimberly, Lisa, and Pam. And of course, Grandma Brenda was there. Combined with the four in the Miller family circle, it was going to be a big celebration indeed.

At 4:00 P. M., they all gathered in the beautiful dining room with the floor of cedar wood and the walls covered with light-brown wallpaper for the blessing. Grandma Brenda said the prayer for the meal.

"Heavenly Father, we thank You for all Your matchless blessings, for blessing us with this wonderful country of freedom and prosperity, and for Your resurrection and miracle working power. We thank You for this food which we are about to eat. Bless it and nourish it for our bodies and bless the fellowship around the table. In the beautiful name of Jesus, amen!"

They then passed the turkey, the mashed potatoes, the dressing, the gravy, the cranberry sauce, the green beans, and the broccoli around the table in order for everyone to be able to fill up their plates. There was iced tea, coffee, milk, 7-Up, and Martinelli's Sparkling Cider available for their drinks. As they ate that delectable dinner, happy and animated conversation broke out among the banqueters with much laughter and many witty jokes and fond memories.

"So tell me, Jitterbug Josh," asked Brad. "What are your plans, now? Are you going to get back into the pop music racket and use your fame and fortune to win millions and millions of people to Christ?"

Donna Applebaum added, "Yeah, I hear that music kingmaker Harry Gates wants to get the group, The Universal Mindset going again."

"No, my friends," said Joshua Randall. "My days of trying to be rich and famous are over. The Lord has clearly shown me that He has a new plan for my life."

"But don't you see what an impact you could make on the world by using The Universal Mindset band as a platform to witness for Christ?" asked Brad.

"The important thing, my friend," said Joshua Randall, "is to be focused on the things of eternity, not on the things of the world that are only temporary."

Grandma Brenda added, "And the really important thing is obedience, much more than just outward success."

"When I was in heaven," said Joshua Randall, "I was told that there are many people who were famous on Earth who are not at all famous in heaven."

"So, do you have any future plans?" asked Mike Applebaum.

"Yes," said the erstwhile music star. "There is a high school down in Visalia that is looking for a choral teacher next year. That sounds like a very intriguing possibility to me. I do know that we're going to have to move into a much smaller house soon and that I'm going to have to find a new job."

"I hope that new school doesn't have any dirty tricksters like Ray Palmer or Greg Darrow," remarked Mike.

Joshua Randall chuckled and quipped, "Yeah, Ray Palmer! You know, he's the one who did that obscene prank against the female sub teacher on that day of chaos in men's chorus in May 1973. The next day, I gave him an ultimatum: either be suspended, (which would have led to his expulsion), or strip down in front of all the men."

"So, what choice did he make?" asked Lisa Applebaum.

"Well, it's a no-brainer, Lisa. He chose the second option. They were laughing their heads off, and to add insult to injury, one of the guys walked by and whacked his bare butt hard."

Everyone roared with laughter as Kimberly Applebaum quipped, "Yeah! And I've heard that Ray Palmer streaked right in the middle of the graduation ceremonies at Campolindo last June."

More spirited laughter erupted from the happy circle of people.

Brad and Pam were sitting next to each other. The spark of romance was as strong as ever between the two of them.

"It's just too bad that your dad has to move to Nashville in January," lamented Brad.

"Yeah, sweetheart! It's going to be so tough, Brad! I'm gonna miss you something awful!"

"I sure hope we get to see each other again."

"Do you think we'll ever get back together, Brad?"

"I hope so, Pam! I really hope so!"

"Will you write to me?"

"I'll try."

"I'm gonna miss the prayer group too."

"Yeah."

Meanwhile, Sid and Mike were talking about the economy.

"Well, Sid. Looks like the market is up a little in the last week or two," said Mike.

"Yeah, we're in a big boom."

"It's going to be interesting to see what happens to the market with this big democratic landslide we've had this fall."

"Yeah, Ford has a tough road ahead of him."

"Who do you think will be the next president in 1976?"

"I kinda' hope it's Ronnie Reagan."

"He's a little too conservative for me, pal. Most politicians are crooked, whether it's guys named Nixon or guys from Dixon."

Sid laughed and said, "Well, I still like Ronnie boy! I think he's an honest man and will be good for stocks and for business."

"Did you hear about the black dude who was in on the plot to kidnap Randy and then turned himself in? I heard his testimony on the news last night. He said this: 'I used to be a communist, but now I'm a 'publican.'"

Pam, who was listening in on the conversation, commented, "The correct word is *Republican!* A publican is one who is a tax collector, and most of them are Democrats—not Republicans!"

The whole room erupted into a tsunami of uncontrollable laughter.

Brad said, "You see that? My sweetheart, Pam over here, has a great sense of humor—just like me—and I'm very humble about it! I'm a humble person and very proud of it!"

Everybody in the room was in stitches after this hilarious joke.

****

LATER THAT EVENING, Joshua Randall and Lila were sitting quietly in the living room, not saying too much, but just enjoying the peaceful togetherness.

"So, tell me Lila. What do you think about the fact that our economic fortunes are going downhill, and that I'm not going to be that rich and famous superstar that I once was?"

"You know what I think? I think it's the greatest thing that ever happened to us. I've got a new and improved Randy Miller back in my life—and now, I have Christ. I don't care if we have to live in a tiny little shack! I'd still be much, much happier than I've been during this whole last year."

"I've finally found the purpose for my life, Lila dear! Now that I have Christ, I have the greatest treasure that a man could ever want. Right now, I'm happier than I've been in my whole life."

"And I'm a happy camper too, my love. I love you so much, J. R."

"And I love you bunches and bunches, sweetheart."

The two of them held on to each other in a passionate and loving embrace.

21.

EPILOGUE

It was a balmy and partly cloudy Friday evening. The mountain scenery over Gatlinburg, Tennessee, was absolutely spectacular with the leaves of the trees on the forested ridges at the height of their beauty, displaying their glistening red, orange, and yellow hues, made even more gorgeous from the reflection of the orange and hazy sunset. The Celestial Prayer Retreat Center was situated on a beautiful forested slope, which provided a stunning view of the lovely resort city that lay below the ridge. The homes, stores, and hotels of this vacation metropolis were interspersed with inviting trees and bushes. The Smoky Mountains could be seen directly east of this entrancing city.

The Celestial Prayer Retreat Center was an extremely lovely place, not only because of its outward beauty, but also because of the sweet presence of the Holy Spirit that resided there. The bedroom units were not luxurious, but they were clean and contemporary in architecture. Inviting paths curved this way and that way, bordered by shady trees, flowerbeds, and benches for the people to sit on and have a time of seeking the Lord. The retreat center included a prayer chapel, a dining room, and a conference convention center with a seating capability of 800. The conference center was covered with dainty purple carpeting. This room consisted of large windows that reached to the floor, providing a spellbinding view of the resort city that lay below.

Tonight, on that Friday of September 26, 2008, there was going to be a festive birthday celebration and reunion of family and friends. During that last weekend of September, two 'homecoming' concerts were scheduled, featuring the singing group The Celestial Singers in the conference auditorium that was expected to be packed full. Randy Miller (now known as J. R. Miller—standing for Joshua Randall Miller) was turning sixty-five today. A special room in back of the main dining hall was reserved for the great celebration. Meanwhile, all the prayer pilgrims would be using the main dining room to eat their supper—that is those pilgrims who were not fasting.

At 6:00 P. M., all the guests were gathered in that lovely back room, seated at a large table with a checkered red-and-white tablecloth on it and a delicious dinner of grilled chicken, green peas, asparagus, mashed potatoes, garden salad, and fresh rolls. There were pitchers of unsweetened iced tea, lemonade, and water. J. R., the guest of honor, was seated at the head of the table. Beside him was sixty-seven-year-old Lila. Both of them had white hair, but otherwise, they looked young for their ages. Their faces were graced with a deep reservoir of wisdom and shone with the presence of the Holy Spirit.

Gray-headed Mike Applebaum, with his wife Donna, was seated next to the Millers. Mike had retired from teaching history several years ago. Brad Applebaum was there. His hair was almost totally gray while his wife's hair was still an attractive brown. Even at the age of fifty-five, the hazel eyes of Pam Applebaum had lost none of their sparkle—if anything, the glow in them and in her face had actually increased. She continued to be the same bubbly, vivacious lady she had been when she was twenty years old. The love between Brad and Pam Applebaum was deeper and stronger than ever. More and more over the years, they knew, without even saying a single word, what each one was thinking. Sitting beside them were their children with their spouses. There was twenty-nine-year-old David Applebaum with his attractive, blonde-haired wife, Leah. Their son, three-year-old Caleb, was seated next to the young couple. David was the senior pastor of Faith Tabernacle Church in Pensacola, Florida. Twenty-six-year-old Mark Applebaum was the second son of Brad and Pam. He was seated by his new bride, Cathy. Mark was a math teacher at Bethel Christian College in Birmingham, Alabama. Next to this new couple was the daughter of Brad and Pam, twenty-four-year-old Linda Applebaum. She worked as a secretary in her home city of Louisville, Kentucky.

On the other side of the table was Jack Miller with his wife, Lucy. He was a used car salesman who resided in Springfield, Illinois. Next to them were Thomas Miller Junior and his wife, Betsy. He was a computer programmer and graphics designer. That couple resided in Jackson, Tennessee. Also attending the party were Hal and Laura Odell who had gotten married on July 3, 1976. Hal was a Bible professor at Nashville Christian Academy. Their two daughters, Marci and Stacy, were sitting beside the couple.

It was a joyful, festive dinner with much laughter, many jokes, and numerous moving stories that had happened to them in the past.

"Well, J. R.," said Brad. "You sure are looking healthy considering your age."

"Thank you, Brad! Likewise, you are looking real good—and your wife's beauty is absolutely stunning! I wonder. It looks to me like you've lost some weight. Are you on any kind of diet?"

"Nope! I just try to eat healthy—a lot of fresh fruits and veggies—and I take those wonderful powdered vitamin/mineral supplements from the company, Life Revival. But the biggest thing is the joy of the Lord in my life."

"Yeah," added Pam. "To walk in close fellowship with the Lord is bound to make anybody healthy."

Presently, Lila walked into the kitchen and returned with an angel food birthday cake with chocolate frosting, blueberries, and blue candles on top. Pam Applebaum walked over to the upright piano, sat down on the bench, and started playing the introduction to "Happy Birthday," while everybody joined in singing that song in the key of F. When the sound of the last chord died out, hearty applause broke out with cries of "Speech, speech!"

J. R. Miller stood up and looked with gratefulness on all the wonderful people who were gathered in the room, tears of joy running down his face.

"I'm speechless," he began. "I just don't know where to begin! Well, I can remember that birthday celebration thirty-five years ago when Lila, Mike, and Donna spent a weekend at Tahoe, 'painting the town red.' You know, I had no idea then that events were lurking in the background that would change my life forever. We stopped off at that New Age Center in Placerville where that apparition appeared to that pudgy old man and prophesized fame and fortune for me. I thought it was going to be a wonderful thing, but I found out during the next year that it was worse than just empty—it was a trapdoor from Satan himself. I'm just so thankful that God is stronger than Satan, and that the devil was totally defeated at the cross. And you know, I am eternally indebted to all the prayer warriors—Brad and Pam Applebaum over here, Pastor Norris, and especially Grandma Brenda—as well as all the others who prayed me out of hell and into the wonderfully fulfilling ministry I've had over the last thirty years. As we're soon to have a very important election, with the race being between John McCain and Barack Obama for president, all I have to say about that is what Ronald Reagan said after he was shot in 1981 and had been wheeled into the hospital: 'I hope that they're Republicans!' No, seriously, things look very hairy right now with the crashing stock market and the high gas prices. Many people can only see the gloom and doom, but I have a different outlook, and it has nothing to do with this present world. There's a great big beautiful tomorrow waiting for us who love Jesus, and to quote another famous line of the Old Gipper, 'You ain't seen nothing yet!' Remember: I've actually seen some parts of heaven, you know. And there's no doubt in my mind that the second coming of Jesus for His Bride is right around the corner. In fact, I really sense in my spirit that I will be alive physically when He comes to take us all away!

"To sum it all up, this is a very, very happy day for me! You are all such beautiful and loving people! I remember those days in 1974 when my name was in lights and everybody dubbed me 'Jitterbug Josh.' It was nothing but a shallow image. But today, I feel like a real person! I have the wonderful joy of the Holy Spirit, my Comforter and Helper, I have a loving wife and a wonderful family, the Lord has opened up a worldwide ministry for me where we've had the opportunity to see thousands of people accept Christ, and I have an awesome hope for the future! I love you so very, very much! Thank you!"

Joshua Randall sat down, and the pageantry of cake eating and opening of presents began. He mused contentedly over the events of the last thirty-four years.

Shortly after that Thanksgiving in 1974, Harry Gates had approached him about starting up the band again, and he had declined, saying, "The Lord is leading me down a different path." Harry was shocked, angry, and said that

Jitterbug Josh was crazy and had gone insane. The news media picked up this story and reported that Jitterbug Josh was quitting the music business because he had "gotten religion."

J. R.'s recovery from his heart attack and gunshot wound was very rapid. By early March of 1975, he was pretty much back to normal health. He had applied for the teaching job at Visalia High School and had been accepted. He found a very nice and spacious home with nine rooms out in the country near the town of Woodlake. It was a quiet and peaceful place with a two-lane road running adjacent to it. It was surrounded by fields and had a lovely patio and swimming pool. The house was encircled by farmland, and the two-lane highway had very little traffic on it. During this time, the Miller family attended Woodlake Pentecostal Holiness Church. Word began to trickle around the area concerning Joshua Randall's testimony of seeing the other side, and he began to get invitations to speak and sing at a number of places: churches, women's conferences, and Full Gospel Businessmen's meetings.

In the spring of 1977, J. R. received a call from the Lord to start up an international music and prayer ministry with a focus on preaching the reality of heaven and hell, and that the coming of Jesus is near at hand. This ministry would be heavily involved in full-time missionary activity. Concurrently, he got a call from a man he had met in his travels with The Universal Mindset. This man, Monty Cole, had accepted the Lord two years ago, and had some land for sale at a very cheap price in Gatlinburg. A run-down bungalow consisting of five rooms was on the property. The Lord spoke to J. R. in a still small voice that this was the place where He wanted him to set up his ministry headquarters. So, the Miller family sold their house near Woodlake, headed east, and set up shop in that dinky little bungalow. J. R. had only two hundred dollars to start up this new ministry, and the Lord told him to give seventy dollars of that money to another ministry. He obeyed, and miraculously, they had thirty people on the team when they started their tour during the summer of 1977. J. R. worked on recruiting the needed singers, orchestra members, and sound technician who were needed to fill out the group. Lila set up shop in one of the rooms in the bungalow in order to book concerts. Miraculously, she was able to book a full itinerary of concerts for that summer in medium-sized churches of all denominations all across America and also in British Columbia. They relied on love offerings to help keep them going. J. R. decided to name his group, 'The Celestial Singers' with the logo, 'heaven is mega, mega real!' They were very successful, and the Lord led them to minister in India for three months in the early part of 1978. J. R. led this ministry, singing and playing acoustic guitar. In that first year, they saw hundreds of people giving their hearts to the Lord as well as many people receiving miraculous physical healings. But when they went to India, many of the team members became sick with parasites because they ignorantly drank the water right out of the tap.

Over the following years, God prospered the Celestial Singers, and the ministry grew steadily. J. R. and Lila were able to build the lovely prayer center on their land during the mid-1980s, and they were able to build a nice eight-room house for themselves in the late 1980s.

Celestial Singers was a moderately sized ministry rather than a big-name group. But they were very effective. The musical style and arrangements were very pleasant to listen to as well as very anointed, and J. R. and the team members were very sensitive to the leading of the Holy Spirit as they concertized and preached the gospel. Over the years, they were able to minister in all fifty states as well as seventy-five foreign countries. This included such places as Greenland, Iceland, England, France, Norway, Hungary, Bulgaria, Romania, Kenya, South Africa, India, Thailand, China, Peru, Chile, Argentina, and Israel as well as many other countries. Thousands of people came to Christ at these concerts, and many were baptized in the Holy Spirit. The places that J. R. Miller felt most at home at were India and Israel. Starting in 1990, the Celestial Singers did a concert tour in Israel almost every year. The Celestial Singers started out with one full-time team. In 1984, they added another full-time team. In 1989, they added 3 summer teams to the 2 full-time teams, and in 1995, they added 2 more full-time teams to make 7 teams that traveled all around the world, sharing the love of God.

A few days after the suicide of Eric Burns, Jan Burns suffered a massive stroke and died almost instantly. Art, her husband and the dad of the wayward communist, was totally grief-stricken. This created a great hatred against communism in his heart, and his political views turned very sharply to the right. He joined the John Birch Society and Liberty Lobby. He died of complications from diabetes in 2003.

Ted Johnson spent the rest of his life as a prisoner in San Quentin. He became insane in his old age and died in 2007.

Scott Williams was tried and sentenced to fifteen years in prison but was released after four years. He went on to become heavily involved in prison ministry and preached the gospel in jails all over the United States, leading many thousands of prisoners to Christ. He also became a very accomplished writer with several published books, one of them being entitled, *The Similarity between Communism and American Slavery*. This book became a bestseller in the Black Political Science sector of literature. In this historical essay, he showed how both communism and American slavery in the South took away the basic rights of men found in the Declaration of Independence: the right to life, liberty, and the pursuit of happiness. He postulated that both communism and American slavery held men under the bondage of fear, crushed the spirits of multitudes of people, and kept them from advancing to a higher standard of living. He said that both systems had been fraught with much physical and psychological torture.

As for Yappy Yellowfield, he was tried and found guilty of masterminding a rip-off scheme in 1977. He had cheated many people out of millions of dollars with his bogus scam that claimed to be a new and cheaper way of supplying electricity to customers. He was sentenced to twenty years in prison, and the new DJ on radio station KROK proved to be a much mellower person.

After Pam moved to Tennessee with her parents, she was able to enroll at Rhema Bible Institute in Oklahoma. Brad and Pam kept in touch through the telephone and letter writing. During the summer of 1975, Brad was able to coax his mom and dad into letting him enroll at Rhema also after he had heard the glowing reports about that school from Pam. The spark between them didn't die down, but instead, it continued to grow. They were formally engaged in December of 1976, and they were married on Saturday, June 18, 1977. They lived in Nashville for several years, Brad working as a salesman at a large Christian bookstore and eventually becoming a part owner of it, and Pam teaching piano and voice lessons at Nashville Christian Academy. In 1982, Brad had a Christian novel he had written published. It became an instant bestseller in the Christian arena. It was called *The Missing Link* and was taken from his essay he had written in 1974 concerning what might the outcome of World War II have been if there had been no prayer warriors. The plot concerned a lady around 1980 who went to church but didn't value prayer very much. An angel took her on a trip back in time to let her live in a world after World War II that had not been under-girded by the prayer warriors to help bring victory for the Allies against Hitler. There were characters that he added to the book who were in the terrible scenario of a world without freedom. In the vision, the world she saw was very much like the world in George Orwell's *1984*. At the end of this terrible vision, the girl comes back to the real world, having learned her lesson, becoming a great prayer warrior. He wrote another bestseller after that, an end-times novel with the title, *The Great Party;* a novel about the Rapture, the Judgment Seat of Christ, and the Marriage Supper of the Lamb. Brad also wrote some lyrics that were set to music and became published. His poem of 1973, "A Heart Aglow," was set to music by Joshua Randall, performed by the Celestial Singers, and eventually became published as well. In 1987, Brad and Pam moved to Gatlinburg where they became the leaders and co-owners of the Celestial Prayer Retreat Center. Christians from around the world came to this retreat center for conferences, conventions, and just to find a place to get intimate with Jesus. It was also the place where the Celestial Singers had their rehearsal camps before they went out on tour.

Brad's parents became Christians just a few days after the near-resurrection of 'Jitterbug Josh.' This miracle, plus the heroism of Pam and Brad, drew them to giving their hearts to Jesus. Over the years, their lives changed tremendously, although Harriet was a more regular church attender than Sid was. They both kicked their smoking habit in the mid-1980s. In 2001, when Sid died and went to heaven, he saw his beautiful mansion with the huge, beautiful golf course in front of it and cried out with intense glee,

"THAT A BABY, PRECIOUS JESUS!" Many a time, he and other saints would have friendly tournaments on this lovely golf course. After Sid went home to be with the Lord, the grief-stricken Harriet moved to Rossmoor Senior Center where she lived out the rest of her days.

Anthony, the atheistic uncle of Brad, died of an aortic aneurysm in 1980 without showing any evidence of ever finding the Lord. Aunt Mary died of breast cancer in 1997.

Doctor Howard Clarvoe, the atheistic cardiologist who insisted that J. R. should have his life support plug pulled, never did believe in God, not even after the miraculous recovery of the singing star. Sad to say, he died of a massive heart attack in 1976 when he was only forty. As he plunged into hell, he screamed in great terror and agony.

Grandma Brenda lived a very long and healthy life. In 1993, when she was 101 years old, she was diagnosed with Alzheimer's disease. Her memory steadily deteriorated until her death in March 1996. Her deathbed experience was an extremely memorable one for those who witnessed it. They could feel the presence of some very holy and awesome entities who came into the room. Suddenly, her face lit up like a light bulb and she exclaimed, "Oh, glory, GLORY, *GLORY!!* I see Jesus beckoning to me and He is so very, very, very *beautiful!!*" She then stopped breathing, but two minutes later, she stirred, opened her eyes, and exclaimed, "Oh, the rapture of it all!! I just came back for a minute to tell you it pays to serve the Lord!! I've just been to heaven, and oh, you have no idea at all how very, very, very wonderful it is!!" And right after that, she *really* breathed her last.

After Carmen Schmidt had her abortion in the fall of 1974, she experienced unbearable depression. Alan, her husband, divorced her in May of 1980. That traumatic experience drove her even deeper into the pit of despondency, and on September 23, 1980, she decided to take her own life. She wrote a goodbye note to her family members, explaining why she was committing suicide after which she pointed the loaded gun at her forehead while standing in her small bedroom. She tried to pull the trigger but was unable to do so; her hand was frozen. She cussed and tried again with no success. The gun slipped out of her hand, and the next thing she knew, she was in something like the most realistic dream she had ever experienced. She found herself in the brightest room she had seen in her whole life. The sense of peace was altogether unbelievable and wonderful. Two men in totally white garments approached her, carrying the most beautiful baby girl she had ever seen. The infant looked at Carmen with eyes full of love, and wonders of wonders, spoke with perfect ease in an extremely sweet and high-pitched voice these words: "Mommy! Mommy! Please don't end your life! I want to see you here with me! I forgive you, mommy! *I forgive you!* I love you so much!"

At this point, the dream ended, and Carmen found herself back in the bedroom with the gun lying on the carpet. She fell onto the bed and broke out into uncontrollable weeping. Three weeks later, she heard the gospel, accepted Christ at a small Christian Missionary Alliance church in Madera, California, and experienced sweet relief from that terrible load of depression. She was remarried to a wonderful Christian man named Don Weston in 1989.

It was Saturday, September 27. The members of the Celestial Singers were gathering at the conference center and setting up their microphones, musical instruments, sound system, and lighting system for the homecoming concerts that would be performed today and tomorrow. At 12:00 noon, the sound system was ready to be tested and tweaked, and by 3:00, the vocalists and orchestra members walked onto the stage for a sound check. They then practiced the songs they would be performing tonight with J. R. Miller conducting the orchestra, singing some solos, and playing the guitar on some songs. Voices echoed through the room as they tested the microphones, speakers, and monitors. "Check, check! One, two, three, check! For God so loved the world—check, CHECK!"

At precisely 7:30, the homecoming concert began. It was a full house tonight with standing room only in the conference center. Seven different Celestial Singers teams were massed together that had traveled all over America as well as many different countries of the world. These teams included 80 singers, 14 violinists, 7 violists, 7 cellists, 12 flute players, 7 clarinet players, 5 oboists, 1 saxophone player, 12 trumpeters, 6 French horn players, 14 trombone players, 7 pianists, 5 string synthesizer players, 5 brass synthesizer players, 7 bass players, 7 drummers, a sound technician, a light technician, and a signer for the hearing impaired. (Each of the pianists, synthesizer players, bass players, and drummers were assigned to play certain songs so that they would all have their turn to perform and their moment to shine.) The outfits consisted of blue suits, white dress shirts, and red ties for the men, while the ladies were clad in beautiful royal blue dresses. Most of the people in the Celestial Singers were in their twenties with a few of them in their thirties.

Oh, it was such a magnificent concert that night! The singers and orchestra sounded so very, very beautiful—the people on stage and in the audience felt like they were hearing the music of heaven! Wave after wave of the anointing of the Holy Spirit was flowing from the singers and orchestra right into the audience! The program started with "Celebrate the Lord of Love" followed by "Sing." J. R. Miller then introduced the group to the audience and did a little 'ice-breaker' spiel. After that, they sang a complicated arrangement of "I Am a Friend of God" with J. R. Miller doing some funky guitar riffs. One of the sopranos, whose name was Ronda, then gave a testimony about the recent trip to Kenya and how she prayed for a blind man who the Lord healed on the spot. The group then did a beautiful arrangement of the Terry MacAlmon song, "How We Need the River." Following this was a song J. R. Miller had received in a dream one night. The name of it was "The Circle of Worship." After that came a peppy arrangement of the song, "Days of Elijah," followed by "Jewish Medley," a group of Israeli songs that included such favorites as "Rejoice, Rejoice!"

The audience was thoroughly enjoying the music and testimonies. One of the men in the crowd was the seventy-three-year-old former pastor of the United Church of the Valley, Kevin Harmon. He had been the one who had encouraged J. R. Miller to become a Mason thirty-five years ago. After J. R. had come back from the dead, he had told Pastor Kevin all about his experiences of seeing heaven, hell, and Jesus on the cross. Pastor Kevin had totally bought into the story that J. R. had told him and had accepted Christ and started preaching the gospel in his church. The congregation didn't like his sharp, pointed preaching, and voted him out of that church. He was able to find another church to pastor in Hayward, though, and stayed there as pastor for twenty-five years after which he retired and moved to Knoxville, Tennessee.

The halftime portion of the concert came where J. R. Miller shared the vision of Celestial Singers and some stories about what the Lord had done on their last trip for about ten minutes. When he talked about his recent trip to Israel, he mentioned the wonderful doctor who had treated him during his heart attack.

"When I was practically dead at John Muir Hospital, there were two doctors who were heavily involved in my case. One of those two doctors, Martin Perez, was a wonderful man. I felt he was a *real* doctor who truly cared about people. It turns out that he found out his Jewish heritage in the mid-1980s, and he ended up migrating to Israel in 1991. His ancestors from Spain had hidden their Jewish heritage 500 years ago because of the terrible persecution against the Jewish people by the Spaniards. He lived in Israel until his death last year at the age of ninety-five. We Christians need to go back to our Jewish roots and realize how much we owe to the Jewish people. They have blessed the whole world."

The Celestial Singers soon came back on stage for the second half of the concert. Their first song was a fast, jazzy piece in D minor with a lot of complicated harmonies that had been written in the early 1980s. The name of this piece was "Heaven." It talked about the fact that heaven is a wonderful place, but until we get there, we need to be busy, preaching the gospel. The next piece was an a cappella arrangement of the hymn, "Until Then," consisting of eight-part vocal harmony. It started off in C major and finished in E-flat major. It was arranged by J. R. Miller and had very gorgeous and majestic harmonies in it. Following this, Todd Sutton, one of the pianists, shared a three-minute testimony. After that, they sang another Terry MacAlmon song, "Precious Lamb of God." Next came the song, "A Heart Aglow," which Brad had written the words to in 1973 and J. R. Miller had set to music, writing the melody as well as putting together the Celestial Singers arrangement of that song. Then came another ballad written by J. R., "Sweet and Lovely Jesus." Then came the pre-invitation musical selection, "Love

Medley," which included "The Love of God," "Oh, How He Loves Us," and "Oh, Love that Will Not Let Me Go." Pam Applebaum had a large soprano solo in this medley, and as she sang those two hymns in the medley, J. R. was brought back to that memorable time outside the movie theater in Rheem Valley when Pam had loved on him and sung those songs. He cried like a baby once again in that concert hall.

The invitation time was very sweet as J. R. shared the gospel under the anointing of the Holy Spirit. Many people wept and worshipped the Lord, and seven came forward to accept Christ. The final song was sung to close out the program. As the upbeat song with its slow, ethereal opening started, Brad put his arm lovingly around his wife and whispered, "Oh, Pammypoo! You did such a fantastic job on your solo tonight! You really ministered to me! Hey. Let's get a bite to eat, Pammypoo, after this concert. Good ol' Braddy, the Baddy Daddy, can give you a real hot time! What do you say? C'mon, we'll paint the town red!"

Pam Applebaum cuddled in closely to Brad, looked warmly at him, and said, "Brad Applebaum, I'll go anywhere with you! I love you and am so glad I married you! You're the greatest!"

The two of them looked lovingly into each other's eyes and held hands as the Celestial Singers sang the last song of the evening. The name of it was "Soli Deo Gloria" (to God alone be the glory).

END NOTES

3. The Revolutionists: 1. Author's translation and updating of the Scripture.

6. Spiritual Vitamins: 1. Words from, "I Surrender All" by Judson W. VanDe Venter. 2. Words are from the hymn, "The Comforter Has Come," with lyrics by Frank Bottome.

15. The Last Chance: 1. Obviously, Brad Applebaum, as well as many history teachers of the 1970s, were unaware of the horrible brutality and inhumanity of many of the Japanese against many POWs in World War II, documented in the non-fiction best-selling historical account written by Laura Hillenbrand entitled *Unbroken*.

16. The Prayer Vigil: 1. Words are from the hymn, "The Love of God," with lyrics by Frederick M. Lehman. 2. This author does not endorse the supposed apparitions of the Virgin Mary that Catholics claim have happened around different parts of the world. However, the author dogmatically asserts that there are many precious Catholic people who are truly born from above and on their way to heaven. Doctor Martin Perez would be a prime example. The author maintains that it's not about this or that denomination, but it's about a vibrant relationship with the Lord Jesus Christ.

19. The Valley of Time Travel: 1. Author's translation. 2. The story of Randy's trip of time travel back to the first century with him witnessing the crucifixion, death, and resurrection of Jesus Christ is based on the Bible accounts found in the four gospels that testify concerning the Passion of Jesus. (See Matthew, chapters 26-28; Mark, chapters 14-16; Luke, chapters 22-24; and John, chapters 18-20).

20. The Circle of Celestial Celebrants: 1. Author's translation and updating of that Scripture. 2. Isaiah 44:6-7, Revelation 1:8. Revelation 1:8 is the author's translation, (the Hebrew words, Aleph and Tav, are used instead of the Greek words, Alpha and Omega.)

Author's reflections

This book is a fictional story, but the message of the book is NOT fiction; it is for real. In the last few years, the book by Pastor Todd Burpo, *Heaven is for Real,* has become a national bestseller and has been made into a movie. I firmly believe that the Lord is behind the success of this book and movie because the experience of the little boy Colton going to heaven and sitting on the lap of Jesus really happened. Also, the testimony of Akiane Kramarik, which is mentioned in that book, is real. Nobody, especially not a girl of twelve, could paint as beautifully as she did unless she was anointed by the Holy Spirit. I firmly believe that the Lord is giving many people a sneak preview of the reality of heaven—and even hell, because the second coming of Jesus is right at the door, and the Lord wants as many people as possible to make it into heaven. I have never personally taken a trip into heaven, but I have done much research about heaven in the Bible and also have read many books that relate the testimonies of people who have been there.

How do we make it into heaven and experience a tiny taste of heaven in the here and now? Well, the Good News can be summed up in four points: 1. God loves you and has a wonderful plan for your life. 2. All of us in the human race are sinners separated from God who are deserving of eternal damnation in hell forever. 3. God became man in the person of Jesus, came to earth and lived a perfectly sinless life, died on a cross, suffered the wrath of God for each and every human being so that we could receive the free gift of salvation, and rose again bodily on the third day. 4. Each of us must repent of our sins and receive Jesus into our hearts as Lord and Savior. Romans 10:9 says, "That if thou shalt confess with thy mouth the Lord Jesus, and shalt believe in thy heart that God hath raised Him from the dead, thou shalt be saved."

Have you received Jesus as your Lord and Savior? If the Lord is tugging at your heart, I encourage you to say this prayer: "Lord Jesus! I am a sinner. Thank You for dying on the cross for my sins! Come into my heart and be my Lord and Savior! I repent of my sins. Thank You for saving me now. I will follow You the rest of my life, and I look forward to being with You in heaven. In Your name, Jesus, amen!"

If you prayed this prayer, I rejoice with you! This is the beginning of a beautiful new adventure for you, and I encourage you to do several things to grow in your relationship with Jesus: 1. Pray to the Lord every day. Prayer is simply talking to God. We pray to God the Father in the name of Jesus. 2. Read the Bible every day. Start with the book of John and then go to Acts and then the other three gospels. 3. Get planted in a good, Bible-believing church where you can interface with other Christians. 4. Get intimate with the Holy Spirit. He lives inside of you and wants to fill you with His power. 5. Tell other people of your newfound relationship with Jesus.

Let me know about your decision so I can rejoice with you. My email is: toddnetlandmusic@hotmail.com. May the Lord God bless you richly!!!

About the Author

Todd Netland is an accomplished pianist, composer, and arranger. He has written more than fifty musical compositions during his lifetime. In July 1982, he joined the Christian music group, Sound of Joy, founded by Art Crane, a retired marine colonel who felt the Lord leading him to start that gospel group. Netland was their pianist with them until they disbanded at the end of 1989. He arranged many songs for them.

In February 1990, he was accepted as a pianist in Jon Stemkoski's Celebrant Singers and ministered full-time with them from June 1990 until the end of 2002. During these years, Netland traveled to forty-nine states as well as more than fifty countries including such places as Greenland, Colombia, Kenya, Tanzania, Uganda, Rwanda, India, China, France, Lebanon, Egypt, Vietnam, and many other places.

During the years between 2003 and 2009, Netland travelled on a number of short-term missionary trips to Peru, Chile, Israel, Jordan, Egypt, Hungary, and Romania with Evangelists Tom and Kay Cox, and also with Pastor Tibor Ambrus, ministering the love of Jesus through his piano playing and personal testimony.

In 2010, Netland rejoined the Celebrant Singers on a part-time basis, playing piano with them up to this point.

Netland has recorded ten solo albums during his lifetime. *Sunrise on the Sea of Galilee* and *Every Day* are still available for purchase.

Todd Netland presently lives in Pacheco, California with his wife, Wendy. He does concerts at various senior centers around the San Francisco Bay Area.

Netland is thrilled at the opportunity the Lord has given him to write this debut novel. He loves to read. Some of his favorite books include Herman Wouk's *The City Boy, The Chronicles of Narnia* by C. S. Lewis, Frank Peretti's *This Present Darkness,* Catherine Marshall's *Julie,* Peter Marshall and David Manuel's *The Light and the Glory,* and Richard Sigmund's *My Time in Heaven.*

www.ingramcontent.com/pod-product-compliance
Lightning Source LLC
Chambersburg PA
CBHW050026030726
47506CB00001B/131